I0818216

AN IMPRINT OF WHAT BOOKS PRESS | LOS ANGELES

ALSO BY A. W. DEANNUNTIS

Master Siger's Dream
The Mermaid at the Americana Arms Motel
The Final Death of Rock-And-Roll and Other Stories
The Mysterious Islands and Other Stories

TERROR ISLAND

A NOVEL

Published in the United States by Giant Claw,
an imprint of What Books Press, Los Angeles.

Publisher's Cataloging-In-Publication Data
Names: DeAnnuntis, A. W. (Anthony W.), author.
Title: Terror island : a novel / A.W. DeAnnuntis.
Description: Topanga, CA : Giant Claw, an imprint of What Books Press, [2019]
Identifiers: ISBN 9781733378994
Subjects: LCSH: Shipwrecks--History--17th century--Fiction. | Sea monsters--Fiction. | Ocean travel--History--17th century--Fiction. | Fathers and sons--Fiction. | Piracy--History--17th century--Fiction. | LCGFT: Bildungsromans.
Classification: LCC PS3604.E17 T47 2019 | DDC 813/.6--dc23

Cover art: Gronk, *untitled*, 2018
Book design by Ash Good, www.ashgood.design

Giant Claw
363 South Topanga Canyon Boulevard
Topanga, CA 90290

GIANTCLAWPRESS.COM

TERROR ISLAND

A NOVEL

A. W. DeAnnuntis

This work is dedicated with gratitude and love
to the memory of my mother,
Marianna Campisi DeAnnuntis
and to the memory of my father,
Alderino DeAnnuntis

and for Mary, again.

ACKNOWLEDGMENTS

This author wishes to thank Chuck Rosenthal and Gail Wronsky for their love and good-humor and encouragement and determined support. Without them, this work would not exist.

TERROR ISLAND

PART ONE

JAMAICA

CHAPTER ONE

CURTAIN OF BLACK and thunderous roar; swirling black water beneath a screaming wind. Black sky and black sea, black as the ink that Europe soon would pour over the globe; black as the oil Europe did not yet need since it had discovered energy in bodies brought from Africa.

Wind shrieking though flashes and explosions; Pierre's world was the coffin he clung to and water in furious motion spinning him invisible and careening in terror.

Blue-white lightning struck, a blast in wailing wind. Rain slashed his face as its glare faded. Tossed about in this dark world, forces battered Pierre as they wished.

Beneath him and just larger than his body, that wooden coffin kept him afloat pelted with icy rain and preserving him from death. He had expected none of this.

Certain that nothing very bad could ever happen to him, and accepting that a father is an embarrassing thing to lose, soon after Pierre read that letter he announced to his mother that he would return his father to her. It took a moment for Gabriella to realize he was serious, and then she assured him he would die. But Pierre accepted his challenge armed with the power of Reason, so he was certain his journey could only succeed and his reward would be Augustus's praise and Gabriella's gratitude. Clinging to this coffin and tossed about over this raging ocean under this black sky with lightning to kill him and monsters to devour him, it all was so unreasonable.

Flash of lightning and crack of thunder, another and another as terror impaled his body rigid against that hollow wooden box. His hands gripped the wood side-handles as his legs squeezed the narrow end of the coffin in a clamping embrace. Suspended over a fathomless ocean lashed by furious rain within this black night, the last thing Pierre wished to recall was the impossibility of miracles; if he was to succeed he would need to do that work himself. Another dagger of blue-white light blinded him and its blast stunned his ears.

In all that rain, Gabriella's dark eyes glittered bright with tears. Pierre was startled to see her so far from home and he was a little ashamed. "What are you doing out here?"

"Should I ask you the same thing or will that make us both look stupid?" Her thick black shoes hovered just above the churning surf. "And you can't even swim!" Wind pulled at those same dark clothes she always wore serving tankards of ale to neighbors from behind the bar at the Captain Hudson. Tendrils of her gray-black hair snaked about her pale face while her dark expression absorbed the weak light. "Does this make any sense to you? All of this water and you can't even swim!"

"Thanks for coming out," Pierre said. "You know how I hate the dark."

"Thanks for nothing. Didn't I warn you? 'Oh mother dear, don't worry. These ships float well and twenty stout-hearted fellows will keep us on course. In no time you'll be holding my letters.'" She snorted and spat just as she so often did behind the bar; a bit more venom for this poisonous sea. "You think old people are stupid."

"Maybe overly cautious."

"Don't mouth-off to me, young man. I told you nothing good would come of this. Augustus is wherever he is because that's where he wants to be. But is that good enough for you? No; you abandon those who love you, just like him. You are gone from us and we are gone from you. You have chosen death and left the method to others."

"If I've chosen death I've failed there too because I'm still alive."

"Want to give odds on how long that lasts?"

"All right, you were right and I was wrong." He hoped simply to keep her there and he would not be alone.

"You smiled when you said everything would be all right. Look at you now, just look at yourself. Young and stupid. You care for no one but yourself and for nothing but your stupid ideas. Like worms these ideas work inside your head. You are here because of the worms in your head."

Overwhelmed suddenly with fear and despair he wailed, "Please, mother, the ship was big and sea-travel is as safe as walking along the street."

Gabriella's upper lip curled into a sneer. "Clinging to a speck of wood with nothing around you but water you can't drink." Those tears filling her eyes began to fall. "Wood isn't hard enough; these ships should be made of iron, like the hearts of our sons."

"Please," he pleaded watching her fade until he stared into darkness. "I have not failed," he muttered, "I have simply not succeeded." At the peak of the next wave he lifted his head and cried out. The only answer was the shriek of the wind. Could they all be dead? Another dagger of light exploded as rain stung his face. He opened his eyes but to no purpose.

From a sea invisible in its fury he looked into a black sky without center or edge, grateful to the Savage whose coffin sustained him within this cosmos of water and terror and darkness.

Completed the day before the creature's attack, Pierre remembered watching amused by the Savage's dread as his thick fingers, scared and dark, carefully joined wood to wood. That coffin now labored in the water so that he struggled to keep his face above the churning surf. Determined to breathe and not lose his grip, his body trembled as his hands clamped tighter.

Blast of lightning and crack of thunder again and again until light and sound formed a screen to surround him. Lightning and thunder, cannon fire and musket fire, blood and fire, smell of burning tar and burning gunpowder and burning human flesh. Screams of dying men filled his ears, but most horrifying had been the creature. The storm did not need to terrify him because there had been the creature. Recalling its fury Pierre lifted his head fearful it was near.

Surf and rain struck his face. Terrified of drowning, his fear of the creature ran deeper. Somewhere in all that darkness the creature lurked. Darkness so thick it filled his mouth as it filled his eyes while the creature waited. The beast thought about Pierre as he thought about that beast.

Gabriella's warning had been as clear and urgent as if she had already seen his dread. Had her anguished concern peered into his future? That concern had made him smile, her instinct to shelter him seemed so naked and so strong. Afloat upon another man's coffin, Pierre suspected her warning had been something more, but that question would remain simply one more thing he would never know.

His only time-keeper the lurch and swipe of his battering sea, time resembled a fluid. High waves sent him spinning until a larger wave crashed over him to pour salt water into his throat. Embalmed within a syrupy darkness, time held the fetid stench of fear. Trembling and breathless, Pierre could only cling to his raft without hope.

Body pressed flat against that wooden box and pounded by brittle rain within a time without time, gradually he began to suspect the waves grew weaker. Buffeted about by wind and wave, had he clung to this raft so long he could imagine relief? Had the curtain of that black sky begun to brighten and was the shriek of the wind less loud? The coffin rose and fell, yet even as the restless sea tossed him about like a twig, waves no longer filled his mouth. Determined to keep his grip Pierre began to experience something that resembled relief. Yet, the brightening light revealed shapes floating near him until what he saw made him wish for darkness.

Some he recognized immediately; yellow shards of planking, massive black hull ribs, portions of masts along with their yards floating like wooden barrels festooned with tattered gray sails and all trailing huge snarls of knotted ropes and pulleys, remnants of all that was left of the ship that had carried Pierre. The more he saw, the less he wanted to see.

The sky became still brighter so that he recognized objects floating further away; sea chests like small coffins, fragments of barrels that had contained their provisions, and even more. All of this assured Pierre that what he remembered had truly happened. He lifted his head again to find the horizon

Its hard indigo was softening to blue, as if day might be passing into night. He hoped then to see even a single human head bobbing frightened but alive and close enough to hale. The wind weakened and at the peak of another wave he lifted his head and cried out. He returned his chin to the coffin and heard only the wind and the sea.

Recalling the creature's attack he imagined its claws ripping into his flesh and he cringed. Though he stared into an empty sea, he saw the creature's open jaws expose a cavernous mouth red as a man's blood and lined with enormous pale teeth. Tipping back its massive head, the beast had unleashed a horrific howl, a wail of torment, and once again Pierre trembled.

This voyage should have been a thrilling adventure of initiation and reunion. Pierre's pursuit of Augustus should have been a tale as exciting as any of those romances he had read as a child. His entrance into this world beyond his own should have ended with the reunion with a man he had not seen in ten years.

Pierre had to believe that Fate had decreed his journey and assigned that beast as his peculiar challenge, unique to him alone. The curse of this creature was Pierre's curse even while it had cost the lives of others. Everything that was about to happen was all that could happen, just as everything that will happen has been determined by everything that had happened and so nothing will happen which has not been prepared for. Each moment can only grow out of the last. Yet he wanted to believe his future still lay within his own hands.

In the end, none of this consoled Pierre; not the day he first saw the beast, and certainly not now, tossed about alone and helpless. Despite his pain he again lifted his head.

Enough fading daylight remained to allow him to make out dark objects floating further away that might have been bodies, and he wondered if the creature could have failed to devour every one. The unbroken horizon became hard and bright to assure him that he was alone and at least for the moment safe from the creature. When the rain finally stopped he recognized this ocean; it was the ocean of his ignorance. He was that speck of consciousness clinging to a delusional thread of sensation and suspended above a suffocating darkness.

Only son and sole support of an aging mother, cast adrift on a mission to find a lost father, Pierre recognized the totality of his failure. The Philosopher says that self-taught is half-taught, but even that level of knowledge was far beyond his own. Insufficient as a son, his effort to locate Augustus perhaps had been hopeless from the start. Though it had not been his intention, he had begun a journey bound to reveal his every weakness and inadequacy and deficiency. A simple voyage from one continent to another had proved his ineptitude. Lying on the coffin, he hopped Augustus never learned this truth.

He imagined himself addressing the man he revered as a persecuted genius and opening his mouth to explain his incompetence. And those words loud within his mind would die, leaving only silence to pass his lips. Even his cries for mercy drifted from him as whispers. I have not failed, he imagined himself pleading to Augustus, I have simply not succeeded. But with a coffin as his only companion, how could he hope even to survive? As Gabriella had come out to remind him, he could not even swim.

The featureless expanse of the sea numbed his thoughts and he gripped the handles of the coffin more tightly. Then he discovered a dull pain at the back of his head. Carefully releasing one of the handles he touched a spot behind his right ear and his fingertips came away bright with his own blood. He was alone and bleeding in the middle of the ocean and he could not even swim.

At the creature's first crushing assault, Pierre had managed to cling to a portion of the bow. When the creature struck again that portion fell into the sea. He held onto it as it descended and then, at the last moment, flung himself free. As he struck the water he felt a blow to the back of his head. What followed he remembered as a confusion of moments. Pierre lived through a dream or dreamed through a life, retaining scars and memories to repent for whatever he had endured.

He recovered to find he had managed to keep his head above the water and then turned to discover the blow had come from a large portion of the bow that now floated beside him. He pulled himself under it and managed to hide. He drifted with it and what he witnessed within its shelter and between broken planks still left him horrified.

Most vividly he recalled the screams of men; their cries for their gods but most painfully for mothers, still rang in his ears. And yet as a counterpoint there were the cries of the creature. With each blow the creature had struck, it howled. Yardarms still draped with claw-ripped canvas sails and tangled rigging fell with a tremendous splash into the sea. Beneath the creature's roar those human cries were pitiful in their tiny desperation before each was swallowed by the screams of the beast.

Eventually the creature appeared satisfied that the ship was destroyed. But Pierre's horror deepened when he watched as, relentless as a shark, the beast began to cruise the scattered wreckage pursuing and devouring each of the ship's company. Pierre still wondered if what he saw had been a hallucination. Billy Bones, first mate, bitten in half, the lower portion of his body falling from the creature's jaws back into the sea; Captain Hawthorne, the upper half of his body protruding from the creature's mouth flailing his arms and screaming in Pierre's direction as if begging for his help; Squire Lancier, his rotund body gripped lengthwise, one of the creature's huge teeth crushing his skull until a stream of bloody mash dripped from its mouth. Men he had spoken with hours before became mere morsels for the creature's delectation. He could not close his eyes hard enough to make any of that disappear. Locked squirming and flailing between the creature's terrible jaws, each of his shipmates had been lifted like some bloody trophy high into the air. Piteous cries were followed by abrupt silence as each was crushed by the monster and disappeared. Pierre had retreated under the wreckage terrified and helpless.

But then, as if late-arriving to a feast, real sharks began to attack those sailors still struggling in the water. Most vividly Pierre remembered young Jack Hawkins, the second-mate, suddenly rise within a plume of water. Lifted high in the air, a shark had clamped its jaws around his leg, but beneath them both the enormous maw of the creature arose open. Hawkins along with that shark gripping his leg became captured together, so that those jaws closed around man and shark and then disappeared. But Pierre had not remained long a witness to all that carnage. Perhaps from the wound to his head, eventually he lost consciousness and did not awaken until, still sheltered by that piece of wreckage, he discovered the creature was gone and evening approached. Fearful his memories might still conjure the creature, he scanned the horizon again.

In the deepening twilight that followed the beast's attack Pierre found himself surrounded by shadows but heard nothing beyond the sough of a gentle sea. When the light was nearly gone he came out from beneath his shelter. Silent for fear of attracting the creature, he drifted hopeful that someone else was still alive. Then something suddenly bumped his back.

He cried out as he turned, but even in that weak light he recognized it. Floating beside him was that same coffin the Savage had worked at the previous week. Pierre had been impressed by the close attention he gave to its construction, even lining the inside with tar and neatly caulking every seam. The finishing touch had been large wood handles attached to its sides.

At the time he had wondered why they were needed. Now lying upon it and gripping those handles with his hands and his feet, he guessed that, like Gabriella, the Savage had had a premonition.

When Pierre had asked what he was doing, he assured Pierre he was preparing for that death which would pass among them as a huge black beast. The Savage had spoken so solemnly and with such certainty that Pierre could not laugh, charmed as he was by his simple-minded superstition. But when finally he clambered onto the top of that long box he felt a deep and embarrassed gratitude, since the Savage would never benefit from his own skill. Soon after all of this the wind picked up, became suddenly stronger and then the storm struck. With that, Pierre experienced true gratitude and wished the Savage well, wherever he might be.

But the cost of his reunion with Augustus must be high, its path must be difficult and dangerous and must take a long time. Obstacles must appear in his path to challenge him and to compel doubt and fear and demand his determination until he needed to reach deeply into himself. And yet from the start Pierre had not suspected any of this. But even if he had, its knowledge would have been useless and might even have caused him to give up, resigned never to see his father again and thereafter burdened by the delusion that he need merely survive to succeed.

Rocking gently now on his unlikely life-raft Pierre again looked around. Though he hoped to see another survivor of its attack, he knew that he would meet the creature again. Nature had shaped a powerful creation upon which to demonstrate Pierre's superiority or to lose his life. Not everyone, he decided, was so fortunate as to have their very own and personal adversary. Still, in all this Pierre did not envy himself.

If he managed to survive he might eventually prove his worth. But terrified and vomiting sea water, he failed to recognize the generosity of this gift. Call him Lucky Pierre.

CHAPTER TWO

ON A CHILL and gray morning in May late in the seventeenth century, Pierre Chanceux awoke in his tiny room above the Captain Hudson in Gabriella's tavern to the patter of rain and the sound of Gabriella in the next room beginning to stir. Through the night a cold wind had rattled the shutters as rain pelted the thin roof over his head. Victim of a hundred voices of recrimination, or perhaps only one voice speaking a hundred accusations, he had tossed restlessly in his bed. Looming over all stood that ghost constant in his own home, the glowering figure of Augustus. When Pierre heard her descend to the kitchen he dressed and followed.

From the doorway of the kitchen he watched Gabriella move about preparing their breakfast. He stepped out the back door and ran splashing across the small yard to that shed Augustus had used as his workshop.

Muddy light from the single window populated the workshop with shadows as dampness released the musty aroma of absence. He surveyed the workshop once again with regret for all of the lost years. Since Augustus's departure, his collection of books and equipment had drifted away in pieces, stolen or lost or sold, and forlorn shelves displayed their absent occupants like missing teeth. In his memory, Augustus leaned over the workbench whining of the importance of his work. Pierre was certain that if he were still alive, he now leaned over a workbench peering hard and whining. This thought made him smile. He stepped to the workbench where he remembered Augustus had stood, filling himself with all of his father that remained. Then he returned to the house.

In the kitchen Gabriella moved about silently and never looked directly at Pierre. When he finished eating he returned to his room and completed packing his sea-chest. Floating alone now on the coffin, he recalled each article he had packed as if by remembering, all might be retrieved from the bottom of the sea.

His morning meal finished and now standing sheltered at the threshold of the Captain Hudson's front door with his white canvas jacket draped over his arm and his packed sea-chest at his feet, Pierre faced Gabriella. In a sudden gesture that frightened him, she took his face between her hands and brought it close to hers. She pressed his face hard and he realized she was about to cry. "Kids!" she hissed. "They all should be born dead!"

He moved her hands from his face. "I'll write every day and mail the letters when I reach Antwerp." Aware suddenly of his own fear he embraced her as fiercely as he could ever remember. In her arms the enormity of what he was about to do came to him all at once and a moment of panic gripped him. But she struggled from his arms and pushed him away. Eyes suddenly dry her expression was darkly bitter.

"I can only fear for you, boy. The world is dangerous, but what you wish for will bring your death. Be sure you write those letters with ink that sea water will not wash away."

He remembered grinning at her words and more bravely than he felt. "Your love will sustain me whatever may happen."

"Ha! Better find something more sturdy."

He leaned into her arms, kissed her quickly on both cheeks, and then picked up his sea chest. Following the path to the street, when he reached the gate he turned. She stood now weeping without restraint. In a strained voice she cried out, "At least learn to swim!" He smiled and then turned and stepped into the street. He remembered wishing it had been a bright, clear morning. Afloat and alone he wondered if that weather had been an omen.

Days before, Pierre had booked passage on a British merchantman, the Bristol. As he followed the street leading to the wharves, he saw through a smoky veil of clouds the masts of ships at anchor pierce the thick sky like the spiny black trees of a distant forest.

Even while Augustus was still behind the bar at the tavern, Pierre's life had been part of the port's routine. Helping behind the bar he met sailors who had filled him with tales of high adventure and low behavior. So when he decided to go to sea and search for Augustus, he believed he knew how his voyage would proceed.

Emerging from the mist like clusters of ghosts, Pierre approached the small crowds of sailors, their women and other passengers. Following the wharves he passed dark cloth bales and pale wooden crates, stacks of blond timber sweetly aromatic, dark casks of corn whiskey and rum piled into pyramids along with shipping trunks of every size packed with stuffs journeying to the four corners of the earth, their brass fittings glinting in the gray light.

The Bristol was the largest ship in port and he had recognized its mast from a distance. Approaching the end of its wharf he then saw the nine men. Their skin was colored shades of brown and each wore around an ankle an ugly black iron shackle. Shirtless in the rain and cold they stood or squatted close together, eyes narrowed with resentment and mistrust. He had seen African slaves arrive at these docks, most in transit but some intended for purchase by local farmers and tradesmen, and that experience always left him disturbed. These men stood as cheerless as the sky and they appeared to be as cold as other men and as frightened. Pierre was seized by their presence and chilled by something that was not in the air.

He had witnessed slave markets held at the end of High Street. He had watched men he had served at the tavern examine a man or woman offered for sale, listened to their battle of commerce, those offers and counteroffers, so that by some invisible hand an agreement was reached of the true worth of a human life. And he had recognized their expressions of that pleasure of the power to choose; the ability to scrutinize another human being and estimate the service that person would perform and how much profit would be made. And he had seen as well that smug grin of having bested another bidder, as if it all were merely a competitive entertainment. Looking at these men on the dock, he understood that their futures had already been written by other men, their lives to be lived at the behest of other men, their existence decided by other men. Though he was warmly dressed Pierre shivered. Suddenly he felt something tug at his jacket.

He turned to discover that an old man sitting on the wet bright paving stones behind him clasped his jacket's hem. Bent with age, his bandy legs stretched before him hardly covered by tattered green breeches, and lengths of dark leather and gray wool were tied around his feet. Pierre somehow had failed to notice him sitting there, but now something seemed familiar about his tanned face, his gray eyes opaque and watery, his lips hanging loosely to display black and broken stumps of teeth. As benighted as he seemed, something about this man startled him. Pierre pulled at his jacket but the old man held firm. He looked up into Pierre's face with a confused awe. In a weak and reedy voice he said, "I do know you."

Pierre pulled hard but the old man was stronger than he appeared. "You have seen the devil's spawn," he said. "Its terror has pierced your heart. What you have seen others see only just before death." He grabbed Pierre's forearm with a grip so fierce and hot it felt encircled by fire. Leaning on Pierre's arm he struggled to stand. But Pierre jerked, pushing the man's arm aside and he fell back to the cobblestones with a quiet sigh. When he sat forward, a look of surprised sadness crossed his face.

As if to himself he said, "I've seen the moons of Jupiter and the canals of Mars, the rings of Saturn and the jungles of Venus. I've heard whales sing and dolphins converse. I've seen birds that swim on ice and squirrels that fly through trees. I've met men who drink the blood of a cow and men who'd starve before eating a cow. It's a strange world and all of it was made by God, so God must be the strangest creature of all." His eyes widened and he gasped as if seeing a ghost. "Beware of your knowledge. Take heed of what you believe you know. Understand that by learning one thing, a hundred things become more obscure. Understand how little you will ever understand. The Devil is a geometer whose currency is false certainty. Beware of the mind that thinks it is thinking."

Nearby a knot of people turned to look and Pierre felt their curiosity fall upon him. The old man was entombed in some drunken delusion that Pierre was too baffled to untangle. He stumbled as he turned to walk away while the man cried out, "Do not go! Listen to your mother. Only death awaits you!" Walking faster, the voice of self-doubt grew loud in Pierre's mind.

He opened his eyes to see the horizon was a hard, bright line of blue and in a cloudless sky as the sun neared its zenith. The coffin floated low in the water so that each swell pushed a wave into his face. He was nauseous with hunger and thirst and the relentless sun burned his eyes. His mouth was parched; his cracked and blistered lips sealed together. The skin on his arms was salted white except for dark channels of his sweat. When he lifted his head he became dizzy.

By the time Pierre reached the boarding plank of the Bristol he had recovered his resolve. Augustus is a great man, a profound thinker who sees past every horizon and Pierre would return him to his rightful place. To do that he would face whatever Fate offered. Clinging flat to the coffin, he reminded himself that at least he had survived the creature's attack. This was something more than failure.

His thirst became its own torture as seawater tempted his broken lips. He tried to suck the sweat from his skin and failed. Sunlight poured like hot oil over his head and it seemed the day would never pass and night would never fall. Exhausted, his eyes were stupefied with swirling colors. He laid his cheek against the hot, wet wood and a ripple of sea water washed over his face. He returned gratefully to a fitful doze.

When eventually he opened his eyes again the sea was utterly calm, but lifting his head he saw a dark rim along the horizon to the west and a gray line becoming darker. Soon it split into a black upper half and a silver lower that reached down to trail like a metal curtain to the sea. The air around him became motionless as a faint hissing sound grew louder; another storm approached.

The first drops of rain knocked like lead beads against the coffin. When they struck the shirt on his back the chill of cold water sent such tremors through him he nearly lost his grip. Carefully he raised his chest from the coffin and straddled its center to balance himself with his legs. Rain drops then fell fast and hard and he shivered. Sitting nearly upright with his hands free, he stripped off his shirt. Pellets of rain struck his naked skin like needles of ice. A breeze blew cold across his chest and he struggled to hold on.

When the storm reached him its torrent fell suddenly. His head tipped back and mouth opened wide, the cold water burned his lips as it cooled his face and eyes. He put his arms into the armholes of his shirt and spread its back. Like a beseeching penitent he held it out to catch the rain and the downpour quickly soaked the cloth through. Relaxing his arms, the center of the shirt's back formed a shallow basin and rainwater filled it. He lifted his arms parallel and angled above his head to direct the rainwater toward his face and it poured fresh and cold into his mouth.

He pulled the shirt from his arms and wrung out as much salt as he could. When it was thoroughly soaked he wrung it out into his mouth. As long as he kept it out of the seawater the cloth would become his canteen. And as if this concern brought it about, the sea began to swell and roll threatening his balance. The rain eased gradually but a strong, cold wind arose. He struggled to remain upright over the coffin, the soggy bundle in his hand held as reverently as a holy book.

When the rain stopped and the clouds broke up, the sun had nearly reached the horizon and the air was cooler. The opposite horizon had faded into dark blue. He held the shirt to his lips as his other hand insured his balance. He sucked the water slowly, turning the cloth to spots where it became concentrated.

As moisture on the shirt's surface ran out, he squeezed it harder to surrender its last drops. But when he nearly fell backward from the coffin, he tried to maneuver to slip the shirt back over his head until a gust of wind snatched it from his fingers. It flew through the air landing far beyond his reach and slowly drifted away.

To his surprise, along the rim of eastern twilight Pierre saw something glint as if a star had come to rest on the horizon. He blinked hard twice but that light remained steady. Eventually he had to admit this might not be a hallucination. And then his fear edged toward panic.

But he was reassured that at least fear was a kind of thinking, and since he was thinking, he must still exist. Though the world, this sea and that sky, even the wooden box he floated upon might no longer exist, if he was being fooled, he must still exist in order to be fooled. Of course, the Pierre that existed still could not swim. So if the water existed, he was in trouble. Gabriella had warned him of this and much else as well.

He had resolved to find Augustus, and his reward was to float alone in the middle of the ocean on another man's coffin hours from death.

Augustus had moved his family from Montreal to the new city of Philadelphia since it would soon become the center of scientific research. But nine of the intervening years Pierre had waited for his father's return. At first Augustus had been excited by the prospect of continuing his studies in a large and sophisticated city. It had taken less than a year for him to grow disillusioned and depressed and his excitement turn to bitterness. Pierre realized then that his father's departure had become inevitable.

The day Augustus announced he would travel to Europe, Pierre was one month short of his ninth birthday. His father sat at the head of their small table insisting his mind was made up. He had received letters from eminent scientists in Europe who would confirm his discoveries, his work would raise a fortune and he would return a rich man. Pierre still remembered the horror on Gabriella's face that night, an expression like none he had ever seen before and whose remnants never again left her face. Years later he still recalled those days before his father's departure as a whirl, but then he was gone. When that old sailor appeared carrying Augustus's letter, Pierre recognized it was time he took responsibility for his father's return. More than a year passed and events intervened but that letter remained a bit of shell inside an oyster and Pierre waited without waiting as its tiny pearl grew. But it began with that letter. He looked down into the black sea and its ghost drifted to its surface.

From afar I wish you good health and satisfactory bowel movements. I write from a rat-hole of a room to assure you of my continued existence. The Dutch are a filthy, mean-spirited and foul-smelling people, but they have not attempted to kill me, which is more than can be said for the Italian, the Spanish, and most assuredly the French. Cold and wet constantly, my condition reminds me of miserable Montreal. I have yet to acquire permanent accommodations so my experiments remain still-born. Paying employment has been harder to find than an honest doctor. I have managed to gain some technical work and thus body and soul remain conjoined, much to my surprise. But the good news: recently I met with none other than Henry Oldenburg, recording secretary for the Royal Society. Though I should not be surprised, he confessed a vague familiarity with my efforts. He is a tall, prissy man with too-thin hands and a cheap smile and he has an annoying way of speaking his language, but truth to tell he appears to know nearly everyone of any moment. He would not agree to sponsor my work but he offered an introduction to a Jew of Amsterdam by the name of Spinoza who, he says, is genuinely brilliant and who Leibniz speaks well of and who has frequent need of assistance grinding lenses. Though it means I must remain in this revolting country, I will contact the man, and if he is half as Oldenburg proclaims I will offer my services. I embrace you and your dear mother. May your digestion be regular and your sleep sound. I think of you both often, and frequently with pleasure. I will write again soon.

– Your father –

PS—do not pay the bearer of this letter as he is a scabrous knave and scoundrel and beneath the contempt of honorable people.

When he had finished reading the letter he began it again, but there had been so little to it that he found he had already memorized it. With nothing more to be learned from it he carried it into the kitchen. Gabriella had just returned from the market. She looked into his face and said, "It's from your father, isn't it?" Without waiting she snatched it from his fingers and climbed the stairs. She was upstairs a long time. He never saw the letter again and she never spoke of it.

The evening the letter arrived Pierre found that he could not sleep. He reviewed every phrase trying to hear Augustus's voice in it, a sound he could not quite conjure in his mind's ear. The words of the letter moved through his mind again and again until they lost all weight and became a series of sounds. As young as he was, he realized he had received his mission though he did not understand what having such a mission meant. The world is a dark and fog-shrouded place and time passed before he thought again about the letter and about his father. But when finally he did, he recognized that his path had already been marked out and its steps defined. The old sailor had given him his destiny without intention or expectation. The dice had been cast, they merely had rolled to a place where Pierre could not see them.

In Augustus's absence Pierre had taken responsibility for Gabriella and worked hard to keep up the tavern but he saw that her best years were passing. Work aged her, but her real torment was the absence of Augustus. Finally it was time to take up that responsibility. Besides, at least he would no longer need to listen to Gabriella's hectoring complaints.

The coffin rocked gently on a calming sea and Pierre relaxed his grip on its handles. The colors of the twilight sky shifted, shards of clouds like bits of torn paper became pink and then blue and finally black. Another night was falling, it's softening light and mild breeze embraced him. The first sliver of light from the moon appearing on the horizon felt as if a friend had returned to keep him company. Afloat beneath its shimmering light he fell into a spiral of despair. Was his fate less macabre than that of those who had been devoured by the creature?

In this despair he thought how easy it would be to slip from his life-raft. He need merely not hold on quite so hard. After all, his fingers had become nearly numb anyway.

His first attempt to accomplish something serious in the large and serious world was about to cause his death. He had needed just a few days to fail. He looked around to admire the result of his ambition; afloat on a sliver of wood in the most abysmal ignorance. On the brink of losing his life, not a shred of its puzzle had been resolved, not the smallest morsel of truth revealed. The miasma of cosmic life had collapsed onto this one tiny point in the center of his nearly infinite ocean. If his end must be pathetic and dismal and ludicrous, there should be a hint to the decision to end it and informed by nothing except crystalline reasonableness.

Yet his heart withered. Thinking about Gabriella and the work she had devoted to their survival, her struggle to maintain the Captain Hudson and how little she would be left with, and tears welled hot in his eyes. He glimpsed the life that was about to end, a flash of all that could have been savored and was about to be lost. Her face appeared before his eyes, her lips whispered beside his ear, and then Pierre retreated from the chasm. If there was a chance of rescue, he might at least be rescued to her and then he might rescue her in return. But tears rolled in waves from his eyes; tears for his dreams and the dreams of others within their dreams.

He glanced up to see that spot of light still hovered on the horizon. When he looked for it again it had become larger and brighter. Bobbing with the breeze he tried to keep it in view. Momentarily it became still brighter, but when the sun at his back dropped below the horizon it blinked out. He waited staring into the dark expecting to see that light again. It must still be out there, something must be there, perhaps even watching him. Had the creature returned for him, the only life it had missed? But it was exhaustion that eventually devoured Pierre so that sometimes he seemed to sleep and then he would wake consumed by fear.

Something was out there and perhaps even watching him, and he did not believe it would bring him any luck at all.

CHAPTER THREE

THICK, KNOB-KNUCKLED hands clasped before her, Gabriella stands at the threshold of the wood-and-stone framed tavern gazing up at Pierre with stunned sadness. The morning sun poised at the horizon casts a golden slanting light. The pink blossoms of the dogwood tree beside the door tremble with a humid breeze that blows her gray-black hair into a wiry iron swirl. He no longer wonders how she gets so far out into the ocean, but only who is watching the bar and has enough firewood been cut.

Water lapped at his face, someone groaned and then Pierre awoke. The sun bloomed full above the horizon and already hot. The sky spun slowly, its motion along with his hunger and the bitter water made him nauseous. And the coffin certainly had begun to sink. He would not criticize the Savage's workmanship but he searched the horizon with the taste of panic in his throat.

Where he had seen a glittering point of light on the edge of the horizon, an unlikely silhouette now perched, and the motion of the sea regularly put it over his shoulder until, glancing back it seemed to move to another spot along the horizon. He wondered if it was moving in his direction and whether he should be concerned.

Stunned with a sudden desire to sleep, his face dropped back to the surface of the coffin as his limbs became numb. A tremor passed through him and he forced himself to lift his head once more. When he found the silhouette again it was closer and now resembled a ship. He was annoyed by his indifference and then his eyes closed.

The old sailor arrived at the Captain Hudson one afternoon in late summer. Heat hung in the air like an invisible fog. Pierre sat on a stool behind the bar dozing over a volume of Euclid. Gabriella had gone to shop for food for their evening meal. He looked up to find the old sailor standing on the tavern's threshold and peering about until he saw that Pierre was alone and then smiled. With his empty right pant-leg folded to his thigh, he made his way with his crutch thumping the wood floor. Pierre had seen one-legged sailors before but the sight still startled him. The old sailor reached the bar grinning.

"A fine establishment you have here," he said looking about as if he might buy the place. "A tight ship, just the sort I like. Offers a welcome of great warmth for an old sailor, if you get my meaning." Then he turned his full attention on Pierre. "I don't suppose you're the owner here, young and bright-eyed as you are."

Wishing the old fool would leave him to his book Pierre explained that the tavern belonged to his mother. But the sailor brightened at his words, asked her name and where she was at that moment. With Pierre's answers, the old sailor's eyes brightened more.

"That's the best of news because it means I've docked at the right birth. And mind you, that after a long and hard voyage. But you won't want to know about that. You want to know why I'm here and what it is I have for you. And when I tell you, you'll want to buy me a drink, there ain't no doubt about that." The old sailor's laugh exposed gray and brown teeth.

"You're not from around here, I know that for a fact."

"Do you, now? I was told you was a clever boy and here you are, bright as fresh paint and clever as a monkey. No doubt about it, I've reached safe harbor."

"I'm glad to hear that," Pierre said, his patience ebbing. "Now as soon as you tell me why you're here, we'll both know."

"Ah, mathematically correct," the old sailor said. A guarded look came into his eyes. "But we're leaping ahead of ourselves, ain't we now. The name is Silver on account of that was the name of my father, the Devil toss him to the deepest hold in Hell. My sainted mother named me John after her brother who died defending England from the Spanish dogs. Not that you'd know about that being so young and all. I first went to sea a cabin boy younger than yourself and the sea's been all the family I've ever wished for. Docked at a hundred ports and found a good reason to leave each one." He laughed quietly at his own joke.

"Quite a story," Pierre said, his irritation rising with his boredom. "I expect you've seen a lot of the world."

"Bright as fresh paint, boy, and that's no bad guess. I could tell you stories make your eyes drop from your head. But that ain't what I'm about today, not at all. I come here on a mission, I have. Some time back a man give me something. I was becalmed in Antwerp last winter. The Dutch are an awful people and smell worse than anything. But the man I'm speaking of weren't no Dutchman, thank God. Met him in a tavern. Though it bothers me for saying it, the man I'm speaking of was adrift as it were, cadging drinks and arguing with whoever'd listen. Clearly an educated man, I felt sorry for him as you might say. The Good Lord don't help one without punishing another, and seeing this man, I thought, the world being what it is, I could be in his shoes before sunset. So I invited him to heave-to and bought him a tankard of lager. Well, no sooner did I do that but at once he become the most pleasant and interesting a table-mate as any sailor could wish. Full of the oddest bits of information, he was. Of course, after a time he become tedious, but this I find common among the better-educated types, if you see my point. Friendly though, and polite. When finally he asked after my affairs and I told him I was shipping out for America, well his eyes got big as doubloons, they did. Like he had to think about it a moment but then he reached into his shirt and brought out this." Suddenly the sailor held a folded piece of paper soiled and wrinkled as though it had traveled far.

"Now, you need to understand," he continued as he held the piece of paper in one hand using it to fan the hot and heavy air, "I'm not one to make a promise lightly, not at all. If I say to you I promise to do a thing, well sir, mark it down as good as done, that's the sort of fellow I am. So when this man says to me, please be sure this gets to where it needs to go, and I says to that man, sir, I promise it will be delivered, well, that was all there was to it."

But Pierre only half-listened because his eyes would not leave that piece of paper the old sailor waved between two fingers.

"And as you be the person I was told about." He laid the paper on the bar and slid it slowly toward Pierre leaving his fingertips resting on its edge,

"I've done just as I promised." He lifted his hand away and the paper lay as if abandoned.

Pierre reached for the paper but the old sailor's hand suddenly covered it again. Leaning forward, in a whisper he said, "No disrespect intended, but I was assured that you was the paying-kind." His grin was sheepish.

Looking into the old sailor's eyes Pierre reached under the bar. His hand appeared and he placed a gold guinea beside the paper. The old sailor's eyes grew large. His hand lifted from the paper and covered the coin. In a moment the hand and guinea disappeared.

"That's exactly the thing, good sir, just exactly the thing, yes it is." His eyes closed and a gratified smile came to his face. Pierre picked up the paper, unfolded it and began to read, but already the sailor had stepped from the bar and hobbled his way to the door. Calling over his shoulder he said, "I would accept that drink were it offered, but it appears you have other matters to attend to so I'll just thank you for your time and for listening to an old sailor's tale." He reached the door and turned. "And please convey my deepest respect to your dear mother." Pierre glanced up long enough to watch him reach the street and hobble off far more quickly than his condition might suggest.

Pierre held in his hand a letter from Augustus dated more than a year before. He read it half-way through before he noticed his hand was trembling.

Waves flowing over the coffin woke him. It was plain his life-raft was sinking. He lifted his head again to search the water around him for a piece of wreckage to cling to but the storm had scattered everything. He decided that even if the silhouette belonged to the creature he could not die a worse death.

Between fits of dozing he watched it approach and by the time the sun reached the horizon its outline was certain. Growing up by the docks, he knew ships from any distance so he recognized this as a four-masted carrack. But most curious was the way the ship seemed to sparkle, as if it was covered with bright metal and the glint from its hull was an effect of the light of the setting sun. But at least this was not the creature. He enjoyed an unlikely sense of gratitude that his end would come by mere drowning.

The hard horizon split the red setting sun in half. He guessed the ship's distance and the angle of its approach and feared it would pass without seeing him. To be saved he needed to attract its attention. He struggled to hold one arm in the air but nearly slipped sideways from the coffin. With possible rescue so near he could not risk losing his grasp of the coffin. But his strength was fading with the light and he had to find a way to attract its attention.

Perhaps by paddling with his hands he could put the sun nearing the horizon at his back. Align the coffin between the setting sun and the ship and then sit upright, he might offer a silhouette of his own. Water lapping over the coffin reminded him it was filling with water.

Slipping his feet through the handles at the lower end he fixed the coffin tightly between his knees. With the water inside as ballast, he raised his chest and slid his hips toward the back end. The front of the coffin lifted. He found that his weight could lift it to poise close to vertical. But even with his feet in the handles, his balance was precarious and he knew he could not maintain it long. He had not stopped sinking, but only exchanged one ineffectual posture for another.

The ship reflected the glare of the setting sun so brightly it appeared to hover just above the water. The light and the strain of following the ship's course forced Pierre to close his eyes. So he needed some time to recognize that the ship had changed course and was approaching. He wondered then who could be sailing this ship.

Captain Hawthorne had said their maneuvers to escape the creature had taken them far south of the Atlantic trade routes. Could this be a slave ship? Or another merchant ship driven off course by the storm? Or maybe even pirates? He had heard stories at the tavern about pirates so he knew to fear for his life. Pirates made unlikely friends and rescue by them could prove worse than death.

As fearful as he might be, that tiny shape offered his only hope. Whatever its crew, it could not be worse than an attack by the creature. Otherwise, his fate was simply to drown, unremarked and unknown. Whatever was about to happen, he could neither avoid it nor step forward to meet it. Tossed about over a bottomless sea on a box slowly filling with water, he measured his future in hours. So, for as long as he could, he waved one arm and then the other as the gestures of a desperate man drowning in air.

With the ship close enough for him to see the flag atop the main mast, he recognized it as a black skull and cross-bones and enjoyed an odd relief; one mystery had been resolved. No longer any point to wondering if his salvation would also be his end since his end was more likely than his salvation.

The ship was still far off when he saw a long boat with several figures in it lower and begin to move toward him. He tried to prepare himself; he tried to say good-bye to Gabriella. He apologized for doubting her, for having failed her, and for all the years he would not be by her side in her old age. And he apologized to Augustus, the cause of his dilemma yet not a culprit, just as Pierre recognized himself, not as the product of a process, but accomplice, if not the playwright then the director of his own misery.

The tiny boat rose and fell against the sharp line of the horizon and he recalled the words of the Divine Descartes. That which is clear and distinct must be true, just as the line of the horizon must be true, regardless of whether a human mind perceives it. He closed his eyes again. The light changed and the color of the sky shifted from blue to a pale green.

The longboat grew larger, silhouettes of the bending backs of its rowers more distinct. The sky appeared to be turning red as the sea turned a bloody violet. He became light-headed, his limbs drained of strength and he fell forward onto the coffin breathing as if he had been running a long time.

Face down on his bobbing raft, he wondered. Despite his father's tutoring nothing he thought had helped him to avoid this fate. Like some lonely explorer following a long-abandoned path, by reading the volumes he had left behind he had tried to pursue Augustus through the thickets and over the rocky precipices of natural philosophy. Its effort left his head throbbing, yet he gained a vague familiarity with thoughts that still befuddled his own. But this fate had found him, and what was about to happen was all that could happen, regardless of what he wished. His reading had seemed to offer a glimpse of a world of possibilities yet he was now surrounded by impossibilities. His reading encouraged him to savor his own thoughts which in the next instant erased themselves to leave a bottomless void cluttered with their fragments.

The cry of a human voice opened Pierre's eyes. The voice was deep and clear and he wondered how such a voice could be contained within his head. Had someone in the longboat called to him? That would demand the longboat exist. It would also demand that it contain existing men. The apparent man at the apparent tiller waved his apparent arm and called out to Pierre.

He wondered if he should wave his own arm in reply. But suppose the boat did not exist and by waving he slipped from the coffin? He leaned forward, closed his eyes and rested his cheek against the coffin. Thinking, he concluded, was hard work demanding much practice and he was no longer sufficient for the effort.

Suddenly something gripped Pierre's arm and pulled it hard. He imagined the creature's huge teeth sinking deep into his flesh, blood running red down his arm and into a sea surrounded by creatures made ravenous by its scent. As it offered no advantage he decided not to open his eyes. The grip tightened and pulled hard. Determined to keep his eyes shut, he held onto his coffin with all of his strength. And then he felt himself fly up into the air.

He opened his eyes and what he saw made him smile. He wondered if he was in the presence of an angel, though he knew that angels did not exist and whether somehow he had entered that heaven which he also knew did not exist. Nonexistence, he suspected, was no impediment to reality.

The angel grinned. "Ah hah! Movement of the eye suggests death is not yet victorious."

Pierre discovered himself lying on the wet and rough bottom of the longboat. Five faces smiled down at him. The face at the tiller came close to Pierre's. "Hang on, friend, you are nearly home."

The rocking of the boat and the rhythm of the rowers let his consciousness drift. He clutched at it yet it slipped like oil through his fingers. His understanding surged and ebbed with the motion of the oars.

Suddenly with a dull, ringing thud the longboat struck something hard. Through his hazy vision he looked up to see that the ship's hull towering over him was painted white to the water line. He smiled, another curiosity gratified. Ropes slithered down toward him. He felt himself rise from the rocking boat and sway in the breeze. Then he sat on the deck of the ship with his back propped against the gunwale.

His legs were useless. Splayed out before him they seemed attachments to his body without significance. Looking up he found himself surrounded by faces studying him with curious sympathy. From the babble of their voices he knew he was being questioned but their words baffled him. He swayed with the motion of the ship but could not disentangle anything from the rest of everything. Strong hands reached under his arms and lifted him. He stood hoping like a drunk that in another moment he would be sober but failed and returned to the deck.

And then he watched stride toward him the largest and ugliest man he had ever seen. He hoped this was another illusion conjured by his fog-shrouded mind.

The man seemed to approach for a long time, as if the deck he crossed reached to the horizon and was covered with molasses. But when he stopped in front of Pierre he loomed over him like a dark mountain. Tall with wide, thick shoulders and wearing a bright green coat the size of a tent, his midnight-black hair long and thick with ringlets sprouted from his head at every angle, along with a black beard even thicker and longer, so that his nut-brown face appeared small in the center of an enormous black halo. But most remarkable his glittering black eyes seemed to pierce Pierre though his chest.

"You have seen the creature!" the man cried, his face so close to Pierre's that his hot breath washed over his face like putrid vapors from Hell. "That creature's been here and you've seen it! Tell me, tell me! You've seen it! Tell me now where it's gone."

Gradually the ship and the faces around Pierre and the sky above him all began to fade to a comforting gray, all except for the sharp black eyes and hideous face before him. The fog became dense and then darker. A space opened beneath Pierre, he felt himself drift down for a long time but he found no luck down there at all.

CHAPTER FOUR

SOMETHING SEEMED to be before Pierre's eyes but unlikely perception and reality were identical and more probable he suffered from a powerful hallucination.

The pitch and sway calmed him; a murmur that was not the sea assured him he may not exist but that which existed was safe. He floated among a wreckage of perceptions adrift within him yet not of him. Moments scattered like pearls from a broken thread; bursts of images left him bobbing on a turbulent surface.

That second angel had been the Devil. With harsh sounds to beat at him like the pounding surf in a storm, that Devil had left him falling face down upon suffocating darkness, a drifting descent. Panic drove Pierre to reach to restrain his plunge back into that black sea. His opened eyes discovered a brightening light.

"Welcome back. Feared we had lost you. How are you feeling?"

Looking about, Pierre discovered he lay in a bunk within a cabin. Suspicious of words he hesitated as if his body might be its own ghost. "If I'm not dead then I must be alive."

Another smiling face laughed. "Dualism is the product of consciousness." Pale, round, blue-eyed, and with a grin so wide Pierre felt himself smile. "On the possibility your confusion is genuine, I assure you that you are alive and safe but for hours you have slipped in and out of consciousness."

Finally Pierre accepted this avalanche of sensation and he turned to look about. The smiling face said, "Our Good Lord has given you into our hands and we will not fail His trust."

"But who are you?" The sound of his own voice startled Pierre.

The man's expression changed from sympathy to relief. "Curiosity will forever dispel despair. As for your appropriate question, I am Aubin Robert D'Arcy, Count de Boulogne. The ship that gives you shelter is called the Revenge, and its captain, who you have met, is Monsieur Henry William Stevenson. That is as much as your mind can tolerate. Like water after a long thirst, knowledge is most useful taken in small sips. But I expect you would enjoy a light meal. Since I do not wish to mock your condition, I will not ask you to wait, but only promise to return soon."

Pierre glanced up through the porthole to see a sharp blue sky. "So my dreams haven't been dreams."

"I can tell you nothing about that."

In a moment images he could not distinguish from dreams cascaded before his eyes. The Count said, "From your expression it is true, you have seen the creature." He left quietly closing the door.

The tiny cabin Pierre found himself within was comprised of four bunks stacked in pairs against opposing walls and a small table between. Raising himself onto his elbow he found his bunk included a padded mattress and its linens were soft and clean. Somehow he had fallen into a world of wealth far beyond his experience. But then he wondered if all this too was a dream.

With a quiet knock the Count reappeared carrying a silver tray. "Considering our effort to rescue you, it would be ungrateful of you to suddenly depart." Seeing the tray Pierre remembered his thirst and reached toward it, but the Count restrained his hand. "Our ship's doctor, Gervase Culbert de Montagne, Baron de Faubourg, will join us to review your condition. His reprimand would be justified if I permitted you to drink yourself ill. So have some of this broth before you slack your thirst for water."

Grasping the bowl to bring it to his lips his hands trembled. Smiling with sympathy, the Count sat down beside Pierre. "Allow me."

Exhaustion overwhelmed Pierre and he fell back dazed. "That would be most appreciated." The Count took up the spoon on the tray and Pierre added, "With respect, you should kindly tell me how you wish to be addressed."

"We make remarkable progress," the Count said. "I am told you Americans are unfamiliar with the protocols of royalty. But you, good sir, demonstrate that the citizenry there is not raised without the civilities. Still, in keeping with the democratic ambition of our ship, kindly address me as Count." Smirking as if he had made a remarkable joke he offered a spoonful of broth to Pierre who accepted and instantly decided it was delicious.

"Since you now know my name," the Count said, "suppose you tell me yours." Pierre introduced himself and the Count appeared pleased. "Undoubtedly this is the first time you have been fed by royalty. So that you may conserve your strength permit me to tell you about ourselves and our mission." Pierre leaned back relieved.

"You have heard, no doubt, of the Convent of the Port-Royal." When Pierre confessed he had not, the Count shrugged. "This ocean which separates us is no mere metaphor. So you are unfamiliar with the treasonous collaboration between our monarch and the Pope in Rome. We are decedents of those true followers of the Good Father Cornelius Jansen who you have heard labeled Huguenots. With our families forced into exile for our faith, we have sworn to establish a community beyond the reach of either despot."

He explained that having been made destitute by the King they decided to build a colony in the New World. "It may seem unlikely to you that we have chosen the villainous Jamaican seaport of Port Royal, but establishment of our colony will please the Lord, vanquish heretics and defy papacy and monarchy in one stroke." His grin charmed Pierre.

"So you pursue King Louis's ships?" Pierre asked simply to exercise his voice.

"Dutch, British or Spanish ships we empty without distinction since each upholds the Papacy's world order." His grin became a leer. "But we prefer the French prize."

"You commit infamies to sustain a house of God."

Sneering, the Count brought another spoonful of the broth to Pierre's lips. "Deprived of our wealth and social standing and with the King's backside turned to us we yearned for reconciliation and were betrayed at every turn." Each word increased his agitation. "But all of that is behind us and our holy mission lies before us."

"It seems I've been saved by traitorous heretics fleeing from cross and crown. Once again I'm the beneficiary of a heathen's charity."

Though he could not guess the reference the Count's smile was bright. "Life's greatest pleasure is conversation with a sharp mind. We are better Christians than either potentate, and our mission will expose their debauchery."

The cabin door suddenly swung wide with a crash to reveal the ugliest man Pierre had ever seen. Recoiling in his bunk, he recognized him as the Devil who had promised to send him to Satan if he did not tell him what he wanted to know. He bellowed, "You wretched piece of a dog's arse; tell me where that creature is before I feed your carcass to the sharks!"

Pierre was too startled to reply but then someone stepped up behind the man. The Count stood and introduced him as Gervase Culbert de Montaigne. A round man, flush-faced and cheery, a fringe of brown-red hair circled a shining pink head. "A better ship's doctor does not sail waters salt or fresh."

The Doctor added, "Certainly better than any of you deserve." Turning he said, "And you, Captain, are just the man I wish to speak to. The first-mate claims we approach an island having both fresh water and animals for meat. As we are in need I ask that we make for it."

"By God," the Captain roared, "that creature is near and you wish to pick flowers. When this flotsam tells us where the creature can be found, that is where we will sail!"

"But Captain," the Count interrupted, "to continue our chase we must have supplies."

The Doctor added, "Besides, this man must rest to give you dependable information."

Pierre then heard the sudden cry of, "Ship ahoy! Ship ahoy!"

Smiling to the Captain, Count D'Arcy asked, "Shall we make this prize our own?"

Captain Stevenson glared from one face to the next until his black eyes settled on Pierre. "Rest and reflect, for tomorrow your memories will become as vivid to me as my own, I will see so clearly into their repository."

With a scolding tone the Count said, "He is in no condition to answer questions."

The Captain fixed the Count with a terrible glance. "It'll be different when the creature devours us. Lying all together crushed and mangled in his gut, you'll sing a different tune."

The Doctor asked, "Does that appeal to you?"

“Can’t say I dumb hate it.”

After a moment the Count said, “We are needed on deck.”

Captain Stevenson crouched down, brought his face level with Pierre’s and stared into his eyes. “We saved that coffin since you don’t seem to have quite finished with it.” His black eyes sparkled in the light from the porthole.

Count D’Arcy placed his hand on the Captain’s shoulder. “We are needed on deck.” He turned to Pierre. “I am certain you will excuse us.”

The Captain stood slowly and seemed to fill the cabin to its edges. His black hair and black beard billowed around his face. Words seemed to gather behind his lips yet he simply clenched his right fist before he turned and left. To the Doctor, the Count said, “Do not dawdle; our guest will excuse your absence.” He followed the Captain and in another moment Pierre heard the Captain bellow orders as their steps overhead moved across the deck.

The Doctor filled a cup with water and from a small brown bottle added two drops. He swirled the cup before handing it to Pierre. “This will help you sleep.”

Pierre glanced into the cup. The Doctor said, “Matters appear in a better light after one has consumed a satisfying meal, believe me on this.”

With another dubious peek into the cup Pierre said, “As soon as I’ve told him what he wants to know your Captain’ll tosses me overboard.” He tried to challenge the Doctor with his glance but the Doctor was not impressed. Pierre drank the liquid back in a single swallow.

“I doubt that. You have Count D’Arcy on your side. He and the Captain will argue over your fate until the Captain drinks himself into a stupor and reveals himself to be a kind-hearted person. Believe me, after several draughts of rum, all will be settled to the Count’s satisfaction.”

“It seems so unlikely such a man is ever kind,” Pierre said. Suddenly dazed he struggled to keep his eyes open.

“Deep in his cups,” the Doctor, “I have seen him forgive the gravest outrage and offer his financial resources to aid his enemy.” He sighed. “It surpasses understanding but he can only fill his heart with goodwill by drinking, just as others drink to empty theirs.”

Pierre watched the ceiling of the cabin tilt and begin to fade. “I saw the creature, I watched it, but what is it he thinks he needs to know?”

“He is certain there is something you have forgotten. Besides, you are the only man who has had contact with that creature and survived."

The words in Pierre's mouth became pudding-thick. "So why did you choose him as your captain?"

The Doctor appeared startled. "In a dangerous situation he is the only man I would want by my side. I have seen him hold off three attackers with a saber and I have seen him shoot out the eye of a seagull with a pistol. But you will see that his heart is as stout as the sides of this ship."

Pierre's eyes became heavy and he struggled to keep them open. "Sleep now," the Doctor said. "Dinner, I promise, will be excellent. Having brought along our favorite chief, our dinners are even better than our luncheons. Meanwhile, if the Count believes I am needed, he is probably correct." He stood and moved toward the door.

Perhaps from excitement, or perhaps from curiosity, Pierre became suddenly alert. "Your Captain seems to believe he could survive a battle with the creature."

Resting his hand on the door handle the Doctor turned. With an expression more amused than curious he said, "Tell me, then; can this creature be defeated by men?"

Pierre's vision grew hazy. "Nothing short of God Himself will defeat that creature. Tell your Captain; if you value your life do everything to avoid it. It will bring only pain and misery and death."

Impressed by Pierre's urgency he hesitated but then smiled. "Still, there is the pursuit of ships and I tell you, man, that is good fun!" With a promise to return later, he left.

Alone, Pierre's eyes became heavy as stones. He had met the executors of his fate and learned what was expected of him. He wondered again if the creature was prowling nearby. With a shiver he considered the wooden planks separating him from its jaws, those rows of enormous, yellow teeth and that throat open in a deafening roar; all came unwilled to his mind's eye.

He awoke to find that the candle above his bunk had been lit casting an orange glow around the cabin. Through the porthole he saw that night had fallen. He sat up intending to stand when he heard sounds through the bulkhead beside his bunk. He leaned his ear against it and recognized voices. The loudest was the Captain's. "I've searched a long time, but never have I been so close to the creature. We should toss the boy out on a line and drag the ocean with him; let the creature get his scent."

Another voice Pierre did not recognize said, "I hold no animosity toward our castaway, but I would prefer to avoid sharing our plunder. Throw him back and be done with him."

Another voice spoke in agreement. "I told you it was a bad idea to pick him up."

The next voice to speak Pierre recognized as that of Count D'Arcy. "The consensus seems to be that this man is a burden and we should rid ourselves of him."

A cold wave of fear crashed over Pierre. He looked about to recognize his luxurious cabin as a charming cage. Then he wondered how much luck he might still possess and whether it would be enough.

CHAPTER FIVE

SILENCE SQUEEZED DOWN on Pierre him until he wanted to call out.

"Remember that he has been given into our care by a loving God." This voice belonged to the Count. "And perhaps he possesses some skill or knowledge to benefit our crusade."

"I know his benefit," the Captain interrupted with a growl. "If ever there was a man born to be animal bait, he is that man. Use him as the Lord intends."

"This ship carries a small crew," the Doctor responded. "If he is willing and clever, considering his predicament I believe he will accept a reduced share. And if he proves to have no value, that other option remains."

In the silence that followed, Pierre hoped simply to recognize the moment when he should learn to swim. Then the Count spoke. "Gervaise gives us sufficient reason to keep him with us until we find reason to be rid of him. By show of hands; all in favor?" Pierre dreaded the silence that followed. "All opposed?" Again there was only silence.

Count D'Arcy said. "Captain, we will add this man to our crew with the understanding that his return to the sea and God's mercy remains an option." The Captain simply grunted. The Count continued, "We will anticipate his contribution to our mission and invite him to sign ship's articles. Unless there is other business, this meeting is concluded." Pierre listened until the shuffle of feet and murmur of voices faded.

Panic clutched at his throat. He tried to stand only to find large, brightly colored lights spinning before his eyes and then he discovered himself sitting on the deck. He reached about to try once more to stand when the door opened.

The Count quietly laughed. "Our prodigal feels well enough to take a trip. What do you think, Doctor? By modern standards this is not a very long journey."

The Doctor responded, "Distant enough to exhaust our guest."

Hands reached under Pierre arms and lifted him to a standing position. The dizzy spin of the room returned and he grabbed the edge of his bunk for balance. "Must be out of practice."

"Or perhaps," the Count added, "it has been too long since you have had a meal. What do you think, Doctor? Is he strong enough to take food?"

"He is overdue." The Doctor turned, stepped back through the door and called up the hatchway, "Denis!" In a moment a reedy, high-pitched voice called in response. The Doctor requested a meal be brought down and then returned to the cabin. "Viscount Denis Hubert-Valentine combines the subtle tastes of a chef with the dexterity of a brilliant swordsman. For as long as you are with us, no one in Paris will eat as well as you."

Pierre returned to his bunk. "And how long might that be?"

Discomforted silence suddenly drifted thick in the air. The Count and the Doctor exchanged glances. The Count said, "It appears we owe him an explanation." Turning to Pierre he said, "We live as if we are our only company and as good as a universe. For this we beg your patience. We guard our venture and no sacrifice is too great, not even that of the life of a stranger, if he endangers the enterprise."

Adopting a light-hearted charm, the Doctor added, "What the Count says with little elegance is that we will help you, yet the limit of our tolerance is any threat to our enterprise. We are hunted men, but make no mistake, we will not fail."

The Count added, "Your best path is to give free reign to your talents and discover which are of use to our mission."

The Doctor continued, "Begin by telling our Captain all you know of the creature."

Pierre was about to confess his confusion when another face appeared at the door. The Count turned with a sigh of pleasure. "Man of the hour, Viscount Denis Hubert-Valentine, and no doubt bearing a king's repast."

Half-hidden behind the large, silver-covered tray he carried, the Chef was short and round with a round, dark-complexioned face and thick, cherubic lips. Pierre detected an aroma so tantalizing he forgot his questions.

In a high-pitched and musical voice Chef Denis said, "Monsieur le Count is too kind." His fingers were short and thick, yet arranging Pierre's platter they moved with swift certainty. Addressing Pierre he continued, "I have prepared this meal so quickly it is barely palatable and I can only hope you will not spit it out in disgust. Simply accept my promise that your next meal will be worthy of the high esteem the Doctor and the Count offer."

Pierre's stomach began to grumble. The Count said, "Were I granted a last meal before death, I hope Monsieur le Viscount would condescend to prepare that meal for me."

Pierre was about to bring a fork-full of potatoes to his lips when footsteps suddenly resounded down the gangway and three faces filled the passage.

"I say," the face with the thickest beard and blackest hair said, "there appears to be a party going on in our cabin to which we were not invited. Does this seem fair to you fellows?"

"No!" the other two agreed. A face with a reddish brown beard and bright blue eyes said, "Seems only decent when a chap uses another chap's cabin for a party, the least he can do is invite the chap to the party."

"And here we are," said the one with black hair, "having toiled and struggled and ready now to enjoy the fruits of our labor we find our prerogative of party-throwing preempted."

In a firm though friendly voice, the Count said, "If all of you have finished demonstrating that even a clever wit weakens with exposure to the sun, let me introduce you to your new cabin-mate." Resting his hand on Pierre's shoulder he made his introduction. "He has agreed to cast his lot with us but has not eaten in several days. So join me for cognac in the galley and allow him your cabin for another hour. There will be time enough for an exchange of lies and exaggerations." His jibe drew laughter from the three men.

The Doctor stood. "Tomorrow he should be sufficiently rested to meet the rest of the crew, so do not plague him with questions tonight."

To the Doctor, Count D'Arcy said, "And will you join us for cognac?"

"Yes!" the others exclaimed.

"I could hardly refuse now, could I?"

The Count turned to Pierre. "While I distract these hooligans enjoy your meal and rest."

Overwhelmed, addressing the friendly faces around him Pierre said, "There's no way to express my thanks. You've saved my life. I'm obliged to you and will repay your help." With a flurry of farewells the door closed and he was alone.

With his first taste he recognized that what the Count had said about the meal was true. But he had hardly finished half accompanied by several droughts of water and discovered his stomach was not yet ready for the rest. A pleasant lethargy drifted over him. Drowsy from the rich food, he considered the wisdom of his decision to find Augustus.

"Too many priests!" he remembered Augustus muttering. "Damn city crawls with the buggers. So many priests and so little justice!" Without turning he said, "Save yourself and keep away from priests." A shadow in the twilight of his own workshop, the tall and narrow man leaned forward over a cluttered workbench. Light from the window near the roof shone onto its brass objects. Pierre stood beside his father's elbow, his head just above the edge of the workbench. In that shaft of light he watched supple fingers of gray skin move about.

"Your mother don't understand things like you and me do," Augustus said on another occasion. "Women are like that, it's time you learned that much. Stay away from women," he said with a bitterness that surprised Pierre. "They're always in the dark and they always want to drag you into the dark with them. And stay away from priests; they only know what you shouldn't do. Women and priests all know how to live your life better than you do." Pierre recalled endless harangues over dinner, lectures that continued until Gabriella tried to silence him, and then they would fight and he would climb the stairs to his room pretending he did not hear and would not remember. When Augustus finally left, the first change he noticed was the novelty of silence.

Augustus's narrow, waxy fingers moved nimble as mice among bright brass cogs and axles and glittering brass balances, hair-thin wire springs and elaborately etched scales, and with such ease Pierre imagined each finger possessed consciousness. The workshop had been stocked with bits and pieces of metal and wood, half-finished devices shelved among others dismantled. Most times, Augustus wore a furrow between his eyebrows as if the world conspired against him but he would outmaneuver its thrusts.

Augustus carried out his work accompanied by a stream of mumbled curses against a non-existent God and His non-existent Heaven. Furious that his life was a demonstration of God's perverse humor, he dedicated himself to penetrating His secret realm and turning that power against Him although even Pierre recognized he never managed to resolve that contradiction. Augustus spent his hours creating devices to detect invisible forces by which the work of God was accomplished, or so he explained to Pierre.

He brought his face close to Pierre's, and even now he felt that discomfort as he had stared back into gray, blood-shot eyes already old from staring into the darkness of his workshop. Augustus wanted something from him, he had understood this even at his young age but never recognized what that might be. And after another moment Augustus recognized this as well. The crease in his forehead faded. "You'd need to live a hundred years to understand and you'll be lucky to live twenty-five. Go help your mother and leave me alone." He fled the workshop ashamed but also relieved that he had escaped unscathed.

On another occasion Augustus had turned suddenly to face him with a frustration that was nearly rage. "Some day you'll appreciate what your old man's done. If you knew what I was talking about, then at least that would be something. But no one in this godforsaken wilderness understands what I've achieved." He studied his own skillful fingers as a smile formed on his lips. In a wistful voice he added, "But Newton will understand. And Leibniz will understand. And Oldenburg and Gassendi. Because all that you see, all that I've accomplished, is extraordinary. But the priests'll understand, too, and they'll do something about it." His smile faded, he turned back to the workbench and placed his face in his hands. His fingers became docile, their eyes closed in a kind of sleep. "And then maybe your mother'll understand. Maybe when everyone else agrees, then maybe she'll understand what I've done."

"So explain it to me!" Pierre remembered himself ask, words that escaped his lips as if they were the only ones in his head and they surprised him. "I'll remember until I understand."

Augustus's eyes narrowed and Pierre trembled. His expression suggested there was a voice between his ears speaking quietly and he wanted to catch every word. He turned back to his workbench. "This device proves the relationship between phlogiston and the aether. Just remember that; remember that your old man understood the aether."

Pierre stared hard first at the device on the bench and then at his father's hands and then again at the device as if his words acquired a glow in his mind. He rehearsed that conversation for days and when his father finally left he repeated those words in his head.

In every other way Augustus was an unremarkable man. What Pierre remembered most clearly was his father's back retreating toward his workshop where he worked in copper and brass as he had even before he bought the tavern. To continue his scientific work Augustus had entrusted the tavern to the barely-capable hands of Gabriella and turned to make those elegant and useless objects he insisted eventually would support his family. On many evenings the lamp in the workshop burned until very late and sometimes Pierre would see it still burning as the sun rose.

In the years of his absence Pierre struggled to know the world of his father's mind, of his devices and the mathematics and philosophy behind them, and he had failed. Scrutinizing Augustus's few notebooks, for long moments he would almost believe he had pierced that world, but in the next instant that understanding would collapse. But he recalled his father's words, not just for the evaluation of his intelligence, but his prophesy about Pierre's life. Had he not been saved by this ship, Augustus would have demonstrated remarkable prescience. Yet it was his decision to find Augustus that had put him in this predicament. This bothered him simply for its annoying coincidence.

A shuffle of feet in the gangway outside his door startled Pierre awake and then the door opened. First through the door was a man with reddish brown hair and bright blue eyes. He looked at Pierre and stopped. "Sorry, old man; are we disturbing your beauty sleep?"

"I'd only just dozed off," Pierre said. He recognized this man and the others behind him as those who shared the cabin.

The man behind him was lightly-bearded over a dark complexion. He stepped forward holding in the crook of his arm a dark brown demi-john and he placed it on the small table in the center of the cabin. "We decided some time had passed since your last drink. And this is very good cognac!"

"As we are fortunate to share our cabin with you, we should at least show the courtesy to introduce ourselves." The man speaking had thick black hair. "I am Lorenzo Marcel, Count d'Antoine and a gunner's mate. To my right," he said pointing to the lightly-bearded man, "I introduce you to Abelard, Duke du Bordeaux and ship's poet. And to my left," he said pointing to the man with reddish-brown hair and bright blue eyes, "Jacques Simon, ship's tailor."

Climbing into the bunk on the opposite side of the cabin, Duke du Bordeaux said, "We have heard little but surmised much about your ordeal."

Taking the bunk below the Duke, Count D'Antoine, said, "Your display of tenacity recommends you. You deserve our congratulations for turning a bit of luck into survival."

Jacques Simon climbed into the bunk above Pierre, uncorked the demi-john of cognac and held it down toward him. "Cheers!" From the bunk across, Count D'Antoine grinned. "You have earned this and our respect along with it."

Pierre sat forward and took a short drink. The liquid burned his mouth as its aroma filled his head and he passed it back across the cabin to Count D'Antoine who took the bottle, sipped and then passed it down to Duke Du Bordeaux. "You slept through a great battle," he said to Pierre. The others in their bunks laughed derisively.

"His Majesty the King of Spain's galleon 'Enbricada'," he continued. "Gorgeous vessel."

Jacques-Simone said, "A cannon shot across the bow and she was ours."

"And rich! Wealth a chore to measure," Duke Du Bordeaux said.

"And cases of cognac," Jacques Simone said from above. He reached down to again pass the demi-john to Pierre, who sipped and then passed it along.

Leaning back into his bunk and closing his eyes Duke Du Bordeaux said, "So tell us what brought you to battle a monster. Recite for us as Ulysses in fair Ithaca."

Briefly, Pierre told the story of his father and of his decision to travel to find him. "This world appears to have another plan for me and the creature seems a peculiar instrument."

Silence followed his remark until Count D'Antoine said, "Your mission demands our respect, and your tenacity deserves our praise. But your encounter with that creature fills us with admiration. As you have seen, our Captain is mad on that subject."

"A dangerous delirium, no doubt," Duke Du Bordeaux said without opening his eyes.

"On the contrary," Jacques-Simone said. "There are good reasons to destroy the creature. Above all it must not be permitted to devour men and disrupt the routes of trade unchallenged."

"Unlikely as this must seem," said Count D'Antoine, "I agree with Jacques-Simone. Prosperity for each and harmony for all demands safety and order. The creature only brings an unprofitable anarchy."

"So tell us," Jacques-Simone said to Pierre, "just what is this creature like?"

"Yes," Duke Du Bordeaux said. "In a fight, what do make of our chances?"

Pierre hesitated. "Earlier, I heard the cry of ship ahoy. The Count and the Doctor explained that you practice a form of piracy. Is this true?"

In the silence that followed Pierre suspected he had asked the wrong question. Glancing from one face to the next he recognized he was among conspirators whose votes were cast with the flicker of an eyelid. Count D'Antoine glanced around the cabin. "It is best that your questions are answered by the most reliable source. Every man on this ship has sworn obedience to our enterprise. By this time tomorrow you will know everything you need to know about us, and we about you."

He paused and Pierre wondered if a response was expected. Then eight bells sounded on deck. Count D'Antoine looked up. "Ah, last dog-watch. You have had a hard day; sleep well and rest easy." Jacques-Simone in the top bunk snuffed out the candle throwing the cabin into darkness.

Subtly tossed sightless within the ship, visions of his moments at sea came to Pierre's mind. He clutched at the frame of his bunk until his fingers hurt. But gradually the cognac aided his slow drift to the bottom of a warm sleep. Ragged clouds appeared on the horizon resembling shreds of gray sails afloat on a black sea. Suddenly he saw Augustus's face peering from between those tatters. Had he considered Pierre stupid or merely lucky, and would he have acknowledged any distinction? After all, Augustus was a scientist and luck is an utterly unscientific concept. There is no such thing as a lucky scientist.

CHAPTER SIX

FROM THE BUNK above, Pierre heard Jacques-Simone exclaim, "Late rising is a certain sign of royal lineage."

"Pay no attention to him," Duke Du Bordeaux said to Pierre from his bunk above. "But if your pinched belly expects breakfast, you had better move faster than I."

Pierre stood to discover he felt almost normal and very hungry. He followed his new shipmates along a gangway with a slowly-dawning sense that nothing worse could happen than what he had survived. They reached the galley and as he took his place at the table Denis, the ship's cook, called out with pleasure at seeing him. "So, my impromptu meal did not end your life after all."

Taking a seat at the end of the bench across from Pierre, Duke Du Bordeaux said, "Unfortunately, the same cannot be said for the rest of us."

"Obviously," Denis answered, "in your case I have pathetically failed." He set a loaf of warm bread at the center of the table and before each man he placed a small cup. From a large spouted pot he filled each with a steaming, black brew. "I must remember to make certain your next meal finally sends you to heaven." He turned and walked back toward the kitchen.

Count D'Antoine called out, "Were that successful it would be a doubly miraculous meal." The others at the table laughed.

Pierre stared into his filled cup. This was not the beer soup Gabriella had prepared for him. The others added spoonfuls of what he guessed was sugar, he lifted the cup toward his nose. Its musky and acrid smell startled him. Duke Du Bordeaux noticed his confusion. "Has Denis' cooking become so bad even we do not recognize it?"

Embarrassed, Pierre cut a slice of the bread. "I confess I'm unfamiliar with this drink."

"Though it may seem to you unlikely," Jacques-Simone said, "it is the rage of all Europe. It is a heathen Moslem brew called coffee and is best taken with a bit of sugar."

"So this," Count D'Antoine said, "is not something offered at your mother's tavern."

Jacques-Simone added, "In London, coffeehouses appear as quickly as mushrooms after a rainstorm, and often two or three share the same the road."

Count D'Antoine then spoke of the range of beneficial effects coffee-drinking has on the body. More confused than impressed, Pierre added sugar to the cup, stirred and, despite its aroma, tasted. He returned the rest of the drink to the table unfinished. Count D'Antoine then smiled toward his companions. "I fear our conversation has descended to the mundane." To Pierre he said, "You missed a thrilling display of grace and virtue yesterday." Turning to the others he asked, "Shall we tell him about it?"

Duke Du Bordeaux laughed. "Like Achilles, you only wish to speak for the opportunity to boast of your own exploits."

"One cannot legitimately boast," Jacques-Simone responded, "without also giving a true and just account of one's actions, can one?"

"One certainly can," Duke Du Bordeaux said, "though one rarely should; especially for you."

"And I suppose," Jacques-Simone responded, "you will wait for others to tell of your gallantry." He surveyed the table in search of confirmation.

"Not so," Duke Du Bordeaux said. "For the poet, the glory is in telling the tale beautifully."

This began a verbal joust that amused Pierre as each boast was trumped by a grander one. Being surrounded by these high-spirits left Pierre relieved.

But he was startled to hear Jacques-Simone say, "Undoubtedly he anticipates our next excursion to Port Royal. With our fair haul, I for one wish only to return to port and all the pleasures thereof." His words were greeted with nods of approval.

Patting Pierre on the shoulder, Count D'Antoine asked, "But what of our newest sailor? Shall he share our prize?"

"Our Captain will never agree," Duke Du Bordeaux quietly said. "Satisfied that by confronting the creature he acts as a sword in the right hand of the Lord, nothing will induce him to share our loot with this young sea-waif."

"Pierre has faced the beast," Jacques-Simone said. "Besides, he was on-board for the attack, though ill and indisposed. Surly as a member of the crew he is eligible for a share."

Count D'Antoine said, "The Captain will insist all this is put to a vote." After a contemplative silence he turned to Pierre. "Perhaps you possess a skill useful to our endeavor."

Jacques-Simone's face brightened. "The Captain could not deprive you of a share if he needed your skill."

Recalling the overheard conversation Pierre could only shrug. "Unless your captain is engaged in some peculiar project, I can offer nothing in the way of a special ability."

Count D'Antoine nodded pensively. "Perhaps there is a skill which you do not sufficiently value or seems of unlikely use. Tell us, assuming he was neither a great swordsman nor a great sailor, what vocation did your father pursue?"

Pierre described Augustus's scientific research and his skill in metalwork admitting some skill in that area.

Jacques-Simone said, "Our friend should be introduced to Monsieur Louis de Montpellier, our ship's doctor of natural philosophy. He complains there is no one in our company to give him adequate assistance." Turning to Pierre he added, "Perhaps you are that man. And helping him might prove jolly sport."

"From what you say," Pierre said, "I assume he's thoroughly trained and deeply read. I can't imagine how my help might prove useful to him."

"He is certainly as deeply read," Count D'Antoine said, "as he is deep in his cups, although his explanations seem as confused as confusing. Still, he might be relieved to have like-minded assistance."

Jacques-Simone said, "The Count may speak with you about him. If he offers to introduce you, be certain you accept."

"There's something else I'm confused about," Pierre admitted. "Your piracy is intended to finance a colony yet you hope to use that wealth to pay for adventures at Port Royal. Can that fortune be employed by both God and Satan?" The table became silent and glances passed among the others until finally Count D'Antoine offered an explanation quoting Augustine whose subtlety left Pierre dizzy. Augustus had never explained theological issues beyond dismissing their platitudes so Pierre was unprepared to consider distinctions which seemed critical to his argument. In the end he simply needed to accept that what they did was tolerable to their god.

"Thus our activities," Jacques-Simone concluded, "are those of souls prepared to accept His grace, but not quite yet. Our behavior reflects our faith that He has chosen us and so in the end we will to fall into His loving embrace, regardless of what we have done or failed to do."

The two bells of the forenoon watch sounded and all looked up. Duke Du Bordeaux stood from the table. "Gentlemen, it is time we joined our comrades on deck." To Pierre he said, "If you are feeling strong enough, this should prove an amusing morning."

Stepping out onto the deck, Pierre was nearly blinded by the light and the piercing blue of the sky. When his eyes adjusted he was startled by what he saw.

Sailors sauntered along the gunwale in pairs and groups in a counter-clockwise motion smoking their pipes and talking, each dressed in a brightly decorative way. Wearing knee-breeches and white, long-sleeved shirts, every man displayed a selection of ribbons of various textures and colors tied around an arm or thigh or around the throat. He turned to watch his cabin-mates affix and adjust similar ribbons. The display in that scintillating light gave the deck an oddly festive appearance.

Altogether, the tidy look of the ship and its crew impressed Pierre. The dark wood decking was as brightly polished as a dance floor and each brass fitting and ivory-pale buckle gleamed in the sunshine. Tawny white sails, bright under the powerful sun, billowed against their yards like fat-bellied clouds. With its sails full out, the mild breeze sped their ship along. He watched men above climb about like spiders through the rigging as the rest of the crew circulated along the gunwales talking and laughing in the open air. Wherever he turned he saw bright eyes and heard lively talk. Despite his lingering weakness he found himself infected by the high spirits around him.

Then Pierre noticed dark shapes clustered beside the foremast and he was startled. Six black men all roughly his own age sat chained together, their expressions combining anger and despair as they too watched the dazzling circumambulation. He wondered how these men understood this display. They presented a disturbing contrast to the smiling high spirits around them. Refugees like himself, tossed up by the same sea and snatched from one fate only to be bound to another, he recognized that their fate was far different from his own. When one turned and stared directly into Pierre eyes, he looked away furiously ashamed.

On the quarter-deck Captain Stevenson sat in a large chair with the Count and the Doctor seated in chairs on either side of him. A sailor stepped to the rail and called the ship's company to order and the men stopped to stand where they were.

Count D'Arcy stood from his chair. "Our capture of the Enbricada has given us a generous windfall. I will now read out our current inventory. To wit: five hundred twenty-eight pounds in gold, eight hundred and thirteen pounds in silver, forty-four bolts of fine chambray cloth, twenty-one bolts of high quality calico, eighteen cases of Madeira port, fifteen cases of Virginia tobacco, twenty-nine cases of Spanish rum, three cases of excellent French cognac, seven cases of Carolina molasses, a small chest of jewels and six African slaves. We owe all this to the skill of Captain Stevenson. So, all hands, three cheers for our courageous Captain."

The crew shouted out their congratulations. In contrast, the Captain surveyed the ship's company with dark distrust. His eyes found Pierre and seemed to bore into his head as if he was the only person on-board.

Count D'Arcy continued. "Appreciated as this harvest is, it leaves us with a question. With our success many look forward to returning to Port Royal and all its pleasures." In response to his leering grin, the crew laughed and hooted.

"Our Captain wishes to continue the pursuit of the creature and for one important reason. That reason is the newest addition to our company." The Count gestured toward Pierre, and all eyes turned on him. "This orphan, Pierre by name, floundered among cruel waves until the Good Lord gave him into our protection. He appears a bright lad, strong-limbed and even-tempered, and I believe he is a valuable addition to our crew. Beyond this, he has one further advantage; he has confronted the creature." Count D'Arcy paused as a murmur passed through the crew.

"So, do we follow the Captain accompanied by our new expert with his knowledge of the creature's habits and continue its pursuit? Or do we return to Port Royal and resume that search at a later time." The rumble of debate reminded Pierre of distant thunder.

Count D'Arcy continued, "To assist our decision we should hear Pierre's tale of his encounter with the creature and what light he might shed on its habits. So I invite him to join us up here. Having heard his tale and learned what we can, we shall then vote."

Debate among the crew of a ship about its course of action was something new to Pierre, and conversation continued as he made his way onto the quarterdeck. Count D'Arcy directed him to a chair that faced the Captain. Captain Stevenson studied him as if uncertain whether he saw an ally or an enemy.

Pierre began by describing the circumstances of the Bristol when the creature was first seen and then began to pursue their ship. The Captain leaned forward, his eyes brightening with interest. Pierre described the ship's crew complimenting Captain Hawthorne's effort to evade the creature, and then described how, when attack finally seemed inevitable, Hawthorne organized their defense. Breathless with the urgency of his memory, he then described how, when the creature raised its enormous head beside the ship, the gunfire exploded from the ship but with feeble result. Captain Stevenson's eyes grew brighter still when Pierre explained that the creature appeared hardly to notice the hail of bullets and cannon shot.

The crew remained silent as Pierre described the creature's first assault on the Bristol and its seemingly methodical destruction of the ship. But even the sea itself seemed to hush while he described the creature's pursuit of each sailor who fell into the sea and how it cruised the waters snatching up survivors as they thrashed until the only sound was the grumbling of the creature.

When he finished his tale no one spoke. Leaning close, the Captain asked, "So tell us how is it you survived when all of those courageous men died?"

Pierre confessed that his memory was unclear as he described how a portion of the ship's bow had remained afloat upside down providing a shelter within which he had hidden. When he finished, the only sound was that of the wind passing through the sails, the creaking of the timbers, and the slap of the sea against the hull.

Count D'Arcy stepped to the quarterdeck rail. "Gentlemen, we are in the presence of a man who has seen terrors we can only dream of, and suffered privations we might not have survived. So I ask three cheers for this courageous sailor."

While he did not recognize himself in the Count's description, to his surprise the crew let out three loud cheers on his behalf. Suddenly both charmed and frightened, he could not decide which sensation was stronger or why. But looking over at the Captain, he found the man staring at him as if certain he hid a secret which needed to be exposed. Though the others saw someone else, the Captain recognized Pierre the Fraud, Pierre the Coward, Pierre the Fool.

The Count continued, "A remarkable tale of a terrifying encounter told to us by a brave man, just the sort I would wish by my side in a crisis. So, with your approval I propose we invite him to sign our ship's articles and join our crew. All who agree let your voice be heard now." A loud 'Aye' seemed to come from every throat. "Anyone who objects, make that objection now." To Pierre's surprise no voice offered objection.

Count D'Arcy turned to Pierre. "We invite you to become a member of our crew. What say you?"

Pierre looked over the crew and then turned to the Count. "I am honored."

"Then swear solemnly to uphold the ship's articles and our glorious mission." A Bible appeared, Pierre placed his right hand on it and swore his oath. A large vellum sheet along with a quill and a capped bottle of ink was placed in front of him. He glanced once at the assembled crew and then added his signature. The Count took it from him as the crew applauded.

"Now," Count D'Arcy said, "how say you all? Shall we follow our Captain and pursue the creature?" The response was hardly a murmur. "Or pursue our secret beasts at Port Royal?" With these words the crew erupted into cheers and laughter.

Count D'Arcy turned to Captain Stevenson. "We will make for Port Royal and in one month resume our pursuit of the creature. Have you any objection?"

Captain Stevenson glanced grimly at Pierre, then allowed his look to travel over the rest of the crew. After a tense pause, he said, "I offer no objection and will speed us to port. There is some wisdom in this since, from this man's description, we will need heavier arms and more of them in an encounter with the creature. But I agree to this on the condition that, having resumed our hunt we will continue until the creature is dead. Whoever objects, speak now?"

After a long moment's silence Count D'Arcy addressed the crew. "We are eight days from Port Royal; eight days to prepare for the battles ahead." To a grotesque wink of his eye the crew laughed loudly. "But first, to clear the lungs and the mind, we will have our morning exercise." He nodded to a cluster of five men who went immediately below deck. "To impress our newest sailor, let us begin with a minuet, followed by a gavotte, and end with a gigue."

Accompanied by the crew's polite applause Count D'Arcy called out, "To your partners." In a moment the men paired into couples facing each other and all turned toward the Count. The five men returned to the main deck carrying musical instruments; a lute, a viola da gamba, a violin, a tambour and a drum. Taking positions on the main deck just below the Count they lifted their instruments.

To the musicians the Count said, "Give us a gentle tuple-time to my mark." With a wave of his hand the Count signaled the beat which was taken up by the player of the tambour. As the first notes sounded the couples bowed to each other and then turned and danced and bowed and danced and bowed, on and on in a slow movement around the deck. On every third beat, partners were exchanged with the neighboring couple as the dance continued.

Mesmerized by the most startling display he had ever seen, Pierre stepped to the rail. Suddenly the Captain stood beside him. To no one in particular he muttered, "Find me in my cabin." He turned and made his way below.

As the music continued Pierre became infected by its energy. He moved to descend the stairs to the main deck when the Doctor took his arm. "By your own account you were three days afloat on that box in the sea. Be patient; there will be opportunities to join the dance."

A bit amazed Pierre said, "This is remarkable. I've never seen anything like it."

Count D'Arcy glanced down toward the swirl on the main deck. "These are the very finest France has produced. Brave and determined, they are also the most civilized and refined, gallant and honorable even in their dealings with women." He clapped Pierre on the shoulder. "You are a fortunate man."

Pierre watched delighted as the dancing continued. Count D'Arcy stepped again to the rail and clapped his hands three times and suddenly the tempo increased, the series of steps changed. He could not resist tapping his foot. The Count turned to Doctor De Montaigne. With a nod they descended to the main deck, exchanged gallant bows and joined the surging dances. Pierre could not resist smiling. Finally he was inclined to agree with the Doctor; given all the likely fates of a man in his situation, his was a most fortunate outcome.

A short, dark and spidery man with a milky white left eye stepped up suddenly beside Pierre. Quietly he said, "Captain wants you in his quarters." When Pierre hesitated, the man's expression hardened. "Now!"

Pierre turned to follow him wondering if his luck had just run out.

CHAPTER SEVEN

PIERRE APPROACHED THE Captain's open cabin door certain he was about to be tossed back into the sea. He found the Captain seated with his broad back to a wide table covered with sea charts and maps, his black cockade hat resting to one side. Still wearing his bright blue brocade jacket, the Captain sat with his back to Pierre and he looked out through a wide window that offered a panoramic view of the turquoise sea beyond. Pierre closed the door and moved to a chair on the other side of the chart table.

Still facing the window Captain Stevenson said, "Kindly wait until you are invited to be seated." Pierre remained standing beside the chair, fear mixed with annoyance increasing. Seen through small window frames, the ocean appeared docile, its furious disorder disguised by rolling swells, generous curves, an imitation of tranquility. On deck overhead the music and footsteps of the men became suddenly loud and the lilt of the music grew lively.

With an exasperated sigh the Captain said, "That will go on for a while." He turned in his chair then to face Pierre. Nodding toward a chair, he said, "I encourage their dance. It keeps them in good physical condition and sustains their morale; no easy thing for snobs like them. Must appear silly to you and maybe it is but it beats curses and sword-play and whoever says otherwise be damned."

Pierre could think of no good response. The music and the thumps and thuds of the men's feet rhythmically stepping on the deck filled the silence of the cabin.

"You take us for fools," the Captain continued quietly and with more sadness in his voice than anger. Again he left Pierre in startled silence. "Certainly you take me for a fool. But I tell you, sir, you will know the truth before you leave this cabin. And then you will tell me the truth and we will both know that it is the truth before we have finished." He stood and walked around the table until he towered beside Pierre. Looking down he said, "We have much to discuss."

Abruptly the music became loud and he glanced up. Hands locked behind his back and his massive shoulders rolling pensively, he stepped back around the chart table returned to his chair and sat down. For a time he stared at the charts spread before him as if in search of words that might prove useful. He leaned back sighing and then looked up at Pierre.

"I owe no man an explanation of my life, nor have any obligation to reveal the reason I sail with these men or under what terms. What little you need to know I expect you have already been told by others. What we will speak of is the creature." He leaned forward and lowered his voice, his gaze seemed to pierce Pierre's mind as his voice echoed within his skull.

"It is my responsibility to give you what you do not yet realize you lack. Because what you possess is information about that creature which is not yet knowledge. You possess information which your senses gathered but you do not yet possess knowledge. Thus together you and I will examine that data until I have shaped it into knowledge. This will be worth far more than your fractured and inconsequential impressions. But to do all of that you must know a bit more than you do now."

"Simply put," he continued, "I have sworn to God and the memory of my loved ones that I will hunt the creature and destroy it, thought its destruction demands my life." He moved his face close and Pierre watched the tiny muscles around his mouth tremble. "Do you understand what that means?"

In response to Pierre's silence Captain Stevenson said, "No, you can't." He searched Pierre's eyes and then leaned back in his chair seeming as puzzled as he was angry. "A man your age can have no idea what such an oath means; to swear your life to a single task. At your age even the notion of life's value is without meaning; you will toss it aside for the glimpse of a woman's ankle or a game of cards or a passage in a book as all will appear the same. Your ignorance is so deep it is without meaning." His dark eyes and grim mouth surrounded by its halo of darkest black hair left Pierre to wonder if he would leave the cabin alive. "Your ignorance is so deep it should embarrass us both."

He turned back to the window as if to address the blue sky and shreds of tattered white clouds chased by the wind. "Despite my disapproval you are now a member of this ship's crew. Therefore it is reasonable to confide the reason for my participation in this venture. In addition, however, by telling you my tale I may gain your help in this righteous voyage. For the tale I tell is as dark as any there have been and because of it I have sworn an oath of vengeance."

He turned to face Pierre again, leaned forward and poised his massive finger tips claw-like on the chart table. "Two years ago the merchant brig Exeter met the creature and her sinking sent to the bottom three hundred bales of cotton, fifty-eight bolts of wool cloth and forty-three of cotton broadcloth, twenty-eight casks of Cuban brandy and fourteen of Jamaican rum and a crew of nineteen souls. Among that crew was their captain, Lucius Stevenson, my father. All of those brave men snatched from the face of the earth as if by the hand of God." He paused and his expression suggested he was watching this abominable act unfold.

"But how do you know it was an act of the creature?"

The Captain sighed as if the question merely added to the effort of his recitation. "Three months later, the captain of the frigate Marbury spied a piece of the gunwale adrift bearing the Exeter's name-plate. According to him there were wide gash marks cut deep into its wood. He did not recognize their significance but I knew full-well that only one creature makes such marks."

He rubbed his forehead as if to dispel an anguished vision. "Each of those men had a family. And as captain, my father was additionally responsible to the owners of that ship. So it wasn't simply my father and eighteen sailors under his command whose lives were destroyed. Perhaps a hundred lives were forever changed by the creature. And when the shareholders of that company owning the ship and its cargo are included, the number grows further still. My wrath is honorable, my vengeance is just and my mission is clear." He struck the wooden table with his fist. "Only blood redeems the misery spawned by the creature." With fury rumbling within his chest he said, "The creature must die!"

Pierre cleared his throat. "You've chosen a terrible opponent."

"That is incorrect," the Captain said firmly. "It is the creature who has chosen me."

"You speak of a dumb animal as if it possessed a conscious will."

"Although the creature may merely be reacting to stimuli, the result is the same."

"Still, despite my ignorance explain to me just one thing. Do you worry that although you abhor the creature's wanton destruction yet you have decided by your piracy that it is proper and justifiable to wreak a similar misery and entail a similar loss of life and property against men as innocent as your father simply to revenge yourself against the French crown?"

Captain Stevenson's eyes grew large with barely suppressed fury. "Your ignorance is stunning, extending even to the ethical realms. This issue you pretend is so important is mere hair-splitting. Our forays only challenge the crown ships of the kings of Europe. As such, those ships cruise the seas in support of oppression. Their potentates may construe our activities otherwise, but attacks against their ships amount to military engagements with the enemy. In any case, we have never injured a man who surrendered to our demands. That ship's captain who chose to resist was dealt with as he demanded. We inflict no injury otherwise undeserved. Concerning that creature, it is not I who has chosen this battle. As my father's son I'm obligated to compensate the families of his sailors, and the law of property decrees I compensate the owners of that ship given into his care. I hope now I have assuaged your delicate conscience."

"So I have joined this company of men," Captain Stevenson continued, "to destroy the creature and to repay that debt owed to the families of the crew and owners of the vessel." Again he leaned forward to bring his face close to Pierre's. "Does my appeal to honor move you even slightly?"

Pierre nodded still uncertain what the Captain wanted from him.

Captain Stevenson's piercing eyes carved into Pierre's. Turning the palms of his hands beseechingly upward he said, "I don't believe you and yet I'm helpless." He studied Pierre's face as if his eyes were hands probing the invisible. "No matter how humble the tool Our Lord provides, I must employ it. This ship and its crew are tools given by God to complete His mission. Now He's sent you to me and I'll use you as I use this ship and crew, according to His commands. You'll be my instrument just as I am His. Will you be the right arm of the Lord? Will you stand beside me and smite the infernal enemy of the Lord? Speak now and forever."

Pierre recognized himself confined with a madman so he nodded in agreement.

"Speak!" the Captain cried, "so that even God may hear you!"

"Yes!" Pierre said. On the Captain's lips a smile grew slowly.

"Good. Now tell me again the circumstances of the creature's attack." He then questioned Pierre on every detail of the Bristol's encounter with the creature that he could recall. Pierre described tactics and weather conditions, the time of day and weapons used, various forms of shot that the cannons fired and how often, where on the creature's body they struck and their result. Captain Stevenson questioned him most carefully on the behavior of the creature when it was attacked and its maneuvers. An exhausted Pierre finally protested his ignorance of anything more but the Captain leaned forward again livid with suspicion.

"Hide nothing from me nor dismiss any memory as unimportant. I must know every detail. As this creature is mortal it must possess a spot of deadly vulnerability where the sufficient blow will result in death. Its behavior under attack will reveal to the observant mind that part of its anatomy it must protect. You have witnessed its reaction to attack. To defeat this creature I must see what your eyes have seen. The most insignificant observation may provide the key to its demise." Then he resumed his interrogation.

Pierre's ordeal seemed to last a long time but finally even the Captain had to concede there was nothing more he could tell him. Captain Stevenson then seemed to relax satisfied with Pierre responses. "That creature is more than clever. The Lord has endowed it with an intelligence superior to that of men and so it must be a direct creation of the Lord, without progenitor, siblings or progeny; a creation ex nihilo and with His purpose branded onto its soul."

Quietly Pierre asked, "If that creature really is a direct creation of God, might we pursue it at the risk of our eternal souls?"

Captain Stevenson's fist came down so violently that Pierre wondered if the table beneath it had cracked. "Can you be so feeble-minded that even the simplest thought eludes you? The Lord has created this creature as a test. It is, first, a test of our wills. Are we determined, despite every hardship, to do the work of the Lord? And second, the beast is a test of our ingenuity. Though it be more powerful than any creature ever walked this earth and we but puny beside it, can we employ those humble wits the Lord has given us to destroy His dark creation? Our Good Lord is watching. After all of the sin and corruption we have wallowed in, are we worthy of His love and care? Now do you understand why we must be implacable against this enemy? Because, like the dark angel Lucifer, though it be a creation of the Lord, the creature is the enemy of the Lord."

The intensity of Captain Stevenson's expression convinced Pierre he was entirely serious and completely mad. He knew he was not as clever as the Captain but he also understood that his life was now in the hands of a furious lunatic. The music on deck grew louder and faster, and in the silence of the cabin it seemed to envelope them and gradually press down.

Answerable to no religion of his own, Pierre had listened to Augustus's diatribes against their twisted logic and so he had acquired a superficial knowledge of theology. "Didn't St. Augustine and Calvin both agree God's love is free and undeserved and therefore independent of our acts? I have an ill-formed understanding, yet could attacking this creature knowing that we endanger these lives given to us by the Lord affect our salvation?" He discovered his hands were gripping the arms of his chair.

The Captain's eyes narrowed, his stare deepened as his mouth grew tight and his lips thinned. "You propose a duel of wits. The Lord offers salvation only to those who act in accord with His intentions. If only this is all that you are capable of understanding, understand that as captain of this ship I know the ways and plans of the Lord." He paused as if waiting for Pierre to understand. "This is that gift given to all captains, all leaders, all those placed by God in positions of responsibility for their fellows. In the exercise of my duty to govern the enclosed universe of this ship I become privy to the will of God. This knowledge is acquired honestly and not with the mumbo-jumbo and sweet-smelling smoke of priests."

Pierre struggled to understand what he was being told. "So what you are saying is, the Lord manifests His will through the actions of the sea captains of the world."

Captain Stevenson snarled with disgust. "Wherever I turn I find arrogant ignorance disguised as profound insight. Your understanding depends upon an organ manifestly imperfect. Do not ignore those superior in knowledge, experience and wisdom. This creature is a divinely intended evil added to the world, not some mere accident."

"My suggestion is less ambitious and so less satisfying, but couldn't we leave intentional evil to the professionals and be content to patch the accidental malignancies?"

The Captain continued to glare and Pierre squirmed under his disdain. The music became still louder and the tempo nearly breathless. "You must tell yourself it isn't cowardice you feel. You tell yourself that, since the creature exists it must have a purpose and the intentions of the Lord, like His ways, are mysterious. And I expect that while your most urgent hope is that it never finds you, you also hope someone else does something about it, just not you." The Captain stood.

Hands clasped behind his back he turned again to face the window and its view of the ocean. "I've conceded our return to Port Royal and the carouse to follow for two reasons. First, because the crew wants it and all that loot is there for them, too. But second, because when they've spent their money they'll feel so ghastly and ill and beaten they'll go wherever they're told, as long as its path leads them away from the port." He turned from the window to face Pierre. "Though believing themselves noble, these men care for nothing so much as debauchery, licentiousness and gluttony. But just for all that, when they've had their fill they'll return to this ship as docile as kittens and as eager to sail as escaped convicts." He grinned and Pierre was appalled by that grimace. "Besides, this visit will give me the opportunity to turn my share into coin. Though you may not know it, there's a Florentine-method bank in Port Royal and what I've put aside to repay my father's obligations is locked in its vault."

Pierre found this odd. "Why would anyone keep money in a city filled with pirates?"

The Captain's broad shoulders shrugged. "Safest bank in the world since it contains the ill-gotten wealth of the bloodiest cutthroats outside of Parliament. My money's safer there than piled under my bed." His attention drifted, he returned to his table, sat down and scowled. "Having signed the ship's articles you'll be offered part of our booty. I warn you now; refuse whatever you're offered. As your share comes out of the rest, accepting will not make you popular with the crew."

Suddenly the music stopped, replaced by footsteps moving along the decks and quiet conversation. Pierre asked, "Will that be all, Captain?"

Captain Stevenson laid both hands flat on the table and leaned forward until his face was inches from Pierre's, scrutinizing as if expecting to see something more than was visible. Pierre wondered how quickly he could get to the door. In a whisper the Captain said, "You're not one of us, are you?"

"What?" Pierre asked with genuine astonishment.

He continued to study Pierre's face as if searching for something he was not finding and whose discovery mattered. "I'll say nothing to anyone but understand that you and I both know you're not one of us." He paused as if demanding Pierre's attention. "I expect that none of the others realize this but now you know that I know. In exchange for your discretion I'll be discreet as well and you'll proceed with us without prejudice. But in my heart I hope to God the creature consumes you before it devours the rest of us."

The Captain turned in his chair to face the rolling blue sea. After a moment Pierre decided the Captain had no further interest in him. He stood and left the cabin.

As carefully as he thought about it, he could make no sense of the Captain's words. He felt certain now that he had reached another world, one superficially similar yet at heart utterly different from his own. Was this what the Captain meant, or did he have something even more sinister in mind? Finally he conceded he could not resolve the question so it was better simply to forget it.

Pierre reached the main deck and was relieved to see men working. Some climbed among the ropes and canvas, others polished brass and scrubbed the deck, and still others repaired canvas with needle and thread or spliced rope with marlinespikes. The men gathered around the mizzenmast ate from dark wooden bowls and from time to time spoke quietly to each other. He spied Doctor De Montaigne step from behind the main mast and head in his direction. Seeing Pierre his eyes brightened and he smiled. "Where have you been all of this time? I thought our performance would have fascinated merely by its consummate artistry."

"Speaking with the Captain."

"Ah," the Doctor said, "so you have had your conversation and now know the secret of his obsession." He grinned as if enjoying a private joke.

Pierre shrugged. "I've seen the creature. Your Captain is crazy and the sooner I get off this ship the happier I'll be."

The Doctor's expression glazed into place, his smile and the creases around his eyes froze into a grimace. But as if shaking himself, he looked up to the sky. "It is just so rare one has the opportunity to enjoy the pleasure of such a pleasant day. I suggest we take a turn about the deck." Without waiting he slipped his left arm through Pierre's right and led him in a stroll along the rail. Pierre wondered what the Doctor thought about luck and the role it had played in his life. He wondered if, after all was said and done, the Doctor counted himself a lucky man. And if so, was he happy about it.

CHAPTER EIGHT

"OUR CAPTAIN IS a rare man with remarkable abilities." Doctor De Montaigne spoke as they walked, but so quietly Pierre needed to lean toward him.

Pierre responded, "He's a menace to anyone within five feet of him."

The Doctor chuckled. "From Boston to Bombay he knows the world's oceans as if their maps had hung over his cradle."

"If you'd seen the creature you'd throw him overboard and hang every sail to make for the nearest port."

The Doctor's smile tightened. "We are not without resources. Let me show you something." Their path took them to the quarterdeck.

At the bulkhead beside the door to the gangway Doctor De Montaigne stopped. "I draw your attention to one of the most profound inventions the human mind has yet produced." Mounted vertically to the wall with small brass straps was a long thin glass tube filled with glittering gray liquid. Along its wooden frame were marked out evenly-spaced graduations. Pierre felt some recognition though he could not recall why.

"Behold our Torricelli tube, a gift to mankind from that dear friend of the divine Galileo, the Florentine Evangelista Torricelli. This ingenious device indicates minute variations in the pressure of the atmosphere. Most remarkably, it owes nothing to the wisdom of the Ancients and represents a contribution unique to modern philosophy." From his expression, Pierre might have thought the man had created this device himself.

"But let me draw your attention to another remarkable contrivance." He pointed to a device that resembled the Torricelli tube and also attached to the bulwark. "Our ship's scientist, Master Louis d'Avril de Montpellier, has provided us with a thermoscope. Invented by the Venetian Santorio Santorii, it indicates the amount of phlogiston in the air." He gestured then to a device projecting into the air above the quarter-deck made up of four arms slowly spinning. "Finally, he has provided us with a device he calls an anemometer. An invention of the angelic Genoese Leone Battista Alberti, it indicates both the power and direction of Aeolus's breath." Pierre could only gaze at these devices unsettled by vague recognition.

Dr. De Montaigne continued, "We have kept ourselves informed of advances in scientific research." Turning to look directly in Pierre's eyes he said, "The true victory of this brilliant century is accuracy of measurement."

Though he resisted, Pierre was impressed. "You seem better informed than even my father was."

"Amazing devices continue to come to the world's attention. By every measure, our science is superior even to that of the wisest of the Ancients."

Pierre laughed. "Forgive my skepticism, but far from the Continent, how do you learn of such advances?"

Doctor De Montaigne shrugged as though the answer was obvious. "This is a wonderful time to be alive and not simply for its discoveries. Researchers now put their experiments before colleagues in their field and collaborate at a distance which allows still others to build on those efforts and thus expand the value of every discovery."

Pierre found his enthusiasm amusing. Whether he recognized this, Doctor De Montaigne continued. "A network of corresponding experimentalists has been established through the Journal des Savants, organized by Denis de Sales of Paris, and the Philosophical Transactions of the Royal Society directed by Henry Oldenburg of London."

Finally Pierre heard a name he recognized. "My father corresponded with Oldenburg." He did not describe those arguments Augustus had created with the Society.

"This network," the Doctor continued, "offers an examination of every experiment brought to its attention. Even unsuccessful experiments are reviewed to discover if an underlying principle has been exposed. Across the globe researchers communicate with each other as if all lived nearby so that the work of one quickly becomes known to others. Even here, our scientist has learned that our glorious brother, Blaise Pascal, has invented a mechanical

Arithmetique, capable of rapid calculations. But as great minds invariably follow parallel paths, we have also learned that the divine Leibniz has created a similar mechanical device for performing such calculations which he calls a Calculus Ratiocinator. Imagine a world wherein such scientific advances are announced nearly every year. Consider the depth of human understanding after just two centuries of such discoveries. Though it must seem unlikely to you, I envy your youth simply for what you will live to see, the knowledge that will be at your fingertips and devices which will extend your efforts further than any before."

"What you describe is startling and your devices are impressive but what value could they have for a ship out to rob from the rich and defeat the powerful?"

Doctor De Montaigne spoke quietly. "Our ship's scientist, Doctor de Montpellier, is convinced that disturbances in the atmosphere indicate proximity of the creature and make it impossible for us to be caught off-guard. He assures us that, according to Paracelsus, imbalances of heat and atmosphere attract malevolent creatures and excite their animal essences, while other imbalances drive such creatures away." Then he stopped. "But I should be more discreet since these devices are just as useful for the pursuit of royal fleets as creatures of the deep."

Pierre shook his head. "You risk a bloody death simply out of loyalty to a madman."

Doctor De Montaigne's expression melted into disdain. "Can you believe we would endanger ourselves on the whim of a man whose origins are so common he could be anyone's offspring except there's a compelling need?" Pierre suddenly glimpsed the grimly imperious aristocrat intolerant of contradiction by a social inferior. "Our mission is honorable and if our captain was Lucifer himself he would receive his due. We pursue his personal revenge as long as opportunities occasioned are exploited profitably and with little risk. Our ship is not called the Revenge for merely romantic reasons."

"Your revenge comes at a terrible risk."

Just as suddenly as it had appeared, that visage beneath the facade was replaced by the calm and jocular Doctor. "And where is there a worthy challenge without risk, eh? When one is determined to establish a colony, one runs risks greater than any posed by some animal."

"And this is the purpose of your journey?"

The Doctor's expression remained friendly. "We will establish a colony to sustain our faith beyond the interference of either Rome or Paris. Who contributes to this is an ally, who frustrates it is an enemy. A distressingly simple calculation, but necessary."

After a moment Pierre said, "So, I'm asked to assist in exchange for my life."

Doctor De Montaigne looked away. "Put it less dramatically and agree that your help is useful but not obligatory. We would be the worst of hosts to demand compensation for having rescued you. We assume your sense of justice will incline you to help us." Pierre could think of no good response.

The Doctor clutched Pierre's arm. "Let us continue our stroll on this bright day as I explain a bit more about our quest and these men engaged by it."

In a narrative sprinkled with allusions to classical myth and intrigues at the court of Paris the Doctor recounted stories of the exiles of individual sailors, their struggles with the king's men, the family fortunes lost, the fathers, uncles, and brothers dead or in exile, and the lovely ladies—mothers, sisters, sweethearts—left behind with their anguish at their separation.

"Until we have established our colony," he concluded, "as it demands a pirate to defeat a pirate, we are a pirate's crew."

"But doesn't shedding the blood of innocent men cast a shadow over your cause?"

The shock on the Doctor's face almost convinced Pierre it was genuine. "Do you take us for savages who sneak about slitting throats merely for sport? Do you imagine we stab and slash simply for the excitement? Were we that, our cause would be compromised and undoubtedly you would be dead."

"It seems unlikely any ship you attack yields merely to your request. Unpleasant as it is, blood is shed in the course of your exploits."

The Doctor looked down and if Pierre had not been certain otherwise he might suspect embarrassment in his voice. "We always regret a misguided commander's insistence he must resist, determined to risk his life in the defense of coffee, beans and tobacco."

"And then?"

The Doctor shrugged and his eyes would not meet Pierre's. "We attempt to reason, of course. We point out the hopelessness of his cause and admit our repugnance at needing to threaten his life. But some appear even eager to offer their lives for the glory of their king. This disturbs us greatly. What, after all, can possess a person to exchange life for a handful of beans and leaves? The Ancients have told us that property is not sacred. What is sacred is honor and trust and friendship and these are worthy of all other sacrifices. Where is there nobility in the defense of property? Where is there honor in defense of material possessions? Eventually all turns to dust, but one's honor is eternal." Chin held high and the expression of his eyes sharp, the Doctor turned his gaze out to the sea.

Pierre asked, "So what do you do in that case?"

The Doctor shrugged. "What must be done." As if Aeolus expressed agreement, a sudden gust of wind whistled through the rigging.

Pierre recalled Augustus's insistence his discoveries were his possessions. Long hours of struggle, expense of materials and the wearying succession of failures justified his demand for profit. He wondered what this braggart standing before him could know about that thankless battle or its desperation. Pierre thought then of what Gabriella had sacrificed to support Augustus's delusional faith. Had those made rightful ownership Gabriella's as well? With this distance of time and miles he glimpsed his parents as strangers determined to possess something greater and more enduring, and these thoughts tossed him into a grim depression. Failure, even unacknowledged, remains failure.

Turning, Doctor De Montaigne grinned. " I must introduce you to our scientist. A fascinating scholar, he will provide the scientific explanations for all I have shown you." Pierre was grateful for the chance to think about something else.

He followed the Doctor down the gangway into the heart of ship. Recalling the scene on deck and the inventory of booty, Pierre asked, "What's led you to trade in slaves?"

Doctor De Montaigne stopped and faced Pierre with a curious smile. "My dear boy, though occasionally harsh, the trade in slaves benefits slaves as well as owners. Filled with superstitions and unthinking credulity, the native African possesses the understanding of a child. Well-treated, he can be brought to a hundred small tasks with useful effect. Besides, the slave is far safer in his farm quarters than out in Nature. And for those whose hearts are open, the word of the Lord can be brought."

"But suppose one becomes a Christian. Is it proper for a Christian to own a Christian?"

The Doctor looked at Pierre a long moment. "Clever lad; I wager you and our good Scientist will get along quite well." He turned then saying, "Shall we go?" Without waiting, he resumed their path.

As they passed along dark and narrow passageways the Doctor continued. "He is a genius, if I may say it. A corresponding member of the Royal Society, he communicates with Oldenberg and Newton and the Mechanist Leibniz. A man of rare learning and penetrating mind, for him the secrets of Nature are laid out like images cut into crystal. You will find he is an exemplar of the angelic nature of mankind."

They stopped before a door indistinguishable from the others where Pierre detected noxious vapors somehow familiar to him. Noting his grimace the Doctor laughed. "Your patience will be rewarded." He rapped firmly on the door and when there was no response he rapped again. After another pause and now obviously annoyed he called out, "C'est moi!"

Pierre heard a sound like the dragging of a heavy object across a wooden floor. Preceded by a long, phlegm-clogged cough, a weak yet angry voice cried out, "Go away!" The Doctor looked down and shook his head before he knocked again on the door.

The bolt on the other side of the door snapped back and the door partly opened. Through that space peered the gray face of an old man, nose large and bulbous at the end, creases pouring down the sides of his face and lost in a bush of wiry, gray whiskers, exposed skin dotted with blackened warts and pale eyes so encased by flesh they seemed surrounded by the drippings of gray candle wax. Through the opened door came a wave of vapor that sent Pierre back a step.

With a sudden smile the Doctor said, "Ah, my friend and esteemed colleague, I hope this visit finds you well."

"And just what's to be so damned cheery about?" The Scientist hawked up a gob of phlegm and spat it onto the floor just beyond his threshold.

"I trust your health is as vigorous as your temper." The Doctor turned to Pierre. "Allow me to introduce Pierre Chanceux, plucked from Neptune's domain and the jaws of that infamous creature." Pierre nodded.

Without glancing at Pierre the Scientist barked, "I curse the devil who tempted me to join this voyage. Your Captain has taken advantage of a homeless scholar with the false promise of facilities to pursue his work. You have cheated me and lied to me and I have no more time for you or this pimple-faced oaf." He slammed the door shut and sent the bolt home with a crack.

The Doctor's grin faded, replaced by something near annoyance. "Genius must have its way," he muttered. "Those possessing rare gifts rarely include courtesy among them." He rapped again, this time more quietly.

From the other side of the door they heard, "I told you and that lap-dog to go away!"

In a pleading tone the Doctor called through the closed door, "But our guest is eager to meet you." His hesitation surprised Pierre. "We wish only a little of your time."

The bolt finally slid back and the door opened. Through its narrow space the Scientist again glared at the Doctor. "Courtesy is demanded where none is offered." With a glance to Pierre he said, "The secrets of Nature are pursued in solitude, thankless and profitless except for those who trouble to recognize them." He was not tall yet he was bearish and wide-shouldered and seemed somehow to look down on Pierre. "So tell me now and be quick; what service do you wish me to provide without gratitude or compensation?"

Before Pierre could answer, Doctor De Montaigne said, "Our guest is familiar with the arcana of your studies and wishes to provide you with useful assistance."

"Oh yes!" the Scientist responded without conviction. "Does a slug assist a flower? Does a fly assist a pile of shit?" Turning his glare again on Pierre he asked, "And just what assistance do you propose to provide?"

Again without waiting, the Doctor said, "He has long experience assisting his father in his studies of nature."

Still looking squarely at Pierre the Scientist asked, "And who might that good man be?"

Pierre said, "You may have heard of him. His name is Augustus Chanceux."

The Scientist's eyes flickered. "That is a name with which I am familiar." Stepping back from the threshold he opened the door wide. "I would very much like to speak with you."

Pierre crossed the threshold and entered the cluttered chamber followed by the Doctor, wondering if finally some luck had come his way and would it help him find his father.

CHAPTER NINE

THE CABIN WAS small, dark and low-ceilinged and muddy light seeped from a single porthole open wide. The reek of its poisonous atmosphere brought tears to Pierre's eyes. Metal instruments of odd shape and description filled every space beside glass containers of colored fluids and devices of dark wood and bright brass. Books sprouting the tattered ends of torn paper stood piled on every level space. Appearing a cave of disorderly storage, to Pierre's surprise he recognized certain instruments and several book titles.

Dr. de Montpellier suddenly turned a grim face to the Doctor. "I am grateful for this introduction but I believe our interview would be best conducted in private."

Embarrassed, Doctor De Montaigne turned to Pierre. "When your interview is finished, please search me out. I am eager to continue our discussion." With a bow he wished Dr. de Montpellier good day and left. The Scientist slammed the door at his retreating back.

"Damned busy-body," he muttered at the closed door. "Whole damn ship cluttered with argumentative fops and small-minded idiots. For what sin am I being punished to be thrust into this perverted coven of the delusional, the ignorant and the diabolical?" He stopped suddenly and moved his large face close to Pierre's. "I do not have a world of time, young man, but your father is known to me and I am eager to hear about his work." Turning, he shoved books and papers aside revealing two large chairs and a small table. Suddenly appearing utterly sober, he nodded toward one of the chairs as he sat.

Leaning forward the Scientist said, "Your father has made a reputation among the leaders of aether theory." Reaching down he brought out a bottle and two small glasses and put them on the small table between them. He filled each glass and then slid one before Pierre. He lifted his glass and nodded toward Pierre. "I drink to your health and to the health and success of your illustrious father." Pierre drank and in a moment recognized Jamaican rum, something Gabriella had kept behind the bar but he had never learned to like. Happily, the Scientist appeared so enamored of it he did not notice Pierre's indifference. He leaned back as thunderbolts appeared to gather below his heavy brow. "Despite the ingratitude of youth and kinship, I hope you are impressed by his achievements."

"He often said that only when we can accurately measure the results of our work will we know its value." He was relieved to recall anything Augustus had said.

The Scientist smiled. "According to what I have read, not only is his theory of the aether buttressed by his devices but accurate predictions of its behavior are attributed to him as well."

Pierre knew his father well enough to doubt this description. Still, he was surprised by his own sense of pride at the Scientist's words and surprised as well that his father had to some degree succeeded. He smiled even as he resented a father too busy to communicate with a family that remained eager to see him again.

"Unfortunately," the Scientist continued, "in most other ways he resembles far too many in his contentious field. He has scandalized every quarter yet his work is such that even those who despise his ranting recognize that his achievements set him apart from an ocean of polished idiots pretending themselves scientists. One must hope his talent and ingenuity will out-shine the defects of his spirit. "

Finally Pierre recognized Augustus. "He suffered under a terrible weight of isolation. His work seemed to fall into a deadening silence of indifference. I suggest he carries himself with as much dignity as his situation allows."

Dr. de Montpellier smiled. "Were he to hear you he would have every reason to be proud of the son who defends him even in his absence." He leaned forward and peered into Pierre's cup. "Drink up, boy." Lifting his own cup he said, "I salute a dedicated practitioner, and the loyal son who guards his honor." He emptied his cup in a swallow and sighed with pleasure.

Pierre drank as best he could with a gratitude he did not feel and then returned the cup to the table. The Scientist refilled his own, drank it back in a swallow and then leaned back in his chair. Pierre recognized his expression, the same he had seen countless times at the tavern.

"Tell me this," the Scientist said, "since you spent time in your father's workshop, do you recognize these devices?" Waving he gestured toward the objects around them.

Pierre surveyed the collection as the Scientist refilled his own cup. "He left us when I was young so my education in these matters is incomplete." He gathered his few memories of what he had seen. "But I recall several of these. Others I can guess about. The rest I simply don't recognize."

The Scientist hesitated. "Your caution recommends you as much as your knowledge. Far too many claim what they do not possess and to the detriment of honest workers. Had you said you recognized them all I would have had to put you down as a liar since several are of my own design." Hands clasped casually around his cup he sighed. "Perhaps Doctor De Montaigne is correct and you may provide useful. So perhaps I am under some obligation to suggest you become my assistant."

"That would be a great honor but it seems unlikely I'd be of use to your work. My education I received from my father, but so little it could hardly be useful."

"Allow me to judge that. My need is for a careful assistant, not a competitive back-stabber." He shifted in his chair and again leaned forward. "I am engaged in work of profound importance. No one among the wooden heads on this ship can be trusted with these experiments. But as an inducement, recall that tolerance of your presence may not be eternal. If you wish to continue with this boat-load of posturing rabble, help me with this work and begin tomorrow."

Pierre's hesitation passed. "I'm uncertain of what I can provide but I'm ready to try."

The Scientist nodded. "So perhaps you will provide help to this old man." He refilled his cup again and held it in Pierre's direction before drinking it down.

With the relief of a challenge survived, Pierre stood and stepped toward the door. "Thank you for this opportunity."

The Scientist dozily nodded. With a distracted wave of his hand he signaled his permission for Pierre to leave. "Return tomorrow," he said, "but not too early, if you please."

Pierre slipped out closing the door firmly behind him. In the dimly-lit passageway he suddenly noticed the stench of the Scientist's rooms. As if a draft from Hell had wafted past him, he hurried along eager to breathe fresh air. And somewhere along the dark labyrinth below-decks he became lost.

With Doctor De Montaigne there had seemed only a few turns but somehow his confusion increased their number and so he wandered. Peering around corners and through half-opened doors he hoped to find someone to direct him. But now the ship seemed suddenly large.

Turning another corner, he heard voices from the far end of the corridor speaking in heated disagreement. He quieted his footsteps to approach a partly-opened cabin door until he could hear the voices clearly. A single voice arose suddenly above the others. He did not recognize this voice but what he heard held him.

"Does His Holiness not understand how close we are to ending this heretical threat? Why set us this new task?" To Pierre's surprise, the next voice belonged to Doctor De Montaigne.

"His Holiness worries less about the fates of his pawns and more about the ultimate victory of the Lord."

"But we are so close." The stranger's tone of urgency surprised Pierre. "The creature we can pursue at a later time. Once we have drawn the fangs of the heretics we will resume the search for that creature and do as His Holiness wishes."

"These speculations are beside the point!" Hearing the Chef's voice also surprised Pierre, as if someone who cooks could not also conspire. "We have received new directives and must proceed as if they had come from the lips of His Holiness himself."

The stranger spoke again but now with a tone of dejection. "Is there a way to inform His Holiness of our changed circumstance?"

"We only have the communiqué," the Doctor said flatly, "given to us by the captain of the Enbricada before his death. An issue so urgent the Holy Office rigged out a ship and crew and cargo and then sent it sailing into the south Atlantic simply in the hope it would cross our path; this should assure us how serious His Holiness regards our new mission."

"What I fail to understand," the Chef stated with as much annoyance as anger, "is why His Holiness would conclude it was more important to give the Lord's blessing to the creature than extinguish heresy?"

“Fortunately,” Doctor De Montaigne said, “we need not waste a moment wondering. Either we aid our mad-hatter Captain and use our new sailor to attract the creature, or we delay its pursuit until we settle the issue of the heretics, find their gold and use it to destroy their colony.” Pierre found himself frozen as if a large hand gradually closed around his throat.

“Why does His Holiness want the creature blessed?” The Chef’s confusion gave his question a desperation that stirred Pierre’s sympathy.

Doctor De Montaigne sighed loudly. “According to the message, His Holiness believes it is possessed by the Evil One and does His bidding; the destruction and loss of life it inflicts is only explained by demonic influence. He believes that released from that possession, its power can be turned to benefit the Church.”

“As members of the Society of Jesus,” the stranger added, “and soldiers of the True Religion, perhaps he has concluded that by bringing this creature to heel we protect our Church’s financial interest dependent on international shipping.”

“But ignore the threat from these Jansenist vermin?” the Chef asked. “Their blight upon the face of Christendom becomes more deadly as their numbers grow. The creature, after all, is not attracting followers, but the Hugenots have penetrated the highest levels of the aristocracy.”

“In principle I agree,” Doctor De Montaigne said. “But we must obey His Holiness.”

The stranger added, “Those men who buried that treasure will never return to claim it so we must suppose it can be left where it was buried.”

Doctor De Montaigne said, “It could hardly be safer.”

After a thoughtful silence the Chef said, “What shall we do with the boy?”

The Doctor said, “Our Captain believes he will attract the creature and we must encourage his belief. If the beast appears, the Captain will change course to pursue it.”

The Chef said, “We should put him under lock and key so that he does not escape.”

“At sea that is unnecessary,” the stranger said. “Besides, I am certain our Captain is prepared to hold him safe. And according to the Doctor, the boy has fallen under the thrall of that lunatic Scientist. Between drink and delusion he will be helpless in his company.”

“I care not one whit for that,” the Chef said. “The distraction the boy creates makes him dangerous. And worse luck, he seems just reasonable enough and clever enough to ingratiate."

"I say, do we need to be rid of him?" Pierre did not recognize this voice either but he was grateful. "Port Royal remains days away. I say we ignore the boy and enjoy the port, and when we set sail, make certain he sails with us."

"And ignore the command of His Holiness?" the Chef asked.

In an ameliorating tone the Doctor said "We can only proceed as opportunity allows."

"Suppose," the first stranger asked, "the creature crosses our path and the Captain decides to chase it?" A sudden panic filled Pierre's chest, the muscles of his legs twitched like the plucked strings of a violin, but run where? "What if he decides it is his last chance and the boy his only hope?" He was surprised he had not recognized this stranger's antipathy, but the tremor in his voice at the thought of meeting the creature almost drew his sympathy.

"There are five of us and an infinite sea," Doctor De Montaigne said. "He will be of no use to the Captain if he falls overboard."

"Your reasonableness recommends your program," the Chef said. "I for one look forward to arriving at our destination in good health and with a heavy purse. With pleasure so near, an encounter with that sea-beast would trigger my darker humors." Suddenly, moving chairs squeaked and groaned. The Chef continued, "We will reconvene as matters warrant."

But Pierre had already turned and quietly begun his retreat along the passageway. Further from the door he increased his pace, took the first turn he found and broke into a near-run until he reached another turn, finally safe from discovery. He stopped to catch his breath, now wondering if he had even a single ally on the ship. He chose a direction and began to follow it, all the while listening for other voices. Thus he wandered.

He turned onto a corridor whose end disappeared into brown twilight. He trod leaning away from boards that creaked under his step. Ahead was a nimbus of weak yellow light he suspected came from an open doorway. When he reached the door he stopped and peered inside.

Lit by two candles mounted to the wall that faced the door and a small mirror between, he watched a shirtless young man leaning over a basin vigorously wash his face. As he appeared preoccupied, Pierre decided to hurry across the open door. But as he was about to move the young man picked up a towel, straightened and began to wipe his face. The towel covered the person's face, but it was obvious that Pierre was looking at a woman.

When she brought the towel down and discovered him reflected in the mirror, she gasped but then turned and strode across the cabin, a pale glimmering shape, to reach the door and block his way. Looking with curious, dark eyes deeply into his she whispered, "Say nothing or I am lost." With a quick, light kiss on his lips, she stepped back into the cabin and soundlessly closed the door.

Stunned, Pierre was desperate for sunshine and open air and the company of others. He hurried ahead heedless of who he might encounter eager to return to the living.

He reached the gangway and in the next moment stood under a bright sky.

The wind blew with a sharp edge and he felt as if he had awakened from a dream. Watching the crew go about their duties his thoughts returned to the young woman. The Scientist's suggestion could not have been better-timed.

He made a circuit of the main deck still wondering about that woman. Had he seen her among the crew and simply not recognized her? And was she a secret guest or perhaps some misdirected stowaway? She was sufficiently confident to leave the door open as she washed. Or had that been accidental?

Exhausted by the day, he completed his circuit of the deck and recalled the conversation he had overheard. If the crew excluded him from their hopeless excursion into the jaws of that creature, Pierre was grateful. As for what might occur as they approached the safety of Port Royal, if the creature was sighted, he would refuse to help and hope he was supported by a few sailors.

He had accomplished a lot that morning; he had been made a member of the crew and then met Dr. de Montpellier and agreed to work with him until they reached Port Royal, resigned to tolerate an old fool.

Then the image of that young woman returned. This time she strode toward slowly, her pale breasts round and high on a chest that narrowed to a small waist and flat stomach, loosened trousers revealing a neat, fleshy navel, the white towel held hanging by her side, advancing and yet frozen in the moment. Her dark eyes had seemed more curious than alarmed. He would find her, too. Before their ship had docked, he would learn who she was.

Between creaking timbers and a rolling sea Pierre wondered how lucky he might eventually become and decided he could become very lucky indeed.

CHAPTER TEN

THE NEXT MORNING, as Pierre followed the gangway preparing to meet with the Scientist, he saw Doctor De Montaigne approach him from the opposite direction. He stopped Pierre with a courteous bow. His smile was good-natured and curious and Pierre hesitated, caught between distrust and embarrassment. "Was your conversation with Dr. de Montpellier all you hoped?"

"My father's work seems better-known to him than to me. And I must have appeared as dim-witted to him as I did to my father."

The Doctor's smile turned to concern. "He finds no mind as subtle as his own. Even here among educated men he cloaks his study in mystery. No man is as boring as one enraptured by his own brilliance." His tone edged to sympathy. "Have you reached an agreement?"

Again Pierre hesitated. "He seems confident I can help so I'll do my best."

Doctor De Montaigne laughed. "You are immodestly modesty. If he invites your assistance it is because he believes you will help him."

"Your flattery is appreciated but not comforting."

Pierre wanted to continue on his way but the Doctor seemed determined to hold him. "Considering your background, can you tell me if his work is significant?"

"Since I don't understand it very clearly I'm the wrong person to ask."

"Nonsense! His explanations, I confess, leave me muddled. Whereas you at least understand his scientific principles." Pierre remained silent. "I suppose by his lights the rest of us are mere blockheads." He then smiled with such despondency Pierre overcame his hesitation.

"If his work is as he says—and inspecting his devices, I suspect it is—

then he is no necromancer; your scientist is the genuine article."

Doctor De Montaigne's look suddenly darkened, as if his doubt had shifted to Pierre, but that shadow passed quickly. "So it is doubly fortunate we plucked you from the sea. Natural philosophy will sing our praises for having brought you together. And your father will have even more reason to be proud of his son."

Like a shard of golden glass, a fragment of sunlight passed slowly across the Doctor's face lighting his eyes. Pierre wondered if he knew of that young woman who now gripped his imagination. If so, the Doctor had no reason to reveal it. Pierre said, "Then I will need to work hard. If I'm certain of nothing else, I know he'll be a difficult task-master."

Doctor De Montaigne's smile broadened. "And you will succeed beyond your best expectations." Then he excused himself and Pierre watched his retreating back until it disappeared around a corner.

The little knowledge he had inherited from his father seemed all that stood between Pierre and a watery death; that same knowledge that had taken his father far from Gabriella and set Pierre on this deadly search. But nothing would dispel the image of that young woman, a nettle to every thought. Relieved the Doctor was gone, Pierre looked around to discover that once again he had become lost.

Overhead, the music of the morning dance accompanied by muffled foot-falls provided an accompaniment to his search. This deck between decks appeared a maze of low, narrow passageways and shifting shadows. Pierre wandered, teased by vaguely recollected corridors. And then a shadow that filled the corridor ahead suddenly approached him blocking his way. Certain this was someone with a sure knowledge of the passages, at first he was relieved. But the shadow took form and he recognized striding toward him Captain Stevenson, moving as if the world's sin burdened his shoulders.

"Just what are you about, wandering down here?" His voice was a whisper but fury resonated from his chest. "A mangy dog snooping around; what do you hope to find?"

"I'm looking for the cabin of Dr. de Montpellier." The Captain's expression of grim disbelief sent panic through Pierre's stomach. He brought his wide, dark face close to Pierre's.

"You don't wander down here, boy. People down here know where they're going and mind their own business." His fierce expression leaned hard on Pierre. "Be like those people."

Pierre said nothing but the Captain reached a conclusion. "You've fallen in with a bad man. I tell you this; your eternal soul is at risk. The heathens of the forest are children compared to his diabolical ways. Keep your distance if you care for that thing you regard as your soul." He suddenly spat. "To keep you out of the kind of mischief that leads to death I'll take you to him, but it pains me. Like I'm leading a virgin to the whoremaster's bed." He turned and began to walk. Pierre hesitated but quickly followed.

The Captain strode the passage as if plowing snow with his chest. He took each turn without hesitation as if the ship's innards were so thoroughly within his mind he could navigate blind. Pierre studied doors and counted passageways but soon surrendered to his own confusion.

In the cool, damp twilight, an erotic tremor suddenly passed through Pierre; the image of that young woman returned. He watched the rolling, massive shoulders ahead and wondered, given his omniscience, how the Captain could fail to know of her presence. Then he wondered if some relationship existed between them. Female relative, or friend in hiding, or in flight? Mistress or perhaps daughter? What Pierre could not believe was that he did not know of her at all. Then he noticed the odor of burning chemicals.

The Captain stopped suddenly, nodded toward the door and then turned with an expression that said he had completed a degrading task and was relieved to be on his way. Pierre waited until his retreating footsteps assured him he was gone and then knocked on the door. He heard the cough he had come to recognize.

The opened door revealed the Scientist wearing a stained red robe and surrounded by a thick, blue cloud. "You're late!" He turned from the door and Pierre followed closing it behind him. "I grew impatient and began this experiment alone." He dropped heavily into a large stuffed chair, lifted a tumbler full of wine from the table by his side and drank. "Foolish decision," he said, drank again and returned the glass to the table half-empty. Pierre explained that he had become lost, but the Scientist seemed not to hear. "I am not very skillful this early in the morning." He belched, leaned back and closed his eyes. "Catch me after midnight and then my skills are satanic." His grin exposed black and rotted teeth. Pierre had to look away. "But you are here now," he added, "so all will go well. Have a seat." He gestured toward a pile of objects so various Pierre wondered if something beneath it might be alive.

He eyed the jumble. "The Captain appears to hold unusual ideas about you." Indecision left Pierre standing beside the pile.

Eyes still closed the Scientist's grin curled into a sneer. "Our Captain represents a portion of the species we all should hope is about to disappear." He opened his eyes slowly, glanced at Pierre and his sneer suddenly into a glare. He leaned forward. "You wish to be my assistant yet are unable to move a few books?" With a swipe of his hand the objects tumbled to the floor revealing the tattered chair Pierre remembered from the previous day.

"When I tell my assistant to do something, it gets done or he is no longer my assistant." With a grunt Dr. de Montpellier leaned back into his chair and refilled his glass and then stared angrily into space. "Ignorance and arrogance form a poisonous brew." He clenched his free fist as if about to strike the air. "We are at war and you had best not forget that. So we deploy our meager forces carefully." He turned. "Do you understand?" His expression was so fierce that Pierre had to turn away in embarrassment.

After a long moment the Scientist began quietly to laugh. "It appears my new assistant has no stomach for a fight. Can that be true?"

Pierre looked up and met his glance. "You have a lot on your mind this morning. I'll come back later."

The Scientist roared with laughter. "Drawing room manners will get us nowhere. But can it be that the man who survived all you described retreats from battle with mere humans?"

Pierre could offer no good answer and the Scientist must have recognized this. He stood slowly. "We have work to do and you have something that remains to be demonstrated." He walked to a table at the far end of the cabin and Pierre joined him.

"Spread about are experiments I have built since the beginning of our voyage. As the path of your father's work demanded he employ certain devices to conduct certain experiments, what I ask is simple. Tell me which you recognize and what you know about them."

Taking up one device and then the next, moving levers or exposing pulleys and springs Pierre said, "He has been gone ten years and it seems some of his work was done far from our home." He moved around the table once and then a second time hovering longer over each device as he chased his memory.

With a nod toward the table the Scientist said, “By considering the devices he made, it should be possible to guess his strategy.”

Pierre struggled to recall shapes, structures of wood and brass and glass, anything that reminded him of Augustus’s devices. In the end he managed to identify four. He returned to his chair wondering if he had completely recovered from his time at sea.

Pierre’s effort demanded such concentration he experienced waves of vertigo. Sight of these devices brought to mind Augustus in mid-gesture, mid-word, mid-life. Light passed through the small window as an iridescence like that through a glass filled with filthy water and evoked the musk of eternal shadow. The Scientist surveyed the devices with a satisfied smile while Pierre fell into a gloom that so filled the space around him even the Scientist noticed.

But instead of attempting to console Pierre, he asked, “Have you ever visited Port Royal?” Startled, Pierre glanced up to meet his eyes and then shook his head.

Smiling he said, “A city where the sun is hot, the rum is cheap, and the women are easy.”

“If you’re trying to excite my enthusiasm,” Pierre responded, “you’ve succeeded.”

“And that will be your downfall. Before your first day has passed you will be broke, poxed, and hung-over. And for the rest of our stay you will cadge drinks and dodge creditors. By the time we sail you will curse that town and all its denizens.” He laughed quietly. “In the best interest of science and your own, you should be confined here until we depart, even if that proved more cruel than being left to float about in the sea.” He shook his head. “But let us resume, at least while you can still remember.”

Mention of those devices tossed Pierre further into his gloom. To distract the Scientist he asked, “Do you believe the Captain will continue to pursue the creature?”

The Scientist shrugged. “Surely he is a madman believing in things he cannot prove and possessing thoughts he cannot name. He wants to bring Nature to the bench of Law and have his suit upheld. Execution of the creature will do nicely and even better if he can serve as executioner. It’s time you understood all of this."

"So he means to keep me with his ship."

"Here he can afford you the luxury of free movement. But once landed at Port Royal, he will be on you like a flea."

"So either escape or be cursed. And if I hope to escape I had better plan now."

The Scientist nodded. "But you will need a confederate to hatch the plot aboard ship and then assist when you have landed."

Pierre became silent and wondered.

The Scientist studied him and then laughed; its unpleasant tone startled Pierre. "We have these instruments to examine. Now tell me," he said carefully lifting one from the table, "what you remember about this."

He responded to Dr. de Montpellier's questions as best he could and decided to make his escape plan later. As he spoke, the Scientist took notes, occasionally stopping Pierre with a question. The effort to recognize and remember and explain proved even more tiring and soon he requested the session end. Annoyed the Scientist insisted Pierre resume the next day. "I will have even more questions and they will be more detailed and specific."

Pierre's mind was a gray jumble and even the effort to keep his eyes open was a struggle. . He glanced away. "Do you believe I'll see my father again?"

The Scientist appeared surprised by the question. He studied Pierre and then returned to his chair. Though he appeared distracted he began to speak, as if by compulsion.

"Whatever is about to happen, we can only try to be ready for it. Knowing this tells us all we need in order to do the only thing we can do, which is survive. Give up the illusions of winning and losing. We win by virtue of remaining alive and lose by the inevitability of death. As for your father, it is impossible to know and therefore it must not matter. You are here now and with no assurance you will ever be anywhere else ever again."

Though exhaustion worked at Pierre in ways he could not resist, what he saw in the Scientist's eyes frightened him. The Scientist continued, "The value of science is its assurance that if we understand a problem correctly, we will recognize that those tools needed to solve it lay within our reach. So cherish my advice even while you disparage its source."

Whether it was exhaustion, or the odors swirling about him, or that weak and dolorous light, or some ineluctable combination, Pierre fell again into despair. Looking around the cluttered cabin, he decided he needed sunlight and fresh air and the sight of men about their work. Forcing himself to stand Pierre said, "Fair enough; I'll return tomorrow." He moved toward the door.

To Pierre's back the Scientist said, "One small but urgent request; share nothing of our conversation. Never forget you are being observed and unlikely to your benefit."

Puzzled, Pierre paused and turned. Dr. de Montpellier tipped his chin down until his eyes disappeared in shadow. "This ship holds secrets within secrets and you are a stranger among conspirators. Your confidence will be solicited and not returned. Go about with a vigilant eye and still tongue and your discretion will sustain you." He refilled his glass and held it to the light. "Because the seas you cross are deep." He emptied the glass in one long draught. When he looked up again his eyes glittered and his grin was painful for Pierre to look at. He turned and left, closing the door quietly behind him

Suddenly he felt free to wander according to his whim and perhaps even find her and was excited by that prospect, as if she clung to his thoughts. He tried to remember the path that had led to her and found he could not, so he chose another as if chance might find her for him. Relieved that a lack of success was not the same as failure, he started off.

He walked slowly observing each mark upon a door or change of color of floor or walls although the weak light disguised every passage's secrets. Despite his efforts, eventually he resigned himself to returning to the main deck. But instantly he discovered that was more difficult than he guessed.

Images of that woman had driven the conversation over-heard the previous day from his mind, but wandering now in twilight its memory returned. The Doctor and the others certainly conspired about something that blended the ludicrous with the treacherous. He wondered if this was the conspiracy the Scientist had spoken of. He recalled the Scientist's smirk when he told Pierre they would use him for their own ends without regard to his and insist he share their battle unconcerned about the danger. He imagined the Scientist asking in what way their intentions were different from the Captain's. With all of this, he wondered about the Scientist.

Granted, the man seemed prepared to share greater confidences with Pierre than the others. But did he actually hold Pierre's life at some value? He needed Pierre's help to learn about Augustus's work but also perhaps to leap ahead of him as well. So would helping Dr. de Montpellier also betray Augustus and aid the theft of his work? If so, then perhaps his weak understanding of that work was his salvation since it assured him that, at worst, damage to his father's reputation would be accidental. Relieved that his good fortune lay in not knowing very much, he found himself smiling. Ignorance might even save him; certainly he possessed that in abundance.

He slowed his pace and reached another intersection where the passageways seemed more brightly lit and then stopped. He took a moment to study the cool blue-gray shadows, chose a passageway and followed but nearing its end he stopped.

Familiarity filled him, and with additional steps that became stronger. He stopped at a door and leaned his ear toward it. Hearing nothing he laid the flat of his hand on it and pressed; it moved inward with silent ease. Before it was half open he knew where he was.

Ahead stood a wash-stand, above it hung a small rectangular mirror, wall-mounted candles dark on either side; this was the same room. On the floor to his left lay a single bunk, its bedclothes bunched as if recently slept in, and to his right was a sea chest painted black. Standing at the threshold leaning into the room, he caught his own reflection in the mirror and found its expression of surprise nearly charming. He stepped inside and closed the door. Standing in the center of the tiny cabin, he listened to the thud of his heart beating inside his ears.

Beneath the smell of brine and the sea, Pierre detected an aroma he assumed to be hers. Her body had left an impression in the rumpled bedclothes over the straw mattress and he only needed to squint his eyes to see her, soft and pale in blue twilight. He discovered himself breathing hard and fast. On the washstand was a small piece of pale soap still wet and the basin was also wet. On the floor below the basin and from the angle of the reflected light he made out damp outlines, like a pair of shoes, of two small feet. He went to the sea chest.

It had no label but its nicks and scratches betrayed a life of long and frequent travel. Attempting to lift its lid he was not surprised to find it locked. This gesture of privacy seemed to make her more desirable. He sat down on the edge of the bunk debating whether to remain and dispel the mystery. But she might not return to her cabin alone and even if she did it was unlikely she would be pleased to find him there. Deciding it was best to leave and plan a return visit he stopped at the cabin door, listened before letting himself out and then closed the door as he had found it.

In the passageway he studied its floor and ceiling and then those doors opposite. Confident he would conjure the space in his mind, he resumed his search certain now of what he must do.

But every certainty evaporated as turn after turn confused him more. Reminding himself that every false path points to the true one, he continued only concerned he not be discovered.

Following a passageway he assumed was wrong, he found himself suddenly standing at the foot of the stairs leading to the main deck. Emerging blinded by sunlight in a cloudless sky, in a moment of distraction Pierre looked up. Figures moved around the sails and in the rigging not far above his head but then he recognized her.

He was certain it was her though he was unsure why. He watched her make her way along the starboard yard of the main mast and there begin to descend. He strolled along the rail to a position that allowed him to keep her in sight while appearing to look out over the sea. She moved easily among ropes and tackle blocks and around broad canvas sheets and so he wondered where she might have acquired such skill. He moved toward the gunwale to reach it just as she did. He was about to step forward when a hand fell heavily on his shoulder.

"Ah ha!" the voice behind him said. "Did you think you could hide your secret forever?" Instantly he recognized Doctor De Montaigne's voice. He turned to see that the Chef stood beside him.

Embarrassed the Chef said, "Our Doctor likes his little surprises." With an annoyed glance he added, "Far more than those forced to participate."

"Spoken like the joyless person you are," Doctor De Montaigne announced brightly. "It is apparent our friend delights in such jolly gestures, if only to dispel the ennui of our voyage."

Pierre glanced up toward the mast but she was gone; another effort failed.

The Doctor continued, "Our friend appears disappointed, Monsieur Le Chef, do you agree? A dyspeptic heart, no doubt. He stands in need of light conversation and strong drink." From his jacket the Doctor brought out a silver flask. The cap doubled as a container and he carefully filled it and handed it to Pierre. "Do not take your recovery for granted. Simply alternate periods of activity with periods of rest." He drank recognizing the aroma of brandy. An expression of concern passed over the Doctor's face that might have been genuine. "Conserve your strength for our visit to Port Royal." He laughed while the Chef could only smile.

To Pierre, the Chef said, "Perhaps it will help pass the time in an agreeable way if we share some useful local knowledge of Port Royal and its glittering surprises."

The Doctor nudged Pierre as if they were conspirators. "Join us in my cabin after supper for a pipe of tobacco and some brandy and we will share our favorite tales."

The strong drink reached Pierre's head quickly. With the rocking motion of the ship and under the bright sun, suddenly he felt ill. "Until then," Pierre said bowing and almost losing his balance. At that moment he would have agreed to anything that sent him below-deck.

Calling to Pierre's back the Doctor added, "And be sure you are on-time for dinner or Monsieur Le Chef will suffer another broken heart."

Pierre waved and lengthened his stride. Whatever the Doctor had given him to drink muffled every thought that occurred to him. He moved down the stairs and along the passageway in a somnambulist's fog, proceeding by instinct until he reached his bunk. Stretched out, a weight he could not name or describe gradually slid like a wet overcoat from his chest and he seemed to become lighter so that in the next moment he might levitate. The sensation was delightful and he smiled. Was luck finally moving in his direction? Could Fortune's smirk be turning into a smile? As the light faded he recognized luck as a silver object afloat on a silver sea but he could not decide whether it moved toward him or away.

CHAPTER ELEVEN

PIERRE APPROACHED THE galley to join his shipmates for their evening meal when he heard Count D'Antoine say, "We can only hope Claire remains mistress of the Cat and Fiddle tavern and that it continues to lack a master." His words drew laughter from the table. All turned to greet Pierre and Duke Du Bordeaux offered a place at the end of the bench. Two other sailors had joined their table and Jacques-Simone introduced them as Guy-Marat of Toulouse and Hugo-Pierre of St. Bois. A candle lantern swung in lazy arcs above their table casting amber shadows over their faces.

"Mistress of the tavern or no," Hugo-Pierre said, "there will be no master for Claire." The rest of the table laughed but Guy-Marat laughed loudest.

"Nor will there ever be," he added. "For I shall occupy that position or no man shall."

Jacques-Simone said, "But what about woman?"

The table laughed even louder as Guy-Marat's face became red; whether from embarrassment or anger Pierre could not judge.

"And what matter to you," Duke Du Bordeaux asked, "so long as she is horizontal?"

From the half-door at the end of the galley the Chef appeared bearing a large tureen, pale steam curling lazily from its open top, and placed it at the center of the table.

Hugo-Pierre whined, "Bouillabaisse again?"

"The best you ever will eat," the Chef announced. "In the middle of the ocean you eat like kings yet complain you should eat like gods." He sneered. "Burdened with such ignorance, how can I be offended?" He then disappeared into the galley.

To Hugo-Pierre, Guy-Marat said, "If our next meal is swill, we will know who to blame." To Pierre he said, "So have you visited Port Royal before?" He was startled to be asked this question and explained that the Doctor and the Scientist each had offered to share their experience of the port. The others murmured smiling.

Guy-Marat said, "Then undoubtedly your first visit should be to the Green Dragon Inn."

Jacques-Simone added, "He must be introduced to Maria-Theresa, especially as she remains a close friend of the Governor."

Chuckling, Duke Du Bordeaux said, "Every tavern-keeper in Port Royal is a friend of the Governor, or he does not keep a tavern."

Pierre's companions then shared tales and observations that suggested they knew every dubious character and establishment of doubtful repute on the island. The details of their reminiscences promised Pierre's visit would provide adventures he could only just imagine and whose recollection would delight him for the rest of his days. Regarding the exploits of a particularly notorious couple, Guy-Marat observed, "One such miracle in a lifetime is as much as most of us can endure."

Nodding toward Pierre, Jacques-Simone said, "I suspect our young friend could sustain such a miracle every day of the year."

"And I expect," Count D'Antoine said, "that is precisely his dream."

"One man's dream," Duke Du Bordeaux said, "usually is another's nightmare, yet there is no one who does not share such a dream."

Pierre ate heartily savoring every spoonful, and drank enthusiastically as his crew-mates educated him about their startling experiences. From these he concluded that Port Royal contained more taverns than churches, more brothels than taverns, more whores than moneylenders and more slaves than freemen. Judged by the exploits he heard they approached a city where a humble seaman might gain a burgher's fortune and lose it again within an hour. He imagined a town where every woman's smile offered sensual abandon, lurid and frenzied delight and a hysteria of pleasure. With a side-long grin Duke Du Bordeaux suddenly added, "It appears we have given our new shipmate too much to think about since he has stained his breeches."

Startled, Pierre looked down to find a dark spot, warm and damp, on his thigh. "I've only spilled some soup," he said. He crossed his legs as the rest of the table roared with laughter.

Duke Du Bordeaux said, "Someone so young should have a guide, if only so he is not swallowed whole by the first saucy tart whose jaundiced eye he catches."

"Undoubtedly," Guy-Marat said, "that is another fate he dreams of."

"We must not," Count D'Antoine added, "allow this lamb to wander defenseless through a wilderness of such eager depravity."

Duke Du Bordeaux said, "Considering your raging jealousy I believe your gravest concern is that this fresh face will leave one less nymph for your amusement."

"Men of your advanced age," Hugo-Pierre said, "often have as much difficulty with their hearing as with the toils of Venus."

"And gentlemen of your age," Jacques-Simone added, "have difficulty with their sight as well. Perhaps our young charge will be kind enough to assist you."

Guy-Marat asked, "So, shall we confine him to the ship for his own protection?"

"Such cruelty," Duke Du bordeaux responded in mock fury, "is typical of your mind. Yet your suggestion has some merit."

After a moment's pause Hugo-Pierre suddenly announced, "Our solution is at hand." When all eyes turned he said, "Put Pierre under the tutelage of the venerable Dr. de Montpellier himself."

Silence filled the small room, followed suddenly by loud approval.

Startled, Duke Du Bordeaux said, "With a single stroke you demonstrate sagacity beyond your obviously advanced years."

Count D'Antoine added, "What could be more appropriate than that Science and Reason curb the wild yearning of young flesh?"

Jacques-Simone said, "It will demand a stout-hearted wench to confront our Scientist when he is determined to protect this pup from temptations to his virtue."

Duke Du Bordeaux turned to Pierre and clapped him on the back. "With this problem resolved we can now plan our own encounters confident you will come to no harm."

To Pierre, Hugo-Pierre said, "Do not look disappointed; you will be the most likely of us to leave Port Royal with your pockets full and unburdened by the pox."

Count D'Antoine added, "Consider the loans we will beg from you when our fortunes have vanished."

"And accompanied by our Scientist," Duke Du Bordeaux said, "imagine all of the obscure knowledge you will imbibe. Yours will be an education of the most rounded and varied contours."

Hugo-Pierre added, "As opposed to the rounded contours which now occupy your thoughts."

To the others Jacques-Simone said. "And perhaps in the company of Pierre our Scientist will appear suddenly attractive to the eye of some undemanding female."

Count d'Antoine chimed in, "Such luck would be more than he has enjoyed since the moment of his birth." The others laughed and gloomily he continued. "Gentlemen, we must be honest. Our venerable Scientist has as much chance of attracting affectionate companionship as Duke Du Bordeaux has of reaching Heaven."

The Duke smirked as he surveyed his companions. "If he hopes to enjoy such delights, this castaway represents his best chance." Turning to Pierre he added, "You may even return the favor our Scientist has provided you. Are you not grateful?"

Certain that any response would only draw more ridicule to himself and Dr. de Montpellier he said, "Since all that you've said seems true and my debt to him is genuine, I'll challenge myself to lure female companionship worthy of him."

Count D'Antoine said, "Our sea-waif appears in reality a shark in dolphin's clothing."

"He displays arrogance enough for a bishop," Hugo-Pierre added.

Duke Du Bordeaux stood at his seat holding his tankard aloft. "Let us salute the confidence of a youth brazen enough to spit into the face of Venus and then demand her pleasure." The others cheered "Here, here!" and then, striking their tankards together, all drank deeply.

Suddenly the Chef's scowling face peered into the galley. "Regrettably, others jealously await the seats you now occupy. Their empty bellies may drive them to actions which in good conscience they would not otherwise engage, and I have no desire to defend my galley from a horde of starving sailors. So be off with you! "

Jacques-Simone said, "Gentlemen, we leave this table to our comrades certain that our shipmate has accepted a grave responsibility."

Duke Du Bordeaux then turned to Pierre. "Please join us and we will continue this conversation."

"Your invitation is tempting," Pierre said, "but I've promised to join Doctor De Montaigne in his quarters."

At the mention of the Doctor all eyes turned with knowing looks. Duke Du Bordeaux said, "You have been invited to join the elect and it would be churlish for us to insist you abandon that appointment."

Pierre stood from the table to discover he had drunk more than he realized. Steadying himself with a hand on the table he wished all a good night and left. In the twilight of the gangway he chose a direction he assumed led to the Doctor's cabin but instantly discovered himself lost. Drunk and confused, he wandered.

Recalling the table conversation, he cringed at the prospect of dragging the Scientist along the streets of Port Royal. If that man had a personal life, he did not want to know about it.

Alone in that corridor he considered the Doctor's invitation and its demand for him to be amusing. Being the object of good-natured mockery by his shipmates was one thing, but the prospect of having to endure similar jests from the Doctor left him dejected. He stopped in the dimly-lit passageway and decided to return to his bunk. Resigned to offering apologies in the morning he turned to make his way back to his bunk, and then he saw her.

She was moving away in twilight and in the next moment turned to disappear. Only a glimpse, he had not seen her face but was certain he recognized her. Softening his tread he rushed to the spot where he had seen her turn.

He followed confident she was near and certain he still heard her footsteps. Further ahead she reappeared under the light of another candle but instantly disappeared into muddy twilight. He quickened his step and entered the next corridor but then stopped.

Despite the weak light this short corridor offered two closed doors on either side and ended with no connecting passages. Stepping silently he followed it examining each door. One appeared not entirely closed and along its edge was a space of absolute black.

He rested his hand against the door and leaned until it yielded an opening just wide enough to pass through. With a step he was inside and his back pressed against the closing door. He waited for his eyes to adjust but the windowless space only resolved into a featureless black. Suddenly arms encircled him and a body pressed against his. He gasped but lips just below his ear whispered, "Shush".

"Who are you?" Pierre whispered.

"No one," the voice replied.

He dropped his arms and his hands discovered flesh, naked and warm. The lips beside his ear sighed. While his hands caressed, his companion's hands pulled at Pierre's trousers. Urgent breathing reached his ear and lips suddenly pressed against his own in a hot, moist kiss. His trousers fell to puddle at his ankles. A cool hand grasped him and their kiss was broken by a sweet, quiet sigh.

Free arm encircling his neck, his companion stepped backward pulling him to follow. Ankles confined by his fallen trousers he stumbled forward, his companion somehow beneath him, and onto a pile of rough cloth half-crouched between her thighs. His heart drummed in his ears. While the arm surrounding his neck tightened to bring his lips to her breast she shifted her hips until she brought him inside. The heavy smell of her skin sent his head spinning. He began to thrust and for each his companion pushed back until she met his pace and then set her own.

At each stroke she moaned softly. Her knees curled and her fingers dug into his back as her moans became deeper. Her back arched, her head tossed from side to side and Pierre recognized that his own moment approached. The tone of her moans moved higher as if she might sing. His moment arrived and then he was spinning, a dizzying fall accompanied by bright detonations behind his eyes leaving him breathless and blind. A squeal from the lips beside his ear made him smile.

Naked from stomach to knees he rolled onto his back breathless, his smile a grin of delight. Sensations crashed about him and their cascade swept away every thought. The darkness was so complete he was not even certain his eyes were open. But he was certain a warm body breathed beside his.

That body lay so close he sensed the heat radiating from her flesh and heard the light, even rhythm of her contented breathing. And so, Pierre drifted.

Afloat above a rolling sea he rocked lazily, his body hummed with a visceral contentment he did not question. He drifted in all directions at once. Time became dense leaving him suspending between moments. He allowed his arm to fall by his side and into empty space.

He sat up to realize she was gone.

At first he guessed she had moved beyond his reach, but in that pitch darkness he heard no sighs, no murmurs, no breathing. He stood pulling up his trousers and waited for his companion to emerge, but in the next moment he knew he was alone. Reaching with arms outstretched he located the door and found it wide open. Resigned he stepped into the passageway and quietly closed the door behind him. He followed this corridor moving toward a candle far ahead and its weak yellow light. At the first intersection of corridors he paused trying to recall his path to his bunk.

Turning once and then again he had nearly reached the end of the next corridor when a booming voice behind him growled, "Hey! You! Boy!" The voice belonged to Captain Stevenson. Pierre stopped and turned. His luck had changed more than once this day, and he wondered if there was any limit to how often that might happen, and if there was a way to measure luck or understand the balance between its likelihood and its absence. He was certain the Captain would not help him answer any of his questions.

CHAPTER TWELVE

"WHAT ARE YOU doing down here?" The Captain's voice filled the corridor as his glower dimmed the light. "Or is that a question impossible for your blighted skull?"

No longer glowing, Pierre shrugged. "I seem to be lost."

"Ain't that the God's honest!"

"It happens whenever I come down here."

"Some situations are hopeless," the Captain growled, "like some people." Pierre could add nothing to that. "There's something you need to see." He turned and began to stride away. Pierre hurried to follow. To his surprise, after two turns they stood on deck.

The night sky was cloudless and glittered with stars and the sudden cool breeze cleared Pierre's head. The Captain led him to the quarter-deck. Standing beside the port rail, Doctor De Montaigne watched them approach and when they reached him the Captain took the telescope from his hand and passed it to Pierre. "Look to the moon."

The moon was full and bright as butter and the horizon cut it neatly through the middle. He put the telescope to his eye. Behind him the Captain said, "Follow the horizon line."

But Pierre saw it even before Captain Stevenson spoke. The hand holding the telescope dropped to his side and he took two steps back from the rail.

"That's all I wanted to know," the Captain said. He removed the telescope from Pierre's cramped grasp and put it to his own eye. "Spotted it just after eight bells. The Doctor was on watch and he called for me. I come up and there it was. Didn't want to be wrong, so I come after you."

Pierre stood very still, his mind feeling as his arm did when he had slept on it. When finally a thought emerged, it was to run away. He turned

"Not so fast, boy!" The Captain's eye remained at the eyepiece. "It ain't coming after us, not just yet, anyway. Seems to just want to keep us in view." Telescope now by his side he turned to face Pierre. "Why would it do that?" His grin left Pierre even more frightened than he had been at the sight of the creature's blunt, square head silhouetted against the moon.

Pierre hesitated. "Didn't the Scientist's instruments tell you it was nearby?"

For the first time, something he said caused Captain Stevenson to pause. He looked at Pierre and a faint smile appeared. "I should have a little chat with our Scientist. His contraptions cost a fortune and he promised if it was nearby they'd warn us." Turning back he returned the telescope to his eye. "You and I need to talk." Pierre hesitated, but the Captain's fist pressed into the center of his back reminded him his ambivalence was irrelevant.

When they reached his cabin the Captain lit a candle, gestured toward a chair and took the seat behind his wide chart table. Still covered with charts and instruments, the table now included remains of his evening meal and a thick, black-bound book. Perhaps it was an effect of the light but to Pierre he looked ancient. An expression came over his face of anguish and frustration. He reached for the book. Pierre recognized it was a Bible.

"I take it you're not much on reading this."

He tried to decide how best to answer and this caused the Captain to smile. "That's what I thought."

"It's just that it's been a long time," Pierre said. As usual in dealing with the Captain, his subterfuge proved worthless.

"And do you recall the Book of Job?"

Pierre pretended to search his memory until the Captain became impatient. "It's about somebody I expect you'd recognize." He opened it and began searching pages. "You and that heathen Scientist wouldn't think to look inside here for anything useful; it's all just stories and not very good ones at that." He turned pages as he spoke. "Myself, I like stories." Then he smiled and stopped. "How's this: 'behold now behemoth, which I made with thee'?" His eyes bore into the page as he moved his lips in silence. "Here we are: 'he moveth his tail like a cedar, his bones are as strong pieces of brass; his bones are like bars of iron." The Captain's eyes followed his finger and he said,

"'Out of his mouth go burning lamps, and sparks of fire leap out. Out of his nostrils goeth smoke, as out of a seething pot or caldron. The arrow cannot make him flee; slingstones are turned with him into stubble; he laugheth at the shaking of a spear. He maketh the deep boil like a pot. Upon the earth there is not his like, who is made without fear.'" Smiling, he closed the book and looked up at Pierre. "Remind you of anyone?"

Pierre looked with surprise at the Captain but said nothing.

"Job; Chapters forty and forty-one." He stared hard at Pierre and then reopened the book. "And how's this: 'Then will I also confess unto thee that thine own right hand can save thee.'" He snapped the book shut, returned it to the table and with a satisfied look leaned back. "Like I said, fascinating reading, this Bible. At least to an uneducated man who don't know nothing of science or philosophy or any of that rigmarole you waste your youth on. For me, this is good enough until the Good Lord makes me smart." Pierre ignored the sarcasm certain the Captain wanted to tell him.

"I'm a simple man and plain-spoke. I say my mind in simple ways. But I've seen things, boy, just the telling of would have you piss your breeches and cry for your momma. I've seen every kind of villainy this side of Hades. And boy, I've seen the good die in terror and the evil flourish in contentment. But I'll tell you one thing; there's a time when evil overshadows evil." He shook his head and sighed, a gesture that surprised Pierre.

"Just like this ship, we sail over an ocean of unimportant evil paid no attention to because it's hardly worth the notice. But sometimes, like a few stray clouds swirling together into a hurricane, that ocean rises up and those uncountable tiny evils combine until they've become a force. I've seen it happen and sometimes I've even got myself caught up inside it. But nothing compares to this creature." Perhaps he noticed Pierre shift uncomfortably in his chair because he added, "Hear me out; I'll say my piece and then tell you why I can't throw you overboard."

He paused, and for a moment the distance between them collapsed until Pierre's face seemed inches from the Captain's.

"I will destroy that creature, and you will give me the power to do it. Because I now know its weakness." He paused again as if considering the rest of his thought. "But I've received my orders from the men who pay me so right now I can't turn my ship to chase." His eyes searched the table and then a slight smile appeared. "Of course there'd be no complaint if the creature attacked us." In the weak candle light his eyes disappeared into black shadows.

Quietly Pierre asked, "And just how do you plan to kill it?"

"Aye," the Captain said with a tone of frustration, "there's the deepest waters." His right hand bearing silver and stone rings on its thick fingers appeared from the darkness to rub his whiskered jaw with an audible rasp. "It can't be destroyed by the puny hand of just any man, we already know that. Your captain's cannons had no more chance against it than a broom against a ship of the line. But what's come into being must disappear from being. At least that's what it says in the Bible. If it can't be killed as the rest of God's creatures are killed, how else can it be forced back into Hell?" He leaned forward, his anguished sigh struck Pierre's face as a gust of fetid air.

"That's when I come back to that ocean of evil and the hurricane of this creature. Chewing it over, it come to me there must be a way to get that stew of minor evils to separate again and retreat like when a breaker crashes against rocks."

The Captain's eyes lighted again. "And that's where our filthy, heathen Scientist comes in. A shipmate of mine once heard of my oath to take the creature, and he was the one what introduced me to that old scoundrel. I explained to your Scientist that I was going for the kill, and he said he had a plan that couldn't fail but that he needed money to finish. So we agreed." He grinned and released a deep and cold chuckle.

"But not the way your Scientist thought. He expected to stay anchored to dry land and spend my money on pussy and wine while I chased over Creation looking for certain death. But me and two of my mates set him straight and helped him see the light. We keep our eyes on each other now while he makes that device that'll destroy the creature."

"And what," Pierre asked even while he feared the response, "is that?"

Captain Stevenson studied Pierre cautiously, as if revealing his plan might somehow warn the creature. "I expect you'll know eventually. He calls it the aether grenade. Your Scientist is a dim-witted man in many ways, but he is a magus when it comes to the subtle forces. He understood my notion of the sea of invisible evils immediately, and he's using it to defeat this powerful evil. And that," he said leaning back as his eyes retreated into shadow, "is why I can't throw you overboard. For this moment, the greater good is that you help him. When his aether grenade's done its work we'll all happily part company. But until then, you're my guest and his device is all what keeps you from filling the belly of a shark."

"And just what," Pierre asked in the hope of distracting the Captain from what he seemed to prefer, "is the aether grenade?"

The Captain glanced at Pierre with contempt. "Understand that I understand what I don't understand. Our atheistic Scientist has his own explanation which I know but don't understand. According to him, it's the nature of the subtle matter that when it's disturbed by the explosion of the aether grenade, whatever holds those invisible evils together will break apart and the creature will evaporate into a dissipating mist of trivial evils. And he promises me it'll never rise against Heaven again. But in case it returns, we'll still have this bomb to defeat it."

In the grim silence that followed Pierre listened to the groan of the ship's timbers. "You say this bomb must explode inside the creature. Just how do you plan to do that?" A grin gradually creased the Captain's face. If the sight of it did not chill Pierre's blood, the low chuckle that emanated from the space around him did.

"Don't you concern yourself about that," the Captain finally said. "Once we've rigged it up, it'll swallow the device as eager as a starved wolf." Beneath his glowering eyes his grin brought to Pierre's mind the image of that wolf.

Pierre said, "You depend on the Scientist to save you with his bomb so don't you worry that his other devices didn't warn you of its presence?"

"Not very much. Besides, asking him about it he'd just make up something I wouldn't understand. Isn't that how it's done by you scientists?"

Pierre nodded. "Maybe you're right."

"He could tell me anything and I'd have no hope of deciding if it was true. But now I have you, you see? With all your book-learning you can explain what he's doing and if his device'll work. You being my eyes and ears, I'll know what he's up to."

"What you're asking," Pierre said, "is that we conspire against the Scientist."

The Captain's eyes widened. "Don't tell me you're worried you'll betray the man?"

Pierre glanced up at the night-blackened window behind the Captain, startled to see the reflection of the face of a frightened man.

"How can you feel loyalty to a man who expects you to tell him your father's secrets? I'm just the captain what saved you from drowning and holds the power of life and death over you."

Pierre could not answer. Instead, he asked, "You've described this ship as a nest of conspiracies and now you want me to participate in one more."

The Captain grinned. "You think I'll tell you how to avoid becoming entrapped? Because I tell you that's impossible. Every life is a network of conspiracies. There is only the matter of choosing or being chosen. You only avoid one by joining another."

"You speak of choice as if it's possible." Pierre's frustration surprised him, as if the Captain had fed him something awful.

"You want," the Captain said, "to remain above all conspiracies; honorable and uncompromised. Bravo and good luck to you, but I promise you'll fail, and in failing you'll betray all and call no one friend. If you succeed you'll regret your success for the rest of your days."

"Hardly the answer I was looking for."

"Remember your father," the Captain continued, "alone and unacknowledged. Leaves his home and family and crosses an ocean just to join a conspiracy. Of course, his probably won't kill a king or overthrow a religion. In fact, all he wants is to remake the entire world. But worse? I tell you, boy, he'll succeed and to everyone's regret."

"Isn't that your problem as well?"

With a bitter grin the Captain said, "Men like me are already dead. Our world has passed into history and I'm just waiting for my turn to join it. Mind you, I'm in no hurry because there are still two or three things I look forward to. Still, this world has moved far beyond where the likes of me can catch up. But your world is here and it's a net of conspiracies whose knots are constantly retying into new arrangements. The trick, if an old man can suggest, isn't to reject conspiracy, but to become part of many. There's no other way to avoid being considered an enemy. You'll only survive by being one of the conspirators."

Pierre could think of no good response and frustration turned his mind to a blank.

"Listen to me now because this is the heart of my advice. That Doctor and his men are weak and foppish schoolboys, and while you dearly wish otherwise they ain't your friends. Despise me for saying it but they use you for their purpose as easily as some whore hired for the night. And once done, they'll toss you aside just as easily. And that Scientist of yours ain't one whit better." Captain Stevenson leaned forward, his scared and creased face exposed naked in the pale light. "You're alone, boy, and don't you forget it. I'm the only one who can help you. Go along with me and I'll see you arrive safely home. But as God is my witness I'll vanquish the creature. To accomplish this He's furnished me only a humble and foolish tool, but I'll use it as best I can." He held Pierre with a glower that turned slowly into a grin. "You see, I'm no better than them others save for one thing. At least I tell you straight out what I'm about. I ain't a good man, but sometimes I'm honest." Pierre sat very still enjoying no comfort from this admission.

The Captain grunted and leaned back again into the shadow. "Our time will come, young master, when together we'll face the creature in its very maw. We'll hurl destruction and our fires'll burn without quenching. And together we'll watch the creature writhe in its death-throes with a heart-piercing cry and watch the life flicker from its eyes. So be of good cheer, and pray from the bottom of your heart that day comes soon."

The Captain stood slowly. With a glance at Pierre he turned and stepped to the blackened window. Hands locked behind his back, he stared out as if there was something there that only he could see.

His presence seemed no longer needed so Pierre stood. With a last glance at the Captain he stepped toward the cabin door. As he reached it the Captain spoke.

"A word of caution. More goes on on-board this ship than you need to know. Think of me as a spider and think of every plank and timber as one of the threads of my web. And just like a spider, I know at every moment exactly how much sail is flying and where each sailor is. So when in doubt, always know that I know. Confine your curiosity and avoid opening doors through which you have not been invited." Pierre held his breath. When he heard no more he stepped into the passageway and closed the door quietly behind him.

In the twilight of the gangway he was tempted to return to his bunk. Yet, after sighting the creature and all the Captain had told him, he was restless and returned to the main deck. He assumed the Captain knew he was there and the thought offered no comfort.

The moon was nearly gone, with only a golden shard above the horizon. Pierre leaned his elbows on the rail. He knew he could not see them, yet he sensed he was being watched by both the Captain and the creature. Annoyed, he was certain the Captain was a madman but he was right about one thing; Pierre was alone. From the danger of the creature, he had fallen into the company of sharks. They circled and he had no idea how to avoid them. Despite a creeping exhaustion he remained beside the rail intoxicated by the air and the velvet darkness.

Could the Captain be right that the creature was pursuing Pierre? It seemed impossible and yet he could not otherwise account for all that had happened. But how could the creature even know of his existence? And then a thought occurred to him that left him frightened; if this creature was genuinely demonic, it might possess the power to know his thoughts. So the Captain might be right; the creature was pursuing Pierre and his presence brought danger to anyone near him. This terrified him; not because of some possible encounter with the creature in some vague future, but the assurance that no matter what he did, he would meet the creature again. More than ever he wished for a speedy arrival at Port Royal, or any dry land.

The white light of the stars cast a silver filigree on the cobalt blue darkness of the sea. He looked down to watch waves lap against the hull of the ship. He wondered whether, if the crew decided the creature was following him, the Scientist would convince them otherwise. He recognized himself stranded on a floating island whose natives appeared friendly in the daylight but could not be trusted after sunset. He recalled the words of the Scientist; he needed to make friends quickly or be prepared to die.

A hand suddenly fell hard across his shoulder. "Be careful, my friend." The voice of Doctor De Montaigne startled Pierre and also reassured him. He had forgotten the Doctor remained on watch and Pierre had not seen him in the shadows. The Doctor added, "I saw that you were alone and wondered if you planned to go swimming."

Pierre smiled hopeful it did not appear a grimace. "I've had enough swimming." He wanted his joke to be sufficient but a glance at the Doctor told him he had failed.

"The cardinal sin at sea," Doctor De Montaigne said gravely, "is to stand beside the rail alone at night. One never knows when something unexpected will send one overboard and with no one about to hear your cry for help."

"It seems," Pierre said, "I'm doomed to make stupid mistakes."

Gazing out over the sea the Doctor said, "Had I not been out here, I hate to think what might have happened." He turned and looked into Pierre's eyes. "The night is a strange land filled with the unexpected. At night one should only expect the unexpected." He turned again toward the sea. "The sun will rise soon; perhaps you should return to your cabin. You will undoubtedly need rest. But sleep well, for I will remain here and watch." He turned and ambled aft to disappear into the darkness.

When Pierre reached the stairway he stole a glance back across the deck. But the Doctor was nowhere to be seen. Or perhaps he was simply watching Pierre. That thought did not reassure him. Whatever luck brought to Pierre, luck would eventually take away.

CHAPTER THIRTEEN

"IS IT TRUE that you're experimenting with some explosive that uses the aether?"

Pierre's question startled Dr. de Montpellier but with a quick grin he regained his footing. "Would that our Captain piloted his tongue with the skill he pilots his craft." After a pause he added, "The destruction of an extraordinary creature demands an extraordinary device"

Pierre said, "He and the Doctor spotted the creature. I'm surprised you weren't told." Startled, the Scientist said nothing. "Last night," he continued, "they called me on-deck and I saw it myself with his glass." Sunlight poured through the open porthole yet the light seemed to tremble and dim.

The Scientist nodded as if something had become clear. "Fair enough; there was always the chance that would happen. What has he decided to do?"

"Seems content to let it make the next move."

"That is unusual. Our Captain is more inclined to act than to wait so I wonder what he has in mind."

"He's annoyed your devices didn't warn him. I asked him about it and that's when he told me about the aether bomb. So what does he think I'm helping you build?"

The slabs of the Scientist's face moved and shifted as if his flesh was taffy and hands pulled it in several directions at once. Half to himself he said, "I am surprised he has not already come to send me and my devices to the devil." In his eyes Pierre saw annoyed concern.

"He admits his ignorance," Pierre added, "as if it was an accomplishment."

"Captain Stevenson is a deep man," the Scientist said, "with more ideas in a moment than most have in a day. His unlettered intuitions suggest a mind always active and observing. So believe me when I admit he displays insight into the heart of reality and I have only begun to appreciate its implications."

"He believes," Dr. de Montpellier continued, "I am constructing an explosive device using the Subtle Matter that will be powerful enough to destroy the creature. Though correct, what he cannot know, and what I will not tell him, is that his insight is incomplete. If my calculations are correct, this device will not only destroy the creature but will likely destroy its user as well." His grin faded and the flesh around his eyes seemed to puddle beside his nose.

"This result is possible because the device disrupts that miasma of Subtle Matter which constitutes the fabric of the universe." His face brightened, the putty of his flesh shifted and pulled. "Thus, destruction of the universe may prove easier than we thought."

When Pierre recoiled, the Scientist said, "So it is too bad you retain so little memory of your father's work." He was surprised by the admiration masked behind the annoyed rumble of the Scientist's voice. "Our device will set the very mountains trembling so it would prove a great value if we knew how to avoid destroying the universe." Faint as it was, the Scientist's excitement faded, replaced by a petulant resentment. "So I must repeat your father's experiments. Fate could only have been more generous if it had sent your father in your place."

"Sorry to disappoint," Pierre said unable to keep annoyance from his own voice. "Maybe when I find him he'll offer to help. But to be honest he is not known for his generosity and so would refuse to share his work."

Dr. de Montpellier paused. "Sometimes it is useful to be honest." He glanced up at the open porthole. "Concerning myself, I should tell you how I came to join this ridiculous voyage. I was living on the streets of Paris, the details of which need not detain us, and the man who introduced me to our captain was a gambler I owed money to, a certain Sicilian chieftain by the name of Mezzanotte, a scabrous blackguard and mountebank clever in the ways that exploit those who are weak and impecunious. When Captain Stevenson offered to pay my debt to Mezzanotte and take me on his ship there was only one answer. In the three months I have been his prisoner I have made some progress but I remain far behind your father's work and have yet to create that device he craves. Thus, when I learned who you were, it was not difficult to convince him you hold the key to his device and will advance my efforts, which may prove true, in a manner of speaking." His grin puzzled Pierre.

"What if the Captain intentionally challenges the creature and demands you produce your weapon?"

The sudden darkness of the Scientist's expression seemed to draw the light from the room. "You are the only one among us with the appropriate experience to answer that." Sudden recollections of the creature's attack chilled Pierre into silence. "And by your expression I must assume you judge our success as unlikely. So we have that much more reason to make certain our Captain is never tempted to do that."

Pierre said, "He believes we can discover what the creature intends to do. He claims he wants us to reach Port Royal but I suspect he hopes the creature will attack. But for the moment the beast appears content simply to watch us and this confuses him. So he wonders what provokes its interest."

Dr. de Montpellier's eyes traveled around the room as if the answer lay somewhere else. "Our Captain knows only two strategies, attack or retreat, so his confusion is inevitable." He stroked his chin. "But he understands the problem correctly; we must know what attracts its attention." He turned to Pierre and his gaze froze him in his place. "Do you have any suggestions on that subject?"

"He asked the same question," Pierre said, "and got the same answer." The Scientist studied him as if expecting more but Pierre simply shifted in his chair.

Finally the Scientist seemed to resolve something. He gestured toward his workbench. "We have much work and little time." He moved so close to Pierre that the reek from his clothing set his eyes aflame. "Because I expect to prove the reason the creature pursues our ship is you!" When he smiled, Pierre had to look away.

"And I will accomplish this by modifying the hypothesis your father has investigated. I suggest the creature pursues us because somehow you have created an imbalance in the ambient aether." He paused as if expecting a response from Pierre, but received none.

"Before you ponder too deeply," Dr. de Montpellier continued, "let me explain the way I understand this. Your father's research confirms that we are surrounded by an invisible cloud of the Subtle Matter swirling about us as vortices whose agitation has otherwise no effect on any material object. I theorize that somehow you are an exception to this rule. Some element of your being, contrary to all theory, interacts with the Subtle Matter disturbing the background aether. Only this explains what I have observed. And further, I speculate that the creature senses the ambient Subtle Matter as a dog detects a scent on the breeze and can distinguish it from all of the turbulent waves of the aether swirling around it. A key to your father's theory is the assumption that undulations in the aether waves occur step-wise at discreet and uniform levels and so it is possible to distinguish one level of it from the next. The vortices are sufficiently distinct to signal your presence and so allow the creature to follow you. Yours is a unique signature in the aether and the creature recognizes you by it." Breathing hard as if his explanation demanded effort, he leaned back, to Pierre's relief. "Thus, I believe you and the creature are bound together; you, by actively disturbing the Subtle Matter, and the creature by its ability to detect those disturbances. Does any of that resemble anything you remember from your father's work?"

Pierre struggled to recall Augustus's explanation of his research, something his father would go on about until he drove everyone from his presence. He had tried to follow those explanations and his weak understanding embarrassed him. Yet he was perplexed that so little of what the Scientist said reminded him of his father's words. He fell into confused memories of ideas he had never understood.

He looked up to find the Scientist standing beside his chair, and he was startled. "Before us lurks the creature and behind us lurks our Captain. We begin with the premise that for the creature, you are an antagonist. At least this provides us a testable hypothesis."

Pierre's mind was a fog-washed gray and the range of his sight shortened as if he observed the cabin through a clouded-over window. The Scientist leaned closer, filling his vision. "Have you heard anything I have said?"

Pierre hesitated. "Does anything you've said offer me help?"

The Scientist's eyes fixed on Pierre and with the slightest nod his muddy face withdrew. "You grasp the situation precisely; I congratulate you."

Pierre said, "What you describe amounts to this: while I'm at sea the beast will find me so my best chance of survival is to reach dry land and anything that gets us to Port Royal quickly is in my best interest. Everything else works toward my demise."

The Scientist's eyes widened. "Our research will be productive."

Dejected, Pierre added, "If I knew an alternative I'd already be gone. As I see it, I risk everything and you risk nothing."

"I am just as eager to avoid the creature as you are, since within its jaws I will become just as dead as you." He displayed the space in his mouth where several teeth once had been. "I offer us both a chance to keep the creature away. It is only part of my theory, but it amounts to a great deal of my demonstration. Which is that by manipulations of the Subtle Matter, that creature can be deflected from its intentions and by that we may be able to chase it away." He recognized Pierre's disbelief. "We will find a way to keep the creature from attacking our ship." He turned and walked to the workbench.

On the workbench stood three rows of clear glass beakers filled with a cloudy fluid in which were suspended bits of different colored metals bound to each other by additional strips of metal. Pierre recalled seeing a similar arrangement within the shadows of his father's workshop.

"You will note," the Scientist said, "I use different metals to determine their properties and reactions. This is based on the observation that metals submerged in certain fluids release small bubbles of atmosphere. I have further attempted to discover whether the atmospheres within these bubbles concentrate the aether. But in these experiments I have observed effects I cannot explain."

Pierre studied the beakers. "How do you expect me to help?"

The Scientist smiled nervously. "My research is limited to trial-and-error. Thus, I need assistance that is meticulous. My hope is that you will recognize experiments which correspond to your father's and tell me in what way he used their results. Am I clear?"

"I understand what you're doing, but don't expect I'll give you the help you need."

"Just do as I ask and let me judge the value of the result. Now, shall we proceed?"

Beclouded by noxious fumes and acrid vapors, Pierre and Dr. de Montpellier worked through the morning. Fingers burned and eyes sore and red, in a series of experiments they observed tiny blue fragments of what resembled miniature lightning between bits of closely spaced metal. When the Scientist asked if Augustus had achieved similar results, Pierre assured him that if he had ever seen the same effect he would have remembered it.

All of this continued for hours, but finally the Scientist announced they had finished for the day and Pierre was relieved. He had become annoyed with the Scientist's imperious impatience when he did not accomplish a task precisely as requested.

Dr. de Montpellier made his way back to his chair, fell into it with a sigh of exhaustion and poured a full glass of wine. He asked that Pierre again return the next morning and speak to no one about their work. At that moment Pierre would have agreed to anything that released him from the lethal cabin, its air so poisonous that breathing was painful.

Pierre fled, worried that in the next moment the Scientist would call him back. By some half-conscious memory he navigated the passageways until he stood on the main deck. Blinded by the sunlight he moved to the rail and leaned out to sea filling himself with fresh air as if he could hardly take in enough.

The wind was mild and, when his eyes finally adjusted, the sunlight etched sharp outlines along every edge of the ship. The horizon was a hard line the color of moss that split the undulant green sea from the hard blue of the sky. At the eastern edge of the horizon, a pale gray shape resembled a mountain of clouds. On deck, the sailors went about their routines while the slaves remained gathered around the main mast silent and staring down. Pierre decided he badly needed to speak with Count D'Arcy.

He searched for him among the sailors, but as if disappointment was a form of permission he decided he was hungry and went to the galley hoping to find something left from the midday meal. Aside from his hunger, this visit offered the chance to consider in solitude the meaning of his morning with the Scientist.

The galley appeared empty and he assumed the Chef must be nearby so he began to search. He had not gone far along the passageway before he heard voices muffled in conversation. He followed the sound until those voices became clear. The passage ended at a storage hold crammed with dark wooden crates. He stopped, determined to remain hidden.

"But they saw the creature last night," a voice said bluntly. It took a moment but Pierre recognized it as the voice of Guy-Marat. "The Captain brought the youngster on deck to confirm. According to the Count the creature is keeping its distance. They watched it for a time and then they went below to the Captain's cabin. He can't decide whether to avoid the creature or chase it. Of course the creature might resolve the question and maybe that's what he hopes for."

"Tossing our castaway overboard," he continued, "would solve two problems at once. We need to be done with him if we want our plan to succeed. As for the Jansenists, they must believe he will help their treasonous plans. It is hard to imagine another reason to shelter him."

Pierre froze. Panic rising, he slipped into an alcove hidden from the doorway that gave him a narrow view of the speakers. To his surprise, Duke Du Bordeaux stepped forward.

"In principle two elements argue against your strategy. First; however delusional, our Captain believes that boy is useful to his pursuit of the creature. Tossed overboard, our Captain will turn the ship around to retrieve him regardless of inconvenience. Second; Dr. de Montpellier believes he knows something useful. However ridiculous we find this, he is convinced the boy has some value for him. So even if the Captain did not turn the ship, the Scientist would insist the boy be rescued." He sighed as if confronted by a distasteful problem.

"I agree." Pierre could not see this speaker and did not recognize his voice. "Raising a hand against him risks discovery."

Guy-Marat said, "But we must prevent the traitors from getting their hands on that gold. Somehow we must reach it before they do."

Duke Du Bordeaux said, "We have had no success discovering where it was hidden."

"I have done my best." Pierre realized this was a female voice and he assumed only one woman was on-board. "But the traitors are circumspect. I have failed to discover if any know its location, so we must assume someone on the island will lead them to it."

"We agreed this might be the case," the stranger said. "But we should assume that at least one of them knows."

"It is bad enough this involves our King's gold," Duke du Bordeaux said. "It adds insult to our injury that they will use his gold to betray him."

The female voice added, "The Pope has met with the German and

Austrian princes and so his meeting with the Swedish envoy has increased irritation on all sides. If Gustavus Adolphus believes he is in the Pope's confidence, then expect him to use his military with Paris in his sights."

The stranger said. "If the Jansenist traitors communicate with the council of Geneva, they will soon be speaking with Gustavus as well."

"We can be certain of one thing," the woman said. "The boy knows nothing of us and I guarantee his curiosity will never be aroused." Pierre was stung by her words. Through that narrow space between the closely stacked wooden crates, her figure replaced Duke du Bordeaux's and he watched her pass back and forth.

Guy-Marat said, "We understand you have taken very good care of him." Several voices laughed softly.

With impatient annoyance the woman said, "The Lord gives each of us different abilities. I am grateful if mine are sufficient for the service of our King."

With a tone of mockery, Guy-Marat added, "Your humble abilities seem more than sufficient."

Duke du Bordeaux said, "This bickering will not advance our plan. We do what we can. Criticism only makes our task more difficult."

In a mollifying tone Guy-Marat said, "I agree, our mission is our justification. So I apologize to our colleague if my remark challenged her contribution."

"My dearest hope," the woman said, "is to conclude this campaign quickly. Although I will do whatever helps our King, I long to return to my sisters."

Pierre watched as, dressed in the clothes of an ordinary seaman, she paced back and forth addressing the others. She turned so that her face was framed in the space between the crates. Anger colored her cheeks and he was immediately enchanted, savoring the shape of her jaw, the fullness of her lips, her small narrow nose, her dark arching eyebrows, and the dark blue of her eyes. Suddenly, as he studied her, he watched her eyes widened. "He is there!"

Though he heard the shuffle of approaching feet, the narrow space made escape impossible. In another moment four figures loomed over him.

Duke du Bordeaux smiled to the others. "Our conspiracy appears to have gained a conspirator."

"As if," Guy-Marat added with annoyance, "we had any such need."

Pierre gathered his courage as he stood. "I suppose it does no good to insist I have no idea what you're plotting, or why." Beads of sweat gathered at his hairline as his eyes moved from one face to the next. "But I assume each of you is now wondering how best to dispose of me."

To Guy-Marat, Duke du Bordeaux said, "His understanding suggests some native intelligence."

The stranger's grin shaded toward a leer. "What little intelligence he possesses must prove a burden since it has not helped him."

"One side!" The young woman stepping between the men as if they were mannequins. Feet spread and hands on hips she stared hard at Pierre's face. Her expression did not reassure him. Quietly she said, "I do not think I have ever seen such a fool from this close."

Annoyed, Pierre returned her look. "Happily, that isn't true." Surrounded by suppressed laughter, her face remained grim. He guessed he should now be worried.

"One must admit," Duke du Bordeaux said, "he does a fair job of disguising his fear."

Pierre said, "There's nothing to disguise. I've faced the creature."

Guy-Marat said, "In your position only a fool would fail to be afraid."

"But my position is the reason I'm not afraid." Pierre forced a smile. "You've stated perfectly the reasons my safety is assured."

"It seems," the young woman said, "he understands." Turning to Guy-Marat she added, "And perhaps all too well."

Duke du Bordeaux straightened. "He knows his greatest threat and what it means."

"Between the Captain and the Scientist," the woman said, "he is without alternative. But were he to understand any less he would soon be swimming with the mermaids."

Looking about at the dark confines of the alcove Duke du Bordeaux said, "This closet is hardly conducive to conversation." He led the way back into the storage hold and Pierre followed with the woman, Guy-Marat, and the stranger following behind.

Guy-Marat sat on a stool near the center of the hold and nodded Pierre to another across from him. The others leaned against or sat on the wooden crates surrounding them. "Explanation of our mission demands some background, but understand that given to us by the King of France himself, our mission is nothing less than the preservation of his kingdom."

"Certainly a weighty responsibility," Pierre said.

Guy-Marat spoke with insistent conviction. "We have begun this voyage determined to prevent traitors from delivering our colony into the hands of the British."

The woman added, "Having purged the King's traitors in Paris, we will not allow treachery to take root in the heathen soil of this new world."

"Abbess Maria's description is more than mere poetry." Duke du Bordeaux spoke from a crate behind and just beside Guy-Marat. Pierre enjoyed a special thrill at learning her name.

Guy-Marat continued, "There is nothing we will not do when his kingdom is at risk."

"But we are trapped," Abbess Maria said. The urgency of her voice impressed Pierre. "Surrounded by heretics and agents for alien kings, the nearest land populated by heathens and with the Devil's own spawn pursuing us by sea, do not mistake us for we are desperate people."

"But we will succeed," Duke du Bordeaux announced defiantly.

"So tell us," Guy-Marat asked, "can we depend upon you to preserve our secret?"

Pierre lied with a smile. "I love nothing so much as the sight of the King's flag snapping in the breeze."

"We can only hope that is true," the stranger said. Abbess Maria's eyes were blue sapphires of suspicion.

Duke Du Bordeaux said, "By your agreement you are obliged upon pain of death to do nothing that puts our mission at risk. Do you so agree?"

Pierre nodded without hesitation. "I'm uncertain how I can help but I'm at your service." When he looked around, he found himself surrounded by dark expressions of doubt.

Finally Guy-Marat said, "Regardless of our suspicions we must be satisfied with your promise. Still, you will forgive us if we do not share more of our plan. Your ignorance safeguards us and your silence will demonstrate your commitment."

From her perch on a low wide crate Abbess Maria said, "The hour grows late. I propose we adjourn." Her eyes held Pierre's.

The stranger stepped forward and in a low voice spoke to the Duke.

"Please inform our friend of how we disperse our meetings. Meanwhile, I will depart first."

When the stranger left, Guy-Marat and Duke du Bordeaux together stepped forward. "We leave separately," the Duke said, "as a precaution against discovery." With a nod Guy-Marat said to Pierre, "We will talk further and dispel the confusion your expression suggests." Then he was gone.

Pierre turned hopefully to Duke du Bordeaux but Abbess Maria stepped forward. "I regret any insult you endured; your efforts will be rewarded." Then she was gone.

"You marvel," Duke du Bordeaux said, "that our company includes a bride of Christ." Pierre could not suppress his smile. "Understand that the Jansenist traitors have hidden a quantity of gold on the island to help establish their colony. The Devil's work stops at no blasphemy. Our mission is so important the King himself requested her aid. Although she is in constant danger, none among us has the strength of character to match her zeal for crown and for cross."

"I'm honored you've shared your mission with me," Pierre said.

"You have given us little choice since we are not yet prepared to kill you. As you value your life simply remain circumspect or we are lost."

Then Duke du Bordeaux was gone and Pierre was alone. Sitting on one of the crates he felt as if he had been holding his breath for a long time. The Captain had been right, and he assumed this was the conspiracy he had been warned about. As he had suggested, Pierre joined their conspiracy, even if reluctantly. In that dark hold smelling of brine he glanced about at the crates stacked around him. The Captain described life as a net, but to Pierre it was a hopeless tangle.

Distracted eyes wandering, he saw it before he recognized it. He had not thought of it for days nor wondered what had happened to it. But captive of devious forces and dark speculation, he stood and moved to it. Jammed upright between two large crates, the coffin took up hardly any room. Even in the dim light he could make out those marks and scratches he had come to know well. He let his fingers trace the swirls of the wood's grain. The tall, narrow box seemed small in this space and he wondered whether it could save him again.

He sat down close to the coffin, as if its presence might prompt useful thoughts. Bewilderment swirled within him. From the vast and powerful sea Pierre had sailed into a harbor so full of sand-bars and piles of rocks he could not find a path to safety.

But at least those rocks most dangerous to him had been revealed. The men who had saved his life were either ambitious heretics of a religion not his own, or secret agents of a king or a pope, and none of these inspired his allegiance. He recognized himself immersed in malevolence with dangers in every direction which he had no hope to avoid. Thus, merely for its simplicity, Pierre was glad he was in the service of the Scientist.

As deranged and delusional as the Scientist was, he was unlikely to place Pierre in danger intentionally. He appeared to hold at least some respect for Pierre as the son of an accomplished rival. Pierre struggled to awake from a confusing dream. Looking about he decided that at least the Captain knew where he was.

He followed the passageway back through the galley while his thoughts returned to Abbess Maria. But when the image of the Captain came to his mind he struggled to dismiss his speculation about their relationship, and failed. He decided it was better to return to the main deck since there might be another conspiracy by which he had not yet become entangled.

But as if he only needed to think of the Devil to conjure him, the Captain suddenly filled the passage ahead. He glowered at Pierre. "I've looked for you," he announced grimly. He turned saying, "Follow me."

Pierre's heart thumped in his chest to the tempo of his footsteps, wondering whether the creature had changed its strategy, and also how luck manages to move since it is not a material substance.

CHAPTER FOURTEEN

PIERRE AND THE Captain reached the sudden sunlight of the main deck to find a group of sailors clustered with Count d'Antoine standing at the gunwale near the bow muttering nervously and staring out to sea. Though Pierre saw nothing, he guessed what the others saw. The Captain handed his spyglass to Pierre. He put it to his eye and trembled.

A sailor behind him asked, "How did he do that?" Another asked, "But why did he do it?"

Grimly the Captain said, "The question answers itself. It understands what we're about and it maneuvers for attack. It means to have us."

"Do you suggest," Count d'Antoine asked with mild amusement, "the creature knows our thoughts?" The humor in his voice startled Pierre and left him wondering if he intended to challenge the Captain.

Though the Captain's eyes never left the horizon he replied flatly, "Laughter assures ignorance. Our enemy has placed itself between our ship and Port Royal thereby confirming its intelligence."

Pierre turned to find that Duke du Bordeaux and the Guy-Marat had joined them. Count d'Antoine asked the Captain, "What do you propose to do?"

The Captain's heavy brow collapsed into a fierce glare surrounded by his wreath of black hair and his eyes shimmered as if peering out from the center of a black cloud. "The only course that remains," he announced. "Finish the job here and now."

Sailors joined those by the rail and Captain Stevenson turned his glare toward them. "Any man who believes we can out-run the creature is a fool!"

Just as loudly Count d'Antoine said, "Call me what you like, but we should run like the devil and force it to chase us." The men near him nodded.

"You prove my point," the Captain said. "Flight is the reaction of the panic-stricken and thus is doomed to fail."

"Evasion, Captain!" Stung by his derision the Count squared his shoulders. "Avoid a superior enemy until one achieves an advantage." His smug grin took Pierre's breath away.

"In flight," the Captain said as if determined to argue, "we concede the choice of time and place of engagement."

"Not if we sail more cleverly than it swims," the Count responded.

"It's already overtaken us," the Captain announced. "Two days ago it was astern fifty leagues. Now it lies ahead and waiting. Only a fool could believe we might outrun it."

With a tone of injured arrogance the Count said, "Our maneuvers will disguise our intentions. And I will show you how."

Murmurs among the crew suggested that Count d'Antoine held the upper hand. The Captain said quietly, "I'll pilot my own ship if you please."

"We should vote." This voice came from among the sailors on the main deck. Another voice added, "Sounds risky to me, Captain." Still another added, "You agreed we'd decide."

"I agreed," the Captain said, "to such a vote when it came to confronting armed ships. But this creature is a force of nature. We also agreed that when threatened by a storm, conduct of the ship would be entirely in my hands." To Count d'Antoine he said, "Is this not true?"

The Count studied the Captain and a small smile appeared that suggested he was surprised by this maneuver. "True, Captain, and just as you say. Were this a violent storm we would trust your ability." His smile faded. "But there can be nothing that has prepared you for this challenge. If you will pardon the conundrum, this natural force is unnatural."

The Captain's face stiffened, and with a fierce glare appeared prepared to assault the Count. "Speak glibly of my lack of experience though I am unaware of any you may have of either piloting a ship or confronting this creature."

Guy-Marat suddenly stepped forward. "He understands conflict with a powerful enemy."

Without turning to look at Guy-Marat the Captain said, "Just not this enemy. And. you, we must suppose, have considerable experience running away. Correct me where I'm wrong."

The Chef who had also joined the crowd said to the Captain, "You misrepresent Count d'Antoine's suggestion. He has reason and logic and his plan preserves our lives."

The Captain growled, "You've become too enamored of your own skin."

From the main deck a voice cried out, "And I like keeping my skin." Other voices cried our 'aye'.

Count d'Antoine said, "Admit there is reason in this request. These men have fought hard to earn their treasure. Injuries have occurred, blood has been spilled. Do not blame any man who wishes to keep his reward from sinking to the bottom of the sea, and himself beside it."

"As part of that treasure is mine," the Captain said, "I don't need to be reminded of its value. But this creature cares nothing for either treasure or justice."

"More reason to avoid and evade," Count d'Antoine continued. "Reason trumps emotion, and passion withers under the light of logic. Our calculation will defeat this animal's desires."

Captain Stevenson snorted with derision. "Calculation is for bookkeepers. No action results from adding two numbers. Your logic is a ruse to justify your cowardice and merely yields the result you desire."

"And you conflate terms in order to blur what is obvious. You disparage our ability to reason but your solution will result in death and without benefit."

The Captain briefly smiled. "So I must assume you've decided this danger is just too dangerous, if you'll pardon the conundrum."

"And I repeat," Count d'Antoine said sternly, "that you agreed any decision involving our ship would be put to a vote and you would abide by its result. Our crew has made its wishes clear."

A voice from the cluster of sailors cried, "It's a long swim to Port Royal, Captain. I like our chances with the Count's plan."

Plowing through the crowd pressing around them, the Captain grabbed a man by the throat with one hand and lifted him aloft continuing in his stride toward the gunwale.

The Count cried out, "Captain! Return to your post!" The command seared the air and came to rest between the Captain's wide, black-coated shoulders. He returned the man to the deck and turned to face the Count.

Feet spread and fists on hips his mouth rippled with surly defiance and in his hooded eyes glittered with contempt.

Almost too quietly to be heard, Captain Stevenson said, "Life, Your Excellency, is a trail of bitter regret. I only hope this crew is prepared for the death you wish to avoid." He turned his contemptuous glare on the gathered sailors, sweeping slowly past each face until he arrived at Pierre's. His eyes locked onto Pierre's as a leering grin came to his face and Pierre hoped he had been the only one to see it. The moment passed and the Captain turned and stomped loudly back toward the gangway. The crew remained silent until the Captain disappeared and then resumed their chatter. Its murmur swelled until the Count ascended to the quarterdeck.

Addressing the crew he said, "Do not believe that evasion will be easy. A predator lives by hunting. If it has chosen us as its prey, we must remain vigilant. Our foe is formidable but our strong backs and the love of God will get us through." A cheer went out shrill and strong that thrilled Pierre. He continued, "From dawn until twilight two men will be posted to the crow's nest. Twelve hour shifts for the rest of us, ready to hang every thread of sail at a moment's notice." His look moved over the gathered faces as sunlight slides over rough terrain. Quietly he said, "Now we must be about our business."

To the sound of naked feet padding across the wooden deck, the crew took up their positions, while Guy-Marat as first-mate climbed to the quarterdeck to stand beside the helm.

Pierre watched Duke du Bordeaux, the Captain's spyglass tucked under his rope belt, fly through the tangle of ropes to the crow's nest. As Pierre stared up open-mouthed to watch, a voice beside him muttered, "Captain wants to see you." He turned to see the man with a milky eye standing beside him. The man hissed, "Now!" turned and ambled to the opposite gunwale.

Certain he knew what the Captain wanted Pierre went below-deck and reached the Captain's closed cabin door. He lifted his arm to knock when he heard the Captain call out, "Come in!" Startled, he opened the door and entered.

Once again Captain Stevenson stood with his back to Pierre and facing the window and the sea. He stood very straight, as if in an argument with himself. Pierre closed the door and remained standing beside it.

Speaking as he faced the window the Captain said, "An enemy is a godly thing." His posture, the angle of his arms and the folds of his black frock coat combined to resemble an enormous black bird. A seagull flying beside the window cried out before flying on. The silence that followed grew loud. "An enemy demands from us abilities we otherwise don't recognize." He turned and sat down in his chair behind his chart table. Elbows propped on the table he placed his face in his hands. Pierre realized he was watching a tired man discover that he was tired. He remained beside the door.

As if startled to find he was not alone the Captain sat up and looked at Pierre. "Please," he said with a forced smile, "take a pew. You've the drawn look of a hunted man." The halo of his black hair moved as a cloud of smoke and his eyes glittered like rubies in pools of blood.

"I no longer wonder," Captain Stevenson said, "that darkness rules the earth or that monsters ravage the land and spite the Immortal God." He sighed with a vague smile. Hands flat on the table he leaned toward Pierre.

"But I do wonder that men believe they can flee both Satan and God." His smile became a malevolent grin. "As if in their ignorance they believed there existed a terrain unknown to both and where they might find refuge." His grin widened. "Such audacity leaves me awestruck."

After a long pause the Captain leaned back. "We are judged by the companions we choose. Of course, on-board my ship one's choice of companion is limited. Still it should not surprise you that in scrutinizing you I scrutinize your companions as well." With another pause he added, "You consort with men whose malevolence you fail to recognize and who will eventually turn against you."

The Captain shook his head as his smile disappeared. "I take no pleasure in witnessing imbecility. Over time I've met men created just to die by the stupidity of others. You, sir," he concluded with a sigh, "are surely one of that tribe."

Pierre said, "Tact and the conduct of this ship must demand discipline." He had not intended it, but the Captain's expression suggested he had scored a point.

Emotions passed over the Captain's face; surprise, annoyance, anger and bemusement followed each other like actors onto a stage. And then he grinned. "I'll say nothing more except to suggest that by challenging me you challenge the least powerful person aboard, but also the only one who does not need your death to complete his plan." He watched the effect of his words on Pierre.

"And I must observe everything, for I will protect my ship. She is dearer to me than a wife and I'd defend her from every danger. But by far the greatest danger comes from her crew. This bizarre, buffoonish and rampaging pirate captain you see is my ship's best champion. But let me get to the point."

"To safeguard my ship I must know my crew better than they know themselves. So I congratulate you for having gained the trust of deranged necromancers, religious terrorists and royalist fanatics. Eventually, of course, these lunatics will cost your life." He glanced up and his eyes latched onto Pierre's but Pierre said nothing. "What I will not allow is any danger to my ship. None is spared who puts her at risk." He folded his arms and leaned back.

"And what," Pierre finally asked, "does any of this have to do with me?"

"Put simply, the alliances you've formed will likely get you killed. But my only concern is that this ship arrives safely at Port Royal. And with my performance the Count has promised to avoid attacking the creature."

This confession startled Pierre. After a pause the Captain continued. "Do not misunderstand; I wish the creature dead as much as anyone. But that will only happen with the help of the Scientist. Why else tolerate your presence?" Expecting a response he smiled when there was none. "If I'm lucky, although I haven't always been, you'll tell me just enough to let me stay well out of the creature's path. Because I believe that creature simply chases you."

Gasping suddenly for air as if drowning in dark water Pierre said, "You can't be serious."

The Captain tented his fingers as he studied Pierre. "For the sake of this discussion, let's suppose you embody some spirit that antagonizes the creature. In that case yours is an existence it must annihilate even at the risk of its own."

Startled to hear the same message from two different people, Pierre scrambled in his mind for a question to change the subject. "Tell me this then," he said, "why the bloodthirsty aspect? What's accomplished by the rage?"

The Captain's grin widened. "Finally! I feared you weren't clever enough to ask that. Although you appear unaware of it, more than a dozen captains across the Main believe ships have been lost to that creature. Put aside the question of which went down because of the creature and which by other causes. My job is to convince those captains I'll rid them of their scourge."

"All the while," Pierre continued, impressed by the audacity of a scheme he began to tease apart, "collecting fees and outfitting ships to run contraband or turn pirate." Suddenly he recognized himself in the presence of a man of substance.

The Captain reached forward, uncorked the flagon on the table between them and filled two cups. He passed one to Pierre taking up the other. Pierre asked, "If you're so eager to avoid the creature, why encourage Dr. de Montpellier to create the bomb?"

He cocked an eyebrow as he sipped from his cup. "I'm surprised this is not obvious as well. I'm long at sea and at the mercy of that creature. I've seen it, albeit always from a distance, but the day will come when, despite my best efforts, it will attack." He paused to sip again. "So if you construct the device he's described, I promise to be extremely generous."

"Does the Scientist know of your plan and his role in it?" Pierre drained his cup.

The Captain leaned forward and refilled it. "I've done my best to impress him with false urgency. But he's a clever man and so I assume he's conjectured my true intentions."

"If he has," Pierre added, "he's kept it hidden from me."

"As he should since he can't know who you might speak to. But to return to my original subject; these fanatics pay me to run them around the Main as if they're in command and for that I'm paid handsomely. So be warned; put my little enterprise in danger and you'll swim back to wherever you came from." As if pleased with his joke the Captain raised his cup and drank.

"Fair enough," Pierre said. Suddenly filled with a vast admiration for Captain Stevenson he added, "But as we're sharing confidences, tell me one more thing. That story about your father; how much of it is true?" He smiled realizing he might have taken their intimacy too far.

The Captain studied him as if measuring something. "In truth he was a medical doctor living in Exeter who drank too much and was having it off with his nurse. Since my mother was deaf she didn't know what was afoot in his consulting room. My life at sea began the day he discovered that I knew what he was up to. Right then he handed me a fistful of cash and told me it was time I made my own way in the world. I was sixteen years old at the time and so weren't intimidated. I still deplore the man and believe he's only done worse by my mother, but I'm not ungrateful."

Pierre said, "And I'm relieved I'm not the only one whose most urgent hope is simply to get my feet back on dry land." Comforted, he drained his cup again. But in a moment another thought occurred to him and so sudden that despite his effort, his expression changed and could not, he knew, be disguised.

Watching him the Captain nodded as his wiry black hair gently waved beside his cheek. "Yes, of course. What do you take me for? I know all about the whore nun."

Overwhelmed by his own confusion, Pierre said nothing and the Captain continued. "I'd be a complete fool otherwise and unworthy to captain this ship."

Pierre sat more dazed than concerned yet beneath his confusion he experienced a sense of betrayal and jealousy.

"Not that I've found," the Captain continued, "participation in her charade difficult. If anything, it's given our voyage a certain comic relief with their dim-witted subterfuges they believe disguise their intentions. She has added spice where all otherwise was bland. And truly she's the only member of our company whose demise I'd resist and whose departure I'll regret."

The world swirled around Pierre becoming soft and pliant, as if objects were mere fog-filled reflections. A turbulence worked at the periphery of his sight while the center remained calm. Had the Captain admitted he knew Abbess Maria intimately, or did he simply want Pierre to assume it? The fog surrounding Pierre grew darker while sound became muffled and thick. Resting his hand on the edge of the table, Pierre began to stand. In the next instant, he discovered himself sitting on the floor. He looked up to see several images of the Captain towering above him, but the Captain was not looking down at Pierre. He watched the candle suspended from the ceiling and Pierre recognized that it was slowly swinging to one side.

Eyes fixed on the lamp, the Captain snarled, "He's brought us about! What the devil does he think he's doing?" He glanced down then and saw Pierre. "Go back to your cabin," he said, "and be sure you remember our bargain. Meanwhile, I need to know what these fools think they're doing with my ship."

Pierre moved slowly, one hand leaning hard against the Captain's table determined to bring his eyes into simultaneous focus. When he looked again the Captain had gone and he was alone.

He reached the doorway and stopped to gather the few wits that remained in his skull. Then, with one hand lightly touching the wall he made his way along what he believed was the passage that would return him to his bunk. With the dim light and slow rocking motion of the ship, he struggled against the temptation to sit down where he was and sleep. But he pressed on, confused and exhausted, passing closed door after closed door, doubt gradually growing that he knew where he was or which way he needed to go even as he wondered if it was possible to become luckier and luckier, and if so, would he realize it while it was happening.

CHAPTER FIFTEEN

PIERRE AWOKE STARTLED to find himself in his bunk and that he had somehow missed the morning meal. He stumbled to the main deck where the crew again stood about broken up into small groups and consumed in muttering debate. The musicians stood to one side bemused, their instruments lying beside them on the deck. The slaves around the main mast watched with mild interest. He moved to a vacant space beside the rail. The Chef squirmed through the crowd and stepped up beside him. "No dancing this morning, eh?" Pierre could not mistake the anxiety in his voice. "It appears once again we are about to spend the morning in debate."

Pierre said, "But the Captain and the Count reached an agreement."

"I hate commotion," the Chef said, "it never ends well."

"Perhaps," Pierre said, "the Captain wants to exercise our brains this morning instead of our limbs." Conversation, he discovered, made the cloudy pain in his head worse.

The Chef shook his head. "I hope your knowledge will aid the discussion." Other sailors drifted in their direction and took up positions within earshot.

Addressing the Chef, Pierre asked, "What's happened that has everyone so concerned?"

The Chef looked about nervously. "The Count ordered a change of course last night and suddenly the creature disappeared and has not been seen since. Surmise has led to speculation. On the suggestion we might not continue to Port Royal the word 'mutiny' has been spoken."

Jacques-Marcel, sailor of the watch, stepped forward and spoke to Pierre as if it was natural for him to report. "I was at the helm at four bells when

Count d'Antoine appeared, took the helm and changed our course to the southeast. Then he told to me to resume and keep to the new course. That's when the creature disappeared. Count d'Antoine headed to the gangway as the Captain stepped out and he was hot, voices got loud. He shoved the Count aside and moved toward the wheel. But the Count said something I couldn't hear and the Captain turned the fiercest look I've seen on a human face and said, 'My cabin. Now!' They went below together. I kept to the course the Count gave me as the forenoon watch came on, gave Hugo-Pierre that course and then went below. And that's all I know until now."

The Chef added, "The Captain and the Count have been locked up together a while."

"Has anyone gone to the Captain's cabin?" Pierre discovered that knowing what others did not left him feeling pleasantly light-headed, unless that was simply the rum. "Someone should find out what's going on."

A wave of murmurs and nods left Pierre oddly excited. When he turned toward the gangway several sailors fell in behind him. They moved only a few steps when Count d'Antoine appeared followed by the brooding presence of the Captain. Pierre's group stopped to watch them ascend to the quarter-deck where they turned to face the crew. The Count stepped to the quarterdeck rail.

"After consultation and prayer the Captain and I have come to an agreement; he remains commander of this vessel save only for navigation, whose responsibility he has prudently given to me until we reach Port Royal. But make no mistake, in a crisis he remains in command with every hand at his disposal." Turning to the Captain he said, "Do you so agree?"

A flicker of surprise crossed Captain Stevenson's face, replaced in an instant by a blackly furious grimace. His nod of agreement resembled a twitch.

"To reach our destination safely," the Count continued, "we must remain out of sight of the creature. So we must stand ready to trim sails as the winds change." His face acquired an odd smile. "Our terpsichorean exercises should have taught us the discipline to coordinate our movements." It took a moment for quiet laughter to fade.

"Our path is perilous and our adversary will yield no quarter, so we will evade. We imitate the fox and avoid the jaws of the lion. And, with God's help, we will return when His Hand favors ours." He surveyed the crew as if searching for a sign. "By a show of hands declare you will give everything to our success."

But the Captain suddenly stood, grasped the rail with both hands, leaned forward and bellowed, "The Devil himself is among you!"

The Count stepped close to the Captain. "You agreed you would not bring this to the crew."

The Captain did not even turn. "One among you the creature prizes above all others."

In the hush following his words Count d'Antoine said, "You must not do this!"

"One among you," the Captain continued solemnly, "knows the creature in his heart. He has been to the belly of the creature and returned."

Pierre did not need to look around to know he was again the center of the crew's attention and how different this experience was.

Turning to the crew the Count said, "Do not be deceived; our Captain has reached a conclusion no reasoning man can entertain."

The Captain cried, "The creature has just one desire." When his bleak glare found Pierre, every other eye followed.

"To pacify this spawn of Satan we must give to it what it desires and then it will leave the rest of us in peace. Fortunately we have that decoy for the creature." The Captain brought his hand, arm extended, slowly to shoulder-height and pointed at Pierre. Even the seagulls became silent. "Toss him over the side!"

Although no one moved in response, Count d'Antoine became pale. Loudly he said, "One would not think our Captain possessed such a sense of humor." A gargled laugh escaped his lips. "He asks us to believe a superstition even a child would find impossible to believe; that our castaway is somehow in mystical communication with the beast." Though his face was gray and waxen he forced himself to adopt a smile that even startled Pierre.

"Under any circumstance," he said, "that suggestion would offer merely an opportunity for scurrilous buffoonery. But our situation now puts a terrible stamp on those words."

Captain Stevenson squared his shoulders to speak when, from the center hold of the ship, the ashen face of Dr. de Montpellier gradually arose and even the Captain became silent.

Sweeping those around him with a disdainful glance the Scientist made his way through the gathered sailors. Whether out of respect for his knowledge, or repulsion from the reeking cloud that enveloped him, the silent crew offered a wide path. At the edge of the quarterdeck he looked up at the Count and the Captain.

"Every terrifying event," he said in a weak and reedy voice, "is an effect for which any cause is possible and all are suspect. Thus the marriage of imagination with credulity leads to nine-tenths of our misery. Despite this enlightened age at the first sign of the inexplicable we do not hesitate to resort to human sacrifice. Thus we sleep in the lap of scientific certainty dreaming of monsters."

"That beast," the Captain bellowed, "is no figment of imagination."

"And further," the Scientist continued indifferent to the Captain, "despite logic we battle our daemons by sacrificing the weakest and least powerful person available. Yet the question arises; by what logic do we eventually arrive at sacrificing captains?" He looked up again toward the quarterdeck rail, and continued.

"The ultimate question remains; if our orphan is sacrificed and that creature continues its pursuit, which of us will follow him into the sea?" The Scientist paused again as if his thoughts were a jungle without a path. The Count appeared relieved but the Captain's fury tinted his dark face to red.

To the Captain, the Scientist said, "An enlightened age can harbor no illusions, particularly that nature can be controlled. Our knowledge is not power. That creature is only slightly more intelligent than a wave of the sea yet its power is beyond our puny efforts to control."

Turning to Count d'Antoine, the Scientist said, "I have no faith your plan will succeed but it has the reassuring benefit of being less bloody." The Count squared his shoulders as if vindicated. "However, we must respect our Captain's concerns and those who share his delusion. So I suggest a compromise. Let us reassure the fearful by restricting this man and keep him at our disposal and accommodate him in our brig." He paused as if awaiting the response to his suggestion. "Less than luxurious, but dryer and safer than what the Captain has in mind."

At the Scientist's words the Count's expression relaxed. The Count turned to the rest of the crew. "This is an arrangement even our Captain can support."

But the Captain's expression only became darker. "I cannot agree, and yet, since it appeals to some delusions of safety, I must not oppose." He paused as if weighing his words. "But I offer this warning; there will be tears of rage when you recall that your salvation was offered and how you blindly rejected it. Your piteous cries will avail you nothing." Glancing furious at Pierre he said, "I will watch you! Have no wonder or curiosity; uncertain who observes your every movement, know that it is I. The creature will be observed by others but you will be the sole object of my scrutiny and it will be as relentless as the justice of God."

To the Captain, the Scientist said, "Our castaway only hopes that your mercy is as god-like as your scrutiny."

Enraged, the Captain raised his arms and brought them crashing down on the rail. "Bloody revenge is my prerogative! Mercy I leave to protectors of the weak, the miscreant and the spineless. As to the sacrifice of one in exchange for the safety of my ship, have no doubt." He turned to the Scientist. "If it is a choice, old man, between your life and this ship's safety, you'll speak with the fishes before your next heartbeat."

The Captain then turned as if admitting defeat. Reaching the gangway he looked once more at Pierre and with such fury that Pierre became eager for the confinement he was promised.

"Well put, Captain," the Count said, his self-confidence returned. "We draw strength from your devotion." But the Captain had already disappeared through the gangway.

The Count said, "I call upon our worthy musicians. Let Terpsichore, the goddess of harmony, inspire the spirit of fellowship as we perform the dance of concord."

The musicians took up their instruments, the tambour was held aloft, sailors found partners and on the count of three all began to dance.

The crew swirled around the deck a turning stream of rising and falling bodies. The Chef stepped up beside Pierre. "Doctor de Montpellier has arranged a satisfactory compromise that deserves celebration. Surely you will not refuse me this dance!" The Chef bowed low at the waist. Terrified, Pierre bowed in return.

"I'm flattered," Pierre said, "but I must meet with the Captain. I have information about the creature he must know. This compromise has cost me little, but even that must be paid in full." With a nod of regret he added, "Certainly another occasion will arise."

To Pierre's surprise, a look of distrust came over the Chef's face. He bowed stiffly. "And perhaps you prefer another. I am a magnanimous man; choose your partner as you wish." He turned, merged into the mingling crew and suddenly Pierre felt as if he had been caught within his own lie. He made his way to the Captain's cabin.

As he approached, Pierre heard sounds coming from behind the door. Moving closer, he could just make out quiet groans, a moan, creaking wood, another moan but in a different voice. He put his hand to the latch and turning it quietly he saw a man's wide back, naked and hairy above the chart table, bisecting a pair of pale thighs. Pierre assumed he should recognize those thighs. Suddenly, from beside the man's left forearm, Abbess Maria's face appeared. She smiled, winked and mouthed the words 'This won't take long.' But Pierre had already begun to close the door.

He stumbled back to the gangway breathless with anger and something else. He walked until suddenly he was bathed in sunshine and surrounded by music and dancing.

Conscious of being watched Pierre moved along the edge of the dancers nodding in time to the music. From out of the swirl, Count d'Arcy stepped forward. Flush, breathless and smiling he said, "You must not reproach us if we serenade you to your new quarters." Startled by this suggestion Pierre realized no objection would be accepted. At a signal from the Count the five musicians stepped forward to take the lead. With Count d'Antoine, the Scientist, and Pierre following, their parade snaked across the deck, down the gangway and then along the passageway. Pierre looked back once to see that, content that all was resolved, the rest of the crew had resumed their tasks.

Arriving at the formidable dark wooden door of the brig, the musicians played a hymn to the glory of the French crown. At its end each bowed to Pierre and left. From a pocket the Scientist produced a large black key and handed it to Pierre. "You should at least control who enters."

Startled, Pierre asked, "How did you get that?"

The Scientist shrugged. "The Captain allows me to store valuable equipment here. Possessor of esoteric knowledge, I believe you fit that description."

The Count added, "Besides, occasionally you will want a breath of fresh air." He turned and sniffed dramatically at the small room. "You should need no permission."

Pierre entered to find a blanket thrown over a straw pallet and two three-legged stools. He lit the stump of a candle the Scientist offered him and fixed it to a shelf attached to the wall. Then he chose a stool and sat down.

Count d'Antoine said, "We will reach Port Royal in a few days. Until then these dolorous accommodations should prove sufficient." Pierre gripped the key in his pocket to remind himself that in a row-boat he still might make Jamaica landfall.

The Count then leaned close to Pierre. In an urgent whisper he said, "As we are alone I must confess that as ludicrous as our Captain's suspicions are, I wonder about the relationship you have with that creature."

His suggestion startled Pierre. The candle's flame brightened as the wood beneath his feet became soft as mud. "I'm startled such a question could come to a rational mind."

The Count looked mildly embarrassed. "A particular connection remains to be demonstrated, yet, even if the logic is weak, a lack of evidence is not decisive."

"But how can I prove innocence when you do not need proof of guilt?" Pierre had run out of patience for this quibble and now yearned simply to be left alone.

The Count shrugged. "Your sensitivity is understandable but we do not need to specify an agent, only the evidence that a supernatural transaction has taken place. Thus, if you and the creature behave in ways which appear coordinated, we are left with few alternatives."

"Alternatives?" Pierre repeated the word as if it was loaded and pointed at him.

"What else could we do to save our ship except give the creature what it appears to want? What about this seems unreasonable?"

"The part where I die in order to save you."

The Count said, "Our Captain's point is well-taken. Either we save you at the ship's expense or save the ship at your expense. Forgive me if this seems unavoidable."

The incredulous look on the Scientist's face told Pierre all he needed to know. He retreated to a corner of the brig clutching the key tighter. He recalled the tavern with Gabriella standing beside its front door, furious and calling him stupid, and wondered how she knew.

"Be of good cheer," the Count said. "We will succeed in avoiding the creature. So settle in; we will certainly know where to find you if you are needed."

The Scientist added. "While you have successfully disrupted my work, my experiments have advanced so that I will certainly detect the creature's approach." He turned to the Count. "I expect he now wishes only to be left alone."

"On this we agree," the Count said. He bowed to Pierre, and Pierre then watched through the door's grated opening as they faded into the corridor's brown twilight. Finally he was alone.

He reminded himself that his objective had not changed; he must reach dry land. Yet thinking this, he recognized he still could fail in his search for Augustus. His thoughts darkened.

Pierre had no good cards in his hand to offer in exchange for his security beyond his collaboration with the Scientist. He had become so entwined among conflicting conspiracies that each regarded him as both a possible ally and also a likely threat and so demanded his aid if only to prevent him from exposing their plans. But in the end he decided that once he was safe in Port Royal he would extract himself from all of this and find another ship to continue his search.

Then a new thought struck him, and one so frightening that he reached out to steady himself. Suppose the Captain was right and some real connection existed between himself and the beast?

As if blooming like tiny explosions behind his eyes, he lurched from one recollection of the creature to the next, half-revealed, half-digested but leaving behind a terrifying residual. Was the Captain right and a real connection to the creature existed? In that case, instead of driven by a deranged instinct, the creature might simply be reacting to a stimulus emanating from himself and which, as a reflex reaction, it could not control. The disturbing conclusion was that the wills of neither party were involved. Their fight to the death was as inevitable as the Earth's movement around the sun. One of the two must die. If he could not succeed in fleeing from the creature he must be prepared to battle to kill it.

The fluttering pale light of the candle tossed his shadow rising and falling over the damp, dark walls. He let his hand rest against the timbers of the hull and felt the rush of water on the other side pressing back. A world beyond his own yet not indifferent to his presence. Could he detect those subtle vibrations of the slow breathing and thudding heart of the creature? Just beyond his fingertips a vast presence knew of his own; a force greater than any waited just for him. He had to agree with the Captain; perhaps in the end it would have been better if he tossed himself over the side, accepted his rendezvous with the creature and so saved the crew from its pursuit.

If all of that was inevitable, then this confinement also was inevitable. The duplicity of the Captain, the uncertain acceptance by the crew, the creature's threat of death, each seemed a portion of some grand but unknowable plan. The possibility events might be otherwise was merely apparent and never actual. No matter what he might have intended, he now sat alone, pursued by a monstrous creature and as far from his father as ever.

Suddenly, from the gloom beyond the door of the brig a voice whispered, "Hey, let me in!" Pierre stood already certain who waited, and went to the barred window in the door. The umber shadow hovering in the weak light Pierre recognized as Abbess Maria. A large, dark blanket was pulled tight around her, her face sweetly framed by its edge which formed a hood. In an oddly pleading voice she said, "He means nothing to me. Please, don't abandon me here in the cold." She peeled back an edge of the blanket. The tangled tuft of tightly curled, pitch-black hair stood out from the ruddy cream of her stomach and thighs. In a moment she wrapped herself again.

Pierre unlocked the door and she slipped past him, and suddenly he was grateful he had not thrown himself over the side. There would always be time for that, and only luck would assure the proper moment. But luck was certainly with him when the blanket slipped from her shoulders and dropped to his pallet. Luck, Pierre decided, was round and without angles or corners or ridges and even warmer than a purring kitten.

CHAPTER SIXTEEN

"DO YOU FIND the Captain so intimidating?" the Abbess asked.

Skin glazed icy with sweat Pierre laid on his back beside her and beneath her blanket staring up at soot-blackened wooden beams and planks. Caught in the drift and swell of a dozing dream, even a simple thought was an effort. "I guessed you didn't need an audience." Caught between jealousy and mockery he tried to seem indifferent and in that he failed.

"Can you believe your sarcasm is inscrutable?" She propped herself on an elbow pulling one end of the blanket across her shoulder and studied his face. "Perhaps you do not wish me to know how grateful you are to be with me." Though he recognized the tremolo of annoyance in her voice, he was so relaxed her words only caused his smile to turn into a grin.

"Such ingratitude!" She pulled the blanket entirely away from Pierre and tightly covered herself with it. Her sudden anger startled him. Caught in some emotional undertow, he was overcome and burst into quiet but uncontrolled laughter which left him confused.

She moved to stand but Pierre grabbed her forearm and momentarily held her. She was stronger than he expected, or more angry than he guessed, and escaped his grasp. Wrapped within the blanket, she stood beside the door. He was relieved he had locked it and hid the key. When she found the door locked she turned toward him hands fisted and rage in her eyes.

Pierre decided that if he needed to defend himself he should probably stand. She swung a fist at his head. He managed to avoid most of the blow so he was more surprised than injured. He managed to restrain her arm from repeating it. "At least let me get my trousers on."

She stopped struggling to snarl, "Too bad you took them off."

"And just what was that between you and the Captain?" He tied his trousers at his waist. "Or should I ask?"

Her back straightened and she looked hard. "What I do, I do for the glory of France and the preservation of King Louis."

"Odd way for a holy person to act."

"As an agent of the King of France I have royal permission to act in defense of his interest and for that I am accountable to no one beyond him."

"But you're some sort of religious person, right?"

Her chin elevated just slightly. "I am honored to be the abbess of St. Januarius Abbey near Toulon and trace my ancestors to Count Robert of Narbonne, a great and holy crusader against the Cathar heresy. Our family has served the crown for more than three hundred years but my gender prevents me from taking up arms. Thus, my service is that which the Lord in His wisdom will allow. But as a soldier of Christ, I too put my body at risk in His service."

Nothing she said made sense to Pierre but her expression could not have been more sincere. "People like you promise not to do certain things. Like having sex with a captain?"

"Or a castaway?" She smiled and he could not decide whether the joke was on him or the captain or the King or God.

"You mean you can't commit a sin?"

She sighed as if resigned to an annoying explanation. On the thickest portion of the pallet she sat down pulling the blanket tighter. "I am as capable as anyone of sin, save in the relief of carnal desire. As my actions preserve our King who is king solely by the will of God and my mission is to safeguard his work as protector of the Pope and his Church, I am granted certain dispensations."

Pierre's mind seemed to go blank; he understood her words yet they made no sense.

She scrutinized him as if he might have descended from another world. "I suppose one must allow for those far from the motherland, so let me apprize you of France's situation. As a result of the War of the Grand Alliance there is hardly a river not clogged with the bodies of the dead or running with their blood. The Spanish crown attempted to extend the domains of the

Hapsburgs but gained only misery. Their days of glory are waning while on the horizon rises the British crown. Our King guards his Atlantic flank while he fends off attacks from the Swedes and the German Princes from the north. It has fallen to us, his servants, to keep those parts of the Spanish colonies if they cannot be brought under the French crown from falling into the hands of Great Britain. This is why the island of Jamaica is important; were it to fall to the British, it would solidify their hold on the eastern Main. But when that island comes into the possession of our King it will threaten British domination of North America. Between New France in the north and our colonies in the Caribbean, the British will need a garrison in North America whose cost will do to Britain what such garrisons have done to Spain."

"Wait!" Pierre said, "What do you mean by 'us'? Guy-Marat and the others or do you have someone else in mind?"

She sighed again with impatience. "Those men were assigned to me, I did not choose them. The organization to which I am a member operates exclusively at the direction of the Pope to defend his allies. Our role is to resolve political conflicts as the Jesuits maintain adherence to Church dogma. Where an ally of the Pope is in danger, he provides our help. Thus, most recently I spent several months in Cologne serving the Palatinate as it suppressed the Augsburg conspiracy. Earlier, I was two months in Ferrara negotiating between the duke of Milan and the Serene Republic of Venice. And before that I was five months in Antwerp settling a conflict with the French crown over the province of Brabant."

"Just how many of you are there?"

"That detail also need not detain us, although honestly I am not certain. His Holiness dispatches us as he sees fit and keeps his own counsel. I can only say that we are an international group with a variety of backgrounds."

"And when you receive an assignment," Pierre said, "what exactly do you do to save these poor kings?"

"Your inclination to sarcasm will not assist you among those whose help you need. And you will always need a great deal of help. To answer your question simply, whatever that crisis demands."

"I'm sure there's more to that explanation."

"Actually, no," she said and smiled. "In fact, that king in whose service we operate never learns of our assistance or strategy so that his claim of ignorance of what has been done is honest. But our efforts almost never demand physical violence. As you see, our arsenal of coercive tools is inevitably sufficient."

"So assassination is almost never on your agenda."

Again Abbess Maria smirked. "Assassination and other forms of violence are delegated to experienced hands. And there are many such free-lance operatives eager to serve."

"Helping the Pope pays pretty well?"

"He possesses his own arsenal of enticing benefits available to those who are willing and cooperative. When a political future hangs in the balance, one cannot have too many weapons. His Holiness will win, but his battle will be costly and arduous and defeats, albeit temporary, are inevitable."

"That its, inevitably the world must embrace the religion of the Pope."

She smiled as if this was the thought happiest she could conjure. "True peace can only come when all worship the same God. Then, laws of all nations will be built upon the same faith and so each nation will resemble every other."

"And just where does your ultimate allegiance lie? With the King of France, or the Pope of Rome?"

She hesitated and Pierre guessed this was a question she could answer either way. "Since they are never in conflict, I can honorably say both."

"But if they were?" he asked suspecting he had caught her.

After a moment she shrugged. "That conflict will be resolved by someone other than myself." Her smile returned.

Pierre did not understand all she had said and recognized almost no one she had named, but from her lips all of it all made sense. "So just what does all of this have to do with you and the Captain?"

She sighed with impatience. "So I must draw every line. He believes he understands the conspiracies on board his ship. I have convinced him that by helping us he will gain a share when we have located the heretic's gold. Suffice it to say he needs demonstrations of good will."

"And how does all of that justify a religious person doing what you do?"

"If you are referring to physical intimacy," she said dryly, "as you recall from your Hippocrates and Galen, desire is a product of the humors, and dyscrasia results from their imbalances. Imbalances are usually controlled through moderation of diet, but the desire for intercourse resists this method. The accumulation of semen clouds reason and the body becomes a burden to the mind. Desire results from a liver imbalance and overabundant blood, and its treatment is to bleed excess from the body. But since that renders the sufferer temporarily incapable of arduous labor another method is called for. Pockets of fluid scattered throughout the body are of little concern until they aggregate into pools. So, the relief of desire is the relief from desire's distraction. I need our captain clear-headed and not confused about his own best interests. He can only be useful if he is certain he is working for himself."

"Sounds like the Captain's theory of evil." Listening to her Pierre wondered how much more they shared. Her explanation left him feeling as if his head drifted in dead air. "I have no idea if any of that is true, so I'll repeat my question: what's with you and him?"

She looked away shaking her dark hair. "Understand he believes he has uncovered something he understands. I assure him he is correct and direct him as serves our purpose best."

The chill in the brig suddenly reached Pierre. He shivered and pulled on his shirt. "Sounds calculated and cynical but I guess that's appropriate. I suppose I should be flattered to be included among such companions." He tried to disguise a pique of jealousy and again failed.

She stared hard into his eyes with an oddly eager smile. "Yes, I expect that is true. And you should also feel profound gratitude." A sparkle like a shard of glass appeared in her eyes and her urgency left him frozen. As if struggling in a dream, he watched himself flounder unimpressed by his performance.

Whether she recognized his desperation or relented from boredom, her expression softened. "I have sometimes been hasty in my judgments. Perhaps I underestimate your sense of awe in my presence and the grand events that have entangled you." Around her eyes came a look as if conceding that his further enlightenment was unlikely and she should be satisfied with what she had accomplished. Her expression softened to lazy good humor. In the tone of a teacher helping an inept student she said, "I am content to dispel the cloud of ignorance surrounding you, especially since you are alive only as a result of my decision."

Pierre's surprise must have been obvious from his expression. Patiently she continued, "I was the first to see you from the crows' nest, and it was I who called out to turn and rescue you." She sighed, lips poised to smile. "From the first, it was I who negotiated your rescue."

"Negotiated?" Pierre asked.

"As you have seen, you arrived upon a complicated stage impossible for anyone who was not already part of it to decipher. Think of it as a play that keeps erasing its earlier scenes, determined to exploit each avenue of drama and complication." She laughed softly and turned to look directly into his eyes. "Even your precious Scientist conceded long ago that this was all too tangled for a rational mind. His demand to be left alone is his effort at self-preservation."

Pierre hesitated, unsure of which question to ask next. "So why intervene for me?"

She sighed even while something like a smile remained in her eyes. "My situation was complicated and your rescue was a precious distraction. Besides, snatched from the jaws of death, you might prove useful to me. The Count pretended indifference but the Captain and the Scientist insisted we pass you, or lose time in their pursuit of the creature. I convinced them you likely possessed useful information. This, by the way, is one of the reasons I like working with men." She stretched and yawned, her movement shifted the edge of the blanket exposing a firm, rose-tipped breast. "They are so easily distracted. Give them a mystery and they will struggle deep into the night to resolve it." She let her arms cross her chest and, eyes closed, she sighed. "I hope you are at least moderately grateful."

"At the risk of exposing my rigid ignorance," he said smirking, "I ask again; why me?"

She opened her eyes and shrugged. "Though I believe the Lord directs my decisions, perhaps it is true that there is such a thing as dumb luck. If you do not believe in God, you must then believe in luck. You may not approve but simple luck may account for your very existence. But what begins in luck can only be sustained by luck. When I was up in the crow's nest and cried out, I could have done otherwise. You might already have been dead, or alive but so seriously injured you could only have been a burden. Or you might have been the worst cutthroat ever sailed the Main. But I rolled the dice." She looked again at him but this time with affection. She slid down to nestle her head beside his shoulder and laid her arm and her leg across his body.

Sighing she said, "You are a wretch at heart, like all men. It is much to be pitied that such a face gives one false hope." Again she sighed but now with resignation. "Something spoke to me; perhaps the same sensation that creature has felt from you." She pulled closer and shivered. "Still, what was done has been done. You and I are here on our way away from the creature and toward Port Royal."

"For some reason I fail to detect pleasure in your decision."

"Because it is not there." Her face was nearly buried in the blanket and her voice was muffled by its folds. "The forces of the anti-Christ are everywhere, but at Port Royal they form a mountain and I am but one soul. Your appearance has neither improved my position nor assisted my struggle."

"So you are not optimistic of victory?"

"My battles may end in defeat, but the ultimate outcome is inevitable."

Though he disguised his doubt with an expression of admiration, he could not quiet a voice in his head telling him she must not be trusted. "So once we've landed, will I see you again?"

She lifted her face smiling, leaned toward him, lifted the edge of the blanket and wrapped it around them together. "Though I am uncomfortable confessing it, I am flattered that question even occurs to you."

"Would you prefer I foreswear all temptation?"

Her eyes widened with surprise. "Do as you will but make no vow you cannot sustain. Besides, what reason could you have?" She hesitated, as if considering which of her many fabulous jewels she could afford to give away. "Dare I hope your suggestion is intended to make you appear more worthy in my eyes?"

With a reflex he instantly regretted, Pierre grinned. "Such might seem appealing but succumbing to the appropriate temptation could provide information that will help find my father."

When a laugh burst from Abbess Maria's lips, Pierre discovered himself enchanted by her laughter. "You have your mission to fulfill so I suppose prudence dictates flexibility, and the few opportunities we might enjoy would hardly engage all of your attention."

"There!" Pierre said. "So I can hope to see you again. I ask no more."

"Ask what you wish, you will get no more." She nodded toward the door.

"Now, allow me to return to my mission."

Grinning playfully Pierre asked, "And what will you do if I refuse and keep you here until I have finished with you?"

"Perhaps I will scream 'till the dowels shake loose from these rafters." Her face suddenly lost all expression. Pierre reached under the pile of straw and retrieved the key.

"I doubt you would do that," Pierre said, "since it would expose your conspiracy." He stood and stepped to the door. Pulling the blanket tight around her she joined him.

"I ask once more," Pierre said. "Why me?"

Her blue eyes were flat and hard. "Why indeed. One certainly can ask that question." She crossed the threshold pulling the blanket even more tightly, leaned forward and kissed him quickly on the cheek. "One might ask it again and again and never reach a satisfactory answer. Sleep well." In another moment she was gone, the soles of her naked feet slapping lightly against the wooden deck. With a final glance toward her dimming shape, he locked the door to his cell.

Pierre dropped onto the pile of straw still warm from their bodies. He remained awake long enough to wonder if all of this had been merely one gigantic mistake, or a series of remarkable smaller mistakes whipped up like the Captain's theory of Evil into a tornado-sized mistake. He wondered about luck and how events mask their luckiness, so that in every instance, no matter its appearance at the moment, it is impossible to distinguish a lucky from an unlucky event until long afterward and with the frigid clarity of hindsight.

CHAPTER SEVENTEEN

IN THE TWILIGHT of his single candle Pierre crouched on a stool as a second supported the plate of his evening meal. And then he recognized the sound of the Captain's approaching tread. He emptied his cup of wine in one swallow hopeful that this time he would withstand the man's glowering presence.

Captain Stevenson's dark face suddenly filled the grate in the wooden door, gleaming eyes of old ivory pinned Pierre to his seat glaring as if he might pass his body between the bars. He then turned the only other key to the brig beside the one in Pierre's pocket. As the Captain relocked the cell door behind him he began to speak.

"We'll be clear about one thing." He turned and brought his face close to Pierre's. "Half the people in that town owe me money." His eyes bored into Pierre's until Pierre had to turn away.

"By my lights," he continued, "you owe your existence to me. But I didn't rescue you, nor have I preserved you, for any reason except what you know about the creature. Four weeks from when we dock this ship'll carry cannons and mortars aplenty, along with a dozen harpooners. Word'll travel back to every ship at anchor that needs to know I'm serious. So no matter how drunk you get or how sweet any face appears, you must keep this secret."

"If all you want is to fool people, why keep me around?"

"Because a good lie is a story well-told with details in their proper place and order. Every deception must appear obviously true. Since you're the main actor in my plan, every lie will fail without you. Is this clear or am I just loading you with too many details?"

"I'm following well enough; I just don't like what I'm hearing."

"Too bad. Just do what I say and our adventure will have a happy conclusion."

"Happy for who, or do I already know that answer?"

"Every half smart boy is smart enough to know what he needs to do. Are you that smart?"

"Smart enough, but just too annoyed to be trusted."

The Captain smirked. "Do anything that reveals my plan I'll know where to find you and what to do when I do."

"A threat like that is unlikely to entice assistance."

"And a threat for a threat," he said grinning. "This exchange of threats is good sport but mine are more durable."

"Fair enough," Pierre said because he knew that what the Captain said was true. "Thanks for the warning but it would be easier if there was a reward for me at the end."

The Captain snorted, folded his arms across his chest and peered down at Pierre. "Your reward is your life, small and trivial as it is, which I have returned to you. More's the pity you receive your reward before it is earned. But you'll remain within my sight, I promise you that." He brought his thick hand down onto Pierre's narrow shoulder and tightened his grip. "So we come to what's brought me." He moved Pierre's dinner platter to the floor and sat down on the stool opposite. "I'm about to let you loose to wander and get drunk and laid and robbed and cut up a bit. And guess why?" When he grinned, Pierre flinched. "Because every moment of every day, I'll know exactly where you are." His grin broadened. "Where you are and what you're doing and who you're doing it with and how much it's costing you. And guess how it is that I'll know all of that?"

Pierre almost smiled. "Because half the people in that town owe you money?"

Still grinning the Captain said, "Always nice to talk even to a half-smart fellow. Reminds me we should use all the faculties the Lord God's provided us."

"If all of that disguises your plan, why do you need my company? If you're avoiding the creature, why risk keeping me with you when you're certain I attract it?"

The Captain looked startled. "Pardon my presumption, but I'd come to believe you'd enjoy that adventure."

Since the Captain appeared earnest Pierre held back his laughter. "I only want to find my father and if I never see the creature again I'll die a happier man. As for you and this ship, I'm grateful for your help but I'll be glad when we part company. Does any of that seem unlikely to you?"

The Captain leaned back, his smile fading to disappointment. "You're right, I shouldn't be surprised you're reluctant to face that creature again. But what I find most surprising is that, after all I've done for you, you won't help my enterprise."

"Your enterprise, as you call it, is doomed; at least that's how I see it."

"Which is why I need your help. When we've landed at Port Royal, you and me'll take a walk to the Governor's mansion and meet his associates. And you'll describe your fight with that beast embellished to the best effect, along with what you've learned of the Scientist's creations. And you'll assure them you are eager for revenge and confident we're prepared and our success assured. Is any of this becoming clear?"

"A parrot would be just as useful."

"But not as convincing. Besides, my associates will have questions."

"You underestimate the value of a parrot; it would at least be easier to control."

"True but not useful. My preparations will cost a good deal. But once they've heard your story, those captains'll be eager to hand over whatever I ask."

"Guessed as much but I'd be happier to help if I was promised a portion of that cash."

The Captain looked at Pierre a long moment. "I've seen wicked men and I've seen fools and perhaps more of one than the other; and I know that both in the end get paid, but the fools last." Just as suddenly as he had arrived, the Captain stood. Striding toward the door, over his shoulder said, "Do what you will but in four weeks you'll be here again with me." He closed the cell door, turned the lock and again brought his face close to the bars. "A net of a thousand threads has fallen over you, so regardless of your wish, in four weeks we will meet again." Boots thudding invisible on the hollow deck, the twilight of the gangway swallowed him.

Pierre wanted to stand except that blood had drained from his knees and he breathed in shallow puffs. The moment he reached port, he would do whatever was necessary to put himself miles from that creature, and the Captain was a lunatic to imagine otherwise. Arrival at Port Royal was the first step to safety, regardless of how many people owed the Captain money.

He had heard of Port Royal, everyone had heard of Port Royal. Every sailor knew it as the richest and most vile city in the Americas. Pierre could hardly contain his excitement.

Working in a tavern in a busy port like Philadelphia, a young man would have heard a good deal about Port Royal until he came to believe he knew something of it. Drifting like an intoxicating miasma along the wharves, tales of greed and lust and blood became amplified from ship to ship, from one sailor's lips to a stevedore's ear, and so a young man might, in dreams, believe he had visited Port Royal. He could assume he would recognize its beaches, pale as sugar, reaching from the edge of bright blue water to a green wall of dark foliage; shadows blending within palm groves as terrains so empty anything could happen within them. A young man with such a background would recognize its portside menagerie where banker and pirate shared the same path, the same woman, the same life, alternately leading and being led along a path too narrow for either to pass, beside a port that lay supine, lapped by the rolling waves of the sea and of those men. And all of that now waited smiling just for Pierre. A terrain where anything could be done and anyone could do it, where anything could happen, grand success or humiliating failure, and fresh opportunities waited within each doorway as an entrance to a new life, every morning a birth. Images of debauchery and delight might dance in the head of such a young man.

Within his cell Pierre began to pace. It could all be true; this maniac Captain could be offering either fair warning or obliging permission. If he was determined that Pierre appear to participate in his next voyage the Captain would do what was needed to keep his property close.

The sigh of shuffling footsteps approached his cell and Pierre recognized Dr. de Montpellier. Muttering, the old man reached the cell door calling out, "Good news, we have the permission. Let me in." Pounding feebly at the door he began to cough. When Pierre unlocked the door, he staggered in. Wheezing quietly he sat down on a stool.

Pierre took the other stool. "Permission for what?"

The Scientist's face brightened. "But of course you do not know, how could you?" He moved closer to Pierre smelling of brine and rum and an unidentifiable chemical that trembled at the edge of his memory. "The

Captain has given permission to bring you as my assistant to help catalogue the island's flora and fauna, physical features and astronomical readings as well as atmospheric." He grinned, broken teeth and all.

Pierre studied him with disbelief. "Can you seriously think I want to be bitten and cut and thirsty and sunburned and exhausted chasing butterflies with you?"

The Scientist appeared startled. "Grant me some common sense. Your services will not be needed every day, and I will never obstruct an adventure you are tempted to, real or imagined. But amongst the hangovers it would be no bad thing to expand the sum of human knowledge as well as your own. And it might prove a pleasant way to sweat out the rum."

Pierre stood and walked to the far side of the cell with panic in this throat. "That's what my father would have said. So I'll ask you; what exactly is in this for me?" His stern glare attempted to convey disapproval; in Dr. de Montpellier's eyes he recognized his failure.

"Our success," the Scientist said in a patient voice, "resides in its being a disinterested act on behalf of Science; an interested act of disinterest. Besides, after three days you will be grateful to be rescued from your own pleasures."

Pierre studied him thinking there's only one sure way to deal with someone who has power over you; agree and then do as you wish. "Let's pretend I agree to this. What do you expect me to do?"

"Quite simple; using a map we will take notes and gather samples. We will follow streams adding details to our map and describe their features. So much here has no place in Aristotle's science that all of the books of science must be re-written."

"Honestly," Pierre said, "it sounds like a colossal waste of time and effort and boring to boot. How could you learn anything useful from counting sticks and rocks?"

The Scientist smiled indulgently. "By this method useful information is gathered. Understand that according to both the Bible and Aristotle it is impossible that trees on these islands could be different from trees of the Old World, because if they are, their existence demands a separate act of creation. As has already been proved, such trees exist, therefore Aristotle and the Bible must be corrected."

"All of that may be true but I don't see myself as the person to do it."

The Scientist waved at the air as if chasing a fly. "Recall that the New Science is based on two habits of thought: reductionism and skepticism. With reductionism, every object or phenomenon is described by its most distinctive qualities. All leaves of trees are green but some have three lobes and some five and others more. The habit of mind we call skepticism demands we disregard the source of information and instead test the information itself. Remember from your Descartes his insistence on methodical doubt. As he pointed out, it does not matter that a thing was said by Aristotle, it matters whether it can be proved. According to the New Science, unless the array of phenomena is infinite, we must eventually learn everything."

Pierre assumed his attention had wandered because what the Scientist said made no sense. "I never heard anything from my father that resembles what you've said."

The Scientist's eyes grew wide and then he glowered. "Because he proceeded intuitively. He made guesses, some of them excellent, at the interpretation of phenomena. But his method was without method. Eventually his research will reach an end, and to make further progress he will need help. His experiments have resulted in clever devices but those have advanced science hardly at all. Forgive me for saying this, but he never understood what he was doing."

"And you do?" Pierre could just contain his anger.

Hastily the Scientist said, "I mean no insult but I recognized his lack of method by the devices you identified. Those which would demand a systematic knowledge, you failed to recognize, while those you did were simple variants derived from earlier successes."

Pierre shook his head even more confused than he had been after speaking with the Captain. At least he had understood the Captain's threats. "I still don't know what you mean but you are wrong about my father's work."

The Scientist shrugged. "Clearly my powers of explanation fail me. But I have a friend in Port Royal, a very smart man who will explain it all to you far better than I."

Pierre was surprised. "You have been to Port Royal before?"

"Only in my mind." The Scientist added, "So I am as thrilled at the prospect of our arrival as you, even if for different reasons."

"Seems unlikely to me."

The Scientist again waved distractedly at the air. "My friend and I have exchanged letters over the years and recently he has found shelter in Port Royal. It is for his benefit that we will carry out our research." His expression darkened. "Do we have a deal?"

Pierre sighed. "You will tire of all that quickly. Or maybe I'm thinking of myself."

Dr. de Montpellier stood; he had won his compromise and he was enjoying it. "You are clever and will give me better help than you think. You have already demonstrated that not everything your father taught you has been lost." At the door he stopped and turned back to face Pierre. "But one more thing." He smiled apologetically. "The Captain expects to keep you under surveillance. I suppose you know this?" When Pierre said nothing, he continued. "Understand that once off this ship I will no longer be responsible to him or his commands." He paused. "And I do not expect you to be, either." He flashed a grin to Pierre, then turned and left.

When the door closed and the Scientist's shuffling footsteps faded, Pierre locked it. Everyone had a plan for him and none resembled his own. Above all, none offered the chance to search for Augustus or to enjoy the company of Abbess Maria. Looked at clearly, the Captain's plan was certain to get him killed, while the Scientist's plan would bore him to death. Added to all that, Pierre was compelled to wonder if he had half-fallen in love with the sexy Abbess.

This suspicion came to him heavy with the weight of regret; of all his visitors, there was only one he urgently hoped to see, looked forward to seeing, and could not quite see enough of. So whichever plan involved him, his own was foremost to find her. Of course he had lied about this to Dr. de Montpellier. But even that guilt evaporated when he decided that the Scientist had assumed his help without thought of his health or his pleasure. Still, the shadow of the creature overhung all, even his determination to find Augustus. So as he lay down on his pallet of straw, he again wondered how complicated all simple things are, and how small his portion of luck might actually be.

CHAPTER EIGHTEEN

STILL DAYS OUT from Port Royal a dank, sweet smell of rotting vegetation drifting on a hot breeze gradually enfolded the Revenge so that at night its perfume seeped into the brig to fill Pierre's dreams. Then early on the morning of the fourth day the call went out they had made land-fall. Pierre left the cell and joined the sailors gathered at the port rail. Rays from the rising sun caught the island's green, tree-covered hills in honey-golden light.

Stepping from their cluster, the Chef approached Pierre with a broad smile. "Our dance has been suspended, there will be much to prepare before we dock. But sight of land is delightful after so many days at sea. Perhaps I can point out to you the various landmarks of interest."

Changing course toward the west the island of Jamaica gradually filled the horizon. A steady breeze lifted them over sparkling turquoise water and they were joined by a pod of sleek dolphins whose glittering gray arching backs beckoned them ahead.

The Chef pointed out the mouth of the Hope River where small boats native-built for fishing with their fishermen black as upright silhouettes, clustered or moved up river. They sailed passed a line of pale sand dunes the Chef called the Palisadoes connecting Port Royal to the rest of Jamaica. Looking back, Pierre saw the profiles of ships approaching the port while other ships passed the Revenge headed out to sea. Further along, the Chef pointed out the gloomy stones of Fort Rupert, the menacing edifice of Birdwell Prison, and further, the white peak of the Court House. Beyond, he pointed to the steeple of the Old Church and the Governor's Mansion and then the line of buildings became more tightly grouped. The Revenge changed bearings again to head north toward the harbor proper where they sailed into the midst of a clutter of ships, some at anchor and others setting sail. Beyond those stood a line of wharves with a ship at nearly every dock and crowds of people gathered or moved among them. Then a dinghy emerged for the clutter of vessels and approached the Revenge; Pierre guessed it was the harbor pilot.

The Chef sighed. "I must secure the galley but I hope my bit of knowledge proved entertaining." He bowed. "I have enjoyed your company and hope we meet again ashore."

"I will look forward to that occasion," Pierre said. "And I thank you for your wonderful meals. I will not forget them." With a sudden smile of pride the Chef crossed the deck and disappeared down the gangway.

As the Revenge approached the dock Count D'Arcy stepped up beside him. "I regret we could not offer you a celebratory farewell." He held out a gray canvas kit-bag pulled closed with a long brown draw-string. "But we collected these for you; merely a change of clothes, a needle and some thread, a jack-knife, a compass and a few coins. We wish you well on the rest of your journey and speedy success in locating your father." Pierre was startled by this gesture.

"I thank you," he said, "and will remember you all for the rest of my life." He was certain he had never before been more sincere. With a sense of loss he could not account for Pierre watched the Count turn and walk away.

The Revenge finally tied up at a dock and kit-bag over his shoulder Pierre stepped shakily down the gangplank. The hot bright sun and noise of the crowd that surged around him left him in a fever-dream until something touched his arm. Looking about he discovered the Scientist standing by his side. He was so startled it took a moment to recognize him. The Scientist glanced at the bag slung from his shoulder nodding. "The best life is one that can be carried over one's shoulder." Although his face was the color of old rice, as he surveyed the crowd and the town beyond, his eyes glittered with an unexpected light. "So, ready for your excursion?"

"More than ready." Pierre's legs trembled and he felt vaguely ill which must have appeared in his face because the Scientist laid his hand on his shoulder.

"Be grateful to be alive and here at this moment. In all human history there will never be anything like it again."

Pierre glanced at him unconvinced and the Scientist added, "It is possible to know something we do not realize we know."

The crowd at the dock presented a confetti of colors bright and dark, a cacophony of voices shrill and strong and all trilled in a confusion of languages. Formally dressed plantation owners rubbed shoulders with stevedores and ordinary seamen. Burly, distraught men and lascivious, smiling women behaved with such familiarity he wondered if each knew everyone else and only he was a stranger. With a sympathy Pierre had not expected the Scientist leaned close. "We will be here some weeks so let's take an amble about the town, gain our bearings and get to know our new home."

Whether it was the odors or heat or noise or his confusion at finally standing again on dry land, Pierre felt suddenly drained and could do nothing except follow the Scientist's lead. "There is only one business here," the Scientist said, "and it appears that business is brisk." When Pierre asked which were pirate ships, the Scientist leaned close and spoke quietly. "Formal labels rarely endure. Undoubtedly there are privateers sailing under marque anchored beside merchant ships from all points of the compass and each is engaged in whatever will prove profitable."

"So some sail for the King of England?"

"One king or another, except for those free-booters who honor no allegiance and remain available to the highest bidder. It even happens that an unchartered privateer sometimes off-loads cargo not entirely legitimate."

"And when they're discovered?"

The Scientist shrugged. "When the price is right uncomfortable questions are avoided."

"So they could all be pirates."

Dr. de Montpellier stopped and turned to face Pierre. "Unprofitable questions rarely profit the questioner." Then he smiled. "Found your land-legs?"

"I suppose so," Pierre said, "or I soon will."

They passed among several buildings and then stood in a crowded thoroughfare. Thrilled by the crowd's excitement Pierre could not turn his head quickly enough to ensnare the swirl around him. When they reached the Customs House the Scientist pointed out the King's Warehouse behind it. "This is Queen Street and immediately ahead stands the Governor's Mansion."

Having grown up in a busy port Pierre was transfixed by everything he saw. Turning the next corner they approached the Governor's Mansion.

The Scientist stopped. "We have reached High Street, the busiest of the settlement. Followed to its end we will cross the Palisadoes and join the main road to the rest of the island."

Beyond the Old Church and its graveyard they passed a market with fruits and vegetables piled high in bright pyramids and then Bridewell prison. The buildings became fewer and between them stood golden sand dunes while beyond those lay the turquoise sea. At the top of a small rise they stopped and turned back to see the town spread out before them. Squinting against the sunshine the Scientist said, "Now you will have no excuse for becoming lost."

"One question," Pierre said. He glanced from the town to the Scientist. "Where do they keep the slaves?"

The Scientist's smile disappeared. "The slave-house is near the docks and is guarded by Fort Charles."

"And are they also sold there as well?"

"Auctions are conducted the first of each month. If curiosity so demands we could walk passed, although I assume the trade in human beings is among the least of your interests."

Pierre shrugged. "I'm just surprised it continues."

"A community remains free to the extent it satisfies the needs of those who have wealth and power. And there is no more certain sign of wealth and power than the ownership of another human being." The Scientist shrugged. "Shall we return?"

As they walked, Pierre felt emboldened to ask that question he had been reluctant to ask aboard ship. "Do you know of the Abbess Maria?"

Again the Scientist stopped and turned and suddenly Pierre wished he had not asked the question. "We should say she is someone known differently by each person who knows of her." As if completing Pierre's thought he added, "None of us is the same person to each person we know. Some turn that to their advantage." After a moment he took Pierre's arm. "Leave it at this; assume you have proved as valuable to her as she has been to you."

Pierre's wounded feelings must have shown in his expression because the Scientist stopped to face him directly. "Did you believe you were in love with her, or she with you?"

Jostled and bumped by the passing crowd, Pierre decided he did not know how he felt, and he hesitated, waiting for those emotions to drop their disguise and stand naked and exposed in all his secret self-interests.

Watching him the Scientist laid a consoling hand on his shoulder. "All of the important questions, if they are truly important, remain unanswered. We wander in darkness bumping into invisible truths feeling them as best we can, guessing at their true size and weight and shape. If we encounter them again, it is only by chance we recognize we have met them before."

They turned and began their descent back along High street to return to the town. Pierre asked, "Where do you think the rest of the crew has gone?"

"After a month spent exclusively in each other's company, it is unlikely they will remain so here. Anyway, I am eager to visit my friend. He will provide useful information as well as accommodations."

"Is he far?"

The Scientist grinned. "Never question the distance when the destination is a soft bed."

He led Pierre down a side street. Glancing further ahead Pierre realized that at the far end two burly sailors were fighting; he recognized the awkward gestures of men who were thoroughly drunk. He recalled evenings at the tavern when drunken friends would fall out and begin to fight. Their encounters were more often comical than frightening. But then Pierre saw something glint in one of the men's hands. In the next moment the other man staggered backward holding his side while his opponent turned and ran. The staggering man screamed for his mother and for God's help before he fell to the ground, and then he did not move. Pierre stepped toward him but a hand on his shoulder held him back.

"We can do nothing and there is only trouble for whoever interferes."

Pierre turned to face him. The Scientist said, "Whatever could have been done should have been done long ago. While you are here mind your own affairs and leave others to mind theirs." Pierre hesitated but then nodded and followed the Scientist.

By the time they passed the fallen man, several people had gathered. The Scientist muttered sympathies loud enough to be heard but did not stop. Pierre was relieved he did not recognize the fallen man as one of his shipmates.

At the next intersection they turned into a smaller street. The sky edged toward pink and lavender. Late afternoon heat weighed on Pierre like a heavy coat and his legs felt like soggy logs. He had to force himself to hurry and not fall behind the Scientist.

"Best step lively," the Scientist said without turning. "Just remember that you will soon be dead and unlikely to do more walking."

The humor in his voice annoyed Pierre, but lectures about approaching death by someone who seemed nearly there annoyed him more. "I expect you think a lot about death."

The Scientist shook his head. "Knowing is all the thinking that subject deserves."

"But you do think about it."

The Scientist's laugh filled the alley. "I thought about it more when I was your age."

Pierre was about to ask if he believed there was life after death when just ahead he saw three nuns approached. To his surprise, others on the street stepped aside, turned their backs or entered the nearest shop, all as if determined to avoid them. He turned to see the Scientist glower. When they reached those women, all three turned to scrutinize Pierre and the Scientist with dark expressions.

"Evening, ladies!" Pierre said in a loud voice. Instead of the smile he expected, the nun closest turned to him and scowled. Grabbing his arm the Scientist pushed him toward an alley. "There are things," he muttered, "more important than death, and those are the things which will hold off death."

"You mean, pirates?"

The Scientist hissed, "Keep your voice down." He shoved Pierre along an alley until it opened into a courtyard. The buildings around them stood three and four stories. The sky above presented an irregular rectangle of thickening blue. The Scientist led him to a roughly-made bench against one wall and sat down. He paused as if listening and then relaxed. Leaning his head back, from time to time he glanced at the entrance through which they had come.

"Pirates," he said, "merely dispense death. Like Royal Executioners they provide death without anger or reflection. But others live on death, on the fear of death. They wallow in death, bathe in it. Death keeps them alive and those who are dying invigorate them, anoint their pleasure and purify their lust. Pirates and the king's men simply distinguish who will die, but priests and nuns need death. If no one died, who would ever call a priest? Do not be fooled; death is distributed unequally and priests do not care who dies as long as they participate."

Nothing the Scientist said made sense to Pierre. "So what are we doing here?"

The Scientist smiled. "If we are very lucky, for a while longer the priests will not know we are here and so we may remain among the living."

Sounds from open windows and doors echoed the rhythms of the living. What Pierre had been told could only be the ranting of a man old enough to envision death. Nothing he said dampened the thrill that came to him of the lives being lived and whose sounds floated on the soft evening breeze swirling around them.

The Scientist struck Pierre's shoulder. "If you do not understand what I have said, perhaps it is premature. But I have developed a powerful appetite. Suppose we find some food."

Finally Dr. de Montpellier suggested something that held Pierre's interest. "And will we also find our lodgings?" His grin was a sufficient answer. Then another question came to Pierre. "And the Captain? What about him?"

"What about him?" the Scientist asked as if the question held only the mildest interest.

"Shouldn't we, I mean, shouldn't I, return to the ship?"

The Scientist shrugged. "In the words of the immortal Rabelais, Do as thou wilt." When Pierre hesitated he added, "I thought I had made it clear; if you wish to return to the ship, be off with you. But this is Port Royal; do as you like and allow others to do the same."

"Does the Captain see things the same way?"

"He is a resourceful man." The Scientist stood and turned to lead the way. "When he decides he wants to see you again, believe me, he will."

They passed along one alley and then another, and Pierre was suddenly startled to discover that they stood once again in the middle of Queen's street. Despite what the Scientist might say to Pierre, resuming a path he once had thought lost felt exactly like luck.

CHAPTER NINETEEN

AT THE END of the street the sun just touched the horizon, while behind Pierre the eastern sky ran to a deepening blue. Fewer people traveled the street and vendors had nearly all packed their wares. Most of their stands built of palm fronds and roughly-cut planks stood empty and packs of small dogs rooted in the refuse piled between them and along the street. By the time they reached an undistinguished doorway with a faint orange light flickering through a window beside the door, the sun was a golden sliver at the edge of a darkening sky.

Inside stood three long tables. Sailors of different ages sat spread among them who watched without curiosity as Pierre and the Scientist entered. Dr. de Montpellier led him to a bench and sat on another across the table from him. A large, dark-skinned woman with thick, dark hair and glittering black eyes stepped from beyond the bar and set platters piled with blackened broiled fish before them. Smiling to the Scientist she said, “Welcome, gentlemen. My name is Margaret and I call my establishment the Windmill. You will forgive me, I’m sure, that I have no windmill.” Her voice was pitched with enthusiasm. “If you have a thirst for it, I have ale today.” He thanked her, complimented her tavern and requested tankards for each of them.

When she was gone the Scientist began to devour his fish as if it had been days since his last meal. Pierre ate his as he looked about, his curiosity an appetite even sharper than that of his stomach. A large and grizzled man sitting alone across the room, his massive head tipped down, roused himself to sip from the tankard before him. His eyes circled the room and came to rest on Pierre. A flat, indifferent expression masked his face, yet his eyes suggested a moment's curiosity.

The Scientist had finished his third fish and Margaret had just placed their tankards on the table before them when he looked up at Pierre with mild surprise. "Something does not agree with you?"

Pierre glanced down at his portion; he had fallen behind the Scientist's pace. "I suppose curiosity has gotten the better of my appetite."

"Never a good thing." The Scientist belched loudly, a sound like water draining from a tub. "Like love, food must be appreciated even as it is being devoured. Contemplation has no place in that scheme and the one can only corrupt the other."

Pierre was about to respond when he saw the dozing man stand and move toward their table. He sat down beside Pierre without introducing himself.

In a deep and rumbling voice he said, "Though we've never met, I believe you men to be honorable shipmates and fair to all you meet, so I'll be blunt and not decorate my words." Though dour, as he spoke the man's face reshaped itself into something resembling a wily elf.

"Let me help you there," Dr. de Montpellier said without glancing to look at him. "I surmise you have shipwrecked for the price of tobacco or of a bed and hope you will find aid."

The man's thick face shifted to a tolerant good humor. "You have me a-right, mates, and I won't give you no trouble. I've had God's own misery and I care not for more. But I must leave this cursed town or Death will be upon me as the next sun rises."

"Death awaits all of us, friend," the Scientist said, "and no man can say otherwise."

"True that is and a scholar you must be for the fine way you have of saying it." The man lowered his voice so that it seemed to come from within the table. "Death dogs the heels of us all though some know that better than others." He turned toward Pierre with a glance that was both sympathetic and dismissive. "Excuse gray-beards like ourselves for we have the deeper knowledge, if you don't mind me saying." Turning back to the Scientist he said, "But what I'm about ain't your garden-variety misery. The evil what pursues me is darker than a moonless night on a stormy sea. There's nothing more to it but leave this island or die where I stand."

Though the Scientist's expression did not change, a note of humor colored his voice. "There is a trouble that only flight can cure and I have been there, too. But we are just poor sailors like yourself and making our way as best we can, so our help is as little as can be."

"You mistake me, mates, and that's the truth." The man leaned back and his dour glance traveled from the Scientist to Pierre as if measuring them both. "Call me Strong Bill," he said, "for that's as I've been known on every ship I've sailed in a life lived on every sea God made. But I've a tale that needs telling."

Dr. de Montpellier turned to Pierre. "Should we hear him out or send him on his way?" Before Pierre could respond the Scientist said to Strong Bill, "But my manners have failed me. As we are all mates here and well-met, we should share a rum to hear you out." As he spoke, the Scientist slid a coin covered by his hand across the table to Strong Bill.

"It was a generous God what led you to this place and smiled at me when He showed you that door. But my tale's so uncanny you'll have drunk your fill and won't believe your ears."

The Scientist signaled Margaret and she approached the table looking warily at Strong Bill. Asking for three cups of rum they sat in silence while Pierre studied the stranger. The calluses on his hands were thick as good leather, scars on his fingers spread like a spider's web and two of his fingers crooked as if once broken and badly healed. His eyes and mouth offered the deep wrinkles of a life spent in harsh sun and salt air. But Pierre was startled by a red scar edged with black of a recent burn the rough shape of a large star on the back of his right hand. Margaret placed the drinks on the table and Strong Bill watched until she was well away before he spoke.

"The time I mean to tell you of was three evenings ago. I was enjoying the company of my good woman in a room not a stone's-throw from here. Me and her, Emilia's her name, we've been friendly-like for a long while. We were abed with a bottle of good rum between us and the world could not have been better to an old dog like myself if my arse was pouring forth gold, if you'll pardon the expression. I tell you gentlemen, she give as much as a poor old sailor could wish for. But I'm here now and there's the heartache."

"What happened?" Pierre asked. The Scientist sat with his arms folded over his chest watching the sailor.

To Pierre, Strong Bill said, "And there it is, young gentlemen, the question

I've asked myself and can't credit the answer. I'll tell you all I remember and hope you've the smarts to knit it together. When the rum was gone and we'd done what we'd hoped to do, my good woman fell fast asleep. And but for her quiet breathing I might've wondered that she'd passed over, she slept so hard and sound. Myself, I was so full of rum and contentment I could've gone over myself and never complained. And pretty soon I drifted into a snooze like you'd think I hadn't slept for a week. So there we were, snug in our bed and dreaming like babies. But then I woke up."

Strong Bill's eyes traveled the room. "Can't say whether I felt it first or heard it, but I woke knowing we weren't alone and opened my eyes already reaching for my good woman. Only she weren't beside me no more. In that darkness it took a moment but then I made them out. Four of them, but with the black shadows maybe more, and all standing like statues around the bed. Except that at the foot of the bed, well, I blinked my eyes so hard I saw stars, but there stood my good except she was sort of wrapped in something that could have been black silk it were so kind of shinny, except I couldn't be sure of any of this 'cause all you could see for certain was her dark hair and I just had to guess it was her and she was being sort of carried like these others planned to take her someplace they had her between them."

"Who was?" the Scientist asked suddenly with a look of grim annoyance.

"Well and there's the trick of it," he said and paused. He stared at his scared hand, fingers spread on the table as if words were strung like pearls between his fingertips. "I admit there was a good bit of rum in that bottle and maybe I sucked up more than my Emilia and it was dark as pitch, as I say, and so I could hardly tell if I was awake so, laugh if you like, but I would swear to the Lord God that around that bed was a pack of nuns."

"Nuns, you say?" The Scientist's eyes were wide with surprise.

"Nothing but," Strong Bill said. "It's a heathen thing to say and I've gone over it in my head a hundred times but there ain't no other way to say it. And like you, each time I think it I ask myself the same."

Pierre said, "You must have been dreaming. That's all that explains." He turned to the Scientist, whose look was fixed on Strong Bill as if trying to see into the man's head.

"In that darkness," Strong Bill continued, "them young faces stood out like pale flames, but it was their eyes what chilled me. The color of melting silver they was, glittering with kind of an icy sparkle. I swear it was them eyes what frightened me most."

Pierre said, "All that rum just confused you."

"You might think that, young gentleman, you just might. Me, I couldn't tell who they were, but rum or no, people stood in that room and they had my Emilia between them and there weren't nothing but for me to do something about it. So I sat up and swung my hand out at the one nearest me and hit something. I don't know who or what it was, but I got this for my trouble." He held out his scarred hand. "It was like I'd put my hand into a fire and I screamed out. I tried to stand and don't you know but something come down on my head so hard I was gone 'til past daybreak. I woke up alone and Emilia was gone."

Pierre held his breath but the Scientist began to laugh, its sound like sawing metal except wet and wracked with phlegm and loud enough to cause the heads of the others to turn.

Finally the Scientist turned to study Strong Bill with mirthful eyes. "A rare tale, old salt, indeed a rare tale. I have heard the best from the seven seas but your yarn beats everything." Another coin appeared under his hand and he slid it across the table to Strong Bill.

His scarred hand moved toward it but stopped midway. "Begging your pardon but every word I just spoke was as true as the Bible. And I didn't tell it for the sake of gold though you're as generous as a spring day and that's a fact."

"What did you do?" Pierre asked.

"You see," Dr. de Montpellier said to Strong Bill, "one of us is curious to know how your story ends." The smile on the Scientist's face suggested his skepticism.

To Pierre's surprise, Strong Bill became flustered. "Now, there ain't no call to mock, if you don't mind me saying so. As to the young gentleman's question, I'll tell you right. I ain't told another soul but I've received only ignorance and suspicion. But I saw you two a cut above the local lot. I hoped you'd take my trouble aright and even offer advice on what I should do next. Because this story, as you calls it, ain't rightly over, not by my lights. For two days I've searched for my Emilia, visited her friends, gone to her haunts, but no one's seen her. Even asked a group of nuns I seen walking the byways. Like the hand of God scooped her off the face of the earth, as you might say. It weren't like she was rich or a raving beauty, though I myself found her better than passing fine. I swear to you both I'd do anything to find her. But what's worse, I ain't slept hardly a wink since that night for fear of what might creepy-crawl through my window, though I've faced men with pistol and cutlass and would do so again. But I fear these creatures, I rightly do, and have no shame of saying it plain."

Dr. de Montpellier's grin faded, and he leaned toward Strong Bill. "That is a weird tale, old salt, and you must not take offense at my saying so. But you say you have not seen the woman again and you want our help finding her; do I have your meaning right?"

"I look for advice, like I said, because it's all as I said and not a lie in it. I'm not an educated man, as you must know, and I've so a little money I don't know where my next meal'll come from. You've been generous to a fault and the Good Lord will bless you for it. But I mean to find her and I'll give anything to do it. And not just because she was so precious. A woman in my company is as safe as if she was sleeping in her own mother's bed. And these women, whatever they are, I mean to get my Emilia back and get my even as well. You see my point, don't you?"

The Scientist turned to Pierre. "So what do you say? Intrigued enough to spend some time finding a woman who may not want to be found?" He turned back to Strong Bill. "Because that is how it sounds to me. Women get lost and found on this island every day, if you get my point. Suppose that is the true nature of the thing. If she has finished with you, all God's angels and saints will not bring her back. Have you thought of that?"

Strong Bill hung his head and sighed, his shoulders dipped and he clasped his good hand over the burned one. "The thought never leaves my head and that's God's truth. But if she's finished with me there's no need of her hiding. I've been in more ports than you can find on a map. If it's like that, I'm enough of a man to say well and good and God speed to you. I ain't the vindictive type, as you might say and she don't need to make a drama of it. No, there's too much of the weird in all this. Truly, I am afeared there's evil afoot, something of the ungodly as you might say. Besides, suppose it ain't just my Emilia the likes of these is after. If you ain't about to help me, well and good but have a care for them others."

"He has a point," Pierre said. "This could be deeper than we can think."

"All right," the Scientist said to Pierre, "let us suppose there is a thread of truth in what he says. How do we find a woman we've never met? Where to begin is our problem."

"I've nothing to pay you with, as you know," a tone of pleading seeped into Strong Bill's voice, "except the sweat off my back and my eternal gratitude. But help me here and you'll have my loyalty for life and I swear that before God Himself."

The Scientist leaned back again and sighed. "It seems we have too much time on our hands and too much curiosity to boot. But I expect you want to see how this story ends. And to be honest, so do I." He turned again to Strong Bill. "It's too late in the day to begin a search for what may not want to be found. We'll meet here tomorrow at noon and perhaps by then our path will appear a bit clearer."

Strong Bill's grin startled Pierre, as if the effort had opened every scar and fissure on his face. But the light in his eyes convinced Pierre the man was moved and grateful. Looking from him to the Scientist, he said, "Aye and I knew you were the mates for me and after my own heart, too. High noon it is. We'll clear up this little mystery and my Emilia'll be back in my arms by nightfall." He stood. "It was a blessing from God what brought you gentlemen to this establishment. A blessing and a benediction upon you both and upon a miserable heathen like myself." He stepped back with a bow. "Until tomorrow, and I'll trouble you no more." He went to the door and left.

When he was gone Pierre turned to the Scientist. "What do you think?"

The Scientist hesitated. "Too little information, but to be honest I will be surprised if we ever see him again."

"So you think it was all just a story to get a hand-out?"

"An elaborate tale for a small amount of money. One thing is certain; that scar is no invention. And his story was more preposterous than it needed to be, so some bit of it might be true." He shook himself and then looked up smiling. "Finish that delicious fish and we will move on. There is a man I need to see. "

"So we will meet him here tomorrow?" Pierre asked, unsure if he was excited or worried.

"We will be here. Whether he will remains to be seen."

Pierre finished his fish with a sudden appetite. When they stood to leave Margaret came to their table. She smiled at Pierre. "You gentlemen enjoyed your meal well enough, I trust."

"It was exquisite, Madame," the Scientist said as gallantly as a bishop as he handed her several coins, "and my compliments to the chef."

"Well then," she said placing her hands on her hips and thrusting out her broad chest, "considering the hour, I expect you'll be needing rooms."

"As it turns out," the Scientist said, "accommodations have already been arranged."

Her shoulders sagged, and though she tried to sustain it, her smile faded. The Scientist added, "But if your beds are as comfortable as your victuals are tasty, I expect this house is always full up." The complement seemed to brighten her spirits.

Smile retrieved she said, "Gentlemen of your quality will always be welcome here."

Outside on the street Pierre asked, "When were these rooms arranged?"

"Never mind, boy, I am not entirely without resources. Now, we must see that man I know." He turned. Pierre hesitated as he watched Margaret make her shapely way toward her kitchen. But then he fell in beside the Scientist wondering about luck and its different forms and hopeful he was at least luckier than Strong Bill.

CHAPTER TWENTY

PIERRE WAS SURPRISED to see the streets even more crowded and noisy than when they arrived. With a glowing lantern lit warmly orange beside every door and a candle burning in every window, the streets were awash in a glow that brightened their way.

Leaving Queen Street they passed along a series of alleyways until they came to a narrow dark blue door, windows above it dark except one on the second floor. The Scientist pounded on the door with the side of his fist, paused and then pounded again. The shutters of the lighted window swung open and a gruff voice cried out, "Away with you or face my cutlass."

"Humble pilgrims come seeking shelter. By the breath of God do not turn us away."

A man's head appeared in the window, his smile bright even in the darkness. "Ah, and it's you, come to plague my mind, drink my rum and empty my purse."

"And front to back that is a heathen lie."

"Well-spoken by a heathen. Seems there is nothing for it but let you in and be done with you."

The face disappeared, only to be framed in a few moments by the opened doorway. After an affectionate greeting, the Scientist introduced Pierre to Brother Guarino Tomasso Sengelese. Brother Guarino said to the Scientist, "Another you have corrupted with your smelly old books."

"This block of wood would not know which end of a book to open, but he is passing clever with tools and potions and seems resigned to learning a thing or two."

"More's the pity for him. Come in before the Devil spies you without your rosary." Brother Guarino led as they climbed stairs. A small, round man with a large square head, thick eyebrows and large, darkly-circled eyes, the fringe of dark hair surrounding his skull became black and grey when it reached his chin, but he moved with an agility that surprised Pierre. The Scientist following Pierre up the stairs said, "Pierre's father is a man whose name you likely have heard; Augustus Chanceux."

Brother Guarino stopped and turned to look at Pierre with mild surprise. "That is a name I am familiar with."

"And not only," the Scientist continued, "does he have a famous progenitor, but he has a tale to tell that verges on the unbelievable, though I believe it absolutely."

To Pierre, the Brother said, "Then it is particularly good that I restocked my rum."

At the top of the stairs they entered a tiny and cluttered room. "Do not move a thing," the Brother said. "This is all carefully organized and arranged."

With hardly a glance the Scientist swept a stack of books and papers from a chair with the back of his hand and sat down. "It is like you to disguise an accident as an intention."

"And it is like you to insist every intention disguises an accident."

Turning to Pierre the Scientist said, "Observe the prevarications typical of the pseudo-intellectual trained by the Jesuits though still just as poor as a monk."

The Brother responded, "Spoken as the true materialist you are." He cleared another chair for Pierre and brought out a bottle of rum and three cups. To Pierre he said, "I must confess I am uncertain what piques my curiosity more, but I am eager to know of your father."

"The fact is," the Scientist interjected, "he has not seen the man for ten years."

Brother Guarino's eyes grew wide and he glanced from the Scientist to Pierre. "Then I suspect you want to know anything I can tell you about him." He shifted in his chair. "Simply put, though I have heard of his work, what little I can tell you is merely that which I have learned on good authority. Which is that, some time ago he passed through Port Royal. I would be happy to make additional inquiries since what I know is less than what you likely desire."

"Have you heard," Pierre asked, "whether or not he is still alive?"

"If something untoward had occurred," Brother Guarino said, "I would have heard." He offered Pierre a smile of reassurance.

"Do you know when he passed through the port or where he went from here?"

"I am not certain, but I believe he traveled to Havana."

"And what makes you believe that?"

"A sort of university has been established near there with scholars engaged in various studies. It seems likely he planned to contact them."

The Scientist said, "I am delighted to hear you say that. A former student of mine owns a large estate on the island. It would be wonderful good fortune if that was what you spoke of and Augustus had found his way there."

"It appears," Brother Guarino said to Pierre, "there is good reason to hope you will learn more about his travels." He hesitated. "I assume that you want to locate him."

"For my mother's sake," Pierre said. "This is what has set me on my journey."

"And it was in the course of that journey," the Scientist added, "that Pierre survived an attack by the legendary creature."

Brother Guarino appeared thoroughly startled. "That is even more extraordinary than the fact that you are the son of Augustus." Pierre assumed this was an invitation to recite his tale so beginning with his departure on the Bristol, he described his adventure as he had for Captain Stevenson. While the Scientist sat back in his chair, Brother Guarino leaned forward, determined to catch his every word. Several times he appeared about to ask a question but then held back. When Pierre reached his description of his rescue by the Revenge, the Scientist said, "And it was there that I encountered this unusual young man."

"A remarkable story," Brother Guarino said. "Foremost because, although there have been rumors, you are the first I know of who has survived to tell the tale."

"It begs the question," the Scientists ventured, "of the nature and origin of the creature."

"One finds the urge to speculate irresistible."

"Even though we lack material evidence on which to base such speculations."

"But we have Pierre's account," Brother Guarino said, "which offers a few nuggets."

"One of which," the Scientists added, "is that the creature exists, and the second its description and how it behaves."

"Yet neither helps us with the two most important questions; where it came from, and whether each sighting was a separate beast. And since," Brother Guarino continued, "according to your account, the creature appears impervious to weapons, another question arises as to what substance the creature is made."

"One is tempted," the Scientist said, "to reach back to Aristotle or Pliny the Elder for clues to the nature of its existence."

"And Lucretius as well," Brother Guarino added.

"That which is unprecedented refuses generalization."

"Of course," Brother Guarino said, "within popular opinion, only error resides."

The men exchanged conjectures until Pierre grew bored and suddenly interrupted asking if Brother Guarino had heard stories of renegade nuns. All humor vanished from the Brother's face. The Scientist folded his arms and sat back watching him closely.

"Now there is a mystery wrapped in an enigma if ever I heard of one. I confess that I have had no contact with those good ladies but they are talked about, I can tell you that."

The Scientist asked, "And exactly what does that talk amount to?"

Brother Guarino rubbed his gray-and-black bearded chin. "Putting aside the usual superstitious rot, you are left with a fistful of pieces that add up to nothing. There is supposed to be a convent of them high in the hills. Apparently they call themselves the Sisters of the Bloody Cross but there appears to be a good deal of the unlikely about them."

Dr. de Montpellier said, "I have never heard of an order of nuns by that name. How have they acquired this reputation?"

"For one thing, no one has ever seen a priest enter their convent when one would expect them to hear Mass. And when a passing peddler offering his sundries is a man, he does not so much as get a toe inside the gates. But every vegetable-peddling or fish-mongering woman, no matter how unsavory, is welcome. And when a group comes into the town, they are always seen entering one or another of the superstition shops; you know, eye-of-toad, gallbladder-of-shark places. What is purchased inside no one will say. Even the proprietors are mum although street-sense suggests they are paid extra for that service. But strangest, folks report hearing the most awful racket coming from the convent at night; screams and such. There is no lack of speculation, I can tell you. When anyone tries to engage one in conversation on the street, they get stony silence and an evil look for their bother. They are a queer lot, no question of that. But what could you expect from a group of women living together and who pray to God every day?"

"We had an encounter and your description seems most apt," the Scientist said. Pierre was about to ask after Abbess Maria but the Scientist continued. "A short while ago we spoke with a man who claims his lady-friend was kidnapped by women he described as nuns."

Brother Guarino's expression turned into a leer. "Nothing surprising there. That sort of rumor surrounds every convent from Cadiz to Calcutta. The kidnapping angle is unusual; those types usually find what they are looking for without stealing. Are you sure your man was not deep in the cask?"

"He admits," Pierre said, "that he and the woman had been drinking, but he showed us a burn scar that could not have been faked."

"What can and cannot be faked," Brother Guarino said, "changes every day. There is always a man with an oddity looking to enrich himself with an amazing tale. I do not suggest your man faked his wound. But a scar is evidence of an injury, not how it was got."

"So you think our friend's story is a hoax to raise cash?" the Scientist asked.

"Put it this way; visions come to men in dreams that cannot be true, yet the dreamer finds them impossible to deny. The mind is a vast ocean. The surface is clearly seen and directly encountered but it is a separate world beneath, filled with creatures whose natures are inexplicable and whose intentions we can never know."

"This surprises me," the Scientist said. "You make the mind out to be a world of constant danger. As if anything hidden must be a threat."

"That which is harmless is of no account. The first goal of all empirical knowledge is recognition of danger. We observe first to neutralize the world through knowledge."

"But this is not how Aristotle saw the world, or the mind."

"Nor is it the way Plato saw it. But the fact remains that the Ancients failed to measure the world in a meaningful way. To them, the mind was an internal actualizing ghost separable from the body. For them, the mind travels within the body as a man rides in a carriage."

"And common experience confirms this account as sufficient," the Scientist said.

"Yet, when we attempt to reach the heart of any question, everyday experience is never adequate. Take the metaphor of the rider and the carriage. To be useful, we must stipulate that the rider is never confused or hesitant and the horse never has a mind of its own. But both of these occur in the everyday world of men and horses. As so often is the case, a metaphor complicates what it is assumed to simplify."

"Holding aside the sufficiency of the metaphor, to be adequate our description must account for significant elements of the phenomenon. It is an unfortunate inclination of the Ancients to account for dreams as impositions from external spirits even when we recognize our dreams populated by people and within settings from our own world."

"The Ancients," Brother Guarino said, "recognized that dreams do not communicate directly but move through the mind like poems, setting alight certain emotions and ideas which then demand interpretation."

"And this is merely," the Scientist said, "another way of suggesting that, because dreams are never completely understood, they shed no reliable light on our experience."

At first, the two men turned frequently to Pierre as if to include him in their conversation, but when it descended into an argument over Aristotle's distinction between substance and extension, a second bottle of rum appeared. Pierre decided that since he could not follow the debate he might at least keep up with their drinking, but even that soon was impossible. The Scientist attempted to persuade Brother Guarino that someone named Leibniz had postulated something about lodestone and the aether, and the Scientist had experimentally confirmed it so that some distinction was transcended which Pierre could not grasp. That second bottle of rum emptied and words began to slur and soon after, Pierre dozed off in his chair.

He awoke with a start to find himself in the darkened room drunk and alone and the two men gone. He wandered into the next room to discover them huddled in a narrow bed and snoring into each other's faces. Befuddled and annoyed, Pierre roused himself determined to shake the fog from his head and left, quietly closing the door behind him.

Despite the late hour the street was even more crowded with noisy travelers, only now most he passed were quite drunk. The spirit of carnival now reigned, laughter and raucous gaiety enflamed every face. He retraced his steps as best as he could recall back along Queen Street and he was relieved finally to reach the Windmill Inn. For a reason he would not consider, he was excited to see the lantern beside the door still lit and a good fire in the hearth.

The inn was crowded and smoky with tobacco and something sweet Pierre did not recognize. He shouldered his way to the bar until he stood before Margaret. Her eyes were glazed and her face glistened with sweat, and it took a moment for her to recognize him, but when she did a broad grin appeared. "Well, I see you managed to slip your father's leash." He was about to correct her confusion over who his father was but then thought better of it and smiled in mild embarrassment.

"We became separated and I've become lost. I hoped your offer of lodgings remained."

At those words her eyes became bright. "Indeed, good sir, the most comfortable lodgings you have ever had the good fortune to enjoy. But pray take that seat beside the bar where I can keep a weather eye on you and I will be your servant in no-time."

He did as she requested and sat back to enjoy watching others do the work he had done for his mother at the tavern. What he did not recognize were the familiarities that customers took with Margaret's person. Hugs and caresses evoked smiles, laughter, teasing protest and amused complaint. He had never witnessed such familiarities with Gabriella. But then he found himself wondering if such things had simply been kept from him. With this he drifted back to the Captain Hudson and he was overwhelmed with a wistful nostalgia. Suddenly, a tall glass of rum appeared before him. He looked up to see Margaret grinning down. "We permit no long faces here, good sir. Cheer up or drink up, the choice is yours as long as the result is the same."

He smiled and took the glass from her hand. "Your kindness is without limit."

Margaret's smile brightened. "I would not go so far as that, good sir. I wish just a favor or two in return, simple tasks a sturdy young man like yourself will accomplish without much bother."

"It so happens I've spent a lot of time doing chores for a tavern."

Grinning, her eyes widened. "Well, there is indeed a fair wind tonight."

"And that is good?" Pierre asked.

"Always go before the wind, good sir," Margaret said. She leaned down exposing the cleavage of her bosom as she brought her lips to his ear. "No matter which way it blows, always go before the wind." She straightened and with a wink added, "Always." She turned and he watched her generous hips sway in retreat as she resumed serving her customers.

Pierre sipped from his glass watching Margaret pass between tables, slip between customers, move back and forth between the bar and the tables, and the more she moved the thirstier he became. Gradually the red-orange light of the hearth brightened and the room became warmer.

In a corner beside the door a man sat with a lute in his hands singing songs, several of which Pierre had heard before, but several were new to him. Songs of danger and bravery, songs of love and loss, songs of pleasure and pain. The songs were lively and customers often joined in their singing. But then he chose a song that was slow and melancholic about home and mother and the life before and the room became silent. Those eyes not on the singer looked out vacantly into space or down at the sand-powdered floor. And Pierre knew what they were thinking because he was thinking the same. When the song ended, without pause the singer struck up something rollicking and lewd and funny bringing smiles to the gathering.

His glass was nearly empty when Margaret appeared. "Surely your drink has evaporated since I have seen you take hardly more than a sip. I will happily refill it," she said taking his glass, "but you must drink all of it this time." When she turned back toward the bar he watched her as if she was the only person in the room.

When she was gone, a man sitting close to Pierre leaned toward him. He was tall, gray and cadaverous with a long face, dour and brooding. In a conspiratorial whisper he said, "You're the luckiest man in this room. I hope you know that, and if you don't, I'm happy to tell you."

Pierre was startled and uncomfortable and blandly responded, "I thank you for that."

The man studied Pierre a moment. "By your expression I assume you don't believe me." Leaning still closer he said, "I wasn't always this old. There was a time when I found myself the luckiest man in the room and, to my eternal regret, I didn't realize it. Of course, that was long ago. You likely think all old men tell tales that are almost never true. And you may be right, thought myself, I see no point in making up adventures when the true ones are good. Just remember this; all you see who are old were once young, and all who you see as young will one day be old. One day you will sit beside a younger man telling him of something from your life and suddenly it'll seem to you as if what you describe had happened to someone else. And that young man will look at you the way you're looking at me now. When that happens, I hope you'll do him the favor of telling him only true things." He glanced over Pierre's shoulder and Pierre turned to see Margaret approach with a full glass in her hand. When he turned back, the stranger had turned away and was talking with someone beside him.

Reaching his table she placed the glass in front of him. "Surely you do not intend to insult my generosity." Her voice took on a scolding quality. "Since it appears the only way to assure your compliance, I will stand here beside you until this glass is empty. And do not test my patience by drinking slowly. Pretend, if you must, that it's a glass of milk poured by your dear mother's hand." She folded her arms beneath her breasts as if she would do as she said. He took up the glass and the hint of a smile appeared at her lips. As he drank her smile grew, so that by the time he finished, she was grinning. "There! That weren't so hard now was it."

He smiled up at her slightly out of breath, the spirits already rushing to his head.

She took the empty glass from his hand. "Now I'll bring you another and this time you may drink as slowly as you wish." In what seemed to him merely a moment she returned with another glass she put on the table before him. When she turned back to the bar, Pierre discovered that everyone in the tavern was looking at him. But none of that mattered. The full glass reminded him he was thirsty and so he drank. In this way he found himself feeling better and better.

He watched Margaret move about the room and the eyes of other men follow her and he began to think of himself as a lucky person. He thought about how luck had dogged his heels. At one instance he was unlucky, but the next he was lucky, but then unlucky again, a see-saw of fortune and how he had walked into this room a stranger but luck had come to his aid.

He wondered about the nature of luck and whether it was possible to acquire more or perhaps hold it aside until it was urgently needed. Did luck flow like water, or blow and drift like snow, or form into blocks and bricks like ice? Or worse, was it like fog that blew and drifted and disappeared only to billow again into a cloud so thick the material world disappeared? And where did luck go when it was gone? Did it evaporated completely, or did it flow elsewhere, to someone else, or was there a place where luck would collect, like a stream of water that flowed into a lake.

But perhaps the word was really simply a name for something common yet inscrutable but so elusive even attempting to grasp caused its escape.

He looked up to realize his eyes had been closed. Aside from three drunken stragglers, the tavern was empty. He stood, and doing so realized he was remarkably drunk. The room seemed to move beneath his feet and the light was painfully bright. He took unsteady steps until a hand grasped his elbow and he turned to find that Margaret stood beside him.

"Surely, good sir," she said smiling, "you are not attempting to leave my establishment without paying." For a moment Pierre panicked. Her eyes glittered and she leaned toward him. In a voice just above a whisper she said, "Your evening's work has hardly begun." Her smile took on a devilish delight, reminding Pierre that the differences of luck were the differences of a moment, but happily for this moment he remained the luckiest man in the room.

CHAPTER TWENTY-ONE

PIERRE'S BODY WAS being shaken. The pressure and throbbing pain in his head suggested he was being beaten with a hammer and the shaking came from the pounding of his head and guessed his nausea had something to do with that pounding. He opened his eyes to see the massive face of Dr. de Montpellier hover like a wrinkled gray balloon just above his. "So the Devil did not take you after all."

"Ah, the Devil take yourself."

"Testy because of your hang-over." The flesh-balloon grinned. "Must have been a wonderful night."

Pierre looked about startled to find himself where he was, and not where he thought he remembered. Fragments of the previous night cascaded past his eyes. The Scientist sat in a chair beside the bed and with his hands in his lap watched Pierre with the shadow of a grin. "Your fetching proprietress tells me you washed up upon her shore so she found a bunk for you below-deck. I offered to pay but she assured me it has been taken care of. I assume you did more than instruct her on the fine points of Aristotle."

"Aristotle and rum," Pierre said. Pain behind his eyes forced them closed against the morning light. "How did you find me? And what in blazes were you and that prattling old crank yelling about?"

"That crank is the finest mind in this hemisphere. And what we prattled on about involved your father. As for finding you, nothing could have been simpler."

He wanted the fog in his head to clear, the mud and foam behind his eyes to dissipate, the pain to subside, if only just long enough to ask the question, "What?" But he could only stare with pain-filled eyes. The Scientist continued.

"From what he told me, it seems your father has continued his work and has become known among the cognoscenti. So, in answer to your most urgent question, apparently he is very much alive." He paused waiting for the effect of his words to take hold but Pierre could only stare and even that demanded an effort.

"Unfortunately, Brother Guarino does not know where he is. In fact, once he left for Havana, he seems to have disappeared."

"Havana?" The word came out more as a croak and Pierre could think of no others to follow it. From the dismal swamp of his mind a vague memory emerged of having heard that suggested the previous night.

The Scientist said, "So your next question is, when do we leave for Havana?"

A light rapping at the door distracted them both. "Enter," the Scientist said.

The opened door revealed a smiling Margaret carrying a tall pewter tanker. "Now, don't you plague him with useless questions. The young gentleman worked hard until the early morning and I don't want him to leave with the wrong impression of my establishment."

"Fear not, dear woman," the Scientist said taking the tankard from her hand and sipping from it before passing it to Pierre. "When he has drunk this he will feel very much better."

"What is it?" Pierre croaked again as he took it in both hands from the Scientist.

"Salvation," the Scientist said, "but you must drink every bit of it." Pierre sniffed at it and was appalled by the aroma.

Margaret saw him wince. "Do not concern yourself with the smell. You'll thank me for preparing it for you just as you have thanked me for the delightful misery you have enjoyed." With a glance at the Scientist she added, "I assume you gentleman will vacate this room shortly. I'll be grateful since it's needed by another." With a final affectionate look at Pierre she closed the door.

"Making new friends is a difficult challenge," the Scientist said. "But youth has that capacity which is eroded by age. Now, drink!" When Pierre hesitated, he said, "We begin to feel better only after we have finished feeling worse. Drink!"

When the brew touched his lips he thought he might be drinking fish oil, but in a moment the smell of fresh flowers filled his nose. He emptied the tanker and with a trembling hand passed it back to the Scientist.

"Good," the Scientist said. "You are now on your way to recovery." With the empty tankard in his hands he stood. "I will return this to our delightful proprietress and divert her with amusing anecdotes while you gather yourself. Join us quickly." Then he was gone.

Pierre reached the public room and he was surprised to see the Scientist sitting beside Strong Bill, their heads close and voices quiet. As he approached, Strong Bill looked up and greeted him. "Now our crew's complete." With a glance at the Scientist he added, "We can begin whenever you're ready."

Dr. de Montpellier laid his hands flat on the table and stood. "Then we shall begin now."

"Where are we going?" Pierre asked.

"It seems," the Scientist said, "we are about to climb some mountains."

"That's the spirit." Smiling, Strong Bill added, "Only a few hills, really; more walking than climbing and no challenge to a young man like yourself. But it does my heavy heart good to see enthusiasm for a long walk."

"A long walk to see some women about a woman," the Scientist said.

The sudden sunlight and heat outside the tavern left Pierre dazed and unsteady. To Pierre, Strong Bill said, "A friend give it to me about a sort of convent in them hills. Seems a good place to start, ask a few questions as it were, but friendly-like."

"Couldn't we start closer to home?" Pierre asked.

"If there's a door I ain't knocked on or a shopkeeper I ain't spoke with, it's only because they just arrived yesterday. Besides, these nuns maybe have a peculiar interest in my Emilia which I ain't figured."

The Scientist interrupted impatiently, "Every search begins with the likeliest suspect. Since he has already visited those, the convent is the next candidate."

Pierre abandoned hope of changing either mind, he just wanted his reluctance noticed.

At the dock behind the Governor's Mansion they hired a small boat that took them across the lagoon and soon reached the road. Though his head remained foggy as they walked, Pierre began to recover. Suddenly he turned to the Scientist. "I must have left that kit bag at the tavern." He felt an odd panic, but the Scientist merely smiled.

"Then you will have a very good excuse for repeating your visit to our delightful proprietress."

Hills that appeared tame from a distance grew sharp and more broken as they approached. They passed shacks and huts and beside their entrances Pierre saw odd arrangements of piled stones, or cooking pots overturned with lids poised on the bottoms. He asked Strong Bill what he knew about them.

"Mystery stuff, if you see my point, all so their gods don't strike 'em dead." When Pierre appeared confused, he continued, "These Africans held onto their heathen ways and at first the priests killed them for it. But they're clever, I give 'em that. Learned just enough Christianity and mated up their heathen gods with good Christian saints. So when the priests come after 'em for their heathen practices, they say they're just honoring their saints and praying to God to keep them safe from the Devil."

"And the priests accept all that?" the Scientist asked.

Strong Bill shrugged. "They think if these heathens do enough praying they'll give up their devilish ways. Besides, these slaves cost quite a bit and them owners don't want to lose their price over a trifle."

"How do you know all of this?" Pierre asked.

Strong Bill slowed and stared down at the path before him. When he looked up his expression was hard and dark. "I don't like remembering, but as you're honorable shipmates, I owe it to you. So the long and short of it is, I sailed a slave ship as a deck hand once, just once, and it was the worst voyage of my life."

"When was this?" Pierre asked, but a glance from the Scientist silenced him.

"Long time ago when I was a lad hardly older than yourself. I was stuck in Liverpool without a berth, you see, when a friend told me about a ship sailing to Freeport. Well, I was broke and down on my luck so I told myself shipping out was better than rotting in England and signed ship's papers. They told me it was a slave ship but I was young and a ship was a ship so I didn't give it much thought. Loaded up with bolts of cloth and metal goods, the stuff you trade for slaves with, we headed to the Gold Coast. Spent a miserable week anchored off Elmina Castle while the captain haggled and between the heat and food and mosquitoes I started to wonder what I'd got myself into. But finally we weighed anchor. And believe me when I tell you, over the following months I never seen so much death and I hope to the Lord I never do again."

"Sounds like a wonderful voyage," the Scientist said. "How many did you transport?"

"I know you mean to lighten the conversation, but truth be told there weren't nothing amusing about any of it. We left with one hundred and ninety-three slaves; men, women and children. The men we kept shackled each to the next, the same for the women and children, though them we let out onto the deck from time to time. Between the weeping and the moaning and all them wailing brats there weren't a quiet moment the whole voyage. And there was that stench so thick and vile you'd have smelled us twenty miles out. We fed them one meal a day, mostly beans and rice and yams, but it didn't matter because the dying started almost right away. The first died before the first week was out. I remember because it was me and another hand was ordered to bring the miserable bugger out of the hold. The captain took one look at him and said he'd starved himself to death. That made a great impression on me, I can tell you. It takes a desperate misery to cause a man to stop eating. Now I wonder sometimes if he weren't one of the lucky ones, 'cause by the third week we was bringing up one every day. Then it was two, and then it was three, when the disease begun to get them. First come the scurvy and then come the bloody flux."

"And their bodies?" Pierre asked. "What did you do with them?"

"Tossed overboard," Strong Bill said. A look between anger and despair spread over his face. "What else could we do? Anyway, the worst was still to come." He sighed, as if the act of remembering demanded an effort. "Three weeks out we was suddenly becalmed. I've seen it before and I've seen it since but it's still the most uncanny thing. The air all suddenly stops moving, just stops. Not a breath of a breeze and that miasma in the hold getting deeper and more putrid. We started to run low on food and water, what was left we held for the crew. Then the pox took hold and we bring up five and six a day. But being becalmed, them bodies just floated beside us, bobbing along like floating statues, like they wanted to stay with us or maybe drag us along with them to Hell. Pretty soon they surrounded us so you couldn't look no place without seeing one. But even that weren't the worst. Sharks followed us almost from the time we weighed anchor and now they circled us like wolves. Sailors made bets on which body they'd go to next. Between the blood and the stench and all of it drifting around us like a great bloody stew even the hard sailors was disgusted. Eventually the captain was at his wit's end. He lowered two boats tied to painter's lines from the ship's bow and had us row looking for a breeze. Under the hot sun that was hard and miserable work. It was one thing to be on deck and above, but being down beside it; rot and decay and words can't draw the picture nor give you the smell. And they just kept dying. The very worst was the babies; their mothers wailing and screaming, some won't let go of the bodies so we had to fight with them. Weak as they were they fought us, they did. So pitiful, them dead babies, some so small you could carry two in one hand. How did the good Lord look down and not strike us dead, each and every one of us, just wipe the earth clean of us? I couldn't understand then and still can't."

He stopped suddenly and turned to face Pierre and the Scientist. Full of rage and despair he said, "Just don't mistake me. I ain't a good person, never have been or will be. I've done more bad in a year than you'll do your whole lives." He looked down at the dust of the trail as if something there might be useful.

"By my lights the Devil's just another name for God because if there's a God, He's the meanest that could be because He contains the nastiness of His worst creation." With a cold-blooded smirk he added, "There's a level deeper than Hell and I know it because I've seen it, I know its sound and its smell. And I'll kill anyone before I end up there again."

He became silent; the three of them turned and resumed their walk each occupied by his own thoughts until Pierre finally asked, "So what happened?"

Strong Bill looked up as if he had been called from far away. "Five miserable days and then a strong breeze found us. But them slaves kept dying and we kept tossing them over the side. We dropped anchor with just a hundred and twelve, and even a good many of them were but a step from death. I'll admit right off I got paid better for that voyage than for the next three combined. But I'll starve 'till there's ants crawling about my mouth before I sail another slave ship. I've done bad things in my time but that there voyage is the only thing I repent of every time it comes to mind, and it comes to mind every day."

After a long pause the Scientist said, "The trade in humans is a brutal mystery. How it can be practiced by enlightened and educate men eludes me."

Strong Bill shrugged but seemed to regain his composure. "It's just the simplest thing to think. Some of them plantations go for miles. Owners are happy to pay a fortune for them strong backs what survive the crossing. Somebody's got to cut all that cane and it won't be one of them, sweating under the sun with a machete in his hand, I promise you that."

The higher they climbed the more difficult their path became. Soon they reached the foot of a high and craggy bluff where it was just wide enough for a single man to pass. Pierre turned back to see the golden peninsula of the Palisidoes reaching like a broken finger into the turquoise sea and with Port Royal at its tip.

As if anticipating his question Strong Bill said, "Don't concern yourself. We'll arrive before nightfall and who knows but there'll be victuals and clean sheets waiting."

Beyond the brow of the hills Pierre sighted the upper stories of a gray stone building surrounded by narrow widely separated windows and topped with a red tile roof. To one side stood a round tower capped with a red bell-shaped top. "That the convent?"

Strong Bill grinned. "I expect it is and an eagle's eye must be yours; the Convent of the Sisters of the Bloody Cross, or so I've been told."

Pierre glanced at the Scientist who shook his head for Pierre to say nothing. The Scientist said, "Quite an isolated place."

Pierre added, "These women seem determined to discourage visitors."

"They'll be left alone, they will" Strong Bill said.

By the time they reached the main gates, the sky had edged toward purple twilight and they could neither have walked further nor returned to Port Royal. Wide as two carriages and a full storey tall, the gates of the convent were dark, scared wood and thick with riveted bands of black wrought iron except for a grilled window in the right gate twice the width of a man's head. Above these gates was a series of wide, short windows that continued around the wall. Set further back, an interior building stood three stories high, and behind that and close to the wall stood the round, bell-capped tower Pierre had seen from a distance. Most of the windows were black but a few were brightly lit.

The Scientist asked, "How do you propose we make our arrival noticed?"

Strong Bill scratched his grizzled chin. "Don't see no way to raise a ruckus if you see my point." Despite the weak light he spied a rock on the edge of the path just larger than his hand. He picked it up and struck the gate with it as hard as he could three times quickly, then paused. "This ought to wake somebody up," he said and then struck three times again. Finally a window just above the gate opened. A figure obscured by the twilight filled the window but the voice was young and female.

"Our gate is closed," she said. "Be on your way and may God protect you."

To the others the Scientist muttered, "Sounds like welcome in any language."

Strong Bill yelled, "We mean to speak to someone in charge."

"You have heard me plain," the voice at the window said. "Be gone!" The window closed with a slam.

"So says thee," Strong Bill muttered. He beat repeatedly against the gate until finally a shadow filled its grilled window.

"State your business," the voice said. Female and young, it was not the same as the first.

The Scientist said, "We need to speak to the person in charge. Is that you?"

"State your need and I will inform the Mother Superior."

He said. "So you are not the person we need to speak to and you mean us to stand out here until a decision is made. This is no Christian hospitality I am familiar with."

The shadow hesitated and then disappeared. Strong Bill said, "Seems either we've been cut adrift or we're about to meet the captain."

To Strong Bill, Pierre said, "Are you sure these people know something useful?"

"I don't know nothing," Strong Bill said. "That's why I'm always about asking questions." In the twilight his grin was grim.

Pierre was about to ask if asking questions always yielded useful answers when they heard a bolt grate noisily back and then the gate opened just enough for a man to pass. Beyond the gate was a black void. Though the speaker remained invisible a voice for behind the gate said, "Enter."

"I guess," Pierre said, "that's their idea of an invitation."

"No matter how rude," the Scientist said.

Strong Bill stepped through the opening and the Scientist and Pierre followed.

They found themselves in a small courtyard. Ahead, a door stood open leading to a small building, its short and wide hallway ended in a low-ceilinged room. Two tall candles at either side provided the only light. At the room's center stood three women dressed as nuns, their faces obscured by black veils thicker than smoke. "State your business and allow us to return to our prayers." It took Pierre a moment to decide the speaker was the one in the middle.

"We have come for shelter and information," the Scientist said. "A friend of ours has gone missing, a woman reported to have been in your company."

"And we was told," Strong Bill interrupted, "that she's here not to her liking, you might say." To Pierre's surprise, Strong Bill seemed as intimidated by the women as he was.

"There is no one here without their consent," the woman said with chilly certainty. "As for your friend, besides yourselves no one has arrived here in more than five days." Pierre was impressed by her flat and even tone, the voice of someone invariably obeyed.

The Scientist said, "You say you cannot help us in our search. Can you at least provide us shelter until morning?"

The three women tipped their heads together and muttered quietly until the woman in the center looked up. "Very well. Our infirmary at the moment is not occupied. We offer this for your nights' lodging provided you agree to be gone by sunrise."

"Not until we've found my Emilia," Strong Bill said, but the Scientist placed his hand on the man's forearm.

"You have my assurance we will burden you no further than our need."

"Once admitted," the woman continued, "the door will be locked behind you and will not be opened again until dawn. Do you understand this?"

"Perfectly," the Scientist said gravely.

"Us being your prisoners, like as I see it," Strong Bill said. He seemed less angry than resentful, as if annoyed at the suggestion of distrust.

"And how about food?" Pierre asked because his stomach had begun to ache with hunger. The others turned as if surprised he was capable of speech.

After a pause the woman in the center said, "You may share in our simple fare. Though not abundant it should prove sufficient."

"That is as much as we could ask, Madame," the Scientist said, "and will be appreciated."

The woman said, "Accompany these sisters." She nodded toward a doorway Pierre had not noticed. "I repeat my warning; our infirmary is provided for your shelter. Do not abuse our hospitality."

They followed the two nuns as directed, though Pierre detected annoyance from the Scientist and Strong Bill.

Passing along a narrow corridor, the room they entered was wide and windowless, three beds along each wall. Ahead against the far wall stood a small altar with a statue of the Virgin, and above it hung the statue of a grotesque crucifixion. The nuns lit the two candles on either side of the statue providing just enough light for them to make their way around the room. They then left and without a glance at the men; the door locked behind them. The Scientist asked, "Are you certain your friend is here?"

Strong Bill grinned with a horrible expression of embarrassment. "Now governor, I don't know no more about these people than you do. The woman who told me to come here is reliable as a stone or I wouldn't have dragged you out." He sighed heavily as if he had already begun to lose heart. Looking around he added, "But we won't find nothing in here. There's rooms inside rooms, or so I'm told, and there's nothing else to do except to look."

"So we just wander around?" Pierre asked. "We won't be much help to anyone if we're caught." After the long climb he was exhausted and the beds offered a powerful temptation. "Let's eat and then wait until morning."

"And wake up with our throats slit?" Strong Bill said, his grin replaced with something close to anger. "My Emilia's here somewhere and maybe she's in trouble and needs help." He stared down wringing his hands. Then with a sigh he looked up. "Anyway, she won't be found by us here talking."

"We need a plan," the Scientist said, "and then be gone before sunrise."

"You think we're in danger?" Pierre asked. The men turned to him without speaking and he decided he had no more to add. To Strong Bill, the Scientist said, "Did your friend tell you how we might find her?"

"She said that if we got here we'd find her."

Startled, Pierre said, "You dragged us all the way up here on that?"

"Instead of us being angry," Strong Bill said, "why don't we just take a look around?"

The Scientist turned to Pierre. "There seems no alternative."

Strong Bill put his ear to the door and then from his pocket brought out a thin metal tool. He knelt down and inserted the tool into the lock. "You travel long enough," he said paying close attention to his work, "you find you've learned things you never expected to. But it's Heaven's own blessing if you have the knowledge when you need it." Suddenly they all heard a loud click. He stood grinning. With a glance at the Scientist and Pierre he turned the handle and the door opened.

It was the Scientist's turn to sigh. "Something is about to begin." They followed Strong Bill as he stepped out into the hall. Pierre wondered if after the previous night he had held back enough luck to see him through or whether his luck was gone leaving his pockets empty.

CHAPTER TWENTY-TWO

CANDLES MOUNTED TO the gray stone walls cast the narrow corridor in a ruddy twilight. Strong Bill led them down stairs, along a windowless corridor and then down more stairs. At the next turn a slit of pale light glowed from beneath a doorway ahead and they stopped. He leaned his ear to the door and waved Pierre and the Scientist passed. At the next intersection a door stood open and peering inside they found the room empty. Large and windowless, its only light came from a single candle mounted to the wall just inside; the room's ceiling disappeared into shadows and nothing suggested its purpose.

"So! You could not be trusted!" They turned to find three nuns blocked their exit. Though veiled, they appeared not to be those they had met.

"Madame," the Scientist said, "We meant no disrespect but we were in need of facilities and somehow we became lost..." The nun at the center of the trio cut him short.

"Lies!" she said. "This is how you repay our trust." Pierre wondered if hers was a voice he had heard before

"No!" Strong Bill said. "Beggin' your pardon but Nature is awful insistent, in a manner of speaking. We've done no wrong. Once we've answered Nature's call we'll gladly go back. Just don't be unfair to us strangers."

Pierre said, "Wait; she's right. We've broken our promise, even if only by accident." Turning to the nun who had spoken, he said, "Just lead us back to our room."

The other nuns seemed to hesitate as the one at the center reached a conclusion. "My sisters will bring what you require and return you to the infirmary where you must remain." Turning to Pierre she added, "But you will come with me."

He turned to the Scientist and Strong Bill. "I'd rather remain with my companions."

They looked back helpless as they followed the other nuns.

"Follow me." She led him out into the corridor and along another penumbral passage, but he nearly stumbled when she stopped suddenly. She opened the door to a room that was utterly dark. Once inside Pierre heard the door close behind them. A light flared from a lit candle and he saw that they stood in a small room filled with dusty, discarded furniture stacked to the ceiling. She lifted her veil and Pierre disbelieved his eyes; before him stood Abbess Maria and she was not pleased. A question occurred to him which he was about to ask but she stole his words. "What can you possibly be doing here?"

Pierre said, "A long story; and you?"

"There is no time to explain," she said. "You all must leave right now!"

"Tell me why."

"Do you always argue when someone attempts to save your life?"

"My life?"

"All of your lives!" Her expression was dark with anger. "I will lead you back to your friends but do not to tell them who I am. Convince them to follow me or there is only death." She paused as if waiting for him to agree. "Now, no more questions. What I have said must be sufficient."

Pierre remained startled by her presence. "I want to know what's going on."

Whispering angrily she asked, "And just who are you to make that demand?"

"Will you remain behind when we've gone?"

Her eyes flashed in a way that startled Pierre. "What goes on here is more ungodly than ever I imagined. Your danger is impossible to explain and I would not be believed if I tried. You must trust me."

She turned reaching for the door latch when Pierre asked, "And what's happened to Strong Bill's woman; Emilia? Will we save her, too?"

Hand still on the door latch, she did not turn. "If I can help her I will, but you must leave." She lifted the latch and opened the door.

Filling the opened doorway stood the Scientist and Strong Bill. Pierre was about to greet them when he saw that behind them stood three nuns, the one in the center without her veil. Addressing her, Abbess Maria said, "Mother Superior! Thankfully you are here." The Scientist lunged suddenly forward and grasped Pierre's hand in his.

"You are safe! We worried about what had happened to you." The woman the Abbess addressed as Mother Superior smiled slowly. Her heart-shaped face was broad and pale, and her luminous eyes nearly black with glints of silver and amber that thrilled and frightened Pierre reminding him of the embers of a smoldering fire.

In a wistful tone she said, "Reunions remind me that humans form relations they come to depend upon. I am nearly envious." Turning to the Scientist she asked, "Is this encompassed in your science?"

The others looked to him and he appeared annoyed. "Friendship is valued even above glory, and loyalty to a friend is most praise-worthy. Does that answer your question?"

"Oh, hardly," the Mother Superior said, "but I delight in the sound of your voice. Perhaps you will read aloud from the esoteric volumes in our library. I am certain my sisters will find that enchanting."

Strong Bill growled, "Talk and talk and talk. My Emilia is somewhere here and if nobody don't tell me where, I'll find her myself and won't be polite." As large as he was and as thick-shouldered and broad-backed, in the presence of the Mother Superior he seemed to cower.

"Brave words," the Mother Superior said. "I might almost believe they could be matched by deeds. But your plot is revealed. I knew you could not be innocent. Still, I promise you will see her soon." To her companions she said, "See that our guests do not become lost."

In sepia and blue twilight they followed silent hallways and climbed steep stairs until Pierre suspected he had followed these gray stone-walled corridors before. Turning another corner his suspicion was confirmed, except that torches now flamed red-orange at either side of the broad doorway casting the room with a weak orange light that left its corners and far edges in shadow. But Pierre was startled to see the many nuns gathered nearly filling the room. All turned to watch as they entered. Strong Bill said, "What in Hell's name is going on here?"

The Mother Superior laughed, a bright, sharp, oddly fractured sound that frightened Pierre. "Your words are almost clairvoyant. But all will become clear and you will see your sweetheart." Strong Bill clenched his fists but said nothing.

At one end of the hall and close to the wall a sort of rectangular altar of polished black stone stood on a raised platform. At its four corners stood thick, red candles, each taller than a man. The room was neither wide nor deep yet its corners appeared filled with shadows. With the arrival of the Mother Superior the nuns moved toward the altar. She turned to Abbess Maria. "We thank you for bringing these creatures into our care. Our community is richer by your help and your loyalty will be rewarded."

Abbess Maria lowered her eyes with a deference that surprised Pierre. "I await my next opportunity to serve you."

To the Mother Superior the Scientist said, "This is a remarkably isolated place to carry on your mission."

"You misunderstand our mission. But our invocation is about to begin and all will become clear."

"And Emilia?" Strong Bill asked.

"You will see her, well and content." Suddenly, the sound of an enormous bell tolling filled the space around them, its bleak tone thick with dread. Turning she stepped behind the altar, its surface level with her waist.

As the final tone of the bell faded, a low and rumbling drone began to fill the room. Pierre turned to the Scientist and Strong Bill but their eyes appeared glazed. That drone became louder and he realized it came from the gathered nuns. Growing still louder, he thought he recognized particular sounds chanted in a language he did not understand.

"Sisters!" the Mother Superior called out. The chanting stopped and all became silent. "Daughters of Beelzebub and Brides of Satan, we gather this night to praise and adore Him. For Nature, in Her glorious and mysterious splendor, is Satan's mistress. To Him does She offer Herself. Eagerly She parts each of her veils inviting Him to know Her. He savors that privilege of access to Her secrets and gifts and He cherishes every one. She offers Him that knowledge denied all others and opens those paths to Her deepest mysteries. Nature has provided Her reward for His ardent and vigorous love. Whether the sky and its stars or the sea and its creatures, She exposes all to Him, and He, in turn, rewards us, His devout acolytes. Eager and passionate in His ardor He shares with us that gift. Science contemplates His Secret Wisdom and that Wisdom of All Secrets. She opens each of Her jeweled and precious books to Him so that His desire will turn their pages. The knowledge She reveals becomes His power. Like that wind which fills the sails of ships, Her knowledge propels Him forward, relentless and irresistible. His Science overcomes all because it is the product of their intimate embrace. She desires nothing as much as His return. Whether His caress is as gentle as a breeze or as forceful as the storm-tossed waves upon the shore, She yearns for nothing as eagerly as His return."

"Satan shares Her wisdom with us becoming that Great Channel through which She nurtures our spirits. He fills us with that which She bequeaths to Him. We bend our knees and bow our heads so that through Him Her blessings will fall upon us. Our path is stony and hedged all around with thorns, yet He protects us and provides us His power. Our battle will be long and perilous, yet our time approaches. Our strength is His strength and as He grows stronger, we grow stronger." She paused, her eyes surveyed the room and a smile grew on her lips.

"But this night He has provided us special gifts. We had planned simply to offer Him thanks for the arrival of our new sister but His generosity exceeds our expectation for He has also sent us these." She paused again and her glance took in Pierre, Strong Bill and the Scientist.

"Our Master has seen our need and provided this sustenance. The old and grizzled one is rich in what he believes is science and will nourish our minds as well as our bodies. The young one is rich in that furious and urgent passion upon which our enterprise depends. The large and battered one is rich in strength and guile and also endurance and so provides that which will sustain our effort. So with all this He has particularly rewarded our love and for all this we offer thanks. Our Loving Guide could not have been more generous. Now, let us pray."

Hands held up and looking upward she said, "All praise and thanks to Him who has brought us together, who sustains and protects us, and who provides for us in our need. Let us raise our hands as we raise our hearts."

Hands open above their heads, in chorus the nuns intoned, "Our God, our King, our Lover, reign over all forever and ever. As Your wish is Your will, may Your will strengthen us for Your greater glory as only You can bring us to Her who most loves us above all."

Pierre leaned toward the Scientist. "What is all this?"

"Nothing good," the Scientist muttered.

The Mother Superior continued, "With our invocation complete we will now greet our newest acolyte. But first I must introduce our foremost guest, that man in search of his love."

Led forward by nuns holding each of his wrists, Strong Bill was brought to stand before the altar and the Mother Superior. Glancing about he growled, "I just come to see she done herself alright."

"And so you shall," the Mother Superior said brightly. "Our promises are not empty, for I ask that she now step forward." Dark shapes along the back of the room stirred and moved until a single shadow, her cowl still covering her face, separated from the rest and approached.

A step from Strong Bill the acolyte tipped the cowl back to reveal the face of a dark-haired woman.

"Emilia!" Strong Bill cried.

At the sound of his voice she smiled and tipped her head to one side in affectionate sympathy. "But of course, I should have known you would worry; my sweet man." She leaned forward. "I hoped to see you. Your generous heart has so cared for me." Her lips approached his and he seemed at first confused but then he smiled with relief. Suddenly she opened her mouth wide and put it to his neck. Strong Bill screamed with pain. Standing upright to his full height he turned his broad, thick body away from her but with both her arms she appeared to cling to him harder.

The gathered nuns leaned forward squealing and trembling mesmerized watching Bill turn his shoulders from side to side as if determined to cast Emilia off. Yet she seemed to wrap herself around him to cling even more fiercely. But then, with furious desperation he tossed his shoulders hard so that Emilia fell to the floor. But with that gesture, a glittering spray of red arterial blood misted instantly into the air over those nuns crowding close to the altar. A scream arose so sharp and ear-piercing Pierre wondered for a moment if he had gone deaf. The group of nuns surged suddenly forward. Those closest leapt onto Strong Bill's back or clung to his arms, with their mouths opened wide writhing and screeching. Strong Bill swayed as he tossed back and forth struggling beneath the black-clad nuns.

The Mother Superior at first stood to one side satisfied to observe but then as if overwhelmed by some temptation, abruptly she pushed several nuns aside to leap into the center of the melee. Bellowing with pain as more nuns climbed onto his massive shoulders and broad back, Strong Bill thrashed about until finally, covered by the roiling and shimmering black-clad nuns, he dropped to the floor.

"This is crazy," Pierre said in a tone of such astonishment the Scientist turned.

The hands of those nuns restraining Pierre dropped away and they rushed forward, but almost instantly that grip on Pierre was replaced. He turned to the Scientist. "We should do something!" He pulled at the hands restraining him until a voice from behind hissed, "This way! Now!" The restraining hands pulled hard and he turned to find Abbess Maria. He saw then that the Scientist had also stepped further back from the writhing pile.

The Abbess led their retreat with cautious steps until they reached the back of the room and a closed door. She said, "Through this door go left. At the end of the corridor go left again, then climb the stairs. This will lead you out."

"Will I see you again?" Pierre asked.

"Fool!" she said, fury contorting her face. "Why do you believe you are seeing me now?" She stepped past him and disappeared into the crowd.

He moved to follow but the Scientist held his arm. "Know when you are favored!" He turned then and passed through the doorway.

Frozen with confusion Pierre hesitated until a nun near him looked up, her eyes locked onto his and then he had no choice.

In the silent corridor beyond the doorway he spied the Scientist's retreating figure. Voices behind Pierre suddenly became loud and he ran; those voices and the patter of rapid footsteps prodded him to catch up. They followed the corridor, but nearing that door the Abbess had described leading outside, two nuns stepped into their path. Pierre ran toward them and at the last instant lowered his shoulder into the chest of the one closest pushing her into the other so that both fell to the floor. As they lay sprawled and screaming he grabbed Dr. de Montpellier's arm and then they were through the door.

Chill, damp air assured him they stood outside the building though still within the compound. Hidden within shadow the Scientist was breathless and struggling. Pierre asked, "Are you all right?"

Between wheezing breaths the Scientist said, "Not until we've returned to Port Royal."

"How do we get out of here?"

"We must try the front gate."

"And avoid more contact?"

"We will storm the gate and hope for a miracle."

"You mean, hope I knock down a few more nuns."

"If that achieves our end, so be it."

Leading their way along the compound wall Pierre could just make out the darkness of the sky against the pitch-black of the walls. He paused every few steps to listen until finally they approached the main gate. The gatehouse was lighted by a single candle within.

The Scientist whispered, "Follow my lead," and then stepped onto the path leading toward the gate. Steps from the gatehouse he staggered and called out, "Help me! Please help!" Two nuns suddenly filled the gatehouse door. One stepped forward, the other stood within the doorway.

In a wheezing and frightened voice he said, "I am being pursued; please help me." He collapsed then to his knees.

The approaching nun said, "You poor man, of course. Whatever has happened?"

Shifting about as he watched all of this, Pierre's foot struck something he found to be a stout tree branch. He picked it up certain it would be useful.

The Scientist said, "My companion has been captured by depraved creatures. We must save him."

"Certainly," the nun said and called out, "Sister, we must help this man."

The second nun stepped forward. "What has happened?"

"Just a moment to catch my breath. Please help me stand."

Taking the Scientist under each arm they began to lift him when Pierre charged from his hiding place with the tree branch held above his head. His first swing knocked down one of the nuns. He turned to strike the other but his blow glanced off the Scientist's back.

"What are you doing?" the Scientist cried. Pierre saw that he had already knocked down the second nun. Pierre turned to deliver a blow to her head.

The Scientist cried, "Behind you!" Pierre turned to see the first nun struggling to stand. Again he swung at her head but she rolled aside and then regained her feet. She charged at Pierre and in a reflex of self-defense he held out the end of the tree branch. It sank into her chest with a nauseating crunch. He tried to pull it from her body when arms from behind suddenly encircled his neck.

He swung around trying to escape but the arms clung to his neck with a desperate embrace pulling him backward. Seeing that the Scientist held onto her legs he shoved his elbow backward into her ribs and, gasping for air, she released him. When he turned she had recovered and moved to charge him again but this time he stepped aside. In one motion he freed the tree branch from one nun and swung it with all his might at the other. The sound of cracking bones startled him as she sank to her knees.

He turned to see the Scientist and the second nun, a gaping and bloodless hole in her back, wrestling on the ground, the nun's mouth open and long teeth reaching toward his neck. Pierre kicked her hard in the back. She released the Scientist and turned with a furious hiss to face him. He was about to kick her again when he saw the eyes of the Scientist focus behind him. He stepped to one side and turned. The nun he had struck with the tree branch stood behind him, the lower portion of her face twisted to one side and her cheek torn away exposing sharp and bloody teeth.

"This way!" Pierre looked up; the Scientist stood beside the open gate. The nun leaped toward the Scientist but Pierre kicked at her leg and she fell screaming. He and the Scientist then raced through the gate and charged into the forest's sheltering darkness.

They ran until Pierre discovered that the Scientist had fallen behind. When he caught up to Pierre he was wheezing and panting. "I must rest, even for a moment."

Pierre looked about; the compound gate was now out of sight. "Only a moment."

The Scientist gasped for air. "They cannot allow their secret to be revealed. Unless their grisly meal has left them sated and docile, they must pursue us."

"Which way?" Pierre asked.

"They will assume we are returning to Port Royal. So we will climb higher."

"But we need to get back to town."

"As our pursuers believe, but once we are safe from their pursuit we will rest until dawn. If I recognize these creatures correctly, daylight will render them passive."

"And if it doesn't?"

Grinning he clapped Pierre on the shoulder. "We will call upon your considerable fighting skills again."

Pushing through underbrush they climbed in utter darkness, stumbling and staggering until they reached a wide ledge. Through its break in the forest the stars glittered as shards of polished pewter. Below them they recognized shrouded by darkness the walls and buildings of the compound.

Pierre sat on the ground and shook his head. "But what was all that?"

"Rest and tomorrow we will return to Port Royal and find Brother Guarino. If he cannot help us he will know that person who will."

Seated on the ground the Scientist leaned his back against a tree and folded his arms across his chest. Staring into stifling darkness Pierre listened for those sounds that they were being followed. Horrors he had just witnessed crowded his mind until his thoughts turned to Abbess Maria, and with that another anguish overwhelmed him. He promised himself he would return to the convent at first light and find her since some luck might still remain with him. That was his last thought before all went black.

CHAPTER TWENTY-THREE

PIERRE AWOKE PANTING in a miasmal terror and opened his eyes to a sky that was a frightening blue. Sitting up, he looked over to where he remembered having seen the Scientist and found the base of the tree vacant. He stood as panic crawled toward his scalp.

"Fear not, we are safe." He turned to see the Scientist. "You earned a night's rest and I would not disturb you."

Suddenly ready to weep Pierre sat down again; sight of the Scientist confirmed all he remembered. The Scientist leaned down resting his hand on Pierre's shoulder. "We have much to do. When you are ready, we should depart." He studied Pierre's face. Before he could speak the Scientist said, "Yes, everything that you remember took place and we are fortunate to be alive. Now we must find Brother Guarino; he will know what must be done and who can help."

Pierre looked up to the Scientist with something large and painful in his chest and wished the man would disappear so he could be left alone. Instead he said, "I suppose there's no help for it." He stood and followed Dr. de Montpellier through an opening in the wall of forest. They found a pale ribbon of a path curtained on either side by forest. Dappled by sunlight, between the trees he could see the turquoise lagoon and then the cluster of buildings that was Port Royal, and then further out to sea a scatter of ships at anchor. The Scientists said, "Happily, our path is entirely downhill."

They reached a spot along the path suddenly familiar to Pierre. Through the trees he recognized the convent. As if anticipating his question, the Scientist said, "We do the only thing we can, and the more quickly we do it, the more help we will provide." No one moved about and he wondered if all had fled and somehow the convent had been abandoned.

"By the way, as I'm remembering it, what was all that the Mother Superior was going on about with the Devil and Satan and science? You think that's what they believe? That science is somehow the Devil's work"

Dr. de Montpellier shrugged and turned away. "Religion makes fools of us all; the question is, does it make us angry, belligerent, bloodthirsty fools, or simply contented, optimistic and passive fools. If science is the Devil's work, then our world and our life upon it is utterly doomed." Then he turned back to Pierre. "On the other hand, this may be something that Brother Guarino has heard about. It will be one more thing about this island we do not know about and he does."

Pierre said, "You have a lot of confidence in Brother Guarino."

"The ignorant must always depend on those who know more."

"What do you believe happened?"

"Belief is of no value here and is likely dangerous. But I suspect we just escaped with our lives and that Strong Bill and Emilia are dead, or perhaps worse."

"Is there something worse than death?"

"That is a topic we should discuss at length someday."

"And Abbess Maria? Is she in danger?"

"If she was able to sustain her disguise, all might remain well for her."

"And if not?"

The Scientists paused. "I find that talking as one walks is exhausting."

A single question beat upon Pierre's mind unresolved. "Did you know she traveled with us?"

"Since it had no bearing on my work, I never wondered."

"And those other conspirators? Did you know about them?"

He hesitated. "They were less discrete than they should have been."

"So I suppose I assumed too much and investigated too little."

The Scientist said, "As we are human we act without sufficient thought. How many of our ills are the result of the one over the other?"

Their path leveled until it reached another opening in the trees. Near its edge a fresh-water spring formed a pool. At the sight of it Pierre discovered he was thirsty. The Scientist said, "We seem safe enough to rest and a drink;

fresh water will revive us." But instead of moving toward the spring the Scientist sat down in a spot of shade leaning his back against a tree. With his eyes closed, in another moment he appeared to be asleep.

Pierre took his time drinking from the spring. Within this gap in the canopy, sunlight poured down to deny his anguish. He wondered if that Nature he had heard spoken of now wished to remind Pierre of its ineffable delight. A breeze played in the tops of the trees; its music assured him the world had regained its course. Yet no matter his thoughts, the face of Abbess Maria hovered above all.

From their very first meeting she had cast him into confusion, but the previous night left him baffled beyond hope. She had proved herself stronger and more resourceful than he and decisive in ways that eluded him. She had claimed to be a member of some group of agents and he wondered if the previous night had confirmed her account. Memories of their encounters aboard the Revenge triggered such a thrill he decided to tell Dr. de Montpellier to return to the port without him because he would go to the convent to find her, regardless of the risk.

Pierre stood from the spring intending to announce his decision and was surprised to see the Scientist standing beside a gap in the forest and staring out toward the sea. "Do you see that?" Pierre followed his gaze and saw nothing.

"Near the horizon," the Scientist said. Pierre noticed a gray-green smudge and after a moment he realized it approached the shore with exceptional speed.

Off-handedly the Scientist said, "I have watched it for some time."

Before he finished speaking, Pierre suspected he had seen something like it before. "I can't be certain but it seems as if..." Then he recognized what he was seeing. "My God!"

"Two independent observers," the Scientist said, "have reached the same conclusion."

The shape drew closer and then there was no doubt.

Pierre asked, "But how can this be?"

"That may be the wrong question," Dr. de Montpellier said.

"And why?" Pierre asked, fear fracturing his voice.

"Another bad question. Whatever its intention, it is on a direct path toward us."

"Shouldn't we sound an alarm?"

"At the speed it is moving it will reach Port Royal well before we would. Besides, what could we do?" Its head and throat became visible above that curl of its own white-foamed wave.

"There must be something we can do," Pierre said. The fear in his voice was tinged with despair.

"Can you rebuff the wind? Otherwise we are helpless." Broad, spiked fins that began at the crown of its skull became visible as the foamy sea-swell grew before it.

The beast approached Port Royal as if brute power had acquired intuitive awareness, glaring down as if it bore the town some sort of grudge. As it approached the first of those ships at anchor, some began to fire cannon at it. Among those, Pierre recognized the white-painted Revenge. He imagined Captain Stevenson barking orders and his crew of sailors running to their cannons. Pierre seemed to watch Captain time his fusillades to catch the creature when it lifted its head and exposed its throat; perhaps he had remembered something Pierre had told him. One shot reached its target and the next sent the creature backward two steps. But then it brought its head low and the next shots glanced off the crest of its skull. It ploughed forward and with a single stroke crushed the Revenge mid-ship; within seconds the ship disappeared beneath the waves.

The other ships also had begun to fire until so many cannons fired that their individual blasts merged into a continuous, jaw-rattling explosion. But the creature was indifferent; one after the next, it crushed each ship at anchor.

Moving closer to the shore, more of the beast became visible until it towered above the harbor, crushing each ship in its path with a casual fury. Its short-clawed forelimbs paddled the air as it rocked from side to side, its open jaws roared and bellowed as ships were shattered into tinder and men shrieking for their lives fell into the sea. Finally it came into range of the cannons in those forts defending Port Royal and they began to fire.

Indifferent to these cannon-shots the creature paused to survey the clutter of shattered ribs and broken hulls of the ships scattered around it before turning to face the town.

That curling wave of seawater the creature drove gained momentum so that even while the creature was still a distance away, that wave crashed into the seawall and spilled over to wash the streets of Port Royal reaching the farthest end of town. That wave then continued across the bay to crash into the foothills with a thump that shook the earth beneath Pierre's feet.

Emerged from the sea with its huge legs now exposed, it plodded forward and Pierre was stunned by its enormity. In some perverse way he found the beast thrilling and nearly beautiful to behold, as if he watched a great living and breathing mountain move. He was astonished by its outsized musculature, the rippling shapes under its gray-green pebbled skin, the way its flesh folded at its joints while its fore-limbs pawed at the air as if only just within its control. But it was the creature's bulk, its utter immensity, which left him unable to do more than stare open-mouthed.

Reaching the shallow bay of the harbor, the creature's tail swung back and forth to crush and shatter ships of every size as indifferently as a dog's tail knocks over a child's toy. Pierre turned to speak to the Scientist but no words would come.

Startled citizens of Port Royal had already stepped from their buildings to see what was going on. Their screams and cries of terror were so loud they traveled even to where he and the Scientist stood. The creature approached Fort Rupert first, indifferent to its sturdy walls and its cannon fire. As if merely curious it brought its head low roaring and snarling like an annoyed cat as if perhaps to intimidate the structure. The creature then straightened and reached one clawed foot forward; the fort's seawall collapsed as if made of sand. Emboldened, the creature trod over the fort until it was simply a pile of rubble. It paused then and roared long and loud before it turned. Following the shoreline it passed the prison and the graveyard and finally reached Fort Morgan.

Larger than Fort Rupert, its walls were higher and thicker and extended further along the shore. Its cannons began to fire, but the creature was no longer curious and approached these fortifications without hesitation. Despite cannon shots crashing into its body, the fort soon was reduced to broken stone.

Further along, the creature reached Fort Charles, the largest and most formidable of the forts. But even if the creature recognized this fort's greater strength, it moved directly against its fortifications. Driven back once by the fury of its cannon fire, the beast again tipped its chin down and strode forward to breach its seaward walls. Standing within the fort's complex of buildings, the cannons could no longer be turned and so only the small-arms from the walls could reach it. This battle too was over quickly; the creature decimated its buildings before pushing its walls out to crumble into the sea.

As if excited to even greater fury, the beast then destroyed Fort Walker almost as an afterthought, and did the same to that cluster of warehouses within its shadow. Then it entered Port Royal harbor proper.

Rocking and swaying the beast surveyed the wharves of the Turtle Crawles and ships tied up there. With the forts destroyed, only these ships continued to fire on the creature. Methodically it strode parallel to the wharf destroying with an indifferent ease each ship it encountered. But then, half-way along the wharf it turned and attacked the buildings of the town in earnest. Its great clawed feet struck land and buildings disappeared in explosions of brown-gray of dust. Moving further into the town, its swerving tail left more devastation, its path a swath of piled ruble. With an animal's attentiveness, it crushed the Merchant's Exchange, obsessing over the details of its destruction. And then with hardly a pause it turned to the meat market and then the Governor's Palace and that put the creature within range of the four huge cannons of Fort Carlisle on the lagoon at the north edge of town. When the palace was reduced to shattered timbers, instead of attacking the fort, the creature paused. Cannon shot from the fort continued to strike but the creature appeared somehow distracted. It lifted its head as if to put its nose to the wind. In the next moment it trod passed the fort and turned north. To Pierre's horror, when it crossed the lagoon it began to climb into the hills.

Without turning he asked, "Can all of this be possible?"

"Since we are its witness, it must be possible."

The creature crashed through the line of trees at the edge of the beach and its wide tail carved a brown-red path toward the hills.

Pierre asked, "How are you at running?"

"Not as good as I wish I was," the Scientist said. "But I have never had such urgent motivation. Which way should we go?"

"Up into the hills," Pierre said, "and hope the climb discourages the creature."

"Nothing seems to discourage that beast but perhaps there is some logic there." Pierre began the climb back along their path.

The Scientist had not exaggerated his weakness; Pierre was forced to stop frequently to allow him to catch up. Breathing the hot, thick air also slowed Pierre until he found the climb exhausting. Still, there could be no question the creature was closing the distance. The earth shook with each of its steps, the sound of crashing trees an odd accompaniment to the shrieking cries that followed.

They reached the spot on their path from which they had seen the convent's compound. This time, black-clad nuns scurried about like ants and the bell in the tower tolled a rapid alarm. Pierre paused hoping to see the Abbess but the creature's approach gave him no chance. With the Scientist wheezing and gasping behind him, he continued to climb. They reached the clearing where they had awakened earlier but the creature was now even closer.

Pierre asked, "Which way from here?"

The Scientist leaned forward gasping for air. "Tell me we are beyond danger."

Pierre peered from the edge of the ridge. The creature's path left a red-brown scar of exposed soil as a nearly straight line through the dark green of the forest pointing in their direction as if it knew where it was going and its progress as inevitable as the movement of the sun. He turned to see the Scientist sitting under a tree mopping his brow.

"We can't stay here,"

"And I promise that I can go no further."

"I'll leave you here if I have to but I won't face that creature twice."

Panting the Scientist smiled. "Do you honestly believe it is pursuing you?" His grin made Pierre even more angry.

"If it isn't, it won't matter, but I won't wait to find out. Now; are you coming or not?"

The creature's roar pierced the air and suddenly it seemed even closer.

"Go that way," the Scientist said pointing toward a peak at the top of the ridge. "From there you will see it coming from any direction."

"Suit yourself!" Pierre turned and resumed his climb. He pushed through the undergrowth, the sound of breaking tree limbs behind him assuring him of the creature's approach. Disguised by the forest canopy his only choice was to continue moving up.

The forest parted abruptly, the sky and sun appeared, and he recognized that he had nearly reached that peak the Scientist had pointed to. He turned to watch the creature's advance but now it no longer seemed to be moving toward him. Then he realized he was looking down on the convent compound and the creature's path led directly toward it. Instantly, Abbess Maria came to his mind. Was the creature in fact pursuing her? Or instead had he led the creature to her? But worse, was she now in danger from this creature because of him? He resisted the impulse to rush back down the path and attempt to rescue her. He reminded himself that, as the Scientist had said, she was smarter than he was, so if there was a way for her to rescue herself she would find it and without his help.

He crouched behind a boulder as if the beast might otherwise see him and from there watched with rising amazement as it reached the convent and then stopped.

Lifting its chin high, its cavernous nostrils flared to sniff the air as if uncertain which direction to follow. Its forearms raked the air slowly and it lowered its snout close to the ground. But then suddenly as if startled the creature lifted its head again and unleashed a furious roar, as if it had discovered something it despised. Huge feet plodding, it strode directly toward the compound and, lifting a clawed foot high, crushed the main building as a child would a paper box. Roaring again and again it reduced each of the other buildings until hardly one stone stood upon another. Then, as if still unsatisfied, it stomped that rubble into powder as if it could not crush these remains enough.

Moving beyond the devastated buildings, the creature then brought its huge tail down on all of it, swiping back and forth as if to disperse even its smallest fragments. For a moment Pierre wonder what could drive a dumb animal to such determined fury. With the compound reduced to powder and splinters, the creature stood motionless and surveyed its work. Astride that devastation it lifted its head and released such a roar, the broad, spiked fins running from its tail to the crown of its skull trembled, as it appeared to address heaven. It turned then and followed its path back toward the sea.

Pierre watched with astonished awe as the beast made its way, its huge tail thumping the ground with each alternate step. Passing the devastated Port Royal it entered the sea and Pierre turned his attention back to the convent. Nothing moved and even the birds were silent. He returned to the clearing where he had left the Scientist.

Except that the Scientist was not there. Pierre searched the edge of the clearing wondering if he had taken another path. He called out and, receiving no answer he assumed Dr. de Montpellier had taken the path down to the port. He stepped to the edge of the clearing when a voice behind him asked, "Has our guest departed?" He turned to see the Scientist emerge from behind a tree, his face as gray as dust.

"Gone back to the sea, or so I hope."

Relief came over the Scientist's face. With an embarrassed smile he said, "I was busy hiding and missed the fun." Pierre described what he had seen and the Scientist nodded as if something was now clear. Pierre then asked, "Why would it crush a convent to dust?"

The Scientist squinted into the bright sky. "Simply speaking, I cannot think what would drive a dumb creature to do what it did."

"Is it following us? Is that even possible?"

"Many explanations may apply to its behavior but only one can be true."

Overwhelmed by confusion and the shock of what he had seen, Pierre moved to the shade of a tree and sat down. The Scientist sat down beside him. Shaking his head Pierre said, "The Captain had called it a spawn of Satan, so is that why it attacked a convent?"

The Scientist hesitated. "Suggesting that either we misjudge the convent or misjudge the creature."

"And neither of those seems possible." Pierre pounded his fist into the hard, dry ground, as if something would not settle in its mind.

After a moment the Scientist said, "Your thoughts have returned to the young nun."

Pierre looked up feeling suddenly caught. "I can't imagine how she might have survived." His despair grew like a wave feeding upon its own motion.

"If it is easy to imagine her dead it should also be easy to imagine she discovered a way to save herself. After all, she succeeded in rescuing us. Had we been sufficient to help, she might have saved Strong Bill and Emilia. We speak of a woman able to enter a hostile organization and remain undiscovered. Is it so hard to imagine she discovered a passage that took her beyond the creature?"

Pierre assumed the Scientist wanted to reassure him, to assuage his conscience and relieve his guilt. What surprised him was that it seemed to work.

But then he recalled the Revenge, the Count and the Captain and the musicians and the rest of the crew; men whose names he knew and those he would never know. They had saved him, plucked at the last moment from the pitiless sea. They had nursed him back to health and sustained him, men who neither knew who Pierre was nor cared. And now he was the observer of their destruction unable to return their favor. He stared at the ground with sightless eyes, his vision filled with faces and scenes as vivid as they were piercing, as sharp and cutting as the creature's cry.

Pierre was startled as the Scientist suddenly began to laugh.

"What are you laughing about?" Pierre's depression turned into anger that edged into fury. He turned to the Scientist. "Stop it! Stop!" But Dr. de Montpellier continued to laugh, and seeing Pierre's anger he laughed even more loudly.

Catching his breath he said, "My boy, just look at us!" His laughter became a breathless wheezing. "No ship, no town, no friends, nowhere to hide, nowhere to run. And you fail to see the humor? I have lost years of hard work along with every possession I called my own. Gone, all of it gone as if it had never been. It is even possible we are the only people alive who witnessed the destruction of the largest English-speaking city outside of London. Laugh, boy, laugh. Laugh yourself hoarse, laugh until your throat aches and your chest hurts. Laugh because you have survived. If you cannot laugh at this you will never find anything worth laughing at."

Pierre's fists clenched and his body tensed about to lunge toward the old man. But staring at that grey and wrinkled face split with mirth, eyes squinting, large, thick body shivering with laughter, his own anger began to drain away. And then it began.

In Pierre's chest and then in his throat slowly moving into his face he began to laugh. And the louder he laughed, the louder the Scientist laughed, and the louder the Scientist laughed, the louder Pierre laughed, so that finally his throat was sore and his chest ached and the muscles of his face hurt and tears came to his eyes. They faced each other mouths wide braying laughter into each other's face until that anguish and despair had drained away leaving a sense of calm while his tears began to dry. He leaned down hands on his knees panting as if he had run a great distance. When he looked again he realized the Scientist was wiping tears from his own eyes as well.

After a moment Pierre asked, "So, what do we do now?"

Dr. de Montpellier shook his head. "What else is there? No port to return to and no ships to take us away, we must walk until we reach Costa d'Oro on the north end of the island and there hope to get another ship. That is, unless you have given up searching for your father and prefer instead to spend the rest of your days here."

"But when we reach this port, where will we go?"

The Scientist paused and then shrugged. "Havana. We can search out that former student I mentioned to Brother Guarino." At the man's name he paused and they both shared the same thought.

"And after Havana?"

The Scientist shook his head. "Europe? Perhaps Amsterdam? Perhaps even London? We will pursue the opportunities that appear and hope we discover your father's trail."

"And this ship; how will we pay for passage?"

"Do not concern yourself. The problem will give us something to think about as we walk. And the walk before us will be long and difficult." The Scientist looked about. "We should start now; making our way through the forest after dark will not be easy."

Pierre looked back and sighed. "At least we should go back and help any survivors."

The Scientist looked down and shook his head. "We are the survivors, boy; we should keep it that way." He turned then and began the slow climb higher into the hills.

"Wouldn't it be easier to go down and follow the beach?"

The Scientist stopped. Without turning he said, "There is an old saying: lead, follow, or get out of the way. The choice is yours." When he hesitated the Scientist said, "Come along, boy. What do you say we go and look for your father?" Then he resumed the climb.

Pierre watched his back as the faces of Augustus and then of Gabriella appeared before his eyes. He followed the Scientist into the forest and did not look back because he knew finally that whatever luck remained with him would need to be enough to sustain him, and he had to hope he possessed just enough luck to find his father.

PART TWO

CUBA

CHAPTER ONE

"BUT YOU'VE NEVER seen the creature?" Pierre tried to keep disbelief from his voice. Captain Diego dela Vega, master of the Esperanza, smiled and shrugged and folded his narrow, nervous hands across his thin stomach. Pierre sat at dela Vega's table with Dr. de Montpellier and the first-mate named Rodrigo. A single, gloomy candle-lantern swayed overhead to cast shifting bronze shadows against the cabin's dark walls. Fierce rain and furious sea beat upon the Esperanza, and the thick timbers surrounding them groaned. The remains of their evening meal including a nearly-empty flagon of wine lay about the table. Despite his annoyance with the Captain, Pierre enjoyed the pleasant glow of a full meal, the first he and the Scientist had enjoyed since they reached Costa d'Oro on the Jamaican coast.

A slim man with a long, narrow face, large, dark eyes and an oddly wide, protruding jaw, Captain dela Vega's heavy uniform edged with thick gold braiding seemed to weigh upon him like a suit of armor on a child. A thick and menacing black whip coiled at his belt. The looming bulk of his dark chair made him appear even smaller. His smirking grin seemed calculated to convey a barely-endurable indifference, as if he knew everything and understood everything, including that which was not yet known to him. His rolling speech and slight lisp seemed to Pierre an arrogant affectation more irritating than an outright insult.

With a patient smile, the Captain said, "I have heard tales but always from drunkards or low and untrustworthy seaman, which I have regarded as worthless. You Señors are the first witnesses I have encountered worthy of belief. So tell me bluntly, is this creature as awful as has been claimed?"

Pierre was certain this man was a fool but he and the Scientist depended on him for their accommodations as well as security. To Pierre's relief, Dr. de Montpellier spoke up.

"Believe us, Captain; we have seen that creature in all its fury. We watched it attack Port Royal leaving not a single brick upon a stone; we watched it destroy ships at harbor, some even larger than this. And more, we watched it climb into the hills to destroy stone buildings as sturdy as any made. We report only what we have seen. I assure you that when you see that creature you will wish you had not. And if it chooses to pursue you, you will pray to the Lord as you have not since you were a child."

Despite Dr. de Montpellier's urgency, the Captain smiled politely, his gold eye-teeth sparkling in the candle-lit twilight. "You are honorable men with no cause to exaggerate, so I can only agree that surely this is an age of miracles. You philosophers conjure remarkable discoveries, and who am I but a humble sea captain laboring in the service of his Glorious Majesty Carlos Segundo, King of Naples and Sicily, Sovereign of the Netherlands, Duke of Milan, Duke of Burgundy and King of Spain. We float upon a vast and mysterious sea. I am regularly challenged by pirates and heathens and heretics and otherwise struggle with mysteries barely within my capacity, but now you bring me one beyond all hope of my understanding. I must confess astonishment at this report."

"Believe us," Pierre insisted. "Once you've seen the creature, you'll regret it."

Though he had remained silent throughout the meal, Rodrigo turned an alarmed glance to the Captain. "Perhaps we should mount a second watch." A broad-shouldered and powerful-looking man, he spoke with a diffidence that startled Pierre.

Suddenly impatient, the Captain responded, "And perhaps we should sound an alarm for every fish that makes a rude noise." His contempt startled Pierre, yet when the Captain turned to face him and the Scientist, that contempt evaporated. "For this earnest warning I offer thanks. While your creature is powerful and diabolical, I believe I am in greater danger of encountering a mermaid." His expression set Pierre's skin crawling. "Be assured that, should your beast raise its ugly head, we will do what we must. So let no dreams of sea monsters disturb your slumber."

"Your assurance is all we can ask," the Scientist said. "Under your protection we will sleep very well."

The Captain nodded as if relieved this subject was settled. "Now, please tell me of your friendship with Don Benito. I have heard his name and been told he lives on the island of Cuba."

The Scientist leaned back like a man intimate with those who are famous and accomplished. "More than a decade has passed since he attended my lecturers at the University of Valladolid, but I recall him as admired for his pride and courage and honest intelligence. Conversant with certain esoteric studies, he wrote letters some years ago to natural philosophers conducting research in the New World inviting them to visit his hacienda. Unhappily, I could not accept his offer then but following the events we have described we now eager to join him."

Though appearing unimpressed the Captain nodded. "Your determination does you credit. Rodrigo tells me you walked across the island of Jamaica, a three-day march."

"That determination," the Scientist said, "was the result of our terror of the creature."

The Captain said, "Let us pretend for a moment that I am an entirely ignorant man. Explain to me how Don Benito's studies coincide with your research."

The Scientist leaned back, this time an expert about to discuss his area of expertise. "While we are uncertain of his particular studies, our experiments have involved the aether. We know that the aether must exist, first because we are assured by Aristotle himself along with Plato and Thales and then repeated by Descartes. But as well, because our experiments demonstrate it must exist. So, we plan to visit him in the hope that others there have resolved particular questions concerning the harmony of the aetherial spheres along with those aetherial winds Ptolemy said did not exist but which Pythagoras insisted had shaped the universe."

"That is all so marvelous," the Captain said. "Yet I must confess I am unable to understand any of it. You say all of this has something to do with a thing called the aether. But how is it I have never heard of such a thing?"

"Indeed, Excellency," Rodrigo spoke up, "it's referred to as the quintessence, that fifth element which fills the space beyond the moon, and it is believed the substance from which the planets are made. Plato writes of all this in the Timaeus. And as our guests point out, Aristotle wrote at length about it. Even Lucretius writes of it in his De Rerum Natura."

The Captain turned to stare at Rodrigo astonished. To Dr. de Montpellier he asked, "Is he correct in what he says?"

The grinning Scientist nodded. "I confess myself impressed; your first-mate reveals a remarkable knowledge of a subtle science."

Turning back to Rodrigo, the Captain asked, "And just where might one such as yourself have acquired such esoterica?"

Rodrigo looked down at his fingers spread on the table and his deference again made Pierre uncomfortable. "It's really of no significance, Excellency. A bit of reading here and there and with little method to the study."

The Scientist added, "But also a man of considerable modesty. Rodrigo appears to have his secrets, but then again which of us is without them?"

With an embarrassed smile Rodrigo responded, "Hardly that, Excellency."

The Captain spoke to Rodrigo with incredulous annoyance. "You told me your father cured hides and never owned his land and your mother was a common woman. In all of that, where could you have acquired such knowledge?"

Rodrigo again studied the top of the table and Pierre watched his jaw tighten. But then a small smile came to his lips. "As one travels one learns. It's simply been my good fortune to meet men such as our guests who've read deeply and yet share even with one such as myself."

"And in these intellectual adventures," the Captain asked Rodrigo, "have you acquired any knowledge useful to the safe conduct of my ship?" Despite sarcastic disbelief the Captain's curiosity had been aroused and he suspected his first-mate hid something more significant.

Rodrigo said. "Please do not exaggerate, Excellency. Those morsels of knowledge hardly amount to a meal and have little value except as amusement."

The Captain said, "Given the circumstances of your birth, the pursuit of such knowledge is the height of self-indulgence. Dare I suggest a man in your station should pursue that which makes him most useful to his betters."

In a conciliating tone, the Scientist added, "The acquisition of knowledge simply for the pleasure of its possession regrettably is a fading inclination in our modern world."

The Captain responded, "So it is best we not exaggerate the achievement that acquisition represents."

"Most humbly," Rodrigo said, "I recognize myself as little more than a parrot with just as little comprehension of the words spoken."

Finally, the Captain appeared mollified; his first-mate had agreed that possession of certain types of knowledge did not justify his holding himself equal to captains of Crown ships.

The cabin door opened suddenly to reveal Pablo, the ship's second-mate, standing in the passageway dripping with rain. "A thousand regrets, Excellency, but the storm has grown violent and Señor Rodrigo's presence is needed on deck."

With sudden exasperation the Captain asked, "Is it the case that my crew is so inept, or so lazy, that a little rain overwhelms their trivial skills?" Straightening in his chair he turned to Rodrigo. "Be so kind as to bring order to their efforts and spare my ship."

Rodrigo stood, bowed to the Captain and then to Pierre and the Scientist, and left.

When the cabin door closed, Captain dela Vega turned to the Scientist. "Imagine the likes of him adopting the airs of an educated hidalgo. As if station of birth was of no importance. He pretends that mouthing a few phrases should convince others to regard him as an educated man. One wonders what this world has come to."

"Perhaps he believes," the Scientist responded, "that knowledge knows no station, but like a seed from a tree, it is merely a matter of falling upon fertile soil."

The Captain responded with mild irritation, "Precisely my point. Such fertility is a matter of blood. Considering his origins, from whence could that facility of thought arise? Were that ability part of his heritage, surely it would have manifest in the person of a glorious ancestor."

"Perhaps," Pierre said, "he's the glorious ancestor."

Captain dela Vega turned a sudden glare at Pierre, but instantly it softened to a condescending smile. "But of course, I must recall that you colonists entertain delusions concerning merit and achievement. Ignore the wisdom of your elders if you wish but prepare for disappointment."

Dr. de Montpellier said, "Interest in questions involving invisible but powerful forces is common. Individuals from many walks of life have discovered a thirst for certain knowledge of the material world. My education began in medicine yet I was enticed to pursue certain questions which that study does not answer. Though most have acquired their knowledge through university education, there are others who, though mere mechanics, have been inspired to create devices that have advanced the study. And I hope it is no disappointment that my own ancestry is no more remarkable than Rodrigo's."

Attempting to appear impressed, the Captain said, "I surmise that great sacrifice has been the price of your hard-gotten knowledge and I congratulate you for its achievement. Low-born as you are, yet you conduct yourself in a way worthy of any hidalgo. But tell me this; though undoubtedly momentous, how will the life of one such as I be improved by these discoveries?"

Pierre asked, "You mean, what's their monetary value?" He had not recognized how the Captain challenged his patience. But before the Captain could answer, the Scientist spoke up.

"Surely that valuation is premature. After all, how might one recognize such value until someone discovers a clever use for that which was pursued merely out of passionate curiosity?"

"I grant," the Captain said smirking, "that you possess many skills, but that of foretelling the future is not among them. Still, you must speculate as to the practical value of your pursuit."

"Instead of speculation," the Scientist answered, "we consider the method itself. Our studies demand the construction of devices of subtle sensitivity. Though products of our own creation and therefore unprecedented, their utility may perhaps be recognized by others who work in other fields."

Pierre watched the lids of the Captain's eyes descend just slightly. Whether the result of disbelief or distrust or simple boredom, he decided not to guess.

The Scientist continued, "As Rodrigo points out, however diverse they are in detail, all speculations agree the aether permeates everything. But particular questions remain; does it blow like the wind, or flow like water? Is it static and motionless like the earth, or does it come into and go out of existence like fog?" Yet finally even Pierre recognized that although the Captain remained in his chair, he had fled. "No one can foretell its use to others who are more clever than ourselves."

Perhaps it was the sharpness of the Scientist's tone more than his assertion but the Captain's eyes fluttered open and he attempted to appear impressed though he succeeded only in exposing his indifference. "I now understand what motivates your journey."

"Our hope is," the Scientist said, "someone there has discovered under what conditions motion among the stars may be the result of their being composed of condensed aether. For this reason we are eager to reach the hacienda and compare our results with theirs."

Shaking his head in disbelief the Captain smiled. "Should you discover a new way to propel a vessel or to communicate between ships, you will earn the gratitude of every captain on the face of the earth."

Pierre was certain the Captain mocked them though the Scientist appeared to believe he was being taken seriously. He said, "But undoubtedly you have yourself encountered many extraordinary men and survived many exceptional adventures."

The Captain appeared relieved finally to discuss his successes, and suddenly he revived. "Commanding this vessel for nearly ten years I have met many outstanding men, but just as many of the lowest and most villainous." Over an interminable hour, the Captain described alternately ludicrous and terrifying encounters. Whether a result of the wine, or the stifling, humid atmosphere, or the tedium of his tales, Pierre struggled to remain alert. So he was grateful this recitation appealed to the Scientist's curiosity.

Sheltered within the drone of the Captain's voice, Pierre's mind drifted back to their dismal trek through dense forests and over jagged hills, peculiar encounters with natives interrupting the continuous assault of biting and stinging insects. As the Captain prattled on, Pierre recognized that, by comparison, the assault of these words was almost enjoyable. But then, in response to a question from Dr. de Montpellier, the Captain spoke about discipline aboard his ship.

"I sail with men who, in other circumstances, I would not trust even to turn my back upon; men so lacking in honor they are no better than dogs of the street. For these I keep Consuelo near to hand." He patted the gleaming black whip coiled at his belt with disturbing affection.

Laughing uncomfortably the Scientist said, "Surely you exaggerate for effect."

The Captain's expression hardened. "The value of demonstration is certainly great but often not sufficient. At that moment mercy is dangerous. Even a small infraction must provoke a vigorous response because, unfortunately, the power of example runs in both directions. Ignore the trivial and substantial infractions will follow. It is in the nature of those low-born that tolerance is misunderstood as license. And among the black ones it is much worse, for their proclivity to violence and betrayal runs deep in their corrupt blood. Nor must I distinguish among sailors; even Pablo has endured Consuelo's kiss, and Rodrigo himself has been compelled to submit. I assure you, gentlemen, I take no pleasure in any of this, but as father to my crew I derive considerable satisfaction. I am severe because our conditions demand it. But I am also just, for in the service of His Majesty nothing less will be accepted."

Pierre listened to the Captain horrified. He had heard tales at the tavern of brutal tortures inflicted for trivial infractions by Spanish commanders on ordinary sailors. But he had assumed they were the wild tales of sailors inclined to exaggerate. Recalling those stories now, Pierre was stunned at the possibility that any had been true.

"You know," Pierre said, "that Spanish captains are notorious for their brutality. Have you ever gone so far as to beat a sailor to death?" The Captain looked darkly at him and Pierre was glad he was not a member of his crew.

"Brutality is relative; compared to what? In the conduct of a ship, what appears trivial may result in the loss of that ship with all hands. Compared to that, injury to a single sailor, no matter how serious, is a small thing. To answer your question, I have indeed ordered punishments and assisted other captains in their duties on-board their own vessels."

"And if the sailor," Pierre continued, "becomes gravely injured, what do you do?"

"The infraction is the responsibility of the sailor, the act of discipline that of the captain. Of course, any sailor's injuries are treated with care, yet it remains in the hands of the Lord as to whether he survives. In the end, we all reside in the hands of God."

"From your description," the Scientist added, "the burden of command is indeed heavy."

The Captain shrugged as if dismissing a compliment. "For generations my people have accepted their responsibility as the sign of that honor with which we have conducted ourselves. The failure of any of us brings dishonor to all, something your friend Don Benito undoubtedly understands. Though I have never met him, I am certain his hacienda is led with complete discipline. No doubt, he surrounds himself with honorable men, and obedience to his instruction is immediate. So I compliment you on the possession of such a friend."

Later, when they had returned to their cabin, the Scientists was exuberant. "Did you hear? Don Benito is known and his work, though misunderstood, is acknowledged even by one such as our captain. As ignorant as he is, he speaks of Don Benito with admiration. Undoubtedly we will be greeted with great warmth."

Though Pierre doubted all this he nodded. "Don Benito invited you to join him, didn't he?" He remained furiously annoyed by the Captain and inclined to distrust anyone that man held in high regard. "I just don't understand these people."

"What is there to understand?" He asked this question as if Pierre was his student and he had confessed an ignorance of arithmetic.

Pierre said, "I met men like him at the tavern. The more they drink the more interesting they become. And being interesting to themselves, they become even more interesting to others. Each person they've met becomes interesting, every event they've witnessed and each thought they've had. But in the end they only prove how unexceptional they are."

The Scientist laughed suddenly. "And perhaps experience has clouded your judgment instead of shaping it. Perhaps, in my desire to ingratiate, I showed an unjustified respect for our Captain. But make no mistake; those with power can use that power on your behalf or against it. We are too close to our goal to risk distraction. If praise of the unworthy is reprehensible, remember that we are his guests and therefore also his victims."

Exasperation cloaked Pierre's thoughts. "I respect you as a man pursuing goals shared by my father, so the arrogance of ignorant men like our Captain infuriates me."

"We must not confuse means with ends. Besides, in a few days we will be free to be as contemptuous of him as we wish."

"In any case, I'll be heartily glad to set foot on dry land again."

The Scientist smiled. "Because of our Captain or because of the creature?"

"The answer to that excellent question I'll leave to your surmise."

Lying back in his bunk and staring up at the timbers overhead, Pierre wanted his annoyance to subside and it would not. But he understood that locating Dr. de Montpellier's friend might demand all of the luck either of them possessed.

CHAPTER TWO

THE MORNING SUN low in the sky beat hot against Pierre's back and a musty, fecund breeze swirled around him as he leaned against the gunwale staring out to sea. The island of Cuba had appeared near daybreak as a green ridge below powder-gray mountains that disappeared into slate clouds and a brightening sky. Since then, their ship had sailed west and just within sight.

From time to time he spied roughly-shaped dugout canoes and, although never close enough to see clearly, he wondered at those dark men who stood solitary holding long poles to propel them. They appeared indifferent to the Esperanza as if it were a piece of large but uninteresting debris. Would any of them respond if Pierre waved, or was he, in their eyes, simply another white-skin; someone to ignore if he could not be avoided and who could only make trouble? The Scientist stepped up beside Pierre and he was surprised by his sense of relief. Nodding toward the canoes he asked, "Know anything about them?"

The Scientist glanced in their direction and then turned away. "Heathens," he said flatly. "Blessed and happy, insensitive to fear or ambition and content to eat each other and fornicate with each other's women. Fortunate if they have never heard of the Pope in Rome, and doubly fortunate if he has never heard of them. What more is there to know?"

"Slept well, I see," Pierre said.

"There are places in this world where sarcasm is punishable by death."

"Be sure to tell me when we get there."

"Better yet, I will not."

Looking past the Scientist's shoulder Pierre watched a sailor approach. Middle-aged, grizzled, muscle-knotted body, face nut-brown and bald but for a fringe of gray-white hair, tattered blue trousers held up with a piece of worn rope black with tar and age. He did not look toward them but moved in their direction. Pierre resumed watching the shore, his expression as blank as he could manage. The Scientist looked down to watch the undulant waves.

Pierre quietly asked, "Friend of yours?"

"We will find out soon enough."

The sailor stopped two steps away and leaned out to adjust a line. To their backs he muttered, "Come forward and stop where I do if you value your lives." Satisfied with the adjustment he stepped away. Pierre and the Scientist watched the sea as if mesmerized by the view.

Without turning the Scientist said, "We should do as he asked."

"Why?" Pierre asked.

"Because the message ran some risk in its delivery."

They watched the sailor walk to the bow, lean forward to tighten a hawser and then begin to coil a length of rope. The Scientist turned to Pierre. "Shall we take a stroll?" They ambled along the gunwale until near the sailor they stopped.

In a few moments, Captain dela Vega emerged from below deck. He climbed to the quarterdeck, stepped to Pablo beside the tiller and peered at the binnacle compass. They spoke, the Captain gestured and Pablo gestured in response, their voices grew louder until Pierre heard the Captain say, "You will return to our course or be flogged!"

Pablo stepped from the tiller and folded his arms across his chest. A big man with a farmer's arms thick as small trees, he seemed to tower over the Captain. The Captain glared up at him as if he was a dog to be brought to heel. Then the Captain called for Rodrigo. Appearing to anticipate the call, Rodrigo emerged from the hold with a weary expression and approached the Captain. Loudly the Captain said, "Put this man in chains."

Rodrigo climbed to the quarterdeck to join him. "I won't do that, Excellency; he's under my orders."

Even from the distance Pierre recognized dela Vega's startled hatred. He turned from one man to the other. "Madness! There is only death in this. Do not forget all what you owe to me."

Rodrigo's laughter chilled Pierre. "But at what cost?"

The Captain turned to Pablo. "Is this about loyalty to Rodrigo or hatred of me?"

Pablo spoke up. "It is neither. As your Excellency provides for himself and Rodrigo for himself, so I must do the same. This is the law, Excellency, older than time."

The Captain looked from one to the other with a furious astonishment, then began to call out names Pierre assumed were those of other sailors, but under the flat, bright sunlight, all stood motionless to watch. Seeing that none would come to his aid the Captain approached Rodrigo detaching his whip from his belt. After two steps a shot rang out. The Captain turned at the sound and his expression of incredulous surprise was almost comical. The whip dropped from his hand to the deck with a thud. Then, slowly he dropped to his knees, fell to one side and did not move again. Under the hot blue sky, a pool of bright red blood spread slowly beneath him.

Around the tops of the masts gulls swooped crying out, but the silence was otherwise complete. Rodrigo then stepped to the fallen man and his movement seemed to release the crew. To Pierre's astonishment, sailors scrambled down from the rigging and ran across the deck toward Rodrigo and Pablo erupting in cheers. Pierre and the Scientist stood to one side as more sailors emerged from below to join the celebration. With the attack by the beast, Pierre had seen blood and death, but he had never seen a man shot and its casual simplicity startled him. When the excitement subsided, Rodrigo stepped through the crowd and approached them.

In a voice loud enough to be heard across the deck he said, "It is not our intention to involve you good men in this. Our dinghy will be given to you to reach the shore close by. In exchange, we ask only that you say nothing of what you've seen."

The Scientist asked, "And what of you and this ship and its crew?"

"Don't concern yourself, Señor. There is an island off Hispaniola where a compatriot will exchange our goods for gold. Then, it will be up to the crew to decide our fate."

Pierre asked, "So you have become pirates?"

"Certainly in the eyes of the monarchs of Europe; we still must decide whether to continue."

The Scientist asked, "And how will that be done?"

"Just as we chose this course, by a show of hands." Looking closely at the Scientist, he said, "This confuses you."

The Scientist shrugged. "Democracy begins in optimism and ends in tyranny. What remains in question is whether that path is long or short."

Rodrigo offered a curious smile. "That outlook is common among men of your class. But as God has given us the strength to achieve this, He will protect our path and preserve our honor." He held out his hand and shook that of the Scientist and then Pierre.

The Scientist said, "We depart as friends and leave you to your fate. We wish you luck."

Rodrigo nodded. "Most times, all one needs is luck." Turning to Pierre he added, "Your father is already fortunate for having such a brave and determined son."

More sailors gathered around the body of the Captain. Pierre had a dozen questions, but finally he resigned himself that nothing would become clear. He and the Scientist had stepped into the middle of a drama whose beginning and end they could never know.

The dinghy was lowered and they climbed down and boarded. With Pierre at the oars they traveled some distance before the Esperanza turned to sail toward the open ocean.

From his seat at the stern the Scientist said, "I would prefer to be gone when the king of Spain's ships take up the chase, so put your back into it before I suffer sun-stroke."

"We'll make faster progress if you take an oar."

"Physical exertion debilitates the mind. Thus, we will more likely survive if you handle the oars while I consider what we should do next. This is referred to as the division of labor."

"Surely, we'll continue on to Havana."

"And just as surely, we cannot reach Havana unless God gives you greater strength."

"How do you propose we locate your friend and his hacienda?"

"This is what I must ponder. Simply keep rowing toward that line of palm trees."

Pierre's thoughts returned to the deck of the Esperanza. "Do you think they'll make it?"

"Make what?" the Scientist asked.

"Do you think they'll survive?"

"Do you mean individually or as a group?"

"Is there a difference?"

The Scientist said, "If they remain together, their chance to survive will increase; isolated, they are doomed."

"Rodrigo said they chose their course of action by a show of hands."

"Having endured brutal treatment from a despotic captain, it was inevitable they would choose a course of conduct that appeared just the opposite."

"But you said they'd end as tyrants."

"Despotism is, above all, decisive. Regardless of how successful a democracy appears, eventually there is a crisis. Whether internal dissension or external threat, that crisis will demand a decisive response and every disagreement will appear intolerable. But regardless of how the threat is dealt with, someone inevitably will believe he has been slighted in its resolution. And with that, the end will begin."

"So you don't believe democracy is possible?"

"The question is whether it can be sustained. It survives as long as its members remain social and economic equals. With sever inequality, democracy merely sustains a disequilibrium even while appearing to assure political equality; all of which amounts to a house of cards."

"I've heard stories of pirates who started democratic colonies. Wealth was distributed evenly along with food and other resources. And some of these colonies have been so successful they attract sailors from other ships. So, were those all lies?"

"It is not surprising such colonies are successful for a time, but democracy demands equilibrium. When balance is lost, democracy is unable to re-impose it because the beneficiaries of that imbalance will democratically perpetuate and expand it."

Pierre rowed and thought. "So, in a society of winners and losers, the winners tilt the table so that they continue to win and the rest continue to lose."

"A clever metaphor but it states the case."

"And you believe a democracy can't be established that keeps this from happening."

"On the contrary, nothing could be simpler. But only in a society in which it is impossible for a loser to awake one morning as a winner, regardless of luck or hard work. And conversely, that no winner will discover himself suddenly a loser. Each would need to agree their current status would remain the status even of their grandchildren."

Pierre considered this. "So this world is as modern as it'll ever be."

"Different colors but same pattern. We are, after all, merely human."

Pierre rowed until his hands were raw and his back sore but finally they reached the breakers. Jumping into the waist-deep surf, he dragged the dinghy toward the beach. "At least you could make the boat lighter."

"The danger of drowning is too acute. After all, what would you do if I drowned?"

The prow of the dinghy finally dug into the bright, yellow sand of the beach; Pierre fell to his knees panting. "Something would occur to me."

"Your confidence is misplaced." Dr. de Montpellier stepped carefully onto the sand. "But we have landed on the island of Cuba and for this I offer thanks."

"Your well-rested brain has considered our situation, so what should we do now?"

"Find the road that takes us to Havana. Once we have reached the city, I will contact my friend."

"So much certainty and so little evidence."

"Propose a better plan."

Exhausted and annoyed, Pierre said, "At least it's a plan, however lousy."

"Meanwhile we will rest here a bit before we begin the trek to the city."

"About how far do you think we need to go?"

"I am only certain that to reach the city we must travel west."

Beyond the edge of the beach they sat in the shade of a cluster of palms. Pierre asked, "What did you make of that scene on the Esperanza?"

"The crew decided they would rather be masters for a moment than slaves for life."

"But they'll be hanged as soon as they're caught."

"Exactly my point. Freebooters for a fortnight, they will sail to a safe port, sell their cargo and live as rich men until their money runs out. Then they will need to decide whether to return to raiding or settle in that port, unless they manage to find a captain not too curious about his crew. Whatever their choice, if their actions are discovered their lives will be forfeit."

"Could their lives have been so awful that living as pirates will be better?"

"Under the Spanish flag a sailor is worse than a slave. Every captain is king of his ship, but Spanish captains are gods, gifted with the absolute power of life and death and with that power they maintain discipline with the harshest punishments. Paid a pittance, a sailor's voyages can last years. The wonder is not that they prefer mutiny to misery, but that such are not more common."

"I heard tales at the tavern but they seemed far-fetched. But you say they weren't exaggerated?"

"It is in the nature of sailors to report what they have heard as if they had seen it. But Spanish captains are notorious for arbitrary brutality, so those stories could have been true."

"Captain dela Vega seemed just an annoying buffoon and hardly such a threat that he needed to be shot."

"In our company he was polite, but we were not part of his crew. Besides, even if he was one of the better captains, more thoughtful or compassionate, he had a reputation to maintain. If it became known he tolerated even small infractions, he would lose honor among other captains."

"And does this friend of yours resemble our captain?"

"If our Captain was the frigid North Pole, Don Benito is the torrid equator, so different in their temperament it will be hard for you to credit. Where our Captain was suspicious, my friend is open-minded. Undoubtedly, he manages his hacienda in a most enlightened fashion."

Eventually they stood and, moving west, followed the beach until they found an opening in the undergrowth that led to a path bright with sand and a calligraphy of fallen brown-green palm fronds. Pierre finally found the courage to ask, "Do you think Don Benito knows my father and his work?"

The Scientist stopped and turned. "Ask the question you truly wish to ask? You want to know if he visited the hacienda and might even be there now." Pierre hesitated before he nodded. The Scientist grinned. "We will admit that anything is possible, including that he has visited. But you received that letter from Europe, so it seems unlikely he is still there."

Pierre could not decide if he was disappointed or relieved. "Others may have heard of him."

"They may at least have heard of his work."

The path widened and they began to pass dark-skinned men and women walking slowly, some with large woven baskets of fruit or vegetables suspended by broad bands of cloth from their heads and resting upon their backs. None glanced up as they passed, their naked feet sent up puffs of tan dust with each step. Pierre and the Scientist followed this path until they reached a cluster of huts that resembled a hamlet.

The Scientist spoke in Spanish to several natives until a portly older man finally responded. After a series of exchanges Dr. de Montpellier turned to Pierre. "It seems we have a full day's walk to Havana and cannot reach it before nightfall, but this man will provide us shelter."

"As long as there's a meal and a bed, this seems as good a place as any to pass the night."

Approaching a cluster of small shacks, a short and fat man, pale and florid with a head of wildly wiry gray hair and dressed in the tattered clothing of a British seaman, emerged from the largest. The Scientist spoke a few words to him and the man smiled. Spoken in imperfect English, the man introduced himself as Miguel. After arranging for beds and meals, the Scientist asked if the man knew of his friend, Don Benito. Miguel's eyes widened but then he shook his head denying he knew anyone by that name. Behind them, a frail woman passed back and forth without looking up. Her profile suggested she was a native of the island. Miguel led them to the largest of the shacks, a wood fire burned low before it. To one side stood four other shacks whose entrances faced the wood fire. Miguel gestured Pierre and the Scientist to a clear space on the ground before its entrance.

Small pigs and scrawny chickens wandering about, and in the still and humid air a strand of steel-gray smoke from the smoldering fire drifted straight up. The Scientist looked around bemused. "We will now partake as the natives do; consider this part of your education. And when we reach Don Benito we will have one more tale to entertain him with."

Pierre was not confident. "Unless we become occupants of the stew-pot."

The Scientist laughed. "These are not the cannibals you undoubtedly heard tales of. Besides, where is true adventure without the aroma of danger?"

At that moment a piercing scream came from behind the shack. Pierre's startled look amused the Scientist. "Our host has sacrificed a young pig in our honor; you should be flattered."

"Or just relieved we won't travel by night."

Soon Miguel returned carrying to the fire a broad dark wooden bowl piled with bloody pieces of meat. The woman set a metal rack across two rocks on either side of the fire and placed the pieces on it. Immediately they began to sizzle and sputter and its aroma drifted to Pierre reminding him how hungry he was.

Grinning, the Scientist said, "Cheer up; we will soon eat from silver plates and sleep beneath clean sheets."

Pierre did not feel better as a result of this promise.

As the meat cooked, the woman placed two long, yellow plants resembling vegetables directly on the coals of the fire. He was about to ask about them when the Scientist asked, "Do you think we have seen the last of the creature?"

Startled, he realized that, since they left the Esperanza, he had stopped thinking about the beast.

"I'm more worried about finding my father."

"No need to be defensive. You remain the only person to have observed it closely."

"But now you've joined me in that dubious distinction."

"Not quite; I have never been close to it and certainly not as close as you."

Pierre growled, "I have no special knowledge of it and nothing to answer that question."

"Not much for small talk," the Scientist said mildly annoyed. "At least admit you are curious to know whether it was after you or those nuns or had simply wandered onto the island."

"If I agreed that it had followed me, wouldn't I claim it's following me because it knew I existed?"

"And that is impossible?"

"So unlikely I won't think about it."

The Scientist appeared amused. "So you no longer wonder if you will see it again?"

"I wonder whether I'll see my father again. Otherwise I can't get far enough away from that creature fast enough." The woman placed on the ground before each of them a wooden platter piled with charred pieces of meat beside one of those vegetables cooked on the coals.

Pierre looked mistrustfully at the platter. He watched the Scientist take a portion of the meat into his fingers and carefully bite pieces off. Glistening fat dripped from his chin. He looked up at Pierre smiling, then glanced down at his platter. "Fingers were created first, forks came along much later." He laughed at his own joke, but Pierre glowered and said nothing.

Between bites of meat the Scientist said, "I was on the road one night just outside Lyon on my way to Paris and without money. Night was falling and a cold winter day was becoming an even colder night. Near twilight a silhouette appeared against the sky, a shepherd leading his flock. Without an alternative I called out to him. Well, one thing led to another, he invited me to share his meal and he turned out to be an interesting man with a curious story. According to him, once as he watched his flock, a thunderstorm suddenly blew up and he needed to find shelter. His flock scattered so he decided to wait out the storm beneath a large tree and trust that his flock would be safe."

"Seeking shelter he discovered a hollow at the base of the tree large enough to allow him to crawl inside. But after a few moments sheltered within, an odd thing happened; as the storm raged he discovered his hair had begun to stand on end. And then suddenly he was surrounded by bright light. There was an explosion and a flash of intense heat. Stunned, when finally he gathered his wits he crawled out of his refuge and looked up. To his surprise, the tree had been struck by lightning and its trunk split and branches shattered. But what intrigued him was his hair standing on end. We mused over this but I recalled nothing to explain it." He paused. "There is some peculiar magic to this cooking; I have never tasted anything like it."

Pierre looked morosely at the Scientist. "Maybe eventually I'll acquire a taste for it."

The Scientist grinned and shrugged his shoulders. He then split open the ash-blackened yellow-green vegetable. Steam drifted from the yellow pulp inside. "You should become acquainted with this plant. It is more delightfully sweet than anything you have eaten." Seeing that Pierre's remained untouched he shook his head. "More misery is spread by fear and prejudice than by all the swords and guns in the land."

Pierre looked away. "At least I know when a gun's pointed in my direction."

"And you fail to recognize when a friend attempts to do you a favor."

"But your point about the story of your shepherd?"

"Yes, of course. Simply put, after we had consumed a sufficient amount of wine we agreed that his hair standing on-end and the arrival of the lightning somehow must be linked. Perhaps it is the Lord's way of warning us that lightning is about to strike."

Pierre resisted an urge to laugh. "Still, you can't establish a link between the two?"

The Scientist nodded. "Nothing connects them beyond their coincidence."

"Not much of a hypothesis."

"Beware, my friend; a lack of apparent connection does not deny a relationship exists. In fact, while it did not occur to me until later, I remember having witnessed an experiment at Paris involving the gem-stone amber. Rubbing it with a wool cloth endowed it with the ability to attract bits of hair. Might that imply a connection between the amber effect and lightning?"

Pierre hesitated. He recalled tricks Augustus had performed involving a piece of amber rubbed with wool and a thin piece of iron suspended by a thread under a bell-jar and how it deflected the iron. "The effect may be similar but without a mechanism there's no connection."

The Scientist eyed Pierre but then smiled. "Very good; you state the difficulty exactly. Perhaps when we reach the hacienda we will find that others have pursued this same question."

Pierre glanced down again at the food piled on his platter and then at the platter before the Scientist, empty except for scraps and the husk of yellow vegetable. "Speaking of time, I'm tired and the hour is late."

The Scientist nodded. "Between rowing and our walk here, I confess I am exhausted."

"But you didn't so much as touch the oars."

"You forget that I encouraged you energetically the entire time."

Pierre stifled his annoyance and laughed. "However that may be, now that we've eaten, tell me where we'll sleep and how we'll pay for it."

The Scientist shifted and reached under his shirt. His hand emerged with a large coin between pinched fingers. "Provided for; and perhaps a bit more."

"Right now, a night's sleep will be more than enough."

The Scientist looked up and Miguel suddenly squatted beside him.

Drawn perhaps by the glint of the coin he grinned obsequiously at the Scientist. They spoke in Spanish and the Scientist struggled to stand. "Our rooms are ready; a cabin for each of us." Brushing sand from his trousers he added, "You have earned a bit of luxury."

Miguel glanced at Pierre's platter still piled with food and his smile faded. The Scientist spoke in Spanish and Miguel nodded as his smile returned. Pierre turned a questioning look at him. "I told him your lover had run off with another and took your appetite with her. I did not want him to feel insulted."

Miguel led them away and Pierre glanced back; pigs devoured his abandoned meal.

Standing paces apart, each shack was just large enough to accommodate a grown man. The Scientist yawned and stretched. "I wish you a pleasant night's rest." Pierre turned toward his and to his back the Scientist said, "Clean sheets and soft bedding tomorrow night." Pierre could not summon the energy to contradict.

Inside his cabin the darkness was complete. Hands outstretched he discovered suspended above the ground and blocking his path a hammock, something he had slept in before and not comfortably. He maneuvered himself into it, managed a secure position and let himself lie back certain he was about fall from it with every breath. He could not relax and he cursed himself and the hammock and even his reluctance to eat that meal offered to him. Fatigue left him eager for sleep yet his mind would not allow him rest. Moments from the past drifted before his sightless eyes like sparkling shards of broken glass, razor-sharp and impossible to grasp without pain and blood. Soon he heard a low rumbling he recognized as the snore of the Scientist, and to his surprise this reassured him. Wrapped in darkness his eyes gradually began to close. Time passed beneath him as an ocean of moments whose shimmering surfaces merged. Suddenly, a sound he did not recognize pricked his ears reminding him that luck is only apparent in hindsight. But sleep soon descended as a curtain and then all became dark, and it would only be a matter of luck if he remembered anything at all.

CHAPTER THREE

WHEN PIERRE OPENED his eyes again the blue sky beyond the cloth doorway's edges seemed to mock his uneasy recollection. He tried to retrieve what he sensed had been a disturbing dream but only odd words and cacophonous phrases accompanied by darkly fractured images appeared, and those fragments evaporated from his mind leaving a gray mist of doubt and fear along with a certainty his dream had frightened him though he failed to recall its details.

He left the cabin and made his way to the smoking embers of the night's cooking fire where he found the Scientist sitting with his back against a tree, eyes closed and hands folded loosely over his stomach. The woman who had prepared their evening meal emerged from the larger shack carrying a mug and a large piece of bread. Pierre sat down beside the Scientist as she handed it to him. He sipped something from the mug both bitter and sweet he recalled from the Revenge; the bread was thick-crusted and sweetly fresh. He looked up between tree branches at a bright sky and decided that whatever had happened during the night and regardless of how little he recalled, this new day would be an improvement.

"Slept well?" Startled, Pierre turned to see the Scientist smiling. Then Dr. de Montpellier opened his eyes. "After a long and exhausting day, I hope you had a long and exhausting night."

Perhaps he recognized Pierre's confusion because he added, "I hope you enjoyed the attention." When Pierre still did not appear to understand, he continued, "Around here, silver buys more than just pieces of cooked meat and a hammock."

An idea gathered slowly until the Scientist said, "I hope you do not feel slighted, because undoubtedly your personal charm would have drawn charming and attractive companionship. I hoped merely to hasten that encounter and assure its outcome."

Finally something occurred to Pierre that made him smile thoroughly embarrassed.

Satisfied, the Scientist said, "I will guess my effort proved satisfactory."

Pierre simply grinned. Dr. de Montpellier continued, "I am grateful for your effort on my behalf and recall the thrill of the exotic, though its experience has fallen far into my past."

"Then I won't need to exaggerate my thanks."

"If another opportunity arises, I will happily accommodate. Now, finish and we will depart for the capital. It would be best to arrive before nightfall."

Pierre sipped his drink. "How will we do that?"

The Scientist settled back against the tree and closed his eyes. "As I said, silver goes far around here. Finish and all will become clear."

Later, the woman returned with a pewter mug for Pierre, this one filled with fresh water. Sight of her reminded him of something and he wondered if what the Scientist believed he had paid for had actually happened. But his memory was a fist full of fog.

"Ready?" the Scientist asked. Pierre looked over to see him standing. "Either you are in deep thought or this languorous atmosphere has infected you, too."

Pierce stood and shook himself. "If it has, I'm escaping just in time."

Miguel appeared at the edge of the clearing leading two gray and black mules by their reins. To Pierre's expression of surprise, the Scientist said, "I repeat that among these natives a little silver goes a long way." Miguel held the reins as they mounted.

Directed to the main road with the promise they would reach Havana before nightfall, the Scientist turned to Pierre. "Let us hope that fortune smiles upon us finally."

"But also hope that fortune is more constant on land than at sea."

"Spoken by someone for whom youth is a burden. Instead, we should recognize how fortunate we are. But let's not distract the mules for they have more than enough to do."

Pierre was content to do just that. He had something to recall and he hoped the trip would be long enough for the obscure to become clear.

Confined between curtains of brown and green foliage, Pierre remained bewildered by the little he recalled of the previous night. Those shards of memory poised at the edge of his mind seemed important to retrieve, yet the harder he tried the less that came to mind, and that emerged distorted, hazy and nonsensical, but bore no resemblance to whatever the Scientist assumed.

The road gradually widened as it passed more villages. Near mid-day, and to Pierre's relief, they reached a small tavern where they stopped to refresh themselves. There the Scientist prattled on to Pierre about the history of the island and its villainous conquistadors. Pierre regretted he could not give him his full attention, but the previous night remained unsettled in his mind. By the time they resumed their journey, Pierre endured a peculiar sensation that something within that dream had concerned the Scientist and its residual dread suggested danger for them both. Though its memory escaped his grasp, because of the dream's dark urgency, like a damaged tooth he could not leave it alone.

Finally the setting sun crouched above the horizon as a scintillating arch of brass over the rooftops of Havana. The dust raised by the Scientist's mount powered Pierre's feet. Pierre watched him wondering how the old man managed, as if he had ridden mules his entire life. Due to the insolvable fragments of his dream Pierre thought he remembered, the Scientist's presence seemed tinged by anxiety. Something within his dream left him unaccountably certain that Captain Stevenson had been right; that beast was Pierre's personal demon, a material adversary unique to him, visible to all but entirely his own.

The creature frightened Pierre but nothing suggested he possessed special knowledge of it, so the insistence it pursued him could only add to his terror. Watching the Scientist sway on his mule unaware of what Pierre could barely remember left him feeling utterly alone. He wondered then whether his pursuit of Augustus would demand another confrontation with the creature. Yet the possibility Don Benito could help him find his father compelled Pierre to continue. Cast adrift, whether at sea or on land, he could only hope that whatever happened, he remained on that path leading to Augustus.

As they approached the towering stone walls surrounding the city of Havana, more travelers joined their path. Unlike Pierre and the Scientist, these were on foot, and dust like a brown-red fog drifted over their path. Under its reddish haze, finally they approached one of the city's gates.

To the Scientist's swaying back, Pierre said, "If Augustus isn't at Don Benito's hacienda I'll need the price of another ship to continue my search."

Dr. de Montpellier turned appearing annoyed. "You have a distressing habit of worrying over non-existent difficulties. Please stop or continue in silence."

Side by side they passed under the bored gaze of several shabbily-dressed Spanish troops. Their pace was slowed by the clutter of bodies around them. Beyond the gate and secure behind its high, thick walls that crowd dispersed, some continuing ahead as others followed streets to the right and left. The Scientist stopped until Pierre caught up.

Reaching him, the Scientist smiled. "You speak as if you expect to continue alone."

"I assume that when we reach the hacienda, you'll remain to join in its work."

Their mules continued forward as if eager to reach what awaited them. "That idea tempts me." The Scientist looked down as if embarrassed. "But I have become curious about your father. Certainly about his work and its progress, but now I am curious about the man. So I would happily wait for a chance to spend an evening in his company."

"That would be a first for him and a different experience for me."

The Scientist nodded as if ready to move on. "According to Miguel there is an inn on the Plaza des Armas where we will find assistance in reaching the hacienda. But we are now within the walls of the most protected port in all of New Spain, so we should rest easy."

"Including protection from gigantic creatures?"

The Scientist grinned. "Perhaps your beast will give us an opportunity to find out."

The buildings they passed at first were hardly more than shacks, but continuing, the buildings took on substance. Doorways hung with tattered curtains were replaced by solid wood, and mud and reed walls became wood and stone. Under a deepening violet twilight Pierre and the Scientist reached the plaza.

Dismounting, they led the mules past a busy food market. The Scientist again stopped passers-by addressing them in Spanish. A matronly woman finally pointed to the north end of the plaza, and the front of a tavern sheltered behind a colonnade.

Inside the tavern, and despite the heat, the air smelled of wood smoke and something sickly sweet, an aroma like that of dead flowers that Pierre found unpleasant. The Scientist said, "Find a seat because this may take some time."

But a man suddenly appeared from behind a curtained doorway and introduced himself as Phillip, the tavern-keeper. Tall and rail-thin, his ribs seemed to prod his loose white blouse. His voice sounded as if it passed between rocks within his chest, and the angles of his cheeks and corners of his jaw appeared tinged with green. His long thin hands were rake-like and his knuckles resembled large, tan pebbles he could not hide. His fingers reminded Pierre of dried and shriveled tendrils. But what bothered him most were large, dark circles around his drooping-lidded eyes. Phillip appeared to spend his life watching others enjoy what he could only desire and possessed by appetites doomed to remain unfulfilled.

The Scientist requested their meal and when Phillip had gone Pierre said, "For a tavern-keeper, your friend is one dismal character."

Dr. de Montpellier shrugged. "It happens to some Europeans with Mediterranean roots. They breathe the atmosphere, indulge in the dietary and sexual menus, and then something happens. Perhaps a deeper heritage asserts itself; something in the blood takes over until they become both docile and devious. Sleeping far into the day, they ramble the countryside deep into the night. I have seen men like him before and so will you."

Phillip returned to place platters of food before them and then disappeared again into the back. The Scientist added, "Our man has offered a vacant room. We can spend the night here and get an early start tomorrow"

"And he knows Don Benito?"

"He says the journey will demand an entire day but we should arrive before nightfall."

Phillip stepped to their table hands entwined one within the other and grinning he bowed oddly at the waist. "Shall I bring you gentlemen anything more?"

The Scientist requested another carafe of wine as Pierre glanced up. When he returned with their carafe the Scientist refilled Pierre's glass. "Drink up. We have reached a safe harbor with a clear horizon and our room is just upstairs. By this time tomorrow we will enjoy accommodations with like-minded spirits." He blinked hard then as if that thought demanded an effort. "Our journey will be long and difficult so our first task will be to locate a guide."

Phillip stepped forward. "I believe I know of a man who will lead you to the hacienda."

The Scientist said, "We hope to leave early tomorrow morning."

For Pierre, the tavern-keeper's expression resembled a grimace. "That journey leads far into the Blue Mountains. I know it well and would be honored to guide you, yet my responsibilities demand I remain here. But a man living nearby also knows that path and I am certain he will be happy to assure your safe arrival."

"Thank you for that," the Scientist said. For some reason, suddenly the Scientist appeared hardly able to keep his eyes open or his chin above the surface of the table.

Pierre turned to the innkeeper. "We need to rest; please show us to our room."

Full night had fallen. Carrying a lighted candle, Phillip led them to the darkened rear of the tavern and up a set of nearly vertical stairs. By that weak light Pierre saw a narrow, low-ceiling corridor with pairs of closed doors on either side. At the end of the corridor the innkeeper opened a door. This room was small with two narrow pallets against opposite walls. He handed a candle to Pierre, bowed and left. Pierre listened to his tread descend the stairs.

"All right, old man," Pierre said with gruff impatience, "there's your bed, make use of it."

"Ah, let the Devil take you," the Scientist said, "and I will take care of myself." He sat heavily shaking his head as if baffled, and then turned and fell backward onto the pallet. By the time Pierre reclined on his own, the Scientist was snoring.

Pierre lay on his back, crossed his arms over his chest and closed his eyes inviting sleep. But his closed eyes left his mind to race. He recalled Augustus in the midst of an experiment; something subtle and intricate he had created to astonish and elicit admiration. It pleased Pierre to think that somewhere right now, Augustus was being listened to by others who understood what he was determined to achieve. Though Pierre had never considered it, he realized his concern for Augustus ran that deep. What he had suspected was merely his self-justification for fleeing the tavern and Gabriella now appeared a challenge only satisfied by returning Augustus to his home.

Entranced by these drowsy thoughts, he had to remind himself what else he might need to do in order to remain lucky.

CHAPTER FOUR

"SO THESE ACCOMMODATIONS were not good enough for you?"

Pierre awoke to find himself sitting on the floor with his back against the door. The Scientist stared down at him, a surly smirk on his lips.

"Bugs," Pierre said scratching his leg. The pain that resulted startled him. He lifted his trouser leg to discover two short, purple-red scratches. He suspected then that he might not have dreamed his encounter, and that worried him. "Glad to see you've recovered."

The Scientist laughed. "Recovery is that ability which permits the young to become old. Now, I wish to pass as I assume some breakfast is waiting downstairs."

Pierre stood and turned to see daylight leaking yellow from under the door behind him. His head felt swollen and tender and even that small bit of light pierced his eyes.

The Scientist said, "You look like I feel."

"Between the bugs and your snoring, I didn't get much sleep."

"With something to eat you will begin to feel better." The concern in the Scientist's voice caught Pierre by surprise.

They reached the common room to be greeted by a man who was not Phillip. Shorter and older than the tavern-keeper, this man had the same cadaverous cast and dark circles around his eyes, and moved with that same trance-like blankness. He introduced himself as Hernando. "I trust you gentleman slept well," he said, but so softly Pierre was not certain he had heard him correctly.

The Scientist responded, "It appears I slept better than my companion. Right now we would like some bread and ale."

Smiling, he nodded but then moved off at such a slow shuffle that Pierre guessed this might take the rest of the day. Yet he remained so tired he was grateful for an excuse to sit down.

With a concerned glance the Scientist said, "Are you sure you are all right?"

Pierre shrugged. "Another chance to practice recovery."

The Scientist grinned. "Life is rich in such opportunities."

After an eternity as measured by Pierre's discomfort, Hernando appeared carrying a tray of coarse bread and two tankards. The Scientist once again assured Pierre they could expect a warm greeting, good food and comfortable beds at the hacienda but he had repeated this so often that Pierre could only nod. An odd lassitude left his body operating a heart-beat behind his mind. They finished their morning meal in silence.

While the Scientist paid Hernando he asked about the guide he had suggested. Hernando grinned, a sight that, with his teeth nearly black and sharpened to points and lips lined with sores, startled Pierre. If the Scientist also noticed, he said nothing. They passed under the colonnade and stepped out into the dusty sunlight. Hernando soon reappeared leading their mules. By his side walked a small, slim man who moved with an obvious limp. He introduced the man as Ernesto. A tall, strongly built African woman followed several steps behind and stood to one side as they spoke. Ernesto's deformed leg held Pierre's attention.

Their brief negotiation complete, the Scientist spoke to Ernesto. "I hope I do not embarrass you if I ask what happened to your leg."

"The price of bravery or of foolishness, Excellency," Ernesto said with a rueful smile, "depending upon your point of view." His face was long and narrow and brown from the sun, but his eyes were bright as shards of violet glass. "Injured in the defense of my King far from here, I walked imperfectly from a battle where many will remain for eternity. But you'll be challenged to sustain my pace." He turned to examine their mules adjusting their straps and harnesses. To the Scientist he said, "It's important we arrive before nightfall."

Riding what appeared to Pierre a spindle-legged mule, Ernesto led them along the same road by which they had arrived. When they passed beneath Havana's gates and gained the main road, the Scientist asked, "But just how did you find your way to this magnificent city?"

Ernesto turned with a smile. "It's good that we've reached the main road, for my tale will demand some time and all of your attention if you hope to learn the truth."

"A good tale," said Pierre, "always takes time to tell."

Ernesto said, "But I will be brief, for as Livy said, brevity keeps the point sharp." After a pause, he continued.

"My tale begins in the province of Extramadura in Spain, in a village so small and vile it could only be an incomplete thought of our Lord's. My father was a mule driver and my mother died soon after I was born. Thus, it was just he and I to struggle together. But my father was a man whose heart was too soft and generous to withstand those injuries that come in this unjust world, and that world delivered one blow more than his sweet heart could sustain. Anguish and humiliation drove him into the arms of our Lord, leaving me, a boy just fifteen, to struggle alone."

"There are miseries," the Scientist said, "we withstand only if they are shared."

"And for that reason I joined my King's army, where I was certain always to have comrades by my side. With my father in the earth, I surrendered my life to my King."

Pierre asked, "Life had been difficult, but wasn't your life in the army even more so?"

"You have it right; that life was hard. But I shared my difficulties with men I came to see as those brothers I'd never had. Indeed, the weight of our burdens forced all of us to shed our prejudices, and prepared us to share the burdens to come."

The Scientist asked, "As a soldier in King Philip's army, can I assume you served under Commander Spinola?"

With a glance of mild surprise Ernesto said, "Since your Excellency knows our Commander Spinola, you must also know that soon after my enlistment I boarded a ship that sailed for Antwerp. You can guess what that voyage was like for a youth raised in a dry and stony land, suddenly afloat upon the uncertain waters of the cold and dismal north. Nothing had prepared me for that misery. When finally we landed, I fell to my knees in gratitude to a merciful God."

Pierre said, "It is not difficult to imagine how such an ordeal tested you."

"But let me not exaggerate," Ernesto said with embarrassment. "Far worse would befall us and very soon. Spinola had assembled a grand army, and we arrived at an encampment whose size astonished all of us. At twilight our campfires seemed to reach to the horizon itself. Ascribe it to my youth, but the sight of those fires thrilled me. Ours was the greatest army on earth and therefore invincible. Despite all, that night I was happy to be alive."

To Pierre the Scientist said, "All happiness departs which is why its pursuit is a destructive delusion." Pierre said nothing, confident he was wrong.

Ernesto continued, "We could no more imagine defeat than stones falling from the sky. On those days when clouds parted and the sun shone, our armor sparkled like a field of diamonds. And so, convinced our victory was ordained by God, we became restless and battle could not come soon enough. We were certain that when we had accomplished our mission we would depart that land of cold and mud and return to the embrace of our fathers."

The Scientist said, "Only with such an illusion can a young man march forth, unafraid."

"Knowledge," Ernesto added, "makes cowards of us all. But there was no time to indulge our fantasies. Eventually, the rain stopped falling, the roads dried out and we began to move. And a sight more glorious has never been seen by the eyes of men."

Their path began to rise and then climb into the mountains.

Ernesto said, "An army is a swamp of lies that circulate as unfettered as mosquitoes, but always trace back to a source as close to the commander's lips as his whiskers. We began each day convinced we would encounter the enemy, and every evening found us certain the enemy awaited just beyond the next hill. At first, we ate hearty meals before taking our rest on that cold, wet ground, but our supply wagons soon emptied, and then we were forced to forage among the local farms. Thus began my education in the true perfidy of humankind. But worse and unknown to us, Spinola was as misinformed about the location of the army of Gustavus Adolphus as the rest of us were."

To Pierre, the Scientist said, "The Swedish army of Adolphus was the best-trained and equipped in all Europe."

"Your Excellency could not be more right," Ernesto said, "though we who slept in mud and dreamed of Spain believed Spinola nearly as prescient as God."

Pierre asked, "But with such an army, how could he achieve anything less than victory?"

Dr. de Montpellier responded, "Spinola possessed the superior force, but Adolphus had science."

Ernesto said, "Your Excellency demonstrates uncanny understanding, but allow me to tell the tale as I experienced it. Though marching makes an army physically stronger, our spirits fell with each mile while our foraging raids on the surrounding farms became vindictive. As if, unable to fight an honorable enemy, we gratified ourselves by inflicting horrors on defenseless farmers and especially their wives and children. Their sons we coerced into joining us, the wives and daughters fared far worse. At first, some of us protested that these farmers were unworthy of our steel, and so it was nothing less than cowardice to rob those without arms and hardly able to feed themselves. And the first time I discovered a group of our troops raping a farmer's daughter, I drew my own sword in outrage. But it's a vicious world that leads us to behave in ways we find intolerable in others. Thus, I found myself an accomplice in acts for which I should have been murdered." For a moment he became pale and glanced at his leg with great sadness. "This curse I'll bear until I breathe my last, but it fails to approach that punishment I've earned."

"You were one among many," the Scientist said, "frightened and confused and hardly more than a boy. Surely, God has forgiven you."

Ernesto looked down. "I can only hope the Lord God will be so generous, but you were not there and so can't know what He knows. I live in fear of death and of God's judgment."

Pierre said, "It is little consolation but I'm sure the Swedes behaved not a whit better."

"That is likely true," Ernesto said and gloomily shook his head, "but our army left a trail of misery that could only be justified by the destruction of Adolphus." He looked around then as if suddenly awakened from a trance. "But it is mid-day and we're near an inn owned by a good friend. We should stop for refreshment."

Glancing at Pierre, the Scientist said, "Only if you promise to finish your tale."

"I assure your Excellencies, there'll be sufficient time to satisfy that curiosity."

At a wide clearing between low hills and beside their road Ernesto led them to a broad low building of dark timbers. Behind it clustered several small and simply built cabins. A tall, bearish man nearly bald with a thick black beard stepped from its main door and greeted Ernesto warmly. Ernesto introduced him as Guido, who then ushered them all inside.

This room was wide with a low ceiling and although it was mid-day its few windows left it gloomy. Beyond the entrance stood individual tables and chairs; at the far end was a cold fireplace. They were now far into the mountains, and Pierre guessed that evenings could be brisk.

From a passage behind the bar appeared two young women who shared a resemblance that led Pierre to guess they were sisters. Introduced as Juanita and Galacia, each greeted Ernesto with a friendly embrace. When Guido requested their meals, the sisters returned to the back. Ernesto then explained that Hernando had hired him as their guide to the hacienda of Don Benito Cerino, and this seemed to surprise Guido. He glanced from the Scientist to Pierre saying he was honored to have such men under his roof, and he knew they were accomplished men because only that sort traveled to visit Don Benito. Turning to Ernesto, Guido added, "Rumor's going around that slaves from the farms are running off to hide in caves in the hills. Farmers are nervous, I can tell you."

Ernesto leaned back. "Building their own settlement and far from the likes of us."

The two women returned carrying platters of food along with tankards of wine, then turned to disappear into the back. Thoroughly charmed, Pierre thought to find a reason to join them.

Guido hesitated and then shook his head. "They leave their women and children behind and even abandon their tools. You'd think at least they'd bring along their families. And if they expect to farm, they'll need tools as well."

Ernesto asked, "Have any been seen since they left their farms?"

Guido again shook his head. "Like they was assumed into heaven." He laughed more from nervousness than good humor. "Owners are frightened, but them slaves' women are just plain mad. They complain they have kids to feed and no one to help. So another rumor's going around that there's a creature wandering these hills and eating them."

At this the Scientist laughed, but Guido turned to him with dark seriousness. "Them stories sound quaint but those are scared people, and mad that nobody gives them an explanation or help. Maybe it's childish, but nobody's offered better."

Embarrassed, the Scientist said, "Pardon my offense. As you say, these explanations appear fanciful but their fear can only be genuine and deep. Still, when confronted by a mystery, assume human actors first."

Guido studied the Scientist but as if he settled something in his mind he turned to Pierre asking what led him to join this journey. Briefly, Pierre explained his determination to find his father and the possibility Augustus had visited Don Benito's hacienda. This seemed to catch Guido's attention and the more he explained, the more Guido appeared to want to know. When Pierre reached the end of his story, Guido leaned back to study him with an admiring smile. "Had I a son," he said, "and we became separated, I can only hope he would do as you have."

Pierre said, "Your encouragement is valuable and I hope you have that son you wish for."

At this Guido and Ernesto laughed. Guido said, "I know you mean that as a compliment so I thank you for your generous wish." Ernesto then turned to Guido and asked about a man named Salvatore. For Pierre's and the Scientist's benefit, Guido explained that Salvatore was a gifted musician who often graced the inn. Ernesto and Guido then exchanged gossip as Pierre and Dr. de Montpellier finished their meals.

When they stood from the table, Guido shook both their hands confiding that it had been a long time since he had enjoyed such company. Standing at the threshold of the inn, he offered the hope he would see them both again soon. They mounted their mules and soon regained the main road. The Scientist then reminded Ernesto of his promise to continue his tale.

Ernesto looked about. "Please forgive me, but while I find it easy to recall those events, they are bitter to describe. So indulge me as I explain what I recall as the nature of war. Among the farmers I'd seen blood and heard the cries of injured animals, and once a mule stepped on the leg of a hired hand crushing the bone; he had screamed for hours. But unspeakable misery overhung our roads like a vicious fog that spread far over the countryside. We wandered; that's the only way to describe our army's movements. Commander Spinola couldn't confront the Swedes, and by avoiding direct attack they weakened us. Gradually, life and time became suspended even while our fury never receded. Life is as fragile as a candle's flame, but just as fragile were any constraints on our behavior short of the blade of another's sword. We skirmished and slept and marched in a haze, and traveled like a swarm of angry bees, spreading havoc wherever we went, though none of that brought us to battle. But then, one night word came down the line that the Swedes were less than a mile away. We'd heard such rumors before, but I tell you, that night we rejoiced. An eerie glee filled us and we drank ourselves catatonic in loyalty to each other, relieved simply that steel soon would meet steel, and with glory at the end of the day."

The road leveled and they traveled nearly shoulder to shoulder with Ernesto riding between Pierre and Dr. de Montpellier.

"And just as we had hoped, as we formed our lines before sunrise, the line of the Swedes appeared as a sparkling fringe along the crest of the next hill. The Jesuits ran about blessing everything in sight. God would help us even if we couldn't help ourselves."

"Insisting this was a glorious day and that we'd be praised by our grandchildren and many other stupid things, our officers moved to the front of our lines. We shivered in that cold, damp dawn but whether we waited five minutes or two hours, we wanted only one thing. And just as the clouds parted and the sun shone suddenly bright, we were ordered to move forward. Some fools even insisted the sunshine was a sign our victory was certain."

Grinning, Ernesto shook his head. "We charged, and then Adolphus showed why his army was the terror of the continent. Men screamed more loudly than horses, steel crashed against steel, guns exploded, and suddenly we were surrounded on three sides. He had set his trap and Spinola then sent us headlong into it. Those Swedes appeared everywhere. And most awful for me, though I swung my sword in every direction and my steel met steel, I don't believe I injured even a single enemy soldier. At one moment I turned to look for the rest of my comrades, there was an explosion and just as suddenly I was face down in mud and darkness with the sounds of battle subsiding." Ernesto paused to tighten a hitch.

"I awoke alone in the cold mud and in horrible pain. Night had fallen and I lay surrounded by the moans and screams of dying men that arose as if from the earth itself. And then came the dogs. At some moment I discovered I had acquired this." He slapped his bad leg hard.

"I next remember being shaken. A purple shadow hovered over me pulling on my breast plate. I tried to raise my sword before I understood I was merely being robbed, but I screamed as much from pain as from fear. Then I recognized the figure was that of an old woman. She stepped back horrified. I can't guess which of us was more frightened but after a moment she returned and knelt beside my head muttering and stroking my face. Then she touched my leg. How she managed that I'll never know; from the middle of my thigh to nearly my ankle was raw and mangled flesh. I passed into unconsciousness and only awoke to discover I had been carried into a barn, laid on a bed of straw and covered with a thin blanket. How she could have managed to drag me from the battlefield, whether she'd done it alone or had been helped, I never learned. My leg was now wrapped with heavy cloth to a piece of wood. I burned with fever, awoke and slept without rhythm. At some moment I awoke to find her again kneeling beside my head holding a bowl of something hot and offering it to me. Weak and confused, I grabbed it and drank even though it scalded my mouth."

Pierre asked, "Did you learn anything about her?"

"Or why," the Scientist asked, "she took you in?"

Ernesto shrugged. "Perhaps she recognized my youth and took pity on me. Or perhaps she was simply one of those souls gifted with charity and had no choice but to help. Whatever the truth, I never learned it. Six days, perhaps less, and I decided my leg had healed enough for me to use. It was then I discovered the sort of leg I was to keep."

Blue-black twilight approached leaving the tops of the trees washed by a bronze twilight. Ernesto continued; "Hobbled as I was, I managed to improvise a crutch. I knew I couldn't repay her, and marauding troops from Adolphus's army might discover me at any time. If that happened I'd be killed, and likely the old woman as well. So, far into the night I left, found the main road and began to walk. I continue to hope that when finally she saw I was gone she felt deep relief. Anyway, after days of painful walking I reached Antwerp, but the crippled man who returned was not the boy who had departed. I was useless for most work, but eventually I found a job as a mule driver and then gradually gained a reputation for my skill. As I prepared one day for a voyage to Valencia, a man approached asking if I would accompany his cargo of mules to the New World. He assured me that once delivered those mules be worth their weight in gold." He began to laugh. It was the first time Pierre had heard him laugh and it had an uncanny, chilling quality. "As you see, I've turned my riches to good purpose."

They continued for some time in silence until the Scientist said, "A remarkable story and you are a remarkable man, but tell me how you came to know my friend, Don Benito?"

"I can only admit to having heard of him." He looked about. "Having assured your arrival, I will be paid well. Once done, I will begin my return journey."

Pierre said, "But you can't possibly return to Havana before nightfall."

"Nothing to concern yourself about, young sir, although I'm grateful for that thought. Only a few miles from the hacienda, there lives a dear friend who'll provide my shelter."

The Scientist said, "Surely, Don Benito would offer you shelter for the night."

Ernesto turned to face them both. "He is well-known for his generosity and I'm certain were I to request it, he'd provide most pleasant accommodations. But in the presence of such a body of educated men I would not feel comfortable. His companions are most erudite and would have little interest in the history of a crippled mule driver."

The Scientist said, "In my experience he despises only the mean or cowardly or foolish, and you are most assuredly none of those."

"Your Excellencies are too kind. Still, I believe I'll keep with my own company. But I thank you for the delicacy of feeling you've expressed."

Further along, they passed a cluster of shacks perched on a nearly vertical rise just off the trail. In front of one Pierre saw what appeared to be a double-headed ax propped upright with its handle stuck into the ground. Beside it stood a pole painted with broad stripes of red and white. Something in all of this stirred Pierre's memory though he could not recall what that could be. He was certain he should know what all of these meant, but that knowledge was hazy and without edges or contours. He looked up to see that Ernesto and the Scientist had continued ahead speaking together quietly, and had not noticed he was no longer beside them. So he took this as permission to gratify his curiosity. He got off his mule and tied its reins to a nearby bush.

As he climbed the path toward the shacks, chickens and pigs wandered past as if he were no more interesting than a stone, but no one emerged from the shacks to greet or challenge him. He reached the ax and pole to discover, resting on the ground between them, a large, white bowl filled with shining triangular black stones. He stared down certain that if he looked long enough he would remember and understand, yet these remained mute and meaningless. Nothing connected that ax, those stones and a painted pole. Yet, somehow Pierre knew they were significant. Despite determined thought, nothing was clear and he gritted his teeth in frustration.

He reached deeper in his memory, but the more he reflected the more frustrating the sensation became; as if these objects refused to be recognized. Somehow they remained beyond reason and no rational process would expose their nature. And the more Pierre considered them, the further they seemed to retreat, and this left him angry. Their resistance to reason was an insult aimed at him, and thinking this made him even more angry. And the more angry he became, the more resistant those objects seemed, until all he wanted to do was knock them over; push them down and let them rot. As if their upright posture was a defiance to Pierre's reason.

He lifted his foot to attack the double-headed ax, when suddenly he was shoved hard to the ground. He turned to find Ernesto kicking at him with his twisted leg, an expression of fury on his face. With each kick he screamed, "Are you crazy? You fool! You dog! You pig! You idiot!" Between these blows, Pierre watched the Scientist struggle up the rise toward them. Blows struck his head and he pressed himself into the soil. Then he heard the Scientist call out. When the blows ceased, he saw the Scientist pushing Ernesto back.

"Have you lost your mind?" the Scientist asked Ernesto. "What has possessed you?"

Ernesto stared down at Pierre with black contempt. Once again Pierre was reminded of the luck that had brought him here but which might take him no further.

CHAPTER FIVE

ERNESTO'S FURY DRAINED away, replaced by a glazed look of weary confusion and then embarrassment. But Pierre's own anger suddenly arose. To Ernesto he said, "What was that about? Did you want to kill me?"

Ernesto paced a small circle with an odd hopping motion looking down and shaking his head. "I am deeply sorry. You are honorable men and the young master didn't deserve my assault." When he stopped moving he looked directly into Pierre's eyes. "You don't understand these things yet they're important and for some of us they're profound."

Dr. de Montpellier said, "I am certain he intended no offense. Still, perhaps you will explain what they are and how it is you know about them."

Ernesto's eyes darted from Pierre to the Scientist, but then as if he resolved something he sighed. "You ask a great deal, yet I'm pleased by your curiosity. Still, the answer to your question will take more than a moment and we still have a way to go."

Returned to their mules they resumed the journey. Ernesto again rode between Pierre and the Scientist.

"For a proper understanding you should speak with a babalawo, for those men gather such knowledge. The little I know I've learned from a woman who took pity on me and comforted me and offered me her bed." Glancing down he slapped angrily at his twisted leg. "Which was more than any white woman would do, and for which I'm grateful enough to respect her beliefs. I've seen what Christians gleefully do to Christians. Though faithful to Jesus and his promise of salvation, yet I've come to believe there're many gods and each deserves respect."

The Scientist asked, "Is she the African woman we saw in your company at the inn?"

"Her name is Theresa," Ernesto said, "and she's been more kind and understanding than any person I've known. She's been better than a lover, she has been my friend. It was from her that I learned what little I know about those objects the young master was about to desecrate."

"They are part of the worship of a being named Chango. He is one of a group of spiritual figures called orishas that have power over the forces of Nature. Chango is a warrior orisha who commands thunder and lightning and fire. Just as in Christianity, the purpose of worship is care for the ori, a word that names more than merely a soul. The ori is a sort of container for ase, the life-force that runs through all things and controls all, including each person's destiny. Believers accumulate ase through the exercise of good character and establish a personal bond with one of the orishias. And the array of orishias is nearly as wide as that of Christian saints."

The Scientist looked at Ernesto with mild surprise. "You have already said many things I do not understand and you seem to know a great deal. Did these figures originate in Africa?"

Ernesto nodded with a flush of embarrassment. "But not in the way you assume. In an effort at disguise and self-defense, each orisha is associated with a Christian saint who provides it a sort of Christian mask. For example, Theresa's orisha is Oya, creator of hurricanes and guardian of the Underworld, and Oya's Christian shadow is St. Theresa."

To the Scientist, Pierre said, "Strong Bill told us something about all his."

The Scientist nodded. "If they are discovered by the authorities, the adherents to these beliefs find themselves in serious danger."

Ernesto looked from the Scientist to Pierre. "There's some advantage in the fact that the Church so poorly educates its priests; their ignorance allows these beliefs to survive. As with Christian saints, a believer appeals to his orisha to act as intermediary to that orisha who controls the force of nature he hopes to influence. By swearing loyalty, the believer can then demand that orisha's help."

Pierre asked, "How does someone become a believer in this Chango god?"

Ernesto and Dr. de Montpellier turned to look at him with mild surprise. Ernesto said, "I haven't explained this properly. Believers don't choose an orisha, an orisha chooses them, but it's up to the believer to discover which orisha has chosen him. The orisha agrees to ride the believer as we ride these mules. This sounds paradoxical, but one gains power over the orisha by submitting to it. By agreeing to be ridden, that orisha assumes responsibility for the believer."

"Pardon me for saying it," the Scientists said, "but that's a distinction without a difference."

"Then let me explain it this way. The orisha rides you but doesn't direct your life. Unlike what I'm doing with this mule, the orisha doesn't direct a person's life, it simply rides along, watching and listening. But from time to time the orisha nudges us with his knee just as I'm doing right now with my mule. Gently, hardly any pressure. And this mule's stupid as we all are stupid. We don't notice when our orisha tries to help us. And because we don't notice, we go our own way with our orisha laughing at our stupidity, or worse. Had I known my orisha when I was in Spain, perhaps I wouldn't have this leg. People refer to those deformed like me as olori-buruku, which can mean both an unlucky man, and a stupid man; unlucky because he's so stupid he fails to heed his orisha. It's a smart religion that knows enough to blur that distinction."

To Pierre, Ernesto said, "Each orisha's related to a specific object, color and number, or that's how it was explained to me." He laughed nervously. "To be honest, their significance escapes me and I never remember which goes with which." He looked down embarrassed. "Through Theresa, this religion saved my life. But I have no desire to share it with others, let alone insist others believe as I do."

With a smirk the Scientist said, "In this day, such an inclination is unusual. More often, the first responsibility for possessing a religion is to demand that others believe as he does."

Ernesto responded, "I've been a believer in that religion now at war in Europe and which demands that some Christians murder others, and I've heard of those massacres of unbelievers in the New World. One wonders that the nature of religion is the demand to kill others."

The Scientist asked, "But can it be called a religion without a dogma? A single person must have authority to affirm its truth."

Ernesto said, "If you're asking whether that religion has a Pope, the answer is no, nor does it appear to need one. It must seem a small and confused thing to call a religion, but believers make it work for themselves, if not for everyone else."

Pierre remained unsatisfied by this explanation, but after their long, steep climb, the three riders reached the top of a high hill. Nodding, Ernesto explained that the expanse spread below them was the Hacienda Verdidad, the plantation of Don Benito Cerino. From where they stood the hacienda appeared impressively large, strongly built and carefully maintained.

Smiling with satisfaction Ernesto said, "Follow this road and you'll arrive at the main gate. Meanwhile, I'll continue to the home of my friend." Turning, he said, "It has been an honor to accompany you gentlemen, and in future I'll recall our journey with pleasure." From the back of his mule he reached to shake first the hand of Dr. de Montpellier and then Pierre. "May all of the gods shield you." He turned his mule and began his journey back along the path from which they had come.

When he was gone, Pierre asked, "Do you think there was any truth in his story?"

The Scientist shrugged. "Most likely just enough to keep it interesting. As to which parts were true I cannot even guess, but his injured leg certainly was not false. As for ghostly spirits, your guess is as good as any, but at least our time passed pleasantly."

The setting sun cast thick blue shadows and their descent along the steep hillside quickly put them into twilight. Reaching the gates of the hacienda they found its buildings shrouded in dark violet. The Scientist dismounted, walked to the gate and using a metal weight shaped like a cannonball that hung from a chain, he rapped hard. Pierre looked about to see that within the arch above the gate were painted, in gold-leaf and green, words which the Scientist translated as, "Follow your Leader." The Scientist was about to rap again at the gate when a small window beside the gate opened. "Who calls upon his Excellency, Don Benito Cerino, and for what purpose?"

"Please tell Don Benito that the eminent philosopher of natural science, Dr. de Montpellier, and his colleague, Pierre Chanceux, beg his hospitality."

The eyes behind the gate traveled from the Scientist to Pierre. "I will convey your message and return with his response." The window then slammed shut.

"Not exactly a warm welcome," Pierre said.

“We should not misjudge. This is an isolated location and undoubtedly Don Benito must preserve his security and the well-being of his guests.”

“Then I suppose we should be relieved such care will be given to our security whenever we’re permitted inside.” He did not intend to sound sarcastic and regretted his words as soon as he said them, but the Scientist smirked darkly and looked away.

Despite a veil of shadows Pierre recognized that, contrary to its appearance from the hill, on closer inspection the gate and walls were weathered and poorly maintained. Mortar between the stones had turned to moldy gray-green powder, climbing vines covered much of what was left, and undergrowth grew high against the walls. Paint on the wooden gate and its frame was chipped and peeling and in places was gone. He had turned to mention this to the Scientist when the bolt shot back and the broad main gate groaned open. The gate-keeper appeared.

In a deep yet thin and reedy voice he said, “If your Excellencies will follow me, Don Benito has asked that I offer you his hospitality. My name is Alonso and I am at your service.” Tall and dark-skinned, each of his bones seemed visible beneath skin which, despite the twilight, had a grayish cast. His coarse black hair sprang from the dusty gray skin of his skull in oddly spaced clumps and hung lank before eyes which were surrounded by dark circles and rimmed with red, making them seem infernally bright.

Leading their mules they followed Alonso on foot. A few steps within the gate they were met by another thin, dark-skinned man who took the reins of their mules and lead them off. Alonso said, “In the morning they will be returned to Phillip at the inn.”

With a note of surprise, the Scientist said, “So, you are familiar with our tavern-keeper.”

“He informed Don Benito,” Alonso said, “that he should expect your arrival.”

Despite the violet haze Pierre recognized that, although the broad, two-story building ahead once had been impressive, neglect had overtaken it. The veranda surrounding its ground floor was broad and deep, but descending vines wove an impenetrable web so that it was impossible to recognize windows and doors, and shadows cast its recesses into perpetual twilight. Even the stone stairs leading to the main door were covered, except for a narrow footpath at the center, with brittle, dead leaves and overgrown with withered vines. Dr. de Montpellier asked Alonso, "Do the guests of Don Benito reside here, or do they occupy another building?"

Alonso turned a doleful look at the Scientist. "His Excellency enjoys their company so he prefers to keep his guests near at hand. As well, this assures him of their comfort and security."

Pierre added, "A lot of effort seems spent on security."

"As is only right and proper for any host," Alonso replied.

"Such security," Pierre said, "suggests considerable danger."

"Our world may appear edenic, yet danger is ever-present." Alonso led them up the stairs to tall double doors. Opening them, a strong odor oddly sweet, the aroma of rotted honeysuckle mingled with a dry, dusty smell he could not name, overwhelmed Pierre and reminded him of the odor of the inn. When the doors closed behind them their twilight turned to nearly complete darkness. With windows only slightly brighter rectangles of gray, it seemed to Pierre they stood in a cave no one had entered for a long time. His eyes adjusted and he saw ahead a wide staircase that climbed into shadows he assumed was the second floor. The Scientist asked Alonso, "Does Don Benito maintain his laboratory in this building as well?"

"For reasons of safety another has been used for research. But after a recent fire, what little of our equipment remains is stored elsewhere. His Excellency is eager to reassemble his laboratory as soon as he can."

The Scientist said, "That is unfortunate. Still, perhaps we will be able to assist." Pierre was annoyed at that prospect but guessed it might ingratiate them with Don Benito.

Alonso led them up the grand staircase and at its upper floor another pair of tall, narrow doors stood closed. On the face of each was painted a circular figure in faded red, eyes wide and mouths grinning with protruding tongues.

"Please wait here," Alonso said. "I will inform his Excellency of your presence." He opened one of the doors and passed through closing it behind him. The corridor running left and right disappeared into utter gloom with closed doors along either side.

The Scientist glanced at Pierre and smiled. "The only certain cure for curiosity is time." Just then the door opened and Alonso emerged, closing the door quietly behind him.

"His Excellency offers his most earnest greetings. He remembers his friend Dr. de Montpellier with respect and pleasure and is grateful for this visit since his presence brings honor to his home. However, he regrets that at the moment he is unexpectedly indisposed. He asks that I accompany you to a room prepared to receive you. He further requests I assure you he will join you for the evening meal. He looks forward to a long conversation and he is eager to learn of your exploits."

"Tell his Excellency," the Scientist said, "we are grateful for his hospitality and hope his indisposition passes quickly. Please assure him we look forward to his companionship."

With a deep bow Alonso said, "Now, please follow me."

To Pierre's surprise, instead of turning to follow the corridor, Alonso led them back down the stairs and then out of the building. They crossed the dusty courtyard to a clapboard cottage painted dark green and several paces beyond the main building. Three wooden steps lead up to its door. From a pocket of his shabby trousers, Alonso produced a key and unlocked it. "His Excellency asks that you consider this your home for the length of your visit and arrange it to your comfort. I will return shortly with a light meal. He requests that you remain here until then. The hacienda is vast with many opportunities to become lost. Finally, he asks that you remember that the evening meal will be served one hour after sunset." Again he bowed and then left. They heard their door lock from the outside and looked at each other.

"Certainly an odd fellow," the Scientist said. "As to why we must remain confined, it seems to be assumed necessary."

Their room was narrow and tidy though its two windows seemed only to add to its gloom, as if nothing within could be seen clearly; a world without sharp edges or clear lines. The room included two beds against opposing walls and a chest of drawers. A circular table with three chairs stood at its center. Deeper shadows disguised corners and spaces where things might hide. Pierre chose a bed and lay down.

Reclining with his arms crossed behind his head Pierre said, "Not exactly as you described but certainly an improvement." Cracks in the ceiling above his head marked a spider web of fine white lines. He tried with his eyes to find a pattern. The near-darkness offered an invitation to doze and even though he struggled to keep them open, his eyes became heavy. He lifted himself onto his elbows to see Dr. de Montpellier lying on his back, eyes closed, his arms crossed over his chest and quietly snoring. He considered doing the same when suddenly the lock on the door clicked back and it quietly opened. He lay back down with his eyes slightly open. Alonso entered carrying a large tray, glanced at the Scientist and then at Pierre and placed the tray on the table. He lingered as if observing something but in the next moment he left, locking the door behind him.

When Pierre was certain he had gone he propped himself on his elbow again and glanced at the tray. On it were oily and glistening pieces of roasted meat beside a pile of bread slices. Drawn by the aroma of the gray-brown meat, he stood and reached for several slices of the bread and then returned with them to his bed. He sniffed at the bread, broke off a morsel and guessed it had the same sweet, dry odor of the room. He put the morsel in his mouth and began to chew. Glancing up he looked again at the greasy chunks of meat and felt himself drawn but then wondered why he hesitated. His ambivalence annoyed him, yet when his thoughts moved to the platter of meat, the impulse to reach for it turned into revulsion. He only needed to think of its taste on his tongue, its texture inside his mouth and grease on his lips, and a shiver of nausea passed through him which he could not explain. He broke off another piece of the bread and stuffed it into his mouth determined not to think about the meat.

He glanced over at the Scientist whose faint snoring was the only assurance he remained alive. Finishing the pieces of bread he was tempted to retrieve more but his eyes again began to feel heavy. He assumed his fatigue was the result of their long journey under a hot sun, so he laid down promising himself he would rest his eyes for only a moment. Almost instantly he fell asleep.

Pierre was only certain he was asleep because he was again in that room at the inn, except that the Scientist was replaced in the bed by Alonso. He laid in the bed with his eyes closed and his arms crossed over his chest. In a low monotone Alonso reviewed their journey to the hacienda, except that instead of repeating the story Ernesto had told, Alonso spoke of Chango and then spoke other names as if he was familiar with each and with their roles. Pierre was frozen into silence anticipating what he was about to hear, yet already oblivious to what he had just heard. This continued as if he was hearing a sequence of tales like some trail of time experienced as space. Then a sound he could not identify distracted him.

Certain this sound was not part of his dream Pierre opened his eyes to find that Alonso had entered the room. The Scientist was sitting on the edge of his bed and shaking his head as if determined to rouse himself. Alonso stood just inside the door speaking to him. It took Pierre another moment to realize that Alonso was inviting them to the evening meal.

When the Scientist finally looked up, there was a dark and haggard cast to his expression, and in their deep twilight his eyes seemed almost to glow. The Scientist assured Alonso he would be grateful for his company. Pierre wondered if eventually he would need even more luck than he already had.

CHAPTER SIX

ALONSO OPENED A pair of tall doors to reveal a long, wide table elaborately laid-out and bearing three lighted candelabra. The table filled the center of a dining room with tall, narrow windows along one side and a high, painted ceiling. A dozen, shabbily-dressed older men sat on either side of the table and all turned to watch Pierre and the Scientist approach. At the head of the table sat the man Pierre guessed was Don Benito Cerino.

"Dr. de Montpellier," this man said in a voice that seemed filled with sand, "too many years have passed, and yet seeing you now under my roof, those years suddenly drop away." His dark red silk military uniform included a stiff white collar that reached to his chin, bright gold buttons and gold braid trim. Around his waist was a wide black belt from which hung a gaudy silver scabbard with a sparkling sword hilt. He sat half-reclining in an enormous chair whose high back of dark blue velvet was topped by a crest of gold-gilt figures of a lion and an eagle. His black hair was long and thick and hung beside his face in greasy ringlets. His face was gray and hollow-cheeked, and his large dark eyes were circled in dark shadow to give him a haggard quality, while its narrowness, his sharp chin and hawkish nose all brought to mind a predator's gloomy stare. A weak smile rippled across his face.

With Pierre following, the Scientist passed behind the seated men until he stood beside the grand chair and its occupant.

Breathless with excitement, the Scientist said, "Don Benito, I am humbled that you recall our last meeting." He bowed nearly to genuflection. Pierre then noticed that just beside the feet of Don Benito, a small, dark-skinned man sat on a small, low chair and watched Don Benito's face as expectantly as a spaniel. Thin and wiry, the man appeared withered and yet ageless. Pierre guessed he was the hacienda's old retainer who Don Benito kept by his side for pity's sake. The Scientist introduced Pierre saying, "He has proved himself an adroit and determined companion. And his father apparently visited you; his name is Augustus Chanceux."

Don Benito's eyes widened and he turned a curious glance at Pierre, "Indeed he visited us briefly a year or two ago. Meeting the son of such an accomplished man is a particular honor." With a wave of his hand that seemed to demand effort, he gestured to a pair of empty chairs to his right. "Please join our humble meal."

"The simplest meal under your roof," the Scientist said taking the chair nearest Don Benito, "can only compare with a banquet under any other." His suppliant tone surprised Pierre and left him oddly uncomfortable.

"Babo," Don Benito said and Pierre realized he addressed the man crouching at his feet, "see that our guests are served."

The man sprang up as if he had been waiting to hear just those words. Grinning brightly he said, "It shall be done." He scurried through a door behind Don Benito's chair.

Don Benito then said, "But let me introduce you to your remarkable colleagues." Beginning with the man to Pierre's right, Don Benito named each along with the topic of his study. And just as Dr. de Montpellier had predicted, together these men represented a wide range of intellectual specialties. Occasionally during this introduction the Scientist made a comment or asked a question assuring the others of his own background. When Don Benito spoke of the man at the far end of the table who appeared younger than the others, he introduced him as Señor Antonio Barbaducci whose experiments investigated a substance found in the earth but which he claimed contains quantities of the Quintessence.

The door behind Don Benito opened and Babo emerged leading Alonso who carried two large platters of bread and meat. These resembled the platter left in their room, except these appeared piled even higher. Alonso's elbow bumped the Scientist's shoulder as he placed the platter before him on the table.

"Don't be stupid!" Babo screeched at Alonso. "Do the thing right! Do what needs to be done!" Alonso flinched at each word. Babo turned an embarassed grin at Don Benito. "Has your Excellency completed the introduction to your companions?"

Don Benito observed him with an indulgent smile. "It is likely our guests know us even better than we know ourselves."

"Not possible!" Babo screeched, then burst into cackling laughter. "No one knows as much as you do. That is why you are our master. The master of knowledge is the master of all!" He took Don Benito's hand and began to kiss it until Don Benito pulled it away.

"Understand that you are in the presence of your master's teacher."

Babo's eyes grew large. He turned to look at Dr. de Montpellier and then scrambled over to crouch at his feet. He studied the Scientist's face as if it was a map to something hidden.

To the Scientist, Don Benito said, "Please tell us what has brought you to our enclave." He then settled back into his chair.

While Dr. de Montpellier recounted their adventures, Pierre watched his companions who appeared to follow his account with a somnambulist's indifference. Each had the same grayish pallor and heavy-lidded expression to their eyes, as if each had come from a sick bed and not yet completely recovered. But when the Scientist described their encounters with the creature, eyes brightened and expressions became nearly animated. The Scientist was so deeply engaged in his tale he hardly glanced at his platter.

At the far end of the table, Señor Barbaducci appeared even more intrigued than his companions. His face seemed less gray-green, his eyes more alert and his attention moved about the room. Pierre reached for a slice of bread, and as he broke it into smaller pieces he noticed that Señor Barbaducci watched his movements. When the Scientist described the creature's attack on the convent, Babo from his place on the floor began to cackle and laugh. The others at table showed no emotion stronger than vague distress.

Glancing at the meat piled on his platter, Pierre found he still could not bring himself to eat any, so very slowly he continued to eat pieces of bread. The others watched the Scientist, but Señor Balbaducci watched Pierre with unnerving care. The Scientist then described the mutiny aboard the Esperanza. Babo began suddenly to pound his fist against the floor and angrily enough to stop Dr. de Montpellier's recitation. Don Benito appeared alarmed but regained his composure quickly.

"I hope," he said to the Scientist as if mildly amused, "you will forgive

Babo. He becomes agitated over any act of disorder."

"But Excellency," Babo said turning a pleading expression on the Scientist, "do you see they had no respect for their betters? They behaved as if they were the equal to their master."

It was the Scientist's turn to be confused. Addressing Don Benito, he said, "I did not know the Captain well but my impression was that he was a tyrant. Although I would not condone such an act, I did not serve under him and so was not the object of his tyranny."

These words simply made Babo more angry. "As God himself made that man captain, so he acts in the name of God and so his acts are God's will. As God is no tyrant, neither can his captain be a tyrant." He half-stood bringing his face close to the Scientist's. "There can be only one captain, just as there can be only one God, on earth and in heaven." He studied the Scientist's face while an uncomfortable quiet filled the room, as if all waited for the Scientist to admit his error. Tension pressed against everyone until Don Benito began weakly to laugh.

"Dear Babo," he said, "our guests have not come here to recite their beads. I am certain that his mind and his soul remain with God."

Babo turned to face Don Benito but instantly turned again to observe the Scientist. After another moment his expression softened. "His Excellency is all-wise and a perfect judge. Poor, stupid Babo is even more stupid then he is poor. The little that Babo knows he has learned from his master. As you were his teacher, you know even more than my master and so much more than me. Poor, stupid Babo, even more stupid then he is poor." He then began to laugh. He spun himself away from the foot of the Scientist's chair and began to cavort beside his master until smiles appeared on the faces of everyone at the table. Pierre glanced at Don Benito to see a withered grin that more resembled a grimace.

Suddenly Babo thrust his face inches from Pierre's. Searching Babo's eyes, Pierre realized the man was furiously angry. Babo's grin faded, as if something had appeared in Pierre's eyes. "Arrogance of mind!" he screeched. Pointing at Pierre he howled with laughter. "He thinks he is thinking!" Pierre felt Babo's breath strike his face and nausea suddenly filled him.

"Babo!" Don Benito cried, and his anger was as clear on his face as it was in his voice. "We will remember what it is we owe our guests!"

Whining and tearful, Babo scrambled back to his side. "Babo forgets. Forgive Babo, forgive Babo." He grabbed Don Benito's hand and sobbing began to kiss it.

Don Benito's expression softened. "The comfort of our guests is a matter of honor and we will do nothing to soil that honor." Tears glistened large in Babo's eyes.

"Poor, stupid Babo, more stupid then poor, more stupid than dirt, more stupid then a stone." Tears rolling down his face clung to his chin. Don Benito extracted his hand from his grasp and stroked Babo's head.

"Calm yourself, my friend, because I know these good people forgive you."

"Yes," Babo said turning to face the Scientist and then to Pierre. "Forgive Babo though he does not deserve it. His master is the best in the world, so Babo is the most fortunate of men."

Pierre glanced at the Scientist who seemed mesmerized by Babo's incantation. He then looked about to the rest of the table. All eyes were on the pitiable sight of Babo crouching at Don Benito's feet; all except Señor Barbaducci.

The Scientist turned to Don Benito. "You have heard our tale and what we have endured to reach you. All of the New World envies the facilities and colleagues you have gathered and are eager to hear of your many achievements."

But even before the Scientist finished, a crest-fallen expression came over Don Benito's face. "Be that as it may, there was recently a fire whose result has been disastrous. Precious equipment was destroyed along with notes and reports and so our research has had to stop. I have written to colleagues requesting assistance and I continue to hope that we will soon replace that which has been lost. Until then, however, we simply mark time."

"How tragic," the Scientist said in a tone so earnest that Pierre was startled. "I hope no lives were lost in the conflagration."

Don Benito sighed and glanced around the table. "Fortunately not, but this tragedy remains beyond our understanding and its cause eludes us still."

Pierre again surveyed his companions, and to his surprise the attention of each was turned away, as if the schoolmaster had asked who among them had prepared his lesson for the day. All except Señor Babalducci, who stared urgently at Pierre.

Dr. de Montpellier's sympathetic sigh was loud. "That is terrible news. But please allow us to help in any way we can."

Don Benito's expression brightened. "Simply your arrival has lightened our gloom and is therefore a prize of great value."

Babo leapt laughing. "His Excellency loves his teacher even more than he loves Babo. His Excellency wants his teacher to stay. Remain with us here, please say you will. Say you will remain with us forever!"

To Don Benito, the Scientist said, "As long as my presence proves useful." Turning he added, "But Pierre is determined to locate his father and I have promised him my help."

Babo turned and glared at Pierre. "Will you steal his teacher from my master? Do you dare to injure my master? My master is wise and he is wealthy and powerful and compassionate and a better man than your father. You are an ungrateful fool!"

"Babo!" Don Benito's voice thundered in the room. "How dare you insult our guests and soil my honor!"

At the sound of his name Babo fell limp as a rag doll to his knees. His retreat to the side of Don Benito's chair took only a moment. "Babo is a fool, Babo is a fool. Punish me, master, punish Babo the fool. Do anything you wish to Babo but do not send him away." He stared up pathetic and pleading at Don Benito.

Don Benito glanced down at him, closed his eyes slowly and sighed. "If their plans take our guests elsewhere, we will enjoy their company for as long as we can and hope they will return as soon as their task is concluded. Their company is precious, but we wish only to share as much of it as we can." He leaned down smiling and stroked Babo's head. Babo leaned his cheek against Don Benito's knee, his eyes glazed with devotion. Don Benito then gathered himself as if just recalling that others were in the room.

"Of course, Dr. de Montpellier," Don Benito said. "Yours is a mission of honor and mercy and we will detain you no longer than you wish to remain. But I invite you to discuss with these wise men the work they managed before our disaster. As you must recall, I am merely a dabbler, curious about all but master of nothing. Knowing my inclination to fanciful lassitude, I invited these men to carry on their own work, and my compensation has been to remain informed of their achievements."

The Scientist said, "I will be honored to do just that." The conversation with his old teacher seemed to enliven Don Benito. Babo, however, glared bitterly at Dr. de Montpellier until he saw Pierre watching, and then his hostility disappeared.

Don Benito sighed with frustration. "If only our laboratory remained available, we would have so much more to share."

"It is encouraging," the Scientist said, "simply to know that research continues and new facts will be revealed. With colleagues such as Señor Barbaducci participating, that research will continue even after us gray-beards have moved on." Pierre glanced over to see that the Scientist had emptied his own plate of meat. He wondered again how others found this food so satisfying they sucked the fat from their fingers. When his neighbor, introduced as Dr. Bartholomew, whispered asking if he could finish Pierre's portion, he shrugged and looked away. The sounds the man made as he ate assured Pierre his gesture was appreciated. He turned to see that Babo had observed their exchange, and his expression suggested more than curiosity.

Don Benito turned to the Scientist and Pierre. "After our meal we often enjoy a musical soiree. Babo has instructed our staff in the musical arts so as to provide light entertainment." To Babo he said, "Have they practiced sufficiently to perform well for us tonight?"

"I have encouraged them to make an extra effort. In the presence of our new guests they have even more reason to play well."

To the Scientist and Pierre, Don Benito said, "Our recital chamber is just down the hall." Though he had appeared shrunken in his throne-like chair, he unfolded himself to stand and his height surprised Pierre. Looking about, Pierre noticed that while each was of a different height and bulk, all shared a stooped posture, a haggard and hungry look and a seemingly sightless stare. But most disturbing, each face bore an expression of yearning, of endless desire and loss, as if each wished more of something he could not describe and whose absence was a soul-eating acid.

The men moved toward the door walking with a sort of convict's shuffle, as if shackles at their ankles shortened their gait so they could hardly lift their feet from the floor. Pierre turned to the Scientist, but he appeared resigned to walking in that same funereal pace. They took a long time to traverse the hallway and enter another large room.

The walls of this room were painted dark green and were unadorned except for dull-silver sconces each composed of three lighted candles hung a few feet apart to provide the room some brightness. The wood floor was bare but clean, and there was no furniture except for straight, high-backed chairs placed against three of the walls leaving the center of the room open. A chair against one wall was larger and more elaborate than the others with a thick cushion on its seat. Don Benito sat down in it with a sigh of relief as if he had walked far. The others took seats until only one remained between Señor Barbaducci and Dr. Bartholomew who, despite his bulk, had a face as haggard as a man marooned on a desert island. Pierre assumed this empty chair was for himself and sat.

By the time Pierre took his seat, several others appeared already on the verge of sleep, and for a few it was uncertain they continued even to breathe. Silence thickened until its constraint became irritating. But then, from a distance he heard a loud thump, like the sound of a knock against a huge and empty barrel. This was followed by another, and then another and then another, sounding at shorter intervals but also louder. Evenly rhythmic, these thumps were joined by the sound of thudding feet. As these sounds approached the door, all heads turned.

Babo appeared first carrying under his arm a narrow, open-ended drum, followed by a line of tall, strongly-built black men, each carrying a drum similar to Babo's but larger. Pounding out the rhythm of their steps, he crossed the open center of the room to the wall facing the seated men. The others took positions along that wall and behind Babo. Then came men holding metal horns, each of a different size and shape. Reaching Babo, they arranged themselves behind the men with drums. Babo struck a double beat and all became silent. With an expression of solemn seriousness he turned to face the seated men.

For a long moment Babo observed the seated men with a bitter grin. He raised his hand and brought it down hard on his drum, one-two-three-four. The drummers at the front of the group exploded in wildly furious pounding, each seeming to play a slightly different pattern as all patterns wove together by Babo's steady pounding; a complex rhythm, frantic and so loud it beat against Pierre's chest. Looking around, where before Pierre's companions appeared a comatose, nearly narcoleptic audience, each now twitched and trembled as if tiny insects crawled beneath their skin to control the wires and springs of their bodies. Hands twitched, arms rose, shoulders swayed, heads tipped and nodded, and for a few their eyes rolled up into the backs of their heads. Pierre was startled to find these pounding beats all but irresistible.

Gradually their tempo increased and patterns of beats wove into even more complex arabesques so that sometimes one drummer's pounding became prominent, and then another arose to overwhelm the last. Rhythms blended so that one called and another answered, bringing to Pierre's mind the sight of sparrows flying about each other in thrilling loops.

Those weaving rhythms soared and spiraled to cast a demented hysteria over the room while scintillating flourishes added to the delirium. The others twitched and wriggled in their seats with increasing agitation, their heads rolling with mouths open and tongues hanging out. Pierre could not resist tapping out an accompanying rhythm with his feet. The drums became still louder in a cacophonous crescendo but then with a flourish suddenly stopped.

Grinning, Babo turned to give an approving nod to the musicians ranged behind him. The men seated around Pierre each seemed to collapse in their chairs, motionless as marionettes with their strings cut, eyes closed and hardly breathing, as if the music had deepened their coma. Even Dr. de Montpellier appeared shrunken and exhausted. Pierre turned to find Don Benito sitting half-curled in his chair staring at Babo with a confused expression. Babo returned his look with a self-satisfied smirk before he turned back to the musicians.

He nodded once and pounded out a quicker series of beats which the drummers repeated. He pounded out another series of beats and the drummers again repeated it. On the third sequence, they repeated it, but at its end the men with the metal horns placed them to their lips and, with a startling blast, began to play. Pierre found the sound piercing and yet sinuously mesmerizing. The horns were pitched high, yet with the accompaniment of the drummers the music acquired a sensually swaying and looping intimacy. Though these rhythms were simpler, the complex phrases and accents of the horns thrilled Pierre. He looked again to see his neighbors even more urgently excited. Hands were raised, arms moved back and forth, heads shook, shoulders rocked and bodies trembled, and even Don Benito appeared possessed, though to Pierre's surprise, tears coursed down Don Benito's cheeks. Anguished sadness so reshaped his face he appeared desperate for consolation and possessed by such heartbreak that Pierre had to turn away.

But Pierre watched Babo pound frantically on his drum while staring at Don Benito, as if the more tears that fell, the harder Babo played, and he would be satisfied only when his eyes had been wrung dry.

The horn music approached a hypnotizing frenzy, players prodding each other with melodic and harmonic extravagances so that no phrase emerged without elaboration, thrilling commentary or distorted reflection. The music became more frantic and the gestures of those in their chairs, swaying and moving and twitching, matched their furious passion. Groans and wails escaped one throat and then another, as if a delicious pain coursed through their limbs that filled their throats and they must burst forth. Louder and brighter, the music resonated within the room until it nearly hurt Pierre's ears. Like a shower of tiny slivers of glass suspended in the air, the music from the horns seemed propelled swirling about the room by the pounding drums. Crashing against the bare walls to wash back and boil against the next wave, this music churned and swirled and throbbed until the next crashed.

Don Benito remained curled in his chair, his hands, fingers spread wide over his eyes, as though he could not tolerate the vision before him.

The wailing horns and pounding drums seemed to play endlessly, phrases changing into new shapes from which more sprang to bounce from the ceiling. The drums thundered with a sound so penetrating it seemed to pierce Pierre's mind without passing through his ears.

And then, at the end of a near-vertical crescendo, all sound stopped. Pierre wondered if he had fallen suddenly deaf; the silence that followed was absolute. He discovered himself panting and breathless. His neighbors had collapsed in their chairs like shapes made of mud not yet hardened. Babo passed a pleased grin from one musician to the next like a master craftsman approving his creation. But when his eyes reached Pierre his expression changed to a betrayed anger of such bitterness Pierre feared he might be attacked. But that expression passed as quickly as it appeared.

Babo turned to those behind him and muttered. Each then put down his instrument and, one by one, approached the benumbed men still collapsed in their chairs. As if prearranged, each took a man under the arm who groggily stood and allowed himself to be led away.

One musician approached Dr. de Montpellier and the Scientist looked up as if relieved. Another approached Pierre. Pierre hesitated but then allowed himself to be helped from his chair and led with the others out of the room.

In the hallway, Pierre saw only the Scientist and his companion before him, the others apparently had been led elsewhere. At the end of the hallway they descended stairs and passed through a side door that led outside the building. Crossing the plaza in a velvet and fragrant darkness, a single burning torch mounted nearby cast hard shadows as they reached the cottage.

Inside, the Scientist was led to his bed and Pierre to his. Each sat down on the edge of his bed and the two musicians left. Pierre waited until the door closed. He called quietly to the Scientist but got no response. He was about to stand when a noise at the door stopped him. With his eyes nearly closed he watched one of the musicians re-enter the room carrying a tray heaped as those earlier had been. He placed it on the table and left. Pierre waited until all was quiet and then stood and went to the Scientist.

Dr. de Montpellier lay motionless. Pierre reached down and shook his shoulder calling his name. He seemed deeply asleep, but after a moment his eyes fluttered open. He looked about as if startled to find himself in the room and breathed heavily as if he had climbed from a deep pit.

"Ah yes," he said groggily, "and what are you doing here?" His eyes slipped from Pierre's face and traveled around the room. "And why are we here?"

"Where do you think you are?" Pierre asked.

At the question, a crease formed between the Scientist's eyes and he looked about and then up again at Pierre. "Somewhere else?" He spoke as if unsure the question could even be answered.

"Remember the music?"

His face took on a pinched and confused look. "Possibly," he said. And then, "Perhaps."

"What do you remember?"

"Waves?" the Scientist asked. "And clouds?" Still confused, he added, "Colors?"

"Do you remember returning here?"

He propped himself up on his elbow and sniffed the air. "I am hungry." He looked around and spied the heaping platter. His eyes brightened and he sat forward. "Thank goodness." He stood and shuffled to the table. "I am starving."

"How can you eat that stuff?" Pierre asked, finally certain there was something wrong with the food which he could not identify. Even the bread did not taste quite right.

Breathlessly the Scientist said, "I could eat this at every meal." With startling agility he stood suddenly, took a seat at the table and drew the platter of piled food in front of him.

"You already have," Pierre said. The sight of the grease already sparkling around the Scientist's lips and on his fingers made Pierre's stomach queasy. "And more."

Dr. de Montpellier quickly ate portions of what had been on the platter and leaned back with a glazed look of satisfaction. He asked Pierre, "Are you sure you cannot be tempted?" But his greasy grin already had begun to fade as his breathing slowed. He looked blearily at Pierre for a moment as if he no longer recognized him. "Perhaps I shall take a nap and rest my eyes." He stood and shuffled awkwardly to his bed, fell back into it, and within moments his breathing had all but ceased.

Pierre looked from the recumbent Scientist to the nearly empty platter. Something was going on, something he should think about and perhaps worry about. But it was late and he felt tired and even a little hungry. He looked at the pieces on the platter wondering if a bite or two would be all right and then he would not feel so hungry. He leaned toward the table reaching for a piece of meat when he heard a sound at the door. In a moment he returned to his bed.

The door opened and Alonso entered silent as a dream and stepped to the table. He glanced at the platter, at the sleeping Scientist and then at Pierre. After what seemed a long pause he took up the platter and retreated to the door. When the door closed Pierre opened his eyes again. But Alonso stood beside the closed door, the platter in his hand and watching Pierre. "I apologize for having awakened you," he said quietly. "I hope all is satisfactory."

"Yes," Pierre muttered, "but I'm very tired." Closing his eyes he let his head drop back.

"Please accept my apologies and return to your rest."

Pierre muttered something and then became silent. The door opened and closed. He thought to wait until Alonso was truly gone, but at some moment he drifted off to sleep, though he did not realize this until he awoke the next morning.

He opened his eyes to see a strip of golden light spread from under the door. He looked across to the Scientist, who remained motionless and in the same position as the last time Pierre saw him. He sat up to find he had a throbbing headache that resembled a hang-over. Despite that pain, he stood. Unsteady on his feet, he reached the door and opened it surprised to find it unlocked. The blast of sunlight struck his eyes and nearly drove him back inside. Instead, he stepped out and closed the door behind himself, as if to erase any path of retreat. If he hoped to discover how much luck remained, this seemed the best way to do it.

CHAPTER SEVEN

UNDER A BRIGHT, sharp sun the hacienda appeared so different from that twilight world Pierre recalled of the evening before that he had to pause. The main building stood surrounded and overhung by large and leafy trees, and though hardly a dozen steps from their cottage, it remained shrouded in shadow as if sunlight could never reach it. On either side and set back stood two smaller buildings that resembled storage sheds. Further back lay the remains of a building destroyed by fire. Except that these appeared to have lain in their abandoned condition longer than Don Benito had described.

Pierre appeared to be the only person moving about. By the position of the sun he guessed it was approaching noon yet he saw no one performing the usual chores. From what he recalled of the tavern, simply feeding all the people he had seen would keep a staff busy. Yet aside from the chirping of birds and buzzing of insects this silence was complete. Despite his throbbing head he descended the stairs and approached the burned-out building.

Thick timbers of its walls and roof lay charred through and black, collapsed into a chaotic pile confined within a low pale stone foundation wall fractured like broken teeth. Yet the debris appeared to have been left with no effort to uncover or rescue anything within. Pierre circled the ravaged foundation searching for fragments to assure that scientific work had been done there; shards of broken glassware or bits of worked brass or fragments of burned documents. But brown-green weeds and thinly sinuous vines flourished undisturbed right up to the ruined wall's edge, while amid the debris small trees had begun to grow. He walked its perimeter bothered by what he did not see and could not find. He turned then to look back toward the cottage, but still no one moved about.

Beyond and to either side of the fractured foundation stood several partly-tumbled down shacks; a small stable and corral that enclosed no horse, a barn from which no cow lowed, a fenced patch of weeds that held no chickens, a pig-sty dried out and vacant. Pierre realized he had seen no cats lurking about and had heard no barking dogs. The more of all this he saw, the less he recognized. He guessed that since they did not raise their own livestock they must buy meat from local farmers. Some distance beyond the buildings stood a tall and broad fieldstone wall festooned with vines and creepers. One of the gates in its wooden double-gated entry stood partially opened; beyond it a glowering forest began. Glancing back toward the main building Pierre decided he was well-hidden and stepped through the gate.

A worn and dusty path that began at the gate was canopied by more tall trees and wound deeper into the forest. On either side the undergrowth stood as dense as a green wall and Pierre could see little beyond its edge. He walked a short distance until he recognized that odor of cooking meat. He realized then that he had smelled it since soon after he left the cottage, and in this open-air that odor seemed peculiarly repellent. But he also found it odd that food was prepared so far from the hacienda. He wondered if it was a special type of game animal that had to be prepared quickly or in some exotic away. Further ahead he saw, drifting above the tree-tops, a faint cloud of brown-gray smoke. The path he trod was well-worn and by its use appeared to lead to something important, so he continued to follow.

But after a few paces, Alonso stepped suddenly from the green wall at the edge of the path, and bearing a somber expression he blocked Pierre's way. "The young master is both curious and brave, for only the brave or the foolish enter alone a forest they do not know."

"Where's that smoke coming from?"

Without turning he said, "Undoubtedly a hunter's campfire and certainly nothing to concern us." He remained as if rooted in the path. "Dangerous beasts have been reported in these forests. It would be best for you to return to the safety of the hacienda. The mid-day meal will be served soon and your host would regret your absence."

Pierre hesitated as if there might be a way to continue their conversation, but then nodded and smiled. "I'm sure you're right. I certainly don't want to offend our host." Resigned that he had learned what he could, he turned and retreated along the path. He was tempted to turn to see if Alonso continued to watch him but decided it did not matter. Even if he was not visible, Alonso remained there somewhere and watching.

He reached the gate to find it closed, but pushing against it he was relieved it had not been locked. Although beyond it no one appeared to be moving about, someone had closed it and that could not have been Alonso. He continued toward the cottage determined to ask the Scientist about all of this.

He had just stepped from behind the foundations of the burned building to approach the cottage when Señor Barbaducci appeared. Recognizing Pierre, he seemed intent on speaking to him. He approached with a slow and shuffling gait, as if he were decades older and kept his path within the shade of the buildings and trees. Pierre wondered if sunlight caused him particular discomfort. Señor Barbaducci stopped within a pool of shade at the edge of the main building and held out his hand to Pierre in greeting. Pierre stepped into the shade to accept it.

"The festivities of last evening," Señor Barbaducci said, "left me no opportunity to speak with you. Dr. de Montpellier's account of your adventures was positively thrilling and I hoped to hear more about them. I was especially intrigued by your encounter with that marvelous beast and I am even more eager to learn about that."

Pierre shrugged. "It remains a mystery to me and I have no insight to offer. My most earnest wish is that I never see it again while my goal remains to bring my father home."

"You are too modest; son of an eminent mind, you must share in that eminence."

"Thanks for that compliment but you speak as if you know my father's work."

Señor Barbaducci looked away as if staring into the past. "I am proud to say that I enjoyed the good fortune to share a table with him some years ago."

Pierre was startled and his mind filled suddenly with questions. But one leapt to the front of his mind. "Exactly where and when did this take place?"

Barbaducci's expression darkened with suspicion but in another moment that expression faded. "Of course, you wish to locate that man who is your father. Pardon my hesitation, but certain interests would prefer he remain silent and his work fade into the twilight. I met with him in Naples just more than two years ago and apparently some time after his visit here. He was reluctant to discuss it, but he appeared to be working for a rather curious individual."

A rush of emotions left Pierre stunned. "And how did he seem to you?"

His expression again clouded as if the question had no appropriate answer and Pierre became annoyed. Señor Barbaducci appeared to struggle as if this question left his mind in a thick fog. Pierre resented this annoying fop, fortunate enough to enjoy a conversation with his father yet unwilling to share its details. Barbaducci suddenly grinned with embarrassment.

"One becomes comfortable approaching every question in its most abstract form, and so it becomes easy to forget that a question about the weather is often simply that. Let me assure you he was in good health and good spirits, although certainly an irascible fellow, furious I suppose, with the silence concerning his achievements. And to be fair, had I accomplished as much as he, I would likely be as irritable. But, with a few glasses of wine he became the most enlightening of men. Though his understanding of these matters appears weak, his theories are imaginative and complex and so his research remains intriguing, particularly considering the level of detail his experiments have achieved. I feel privileged to have been in his company and shared his ideas. When I met with Leibniz and told him of our meeting, he pressed me for details."

Mention of that name suggested a memory for Pierre, though he could not relate it to anything. "Thanks for your kind words and for sharing the memory of your meeting. It's been more than a decade since I last saw him and I think about him often."

Señor Barbaducci bowed with a gracious smile and squinted up at the sky. "The heat of the day has begun to tire me. Perhaps you will join me inside for a cooling glass of wine."

Pierre hesitated. "I should check on Dr. de Montpellier, but perhaps we can meet later."

Barbaducci bowed again and retreated toward the main building. Watching his progress, Pierre spied, framed within a window beside the main door, the face of Babo, and he was certainly watching. Startled and then annoyed, Pierre turned and retreated to the cottage.

He entered to find the Scientist sitting at their small table eating. At the sound of his entry Dr. de Montpellier looked up as if he had been caught doing something embarrassing. Defensively he asked, "And just where have you been?"

Pierre laughed. "While some slept the morning away, I was out exploring."

"Fascinating," the Scientist said. His attention returned to the food on his plate.

"Actually, it was." He was about to describe his encounter with Alonso but then thought better of it. Instead, he recounted his meeting with Señor Barbaducci. He summarized their conversation and his report of having met with Augustus. The Scientist's thoughts had seemed entirely taken with his food, but suddenly he looked up and turned to Pierre.

"Did he say where and when their meeting occurred?" For the first time since they arrived, the Scientist seemed almost curious and so, Pierre told him what he had learned.

"Did he name the man Augustus worked for?" When he said he had not, the Scientist's brow furrowed and his attention seemed to drift away. "That would be useful to know." Then as if remembering that Pierre stood beside him, he added, "Perhaps you should resume your conversation to learn that detail."

"Why's that so important?"

He looked at Pierre and opened his mouth as if to speak, but instead he yawned, his eyelids sagged and his eyes lost their focus. "I thought I had slept well but now I can hardly keep my eyes open. Our travels and late evenings perhaps have caught up with me." He stood carefully from the table. "This languid atmosphere is hard on my nerves. Unless my presence is needed I will take a short rest." With that he dropped onto his bed, slowly turned onto his back, and within moments his eyes closed and he breathed quietly.

The sight of the Scientist sleeping tempted Pierre to do the same, but his question puzzled Pierre. What point might there be to knowing who Augustus worked for several years before? He stood from the table intending to search out Señor Barbaducci when he heard quiet knocking on the cottage's door. He opened it and Alonso filled the frame. "Pardon this intrusion but Don Benito begs your indulgence and asks if you would spare him just a few minutes of your company."

Recalling his encounter with this man in the forest earlier, Pierre hesitated. Alonso continued, "If I may suggest, Don Benito is urgently curious to hear of your remarkable adventures. It might appear rude to ignore such a small request from one's host." With that steely point to his invitation Pierre knew he was trapped. Glancing back at the sleeping Scientist, he followed Alonso. They crossed the courtyard and entered the main building and Alonso led the way up the stairs. At the closed doors he knocked quietly. Responding to a sound from within he opened the door and stepped back to gesture Pierre inside.

Don Benito sprawled in another broad, high-backed chair. Sitting on a small, three-legged stool by his right knee, Babo watched with a humorless grin as Pierre entered. Don Benito's smile followed Pierre as he took a seat in a chair directly across from his own.

"Thank you for coming," he said, but in such a weak voice Pierre assumed his ailment had grown worse. "I feared your explorations would occupy you for the rest of the day." Pierre winced, wondering how literally he should take the man's remark. "As you have discovered, aside from our research and our musical diversions, ours is a prosaic life and each other's company is all we require." Babo scrutinized Pierre as if his slightest twitch might reveal something dangerous.

"In brief," he continued, "we hardly qualify as adventurers. Except, of course, in the realm of science; adventurers of the mind, if you will. So I confess your adventures as Dr. de Montpellier related them sounded thrilling, and I cannot imagine a more terrifying experience. So I invited you here foremost to know better the son of our colleague in study, but also to hear more about this amazing creature."

Babo's sudden, high-pitched cackle startled Pierre. "Can you honestly expect us to believe such a fantasy? Because it is scientifically impossible."

"Now," Don Benito said soothingly, "do not insult our guest. As the companion of our dear friend, we will not contradict him no matter how unlikely his story seems. In any case, it appears he absolutely believes his tale." Casting a narrowed look on Pierre he asked, "Do you?"

Pierre hesitated, certain that nothing he said would be believed but determined to report what he knew to be true. "If that tale had been told to me by someone else, I'd be just as skeptical. So, let me assure you that everything I've said is an honest report of what I've seen. I can't explain the creature, but it has the power to destroy ships and the appetite to devour men, just as I described. And I've watched it climb out of the sea to crush buildings larger and sturdier than this. I've seen all of this with my own eyes, though I hope never to do so again." He spoke so earnestly that his report left him breathless.

Don Benito smiled as if Pierre was a schoolboy who had successfully recited his lesson, but Babo watched him with deep suspicion and then snorted. "Just a hair-raising tale told by a drunken sailor to entice some young woman to bed. Can you expect us to believe even a shred of it?"

"My account is no invention!" Pierre felt himself becoming angry. "Unless you accuse me of lying!"

Don Benito said, "Our guest is correct, Babo. Apologize at once for your unjust remark."

"But Excellency, this can only be a fabrication."

"You have accused him of lying, Babo, and you will apologize immediately!"

He cast a bitter look at Pierre. "I hope the bluntness of my speech has not caused you any insult, for none was intended. Kindly forgive my words." His smile resembled a snarl.

Don Benito said to Pierre, "Now, with your permission I would like to learn details of this creature. For example, how tall does it appear to be?"

"I claim no deep knowledge but I assure you it stands taller than the highest mast of the largest ship I've ever seen. And I only report what I have seen with my own eyes."

Babo laughed with acrid derision but said nothing.

Suppressing an oddly frightened glance toward Babo, Don Benito continued, "Would you say it more resembled a lion, or a bull, or perhaps a griffin? In short, what beast that we might recognize does your creature resemble?"

"No creature I've ever imagined. Its color is a dark green mottled with brown and appears to be covered with wide, thick scales like that of a fish. Its head is nearly square and its snout is broad but short. As best I can judge, it resembles an enormous lizard with huge and powerful hind legs that enable it to stand almost upright. Its forelegs are much smaller and tipped with huge claws that it uses as a man might use his arms."

"And I suppose," Babo added with angry good humor, "you will tell us it has a tail with which it hangs from trees and ensnares men."

Annoyed, Pierre said, "The creature has a gigantic tail but I know of no tree large enough for such a feat, nor have I seen it use its tail to grasp men as a snake might. But its tail is so large and powerful the beast used it to destroy stone walls not less than ten feet thick and just as easily as you push over an ant hill. I repeat, I've seen with my own eyes everything I describe."

The two men studied Pierre with bemused astonishment as if, regardless of the truth, they saw that at least Pierre believed his own words. Don Benito asked, "And did Dr. de Montpellier observe all of this as well?"

"Yes, although days before those events, I encountered the creature and Dr. de Montpellier was not present." He then described the beast's attack on the Bristol and his narrow escape. They listened with obvious astonishment as he recalled his shipwreck and the terrifying ordeal at sea that ended with his rescue by the Revenge and introduction to Dr. de Montpellier.

Don Benito studied him with a quizzical expression while Babo's suspicion appeared simply to deepen. Don Benito said, "Your tale defies every other I have ever heard. I congratulate you for your resilience and determination. Your adventure can only bode well for your future. Clearly, you are destined to survive when others do not."

"Yes," Babo said, "a survivor." He laughed then, a sound that enraged Pierre.

"I've only spoken of what has happened and as accurately as I can. But Alonso suggested you have information about my father. For nearly ten years my mother and I heard nothing from him, so you can understand that I'm eager to learn what I can."

"Ah," Don Benito said turning to Babo, "finally a topic far more congenial and rewarding." To Pierre he said, "Augustus Chanceux visited us briefly just more than three years ago and before the great fire. Over several days he impressed us with ingenious experiments and demonstrations. He is remarkably skilled and as nimble with his hands as with his mind. According to his own report he had been investigating the phenomenon of lightning, convinced of some relationship between the lightning and certain curious properties of amber when rubbed with soft cloth. He also seemed intrigued by a curious type of stone he carried with him which he had found in his travels."

"Cranky and ill-mannered," Babo blurted out, "he insulted his Excellency every day."

Don Benito's laugh was tinged with embarrassment. "Babo exaggerates. Men with complex and insightful minds often neglect their social skills. It was a privilege to enjoy his company despite its brevity."

"Had he not left when he did," Babo said, "I would have chased him away myself."

Don Benito's laughter this time contained more irritation. "We have never asked a guest to leave and would not have done so of your father. Babo shows an excessive sensitivity to my honor, but it would have been a larger insult to ask him to leave than to exercise patience on his behalf." Babo looked angrily up at Don Benito and this confused Pierre. Don Benito extended his hand and Babo sneered but remained silent.

"With respect," Pierre said, "in what way did he give insult?"

"He refused our hospitality!" Babo said, and so furious his shoulders shook as he half-stood from his stool.

Again, Don Benito smiled indulgently. "Our meals apparently did not agree with his digestion."

"He demanded fruit and vegetables and cheese and bread," Babo snarled. "As if there is any manliness or honor eating such filth."

"Babo's fastidiousness extends to many areas," Don Benito said and then yawned as if that issue was of no interest. "I repeat my gratitude for this interview, but I begin to feel the need for a brief rest." He stood slowly. Babo sprang from his stool to take his place by his side. "Thank you for this diverting conversation. I hope to continue it, since so many questions remain." From Don Benito's side, Babo gestured that Pierre had been dismissed and should leave.

Outside in the corridor, Pierre paused beside the door and listened but heard nothing more than the quiet closing of a door within. The building then fell silent. He descended the stairs reviewing what he had learned about his father's visit and wondering what it had been like for him to have been there. Beyond the front door he crossed the veranda to reach the top step of the stairs when a voice behind him quietly asked, "Did you enjoy your interview?"

Pierre turned to see, deep in the shadows of the veranda, Señor Barbarducci sprawled in a large chair. And in the chair beside him sat Dr. de Montpellier. They smiled at him like conspirators. Pierre wondered if this was luck or merely its counterfeit.

CHAPTER EIGHT

DESPITE THE PASSAGE of years, Augustus's studies continued to elude Pierre and he resented this. Dr. de Montpellier had answered some questions but his knowledge was second-hand and indirect. Despite what he had learned from Brother Guarino at Port Royal, Pierre remained on an island of speculation surrounded by the ocean of his own ignorance and the tide was rising. As uncomfortable as his interview with Don Benito had been, as he descended the stairs to the front door, Pierre felt he had learned something and so was optimistic.

Augustus had been determined to control Nature. Not as a necromancer, because he abhorred every mysticism, but as a modern scientist working with modern instruments that generated useful information in support of a rational hypothesis. When Don Benito mentioned his devices, Pierre recalled those tricks that had mystified him and Gabriella.

A trick Augustus seemed particularly fond of was to rub a piece of amber with a bit of rabbit fur and then bring the tip of his finger close to the amber until a bit of light leaped to his finger. He repeated this trick once, telling Pierre to hold out his finger. When the bit of light leaped to it, Pierre felt a sharp pain and cried out.

Augustus snarled for him to stop whining before he explained that the light was miniature lightning. Pierre was old enough to know that lightning was loud and bright, while that bit of light could hardly be seen and made no sound. Augustus recognized that Pierre was baffled by this, so he rubbed the piece of amber again and sprinkled filings of iron from a packet onto the table. To Pierre's confusion, when he passed the amber over the lint, instead of giving off a bright spark, it followed the amber, and when he brought it close, the filings jumped from the table to cling to it. Augustus leaned back with his arms folded. “So what do you think of your old man now?” he asked. Pierre knew this was a trick but he could not see how it had been done, or why, so he said nothing.

From what Pierre had heard, his father had impressed Don Benito and his colleagues with these tricks, though at least they had understood his hypothesis. Adding what he had heard with the little he remembered, all of it appeared to want to cling together, like the filings wanting to join the amber and suggest a pattern. That pattern, like a ship in the fog, seemed about to emerge so that in the next moment he would see what his father saw. But at the sound of Señor Barbaducci’s voice, that hope evaporated like a dream at waking.

“Enlightening,” Pierre responded. “Hope I’m not interrupting.”

“On the contrary,” the Scientist said. “my prattle has nearly put him to sleep.”

Señor Barbaducci said, “In fact, our conversation has been illuminating and I am grateful.”

To Pierre, the Scientist said, “Though I envy the time you spent with him, tell us what our host found to talk about for so long?”

“He seems fascinated by the creature.”

“Ah, yes,” Barbaducci said, “your infernal beast. I confess I have asked Dr. de Montpellier about it and he has offered some intriguing conjectures.”

“Its nature and origin,” Pierre said, “remain obscure. At least to me.”

The Scientist added, “But we are certain of its power and its taste for human flesh.”

Señor Barbaducci said, “Speculation on my part is mere ignorance. You have seen the creature while the rest of us lack even that knowledge.”

“If distance is a criterion,” the Scientist said, “then Pierre is the only one of us qualified to offer a reasonable hypothesis. He has all but touched the creature.”

Pierre shrugged. “I know as little about it as I would if I’d simply seen a drawing.”

The Scientist said, “Fortunately for everyone, the creature has returned to wherever it came from, and we can only hope it remains there.” Turning back to Pierre he asked, “What other topics came to light in your conversation?”

“He was generous with his memory of my father’s visit. Apparently he enjoyed it more than Babo did.” He was surprised to see Señor Barbaducci wince at the mention of Babo.

As if to disguise his discomfort, Señor Barbaducci said, "I am curious as well to learn about his visit."

Pierre said, "My ignorance about his work embarrasses me, but I recall his demonstrations of the aether effect and apparently he repeated those during his visit."

Señor Barbaducci said, "What interested me was his assertion that certain black stones concentrate the aether swirling around us. He claimed their power could only be the result of intense contact with the aether." He glanced about, embarrassed. "Of course, we had consumed several bottles of wine by then, but he insisted a material connection must exist between the lightning, those stones and the amber effect." He shook his head. "He confessed these were mere intuitions but he was confident the proper instrument would provide evidence."

Pierre asked, "Did he think the stones are physically changed by contact with the aether?"

"He was evasive, admitting that physical examination had revealed nothing. He claimed that new combinations of lenses had been developed in Europe and he seemed confident that with such a device he would identify changes in those stones, especially since contact with the Quintessence must leave a mark on any sub-lunar object. The search for such a device may have been the reason he traveled to Europe."

Pierre said, "I'm impressed he felt confident enough to discuss so much with you, and I'm grateful for having shared it with me."

Señor Barbaducci looked away. "I am an imperfect scholar in these matters. Whether it was because my curiosity coincides with his, or simply because I did not laugh at his speculation, he seemed to feel sufficiently comfortable to share ideas for which he could provide no proofs."

Pierre asked, "And do you have some other knowledge of the natural sciences?"

Before he could respond the Scientist turned to him asking, "I am curious to know how you found yourself on this fair island." Señor Barbaducci shifted uncomfortably in his chair but then his expression softened.

"That is an unlikely tale which I will trim of extraneous details and simply say that I did not arrive where I had at first intended. Having completed studies at university, a business acquaintance of my father's suggested that his brother in Marseilles would use my knowledge of languages and mathematics. For this reason, my uncle sent me to Naples to negotiate with a Spanish business acquaintance." Turning to Pierre he added, "That is where your father and I enjoyed our conversation. But after just a few months, a letter arrived announcing that my uncle's business had collapsed and his creditors were taking everything. Expressing his regret, he enclosed money sufficient for my return to Paris, and I planned to do just that. Yet I was young and now unemployed in Naples with money in my pocket. On a whim I bought passage to Barcelona to visit a friend with whom I had shared many happy hours at university. When I located him I learned he was sailing for Mexico City where he expected to raise a fortune. Although he knew I had few resources, he suggested it would be a greater adventure if I joined him. He convinced his parents I would be an asset to his venture, so they provided for my passage as well. Two days before we were to depart, my friend's father took me aside asking that I keep his son from falling into ungodly ways. This seemed an innocuous promise, but within two months my friend had discarded his good intentions and adopted a life more corrupt than even I could have imagined. Like all great cities, Mexico City is a wonderful place if one has money, and a terrible place without. He begged me to remain and share his resources even though he seemed the only one who did not realize those resources were running out. Instead, I asked him to underwrite my journey to Havana. It was while in Mexico City that I learned of this community of scientists. I tried to convince him to join me, but he had taken up with a charming though worthless young woman, and had given himself over to a measureless debauchery. He expressed regret I wanted to leave, handed me a fistful of money and wished me a safe voyage. As I had only the resources for the journey here, I accepted necessity and have remained. Regarding my friend, I have heard nothing of him but continue to hope he has abandoned that life he had adopted."

The Scientist nodded. "Life is nothing if it is not an adventure. I congratulate your decision to join Don Benito's colony. Have you managed to participate in research?"

"Alas, our research has all been verbal and hypothetical. You have noted that ours is an oddly somnambulistic colony. With the laboratory destroyed, several of us meet each week to discuss possible projects, though our meetings have become erratic and difficult to repeat. One has been scheduled for later today. Perhaps I will manage to entice you to join us." He leaned forward and quietly added, "Fresh blood would infuse our efforts with an energy we seem to have lost."

The Scientist smiled. "Then we must certainly join your meeting."

Pierre asked, "Has there been progress rebuilding the laboratory?"

Señor Barbaducci's expression became wary. "Despite appearances, there seems an active effort to discourage just that." He looked from the Scientist to Pierre in a way that seemed to suggest something, although Pierre could not think what that might be.

But this information surprised Dr. de Montpellier. "Has Don Benito's enthusiasm gone?"

"On the contrary," Senor Barbaducci said. "He remains keen to encourage although others appear less enthusiastic." He glanced about and leaned forward. "I will share this with you; the cause of that fire was never identified. Certainly a lack of explanation does not mean a nefarious design, but several wish we knew its cause to assure ourselves it was not intentional."

Dr. de Montpellier asked, "And who might have been responsible?"

Señor Barbaducci looked at him alarmed. "Did I say the fire had been intentional? Because I have no reason even to guess that was the case."

The Scientist said, "From what I recall of Don Benito, such a thing seems impossible. However," he continued turning toward Pierre, "perhaps there is a way we can resolve that."

Señor Barbaducci looked hard at the Scientist who returned his gaze with equal determination. "We should return to this topic later and with greater profit." He yawned. "For myself, at the moment I believe a brief siesta is in order." He stood. "This has been a most diverting conversation. And I hope you will join our colloquium this afternoon."

Barbaducci had turned toward the main door when Dr. de Montpellier said, "One more question; I cannot account for a certain lethargy that seems to affect all of us. Perhaps there is a miasmal swamp nearby that is the source of certain vapors."

Señor Barbaducci nodded. "That is an interesting speculation; we may find an opportunity to test." And then he was gone.

Dr. de Montpellier turned to Pierre. "Over the years I have found that one is often told more than one hears." He yawned. "But there is no need to speculate about that lethargy."

"Like the aether," Pierre said, "we know that it exists because it must."

The Scientist turned to Pierre. "Perhaps we should follow the doctor's example." He stood. When Pierre did not join him, the Scientist said, "I will join you at the mid-day meal."

Then Pierre stood. "I'll walk with you as far as the cottage." They descended the steps and crossed the sun-bleached courtyard. Approaching the cottage, the Scientist quietly said, "I confess I am certain that something about all of this is not as it appears."

Pierre stifled a laugh. "I wondered how long it'd take you to figure that out." He was tempted to say more but he knew his sarcasm would not be appreciated.

Within a few steps of the cottage door, in a low voice the Scientist said, "This seems a fine opportunity to survey that workshop. Care to join me?"

Surprised, Pierre nodded. "You've guessed my intention."

They ambled toward the devastated building where they made a slow circuit as the Scientist looked it over. At its back they found themselves out of sight of the main building. The Scientist said, "Your sarcasm has never been helpful." Pierre responded with a quizzical glance and the Scientist completed his thought. "You, too, have noticed an uncanny atmosphere here. Something is in the air and I cannot guess what it might be or who is responsible. I find myself empty of ambition. Something is being disguised and I cannot put my hands around it. This devilish atmosphere drains me of every faculty." He glanced about as if the source might be near.

Pierre said, "And since you seem curious, I'll tell you that earlier I had an interesting encounter." As they moved among the out-buildings, Pierre described his meeting with Alonso and what he had seen.

When he finished the Scientist nodded. "All of this deserves further examination."

Pierre gestured in the direction he had followed earlier. "The gate's that way." At the foundations he said, "Notice the condition of this debris; as if no one has tried to rebuild."

The Scientist said, "We should continue quietly since we are likely being watched." Reaching the gate they found it locked. "Perhaps your adventure displeased someone."

"Think there's another gate?"

"We will only learn that if we search."

Under the hot sun and to the droning buzz of insects, they followed the wall past a tangle of undergrowth and reached a corner of the wall that turned back toward the main house. A few steps beyond more undergrowth they discovered a gap where part of the wall had crumbled.

"So much for our security," the Scientist said. Pierre pushed through bushes and vines and climbed over. The Scientist awkwardly followed.

Pierre led him back beside the wall to that path beyond the gate leading into the forest. "I didn't walk very far before I met Alonso."

"We should know soon enough if anyone is lurking in these bushes."

Further along the path they detected that strong odor Pierre had noticed earlier. Pointing to the plume of smoke rising ahead, he whispered, "I met Alonso near here." To his annoyance the Scientist yawned deeply.

"Something," the Scientist confessed, "in this cursed atmosphere causes one to tire after the least exertion."

"It can't be due to a lack of sleep."

"Let us proceed in silence and I promise I will not yawn."

Almost immediately they heard voices ahead. They slowed and followed at the trail's edge. When the voices became clear, the Scientist signaled Pierre to stop. Invisible ahead they heard a voice that could only belong to Babo. "Andre captured more so why is there a delay?" Pierre glanced at the Scientist.

A second voice responded, "It is these visitors." This voice was unknown to Pierre but he assumed it belonged to one of the musicians.

"Damn your excuses!" Babo said. "Do what needs to be done! I will deal with the visitors in due time. Follow my instructions and leave the rest to me."

Certain this voice belonged to Babo, Pierre was startled to hear him speak with such authority.

"We will make the effort," the other voice said. "But we need help."

"Fool!" Babo said in a voice rich with acid contempt. "These woods are filled with slaves. Do what needs to be done or plan to join them."

"As you wish," the second voice said clearly intimidated. "But we still need help."

“The others have their own work. You will receive no help. Am I clear?”

Pierre heard no response and guessed this conversation was over and Babo would take this path to return to the house. He touched the Scientist’s arm and nodded toward a clearing just beside the path. They stepped into it and hid. A moment later, Babo appeared. They watched him pass and disappear toward the hacienda. When he was gone they stepped back onto the path.

Pierre looked in the direction the voices had come from. The Scientist said, “Is this wise?”

“The only way we’ll find out what’s going on is to see it ourselves.”

“Suppose we are discovered,” the Scientist said. Pierre realized the man’s eyes were heavy with sleep.

He said, “Go back if you wish, but I mean to resolve this.” The Scientist hesitated and that surprised Pierre. “Go,” he said. “I’ll take care of myself.”

“No,” Dr. de Montpellier answered. “If I turned back now and left you here, I would never be able to sleep.” And then he smiled.

Pierre led them silently along the path. Ahead they heard the same voice as earlier speaking quietly and now joined by at least one other. A few steps further, he discovered he could just glimpse through the screen of undergrowth the source of that smoke. He signaled the Scientist forward because he did not want to believe his own eyes.

The clearing was surrounded by a stockade of tall, thick upright logs and the dusty path led directly into its entrance. Within, suspended along the inside wall hung butchered human body parts. Two men passed back and forth, sometimes empty-handed, but often carrying something that resembled a human arm or leg or part of a torso. Pierre turned to Dr. de Montpellier as if hoping for contradiction. The Scientist stared with his mouth open.

Stunned and dazed, Pierre stepped back and something under his heel snapped with a crack. A man passing the opening to the stockade stopped to look in their direction while they crouched down and waited. He continued to stare, his expression fixed as if he saw Pierre watching him, and Pierre held his breath. After a moment a voice within the stockade called out, “What’s wrong?”

When he said nothing, the invisible voice said, “Babo will be angry if our delivery is late again.” Forcing himself to turn away, the man moved from the entrance and out of Pierre’s view.

The Scientist whispered, "If you have not seen enough, I have." Pierre felt him step back. Wrenching himself from the sight of those hanging limbs, Pierre silently moved back to join him. Soon they reached the path out of sight of the stockade. They followed it quickly, until they were certain they could no longer be heard. Then, as if only tension and the fear of discovery had held them back, each of them vomited violently into the bushes. Panting, the Scientist said, "We must return to the hacienda and prepare to leave."

"What about the others?" Pierre asked. He was thinking about Señor Barbaducci but even as he came to mind he asked, "Do you think any of them know?"

"What is there to know? Why would they even wonder?" When Pierre turned, all evidence of the Scientist's somnolence had disappeared. Pierre began to speak, but the Scientist stopped in the middle of the path and turned.

"No more questions," he said with a decisiveness that startled Pierre. "Those must wait until we are far from here. My concern now is with Don Benito."

"You think he doesn't know what's going on in his own kitchen?"

"I can only hope that is so. Otherwise, all is lost and he will perish with the others, as he should. We must return to the hacienda before our absence is noticed and tell no one what we have seen."

Making their way back over the broken wall they found the courtyard still abandoned and walked directly to the cottage. Inside, each began to gather their things when the door suddenly opened. Filling its frame was Babo, and behind him stood two other men.

"Leaving us so soon?" Babo's twisted grin did not reassure Pierre. "It would be rude to depart without saying farewell to your generous host." He paused. "Please come with us. I am certain Don Benito will be sorry to hear of your decision."

Pierre glanced at the Scientist. The Scientist said, "Thank you for your advice. As I think about it, you are quite right. We will gather our belongings and join Don Benito shortly."

Babo's smile disappeared. "My suggestion may seem unkind, but a man of your advanced years might forget his intention, as appears to be the case here."

The Scientist smiled with embarrassment. "You have other responsibilities and we do not wish to detain you. Perhaps you can return in half an hour to escort us to Don Benito."

"As you suggest," Babo said, "I have many duties and my time is valuable. Instead, let me assign Pablo here," he nodded to one of the men behind him, "to remain until you have finished. He will make certain you do not become lost on your way to Don Benito."

The Scientist looked from Babo to Pablo and then to Pierre. "As I think of it, that is a very reasonable arrangement. You have our assurance we will join Don Benito very soon."

Babo eyed the Scientist but then smiled. "I shall inform him to expect your arrival. If you need assistance Pablo will be happy to help." He turned to Pablo and spoke in a language comprised of clicks and grunts so exotic Pierre could not even guess its meaning. Then he left.

They resumed gathering their things but after a moment, the Scientist turned and addressed Pablo in French, asking, "Do you speak French?" Pablo's expression of confused surprise appeared to make the Scientist angry. He asked again, "Do you speak French?" Pablo's surprise turned to alarm. This time with an impatience that bordered on anger, he asked, "Do you speak French?"

When his request still drew no response he muttered in French to Pierre, "I assume this man has been told to not let us from his sight, so we have only this opportunity and I will say this just once. We will conduct ourselves as if we knew no more than the others. Stay beside me and follow my lead." He stared urgently into Pierre's eyes. "Remember that the hardest thing is to behave as if you do not know what it is you know." He paused. "Be brave; our knowledge is our only weapon but used wisely it will be enough. If you understand, simply nod." Glancing at Pablo he nodded. The Scientist turned to Pablo as if to say they were ready to meet with Don Benito.

They followed Pablo across the courtyard and into the main building. In the reception room at the top of the stairs they found Don Benito sitting in his regal chair but slouched far down, his eyes half-lidded and appearing even more somnolent than Pierre had seen him earlier. It took a moment for their presence to penetrate his lethargy, but then his smile grew. Babo said to him, "Our guests have decided to depart. It seems their affairs will take them far from our company." Pierre turned to see that another man he remembered as one of the musicians stood at attention beside the door and watching.

Don Benito's grin faded. "It is rather late in the day to begin a journey. The nearest village is several hours away. Surely, it would be best if you began your journey at daybreak."

"Exactly my suggestion, Excellency," Babo said. "I could only wonder what might so suddenly cause them to leave." He turned to face the Scientist.

"Of course," the Scientist said with surprise. "Once again, my impulsive disposition has caused offense. A spontaneous decision to visit, followed by an impulsive decision to depart; we thought only of ourselves. I hope to assist Pierre locate his father, and since it appears we have gleaned as much information as we can here, my thought was to continue his pursuit. But there I failed to consider the offense I might create. As you suggest, the hour is hardly appropriate to begin a journey, so we are grateful for your saving us from a journey made more dangerous by the approaching night. So happily we will enjoy your hospitality for one more evening."

"There you are, Babo," Don Benito said with lazy relief, "a perfect ending to an all too brief visit."

Babo said, "Let me suggest, Excellency, that in honor of our guests we organize a special dinner to mark their departure and convey our regret they must leave us so soon."

The Scientist said, "That is too kind. We would prefer to depart with the least disruption, so allow us to take our leave as unnoticed as our arrival was sudden. Famed for your magnanimity, permit us this small favor."

"His Excellency will hear nothing of it," Babo said with surprising firmness. "Dine with honor tonight and depart in the morning with our regret and best wishes."

Pierre turned to Don Benito and he was startled to see the man appear intimidated by his servant's announcement. But Don Benito gathered himself in a moment saying, "Surely you can allow us this gesture of respect and friendship."

The Scientist bowed deeply. "As that is your wish, we can only oblige. Meanwhile, we are rather tired and request a period of rest to prepare for the evening's activities. With your permission, we will return to the cottage."

Don Benito was about to respond when Babo spoke up. "Excellency, our guests have had no opportunity to spend time with the fine minds gathered here. As they are about to meet, perhaps our guests can be persuaded to address their meeting. It would be unfortunate for the others to miss a chance to hear from Dr. de Montpellier. Would you agree?"

Don Benito looked from the Scientist to Babo with a concern that caught the Scientist's attention. Dr. de Montpellier said, "I can only offer our gratitude for such an honor but I have no remarkable ideas for these men. Still, if you believe I can advance their research, I am eager to do so."

"Excellent," Babo said without turning to confirm Don Benito's agreement. "Your colleagues will be happy to hear your thoughts."

"Undoubtedly, I will benefit more from my participation than they will."

Don Benito's confused look passed from the Scientist to Babo and then back to the Scientist. Sensing an agreement had been reached, he smiled. "I am pleased you can accept our invitation." Turning to Babo he said, "Arrange for them to join the others."

Babo turned suddenly upon Don Benito with an expression of impatience, but in an instant it melted into acquiescence. "Of course, Excellency, leave everything to me. It is time you retired to your rooms for your siesta."

"Thank you, Babo. You are quite right, I am suddenly rather tired." Don Benito carefully stood. Smiling once again to Dr. de Montpellier and Pierre he said, "Though I regret I will not join you, your colleagues will enjoy your participation. Meanwhile, I look forward to this evening's festivities." Bent like a man twice his age, he stood taking Babo's outstretched arm and shuffled toward a side door.

Babo turned to the Scientist and Pierre. "If you gentlemen will follow Aurelo." He nodded toward the man silent beside the door. "The others have already begun to gather."

The man named Aurelo led Pierre and the Scientist through the main door, and reaching the corridor they turned to follow it nearly to its end. Pierre recognized that, whether he wished for it or not, once again his luck was about to be tested.

CHAPTER NINE

WITH AURELO LEADING, they arrived at the room where they had witnessed the musical presentation. Inside, a long table stood in the center of the room with chairs along both sides and most were already occupied. Seated at the head of the table and gloomily facing the door was Dr. Bartholomew.

All heads looked up as they entered but most betrayed only a sleepy disinterest. Among them sat Dr. Zachariah, Señor Barbaducci, and Brother Flavius. Looking about, Aurelo said, "These gentlemen have been invited by Don Benito to participate in your meeting." Message conveyed, he turned to Pierre and the Scientist. "Until dinner." He bowed and then was gone.

To Dr. Bartholomew, the Scientist said, "Forgive our interruption but we have only just learned of this meeting. We are flattered simply to join this group of remarkable minds. Please continue as though we were merely curious observers."

Despite this assurance, Dr. Bartholomew's broad, pale face flushed bright with embarrassed confusion. He looked down to a large book open before him and flipped pages as if trying to regain his place. "We had just begun to discuss the intriguing notion of Democritus's atoms." He licked his thick lips several times. Glancing toward the thin man on his right midway along the table he said, "Because, aside from Dr. Zachariah here, we find ourselves in some confusion. Perhaps there is a something you can add."

Choking back his annoyance, Pierre found this gathering pathetic, resembling a group of old men snoozing under a tree. The Scientist said, "My imperfect understanding of that complex concept can only spread darkness instead of light."

Dr. Bartholomew tried to summarize their discussion and those points still unresolved. Dr. de Montpellier appeared to follow his explanation with a fierce curiosity.

Still, all this left Pierre appalled. He could not force from his mind the revolting sight they had just seen and was eager to abandon these educated dullards to their fate. Ignorance of science was nothing compared to an ignorance that was diabolical but had not left them compelled to its resolution.

Yet, to his surprised confusion, Dr. de Montpellier joined in their discussion offering insights and quoting ancient authors as though all was as it appeared and he had not seen what Pierre still could not force from his mind's eye. Their discussion touched principles that also applied to Augustus's experiments, but Pierre's curiosity about those had vanished. Recalling Babo's account of Augustus refusing their meals, Pierre wondered if he had guessed what Pierre now knew to be true. Was that what had led Augustus to flee and so earn Babo's contempt? His father left the hacienda before the fire but Pierre wondered whether what he had seen within the stockade was somehow related to that fire though he could not surmise how this horrific state of affairs could have come about.

His anger simmered into a furious panic and he struggled to resist flight. Despite his mind's revolt, Pierre heard questions worthy of discussion and occasionally his curiosity about atoms and the void resurfaced until his thoughts returned to what he had just seen. The Scientist had insisted they must leave the hacienda as soon as possible, yet he was prepared to remain and participate in this meeting. As if tiny snakes flowed through his veins, Pierre struggled to remain in his chair. The deception the Scientist seemed determined to act out frustrated him until anger clotted in his throat.

As the others prattled on about atoms, Pierre anticipated their return to Havana where they would notify the authorities. He assumed that, even with Don Benito's exalted status, at least a few in the city would be eager to punish the miscreants responsible. Thinking this he remembered Phillip and wondered if somehow this corruption had already reached the city. If that was the case, it was likely this villainy went even deeper than he could guess.

Several times Pierre was tempted to interrupt and insist they needed to leave, but the Scientist was so deeply engaged in their discussion he wondered if somehow the Scientist had forgotten what they had just seen.

The door suddenly opened and Alonso filled its frame. He looked about with an impatient disdain. "Don Benito apologizes for this interruption and asks that I remind you the evening meal will be served shortly. Please reconvene in the dining hall. He looks forward to your presence." He grinned as if his invitation was an order in disguise and they all knew it.

Dr. Bartholomew cleared his throat. "Our topic will remain unresolved, but on behalf of all here I thank our newest participants for their help. I declare this meeting adjourned."

Even those who had appeared to be sleeping looked up. To Alonso, Dr. Bartholomew said, "Please assure Don Benito we will arrive promptly."

Alonso again looked about as if to confirm their agreement. "I will convey your words exactly as you have stated." He departed leaving the door open behind him.

As they filed out of the meeting room, Señor Barbaducci said, "I do not recall an occasion when his summons was so urgent. Can we suppose he has an announcement to make?"

Dr. Zachariah said, "That seems the implication."

Brother Flavius added, "Perhaps the devices from Granada finally have arrived and we will resume our experiments. It would be a wonderful relief to return to the laboratory; this talk is interminable, and I for one am heartily ready to resume work."

"We will resist speculation," Señor Barbaducci said, "especially as I find myself suddenly very hungry."

Dr. Zachariah said, "We can at least be grateful to our host that we have never lacked for sustenance." Then he laughed.

Señor Barbaducci said, "In my experience I have never been better-fed." Hearing this, Pierre's stomach began to churn. He glanced at the Scientist who dolefully returned his look.

Even those who had appeared asleep during the colloquium looked around with bright eyes at the announcement of the pending meal, and several moved so eagerly they nearly overtook the leaders of the entourage.

Entering the dining hall, they found candelabra lighted among the places laid even though twilight had not yet faded into darkness. Those who had not joined the colloquium were already seated and watched the door to the kitchen. A drowsy atmosphere seemed to cast a blanket of labored breathing over the room. Oddly, the table servants stood lined against opposite walls, their faces empty as if awaiting orders they were certain would come. Others passed through the room without apparent purpose, except to recount diners and note who was present.

Between appearances of scurrying servants, Pierre turned to the Scientist and in a whisper asked, "After what we saw, why are we still here?"

With a darkly determined voice he responded, "There is one thing I must know."

Pierre was about to ask what that was, when the side door opened and Babo appeared followed by Don Benito. He led Don Benito to the tall, padded chair at the head of the table and then took the smaller chair beside him. His grim expression turned first to Pierre and then to the Scientist, but then turned a bright smile to the rest of the table. Servants appeared one after the next carrying platters piled with sizzling meat and thick slices of dark bread. Pierre could barely keep horror from his eyes. When a platter was placed before him, he had to look away as an icy wave of nausea passed through him.

The others, however, immediately began to eat what had been put before them with unembarrassed enthusiasm. From his chair beside Don Benito, Babo smiled watching the food consumed. Even Don Benito, eyes half-hooded with sleep, ate as if he could not fill his mouth quickly enough. But when Babo's gaze turned to the Scientist and Pierre, his smile was replaced by a suspicious snarl.

"It appears," he announced as if speaking to the entire table, "our newest guests remain unsatisfied by our humble fare." His sarcastic tone even attracted Don Benito's attention, who looked up sleepily from his platter, first at Babo and then at Pierre and the Scientist.

"I hope," Don Benito said slowly, "there is nothing amiss."

Dr. de Montpellier looked about embarrassed. "Perhaps we consumed too much at the mid-day meal."

"This seems unlikely," Babo said, "since neither of you joined us." Though apparently unnoticed by the others, the edge of his voice startled Pierre. He reached for the large, pewter fork on the table by his right hand as if about to begin to eat.

"As a matter of fact," the Scientist said, "we found the opportunity to visit your kitchen this afternoon. It was, I assure you, illuminating." A growl entered his voice as if he was determined to be heard clearly.

Don Benito looked up seemingly distracted by the conversation but Babo glared at the Scientist. "That could not be possible," he said. "I was busy there all afternoon; had I seen you I would remember."

"Oh, but I must contradict. We looked around quite a bit." The Scientist paused. "But perhaps you are right. As I think about it, it was not the kitchen but the abattoir we visited. You know; the stockade in the forest where bodies are butchered and skinned before broiling."

Babo no longer tried to disguise his anger. Don Benito seemed finally to notice a debate in progress and turned to Babo. "What can he be referring to?"

"I cannot say, Excellency, because I cannot know. The forest is deep and has many mysteries. I was not with him and do not know where he went."

In a voice soft with concern, Don Benito said, "Dr. de Montpellier, I would be grateful if you explained to what you are referring."

"I assumed my explanation was unnecessary since I believed you were already aware of it. I am therefore greatly relieved to discover I was wrong."

"I beg you," Don Benito repeated now seeming concerned, "please explain yourself, for I would not ask about something I already knew."

"Excellency," Babo said, "this man is a fool who flaunts his ignorance as knowledge. He knows nothing." Don Benito turned to Babo with an expression of confusion and surprise.

The Scientist said, "I will simply tell you what we saw, and you may judge its worth. Pursuing a curiosity we followed a path that led into the forest. We had not walked far when we came upon a stockade. Its gate stood open and we were free to observe. Within a short time we saw what neither of us could allow ourselves to believe. We waited and watched in the hope we would see something to prove us wrong. Unfortunately, that did not happen." He stopped speaking and sat back.

From his chair at the far end of the table, and as if something in the account, or perhaps its tone, left him suddenly alert, Señor Barbaducci said, "Please tell us what you saw."

Dr. de Montpellier hesitated. "Don Benito, from our arrival I was impressed not only by the quality but also the amount of meat served at every meal to so many men. After all," he continued, looking along the length of the table, "there are quite a few of us and our appetites are considerable. Without giving this matter much thought, I assumed we would find nearby a sizable corral of animals; pigs or goats or sheep or even cattle. But we have seen none of those. So, let me ask where you find such portions of meat."

Don Benito looked drowsily around until his eyes set upon Babo. "Explain to Dr. de Montpellier how we are supplied."

The fury on Babo's face forced his words through clenched teeth. "Local farmers provide us with fresh meat every day for which they are generously paid." Though he remained seated he panted furiously.

The Scientist said, "I would like to believe that, Don Benito. Unfortunately, what we saw suggests something far more disturbing." He hesitated and turned to face the rest of the table. "With our own eyes we saw, hanging from those walls, the limbs and parts of human bodies!"

The silence that followed his words was absolute; as though the weight and significance of those words only gradually made its way through the air to enter each fogged and befuddled mind.

Babo's sudden laughter exploded to cut through the silence. Don Benito, a sharp glitter suddenly in his eyes, turned to him. "What can he possibly be talking about?"

His cackling laughter echoed about the room. "Excellency, must I answer such an absurd assertion?"

Don Benito asked, "But what could he have seen that could lead to this confusion?" There seemed as much doubt in his eyes as in his voice.

"We both saw it," Pierre added. His heart pounded in his chest. "We stood several minutes watching, heard him issue orders and then watched him leave."

"How can I respond," Babo asked, "to an accusation I know is not true?"

The Scientist said, "He described what we saw as the body parts of other slaves."

"It is impossible to refute such scurrilous delusions," Babo said. Laughing, he sat down.

"I remind you," the Scientist said to Don Benito, "that we both saw this. But tell me this; how much are these natives paid for what they supply?"

Don Benito looked down at Babo. "I am assured they are paid well."

The Scientist continued, "And shall I surmise it is Babo who distributes these payments?"

Babo stood again. "Finally, we learn the real charge; a man such as I cannot be trusted to execute his master's orders."

"With respect," Don Benito said, his tone suggesting his self-assured arrogance had returned, "financial wrong-doing is the least of these allegations."

"But Excellency," Babo pleaded, "what but jealousy of your trust could lead to such a suggestion?"

"I wonder that myself," Dr. de Montpellier said.

Don Benito looked about the room as if a resolution to the question might float in the air. "As there remains some daylight, we should follow Dr. de Montpellier and discover how his mistake could lead to his gruesome suggestion."

Babo turned suddenly and with one nearly invisible gesture slipped Don Benito's sword from its scabbard and thrust it through his chest. Pinned upright to the back of his throne, Don Benito's eyes filled with pain and surprise. In another moment, eyes still open, his head arched back with a quiet gasp. Señor Barbaducci half-stood, but Babo's glare forced him back into his chair. Others at the table looked up stunned but remained motionless.

With a vicious grin, Babo stood over the dying Don Benito and addressed him directly. "Such a proud man, son of a proud race and so certain you are superior. Your pale skin endows you with all the gods permit a human to possess. The rest of us are left to your disposal, to do with as you wish since you are our superior and know what is best."

Don Benito's pitiful eyes could not leave Babo's face while bloody foam appeared at his lips. Babo leaned forward until his face was inches from Don Benito's, and for a moment it was as if they were alone together. "Something must be carried and we carry it. You want land and ours is available. What else do we have? What is left for you to steal? So when you find yourself hungry, why not eat us? Is our flesh not as good as that of your pigs or goats? At least we have the good grace to spare you the effort of the chase, and die quietly."

Babo's manic laughter cut brightly through the air. With startling agility he leapt onto the center of the dinner table and began to dance. Nimble as a machine, he tipped with his toe each of the dinner platters and their contents into the laps of the diners. "You can enslave us," he said tipping a plate, "steal our land," and tipped another, "rape our women," and tipped another, "murder our children," and tipped another plate, "force us to build your churches," and tipped another, "whip us to grow your food," and tipped another, "even force us to worship your God." He tipped several more plates and then stopped. With mock surprise he asked, "But you cannot eat us?" He paused to survey the table. "Is this where the grand hidalgos find their limit? Can it be that our flesh is so vile it is even unworthy of your lips?"

Suddenly, the room filled with a blinding silver flash accompanied by the crack and dying rumble of thunder. Sounding like a cascade of pellets, rain began to beat loudly against the windows. Babo looked about, but then turned back to Don Benito. "You see, Excellency, even your god recognizes the justice." Don Benito's eyes gradually closed though his mouth continued to move, as if there were words he must expel before death. Grinning Babo said, "Go ahead, old man, we are all still listening."

Don Benito's eyes fluttered closed and Babo began to straighten when beneath the hissing torrent of falling rain there was a loud, dull thud that was not thunder but so powerful it rattled the objects on the table. All including Pierre and Dr. de Montpellier looked up.

Babo turned to the men standing against the wall. "Take them!"

In unison each stepped behind one of the seated diners, grabbed with one hand the hair of the man seated before him, and pulled back exposing his neck. In their somnolence their eyes merely rolled back, but otherwise each remained docile and motionless. Only Pierre was quick enough to stab blindly back with his fork to strike the hand trying to clutch his hair. That man screamed and released him, but Pierre had already turned and stabbed his fork into the forearm of the man clutching the Scientist. Together they shoved backward pushing aside the men behind them. With three steps they had passed the befuddled and pleading eyes of the others and approached the door.

Babo screamed, "Stop them!" and for a moment, Pierre and the Scientist hesitated. Hopping down from the table he moved toward them when the ground thudded and shook again, and this time louder. Then they heard a roar like that of an enormous and enraged animal. Pierre recognized this sound instantly, and it left him even more frightened than he was of Babo.

As if the sound had released them, Babo looked again at his men. "Finish them!" he said. Pierre and the Scientist stood frozen at the door. With a single simultaneous motion knives appeared flashing and then blood in scarlet blasts arced from those throats high and bright into the air. But before Babo and his accomplices could survey their work, the ground shook again, followed by another screeching roar, and this sound was still closer.

Grabbing the Scientist's arm, Pierre dragged him through the door. Behind them Babo screamed, "Stop them!"

He led the Scientist along the corridor and down the stairs. The sound of feet pounding angrily followed. Beyond the main door, they dashed into a cascade of pelting rain that fell in silver sheets as flashes of lightning and explosions of thunder surrounded them. They splashed through mud to cross the plaza and pass through the main gate where they followed a slick path upward and into the forest. Pierre paused to glance back.

Waving Don Benito's sword above his head half covered in blood in sheeting rain, Babo led his cohort to pursue them and they were catching up. Then they all heard that roar again, a screeching, bellowing sound full of fury and rage and drawing closer still. Needles of rain beat against Pierre's face as he looked up. Despite the rain and darkness, above the tops of the trees and beyond the next hill, the massive head of the beast suddenly appeared, and his yellow-green eyes met Pierre's. Pierre knew now that his luck had finally run out.

CHAPTER TEN

BABO AND HIS MEN stopped and turned to see the creature tower over them and they froze where they stood. But Pierre knew better. Clutching the Scientist's arm he pushed through the undergrowth and then they began to climb. Silver flashes of lightning revealed a hill ahead. Pursued by the sound of the creature's roar, the crash of falling trees and the added screams of terrified men, they climbed through the rain until they reached a level space where they stopped to look back.

With furious roars in pursuit of Babo and his henchmen the creature crushed and collapsed each of the buildings of the hacienda. As a chicken snatches seeds from a barnyard floor, it grabbed up between its jaws one screaming, writhing body after the next casting trembling shadows against a black sky. Pierre watched all of this in terrified memory of the assault on the Bristol. But when he saw Babo caught within the creature's jaws rise in silhouette he enjoyed an unnerving pleasure. Against that black sky, the creature swayed and Babo's limp arm gestured toward his men as if he was ordering them to follow.

The panting Scientist said, "I would prefer not to join them." Pierre wrenched himself from the grotesque sight and they resumed climbing higher. Thick undergrowth forced them to crawl through mud, between bushes and over rocks slick with rain. Screams of those men dying behind them gradually became sporadic.

The ground began to rise more steeply, and despite his effort the Scientist fell behind. Pierre tried to keep him close yet the creature drew still closer. When finally he reached a rise that put him above the treetops, he stopped to locate the creature. The Scientist caught up but then sat down hard and spoke with rasping gasps. "This weakness can only be the result of that corrupt food. My legs have no strength, I can hardly draw a breath and my head swims."

More tree limbs crashed and their sound drew closer. Looking back, Pierre discovered that the creature had turned toward them. "It's following our trail; we need to move faster."

"Following us?" the Scientist gasped. Wide-eyed, he got shakily to his feet. "We must climb beyond those hills and onto the other side."

Pierre followed a mud-clotted path higher as the Scientist struggled to keep up, but the sound of the beast drove them both. Draped by darkness they reached ground covered by large rounded stones and stumbled. The Scientist called out, "We must move faster."

Despite the slick stones, Pierre pushed ahead, and grunting and gasping the Scientist followed. Tree branches whipped at Pierre's face, his hands were cut by thorns and by rocks when he fell, but he was reassured by the rustle of bushes that the Scientist still followed. The ground rose suddenly and so steeply that Pierre could only continue on his hands and knees. Then he spied something on the side of the hill that appeared in deeper shadow. He called out, "Looks like a cave."

At the possibility of shelter Pierre scrambled until he found himself crossing another slope covered by small stones that slid under his feet. He tried to climb faster as he heard the Scientist reach this gravel, though by that sound the Scientist's progress was slow. He climbed further until the field seemed to level. Standing upright he sprinted to the opening of the cave looming black ahead. Again he stopped and looked back. Now merely a black shadow, the Scientist crawled on his hands and knees over those glistening black stones. Suddenly, the head of the beast loomed up, its yellow-green eyes glittering by a flash of lightning. Within a few steps of the cave the Scientist turned to look back in horror and then cried out to Pierre, "Go, go!" Pierre hesitated but then sprinted into the cave.

Just within its shelter he stopped and turned to watch the creature's head descend, jaws open, toward the Scientist. He heard his own scream reverberate within the cave just as the Scientist screamed, until its jaws closed around him. Illuminated by a crystalline flash of lightning the beast lifted its head and between its jaws the Scientist rose in the air. It tipped its head back, opened his jaws and he disappeared.

Suddenly furious Pierre leaned down grabbing rocks that came to his hands and hurled them at the creature until it roared and turned its head toward him. He turned and dashed deeper into the cave. The creature roared its frustration and that sound shook Pierre's body to his bones.

Within the cave's shelter he stopped to catch his breath. Using its clawed forelimbs, the beast scratched at the edges of the cave as if determined to widen its opening. Within the cave, rocks and dirt fell, forcing Pierre back. It clawed and more rocks fell and he moved further back hopeful the cave was deep enough.

Eventually, the beast gave up clawing and brought its snout noisily to its entrance and Pierre assumed it smelled his presence. He turned back to peer deeper into the cave and saw only black. Moving, he sensed the cave grow higher and wider around him. He glanced back to see the head of the creature fill the entrance. Guessing himself now safe he sat down on the cave floor. The creature's roar echoed around him as it might inside a cathedral.

Though Pierre would need to follow the cave to be certain, he hoped it extended far into the hill. After a time he stood and, with hands outstretched, cautiously stepped forward into its darkness. His foot struck what he hoped was a rock, he stumbled once and then again, until he decided to slide his feet along the sandy cave floor. Whenever his foot struck something, he used his other foot to reach beyond it. For what seemed a long time he continued forward until the entrance behind him appeared a deep violet spot on a black curtain, and then he felt safe enough to stop. He found a low boulder and, with his back against it, he sat on the sand.

Reaching his hand up to touch his face, his fingers came away wet. He guessed it was rain or perhaps water dripped from the cave ceiling. But then he suspected he was weeping. Memory of the Scientist's last moments came suddenly to mind; his open hand had reached toward Pierre as he rose, lifted up from the earth and life and being itself, gone now and never to return. Something opened in Pierre, and in that darkness everything within tumbled out to spread before him.

Back at the cave's entrance the creature roared, and although far behind him its sound filled the invisible space. It seemed to be waiting for Pierre as if it knew eventually he would need to leave. But just as surely as Pierre occupied this space within the cave, the Scientist now occupied a place within the creature. He hoped the Scientist was dead, and not sitting inside its gut wondering why Pierre was not helping him. He considered marching out of the cave to allow the creature to take him if only so he could join all those others.

Pierre moved to stand and the creature roared again. He wondered if the beast heard his sighs and recognized his despair. Then something passed weakly across his face like the beat of a bird's wing that he suspected was a breeze. In the next moment he felt it again, and then he was certain. He turned; a draft of air carrying the scent of the sea seemed to come from deeper in the cave. Assuming it could only enter from another opening, he hoped that in all that darkness ahead there was a passage large enough to allow him to escape. That draft also suggested why the creature remained at the entrance; it carried the odor of his terror. Pierre would need to follow this cave to its end sustained only by the faith it would allow him to escape.

He stood from beside the boulder and moved forward. Despite his caution he stumbled often and once cut his hand badly enough to bleed. But at least he was in no hurry.

Pierre had never regarded patience as a virtue, yet to escape he would need to be more cunning than the creature but also more patient. Because it was no longer enough to elude its clutches; he must eventually defeat this beast because finally he was certain it was determined to kill him. More than bad luck had brought their paths to cross. That first encounter could have been the result of chance, but at Port Royal it had trudged ashore and climbed hills to pursue him. He could think of no reason why this should be, but reason no longer seemed useful.

The beast had killed many in its pursuit of Pierre and seemed eager to kill more. He could not guess how his search for Augustus had entangled him with it, but if Pierre hoped to find him, he would need to vanquish it. He laughed suddenly and loudly enough to echo in the invisible expanse of the cave.

Sightless and unable to guess how far the cave reached, fatigue became Pierre's only measure of progress. He guessed it was near midnight, so if he hoped for a glimpse of light he would need to wait. Doubt and confusion and exhaustion finally brought him to a halt.

With his hands outstretched, he found another boulder to lean against and sat down again on the sandy floor. His tattered clothes gave him no protection against a damp chill. He closed his eyes for a long moment but then opened them to recognize the very slightest brightening of the absolute darkness. He saw nothing when he brought his hand before his eyes, and he hoped that when the sun arose, light somehow would reach him. But in such darkness he could not distinguish wakefulness from dreaming, so he had no way to be certain when his thoughts became dreams.

Despite the darkness, or because of it, he found himself surrounded by vaguely luminous presences like clouds of the deepest glowing blue-green fog. He recognized these clouds as all those he had known and met, and all of them glared at him angry and accusing. Person after person, life after life, surrounded him as sentinels aglow within his darkness. He had failed each, even including that beast, since all it had needed him to do was stand still and be devoured.

"Happy now?" He had not wanted Gabriella's advice and he was not eager to hear her opinion of his failure, but with the Scientist gone he found himself defenseless against her disdain.

"I'm unhappy and can't think of a reason to be happy, but you already knew that."

"When it came to you I always just knew. You're in trouble with no idea what to do about it. But this is your dream, so I only know what you know."

"So I can't expect to learn anything from you; is that what you're saying?"

"True and not. You've conjured me as your interlocutor. Speak your ideas aloud and, if you're lucky, which you never are, maybe you'll recognize something useful."

"So I still need to figure out what to do next, but you'll tell me if I hit on a good plan."

"Keep thinking that and you'll be here a long time. But it could be as you say, you never know, it might work out just like that. Or, then again, maybe not."

"And how will I know?"

"Trust me, at best your chances are fifty-fifty; anyway, by trusting me you're only trusting yourself, and we'll agree that hasn't worked out all that great so far."

"Well, answer me this; is the creature chasing me?"

"Don't know and can't tell. What do you think?"

Pierre sighed. "After everything, it seems likely."

"If it seems true then it might be so."

"Simple agreement isn't helpful."

"You forget it's you agreeing with yourself. Besides, it sounds like you have doubts."

"And I'm afraid. Because if it's true, it means I'll see that creature again."

"That's something else you already believe; you just want me to say it isn't."

"Okay, all right, you've won another round."

"And you're still just as lost as you were. But don't feel sorry for yourself. Unless you decide to sit here until you die, which might be a temptation, eventually you'll need to make a move. But you've always been good at quitting when things didn't go your way. Not like your father; arrogant, obnoxious and self-obsessed, but he never quite once he put his hand to something."

"Why is it that every time you compare me to him, I come up short?"

"That's the great thing about feeling sorry for yourself; it only needs an audience of one."

"Stuck in a cave with a creature trying to eat me, and you're telling me to cheer up."

"Imagine how bad you're going to feel after it eats you."

"I've always been able to count on you."

"Your father left me and I made the best of it. I took nobody's charity and never shared my bed with nobody I didn't like. You won't find him because he don't want to be found. But even if you do, it won't matter because he won't come back. What's for me to feel cheery about?"

"Maybe I'm learning where the self-pity comes from."

Gabriella's laughter glittered in the darkness. "Your father would be so proud."

"Okay, so you're right. At least he tried, and probably he's somewhere still trying."

"Sounds like you've answered your own question."

"True and not useful." The Scientist's voice was so sudden it startled

Pierre.

Pierre said, "I know you're dead and can't help me, but I'm glad to hear your voice."

"You merely remember my voice, but if that makes you feel better, then I am glad."

"And you're as likely to help me as Gabriella."

"As she said, this is your dream. We can't know anything more than you do."

"So you're just another interlocutor, too?"

"The choice of interlocutor shapes the interior dialogue by limiting the range of answers."

"I don't see how that follows but tell me this; is the creature chasing me?"

"That depends; if it is, it's doing a poor job. Perhaps it pursues something else and you just keep getting in the way."

"In the way to what?"

"Ah, you have just asked a question you cannot answer, so how could I?"

"Fair enough. It's up to me to line up the elements and see where they lead."

"That assumes there's a pattern, and right now that's a question. You will need to work harder than that."

"Meaning exactly what?"

"Meaning, you need to create a hypothesis and then test it against evidence."

"That's a lot like work."

"Hard but not impossible. Besides, something may become apparent that is not so now. Even a tested hypothesis that fails at least suggests a limit to speculation."

"If my hypothesis is that the creature's chasing me, what would confirm that?"

"Reviewing your memories, you recall nothing to confirm or contradict."

"And I'm just as confused as ever."

"On the contrary, you now know that you do not know enough; be grateful for small victories since larger ones may follow."

"Sounds like optimism."

"That and self-confidence, though delusional, are necessary if you hope to succeed."

"Then my second hypothesis is that the aether can be harnessed to defeat the creature."

"Congratulations; far more interesting. But you have even less evidence to support it."

"And what sort of evidence would do that?"

"Your father's convictions are not evidence."

"What about his experiments? And Señor Barbaducci's certainty?"

"Merely assures that your belief is shared by others. Useful but still lacks evidence."

"But Señor Barbaducci described a mechanism as well."

"And that, if clearly stated, also might prove useful."

"He said that experiments using the amber and those of the lodestone shared an underlying principle."

"Commendable for its clarity but just an intuition. And he agreed with your father that dependence on intuition for anything more than suggestion will fail."

"And an experiment that can't be repeated has no value."

"You claim not to understand his work yet you understand its most basic principle."

"I also know I have no resources for an experiment. And with you gone, no one to help."

"That is all literally true but hardly decisive and perhaps just temporary. At worst, your progress will demand smaller steps. As for a colleague, you need to become the expert on this subject. If that is burdensome, it also offers freedom to choose experiments and interpret results."

"Fair enough but that answer has no value."

"You complain that I have not told you what to do, but in fact I have explained to you what needs to be done first."

"Assume I'm stupid and remind me."

"Intuitively you have concluded that the hypothesis as stated by Señor Barbaducci is promising, so you must begin with a clear statement of that hypothesis."

"I am happy to restate my speculation," Señor Barbaducci said, and the sound of his voice also startled Pierre, especially as he had not known the man well. "The aether possesses a power that can be conserved and directed. Though Augustus's tricks appeared trivial, this is what his experiments suggest. Rubbing the amber gathered and stored the aether, and bringing a finger close triggered some mechanism to expel it. How these effects come about and why the aether behaves as it does remain problems but suggest the most profitable line to consider."

"And how will that help me defeat the creature?"

"I have explained how the aether appears to behave, and you ask how it might help you defeat the creature. These are two separate questions. Anything beyond what has already been demonstrated will demand work on your part."

"I speculate that gathering and expulsion only occur under particular circumstances."

"At least a testable hypothesis. You only need to reproduce the circumstance. I suggest this will prove useful in designing an experiment on a larger scale."

"Expanding the scale will enhance its usefulness?"

"That may prove to be the case, but just as significant, at a larger scale the mechanism involved may become easier to recognize."

"So I need to escape this cave and, however I manage that, in the end I'll need to destroy the creature or it will destroy me. But in order to destroy it, I must first discover the nature of the aether. Is this what you're telling me?"

"You must not depend on others to answers such questions. The beast is a destiny and your future is held hostage until you resolve this."

"That creature is your destiny, assigned to you even before your birth." Pierre did not recognize this new voice or even whether it originated within his mind. Though certain of those others, this voice seemed to emanate from the walls of the cave as if perhaps arising from the bowels of the earth itself to enter his mind.

"I can't believe what you're telling me; that futures are already written with roles assigned and fates predestined. But if I did, I probably wouldn't be stuck here right now."

"Of all the numberless fools I have encountered, you are the grandest. Surely, as Elegba has said, you are olari-buruku. Eleggua warned me even as Oloddumare placed your life in my hands. Eshu-Elegba warned me as well, but he must not be trusted since his greatest trick is to tell the truth. At Orumilla's request, Oya sends this draft of a breeze to give you hope. But it is put to me to decide whether you are worthy, and then make help available to you when you have achieved understanding. Meanwhile, Eshu, as protector of travelers, continues to hold his hand over you. As orisha of the crossroads, he has overseen your path and continues to guide your journey."

"I don't know you and don't understand what you tell me. My dream has been the echo of my experience, but here you tell me things of which I have no knowledge. You name persons unknown to me and speak in a language I've never heard before. You are a stranger to me."

"There is little you now know that will be useful to you in your next encounter with the beast, but knowledge is vital to your success. Be confident that others will add to it. You will accumulate insight and so gradually approach understanding. Darkness abides but slowly it will dissipate as your vision sharpens, until all that you know will be all that you need to know in order to fulfill your fate."

"To believe you I must know who you are."

"Truth is true regardless of its source. You already know that answer though you do not recall it. As has so often been the case in your short life, you have been given knowledge that you dismiss as worthless and you will do the same with all I tell you now. But that is of no consequence, for all that I have said will come to pass even though my words escape your mind as water escapes from a broken bowl. What is important is that you destroy the beast, because it can only die by your hand."

"Are you saying that unless I defeat the creature it will continue to kill?"

Pierre opened his eyes in darkness. He could not guess how much time had passed but he decided that since he was awake he should stand and move on. He reached out to help himself up, and at that moment he awoke. He opened his eyes to pitch black but almost instantly he located the breeze.

On the chance he was awake he reached out his hand and used the rock behind him to stand. He considered returning to the entrance of the cave and see if the creature had wandered off. But that trek through his uncertain darkness could prove a waste of time. He might reach the end of the cave only to discover it still blocked by the creature. He turned in the direction he thought the draft was coming from and carefully began to move.

Sightless in that darkness, the boulders in his path seemed so large he had to feel his way around them, but moving in this way robbed him of his fragile sense of direction. He was forced to stop frequently and then stand motionless waiting to sense the breeze again and regain his path. So he spent as much time standing still as moving forward, never certain of his direction or progress. For all he knew, he could be walking in a large and pointless circle. This thought made him smile. His uncertainty reminded him of the way he felt when he thought about his father's experiments.

What Augustus had explained about the aether came imperfectly to his mind. Parts appeared but then became obscured, like boulders at a rising tide. He moved forward, in his thoughts as well as his actions, certain of nothing except his uncertainty. From time to time he lost his sense of that draft blowing past, and sometimes he became so disoriented he feared it had died and he was utterly lost in the cave's baffling darkness.

Impatience began to gnaw at Pierre as he became irritated at this confinement. Darkness defeats every disguise, hiding everything except light. But darkness is flat and unrelieved, featureless and without texture. He was surrounded by things he would see if only he could dissipate this darkness, and he longed to see them. He inched ahead, his feet sliding over sand and gravel, leaves and twigs and things he did not want to know, the murmur of his movement lost in the cavernous silence. His frustration was corrosive, biting so deeply he wanted to call out. Straining against the deepest dark yet hopeful for light, he pushed forward.

He stared ahead so long and hard determined to force the darkness to yield that he failed to notice when his darkness was no longer absolute. He did not recognize its dilution until he turned to look back in the direction he had come. And then he saw that just ahead, the slightest nimbus of blue stained the purity of the black. But that halo was so faint he willed himself to ignore it, like a thirsty man in the desert determined to ignore what he fears can only be a mirage of water. Moment after moment Pierre pushed forward hopeful that what he saw was light, since whatever light he thought he saw remained so feeble it failed to keep him on his path.

Then, suddenly, the light was bright enough for him to pick out deeper shadows and vaguely recognize shapes. Oddly, by it the cave appeared more narrow than he had guessed. That light faded but then brightened again, and reflexively Pierre moved forward determined to advance as far as it allowed. After several steps, just as suddenly that light dimmed but now he was certain it was ahead and he simply needed to pursue it. In his darkness he found a boulder and sat down against it convinced the light would brighten again.

The air moving softly against his face smelled of the sea and he wondered if the cave ended under water, and this quality of light was the result of it needing to pass through water. He stood a moment hoping to hear crashing surf. But was that simply one more thing he should not wonder about? Just as he should not assume the cave ended under water, or with an opening only large enough for air and light to pass through. Sitting on cool damp sand beside a boulder he closed his eyes and then opened them to assure himself that what he saw could only be light.

The light brightened again and Pierre was determined to make as much progress as it would allow, so he stood. A half-dozen steps and then more, and that light remained. Beyond another large boulder he reached a clear space and could just recognize a glow from the sand before him. He moved forward as this light remained bright, his progress more certain and his feet treading firm ground.

From a sheen of light reflected from a wall, the cave appeared to bend. When he reached it, to one side he saw blue sky before he realized he had reached the opening to the cave.

Leafy underbrush tightly woven covered the entrance and he had to force his way through, but suddenly he stood under sunshine so bright it stabbed his eyes. Closing his eyes he invited the sun to warm his face. Opening them again, he found himself far up a hill and above dense forest, and the sea a glittering turquoise smear further off. The undergrowth was thickly tangled yet he pushed forward eager to reach the beach.

Exhausted, thirsty and hungry, Pierre stumbled through undergrowth and down the hill. The Scientist returned to his memory unbidden; his scream of terror, the way his free arm waived as the creature's head rose into the ink black sky, and then how he had disappeared. He slowed as anguish squeezed the breath from his throat. The Scientist had saved Pierre from himself and despite his pedantic knowledge Pierre had come to admire his good sense. And he had been Pierre's last link with his father. From here he would continue his quest alone and, despite the sunlight and warm breeze, that prospect frightened him. But this sky above and that sea beyond all beckoned Pierre and he would not resist.

CHAPTER ELEVEN

PIERRE'S STUMBLING DESCENT from the cave to the beach took so long that by the time he reached it, the sun touched the horizon. Cooled by wind from the sea, in a gathering twilight the pillows of sugar-white sand appeared ghosted by purple shadows as if piled onto a huge purple bed. Furiously hungry, his deepest desire was simply to sleep without dreams.

At the white-sanded beach, he followed the high-water line of broken seashells and dry seaweed until he found a spot sheltered behind a thicket of rushes that whispered with the breeze. He knelt feeling the warmth of the day's sun reach up through the sand, but knowing that his next decision would need to bring him food. Thinking about food reminded him of the hacienda, which brought to mind Don Benito and Babo and Señor Barbaducci and the smell of burning human flesh and of Dr. de Montpellier and of the creature. With his head resting on his arm he laid down and those were his last thoughts as thought itself faded. Happily for Pierre his sleep was deep and dreamless.

He awoke to a sky dotted with the rosy clouds of sunrise. His first sensations were the twisted gnawing of his stomach and a thirst that left his lips cracked. He looked about for something that hung from a tree which he might eat but luck was not with him. Following the beach, he found a narrow stream that cut a sparkling channel into the white sand as it emptied into the sea. He followed it upstream to a shaded spot where it formed a pool. He dropped to his knees and drank until he fell back breathless. The water left him feeling less hungry but now he needed to find food.

Pierre knew that eventually he must return to Havana, and to find his father he would need to find a ship that would take him to Europe. A sympathetic captain might hire him to work his way across, and then his good fortune would be those chores he had learned at the tavern. But the more he considered continuing his search the more discouraged he became. He had learned something about Augustus yet had had no luck locating him. So perhaps it was better to return to home. He had uncovered hints of his trail and had met men who praised his work. But then, imaging the embarrassment over the failure of his plan to find Augustus, that temptation evaporated. So, following the beach, he began to walk.

To return to Havana he hoped he only needed to turn his back to the rising sun and follow this beach. He tried to recall the path he and the Scientist had taken to reach the city and failed. Then, some way along, he spied a group of men sitting clustered together in the soft sand, a small boat beached nearby. Guessing they were fishermen he approached hopeful at least one spoke English.

Around a small driftwood fire several silver-gray fish mounted to spits of twigs were propped with one end buried in the sand roasting over black and orange coals. Pierre stopped a few paces away. One by one, each turned in his direction and then turned back. Speaking slowly, he explained that he had walked a long time, trying to reach Havana, and then he paused. They said nothing to each other, but then without turning, one said in clear English, "That way," pointing in the direction he had been walking. In his relief he thanked him. After a moment, he repeated that he had walked since early morning. They remained silent until an older man turned toward him holding one of the roasting fish by its twig. Pierre stepped forward to accept it as two of the men moved apart to offer a space. He thanked them, took the fish and sat down.

In a language Pierre did not recognize the men traded quiet remarks as they ate. He wondered if they spoke about him, but his hunger was such that he ignored that possibility. When the fish were eaten, the men passed around a large gourd. It reached Pierre and he was relieved it was filled with cool, sweet water. Again he offered thanks, making certain he drank only as much as the others. The men then stretched out on the sand lying on their backs or with their heads pillowed by their folded arms. They remained this way for some time and Pierre dozed.

When the older man eventually sat up, he said something to the others. They all stood and then Pierre stood as well. They turned toward the boat and to their backs Pierre called out good wishes for their fishing. They all stopped and turned to face him. The older man offered a blessing on his journey as the others waved farewell. Pierre watched them push the boat into the sea and then he resumed his walk.

Despite the constant breeze he found he soon dripped with sweat. He kept to the shade of the tree-line, but by the time the sun was overhead he wanted badly to rest again. He forced himself to push on, and as a reward he found a place where the beach passed close to a road. He took to this road relieved its firm surface made walking easier. He began to pass others, and eventually recognized this as the same road he and the Scientist had followed to reach the city. But it was not until dusk that he spied, small and in the far distance silhouetted against a purpling sky, those dark shapes of the towers and rooftops of Havana. And seeing this he recalled the inn run by the man named Guido that he and the Scientist had visited. Walking further despite the deepening darkness, he reached that widening beside the road and recognized the inn. Stepping through its front door, he was relieved by Guido's cheerful greeting. "What a pleasant surprise! We feared you and your friend had died."

Pierre asked what he meant and Guido explained that the city was alive with a story that Don Benito's hacienda had been destroyed in an earthquake with all its occupants killed. Certain the true story would not be believed, Pierre simply reported that he had escaped the earthquake but the Scientist had not. Solemnly, Guido expressed deep regret before asking what he planned to do.

"There's no reason for me to stay so I'm headed to Havana looking for a ship."

Guido's eyes widened. "All ships are confined to the harbor. Some sea creature has been spotted and the Viceroy sent out a fleet to deal with it."

Pierre shook his head. "I've heard something about that," he lied, "but his plan will fail."

Guido smiled indulgently. "His fleet has many fighting ships. In any case, it seems you'll remain among us a bit longer." Looking Pierre up and down, Guido guessed aloud that he wanted shelter, but having lost his personal things he had no way to pay and no idea what to do next.

When Pierre nodded, Guido grinned and patted his back. "Young and strong, there's always work for the willing." He asked what sort of work Pierre could do and he described what he had done at the tavern. Guido's expression brightened. "This is a fortunate day for us both. I have work and you have experience. Work for me in exchange for bed and meals."

Pierre smiled with relief. "But how will I get a ship?"

Guido's look darkened. "For most, my offer would be generous." Pierre waited as he appeared to consider the question. "Let me suggest this. Even when the port re-opens, there won't be another ship to Europe for a month. Work for me for that time and when the next ship is scheduled, I'll provide for your passage. Is that sufficient?"

Pierre hesitated. "I must depend on your promise."

Something flashed in Guido's eyes but then he laughed. "My promises are written in stone; ask anyone."

Pierre nodded. "You have a new assistant," he said and they shook hands. Galacia suddenly appeared carrying a platter of broiled fish. He smiled at the sight of her but did not catch her eye before she went

"As it's already late, eat while I explain how things are and then we'll go to your cabin."

Guido described his customers and the work they did, then described the villages beyond, naming some of the farmers in the area. As Pierre finished his meal Guido said, "There's much to do, so it's well that you turn in early."

Stepping from the back door of the inn into the deepening night he followed Guido to the cabins he remembered, and to one near the back entrance to the kitchen. He saw Juanita and Galacia walk together from one of the cabins to the kitchen and neither turned to look at him.

Inside the cabin Guido looked about. "Could use a clean-up, I suppose, but it'll do you for the night." He turned to leave, but at the curtained doorway he stopped. "First days are always hard, but my bet is that you'll enjoy working here." Then he was gone.

A hammock was strung across the center of the room. On one wall was a shelf formed of sticks tied together beside two nails to hang clothes. The floor was sand and there were gaps in the walls but that hammock held his attention until it was all he could see. He climbed into it and began to sleep even before he closed his eyes.

And he was back inside the cave, except there were small sources of light wherever he looked. Whether candles or lanterns or something else he could not tell, but they gave the cave the look of a cathedral at midnight mass. He sat on a boulder near the cave's center, and around him forming a circle were smaller boulders spaced as evenly in the pale sand as numbers on the face of a clock. Something was about to take place that involved him. The mutter of voices was so quiet he could not make out words, but the inflections suggested an exchange without conflict. The speakers remained disguised, their faces as invisible as their intentions. He tried to stand but he could not see the ground beneath his feet; the black shadow surrounding them was a pool of ink within which they disappeared. Then he felt a blanket of warm air cover him, or perhaps he sat in a well of intoxicating air with the fragrance of a thousand flowers. He felt light-headed, as he might after drinking a glass of warm rum. The lights dimmed disguising the features of the cave. Someone tapped his shoulder from behind. He turned as his eyes opened to darkness.

The cabin's doorway was filled with indigo light and the night sky beyond the cloth-hung entrance was a velvet wall, but he was not alone. Embraced by the hammock he struggled to turn himself. A female voice whispered, "Be still!"

The voice speaking from the darkness seemed familiar. "A word," she said, "and then I go." He was about to speak but she continued, "The creature cannot find you here. For the creature you have become invisible. Sleep well, for you will remain safe for as long as you are here." A motion in the darkness, the curtain doorway shivered and he was alone again.

Pierre tried to think about what he had been told, and wondered who had told it to him, but that fragrance of flowers overpowered him again until he was certain he floated on an ocean of flowers.

When he awoke again the doorway was pale blue and he was being shaken roughly. A growling voice said, "I do not pay you to sleep! I told you to be ready to work early." He looked over to see Guido pulling at one end of the hammock. With a malicious grin he said, "Join me quickly and know this won't happen tomorrow." Then he was gone

Pierre met Guido in the dining room and found a meal of bread and a mug of something warm, dark and sweet that he recognized as coffee. Galacia appeared and from a pewter pitcher refilled his mug. She never looked at him and when his mug was full she disappeared as silently as she had appeared. Guido then explained to Pierre what he expected him to do and when.

Later, he had to admit that Guido at least had been honest; his first day was hard. He performed familiar chores along with others that were unfamiliar. Whether it was the vegetables he prepared or the drinks he served or the chatter he heard, this world only somewhat resembled his own.

Approaching midday and just as Pierre had been told, men began to arrive alone or in pairs. Yet these men were alien to him; more farmers than sailors, more likely to sell produce than kill time to wait for a ship. Talk more often about the price of beans than schedules of ships; of the weather more about crops than sails. Pierre was certain the only gold any of them would see would be what they were paid selling their plantains or pigs.

It was late in the afternoon when the dining room finally emptied. Looking up from the long day, Pierre discovered himself exhausted. Until then he had thought of nothing except the work at hand, had cared for nothing except the next customer. As he walked between rooms, Guido stopped him, took his arm, led him to an empty table and sat down.

With a grin he said, "You look like you've been punched by a hundred fists. I told you it would be a difficult day and I was not wrong, was I?"

Pierre smiled but said nothing. Galacia once again appeared with a platter of bread with a small piece of meat and a mug of ale and placed it before him. Reaching for the drink Pierre asked, "So how did I do?"

Guido shrugged. "Well enough for me to keep you around." He paused. "At least for another day." Pierre nodded, too tired to be amused.

"The afternoon was difficult but the evening will be even busier. Usually I take a siesta until early evening, but since so much is unfamiliar I'll help you and you'll be permitted to retire early. I assume you approve." Pierre simply nodded and continued with his meal.

The rest of the afternoon he hauled water and firewood and when the storage bin for the wood was full, he spent the remainder of the afternoon splitting more. All the while he looked for a chance to speak to Galacia. For some reason he felt certain it was she who had come in the night to deliver his unlikely message, though he could not say why. But she never turned to look.

Twilight faded toward darkness and men began to arrive to eat, and more often to drink. Guido greeted each by name from behind the bar as they came through the door, and sometimes stepped out to visit among the tables.

The evening had deepened when Pierre noticed a group of men clustered at a table near the back of the dining room playing cards. Their voices gradually became sharp, though Pierre was so tired he did not care. Despite his disinterest, he noticed that from time to time one or the other of the cousins disappeared through the back entrance and he would not see her for a while. But watching anything beyond his immediate chore was just more unnecessary work.

Still later, a man arrived with a guitar slung over his shoulder by a length of rope. Guido greeted him as Salvatore. Small and spindly with a thick ponytail of gray and black hair, a hawkish profile and dark circles around his eyes, he struck Pierre as the saddest man he had ever seen.

Salvatore sat on a stool beside the bar as Guido poured a drink. Swallowing the drink in one go, he crossed his legs to rest the guitar on his thigh and began to strum. He looked about until certain the room was listening and then began to sing, and even the card-players stopped their game. In a rasping, high pitched but quiet voice he sang a song that began: "Her power is in her eyes." A plaintive lament, he described how the woman he loved delighted in his pain since she was without mercy, and that in order to end his misery one of them must die. The men at their tables appeared riveted to his voice. Pierre had heard such songs before, it seemed as if every singer knew several, and he wondered how men like these found themselves so often heartsick for a woman who did not love them. But he was glad for Salvatore's singing since while he sang no one requested his service.

When Salvatore finished, some of the men smiled and nodded to each other and then the room buzzed with quiet conversation. His fingers continued to strum as he looked about, and when Guido refilled his glass he smiled, stopping just long enough to drink. His next song began: "He cannot love her as I do." He explained that the woman he loved was in love with another, but her new lover could not know how wonderful she was and how, for the singer, the world began and ended in her, and so how unworthy this new lover was. Pierre marveled again that in these songs, love was always complicated and brought pain.

When Salvatore finished, silence filled the room like a pent-up sigh. Each man seemed to sit alone with his thoughts, as broken hearts seemed to bleed across the floor. Guido passed another drink to him and patted him lightly on the shoulder muttering, "Very good, very good."

Salvatore continued to strum, his fingers moving among the strings. Different men stepped up to offer greetings and insist Guido charge them for Salvatore's next drink. Salvatore took a few moments to re-tune his guitar, and then with a flourish he played a song that began: "No cloud in the sky foretold their fate." A song of a voyage, this was another sort Pierre had heard sung at the Captain Hudson and so at first he paid little attention. But as the song progressed, Salvatore sang of a terrible creature that, with each added detail, gradually became one he feared he recognized. When Salvatore reached the climax describing the creature's attack on a ship, Pierre felt certain the song was about the beast he had encountered. Salvatore finally brought the song to a close, and Pierre wondered how he might know of it.

The silence again was absolute. Pierre searched the faces of the others for a sign they had heard this song before, but it seemed just another tragic tale of sailors lost to a heartless sea. He was about to ask where Salvatore had learned this song, but before he could do so, Guido tapped his shoulder. "You're needed in the back."

He reached the kitchen and Juanita asked him to bring more water and wood. The wood-bin and the water barrel stood some distance from the back of the building, but the light of the full moon brightened his way. Approaching the wood-bin, he heard a noise and froze in place. But hearing nothing more he continued to the wood-bin and loaded his arms. He turned to return to the kitchen when he heard a sound again, this time followed by a woman's laugh. Nearing the backdoor to the inn he heard quiet voices behind him. He turned to see Galacia leaving one of the cabins followed by an older man Pierre recognized as one of the card players. He continued into the kitchen hoping he had not been seen. With the wood replaced and the water barrel refilled Pierre returned to the dining room to discover the card-players had gone. Only Salvatore and three customers remained. Guido was cleaning up behind the bar.

He told Pierre to clear the tables, take the lanterns to the kitchen and then go to bed. "You've had a rough day but you've done well and I'm grateful for your help. But tomorrow will be another early and difficult day." Then he clapped him on the shoulder. Pierre was so tired, the image of his empty hammock glowed before his eyes.

Over the days that followed he learned where everything was stored, who delivered the meat and bread and wine and ale, the tableware and the candles, along with the responsibilities of the others. But it took more than a week for the mystery of the young cousins to deepen.

Early one afternoon a customer Pierre knew as Marko entered the dining room. Guido was off somewhere, so Pierre stood alone behind the bar. Marko told him he needed to speak with Galacia. Pierre told him he did not know where she was. This made Marko angry and he insisted Pierre find her. Pierre searched every room in the inn, and then left the inn to search the cabins. Approaching the first, the curtain to another was pushed aside, and Guido stepped out followed by Galacia. Pierre stopped, unsure what to do next. When Guido saw him he stepped forward.

"What is it now?" Guido asked as if expecting a question concerning Pierre's duties.

"Marko wants to see her," Pierre said nodding toward Galacia. "He seems upset."

The expression of bored indifference disappeared from Guido face, replaced with genuine anxiety. "What does he want with her?"

Pierre glanced once at Galacia who hovered at the edge of the conversation. "I don't know, but he's waiting beside the bar." Pierre then turned and was startled to see that Marko had followed him and approached from the back door of the inn. He was looking at Galacia and he did not appear happy. She did not seem pleased to see him either. Guido stepped into his path.

"Marko!" Guido said with more enthusiasm than usual, "it has been too long. Have you been spending your money at Callistos', or is it at Rachels'?" He laughed as if he was sharing a favorite joke, but Marko did not smile and his eyes never left Galacia. In his expression there was a kind of pleading frustration close to anger. Her eyes darted avoiding Marko's, and she seemed desperate to be somewhere else. The silence weighed on all of them. Pierre was more confused than panicked and tried to think of a place he could disappear to.

Guido finally said, "My friend, let me buy you a drink." He took Marko's arm but Marko did not even look at him.

In a dark voice he said, "I need to speak with her. Alone."

Guido's expression hardened. "She's busy right now with chores she needs to finish."

"You don't understand," Marko said to Guido though his eyes never left Galacia's face. "I need to speak with her now!"

Guido suddenly grinned and clapped Marko on the shoulder. "My friend, she has work to do, why not let her do it." He turned then to Pierre. "You two go back to work while I speak with my old friend."

Pierre turned with relief toward the dining room, but Galacia was already walking in the same direction and more quickly, so he did not catch up until they were inside the kitchen. He asked, "What was that all about?" She said nothing and busied herself sorting cutlery, studying them as if unsure what should be put where. Beyond a nod and a smile, Pierre had yet to speak with either of the young women and assumed theirs were conventional duties, but his curiosity had been struck. The waters he swam in suddenly seemed far deeper than he had guessed. When she did not respond he said, "Just tell me if this is none of my business."

She did not look up and he assumed she would ignore his curiosity but after a moment she said, "Juanita can explain better than I can." As so often was the case, the less Pierre knew the more curious he became. He left Galacia and busied himself in the dining room hoping to find Juanita.

Then Marko passed through the dining room, an expression of angry despair on his face. Guido appeared in the dining room. Seeing Pierre, a look of barely contained anger appeared. "Never leave that bar unattended, and I don't care if God Himself comes in. And if anyone comes in asking for Juanita or Galacia, you'll say you've been told they're visiting their families. Think you can do all that?"

His fury left Pierre stunned and unsure what had happened, but he was clear about what was expected. Guido glared a moment longer as if to impress upon him how serious he was and then returned to the kitchen. Pierre did not see either cousin for the rest of the day and that evening's customers kept him so busy he had no opportunity to think about them. It was another two days before he had a chance to satisfy his curiosity.

The afternoon had been busy with more customers than usual, but eventually they were gone and Pierre finished cleaning up. He was about to return to his cabin for his siesta when he saw Juanita walking toward another of the cabins. He hurried to catch up with her and walked beside her attempting idle chatter about the day and the work and the customers, but none of it held her attention. Finally he mentioned Marko. This slowed her pace though she still did not look over. He confessed his curiosity, telling her that when he asked Galacia, she told him to speak with her. She stopped walking and looked into his face. "What do you want to know?"

The bluntness of her question surprised him, but it also emboldened him. "What put Marko in a panic?"

She looked down as if her thoughts lay in the stony dust at her feet. "What you ask demands time to explain." She hesitated as if enduring an internal debate. "Before the evening meal I will visit and tell you our story, and then I will answer every question you ask." Without waiting she hurried away. He had not expected this, but the moment she disappeared he felt a sudden thrill. He did not know what he expected but he was convinced it verged on the extraordinary and he was excited by the thought.

That day seemed to pass so slowly he wondered if time was passing at all. In the midst of the busiest times he found himself wondering why the light hardly changed and the birds moved across the sky as if walking and moments seemed like fragile eggs about to burst. But finally the morning did pass, and as his siesta approached Pierre planned to hurry to his shack and wait for Juanita. Just then, Guido stopped him and took him aside. "You must run an errand, a matter of some delicacy. As you're a white man and honorable, you're the only person I can trust to do this."

Pierre said he was flattered by Guido's trust but he was exhausted by the morning's work and asked if the errand could wait until the next day.

Guido did not smile. "This errand can't wait even for a few hours. I ask this as a favor, but remember that you're here as a favor from me. I wouldn't ask this if I didn't need your help." Pierre was caught and he knew it. He could not believe his bad luck and wondered if it was Guido's intention to keep him from speaking with Juanita. In the end he decided his complaint would only irritate Guido, and nothing good for Pierre could come from that.

CHAPTER TWELVE

PIERRE'S ERRAND, as Guido described it, demanded a two-hour journey to the dusty, sun-blanched streets and cool, shaded alleys of Havana. A sealed envelope needed to be delivered and he knew nothing more than that. He was given precise directions to reach its destination, about a mile within the main gates and just beyond a certain plaza. Still hoping to meet with Juanita, he was determined to complete the errand and return to the inn by evening. But Guido had given him this assignment so spontaneously he had no chance to plan beyond that.

His directions had seemed clear when Pierre received them, but within Havana quickly he found himself lost. By the time he reached the city its streets were deserted for siesta, so he wandered until he became so confused he could not even to retrace his steps. Wide, straight streets suddenly buried themselves among knotted alleys and anonymous plazas turned into cul-du-sacs without exit. Narrow passageways wound in baffling patterns that fed back on themselves. Though never certain, he suspected his path re-crossed itself. The city was suddenly so baffling he feared that in the next moment he would disappear within it. Finally Pierre was eager to confess to his confusion, if only he could find someone to confess to. But every door appeared locked and windows tightly closed. He wanted a human face to speak to, and maybe get directions. Being lost had not worked well for him, and it seemed unlikely to do so in here.

Time passed as he wandered, certain nothing would help unless someone stepped forward prepared to return him to the proper path. Whether out of pity or humor but most likely because time passes as water flows downhill, the passage of time finally relented. And just as the flow of water casts objects onto its banks, the passage of time tossed someone across Pierre's path. And as with every gift of time, it was up to him to recognize its value. Time had put a person in his path, but not someone he recognized as the key to his future.

This man lay sprawled on his stomach in the street within the shade of a doorway apparently asleep with his head resting on his folded arm and in a posture suggesting he had a lot of experience sleeping in doorways. He was dark-skinned but whether from exposure to the sun or from a mixed heritage Pierre could only guess. He appeared so completely relaxed Pierre suspected he was either dead or so drunk he was in a coma. Assuming a drunken stupor he stepped past him certain that sleeping dogs are best left sleeping.

"Hey, ya asshole." Pierre heard this croaked insult when he was three steps beyond the sleeping man, so at first he was not certain it was directed his way. When he heard, "Yeah, I'm talkin' to you," he turned and walked back to where the man lay.

Laying on the ground propped on one elbow, round-faced and blue-eyed, lank blond hair hung all around his face. He watched Pierre approach until he was two steps away when with a suddenly cautious smile the man added, "Listen, governor, it's just a manner of speaking, is all. Just another way of saying good-day and how's your mum. Nothing more, governor, nothing more."

Pierre said, "I'm trying to find an address; can you help me there?"

"Well now," he said as his subservience slipped away, "that all depends, now don't it. I'm a man of parts and know a bit of this and a bit of that. Might be I could help you out; that's possible. But one question; what might that help be worth, if you don't mind my asking."

Pierre was caught between relief and anger. He reached into his pocket and brought out three small coins, all that he had, and held them out. "That much and not a bad price."

The man craned his head up to scrutinize the coins. "Seems you're as bad off as me." He paused. "Now that I think about it, you're worse off; you have a job." His open-mouthed cackle revealed a set of gray-green teeth.

"At least I've got a place to sleep," Pierre said though he could not see how the man had guessed about his job. The man just laughed louder.

"Bet you do and three meals a day. And for that you work your balls off. Am I right?" He laughed louder when he saw Pierre's embarrassment. Sweeping his arm about he said, "Behold my palace, and I didn't work a second for it. Here you are with your job and you're lost. At least I know where I am, and it didn't take no boss to tell me."

Pierre panted with frustration. "I've no time to waste, old man. Tell me how to find this address or someone else will."

"Let's not get impatient, governor. It's just a way we get to know each other so to speak. And besides, just who're you calling old?" Finally he began to stand. This took some moments, a careful rearrangement of limbs, a shifting of weight, a propping of one hand against a wall with the other against a door frame, some flexing of knees and several grunts. When he stood he was nearly a head taller than Pierre and appeared only a few years older, though subject to a good bit more wear. "Now, which of us is the old man, eh?"

Pierre looked along both sides of the street hoping to see someone else he could ask for directions, but the street remained as empty as the face of the moon. "I've wasted enough time. Help me out or I'll find someone who can."

"Tell you what, and I only make this offer because I like you, I'll take you to that address myself, and no funny stuff. Just give me them coins you was flashing as sort of a retainer fee so we have like a contract. Deal?"

The passage of time now worked against Pierre. He assumed he had already lost his chance to speak with Juanita. "Okay," he said. "Let's go."

"Soon as you hand over them coins."

"Get me where I need to be and I'll pay you then."

The man hesitated but then he smiled. He pushed himself from the wall with his elbow and got both his feet beneath him. "You're a bright lad who knows how to drive a bargain. I like that. Let's go." Putting one foot in front of the other as if the act demanded forethought, he began walking in the direction from which Pierre had just come.

Pierre asked, "You sure you know where you're going?"

Without stopping he said, "If I don't, don't pay me. Anyway, I could tell you was a sailor stranded on dry land the minute I saw you." He stopped then and faced Pierre. "Name's Joshua but my friends call me Shark." Pierre nodded and introduced himself.

"Well now, Mister Pierre, let's just see how close you got to where you wanted to go."

He followed Shark past doorways and along alleys he remembered, but then he turned to find himself in a small plaza he had not seen before. Another half dozen steps and they stopped before a wide, closed door painted bright blue green. Smiling, Shark nodded at the door. "This is my town, Mister Pierre, and it might as well be my living room."

Pierre rapped hard on the door. After a few moments it opened to reveal a small, dark-skinned woman of middle-age dressed in the black clothing of a servant. He handed her the sealed letter. When she saw the wax seal her eyes widened enough for him to assume she recognized it. She reached into a pocket and produced a large, bright coin which she passed to Pierre and then closed the door, sliding the bolt into place with a crack.

Grinning, Shark said, "Well, ain't we special. By rights half that coin's mine." Pierre was tired and annoyed. He reached into his pocket, brought out the three small coins and passed them to Shark. "A deal's a deal. Thanks for the help but I've got to get back."

"Bet you do." Shark's voice bled sarcasm. "I hear somebody's got to get back, I wonder who's holding the whip."

"Thanks for the concern but I can take care of myself."

"You're a sailor on dry land and all you want is a ship. Kid yourself, but you don't kid me. Go ahead and tell me you ain't."

Pierre stopped. He could not walk and debate at the same time. "Okay, I'm looking for a ship. What's it to you?"

Shark laughed. "See, I know a few things, like about ships. You want a ship, I can get you a ship. You think I can't?"

"Harbor's closed," Pierre insisted "because of that sea monster. Nothing's going out and nothing's coming in. See, I know a couple of things, too."

Again, Shark laughed. "Harbor's been open for days, that's how much you know."

Pierre hid his surprise. "All right, since you know so much, any ships going to Europe?"

Shark's expression became smugly mysterious. "Could be; could even be there's one weighs anchor in two days. Could even be I know the captain. Could even be I plan to sign on myself. Now, how much is all that worth to you?"

His decision demanded less thought. "I'll give you half of what I just got."

"Tell you what," Shark said. "Give me the coin and I'll be sure you're on that ship."

"Half the coin," Pierre said. "Otherwise I've got a job I need to get back to, just like you said." He turned and took a few steps when Shark called out.

"Okay." He stopped and turned. Shark said, "You drive a hard bargain and that's no lie. Ready to go?"

Pierre thought about Guido and about Galacia and Juanita and then nodded. The work at the inn was not awful, but he wondered who might kill who first. But worse, why would Guido tell him the next ship to Europe would not leave for another month when a ship would set sail in two days? Was that to keep him around? But now Pierre was about to put his fate into the hands of a stranger. And even if he got a ship, could he be certain he would reach Europe? He was rolling dice that kept disappearing. He nodded and turned to follow wherever Shark led.

Whether it was because Shark's cobwebs had cleared or because he saw money at the end of their trek or because they headed through a terrain he felt comfortable in, he seemed to brighten with each step. Then he began to share stories he claimed were true. Pierre did not believe them, but they were interesting and filled the time until they reached the harbor.

"If it hadn't been for the earthquake at Port Royal, I'd be in Vera Cruz right now and richer than the King of Spain, Lord curse his bones." When Pierre asked about the earthquake, Shark seemed surprised he had not heard that, several months before, the entire city of Port Royal had been flattened. It took a moment for Pierre to recognize this was the same story he had heard from Guido and so the destruction of the city had not been connected to that beast terrorizing the seas around New Spain. He said nothing.

"Our ship was three days out," Shark continued, "and then all kinds of stuff started to float past. At first we figured it was from a storm, but then the bodies began to show up. The captain decided to continue, but reaching the harbor there weren't nothing left; like the edge of God's glorious hand had swept it all away. We was to trade cloth and finished goods at Port Royal for slaves we planned to sell in Vera Cruz and for a pile of gold. Instead, low on food and water and a crew itching to get paid, our captain landed us here where that cargo was worth pennies."

"Couldn't you trade the finished goods for slaves here and then sell them in Vera Cruz?"

Shark spoke as they walked. "Like I said, them goods weren't worth as much here as at Port Royal, and so we couldn't earn enough to buy many slaves. When we landed, the captain paid us off but a tenth of what he'd promised." Turning to Pierre with a broad grin he asked, "So what's the big hurry to get yourself to Europe? Girlfriend, I'll bet."

"I expect you lose a lot of bets," Pierre said. He described his search for Augusts leaving out all of the interesting parts, particularly his encounters with the creature. Shark nodded from time to time, but Pierre assumed that, since there wasn't a girl in his story, he paid little attention. They entered the harbor district where masts of ships at anchor towered above the rooftops. He was relieved that Shark seemed as good as his word. Approaching the docks, Pierre saw that hum of activity he recognized. Stevedores ran from ship to ship, lines of black slaves stretched along the docks and every vessel was loading or off-loading cargo. He was reminded that the world continued to move and its schemes reached conclusions even while his was frozen in place.

They ambled along the dock and Shark gave each ship they passed a history of its most recent voyage, a biography and character-analysis of its captain and a description of its cargo. Pierre was impressed; Shark's knowledge seemed encyclopedic and its recitation the equivalent to a history of New Spain in the Caribbean. They had nearly reached the end of the dock before Shark pointed to a ship he called the Intrepid. "Our new home," he said, as proud as a farmer at high summer. Pierre hoped he was mistaken because from what he saw, he would have been impressed if the ship made it safely to the edge of the harbor.

Men climbed busily all over, hanging from slings scraping and painting the hull, pounding oakum into the deck or climbing the rigging to replace ropes and canvas and pulleys. Pierre asked, "Are you serious?"

Shark explained that the Intrepid had recently been rescued from pirates. Originally a French ship christened the Bon Vivant, it had shipped cargo between the Cape Verde Islands, Europe, and Caracas. It had been captured off the coast of Bermuda by Red Albert, the one-legged British freebooter, and re-christened the Happy Shopkeeper, its crew captured or sank three Spanish merchant vessels and a French war ship. The commander of a Spanish galleon, the L'enfant dela Rosa, eventually captured and re-christened the ship the

Intrepid disposing of its crew in a way that did not need to be described. The ship was being prepared to sail to an island off Hispaniola, where its crew, along with a company of carpenters, would careen, repair and reseal it from keel to binnacle. "So's you might almost think she was brand-new."

Pierre said, "That could take a month."

"Maybe" Shark said. "But a month of sailing at decent pay plus room and board, and when you're finished you'll know what kind of ship's beneath you."

Pierre hesitated. He would gladly pass up all that heavy lifting and instead return to work for Guido for those six weeks, but working for a captain to refurbish his ship and getting to know its crew had advantages. And no one can know what the future will bring.

Pierre asked, "So where do I sign up, and when do I meet the captain?"

Shark clapped Pierre on the shoulder. "That's the spirit; quick decisions are always the best. And the captain's name is Hitchens"

Shark led the way up the gangplank. They found Captain Hitchens in the hold directing the loading of provisions and material. A small, round man with a fringe of red hair around a reddish and nut-brown skull and thick, red sideburns that reached to his clean-shaven jaw as if a fringe was all he could afford. Despite his girth he moved quickly and his barked orders resounded from the timbers. A whirlwind in the midst of activity, eventually he turned and spotted Shark. He exploded in a fury and charged over to him.

"Are you looking to die, you walking piece of the Devil's shit?" Though the Captain was shorter than Shark, he looked up at him with an anger that even frightened Pierre.

"Now Douglas," Shark said with a smile, "I said I'd be back and with a new sailor. And so I am and so I have. You can't have no complaint against me now."

"And the money! Where's my goddam money? And don't called me Douglas!"

Turning to Pierre, Shark said, "I introduce you to Captain Douglas Hitchens, late of New York and presently master of the Intrepid."

The Captain glanced once at Pierre and then turned back to Shark. "You said you'd double my money. You promised nothing could go wrong. You said you'd make me a rich man or die in the attempt. Since you ain't dead, I must be as rich as the Pope himself."

Shark said, "Word has it you weigh anchor at sunrise tomorrow."

"What's that to you? Unless you've got my money, don't expect to see the sun rise."

Turning to Pierre, Shark said, "A good captain uses hyperbole in his arsenal of leadership; it always grabs the attention of his men."

"Dealing with you," the Captain said to Shark, "I should have a gun." Despite his bluster, Pierre sensed his fury begin to fade. If that was the result of Shark's patient good humor he had succeeded, and again, Pierre was impressed.

Shark asked, "Signed a full crew yet?"

The Captain's thick, red eyebrows converged in furious concentration but he said nothing.

"So you must be glad to see us." His self-satisfied grin made Hitchens more furious.

"Even if I was one sailor short and hauling a cargo of gold, you'd still never get a berth."

Shark continued to grin. "We've got errands but we'll be back at sunset, and you'll be happy to see us."

"The back of you is all I want to see. And if your friend has any sense, and I doubt that since he's with you, he'll lose you quick as a bad cold. Especially if he hopes to avoid becoming dead."

But Shark had already turned and begun to climb from the hold with Pierre following. Over his shoulder he called back, "No need to put a candle in the window, but it'd be nice."

"Don't come back without my money!"

Shark chuckled all the way down the gangplank. Following back along the docks he said, "His money's long gone and he knows it, which is why he'll sign us. He needs to keep an eye on me in case I know how to get his money back."

Pierre asked, "And how does that work for me?"

Shark stopped and turned. "As soon as you hand me that coin, I'll get you signed up."

"Wait," Pierre said. "First I get signed, then I give you the money."

Mildly surprised Shark said, "Hardly seems fair. I might even think you don't trust me."

"After meeting the Captain, I'll hold onto that coin until I've gotten to know it better."

"Suit yourself," Shark said, though Pierre assumed his indifference was a mask. He followed Shark through the busy side-streets near the docks until he stopped at a ship's chandler named Domenico. "Left something with him I need to get; won't take a minute. After that I'll take you to a place where your coin will be respected and proper-spent."

The shop stood at the furthest corner of a small, thickly-shadowed plaza, a dark green awning shaded its front. Inside was as dark as a confessional, a cluttered, crowded cave piled from floor to ceiling with everything that might be useful on-board a ship.

"If you don't got no money, just go back as you come." That voice seemed to surround them. It took Pierre a moment to discover a small-framed man with lank and greasy black hair, hard black eyes and sporting a salt-and-pepper beard that reached to the middle of his chest emerge from deeper shadows behind a tower of sailor's sea-chests. He guessed he and Shark had been watched from the time they entered the plaza.

Shark said, "I wouldn't be here if I didn't."

Domenico eyed Shark as if Shark's head might explode. "All right, let's see it."

Shark turned to Pierre. "Let him have that coin."

He looked from Shark to Domenico and then back to Shark. "Not what we agreed to."

"You're a sailor on the Intrepid, just like I promised. So, now it's your turn."

"I haven't been signed on, so that coin stays in my pocket until I do."

"A bit formal, ain't we? You're as good as signed. In fact, there's hardly any chance you won't be. How's that not fair?"

Domenico asked Pierre, "You owe this guy money?"

"We have a deal."

"My advice? Hold onto your money. Take it from a guy who knows. If you've got a deal with the likes of him, you make sure he holds up his end all the way through."

Shark said, "Without that sea-chest neither of us'll be able to sign on."

Pierre said, "From the reception we got from Hitchens, there don't seem much chance we'll sign on, seaman's chest or no. Besides, you still owe him that money."

"That's my worry." Shark said and Pierre heard impatience enter his voice. "You think he'll sign before he's got his money, you're dreaming. Only reason he'll sign you is he thinks there's money at the end."

"Don't do it, young fellow," Domenico said to Pierre. "You look like you might be a little bit honest. Only way to hold onto your money is never let it leave your pocket."

Shark sneered. "Don't listen to old farts, they only stink and with nothing to say."

"Who you calling an old fart?" Domenico's face became red and things were about to get unpleasant.

Suddenly handing the coin to Domenico, Pierre said, "Take what he owes you out of that." At its sight, Domenico was caught in mid-phrase, his lips opened as his eyes grew large.

"You sure you want to do this?" he asked plucking the coin from Pierre's palm. He looked it over, tested it between his teeth and looked again at Pierre. Without waiting for his reply he disappeared into the darkness of the shop. Shark clapped Pierre on the back.

"You won't regret this," he said. "I'm a fair man and as good as my word."

"Seems you're the only one who believes that, so I'll leave it to you to prove me wrong."

Domenico reappeared carrying a seaman's chest painted black and chipped and scarred. He handed a fist-full of small coins to Pierre. "It's what you get for hanging around with the likes of him. Be off with you both before minds start changing." But Shark was already at the door, the chest balanced on his shoulder.

Without turning Shark called out, "You're a good man, Domenico, and I don't care what your wife says."

To Pierre, Domenico muttered, "You're associating with the wrong type." Then he turned to disappear among the shadows of his shop.

Outside, Pierre found Shark beside the shop's front door squatting over his sea-chest that rested on the ground. He pulled out pieces of clothing as though something important was at the bottom. Finally, he brought out something wrapped in a worn gray shirt. He peeled back just enough of the shirt to flash golden in the sunlight. He sighed with relief, re-wrapped the object, shoved it deep into the chest replacing everything else and closed it. "We're okay now," he said without looking up, "we'll be fine." He stood, hoisted the chest onto his shoulder and turned smiling to Pierre. "Ready for something to eat?"

"Just what was that?"

"What was what?"

"In the chest?"

Shark gave him a comical expression of surprise. "You mean the thing in the chest? Oh, just the thing what's going to get us in good with Captain Hitchens."

Pierre considered asking for details, but Shark was already headed off and this seemed a bad place to become lost.

Away from the plaza and back into the maze of streets, Pierre followed Shark to a narrow building identical to its neighbors. Without knocking he entered and called out "Estella!"

Inside, to the left stood a shadowed staircase up to a second floor and to the right, four small tables with chairs around them barely contained within the room. The air was thick with the odor of roasted meat and cooked vegetables. Pierre began to think of food, but over his head he heard footsteps cross a wooden floor toward the stairs. At the top of the stairs the footsteps stopped, and suddenly something large and dark flew through the air down the stairs that hit Shark on the shoulder. When it fell to the floor it shattered into several large pieces; Pierre guessed it had been a ceramic chamber-pot fortunately empty.

"Hey!" Shark cried out toward the top of the stairs. "Always throw things at people before you feed 'em?"

"Starve!" a young, female voice cried out. "And then die! Just get out!"

"I've got a guy with me who's got money and we want something to eat."

"If he's with you he won't have money for long. Take yourselves out of here!"

"But we need food!"

"I know what you need and I hope you get it! Now go!"

Shark rolled his eyes for Pierre's benefit, as if to say, 'What can you do.' He hoisted the sea-chest onto his shoulder and led Pierre back through the door. "I was afraid that was going to happen, although I'd hoped by having company our reception would have been civilized."

"Let me guess; you broke a promise"

"I'm confused sometimes by what people think. Makes me wonder if there's any thinking going on at all."

"You told her you'd marry her."

"It was just a manner of speaking and a long time ago. Besides, how could anybody believe what I said, given the usual situation I find myself in? I mean, how honorable can a promise be when a gun's held to your head?"

"My guess is it wasn't that melodramatic."

"Thanks for being wrong."

Shark led Pierre along more twisting streets and gloomy alleys. The sun had nearly set and alleys were bathed in twilight blue, while the tops of the buildings were still washed in gold.

"Where are we headed?"

"In case you didn't notice, this town has more than one place to eat food in."

"This time, think of someplace we won't be thrown out of."

"Being thrown out is something you want to get good at."

Pierre had had his fun at Shark's expense, and now he was ready to follow wherever a meal would be found. Turning a corner, suddenly they stood before a brightly-lighted storefront. Inside were tables and two were already occupied. "Okay," Shark said with resignation, "in this place they're going to expect us to pay money. You still have what Domenico gave you?"

"I still have my money and you have more of it."

Shark reached into his pocket and brought out the three coins Pierre had given him. He handed them back. "Right and fair enough, you're holding all the money for now."

Pierre thought of several reasons to disagree, but instead followed Shark into the inn and sat down. Food and drink were brought to them as Shark spoke.

"I'm not such a bad guy, but this world don't reward saints. Nobody asked me, but if I'd put this world together, I'd have made it so the good guys got most of the breaks. As it is, the good guys usually die first. So, sometimes I say things what ain't true and make promises I can't keep, but I ain't out to hurt people and I never take what the other guy can't afford to lose."

"I guess that's sort of a code."

"There you are, you have me exactly. It's a code and I do my best to live by it."

"And how does that help Captain Hitchens?"

"That's different. He ain't a pal, he's a boss. Different codes between pals and bosses. Besides, the offer was that what money he gave me, I'd get him something worth twice as much. Not a deal most can refuse."

"So is that the thing inside the sea-chest?"

Shark grinned and with his hand tapped the chest crouching beside his leg. "Caught me by surprise, but the guy was in trouble. So I helped him out, just like I did Captain Hitchens."

"You're just a nice guy and can't help yourself."

If Shark recognized Pierre's sarcasm, it did not appear in his expression. "It's the only way I can justify the code. See, its one thing to make the promise you can't keep and another thing to not even try. I don't always do like I promise but I always try."

"And how did that workout for Estella?"

Shark's expression suddenly went sheepish as pink appeared under the skin of his tanned face. "That takes us to a place where all bets are off and anything goes."

"Is that how you explained it to her?"

Shark shrugged clearly perplexed that a discussion he had begun was going badly wrong. "The Intrepid's on a run to Bermuda just as soon as them repairs get finished. If you're smart, you'll figure out a way to make some money out of it."

"And if I'm not?"

"Remember one thing: if there's a way to make money out of something, somebody's about figuring it out. And if that person ain't you, you'll lose. So, if you're clever enough to figure it out, don't waste your time thinking about it. By the time you've cleared it with your conscience, somebody else is walking away with the loot."

"Sounds like you've already got something in mind."

Shark's sly grin bloomed like sunrise through a morning mist.

CHAPTER THIRTEEN

WHETHER BY TREACHEROUS sailors or blood-thirsty pirates, roving crown ships or unscrupulous competitors, dishonest captains or inept carpenters, confused navigators or simple bad weather, this world was a conspiracy aimed to keep shipper and receiver apart and the exchange of goods for capital a matter of willfully suspended disbelief. Shipping was a socially revered form of gambling, with the investor's capital the ante that allowed the game to continue. Regardless of skill or knowledge, a captain rolled the dice each time he weighed anchor. So when he had an intuition about the future of events or of men, dismissing it courted disaster, and at sea that was rarely less than total.

Every captain understood there were more captains and more ships beneath the sea than floating upon it, and that among those were better captains and better ships lost forever. So a captain's success depended entirely on luck, the one thing he could never control. By that, every captain depended upon intuition. Whether the behavior of the wind or of a man, each had to understand what others could not even see. Every captain needed to believe he would succeed where others had not. Because every captain had behind him an army of investors he was expected to reward.

The fate of his crew was one thing, but the fate of those investors was separate. Although they also depended on his leadership, their capital gave him his ship and every inch of line and sail, every rib and nail, along with the pay of his crew, from first-mate to cabin boy. Though all these connections were multileveled, at the apex stood the captain, his hands controlling every lever. And his most powerful lever was his intuitive intelligence.

Though Pierre understood all of this, Shark explained it to him as they ate their meal as a prelude to his insistence they find out who Hitchens' investors were and how much money they were willing to spend. When Pierre asked what value that could have for them, Shark shook his head.

"The Intrepid's a tub. Last voyage she hit a storm, and by the time she limped back to port more sailors was below bailing as up in the rigging, and most of the cargo was lost to water damage. If Hitchens thinks he'll cross the Atlantic, that ship'll need a lot of work along with a gang to do it. Find out who puts up the money and we'll know how to cut in."

"And I take it you know how we'll do that."

Shark shrugged. "Not yet; but when money changes hands there's a space between giver and receiver. We get into that space and we'll peel off a bit as it passes between hands."

"And you've got no idea how we might do that," Pierre said. "Am I right?"

Shark shook off his embarrassment. "We won't know until we know. All I'm saying is, dimwits is throwing money at a ship what won't float across this harbor. What do they expect to make and how do they expect to make it?"

Pierre said, "Okay, so tell me when I can sign-on."

"First thing tomorrow. But there's an evening ahead and I know just the place to go. Let's settle up the bill." He glanced about and with a wink whispered, "Stick close."

Shark signaled he was ready to pay but before the cook reached their table, suddenly Shark got a pained look on his face, began to gag and choke and then his face became bright red as his eyes bulged. He clutched at his throat looking frantically about and then began to wretch. The cook, a round, dark-faced man, stood to one side watching Shark with terror in his eyes, and turned his look to the others at their tables who watched his distress. Shark tried to say something to the cook, but abruptly he stood and rushed to the door. Stunned, the cook turned to watch him. Pierre stood, grabbed the sea-chest and ran through the door as a bellowing voice followed.

Outside, he passed the sea-chest to Shark. The cook appeared at the door shouting and then they ran. Pierre was startled by how fast Shark could run with its weight on his shoulder.

With Pierre's eyes pinned to the middle of Shark's back they ran down one dark alley and within steps turned down another, followed for a time and then turned down another. They ran until Pierre could hardly breathe, and then ran more until they reached a small, deserted plaza where Shark finally stopped. Panting he turned to Pierre and began to laugh. "Admit it," he said, "the food weren't all that good."

Pierre asked, "But if it had been better, you'd have paid?"

Shark shrugged. "Some tricks you only get to play once."

With the chest on his shoulder and twilight deepening he led Pierre to an alley out of the plaza and followed it until they reached a wide and busy street, each window lighted by a candle that brightened their way. Pierre asked again where they were going and Shark simply said he would be glad when they arrived. After more twists and turns they stopped at the darkened door of a narrow, two-story building. To Pierre he said, "Give me that money and I'll double it."

"It's all I've got."

"Then you'll be glad to double it."

"And how do you plan to do that?"

"The old-fashioned way," Shark said. "With cards. Now give it to me."

"So, you're going to gamble it away."

"Didn't I just promise I'd double it?"

"But you said you were going to use it to gamble with."

"The way I play, it's hardly a gamble. Now give it to me."

When Pierre still hesitated, Shark put the sea-chest down. "Oh hell, we've got a ship in the morning. Even if I lost it all, which I won't, there's the Intrepid; remember?"

Pierre liked the money being in his pocket, giving him a sense of security that Shark's promise could not match. But Shark appeared determined, whether his confidence was justified or not. Pierre fingered the coins in his pocket, separated the largest and handed over the others.

Shark scrutinized the coins. "You're holding out; I need all of 'em for this to work."

"So you expect to lose it all."

Shark shook his head. "I told you; the way I play it really ain't gambling."

Pierre hesitated but then brought out the last coin. He reminded himself he had arrived without money, and there would be a gratifying symmetry to leaving as he had come.

With the coins in his pocket Shark rapped hard on the door. In a moment a tall, muscular black man, head shaved clean and a ring with a red stone in his ear, opened it. Glancing once at Shark, he began to close it again.

"Wait, Henry!" Shark said, "I've got money!" He brought out the coins Pierre had given him. Henry looked at the coins shining nested in Shark's palm and then glanced at Pierre. He opened the door and stepped back from the entry.

Shark led the way up dark, narrow stairs as if he knew the building well. On the second floor he stopped at a closed door and knocked lightly twice. This door was opened by a slim, old man with a gray beard and forlorn dark eyes. Grinning, Shark reached forward and shook his hand. "Isaiah, it's good to see you." Isaiah looked from Shark to Pierre and then back to Shark with gloomy indifference. Shark said, "He's with me." Isaiah stepped back and Shark led Pierre into the room. Inside, five men sat around a large, round table. They all looked up.

The thick-set, older man in the chair facing the door grinned at the sight of Shark. "Hope you brought serious money this time."

"And I hope you've got enough to make this visit worth the trip."

A man wearing a red beard but otherwise nearly bald, asked "Your friend sitting in?"

"My banker; name's Pierre Chanceux and he hails from the formidable metropolis of Philadelphia." Turning to Pierre he said, "Since pretty soon you'll be holding their money, I should introduce these gentlemen to you." Pointing to the older, heavy-set man Shark said, "Our host is Josiah Rollins, to his left is Benjamin Duquesne, to his left sits Rolland Clotard, to his left Juan-Carlos Piso, and to his left with his distinctive red beard is Henrik Vandervoort."

With a broad laugh Josiah Rollins said to Pierre, "And if you can recall all of that after your second drink, there'll be a third for you."

To Rollins, Shark said, "I invited him to watch me win."

Clotard said, "Then I hope he's ready to be disappointed." The others at the table laughed. Shark laughed as well but without pleasure. He handed the sea-chest to Pierre. Isaiah moved a chair to the table and Clotard and Piso made room between them. While Pierre took a chair against the wall, Shark sat down and piled his coins in a stack before him. "Whose deal and what's the ante?"

Benjamin Duquesne said, "My deal and seeing as how it's been a while and you brought your banker, we'll start easy; one schilling." He tossed a coin to the center of the table. The others did the same and Shark added his as well. Then he dealt the cards. Pierre had seen enough card games at the tavern to have a vague idea of how it was played, but he had never enjoyed it. Now he regretted his ignorance.

The players studied their cards as Clotard said, "With them ships back what the Governor sent out, and the harbor open for business again, I hear the Argo and the Paloma sail at sunrise." Piso raised the bet to two schillings and asked for two cards. Following Piso, Vandervoort said, "There'll be a regular jail-break, what with all them ships waiting to sail. In two days there won't be enough ships left to make a card game."

Rollins followed asking for one card. "Fine by me; brings in the fresh blood, if you get my meaning. In four days, every ship east of the Antilles'll be fighting for a berth, and every sailor fighting to spend his money." He leaned back.

Shark matched the bet and asked for a card. "Hear anything about the Intrepid?"

Vandervoort studied his cards and smirked. "That wreck! Hitchens'll spend all his money and half the rest of his life getting it in shape."

Clotard said, "I hear he sails in the morning headed to Matanzas for repairs."

Piso asked, "Does he got a full crew?"

Vandervoort said, "Won't need it as long as he's got enough carpenters."

Duquesne said, "With them wrecks off Vera Cruz, there ain't no cheap carpenters."

Shark said, "They come cheaper if they ain't carpenters." The others laughed. The bet went around the table again, Vandervoort raised, the bet continued. When Shark's turn came he asked for one card. "What'll Hitchens do when he gets his ship afloat?"

Others at the table looked at each other. Duquesne said, "When the Viceroy closed the harbor, an army of slaves was headed to San Juan. Maybe he wants to make the cost on one trip."

"So he's fitting out for slaves?" Shark asked.

Piso said, “Sounds like somebody’s looking for a ship.”

“Could pick worse,” Shark said. “Slaves pay good. Especially in San Juan.”

Piso said, “More money for more work. Heard about the Salient?” Shark said nothing. “Four days out of Cape Verde she’s becalmed. After two days, the captain put a dozen of his cargo to oars. Pretty soon the rest of the cargo got loose, captain and crew except the navigator was killed, cargo sailed back to Cote d’Ivoir, scuttled the ship and disappeared into the jungle.”

Duquesne added, “And that crew never got paid.” The others at the table laughed.

When the bet went around again, Vandervoort raised, Piso and Clotard folded, Duquesne called and won the hand. Raking the coins toward himself, to Shark he said, “Seems like old times, me winning and you losing.”

“One hand don’t make a night,” Shark said. He sounded determined though Pierre had doubts.

The deal moved to Clotard, the ante remained a schilling. The others studied their cards and Shark said, “I hear the Confidence sails for Spain in a week.”

Vandervoort looked up. “Captain Delgado says he won’t wait for the armada. Says he’s safer on his own.”

“From pirates?” Shark asked.

Duquesne said, “They say Tom Tew’s cruising the Caribbean again. Raided the Virginia colonies for weeks but there was a storm and he near went down off the Carolinas.”

Clotard said, “I hear the Viceroy put out that sea monster story to scare captains into staying with the armada.”

“And why not?” Duquesne said. “They pay the fees and the Viceroy makes the money, even if the armada’s attacked.”

“Sounds like a good deal for the Viceroy,” Shark said.

Vandervoort grunted. “You’ll want an armada if Tom Tew’s off your stern.”

The bet went around the table, Duquesne and Vandervoort folded, Piso raised and Shark called. Piso grinned collecting his winnings. Shark’s stack of coins had reached a disheartening size, but then he won the next hand and things seemed to look up.

For the following hand, the pot grew large enough so that if Shark won he would fulfill his promise to Pierre. But he failed and his stack became even smaller.

Finally the deal came to Shark. With just four coins left he kept the ante a schilling. Vandervoort had the largest stack and Pierre assumed eventually he would force Shark out. But when Shark took two cards Pierre detected a shade more confidence in his grin.

"Dealer's got something good," Clotard said. Pierre guessed the others had noticed Shark's optimism.

Vandervoort said, "He better if he wants to keep his seat."

Shark said, "You should do so good."

Vandervoort said, "And maybe I will." The bet went around again, he called and won the hand and Pierre's coins were gone. To Shark he said, "Taking money from you makes my day." He tossed a coin to Isaiah and asked that drinks be brought.

Rollins turned to Pierre. "So your name's Chanceux and you're from Philadelphia? You wouldn't perchance be French Canadian?"

Startled, he nodded. He asked, "Your father's name wouldn't be Augustus, would it?"

He was even more surprised and said that, yes, that was his name. He was about to ask how he guessed this when the door opened. Isaiah entered carrying a tray of drinks followed by Henry. He placed the tray at the center of the table and returned to his chair against the wall. Henry stood beside the door. Rollins stood and stepped to the window. With a finger he pushed aside the curtain and stared out.

"Shark, my friend," Rollins said with his back to the room, "it's been a real pleasure seeing you after these many months. When you walked through the door I said to myself, it's good to see my friend Shark is back. But when you sat down and put that bit of money on the table asking about a ship, I said to myself, here's a man on a mission and he'll do anything to make his little pile bigger. So I watched you. I hope you're flattered."

Rollins then turned from the window smiling and walked slowly around the table until he stood behind Shark. Leaning down he whispered, "So I watched you deal an entire hand from the bottom of the deck." He brought his lips close to Shark's ear. "And the worst? Even then, you still couldn't deal yourself a winning hand."

Shark's eyes went large, he looked around until he saw Pierre and weakly he smiled.

"Henry," Rollins said to the man beside the door, "please escort our guest downstairs to the library. On the second shelf of the bookcase there's a volume on the rules of card-playing. Undoubtedly he would value a review. With your instruction, of course."

Henry stepped beside Shark's chair. Shark looked around as his smile faded. He stood and turned, Pierre stood as well but Vandervoort's large, thick hand came down on his shoulder. "Your loyalty does you credit but this matter is strictly between Shark and Henry."

Shark said, "It's always a privilege dealing with you, Josiah, even when it isn't a pleasure." Henry followed him through the door.

When they were gone, Rollins turned to Pierre. "So you're the son of Augustus Chanceux. A remarkable man, I assure you. But you're wondering how I know of him, so let me tell you a story. About a year ago I found myself in Naples. After a bit of this and a bit of that I'd become entangled in a complicated situation with a certain individual. That man's representative was none other than your father. And through his efforts I was spared an embarrassing loss of money and prestige." He grinned. "Now, the individual he represented was a certain Don Giovanni d'archangelo Mezzanotte, a powerful person indeed. In addition to running an occasional errand or managing a negotiation, I'm told your father calculated odds of success for his enterprises and has proved himself useful." He leaned back. "Quite a story, eh?"

All of Pierre's questions suddenly came down to one. "Where is he now?"

"That I'm sure I can't help you with," Rollins said. "I can tell you Mezzanotte has since moved his operation to Sicily. Says he likes the climate, but that's all I know."

Pierre hesitated and then stood. "I suppose I should go and find Shark."

"As you wish." Rollins leaned forward and spoke quietly. "But understand one thing. Shark is a valuable companion while the sun is shining and the weather is fair. Otherwise he's a dinghy without oars. You may reach the beach safe and sound, or you may end up in splinters on the rocks. With Shark, you can just never know." He reached into his pocket. When he brought out his hand he flipped a large coin toward Pierre. Pierre caught it awkwardly. The coin was worth slightly more than the money he had given Shark.

"Consider that a gift from your father and do yourself a favor; don't let on to Shark that you've got it. I promise it'll last longer that way." Pierre looked around the room, the other men looked at him without expression. He hesitated but then turned to the door. As he opened it, Rollins called to his back, "Good luck."

Pierre descended the stairs and reached the first floor but found no one there. He stepped out onto the street and did not see Henry or Shark. He took two steps back in the direction they had come when, from the alley beside the building, he heard a sound. He peered into it until his eyes adjusted to the darkness and saw a pile of clothes. He studied it a moment and it moved.

From the pile Shark's face appeared. Smiling nervously he said, "Ah, it's my friend." The bruises on his face disguised his relief at seeing it was only Pierre.

"Can you stand up?" Pierre asked.

"Oh probably," Shark said and began painfully to shift around. "He never hit my legs." It demanded effort but eventually he stood unsteadily. "You're looking at me like I'm supposed to apologize or something. Things didn't work out like I'd expected, so what."

Despite Shark's discomfort Pierre smiled. "You're right there, but my conversation with Rollins was very interesting."

"Well then," Shark said wincing as he stepped out into the street, "my apology ain't necessary."

"Not necessary," Pierre said, "but it's appreciated. After all, thanks to you we're broke."

Awkwardly Shark hefted his sea-chest onto his shoulder. "Broke we are, just as the good Lord made us. But at least we've a place to sleep. Let's go."

"Mind telling me where we're headed?"

"To the only place that'll take us."

In a short while they reached the foot of the gangplank of the Intrepid. Shark led the way. The sailor on watch greeted him by name and soon they stood in Captain Hitchens' cabin. He was rumpled and red-eyed and Pierre guessed drink and sleep. The Captain fell into a chair with a snarling grin. "Must be my lucky day, again."

"You couldn't be more right," Shark said brightly.

"Seems somebody's already done you a good one." A shard of contempt seeped past the Captain's grin.

Shark shrugged. "Every transaction risks misunderstanding. Despite these trivial injuries, the transaction proved successful. I have," he said patting the sea-chest, "what you want."

The Captain said, "What I want won't fit inside that," but curiosity edged his sarcasm.

"You're about to see how wrong you can be." Shark squatted down by the sea-chest, opened it slowly, rooted around as if uncertain where his prize might be, but then with a sigh of satisfaction he brought out that thing wrapped in a worn shirt. With a glance at the Captain he peeled away the shirt to reveal an object about a foot long, half that wide, fairly thick and made of gold, but with a figure of such eccentric design Pierre found it repulsive.

In an instant the Captain's expression melted into delight.

To Pierre, Shark said, "Told you we'd be well-received."

"Where'd you get it?" Hitchens asked, though his eyes did not leave the object.

"You're the last person I'd expect to ask that. Especially with the business you're engaged in."

"Complexity breeds money," the Captain said. "So hand it over."

"Happily," Shark said, "except we expect to sign on tomorrow and need bunks for the night. As I've provided this service and you've agreed to take us on as crew, let us sleep here."

The Captain's expression changed suddenly, a suspicious glint in his eyes. "I give you all that money and you wash ashore beaten and broke and asking for a favor."

"Let's not forget this trinket." He took up the worn shirt and re-wrapped the gold figure.

The Captain's annoyance was replaced by alarm. "Haste is no substitute for thought, especially in business." His forehead wrinkled, he seemed to be thinking and the effort gave him no pleasure. "You have a deal; hand it over."

"Not so fast," Shark said. "We sign ship's articles and then I hand it over. Seems fair."

Like a wave breaking over rocks, fury exploded over the Captain's face. "What kind of cheating deal you running here?" His voice got louder as his face got redder. "You got a hell of a nerve showing up with that crap story. I should call José down and we take what's mine."

"You could," Shark said. "But it won't say nothing good about your word now do it?"

"You talk about trust like it's something you know."

Shark said, "What I know is I've got what you want and you've got what I want. Makes it a fair deal for both of us."

Hitchins looked from Shark to Pierre and back again, but even Pierre knew he would relent. "You're a no-good piece of shit and I'll remember this next time, you best believe that."

"You deal with me because I'm the only one you trust." Shark held out his hand. "No hard feelings."

The Captain glanced down at Shark's hand as if it were a tarantula but shook it with a resigned sigh. "Just make sure it don't fall overboard."

"Couldn't be safer," Shark said. "Besides, my friend here'll keep an eye on it."

"Just what I need," the Captain said glancing at Pierre, "one more friend of yours."

Shark led the way before the mast and below deck to the crew's quarters. Even before they reached their bunks they heard the snoring of sleeping men. Shark whispered, "Take your pick." He tossed his sea-chest onto an empty bunk. "This one's mine." Pierre chose a top bunk far from the others and near the door. He stretched out on his back, folded his arms behind his head and stared up at the twilight and shadows.

Finally he could consider what Rollins had told him about Augustus and it confused him. Though Augustus never succeeded in teaching mathematics to Pierre, he had a certain talent. If someone had told Pierre he had plotted the path of a star or the course of a falling stone, he would have not have been surprise, but probability theory was different. Despite his curiosity Augustus had never shown much skill or enthusiasm for it. Pierre knew only enough about it to know he knew nothing though he remembered Augustus saying that probability was a window on what the world was thinking about and what it favored or disfavored even while it disguised its ultimate decision until its moment transpired. "Ignorance of probability," he said, "is why people created God; the antidote to the unlikely."

But Pierre was just as curious about his collaboration with this Mezzanotte. He could not guess why he might need the help of someone like Augustus to calculate probabilities. Otherwise, Rollins seemed to suggest something about the man was not legitimate. Pierre had never known Augustus to involve himself in anything with even a taint about it, but perhaps the passage of time and the effort of struggle had changed that. What gave him hope was that Augustus might be with Mezzanotte somewhere in Sicily. Though this report was from over a year before, if Augustus was alive and healthy he was probably in trouble, so Pierre's quest had a reason to continue. Knowing this gave him a conscience clear enough to sleep with.

The next morning they climbed to the main deck. Captain Hitchins sat behind a small table beside the mizzenmast, the ship's log open before him. He watched them approach with bitter annoyance.

Shark said brightly, "Good morning, Captain. Ready to sign your newest sailors?"

"A deal's a deal," Hitchins said. "Just put pen to paper and make everything all official-like and above board."

Shark set his sea-chest down beside the table, took up the quill and laboriously made his mark. Then he passed it to Pierre. When he finished, Shark opened the sea-chest and brought out the precious object. Handing it to the Captain he said, "Time to pass this to its new owner."

Satisfied pleasure spread like sunshine over Captain Hitchins's face as his hands reached out greedily for the object. The moment he had it he unwrapped it. Under the sunlight, the gold figure emitted a shimmering glow. The Captain could not take his eyes from it.

"Well now," he said, "if it ain't the handsomest little article, I swear." When he turned to Shark, there was in his face such undisguised greed Pierre had to turn away. "Now it's time you two did some work. Mr. Wallace!" he called out. A tall, slim-built blond man of some years popped his head up from the open hold. "Take these two below and tell them what needs to be done." Turning to Shark and Pierre he said, "Meet your first-mate, Mister Wallace. Time you earned money like honest men. Now, out of my sight the both of you."

Wallace said, "This way, gents." His wide face was as blank as a ship's rib.

In the shadowed twilight Pierre recognized men he had seen sleeping the night before. Mr. Wallace said, "We've got more coming aboard, but for now you'll help with storage." Around them and scattered throughout the hold were barrels black with tar, tan bales of oakum, enormous bolts of white canvas, pale coils of line, fresh-cut and aromatic yard arms, ribs and planks of various lengths, block-and-tackle sets, hogshead barrels festooned with whitewash and paint, and a hundred other of the things needed to repair a ship. To one side stood barrels of salted pork and dried beans, wooden casks of water, crates of flour and the other victuals to feed a crew of sailors. Wallace returned to the main deck while Pierre and Shark joined the other sailors in the sweaty work of sorting cargo and tying down the hold.

As they worked, more material was lowered into the hold, while by ones and twos new sailors joined them. By the mid-day meal, the ship's complement of sailors and carpenters appeared complete. Their meal was simple and brief and afterward more material was sent down into the hold. Beside the rest of the crew, Pierre and Shark pushed and packed and stacked and stowed until there was hardly enough open space for a man to stand. As evening approached, the last supplies were stowed away and the hold became full.

Pierre was certain he had never worked so hard. His hands were cut and bruised by the barrels and planks, his back was sore and his arms and legs trembled from exertion. Shark, meanwhile, appeared bright as a sunrise, as lively at the end of the day as he had been at the beginning. Chatting in an amiable way as they worked, before the day ended Shark had learned each sailor's name and had offered most of them various forms of advice. Pierre was simply relieved their day was over, but for Shark, it seemed his day had just begun. Over the evening meal he coaxed personal histories of several of the sailors and held them enthralled recounting story after tale. He appeared determined to keep these sailors amused and entertained, but Pierre returned to his bunk and was asleep almost before his head touched his pillow.

CHAPTER FOURTEEN

THE INTREPID WEIGHED anchor at dawn and sailed past Castelo del Morro just as the sun peered above the rooftops of Havana. A clear morning with a good wind, they sailed east into the rising sun. When the harbor had dropped away, Captain Hitchens appeared on the aft-deck to set their course and then called all hands to order.

"In two days we'll sight Matanzas and nightfall should find us well-beached. We've got two weeks to make this ship ready for crossing. We've got plenty of supplies so I expect every man to pull his weight and more. The investors spent a pile of money and they're owed a handsome return. Make this ship ready in less than fourteen days and expect a bonus. Nothing's fairer than that and I'm nothing if not a fair man. So, are you with me?" Mr. Wallace led a weak cheer from the crew, but Pierre supposed he was relieved to hear any cheers at all. Preliminaries concluded the Captain returned below as Mr. Wallace read the crew their assignments.

Pierre could claim no skill useful on a sailing ship, so he was surprised when he was assigned to splice line and tie-off rigging. But after a quarter-hour's instruction, he spent the morning sitting on the deck with the sun on his back and a marlinespike in his hand twisting lines as thick as his wrist. From time to time he looked up to watch sailors pull down rotted and torn sails. Others repaired those sails that could be salvaged, and cut into strips and then bailed those they could not, replacing them with new from the hold. Some carpenters cut and replaced rotted or cracked planks of the deck, others pounded oakum and pitch between the planks. By the mid-day meal, Pierre discovered he had become skillful at his chore. Mr. Wallace must have noticed as well because he sent him to a crew repairing lines to the mainmast. But later, when the Captain returned to the deck and saw him pulling line, he became angry and ordered Pierre sent to the hold. He arrived to find Shark working with three other sailors sorting ribs and planks. It was hard, sweaty work in a dark, dank space and he assumed they were both there as punishment for Shark's blackmail. He guessed the rest of the voyage might be like this.

As Hitchens promised, the bay of Matanzas appeared just passed midday two days later. They dropped anchor off the small island of bright sand and scattered palm trees. By evening the upper sails and their rigging had been repaired or replaced and the deck planks were solid. At sunrise the next morning the crew, including the Captain, rowed ashore to the island. Pierre had heard men describe the careening of a ship, but as Philadelphia had proper dry-docks he had never seen it done. He stood with Shark on the beach in the shade of a cluster of tall palms.

"Captain's saving himself dry-docking fees dragging us out here and this careening bay's pretty well-known." Pierre then asked what to expect. "He's brought us as close as he can to the beach at the highest tide. We'll tie-off a block and tackle to the top halyard and to one of them trees. Tide'll go out and the crew on the halyard'll pull the ship over to one side. Then it's a race before the tide returns. It's a miserable way to work. What with being chased by the tide and then waiting 'til it goes out again, it always takes longer than it should. But dry-dock fees ain't cheap and he's saving a pile."

Just as Shark had described, a block-and-tackle was tied to the stoutest tree close to the beach. The halyard was rowed out to the Intrepid and tied near the top of the main mast. The whole crew then manned the halyard as the tide went out. To set cadence Mr. Wallace sang a chantey and they heaved to expose the port side.

Gangs of men then swarmed the hull beginning at the keel scraping barnacles, spreading pitch and checking for rotted or broken planks. They worked quickly in a race against the rising tide, and as it returned, the ship began to right itself so that gangs shifted to work higher along the hull. When the Captain was satisfied, the process was repeated on the starboard side.

Pierre worked among men working, an experience that was new to him. Each gang had a boss and every task had its skill and so, between blasphemous curses and coarse jokes, work was done. In order for carpenters to replace worm-eaten planks while the other carpenters cut and shaped replacements, they were suspended by ropes from the gunwale. Scraping the hull of old paint and barnacles, caulking between planks with oakum and tar, applying paint, setting canvas, running out line; each task needed a coordination that obscured individual efforts to blend into a gang's achievement. After the evening meal the sailors slept on the beach under the stars.

With the hull scraped of barnacles and its cracked or rotted planks and ribs replaced, caulked, tarred and painted, the crew began to refit the interior. Weak timbers were replaced and interior walls added or moved. As material was removed, the hold itself was refitted.

After eighteen days the Intrepid hardly resembled the ship Pierre had signed onto. The evening the last cleat was nailed down and the last bit of rigging hoisted, Captain Hitchens stood before his crew for another speech. With words of congratulations he assured them that although there would be no bonus there would be a double ration of rum all around. Then he announced they would sail for Freeport the next morning and complete the refitting on the way. He promised that a shipment of tobacco was waiting, along with sailors to replace the carpenters. "When we deliver our cargo in England, there'll be shares for each of you."

Just before sunrise the Intrepid weighed anchor heading northeast and over the several days of sailing the last of the repairs were finished. But Pierre found himself constantly under the baleful gaze of Captain Hitchens who scowled each time he saw him. Once when a line to the foremast got loose, he insisted to Mr. Jefferson, the second mate, that Pierre had been responsible. On another occasion, when the cook complained the supply of rum had been pilfered, he speculated the culprits had been Shark and Pierre. Thus, well before they reached Freeport, Pierre was certain his grudge against them would not change before they reached England. Meanwhile, Pierre became friends with two Portuguese carpenters who added to his skills working with metal. Augustus had taught him to cut, bend and drill brass, but always handed ironwork to someone else. Pierre guessed this was a skill he possessed that Augustus did not.

The Intrepid docked at Freeport soon after sunrise and the Captain ordered the crew to begin loading the cargo of tobacco packed in fifty pounds wooden cases. The crew grumbled that, after the work of refitting and repair, they had earned time ashore. Mr. Wallace suggested he hire some of the stevedores prowling the docks for work. The Captain complained about the expense and about his sailors being paid to do nothing, but in the end he agreed to exchange money for time and stevedores joined the crew. The sun moved higher and the heat in the hold became stifling as it filled with a fog of tobacco dust that left Pierre wheezing.

Meanwhile, Mr. Higgins, the boatswain, proved he deserved his exalted position as he adjusted work details, doling out rest periods while reminding the rest the work was not difficult and they would finish by night-fall. Still, the stevedores helped more than his words and finally the cases were loaded.

Over the evening meal in the galley, a big and broad, red-haired Dutchman named Ruk who had joined the crew in Freeport said, "You men all think this be easy voyage but you keep a weather eye open if you know what's good for you 'cause it come on you sudden and then it be the end and this I know. Strange things happen in these parts. I don't want this voyage but I'm a fool what can't say no to money. So hear me good; last ship we sail these waters and there was a terrible thing in the water, most terrible I seen and I seen plenty things terrible. So I tell you boys it's out there and I seen it and never want to see it again."

A sailor named Cranshaw said, "If it don't got a mermaid in it, this'll be a pretty bad story." Another sailor laughed but Ruk remained grim and did not even turn to look at him.

"Clear day, ship's flying like the hand of God's behind us. Midday meal's finished and me and two others on deck to take a pipe. The mizzen-watch calls something in the water, we look but there don't seem nothing to see. Others join us, there's a good argument and then the watch calls out whatever's out there's coming on fast."

Higgins said, "If it's moving fast it ain't no mermaid what's seen the likes of you." Two other sailors laughed but Ruk continued as if he was seeing it all for the first time.

"I'm saying it was moving fast, ain't I? This is what happened: first-mate gets called, cranky bastard named Gustafson. He's angry 'cause we dragged him from the galley. He makes fun, says it's just a log and we all is afraid of shadows. But he looks for another minute and then orders the captain be called."

Cranshaw said, “Hey, let me guess; he says it’s a log.”

Ruk ignored him. “Captain Schmidt was young. Not much experience but plenty smart. Looking don’t give him a clue, but for sure it’s coming on fast so he orders guns loaded. We’re shipping silver and tobacco, you know, and we’ve got eight-pounders fore and aft.”

Higgins asked, “This the Captain Schmidt out of New Amsterdam?”

“No; I know him. This man hails from Portsmouth. Young as he is he’s a cool customer, changes course a time or two to see how things stand. Sure enough, it’s following us and getting close. Finally he orders his spyglass brought and takes a look, and right away he orders all sail hung and calls general quarters.”

When Ruk said this, the rest of the table became silent and all eyes fixed on him.

“I tell you that last spinnaker unfurls, it’s like I might push this tankard. Cruising at that pace, most times whatever trails us falls well-back.” He paused to let his words sink in. “All the while the Captain just looks with his spyglass. Then he come down from the quarterdeck, passed the spyglass around asking who’s seen it before.”

“Guess it weren’t no mermaid,” Cranshaw said but no one laughed.

“My turn come, and what I see makes me wish I was blind.” Ruk paused and the only sound in the galley was the creaking of the timbers. “Big it is, fills the glass. Ugliest animal in Creation. A devil-thing all scaly like a big snake and black like the heart of Hell. But it’s tall as the tallest mast you ever seen and makes the loudest roar you ever heard. I tell you, mates, you see it you’ll say your prayers and that’s no lie. Fire shoots out its eyes, mates. And skin from its head and arms like great black wings, like it’ll fly when it’s ready. And its teeth...”

Pierre listened more captivated than the others, startled to hear from a sailor who had seen the creature. But when Ruk claimed fire came from its eyes and bat-wings from its arms, something made him mutter, “No! It wasn’t like that!” All eyes turned on him.

Most were startled, but Ruk’s eyes went dark with anger. “You calling me a liar, boy? You saying I ain’t seen what I seen?”

Pierre searched the other faces at the table. “That can’t be right.”

Ruk moved to stand, anger boiling into fury. “You don’t know nothing, boy, and you tell me what I don't know. Better hope you ain't, boy. You ain't big enough to call me no liar."

Shark stood suddenly. "He means the Lord couldn't allow such a creature to exist."

Ruk seemed more confused than calmed. "I don't know nothing about what the Good Lord wants, I only say what I seen. And I ain't guessing; I seen it clear as I'm seeing you."

"Hell of a tale, Ruk," Higgins said. "I heard whoppers before, but yours beats 'em all and that's a fact."

Ruk stood and he seemed to fill half the galley. "Make fun if you like, but nobody don't call me a liar." He glared at Pierre. "I know how to deal with them what calls me so!"

Smiling Shark said, "Nobody's calling you a liar, Ruk; least of all my friend."

Ruk stared at Pierre. "I don't talk of what I ain't seen like some people. Who calls me a liar has a fight on his hands, sure enough."

"Good to hear," Shark said. "Since nobody called you a liar, we won't have no fights." Turning he said, "Think I'll step out on deck and give this meal a chance to pass through." The others chuckled, all except Ruk. Shark did not wait and he led Pierre from the galley.

When they had gone far down the passageway, he pushed Pierre suddenly hard against a bulkhead, grabbed his shirt by the collar and brought his furious face close to Pierre's. "I don't know how you've lived so long, but you call them that are big and ornery liars and you won't celebrate a lot of birthdays."

"He had it wrong," Pierre protested. "Fire didn't come from its eyes and it didn't have bat wings and it couldn't fly." He was in a panic though he could not have said why.

Shark said, "You want to fight over a tall-tale told by a drunk sailor, say your prayers 'cause you'll get lots of practice. Just don't expect me to cover for you again." Then curiosity came into his voice. "You talk like this ain't something Ruk made up."

Pierre felt suddenly caught, unsure he wanted Shark to know how much he knew or how he came to know it. He shrugged and grinned. "It's just a story except I heard it different."

Shark studied his eyes. "You sail too close to the wind and that's a game you can only lose."

Pierre nodded. "I'll mind my manners." He paused. "Thanks for the help."

Taking a step back Shark said, "With that guy you'll be in trouble for the rest of the voyage. Steer clear of him and you'll stay healthy." Pierre nodded because he knew that what Shark said was true. He would do whatever he needed to avoid Ruk.

The Intrepid was a week past Bermuda headed northeast into a rough sea and Mr. Wallace ordered Pierre into the hold to check the cargo. When he reached it he found that the crates and barrels that had come loose were more than he could handle. He reported to Mr. Wallace who ordered him back and promised help. Soon after, Ruk appeared in the hold. He saw Pierre and his eyes brightened. "Wallace don't tell me to help a man what calls me a liar."

"I never called anybody a liar," Pierre said and laughed. "Least of all you."

His remark made Ruk more angry. "You laughing at me, boy? I'm so funny to you? You think I'm a fool?"

"No," Pierre said determined to keep panic from his voice. "You got me all wrong."

"You think you're smarter than me, ain't you," Ruk said breathing hard, anger building in his voice. "Just a dumb Dutchman what you make fun of. Book-learning makes you better than me. Ain't you just the smartest guy. Bet your mama loves how smart you are."

Pierre realized the man would be angry no matter what he said. "You've got me wrong and I don't know how else to explain it."

"I'm good as any man," Ruk fumed, "and a lot better than some."

"You'll get no argument from me," Pierre said. "Now, let's tie this stuff down and get out of this smelly hole." He laughed again but something seemed to make Ruk furious.

"I deal with people like you," Ruk said. "Been dealing with your likes all my life. You think you're tough but I show you what tough is." He rolled his shoulders forward, balled his fists and stepped toward Pierre. "This is how we do a man what calls us a fool."

Panic clutched Pierre's throat and he stepped back. "I got no fight with you." He looked about for an escape but Ruk blocked the only passageway. He took another step back and suddenly he pressed against the bulkhead.

"Step back, because I won't go down easy."

Ruk smiled as he took another step forward. "Call me a liar and then threaten me like I be scared of the likes of you. With my bare hands like a twig I break you, tough guy, see if I don't." His panic became terror. Ruk reached his hand toward him as Pierre spied a marlinespike lying on a crate of tobacco. In one motion he grabbed it and slashed at Ruk's face. Ruk cried out, grabbed his cheek and blood oozing between his fingers he took a step back. He brought his hand away and stared startled at the blood. Suddenly wild with fury, he reached out and charged at Pierre. Terrified, Pierre stepped to one side, but his arm did not move as fast. Ruk's chest pinned Pierre's shoulder and fist to the bulkhead, marlinespike's blade out. With a sickening grunt it sank into Ruk's chest to the hilt, something thick, hot and wet suddenly oozed over Pierre's hand and dripped down his arm.

Ruk turned his face slowly toward him, his anger replaced by astonishment. His lips moved, his eyelids fluttered and then closed. Still clutching the marlinespike to his chest he sank to his knees, rolled to one side and did not move again.

Gasping Pierre stepped away from the motionless body. Beside Ruk, blood leaked into a bright red puddle. He looked down, his hand and arm were covered in the same red blood. His knees gave way and he dropped to a sitting position on the deck. He stared at Ruk trying to take in what had happened. He repeated to himself that Ruk was dead and he had killed him, but that notion slipped from his mind the tighter he tried to grasp it. The desire to run away overwhelmed him, even while he knew there was no place to hide. His panic left him frantic and motionless. He tried to get his feet under him to stand and he failed.

A moment later Mr. Wallace stepped through the passageway, saw Ruk's body and almost to himself muttered, "What in hell's happened here?" He turned to Pierre as over his shoulder he called out to Mr. Jefferson. "Stay with this man while I go for the captain." He looked again at Ruk. "I'll get some men to swab this mess." Then he disappeared down the passageway.

"He attacked me!" Pierre said as he managed slowly to stand. His words to Mr. Jefferson came out in a rush. "He came at me. He wanted to kill me. I just defended myself."

Gloomy with doubt Mr. Jefferson said, "There'll be time enough for all that." He glanced over at Ruk. "Mean bastard; figures he'd end like this." He glanced into Pierre's eyes, his expression as flat and blank as a pond in August. "Shame to hang a man what disposed of trash like him; real shame." Mr. Wallace reappeared with two men carrying iron shackles. At his orders they attached them to Pierre's wrists and ankles.

Captain Hitchins stepped suddenly into the hold, his face red to the crown of his bald head and furious. Arms flailing he turned about as if he might explode. "What's happened here? Why isn't this man in the brig? What're you all standing about for?" He sputtered and fumed as Pierre in chains was led toward the passageway. The Captain turned to Mr. Wallace. "Get that man ready for burial and clean up this mess; my cargo don't need blood on it." He looked hard up and down at Pierre standing beside the passageway. "Too bad it's been a while since we had a proper hanging; a man gets out of practice."

Mr. Wallace said, "Begging your pardon Captain, but it might be best if we had some kind of trial first. Reassures the crew."

The Captain turned on Mr. Wallace as if he had been bitten by a snake. After a moment he said, "Long as its quick; I've got a ship to master and cargo to deliver." Storming out, over his shoulder he cried, "Captain's mast! Call all hands! Trial starts as soon as this man's brought to the main deck."

Pierre turned to Mr. Jefferson. "I defended myself. He attacked me. I tried to fend him off and he kept coming. I cut his face but he kept coming."

"It happens like that sometimes," Mr. Jefferson muttered. "You'll have a chance to explain, though it won't be enough for the Captain. He takes this sort of thing personal." He prodded Pierre in the back to head him along the passageway.

CHAPTER FIFTEEN

PIERRE REACHED THE main deck under a sky whose bellies of gray clouds appeared to touch the sea. The rest of the crew gathered about the main deck in groups and muttering. Beside the main mast stood the same chair and small table he had approached when he signed the ship's articles. Mr. Jefferson attached his shackles to a ring at the base of the mast. Every face returned his look as blank as a puddle and each gaze quickly slid away. He watched Shark make his way to the front of the crowd.

Ruk's bloody body was carried forward on a plank of wood by four sailors and laid by Pierre's feet. A grumbling murmur passed among the crew and continued until Captain Hitchens appeared. He wore a dark blue captain's uniform and under his arm carried the enormous tan ship's log and a black Bible. He surveyed the crew until all became silent.

"Hear ye and all that! My sailor's been murdered and this is the man what did it. But we're going to have a trial before we hang him, so let no man say I ain't fair and don't follow the rules." He glared about as if defying contradiction and then sat down. "Now, we'll hear what this miscreant has to say before he's strung up so you'll know what we're hanging him for." In the silence that followed, Pierre listened to the breeze whistle through the lines and the gentle thump of billowing canvas wondering if his life was about to end on this ship under this sky.

"Right then," the Captain said, "let's get started." Turning to Pierre he said, "Tell us what happened and don't lie or say anything false." He held the Bible toward him. "Put your hand here and promise." Pierre reached toward it as far as his shackles allowed. When the Captain realized he could not reach the Bible, he looked angrily at Pierre as if this breach of protocol was also his fault. "Just promise and we'll dispense with the formalities."

Pierre so promised and then recounted the events. At the end, the Captain looked out over the crew and asked if anyone had a question. After a long silence a sailor at the back of the crowd asked where Pierre had gotten the marlinespike from. He repeated that it had been lying on a crate of tobacco. Another asked who the marlinespike belonged to and Pierre said he did not know and a murmur went through the crew. Someone asked that it be passed around, but when it had been, no one spoke up to claim it.

His impatience at its limit, Captain Hitchens sputtered, "What difference do it make who it belonged to? We know who was stabbed and who done it. Stabbings got to be done with something and we got it. Ask a useful question or I'll pronounce sentence now."

Shark spoke up suddenly. "You say Ruk was about to attack you. Why'd he do that?"

The question left Pierre confused. Shark knew that Ruk had threatened him, so it took a moment for him to realize he wanted the argument described. He repeated it insisting Ruk refused his explanation and threatened revenge. Shark then asked, "Anybody else hear all this?" He said that several others had heard but he could not remember who.

"So you figured Ruk wanted to kill you all along and just waited for the right chance?"

Pierre answered yes, as if he understood Shark's intention.

"So when you saw it was just you and him in the hold, you figured you was in trouble?"

"Of course," Pierre said. "He said he'd get revenge."

"So tell us this," Shark continued. "You say when he first come at you, you cut his face with that marlinespike you stabbed him with. Why didn't you just stab him straight off?"

Pierre looked around. "I figured if I cut him he'd know I'd do it. I just wanted him to leave me alone."

"So what you're saying is, you cut him to warn him off."

"That's true," Pierre said though he remained unsure what Shark was getting at.

"You knew the man hated you, so when he come at you, you cut him to chase him off. But you did that before you stabbed him. Is that how things went?"

When he hesitated, Captain Hitchens said, "Speak up! Is that how things stood?" Pierre nodded before he said, "Yes."

The Captain looked hard at Pierre. "I'm still for hanging you just because he was a friend and you've left me short a sailor." He looked down at the deck as if his troubles were mice scampering about indifferent to his presence. "I don't like this one damn bit."

Shark said, "So tell us this; short of getting beat up, was there anything else you could've done to keep this from happening?"

Pierre's confusion deepened and he hesitated. "Ruk was a big man and he come on me fast. If there was something else to do, he didn't give me a chance to do it."

Captain Hitchens said, "We need a yes-or-no answer here, just so we're clear."

Pierre said, "No. He stood between me and the passageway and he come on me like he knew what he wanted to do so there wasn't anything else I could've done."

Another sailor asked if Ruk had ever threatened him with a weapon like a knife before and Pierre said he had not. "He said he could break me like a twig with his bare hands and I believed him."

The sailor continued. "But he didn't have no weapon; no knife or gun. Is that right?"

Pierre looked around suddenly feeling caught. "He was big enough to do what he wanted; he didn't need a weapon."

Pounding the small table with his fist Captain Hitchens said, "That ain't what the man asked! You stabbed an unarmed man; that's what he's saying."

Pierre looked around and then nodded. "Right, he was unarmed."

The Captain said, "So you stabbed an unarmed man. If you didn't, we wouldn't be here." The crew became silent as he looked them over. "Anything anybody ain't clear about?"

Suddenly Shark said, "I got one more. You didn't carry that marlinespike down to the hold with you, is that right?" Pierre nodded and Shark continued. "So, it weren't like you planned to stab him. It weren't like you went there even knowing he'd be there, is that right?"

"Right," Pierre said. "If I'd known I wouldn't have gone myself."

"All right, all right," Captain Hitchens said. "My patience's run out and I'm finished hearing about this. Unless somebody's got a useful question we'll put it to a vote. Last call." In a silence amplified by the whistling wind and the sigh of the sea, sailors looked around as if hopeful someone else would speak. Suddenly above their heads the watch in the mainmast cried out, "Sail-ho! Sail to starboard!"

Mr. Wallace along with the rest of the crew rushed to the starboard side, and Captain Hitchens looked around as if there was something to see. Finally, to the watch he cried, "Flag!" The watch hesitated before he answered "No flag!"

"Gunners!" Captain Hitchens cried out, "To your posts! All hands to station!"

Mr. Jefferson said, "Captain, what'll we do with these?" He nodded toward Pierre shackled to the mainmast and the dead body of Ruk.

"Leave them; we got work to do."

Shark stepped forward. "Begging you pardon but we'll need all hands. Maybe you should release this man."

The Captain looked from Shark to Pierre to the body of Ruk to Mr. Wallace and then to the ship now visible and approaching fast. Then he did this all over again. Confused, he turned to Mr. Jefferson. "Maybe we'll get lucky and their gunners'll do the deed for us." Then he rushed to the forward gun.

Shark stepped over to Mr. Jefferson and muttered, "Let him down and I'll make it worth your while." Mr. Jefferson looked to Hitchens standing beside the forward gunner and then at the ship growing larger. "In a few minutes none of this'll matter." He went to the quarterdeck and joined the rear gunner.

Abandoned beside the dead Ruk, Shark said to Pierre, "Good luck!" and joined the rest of the crew at the rail.

With his hands shackled and anchored to the mast, Pierre could only look from Ruk's body to the approaching ship. He decided that if his life was about to end, at least he would have an excellent view of what happened next.

The ship approaching was a lanteen-masted caravel with twelve guns port and starboard. Its crew reefed its top and main sails and approached to within a hundred yards. A man on the mystery ship's quarterdeck called out, "Surrender and be boarded or die!"

Captain Hitchens responded, "Go to hell!"

The man cried, "Fire!" In the next instant the Intrepid's forward gun, the forward gunner, the forward gunner's mate and Captain Hitchens himself, all flew like rag-dolls in different directions to disappear beneath the sea. It was as if the bow had been swept suddenly clear with no other damage to the ship. The man on the mystery ship called out, "Surrender or be sunk!"

All eyes turned to Mr. Jefferson aft on the quarter-deck. It took a moment for him to realize he now commanded the Intrepid. He looked about as if someone might step forward to make the decision for him. When no one did, he turned to the rear gunner calling,"Stand down!" To the other ship he called out, "Come aboard!" The crew stepped from the rail and watched the other ship lower a boat. Soon, sailors of the mystery ship stood on the main deck.

A tall, broad-shouldered man wearing a bright green coat and a green cockade stepped forward and saluted Mr. Jefferson. His long and flowing dark hair was tied loosely with a scarlet bandanna. His strong, square chin and sharp dark eyes gave him the appearance of peerless authority. To Mr. Jefferson he said, "My name is Captain Rochelle, master of the Laguna." He held out his hand, and warily Mr. Wallace shook it. "It's too bad about your captain but some men are unable to use the sense the Good Lord gave them. I'll take command of this ship but I promise you and your crew will not be harmed."

Mr. Jefferson introduced himself and Mr. Wallace. Captain Rochelle then saw the shackled Pierre and the body of Ruk. When asked, Mr. Jefferson explained what had happened and what they were about to do. Captain Rochelle said, "You say testimony's been taken from this man and the witnesses have been heard. Has the crew made its decision?"

When Mr. Jefferson said they had not, Captain Rochelle turned to the rest of the crew. "Since you have witnessed this trial, you have a decision to make. Do you agree?"

Mr. Jefferson again looked about confused and when no one stepped forward to contradict, he shrugged. Captain Rochelle said, "Let's hear what the crew thinks." Mr. Wallace took his turn to look around as if he had never been asked to do this before. His hesitation made Mr. Jefferson impatient and he ordered a secret ballot. Shark suddenly called out for a show of hands. This left Mr. Wallace and Mr. Jefferson even more confused, but Mr. Jefferson agreed. So, by a show of hands it was resolved that Pierre should be freed, that Ruk's death was the result of self-defense and Pierre had not violated ship's articles. With this, Mr. Wallace released his shackles.

Shark stepped forward and shook Pierre's hand. "I knew you'd be okay when he agreed to a show of hands; sailors don't like to be seen ordering another sailor killed." He smiled with a hint of pride. Captain Rochelle called for the crew's attention.

"As Mr. Jefferson has wisely surrendered, I hereby take possession of this ship and its cargo. Though your ship has been captured, since none of you raised a hand against us you are all free men and may go as you wish. But the Intrepid's now our consort and she'll need sailors. We're an egalitarian crew and I'm ship's master by its agreement. Any sailor willing to swear to our ship's articles can join us; those who wish to move on will do so unharmed. We sail to Santo Domingo where you'll be free to sign onto another ship. Our only condition is that you sign a charter you won't speak of this or join in any attack on our ship." The Captain waited for a response. "Your decision demands consideration; we'll withdraw to the Laguna. Provide your decision in one hour." With a last look at the crew, he and his sailors returned to their boat and rowed back to the Laguna.

Soon it was agreed who would to leave the ship and who was ready to join the Laguna. But several were uncomfortable with each choice, protesting that since they had not resisted, ships of every crown would pursue them as pirates and they would be turned away from every port. And if they met a crown ship before they reached Santo Domingo, they would be treated as pirates themselves. Pierre, meanwhile, had already decided to join the Laguna.

Mr. Jefferson spied the Captain's boat returning and called for a vote. Pressured with a deadline, most agreed to join Rochelle, while five asked to be put off at Santo Domingo.

Mr. Jefferson announced the crew's decision to Captain Rochelle, and upon hearing it he smiled. "Thus the seeds of freedom are sown. You've made this decision based on your needs; for this I congratulate each of you." He ordered the crew to form a lines where each was then offered articles to sign. This done, he announced that Mr. Jefferson would join the Laguna, replaced at the helm of the Intrepid by a member of his crew for their voyage to Santo Domingo.

During all of this, Ruk's body had remained beside the main mast. The Captain ordered Mr. Wallace to organize a burial crew. He chose six sailors and soon the body was sewn into a shroud of stained, old canvas along with some bits of scrap-iron. The Captain then called all hands forward. With a solemnity that caught Pierre by surprise, he led the crew in a prayer placing Ruk's soul in the hands of the Lord. He then asked for silence as Ruk's body slid from the deck of the Intrepid and disappeared beneath the waves.

Pierre watched all this certain Ruk had hated him and likely would have killed him. But Ruk was dead by his hand, and so he wrestled with an uncertain sense of guilt. An unbeliever, he wondered at the belief in a merciful afterlife, although he agreed it was a nice idea. Still, Ruk's death seemed to end something for Pierre even if he did not know what that was. The transfer of sailors was quickly complete, anchors were weighed and the ships set sail together. Returned to the crew, Pierre soon found himself too busy to think about more.

A surging wind sent the Intrepid cutting across bright clear waves beside the Laguna and the exhilaration of sailing beside another ship caught Pierre by surprise. Each sailor stepped a bit more lively and addressed each other with more respect. So he found himself almost excited to be with his ship.

At the evening meal, Gustav, the Laguna's first-mate and now master of the Intrepid, joined Pierre and Shark and three other at table in the galley. A slim, friendly and youngish man with a quick smile, he spoke with calm and good-humored competence. "I've sailed with the Captain a good while and a more honest, honorable and fair man I ain't never sailed under. But he's also one lucky sea dog and if there's one thing I want from my captain, that's it." He chuckled quietly. "Once off the Tortuga Straits we was boxed in by three British crown ships. Cannons seemed to fire at us from every point of the compass, but the Captain was cool enough and talk about lucky. In all that smoke he sailed so them British ships fired into each other until one went down. By then we was out of range with hardly a man dead and just a few more injured. He's a lucky sailor, I can tell you, so I count myself lucky to sail with him."

Shark shook his head with a quizzical smile. "You can't be too lucky in this life, not by sea nor land." The others nodded and Pierre nodded with them.

"Lucky he is," Gustav said. "But he deals fair with a sailor and I'm lucky there, too. A sailor once said I stole money from his kit and another swore he seen me do it so the crew was pretty sure I done it. There weren't nothing to any of it but it come to the Captain and he grilled me like a side of pig.

I stood my ground until somehow he figured I spoke the truth, so he went after the men who accused me. And I'll tell you what; in fifteen minutes they was accusing each other and I was off the hook. Next day, they both took ten lashes at the mast for false charging a fellow sailor. It didn't make me feel good seeing them two whipped, but it proved I weren't a liar. Honor ain't just an important thing, it's the only thing a man's got. But to keep it he's got to be free to do what adds to it and avoid what hurts it."

A sailor named Hugo asked what the Laguna's crew was after. He smiled. "Just the ship, the crew, the arms and powder, the gold and the cargo. We go after merchantmen and don't hurt nobody if it can be helped. You seen our gunners, and that shot weren't nothing special."

Shark laughed. "So you don't leave much when you're done."

Gustav said, "Except for the honor of the captain and his crew. It ain't no dishonorable thing to surrender to a superior enemy. Been there plenty of times, so you can take my word."

Another sailor named Frederick asked what he meant. Gustav said, "Before I sailed with the Captain I lost more battles than I won and seen the inside of more brigs than I can count, and each of them was the awfulest you can imagine."

A sailor named Howard laughed saying he expected Gustav must be rich by now. Embarrassed, Gustav looked away. "We done all right." He then asked what Gustav planned to do with his share of the loot.

"The Captain don't want us thinking like that. Says it's the act and not the result what deserves the closest thought. For him, thinking about the end confuses a man about the means. He says a man should think about how to preserve his honor, and honor ain't in what we have but in how it was got. So, we worry about what we do and what it says about our honor."

Howard asked, "So you don't know what all you've got or what you'll do with it?"

Gustav grinned nervously. "Put it this way; there's an island southeast of Madagascar we kind of made our colony. Built houses and a dock and such and even recruited some farmers. It's kind of our own little country. Anyway, we like it pretty well."

Shark said, "I don't suppose you'll tell us where it's at."

Gustav shrugged. "Don't need to; we'll get there soon enough."

"So this island," Frederick asked, "do it got women on it?" The others muttered and laughed and even Pierre smiled.

"Enough," Gustav said, "and some are even young and pretty."

Then Pierre spoke up. "Sounds like you plan to settle down there when you've done pirating." Gustav nodded and Pierre asked, "Since you don't know what you've got, how'll you know when you've got enough so you can quit and settle down?"

Gustav looked down for a long moment. "We'll know, and then we'll never look back."

"And never look back," Shark repeated quietly, as if the phrase itself enchanted him.

"That's the point of honor," he continued. "A thing done proper-like, there ain't no need for regret. You done your best in the best way you knew and for the best reason."

Pierre said, "So you figure you're free of the past." When Gustav said he didn't understand what he meant, he said, "Like this island; you believe that regardless of what you've done, acting to preserve your honor means you'll never need to regret anything."

Gustav studied Pierre with half a smile. "I'd answer yes if I knew where that was going."

Pierre shrugged. "It's just that there's this man who says everything that is, is a result of what was, and that everything that'll be is a result of everything that is. The point being that results of our actions already connect us and in ways we can't ever know."

Gustav turned to Shark. "Your friend talks like he's read a book."

Shark laughed. "I tell him it don't do no good, but he thinks there's some point to it."

Gustav nodded thoughtfully. "He's young; he'll get over it."

"With or without books," Hugo said, "it's a nasty world and no way out of it but one."

Gustav sighed. "Truer words were never spoke."

Pierre said, "So tell me this; you settled down with your money and women on this island, think you'll ever wish you were a pirate again, cutlass in hand and gunpowder in your nostrils? Ever wonder about that?"

"Honestly?" Gustav asked. "No."

"Sounds certain," Shark said to Pierre. "Seems he answered your question pretty neat."

Pierre continued. "But if you're no longer free to do it, what can your freedom mean?"

Frederick said, "Choosing not to do something is different from being forced to do it, and I know an old salt chained up in Bristol prison who knows that difference."

Remembering his father's words Pierre said, "It's a feeble concept that can only be defined by its contrary."

Looking at Pierre, Gustav's eyes narrowed. "Now that's something you don't think up climbing through the rigging."

Later when they had retreated to their bunks, Shark said, "Until we're off this ship you need to stop getting yourself into jams; know what I mean?"

This caught Pierre by surprise. "You think I was jammed up?"

Shark shook his head as if certain they spoke different languages. "Honesty is a virtue nobody likes, and telling people what you honestly think makes nobody grateful. Guys like you don't think this way, but people appreciate dishonesty if it saves them from having to be honest."

Pierre asked, "And what about you?"

Shark shrugged. "I hate honesty as much as the next guy but I can take it standing up, if that's what you're getting at."

Pierre grinned. "That pretty much covers it."

Secure in his bunk within their sleeping ship, Pierre wondered if he was free to think about freedom, and he was relieved that he fell asleep before he found an answer.

CHAPTER SIXTEEN

SIX DAYS LATER and still under a gray sky of dismal clouds they docked at Santo Domingo where the Captain put off the sailors of the Intrepid who wanted to leave and ordered the ship refitted with additional guns. Because of the work already completed this demanded less than a week. Walking the city together, Shark made certain Pierre was amused. Meanwhile and to his surprise, his skills had become so valuable he was assigned to nearly every work-gang.

As the work approached an end, Captain Rochelle announced that the Laguna and the Intrepid would sail for Bermuda where the Intrepid would continue north to raid ships along the American coast and the Laguna would sail east after ships out of the Azores and after a month they would rejoin at Freeport harbor. The last night in Santo Domingo, Pierre was told he would remain with the Laguna and he was relieved that Shark would be part of the same crew.

With fair weather and strong breezes filling the sails of the two ships, after three days they reached Bermuda where they took up their separate courses. The sun was high in a deeply blue sky as Pierre sat with his back to the quarterdeck next to Sandoval, a carpenter originally from the Laguna. In the days after the Intrepid's capture Pierre found himself working beside him, and he turned out to be someone Pierre enjoyed talking with. Along with his skill working in wood, Sandoval had read a few books including several concerning what Pierre was curious about. He was flattered by Sandoval's approval of his search for Augustus. So he relaxed in his company and one day asked him how he had become a pirate.

Sandoval was a short, strongly-built man with thick, curly black hair and hard dark eyes, and his smile seemed to compress his face. "It weren't like I set out for that. I went to sea young on account of there weren't no other work, and served under a lot of captains since then but I was always a loyal, honorable and hard-working sailor, or tried to be. A year ago I'm stranded without a ship in Havana and a friend signs us onto the Olympia out of New York, Captain Charles Claggart master. We was to run a load of timber from Havana to Barbados and then collect a shipment of molasses for Savannah. The Captain promised we'd pick up another cargo there. Myself, I'd been on enough voyages that went that way. We weighed anchor with a full crew; the usual mix of the useful and useless and nothing special about it. Two days out the Captain calls us all on deck saying something's been stole from his cabin and he'll get to the bottom of it. Seems his wife made up a chest filled with his favorite food, but somebody'd broke into it and stole some. We'd only just left Barbados and nobody was starving so this don't make much sense. Besides, what's worth breaking into a Captain's cabin to steal? But he's sure and furious and swears he'll find out who done it if it takes the rest of the voyage. Next morning he goes down the line, asks each sailor what he knows. Of course, we all say we don't know nothing about any of it. Most of us figure this is just about him scaring the rest of us into listening to him; I've served under a couple of those, though it never turned out good."

"Anyway, he turns up nothing and gets furious. Next day he calls us all again, saying three sailors know all about it and he names them and orders them to tell what they know. They're as surprised as the rest of us and say they don't know nothing, but that just makes the Captain madder. He orders them shackled, each to a different mast, so time and hunger'll loosen their tongues. Real respectful-like, the first-mate says this'll upset the crew and never solve the theft. But that just gets the Captain hot and he tells him to follow orders or be ready to join 'em. The first-mate does what he's told, but the Captain's set himself against the crew and we know this can't end well. Them sailors stay shackled for a day and a night, so by the next day they're miserable and angry. But worse, the sight of them chained up works on the rest of us."

"We ain't a bright bunch, but seeing men chained up who're neither better nor worse than the rest of us, it don't take much imagination to see ourselves in their places. So before the sun starts to set the talk begins. By twos and threes, that's how these things go. I seen the worst of men suddenly realize what's going on and join the group. A sailor they wouldn't piss on if he was on fire suddenly becomes a man they'll risk their life to protect. What's oddest is, Claggart's an experienced captain and should know he's destroyed his chance for a smooth voyage."

Pierre asked, "Did he ever say how he was sure of this theft? Evidence or something?"

Sandoval shrugged. "He's the captain so he don't need any of that. Being captain, whatever he says is true. That's how captains are; they're right no matter what."

Pierre said, "I suppose, alone in the middle of the ocean, that makes sense."

Sandoval nodded though Pierre wondered if he was convinced. "That night the talk goes around and candles burn, I can tell you. Only sailors who stay away from all this palaver is the first-mate and the second-mate. As officers, they're loyal to the Captain, whoever he is, and they'll see this voyage through. They swore oaths, after all, and its them oaths they're loyal to. Next morning, the shackled men are worse than miserable. Burning sun, no food or water and there'd been the nights. But the worse-off they get, the madder the rest of us get. Sailors go to the first-mate to plead their cause but he says there's nothing he can do. By now we're hot for something to be done, so the plots get serious because any one of us could be next. Worked ourselves into a terror, I tell you. By then, the only people who ain't part of the mutiny's the first-mate, the second-mate, and the Captain himself."

"At four bells the Captain orders all hands on deck. Nobody steps forward to confess so he orders them miserable sailors ten lashes, and another ten if they don't talk, and then swears this'll go on until somebody talks. Of course, this just makes us even madder. He orders the first-mate to start with the first man and he does, but after two good ones he stops. The Captain's surprised and orders him to continue. The first-mate turns to him saying the punishment's wrong and he won't do no more. It takes a second, but the Captain gets red in the face and orders the second-mate to shackle the first-mate with the others. But he don't move, either. The Captain repeats the order but the second-mate says he's with the first-mate and won't do it."

"At first the Captain lets loose all around him, but then suddenly he stops like finally he sees he's surrounded by enemies and nobody'll follow his orders. You could see his face change, getting even redder like he might explode, but there's nothing he can do. Finally the first-mate tells him the crew's about replacing him. The Captain gets so mad he can't talk. But he looks around like he knows what happens next because he gets real calm. Quiet-like, he asks the first-mate what he's about. Just as cool, he tells him he'll be set off in a boat with provisions along with whoever wants to join him. The Captain complains they'll drown before reaching dry land, but the first-mate says he's a good enough sailor and won't have no trouble. In the end, four sailors along with the quartermaster join Claggart in the boat."

"But why did those men join him? I thought they were all part of the mutiny?"

Sandoval shrugged as if the rest of the story was obvious. "Maybe they figure we'll be caught and hung for mutiny and don't want no parts of that. Or maybe they're loyal to their oaths and won't do nothing to hurt the captain."

Pierre said, "I guess an officer's always an officer."

"Unless he ain't, but I expect that's how they saw it, too. Anyway, as the boat's being made ready, the Captain stands at the quarter-deck rail swearing he'll see us all chased down and brought to the King's justice. Then he smiles saying he can't hardly wait to see us swing from a gallows. I expect right then, each of us started thinking about his own neck. But when the boat's lowered, like we'd all just woke up from the same bad dream, we start to jeer and hoot and send him to the Devil. Once the boat's off, first thing we do is make the first-mate captain, and the first thing he does is rename our ship the Laguna. And what's the best part? The first-mate was Captain Rochelle and the second-mate was Mr. Gustav. We've had plenty close-calls since then, but nobody's ever said they was sorry, and that includes me. So when anybody asks, I say Captain Claggart made a pirate of me." He laughed quietly shaking his head.

"And what happened to Claggart?"

Sandoval's smile became rueful. "Him and his crew landed safe in Savannah just as Rochelle said. Claggart sails direct to London and the Admiralty court declares us all mutineers. So now, the best of the British navy's after us. We first spied the Intrepid thinking it was British until we got a better look."

Pierre asked, "So what'll you do if you meet up with a real British warship?"

Sandoval laughed. "Run like the Devil's behind us. And if that don't work, run faster. A good pirate runs before he has to fight, so we do a lot of running." He laughed louder.

"Once off the east coast of Madagascar an Indiaman sails into view. She's sailing low in the water so we're sure she's loaded to the gunwales with loot. Captain Rochelle ain't convinced but his crew's ready and it's been near a month since we found a good prize. We maneuver to attack, but two more pop up on the horizon. Your typical Indiaman don't got many guns so we're sure in a fight against one we'll win, but against three we're done. The Captain don't hesitate; we swing about and put them ships to stern. But, instead of being happy we cut off the attack, they chase us. That catches us by surprise, I can tell you. We hang sail thinking they'll drop back quick, but don't they do just the opposite? They hang more sail and then they're catching up. Captain has a palaver with Mr. Gustav and the gunnery mate. We make a quick turn to port, a ship on their flank peels off after us, but we put enough distance between him and that ship in the center of the line. Lucky Rochelle, we catch a wind change to make another turn and the Laguna sails between the two of them in the opposite direction. We pass and let loose with all our cannon, port side on the one, starboard side on the other. Caught 'em by surprise, I can tell you, because we get no answering fire. We get off two volleys before they're astern, and the damage puts them both in enough trouble so they can't follow. That day we was happy just to have a ship under us." Then he leaned toward Pierre. "Always remember, running saves lives, especially your own. And it never hurts to be lucky."

CHAPTER SEVENTEEN

THREE DAYS OF clear skies and fresh breezes convinced Pierre he was on his way to finding his father and this certainty lightened every chore. He sat one day beside Sandoval at the foremast when he told Pierre they were about to cross the Devil's Line. When he asked, Sandoval told him it was called the Devil's Line because of the devilish things that happen there. He asked what sorts of things and Sandoval said, "Things grown men don't talk about. Weird shapes afloat, puffs of light like clouds of colored smoke, islands what disappear when you get close, and big ugly beasts." He grinned and shook his head. Looking into Pierre's eyes he said, "You hear some things from sailors, you really do."

Pierre said, "But you don't believe any of it?"

"Put it this way; a man sometimes sees a thing because he don't want to see it, just like sometimes he sees a thing because he wants to see it. At sea, things like that are always hard to say for sure."

Pierre hesitated. "So if you saw something that wasn't there, which would it be; something you wanted or something you feared?"

He turned with a curious look. "How'd you get to asking such good questions?"

"Answering a question with a question don't answer the question."

"Now that's for sure, ain't it."

Pierre asked, "So is that your answer?"

Sandoval shrugged. "Some questions just don't got good answers. But what about you; what would you answer?"

"Easy," Pierre said, "the thing I most feared. But I could be wrong there, too."

"You see," Sandoval said, "some answers ain't answers." He stood. "Anyway, you give me something to chew on and I ain't sure I'm glad or annoyed."

As Sandoval walked away Pierre wondered about this Devil's Line and whether it might be the haven for the beast. He tried to recall if the Bristol had been attacked in the general area of this Devil's Line and could not. He wondered then about Ruk's account and whether that attack took place in this same area. But the attacks on Port Royal and Don Benito's hacienda on the island of Cuba both happened far from this Devil's Line. He was tempted to warn Captain Rochelle about the creature, but if he did that, unless it made an appearance he would be mistrusted for the rest of the voyage. Still, he liked Sandoval's story and its suggestion of the inscrutable; an intimation that the impossible was likely and the improbable inevitable.

Then, several days after Sandoval told his story and just after a cloudy sunset, out of the deepening twilight a twin-masted ship suddenly appeared astern the Laguna and running somehow with reefed sails. Mr. Gustav looked it over through the spyglass and saw no sailors about. The Laguna's crew wanted to pursue the ship until the mizzen lookout called out that it had turned. Surprise rippled through the crew and Captain Rochelle was called.

He reached the helm and after a glance ordered a change of course as if daring the ship to follow. But when it did the same, the crew's greed turned to alarm. The Captain ordered another change of course and so quick and neat the Laguna suddenly was astern the mystery ship and drawing close. Mr. Gustav insisted the crew was hiding below-deck and he wanted to fire on the ship and provoke them into showing themselves. But the Captain said he wanted to see them make the next move and he did not need to wait long. The mystery ship turned suddenly hard to port and quickly was again astern the Laguna. Then, in a maneuver that startled Pierre, Captain Rochelle made a turn that set the Laguna to approach the mystery ship's starboard. To the crew's surprise the mystery ship allowed the Laguna to approach.

Mr. Trevor, the quartermaster, wanted to board the vessel saying he was certain there was treasure to be gotten. When asked how he knew, he insisted ghost ships always carry treasures and that's why they're ghost ships. But Mr. Gustav argued against, saying that if it was a ghost ship it could disappear as quickly as it had appeared and then where would they be. The Captain followed their conversation without conviction, reluctant to take the risk but also reluctant to deprive his crew of loot. He told Mr. Gustav to form a boarding crew under the command of Carlos. Henry, Pedro, Alfonso and Pierre completed its crew.

The Laguna neared the ship's starboard and the Captain ordered the longboat and its crew lowered. When the crew reached the mystery ship they tossed grappling hooks and tied up to climb to the deck. More curious than frightened, Pierre climbed aboard last.

Under full night of dense clouds the deck was black as pitch and, except for the slap of the sea against the hull and the groaning of its timbers, silent. Reaching the main deck the crew waited beside the gunwale expecting sailors to emerge from below determined to defend their ship. No one appeared, but Carlos still assigned Alfonso to remain on deck as guard. Then carrying a lighted lantern, he led the rest through the black maw of the gangway.

Pierre entered behind Henry while Pedro followed behind him. But once across the threshold, the light from Carlos' lantern disappeared and suddenly there was no one in front or behind him. It seemed Pierre had only advanced a few steps, so he turned expecting to rejoin the others but he found himself alone. In that darkness suddenly he was utterly confused. He reached out his hand until it touched a wooden bulkhead and the timbers overhead. They were wet and slimy as if they had been underwater and for a long time. Continuing ahead Pierre reached an overhead beam that was cracked near to splitting. He still hoped his eyes would adjust to this darkness, but nothing became clear and he seemed to move through a dream. He was tempted to call out but resisted, fearful he would alert the mystery ship's crew. With his hands extended he moved blindly along the bulkhead, determined to reach dry timbers and hopeful that then he would be on the path back to the main deck. Then his hand discovered a gap.

He reached out his foot to be sure the deck continued beneath him, and moving further he detected the frame to a passageway that he expected would lead to an exit, so he continued forward until he reached a corner. Moving his hand along he reached another corner, turned and moved to discover another corner. He turned again, certain he would return to the passageway, but to his surprise, after several steps he reached another corner. Now without any certainty of direction he followed the bulkhead still hopeful he would return to the passageway, but again he reached a corner. He wondered how he managed to miss that passageway he was certain was there, and continued confident it must be just ahead. So when he failed to find it, he began to panic. Reaching another corner, he decided to resolve his confusion by crossing to the opposite corner. After three steps his foot reached into empty space and he fell forward with a scream.

But he was startled that his fall was short and left him half-sitting on a pile of something soft and wet and smelling like the inside of a sailor's shoe he hoped was seaweed. He listened, wondering if his cry had alerted the mystery ship's crew, but he had no way to judge the continuing silence and this frightened him. He sat forward and cautiously reached his leg down expecting to find the deck. But his foot touched water and then sank. The water was frigidly cold, but halfway to his knee his foot touched wood. He slid his other foot down beside it and then stood. With a shock his head bounced hard against a beam. Wherever he was, the timbers overhead were so low he could not stand straight. The water surrounding his legs seemed to be getting colder. He leaned forward and reached out his hand. Moving his feet slowly ahead, his forehead banged against another beam. He reached up and beyond it to discover still another. Reaching past that one he found the ceiling beyond was higher. He contorted his body through what he imagined to be an entrance to its open space. But the overhead beam suddenly dropped to trap his thigh and hold it firmly but not painfully, as if his leg was wrapped in a passionate embrace.

He tried to lift the beam but he could neither move it nor squeeze out from under it. He was trapped and helpless in absolute darkness below the deck of a ship from nowhere. He was about to call out when a cloud the color of dark smoke appeared before him that was only just brighter than the absolute darkness. He blinked his eyes hard but that cloud remained. Then, as if coming from within the cloud though seeming within his head, a voice quietly said, "Do not fear." This voice seemed familiar though he did not recognize it. He looked about but aside from that shapeless cloud his darkness remained complete. Trying again to lift the beam the voice said, "You are not here, this is not real, you are in no danger."

He was certain the speaker stood nearby but looking about revealed nothing. The voice said, "Iron against iron, you will prevail. Decisions have been made, your path is laid and its steps charted. Danger surrounds you yet you will come to no harm. Allies approach though you will not recognize them until their mission is fulfilled. Your quest will not end here; your prize eludes you as your heart fails you and distraction rules your mind. Light and darkness are not, space and time are not, you see what is not and that which exists you are unable to see. Release your mind; what you believe can only harm you. Your escape is imminent. Though your voyage will be long you will reach firm land. Birds will speak your name and men will solicit your thoughts, mountains will explode and night will become day. But beforehand, the sky will join the sea and the world will turn upside down. All of this must come to pass before your quest is rewarded. Fear nothing for there is nothing to fear. No matter the darkness, light approaches."

Suddenly and muffled by distance, he heard the thunderous roar of the beast. Panic opened his eyes wide. Above him, specks of silver became stars glittering down. Somehow and at some moment, the sky had cleared, and cool evening air washed over his face. Henry said, "We'll carry it over to the Laguna."

Alfonso said, "There's too much, we need more hands."

Pedro said, "We should ask the Captain; he'll know what's best." In the darkness of the main deck Pierre managed to stand. Alfonso and Henry stood at the gunwale holding cloth sacks he guessed contained treasure.

Henry said, "At least we'll take these back; give the crew a taste of what's waiting for 'em." He and Alfonso moved to lower the sacks to the longboat and Pierre said, "Don't do it!"

In the starlight all faces turn toward him. "This ship's cursed and so's its cargo." When no one spoke, he continued. "Lift even a single nail and we die."

Henry laughed. "Spooks and ghosties won't keep me from this gold. Stuff's piled here for the taking and that's just what I'm doing."

Pierre said, "It's poison! You want to spread that poison to the Laguna?"

Pedro said, "He's got a point; this ain't no ordinary ship. I want this gold as much as you but I won't die for it. Let's leave it and check with the Captain."

Muttering and head-shaking followed, but the crew agreed and the sacks were returned to the deck. Henry laughed calling them all cowards and fools and warned that following Pierre's advice would cost them. Then he announced he would stay behind and guard their loot for them until they came to their senses. Standing beside the gunwale, he watched the rest of the crew climb down to the longboat and cast off to row back to the Laguna.

The longboat had reached halfway between the two ships when suddenly there was a low, clear rumble that only Pierre recognized. The rowers stopped and looked around. Aside from the wind and the slap of the sea against the sides of their boat, their attention was rewarded with silence. Carlos said they should continue on to the Laguna but Pedro wanted to go back for Henry first. After a moment Carlos said it was more important to report to the Captain.

They tied up beside the Laguna and the crew reached the main deck to find the Captain and the rest of the crew waiting. Carlos described what had happened and what they had found. Hearing of the loot, the crew insisted they return and grab as much as the longboat could carry.

They turned then to hear what Captain Rochelle thought, and he hesitated. "Seems like easy taking," he said, "and it's been awhile since we had a prize. You men know I fear no living man, but that ship maneuvers without a crew; it ain't ordinary. So truly, I fear its cargo'll put the Laguna in danger." They all again heard a low and distant rumble that could not be thunder. The Captain ordered Carlos and his crew to return and fetch Henry but leave the loot. They went over the side, climbed down into the longboat and were about to release the lines when, from the mystery ship, Henry cried out. They turned to see at the very top of the derelict's foremast a tiny and sparkling white light like the tip of a candle flame.

Pierre and the crew froze at their oars to watch that glittering light almost imperceptibly begin to descend the foremast. But they were astonished when suddenly a light appeared at the top of the other mast. As slowly as dripping molasses, both lights descended their masts together until they reached the first yards, where they astonished the crew by spreading along their tops. The lights then continued to descend following the lines of their rigging until the upper part of the derelict glittered with countless sparkling white lights. Scintillating against the black sky, these lights continued to descend to outline more sails and their yards and glitter along their lines to festoon the rigging. But when the lights reached the last of the yards and continued to descend following the masts to approach the main deck, Henry began to scream for help.

His cries seemed to release the longboat's crew from a mesmerized slumber, and they began to row frantically for the derelict. With pitiful cries of terror, Henry screamed for them to hurry. Those sailors still on-board the Laguna remained at the gunwale calling back that help was on the way. The light continued to descend, and when it reached the main deck it seemed to flow in all directions until it reached the gunwales. The crew then watched horrified as Henry himself took light, scintillated as if encased in cold fire. Illuminated, he gestured wildly for a moment in terrifying silence.

Despite Henry's silence, the crew of the longboat continued to call out as they rowed. That light gradually dropped beyond Henry and passed the gunwale. Then, at the moment the light reached the waterline, the entire ship suddenly became blinding bright. In the next instant and without any sound the ship disappeared, though its outline in light continued to sparkle, a glittering afterimage that hovered for several seconds above the sea where the ship had been until each of those lights blinked out.

The stunned crew of the longboat resumed rowing and began to call out Henry's name. Reaching the site of the derelict and finding no one in the water, Carlos announced that Henry must be truly gone and ordered the longboat to return. The crew rowed the longboat back in silence and reached the Laguna; its crew returned to the deck as the longboat was then hoisted aboard. Carlos was reporting what he had seen to the Captain when suddenly they heard that same low rumbling roar, its sound now closer, and it froze each at his post and frightened Pierre. The Captain ordered the crew to the masts to hang all canvas and gave Mr. Gustav a course to steer. Even before the crew reached the yards, the Laguna began to move.

Shark turned to Pierre curious and angry. "You know something about that, don't you." When he said nothing, Shark said, "It's in your face, like you seen a scorpion crawling up your arm." When Pierre said nothing Shark's look turned to concern. "Think we'll get away?"

"Maybe that's the point," Pierre said. "What's the danger?"

Shark laugh resembled a snarl. "Sure, right, play dumb but you already know. You want me to keep quiet, that's fine. Just don't be thinking I'm dumb, too."

Pierre hesitated. "I hope we'll get away, but if we do we'll be the first."

Shark asked, "That bad?"

"If there's anything good about it," Pierre said, "I never heard it."

Suddenly, a sailor in the rigging cried out, "The wind!" It took a moment to realize in all that darkness but the wind gradually weakened as the sails lost their shape. In a few moments the only sound was the slap of the sea against the hull and the groan of the ship's timbers. Sailors looked at each other. Then, once again, they heard a low rumbling roar that seemed even closer.

Captain Rochelle gathered his officers on the quarterdeck beside the helm. Pierre again resisted the temptation to warn them of the danger. They heard that low rumbling sound again and there could be no doubt it had drawn closer still. The Captain and his officers debated whether to wait for the wind to return. The officers suggested they wait until sunrise to give the crew a rest. But the Captain was not convinced they had that much time. He turned his spyglass in the direction of the sound though he had little chance of seeing anything. Finally he called out to Mr. Gustav and Mr. Trevor to lower both longboats. Each was tied by a line to the ship's bow. When their crews reached the ends of their lines, those lines leaped sparkling from the water. The officers in each called out the stroke and they began to tow the Laguna to find a fresh breeze. Shark and Pierre were assigned to Mr. Trevor's crew.

The sailors cursed each other and the wind and the sea and their kings and their gods as they pulled hard on their oars. Mr. Gustav called out his cadence in an echo of Mr. Trevor's, and the sound traveled over the placid sea as easily as across a dinner table. Very gradually, with each stroke, the Laguna began to move and then gain speed. But the crews once again heard the low, rumbling roar. With that sound seeming even closer, arms and backs grew stronger although hearts quailed. But the officers did not need to tell them to pull as though the Devil himself was chasing them since each sailor now believed this was true.

No sailor pulled harder than Pierre. He rowed until he could no longer feel his arms from their pain, until his thighs were burning ropes, until his back was wrapped in broken glass. He rowed as if prepared to tow the Laguna entirely by himself. He was certain the creature pursued only him, wanted to devour only him, but that it would destroy the Laguna to do it. So Pierre rowed.

The sailors rowed until a thin line of powder blue appeared on the eastern horizon. The watch in the mainmast saw the top main fill and then snap as it reached the limit of its rigging. "Wind's up!" he cried, but even before his words reached the longboats, the rest of the sails began to fill. The Laguna gathered speed and soon it was abreast of the longboats. The sky brightened as the exhausted crews along with their boats were brought on-board. But a bank of inky and ominous clouds had appeared at the western horizon and threatened more trouble. Then, just as the rim of the sun peered over the eastern horizon, a tiny black silhouette appeared.

Captain Rochelle stood at the quarterdeck rail with the spyglass to his eye. Mr. Gustav and Mr. Trevor stood beside him. From the main deck Pierre watched the Captain pass the spyglass to his officers and they spoke together, and he realized he had been here before.

Pierre had watched before as fear and confusion overwhelmed a ship's command until desperate flight was inevitable. He looked around at the other sailors, imagining each floating face down among shattered timbers, some without arms or legs and some missing heads. He looked up to the mainmast guessing where it would break and which portions of canvas and rigging would remain attached. The Captain stepped down from the quarterdeck to stand before the mainmast and addressed his crew.

"Whatever's chasing us," he called out, "is getting closer. We'll hang canvas and chart a course for the nearest harbor. We'll out-run it if we can, escape it by maneuver if we must, and pray for the Good Lord's protection." When he finished no one spoke. Then Mr. Gustav called out, "All hands to the rigging."

As they moved to the foremast, Shark turned to Pierre. "Is it that bad?" He did not answer but reached the rigging before Shark and climbed. By the time he reached the first yardarm Shark had caught up. Over the sound of the rising wind he asked, "Is that thing what you and Ruk argued about?" Pierre continued to climb. Shark yelled out, "You know more about it than you're telling."

Pierre climbed to the next yardarm and then waited for Shark to catch up. "Ruk said he'd seen it, but by his description he had to be lying. I was stupid to challenge him but I knew what I knew."

Shark said, "So you done the right thing, even if by accident."

Pierre shrugged. "If that's how you see it, then fair enough."

The sun perched fully above the horizon and the rising wind pushed the

Laguna ahead at a good pace, but the black clouds to the west climbed higher in the sky growing thick. Captain Rochelle kept the cloud-bank to starboard as if determined to skirt the oncoming storm.

The crew of the Laguna tacked and trimmed and managed to stay just ahead of both the creature and the storm even while each continued to approach. Pierre performed his duties with a rising sense of doom. He was determined to say nothing of what he knew, yet time after time he watched the Captain issue ineffective order after useless command, unaware that in the end those orders would not save his ship. Pierre's fear beat against his chest.

The Captain set the Laguna's sails to gain distance from the creature, so it was the storm that caught them first. As the wind began to swirl he ordered all canvas reefed and tied down. Pierre climbed guessing the Captain recognized the storm would be more serious than he had first thought. He helped to reef the sails of the foremast and then was sent up the mainmast to help that crew. The wind whipped about growing stronger, leads flapped in all directions, sailors reached and swung and spun high above the main deck, but despite its reefed sails, the ship began to pitch and roll. Suddenly, with a horrifying shriek a sailor named Cummins fell from the yard beside Pierre's, dropping like a stone to land in the churning sea with hardly a splash. In the gathering maelstrom he disappeared.

The rumble of distant thunder shook the Laguna. The squall-line of rain like a screen of silver became visible. But the sails of the mainmast now were reefed and tied except for the main sail that Cummins had been tying off. Since Pierre was closest, Mr. Trevor ordered him to finish. He reached the sail to find that in his panic, Cummins had folded the canvas in the wrong direction and its tie was trapped within. So, on the tallest mast of a rolling and heaving ship and knocked about by the wind of an approaching storm, Pierre struggled to unfurl part of the sail. The squall-line drew closer and the wind became stronger still.

He grasped the tie between his teeth as he tucked the last fold and with one hand gripping the yard and the other prepared to pass the tie around the reefed sail. Suddenly he smelled a harsh and acrid odor and noticed over his hands and forearms a faint blue glow. He shifted to pass the tie around the sail when a blinding light surrounded him and then a deafening crack left the world utterly black and silent.

For a time Pierre felt his body wrapped in warm velvet within a sinking, drifting space. When he opened his eyes again, his world was upside down. Then he recognized Shark, except that Shark was looking down and appeared upside down. Shark smiled and moved his lips, and Pierre heard him say, "Welcome back, mate. Thought you'd crossed over." Pierre felt the violent pitch and roll beneath him and then discovered himself in his bunk below deck.

Pierre bleated, "What happened?" His throat was as sore as if he had been screaming.

Shark said, "Hit by the lightning, or something like it, and it looks like you didn't die. I climbed to get you down. Otherwise, the storm's still blowing hard."

Pierre's head throbbed and his neck felt as if it had been hit very hard. Slowly he sat up. "Lightning?"

"Prettiest sight I ever seen," Shark said. "All them lights and colors. And that sound, like the crackle of burning meat. We figured you was dead, but you didn't fall so somebody had to get you. Not my choice, you can bet. Mr. Gustav sent me up. So next to you, I'm the luckiest sailor on this ship."

"So I suppose I owe you my life," Pierre sheepishly said. "But why didn't I fall?"

Shark shrugged. "Arms and legs wrapped so tight I almost needed a marlinespike to get you down." He smiled at his own joke and then patted Pierre on the shoulder. "Feeling alright?"

"Pounding head and a sore throat, otherwise not bad."

"Good," Shark said, "because the Captain wants all hands. But at least you won't be doing no more climbing tonight."

"Why do I doubt that?" Pierre asked. He stood bracing himself against a bulkhead with his hands as the ship rolled beneath him. He stepped out of the gangway to wind and rain that slapped hard at his face. Sailors ran about the deck screaming orders and directions as others stood by the rigging taking in or letting out line. Captain Rochelle stood on the quarterdeck staring out to sea. Pierre followed his line of sight until he saw the creature.

Still distant, in the rain and darkness and with only its head visible to its throat above the waves, the creature was difficult to make out but it seemed to approach the Laguna cautiously. Mr. Gustav joined the Captain on the quarterdeck. Pierre believed he knew what they were discussing. Watching the frantic activity on the main deck, he hesitated only a moment before he climbed to the quarterdeck and approached the Captain and Mr. Gustav.

"Begging the Captain's pardon," he said, "but you should load your guns." He yelled over the wind as it screamed through the rigging. "When it opens its mouth, fire into it."

Angrily Mr. Gustav said, "Back to the main deck, sailor. Leave the conduct of the ship to the officers."

Pierre ignored him and addressed Rochelle. "With respect, shot anywhere else won't even bother it. Unless we get away it'll destroy this ship and devour every hand on board."

Captain Rochelle stared hard at Pierre and under his gaze Pierre felt as if his head was filling with air. "You're sure about this?" Pierre nodded without hesitation. The Captain studied him a moment longer. "I won't ask how you know, but you're sure this'll save us?"

Pierre shrugged. "Nothing else'll work, but there's a chance this might."

The Captain turned to Mr. Gustav. "Order gunners to their posts, guns ready to fire on short fuse." Mr. Gustav glanced once at Pierre and then called out for the gunners and gave their commands.

Although still well out of range, the creature continued to approach. The Captain turned to Pierre. He glanced about to see that the others were beyond hearing. "Tell me what you know."

"I only know its danger and its destruction. Beyond that, I'll tell you what doesn't work but I have to guess at what will. Fire as soon as it's in range and keep firing."

"There's no other vulnerable spot on its cursed body?"

"Its open mouth is just a guess; maybe its throat and maybe its eyes. Shot fired anywhere else'll do nothing." Looking hard at the Captain, he said, "That's all I know."

He studied Pierre a moment longer. "I wonder why I doubt that." Rain and wind whipped at their faces as lightning flashed and thunder boomed and crashed around them. Standing beside the Captain on the quarterdeck, Pierre wondered if his swimming was about to be tested again.

While the crew watched the creature, the storm suddenly grew ferocious. The wind roared, the Laguna began to heave and roll, and Pierre gripped the quarter-deck rail to keep from being swept away. Thick, foamy waves crashed across the bow to wash over the main deck. Shimmering sheets of rain fell so dense he could no longer see the bowsprit and heard nothing beyond the shriek of the wind and explosions of thunder. The sky was utterly black and it was impossible to know the direction they sailed. The ship rolled from side to side until Pierre feared the Laguna would capsize. Then the storm grew worse.

The wind screamed through the rigging as thunder exploded around the Laguna like exchanges of cannonades. Flashes of lightning etched the masts and rigging in hard white outlines that blinked instantly out. Mr. Gustav and Mr. Trevor joined Pierre and the Captain on the quarter-deck. Yelling to each other over the fury of the storm, Mr. Gustav told the Captain that although the gun-ports along with the hatches were battened and sealed, the Laguna was taking on water. The Captain asked how long the ship could hold out. The officers agreed that unless the storm subsided soon, the bilge would take on enough water to capsize the ship. With sails reefed and hatches tight, all that could be done had been done, and with the Captain beside the tiller, their only hope was to keep the bow headed into the wind.

Though Pierre could not guess how long the storm raged, at some moment he realized the rain had begun to ease and the wind to abate. As the storm weakened he turned to look for the beast. The violence of the storm had obliterated his terror of the creature, but with the storm's passing that terror returned. The western horizon gradually cleared to show a line of pale blue. Captain Rochelle must have had the same thought, because with his spyglass he slowly swept the horizon all around. By the time the rain was a gossamer drizzle, the Captain decided the creature was gone and the Laguna was safe. When the rain had all but stopped and the wind slackened to a fresh breeze, he ordered all hands back into the rigging and all canvas hung for speed. Mr. Gustav and Mr. Trevor left the quarter-deck. Captain Rochelle turned to Pierre and ordered him to accompany him below. Pierre followed him to his cabin already certain of what would follow.

CHAPTER EIGHTEEN

THE CAPTAIN CLOSED his cabin door. Sighing heavily, he stepped around his navigation table and sat down in his chair. Then he gestured for Pierre to take a seat. He stared hard at a spot on his table as if giving many things a great deal of thought. His expression darkened as he looked up at Pierre. "Tell me all you know and I'll judge its use." But he appeared transformed; as if, in place of the commanding and confident leader sat a man struggling with forces he knew were far beyond to his own.

"I've told you pretty much everything. How I came to know it can't be useful." Pierre wondered how much he could afford to explain.

The Captain glared. "You'll tell me what I want to know or you'll swim a long way."

Pierre saw himself cornered; tell the Captain too much and he could decide the creature pursued him personally, and then Pierre had no doubt he would need to swim a long way. So he described only those encounters with the creature that were far apart in location and time.

The Captain listened with anger at the edge of his face. When Pierre finished the Captain looked at him as if trying to decide what he had learned. "I suppose it must be true." Pierre said nothing. "Discretion is the better part of valor." His glare softened. "I can't decide whether you're more frightened of that beast or of me. So to help you, if it's a choice between you and the survival of this ship, there'll be no decision to make. Still, you tried with what little you know to save us, and for that I'm grateful. But if you put us there in the first place, I'll know what to do." Again the Captain paused as if looking at Pierre would yield one more detail critical to his decision. "If we meet it again, I'll throw you at it before I waste a cannon shot."

Pierre hesitated. "Thanks for that warning." He stood and went to the cabin door.

To his back the Captain said, "Just remember my promise."

When Pierre reached the main deck, Shark stepped up to him. "What was that all about?"

He thought to describe their meeting but instead he said, "The Captain thinks I should practice swimming." He laughed, hopeful that Shark would get the joke.

Shark studied his eyes a moment. "Good advice for any sailor." Pierre was relieved he asked nothing more.

Over several days of clear weather the Laguna followed a northeastern course. Then, in a morning's soft light, a sail appeared on the horizon. The Captain ordered top canvas reefed and set the watch in the mainmast. The watch identified a corsair showing Dutch colors. The Captain ordered French colors run out. Then he ordered a change of course to intercept the ship with gun ports closed and starboard guns loaded. The corsair approached quickly and the Captain ordered most of the crew sent below, and for the quartermaster to arm them with pistols and cutlass. A few sailors continued to move about the deck and in the rigging so that, with its top-most sails reefed, the Laguna appeared in distress. Below deck, Pierre and Shark huddled with the rest of the crew watching the quarterdeck through an open hatchway.

Shark explained to Pierre that the corsair rode high in the water suggesting it carried little cargo. The Captain joined Mr. Gustav and Mr. Trevor on the quarterdeck where they watched the corsair draw closer. Pierre guessed that, with little cargo, they would not risk attempting its capture, but Shark said they could always use the ship as a consort. Meanwhile, the spyglass passed among the officers. The Captain then told Mr. Trevor to order gun crews to load the port-side guns as well. To Pierre, it seemed unlikely that once fire was exchanged from either port or starboard guns, the Laguna would be able to turn to use its additional guns. But in the next moment the Captain's decision appeared prescient, because a second corsair appeared on the horizon. As much good fortune as they might have, the odds were suddenly against them. The first ship approached quickly as the other maneuvered the Laguna between them. Seeing this, the Captain laughed suddenly harsh and loud and ordered the skull-and-crossbones run up the mainmast. At the sight, the ships maneuvered directly for the Laguna.

Crouching in the hold, Shark nudged Pierre. "Ever do this before?"

"No," Pierre said, glumly.

"Two things to remember. First, hold your cutlass upright. Chances are the other guy'll swing like he's chopping at a tree. You'll block every stroke and maybe save your life."

Pierre hefted his cutlass upright and found that maneuvering it was harder than it appeared. "What's the second?"

"He's as scared as you are."

Pierre decided that was impossible. In the narrow space he manipulated the cutlass as Shark watched. "One more thing; keep your pistol tucked away and don't bring it out unless I'm about to be killed." He grinned. It took Pierre a moment to recognize his joke.

"And will you be saving yours to help me?" Pierre asked.

"Hell no," Shark said. "But remember that once fired there's no chance to reload."

Just then the cannons on the port-side lower deck fired in sequence with a deafening series of blasts that shook the deck beneath Pierre's feet. Bitter black smoke billowed up into the hold suddenly engulfing Pierre and the rest of the crew. An instant later the entire ship shook and trembled. One after the next, cannon shots from one of the attacking ships pounded against the hull. Another volley from the Laguna and more smoke poured into the hold. Pierre listened as, on the deck overhead, men ran about screaming and responding to orders. The black acrid smoke was so thick he could only just make out Shark standing nearby. Guns fired and the Laguna shook again. Cannon fire was followed by cannon fire as shot pounded against the hull. The next blast was accompanied by what sounded like a shower of hail raining down on the deck overhead. From the cries of sailors he guessed that round shot had raked the main deck. Cannon shot then blasted into the Laguna's starboard side. Answering fire sent more smoke billowing into the hold even thicker and more acrid. A blast of heat followed like a wall rolling over the men around him. Pierre struggled to breath.

Suddenly Mr. Trevor cried out to close ranks and then sent all hands up. The men around Pierre including Shark screamed curses and waved cutlasses as they climbed to the deck, and Pierre discover himself doing the same.

He stepped through the gangway and the smoke and noise and sight of blood on the deck overwhelmed him. But whether with fear or panic or confusion, cutlass held high Pierre charged into the largest knot of battling men swinging at the nearest sailors. Often enough his cutlass struck something and he resisted looking at what his blade struck.

Somehow, despite the smoke and gunfire and fallen bodies, he managed to make his way through the knot of men to the starboard rail. In a pause he looked up to the quarterdeck. A cluster of the invading sailors were battling Captain Rochelle. The Laguna's sailors closest to the quarterdeck were caught up in their own fights, so Pierre climbed to the quarterdeck and attacked the Captain's opponents from behind. His blade struck several fighters who became confused. As they turned retreating from Pierre, Captain Rochelle cut them down. Sailors screamed and cursed as they swung hard at Pierre. Following Shark's advice he parried their cuts and blows long enough for the Captain's blade to attack. Gradually, he and the Captain cleared the quarterdeck of fighters, but a glance at the main deck revealed that more sailors from the attacking ships were boarding. The fiercest fighting was around the foremast and the Laguna's defenders were losing ground. He glanced back at the Captain who began to fight his way there. Pierre followed defending his back. When they reached the mainmast, the Captain ran up a white flag. Very quickly the battle ended.

Quiet descended as the invading crew stripped the Laguna's sailors of weapons. From the first of the attacking corsairs, a longboat was lowered and mid-ships stood a man dressed in brightly colored robes and wearing a sparkling turban. When it was halfway between the ships a murmur passed through the crew; "Mustafa al Harum!"

The longboat reached the Laguna and the man climbed to the main deck. Pierre was surprised to see he was short and compact and not nearly as large as he had appeared in the longboat. With calmly measured strides he stepped over the blood and around motionless bodies, reached the mainmast and confronted Captain Rochelle. Older than the Captain who towered over him, his dark-skinned face was wreathed by a tightly-curled, coal-black beard, yet his lively eyes gave his expression a jovial quality.

"There is no shame," the visitor said, "in defeat by Mustafa al Harum. You and your crew are now safe. Valiant battle leaves many injuries. Tend to your injured, Captain, and I will send one of my doctors to assist you.

Meanwhile, you will pardon my crew as we look after our wounded as well." He turned and signaled to one of his sailors and spoke to him quietly. The sailor went to the longboat and was rowed back to his ship.

Rochelle unstrapped his cutlass and handed it to him. "All the world knows of the courage of Sheikh Mustafa al Harum and also his compassion. My ship and crew are at your disposal."

Taking the sword, the Sheikh passed it to his aide. "I commend your wisdom and restraint. Survey your damages as it is my desire that your vessel join my fleet."

The Captain said, "You'll find my crew loyal, brave and honorable. As you have spared their lives, those lives are now yours to command."

Surveying the main deck the Sheikh said, "You will honor me by joining my staff. Though we are now far from our course, we sail for the Azores. Once we have landed, those of your crew who so wish will be permitted to sign onto other ships. I hope you approve."

Turning to be heard by his crew the Captain said, "I am honored by your invitation and I encourage all of my crew to join me. But many have wives and children so, to those sailors I say, help those who mean the most to you and assist those who need you most."

Sheikh Mustafa smiled. "Thank you, Captain. Now, please join me onboard my ship as we have much to discuss." The Captain turned and spoke quickly to Mr. Gustav and Mr. Trevor and then the two captains made their way to the longboat. Within a few moments that longboat was being rowed to Sheikh Mustafa's ship.

Pierre felt a slap on his back and turned to see Shark behind him. "Pretty exciting, eh? Fight like the devil and then meet the devil himself." He shrugged, his sense of time had dissolved and he was no longer certain even of what had happened. He knew he had fought hard to protect Captain Rochelle. Now, it occurred to him that others had noticed his actions. He turned to Shark and was about to ask how things had gone for him when he discovered a long, deep cut on his own left arm. Raw flesh and rivulets of blood, the wound ran half the length of his upper arm ending just above his elbow. Suddenly his arm felt wrapped in fire.

With a pained expression Shark said, "You should probably get that looked after."

“Yes,” Pierre said, “I should probably do that.” He turned toward the temporary dispensary when the deck shifted beneath his feet, the masts and rigging spun over his head and suddenly he stared up at clouds. Then all went black.

His eyes opened again but he did not recognize the face staring down at his. In accented English, the man said, “You are strong and brave.” His smile gleamed against his dark skin, his black beard covered much of his face but his large black eyes assured intelligent good-humor.

“What happened?” Pierre asked. He raised his left arm and pain was sudden and furious.

“Your wound will heal without permanent injury, but it will take time and will cause you pain. It will also leave you with a glorious scar. I have been told it was acquired defending your captain. Thus, your wound is honorable and glorious and he will reward you richly.”

Pierre glanced up unimpressed. Smiling the man added, “Pain ends but honor and glory are eternal. Though you may not believe it, I envy you. Most especially your courage.”

Pierre said, “Don’t let the blood and guts fool you. I’d have let my captain die if it’d prevented this.” Then he asked, “Are you one of Sheikh Mustapha’s crew?”

The man closed his eyes reverently. “I have had the honor of serving him for nearly two years. In that time there have been many battles in which he has been victorious. Unfortunately, his sailors have been injured and some have died. My knowledge of medicine has come to me by his grace who saw to it I was educated in Baghdad among the wisest physicians. It is to him I owe all honor and gratitude.” His expression softened. “Feeling strong enough to stand?”

Pierre sat up, waited for a wave of vertigo to pass, and looked around. Men lay on pallets all about him and some injuries appeared terrible if their wrappings were any sign. Carefully he got to his feet. “Many sailors need your help and far more than I do. I thank you for your patience and care. But please tell me to whom I owe this great debt.”

The man introduced himself as Mohamed, and Pierre introduced himself and then offered his right hand in friendship. “If ever you need my help, know that you’ll have it.”

Mohamed bowed. “Until we meet again, may Allah Most Merciful bless you.”

Pierre made his way across the main deck. Pedro, Mr. Trevor and Carlos sat together beside the foremast. Seeing him approach they moved apart to offer him a seat. "So," Mr. Trevor said, "our company is honored by the hero of the day."

Taking the offered seat Pierre laughed nervously. He could not recall ever having been the hero of the day. "Enjoy it," he said, "because next time, someone else'll have to save the Captain." Their laughter reassured him. Shark appeared and took a seat at the end of the group.

"What do we think?" he asked. "Is everybody staying with the Arab?"

Mr. Trevor said, "It'll be a wild ride and I wish I could, but my old lady and her brood need to take all my money from me from time to time, and I hate to disappoint."

"You really think," Pedro asked, "your old lady even remembers what you look like?"

Carlos said, "Bet she remembers what your money looks like."

Mr. Trevor said, "Maybe I should just send the money and save myself a voyage."

Turning to Pedro, Shark asked, "What about you? Anybody waiting for your money?"

"Believe it," Pedro said. "A mother and sister who haven't seen me in two years. Money or no, staying with the Arab would keep me at sea a good while." He became wistful and Pierre suspected he genuinely missed his family. "On the other hand, there's that farm with rocks big as coconuts to crack a plow and mules what won't work worth a lick and crops with bugs and neighbors and the less said the better about them. At least the Arab won't put me behind a plow." There was less laughter then head-nodding.

"Steady work ain't always the best work," Carlos said. "I worked a dozen jobs, and I tell you a man needs to be out and on the move with a hill to see what's on the other side of and with men who'll only rest in their graves. He needs a life where something's at risk and something's to be won." Turning to Pedro he said, "Walking behind a plow, a man might as well be the mule, there's so little difference." More nodding as the group went silent.

Suddenly Shark said, "But let's not forget the women."

The remark triggered quiet chuckling and guffaws. Turning to Mr. Trevor, Shark asked, "You sure your old lady is still your old lady?"

Instead of smiling, Mr. Trevor's face grew suddenly red. He stood up with his fists clenched and moved toward Shark before Carlos grabbed his arm and held it. "Pay no heed; he's just a boy and a fool to boot."

Mr. Trevor said, "He should shut his gob if he wants to live to be a man."

Shark jumped up, his expression set for a fight. "Say that again and I'll give you the proof. Not sure who's a man and who ain't, I'm happy to demonstrate."

Pedro stepped toward him. "I'll take that bet." Shark turned to face him, knees bent and hands closed to fists.

"Then let the lesson begin," Shark said and shoved Pedro's shoulder hard. Pedro raised his fist about to strike when Mr. Gustav appeared.

"Looks like you fellas just ain't got enough of the fighting," Mr. Gustav said with a bitter smile. "Truth be told, me neither. Hope this ain't a private party, 'cause I'm ready when you are." His gaze was hot as his eyes moved from Pedro to Shark. "Who's feeling lucky today?"

The men exchanged glances with as much surprise as anger. Mr. Gustav's expression turned to mockery. "Maybe you all need to go home to your women. Maybe their skirts are big enough to hide behind." Shark and Pedro sat down again. No one seemed able to look Mr. Gustav directly in the eyes. Suddenly, the call went out, "The longboat! Captain's headed back." The sailors stood and moved to the rail. Pierre joined them, but at the rail he stood to one side.

Mr. Trevor said, "Looks like Lucky Rochelle's luck finally run-out."

Mr. Gustav said, "Don't even think it. He's still got a crew with a ship under him. Banged up and shot up, but we're still his. Mustafa will negotiate, but the Captain's got something to negotiate with."

Carlos said, "Ship and crew or not, at least it was him what captured us. Anybody else'd shot us, burned us and set us adrift. Those of us left'll see the top-side of another ship."

After a moment of brooding Shark said, "Maybe, but then again maybe not. It's a long haul to the Azores. We run into crown ships, the Laguna'll be the first to go and you'd better believe that."

Mr. Gustav laughed. "Always the optimist, eh?"

Shark shrugged. "My skin's something I think about a lot."

Watching the longboat approach, Pierre wondered why Shark had been eager to fight a man twice his size where he had no chance of winning. Was it just residue of the battle, or resentment it had been lost, or anger he was no longer master of his fate and forced to answer to the Arab? The rising and dipping oars of the longboat glittered in the sunlight. Perhaps it was just the absence of the Captain, leaving them abandoned and without ballast.

As the longboat drew closer, he wondered about what Carlos had said about those things a man needs. Had he really been so eager to find his father, or had that been just an excuse to leave the Captain Hudson and see the bigger world? He had agreed that Gabriella would be able to run the tavern with whatever help she could find but he also knew she would spend her time worrying about him and about the people he found himself among and if perhaps at that very moment he clung to the edge of disaster. The thud of the longboat's prow against the hull of the Laguna startled Pierre from this reverie and he was grateful.

The Captain climbed on-board and first one sailor and then a second and then the entire crew began to applaud. He climbed to the quarterdeck and smiling stepped to the rail.

"Sheikh Mustafa's first words were to compliment you all for your courage. He assured me I am fortunate to have such men under my command. And I acknowledged how fortunate I know myself to be. So, thank you for your courage." His crew answered with more applause.

"The Sheikh assures me that, although all are invited to serve under his flag, any among you wishing to return home will be permitted to do so. On arriving at Tenerife, the rest of us will then sail for the Sheikh's base in Tunis. Meanwhile, he's begun to load our booty onto his ships. His second-in-command will master the Laguna for the rest of the voyage. In exchange, I will sail with the Sheikh as his hostage to your good behavior." This pause was met with silence.

"The loss of our loot burdens those hoping to carry home a portion. Just remember that your lives have been spared, a gesture your loved ones will appreciate. However, to ease this burden, he has agreed that when we dock, my share of the loot will be distributed among you. So whether you continue with the Sheikh or choose to go your own way, you will not end this voyage with empty pockets." This brought noisy applause.

"Now, I will rejoin the Sheikh for our voyage to Tenerife. However, I have a last announcement. Mr. Chanceux," he said looking at Pierre, "please join me here at the rail."

All eyes turned on Pierre. He discovered Shark looking at him with an odd grin. Those around Pierre cleared a path for him to the stairs to the quarterdeck. As he made his way, sailors reached out to pat his shoulder. He stepped up beside Captain Rochelle.

To the crew, the Captain said, "It has been rare in my life that I find myself obliged to another for saving it. But in this instance, I do it with gratitude and pleasure. Mr. Chanceux," he said turning to Pierre, "as captain of the Laguna, I thank you for your timely and vital assistance. Your courage preserved my life and assured the safety of my ship and crew. On their behalf, I offer you my sincerest thanks." The crew cheered until the Captain continued.

"In appreciation, I invite you to join me as my adjutant and guest of Sheikh Mustafa aboard his ship. I hope this is acceptable to you." This startled Pierre, but when the Captain held out his hand he shook it warmly.

Again addressing the crew, the Captain said, "In parting let me repeat my gratitude for your service. Although I am certain of the Sheikh's skill, I offer you my wishes for a safe voyage, and I look forward to seeing you again when we arrive at Tenerife." He turned and, to loud cheering, led Pierre to the gunwale and the longboat. Pierre glanced at the faces around him. Shark, to his relief, smiled with unembarrassed enjoyment. But when he saw the face of Mr. Gustav, he found a darker look. Whether it was resentment of his elevated status or worry over his Captain's treatment, Pierre could not tell and suddenly he wanted to ask but could not.

While he and the Captain climbed down to their longboat, Pierre saw three longboats leave the Sheikh's ship headed for the Laguna. Along with rowers, each carried three more men. Near the halfway point between the two ships, the longboats passed in opposite directions. Despite the presence of the Captain and rowers and the Sheikh's ship ahead, he had an uncanny sense of being alone again in the middle of the ocean. The sensation came with sudden and unbearable clarity as he recalled clinging to his coffin. He turned to Captain Rochelle.

"Many men," Pierre said, "fought harder than I did, and many were more seriously injured. Though I'm not convinced I deserve it, I'm grateful for your praise and flattered that you wish me to accompany you. So, before I embarrass both of us, tell me what I should know about the Sheikh and life aboard his ship."

Captain Rochelle laid his hand lightly on Pierre's shoulder. "My friend, no one else came to my rescue and no one else was injured in my defense. As I see it, this is the least I can do to acknowledge my debt. Were it not for you, I would be closer to Hell than Heaven. As for the Sheikh, he is known as the most ethical and tolerant of men, despite the despicable religion he follows. I confess that, as the Lord decreed I must be defeated, He could not have found a more honorable opponent. As for life aboard his ship, like every adventure, watch what others do and adopt their ways. In any case, I look forward to your companionship."

The longboat thudded against the hull of Mustafa's ship and with the Captain leading, Pierre climbed aboard. Awaiting them on the main deck stood the Sheikh surrounded by a retinue of tall, brightly-dressed guards. Pierre saw no smiling faces except that of the Sheikh, but his expression was beaming. As soon as Pierre and the Captain reached the deck he stepped forward and embraced him. "I trust all went well and that your crew is satisfied with our plan."

"But of course, Excellency. They are loyal, but they understand how generous your treatment of them is. There is disappointment over the loss of loot, but your offer to share mine with them has relieved some anxiety." Then, with effusive praise for his loyalty and valor, he introduced Pierre. The Sheikh scrutinized him as if he suspected he might be a talking dog.

Glancing at the wrapping on his arm, he said to Pierre, "I believe a member of my staff tended your wound. I recognize the skill with which it has been treated. I hope it is satisfactory."

Again the uncomfortable center of attention, Pierre thanked the Sheikh and praised his treatment. Turning to the Captain, Sheikh Mustafa invited them to his cabin for refreshment while the loot was transferred to his ship. He assured the Captain they would weigh anchor the moment this was done. Followed by one of his guards, the Sheikh led them below.

Following one passageway and then another, Pierre was impressed by the craftsmanship on display. Where he had expected rough timbers and planks he saw polished woodwork. Where he expected crude ironwork, he saw carefully detailed and polished brass. Where he expected darkness and gloom, lighted lamps perched in every corner. All of it dazzled him but he was even more surprised when they entered the Sheikh's cabin.

This cabin appeared enormous, its crafted wood and brass even more detailed and carefully finished. Alternating with brass and panels of decorated wood hung tapestries of subtle colors composed of curving lines and flourishes. Where he expected to see chairs, there were large, brightly-colored pillows. A large lamp of brass made up of small pieces of colored glass hung above the center of the cabin; smaller versions stood in the other corners. To one side stood an object he did not recognize; its top was a small brass cup supported by a slim column of dark wood studded with pearls and gemstones and ending in a glass globe the size of a coconut. Coming from this were four long, flexible tubes equidistant from each other and each ending with a brass mouthpiece. He was studying this when a quiet rap on the cabin door announced the arrival of what the Sheikh had referred to as light refreshments.

The tower of food piled on the silver tray that entered the cabin almost hid the two men carrying it, and the aromas drifting from it stirred Pierre's senses. In a moment his stomach was churning with hunger, and all he could think of was to begin to eat. The men placed the tray on a small stand on the floor and then arranged three pairs of stacked pillows around it. Bowing to the Sheikh they retreated from the cabin.

"Please," he said with a smile and gesturing toward the pillows, "my chef is very-well practiced."

Pierre sat uncertainly on the pillows and watched the Sheikh and the Captain closely. They exchanged remarks about the food and its preparation. From what he could gather, the Sheikh's religion was strict about what one could eat. He looked around for a platter of his own to spoon his portion of food onto, and knives and forks to manipulate, and their absence surprised him. With another rap on the door a man appeared carrying a tray with a large, bright brass carafe and three gold cups.

"Ah," the Sheikh said with his eyes wide and smile broad. "Now we can begin." He then described for the Captain the foods before them, highlighting the subtle blends of spices and flavors and the way the lamb had been prepared. But he spoke in such a casual way it was as if he was thinking aloud in the company of an old friend. He demonstrated his method of enjoying the meal, but as if he merely described his own idiosyncratic technique. Instead of using forks and knives, he and the Captain took their portions directly from the tray using the fingers of their right hands or small pieces of round flat bread stacked to one side on the tray.

The conversation about food and its styles of preparation continued, and Pierre did his best to follow while he practiced eating with his fingers. With the first few bites he found the food sublime. To the Captain, the Sheikh said, "It appears your companion has become a convert, at least as far as our food is concerned." The men chuckled as Pierre shuttled food into his mouth. The conversation then moved to foods in different regions of the Mediterranean and how religion shaped what was eaten and how it was prepared. Pierre sipped from his goblet relieved to discover it was filled with water. The Sheikh must have noticed this because he said, "My people avoid all beverages that contain alcohol." He then resumed his conversation with the Captain. They continued in quiet tones so that between the heavy food and the subtle motion of the ship, Pierre began to doze. If the two men noticed, neither spoke of it, but allowed the conversation to wander as the ship rolled lazily at anchor and Pierre's mind wandered with it.

So when Pierre heard a series of distant, powerful explosions, he assumed it was inside his head. But at the sound, the Captain immediately stood. "We're under attack!"

But Sheikh Mustafa remained seated and unperturbed. "Please, Captain, do not concern yourself. My men are well-trained and capable of handling the situation. Now, let us resume this meal and our conversation."

In astonishment Captain Rochelle said, "Your ships are under attack!"

"A minor skirmish no doubt. Nothing my crew cannot handle efficiently. I am certain of the men under my command."

But by his expression, Captain Rochelle remained concerned. The Sheikh glanced from the Captain to Pierre and then to the Captain again. With a loud sigh of resignation he stood. "As you seem unable to put this from your mind, I suppose I have some obligation to satisfy this curiosity. Follow me." When he opened the cabin door, the guard stepped forward, but seeing the Sheikh he stepped back and took his place behind him as they followed the passageway.

Pierre was the last to step onto the main deck but the Captain had already begun to protest loudly. "What are you doing? You gave me your word. How can this be?" It took a moment for Pierre to realize what was happening, and when he did, the horror overwhelmed him.

The Laguna was burning, two of its masts were down, large portions of the main deck were shattered and most of the quarterdeck stood as a pile of broken ribs and fractured planks. As Pierre watched, the Sheikh's consort ship sent two shots into the Laguna's hull at the water line. The Laguna rolled hard to port and then disappeared beneath the waves. Though he looked closely, Pierre saw no one in the water, or at least no one alive.

PART THREE

SICILY

CHAPTER ONE

CAPTAIN ROCHELLE RUSHED at the rail as if he might dive into the sea and swim to where his ship had just disappeared. But at the rail he stopped and then turned, glaring and furious, to Sheikh Mustafa al Harum. "You gave your word! This is an outrage! An outrage!"

"Now Captain," the Sheikh said in a calming tone, his face wreathed in patience, "it was not a firm promise. More an aspiration, I confess. But can you be so naive?" He shook his head as if weary with the burden of his wisdom. "Your men demonstrated they could not be trusted and had no honor. How could I not assume the moment they became disenchanted and saw the opportunity, they would turn on my officers? After all, could their promise be any more reliable than my own?"

Fury suddenly quenched, a haggard look came to the Captain's face. "That crew included your own sailors."

Turning to look out over the sea, the Sheikh shrugged. "Those men now stirring your sympathy had failed me in the past and undoubtedly would do so again. They revealed themselves useless by their dishonor, and dangerous by their pleasure in deception. Men, I promise you, unworthy of your concern and not a whit better than your own." He turned back to look carefully into the Captain's eyes. "Your concern speaks for your humanity, but I assure you it is misplaced. We will both live longer lives because they are dead." He glanced again toward the spot where the Laguna had disappeared. Except for shards of wood and tatters of sail, the sea was a featureless blue. Pierre recalled Shark and Mr. Gustav and Mr. Trevor and the others; their images swirled in his memory and voices echoed in his ears, and his sadness surprised him.

"I must suppose," the Captain said, "you have a similar plan for us."

Pierre was startled by Sheikh Mustafa's laugh. "Do not concern yourself, you are far too valuable. In any case, you are my guests aboard my ship by my invitation. By every rule of hospitality, your safety is my only concern. And since the value of your ransom will depend upon your condition, my best interest is to preserve your well-being."

The Captain's expression became hard and his voice level. "Aside from the British Navy, who would pay my ransom?"

"Your humility is as commendable as your achievements are well-known. And to be clear, I have no association with the British Navy. Though the party which provides your ransom remains to be identified, be assured that several will learn of your presence with great interest." Captain Rochelle's startled surprise unnerved Pierre. "Be of good cheer; Captain, our treasure is safe and we need share it with no one."

The Captain's face froze with surprise. "Our treasure?"

This time the Sheikh's laugh was a rumble of deep pleasure. "Surely you cannot imagine I sent that to the bottom of the sea. Though its value is not quite sufficient to make either of us kings, grant me some common sense. The attack began only after everything of value had been removed. Miscreants aside, my sailors are well-trained and so our treasure remains safe."

"Our treasure?" Once again startled, Pierre was less surprised than the Captain.

"As we are partners, we will share the Laguna's cargo evenly. Do you agree?"

For the first time, Pierre watched resentment enter Captain Rochelle's eyes. "Now that is remarkable; you call us partners while holding me for ransom and then insist on a share of the wealth. An odd partnership indeed. At the very least, your portion should satisfy your greed."

The Sheikh's expression lost its humor and the tone of his voice dropped. "Greed is a harsh word, Captain, but again you can only be intentionally naive. Your treasure I already have, and your ransom will add to it. If I was not certain it would be substantial, well, one might ask why I keep you alive."

"Honor," Captain Rochelle said darkly.

Eyes suddenly bright the Sheikh said, "Indeed; in the end there is only honor. Even in the dishonorable act of sinking a ship and drowning a crew, there must be honor." He paused. "But let us return to my cabin and continue this conversation in comfort."

Captain Rochelle said, "I believe Pierre and I would prefer to be shown to our cabins."

"Ah Captain," the Sheikh said, "a pique of surly annoyance hardly reflects well on your reputation." He bowed. "But it will be as you wish. I must inform you that due to our close quarters, you and your companion will share the same cabin." With a glance toward Pierre he added, "I assume that is satisfactory." He turned to the guard beside him and spoke quietly, then turned back to the Captain. "Please follow Ahmed to your quarters. And I hope you will take your evening meal at my table." He stepped close to the Captain. "Believe me, upon reflection you will recognize that my decision is best for both of us."

The Captain said, "For everyone except my sailors."

The Sheikh hesitated and then bowed again. "Until this evening."

The Captain and Pierre followed Ahmed below deck and along a series of short passageways forward until they reached a door with a carved wooden lattice opening. Ahmed produced a large iron key, turned it in the lock and stepped back. The Captain and Pierre entered, and Pierre was again impressed at how well-built and carefully kept this cabin was. Along with two tidy bunks there was a chair and small table in its center and fitted cunningly into the bulkhead stood a finely-carved wooden cabinet with open shelves. Ahmed closed the door behind them. A look of surprise came to the Captain's eyes as they heard the door being locked, followed by his quiet retreat. Pierre said, "So we're prisoners after all."

Captain Rochelle nodded. "A point to raise with the Sheikh."

Pierre asked, "Do you think we're in danger?"

The Captain shrugged. "We can only bide our time and see what happens. Meanwhile," he said climbing into the upper bunk, "it has been a busy day and a siesta before dinner might be just the thing." He stretched out on his back, folded his hands over his chest and closed his eyes. "It would be well for you to do the same."

Pierre said, "So much for our honorable and compassionate host!" The sight of the destroyed Laguna would not leave his mind, its sailor's faces hung as lanterns behind his eyes. "Despite what he said, good men died on that ship."

The Captain sighed. "Good men die every day."

"But you owed your life and wealth to them."

"Not every debt acquired in this life is paid," the Captain said. "If you wish to prick my conscience you will need to try again."

"So I'll suppose," Pierre said, "that thought is sufficient to allow you to sleep."

"My ship has been sunk and my crew is dead and there's nothing to be done about any of it. Unless you believe that by brooding over a loss, something may be returned from the sea."

Pierre hesitated. "At least we know our Sheikh is capable of deep treachery."

"True knowledge is always hard-earned."

Pierre said, "But we know he mustn't be trusted."

The Captain again sighed. "As we are his prisoners, faith and trust have no place."

A dozen questions badgered Pierre until finally he asked, "After all that's happened, where do you think we're really going?"

With his eyes still closed the Captain said, "The short answer is, wherever he decides to take us. But since he needs provisions, I expect we will continue to Tenerife." He sighed. "Do you think you can sleep now? Or at least that one of us can sleep?"

Pierre hesitated. "Think this ransom business will take long?"

"Just between us, and this may surprise you, I believe it is I who will be ransomed. As for the ransom, I have known some to continue for years. Now, I will entertain one more question and only one."

Pierre said, "I'm wondering how I'll get back to finding my father."

The Captain sat up, propped himself on his elbow and turned to Pierre. "Resist that question. Your determination has gotten you this far and will not abandon you now. Avoid the temptation to doubt. You will know what you need to know the moment you need to know it." Laying down again he added, "Learn to recognize when nothing more can be done."

Pierre wanted to be reassured and was not. He was relieved to recall that his journey had introduced him to people who had met Augustus and had told him something about him. He climbed into his bunk and laid back. Behind his closed his eyes, memories and fears scattered across his mind, his brooding continued and he did not notice when it stopped.

When he opened his eyes again the Captain was saying, "If you are as hungry as I am, you should rouse yourself. The Sheikh may misunderstand your absence."

Pierre stood slowly and turned to see a sailor standing beside the opened door. "I wonder," he said, "if he can be convinced to stop locking us in."

The Captain nodded. "That should lead to an interesting conversation."

They stepped out into the passageway and the guard locked their door and pocketed the key before leading them to the Sheikh's cabin. At his door, the Sheikh greeted them smiling

Captain Rochelle said, "We are flattered by your concern for our safety but is it necessary to lock us inside our cabin? How might we come to harm?"

The Sheikh's smile disappeared. "You have never been further from danger than you are now on my ship."

Pierre asked, "So why is our cabin door kept locked?"

His glance moved to Pierre and by his expression he might have thought he had heard an obnoxious sound. "My young friend, do not question when you are being treated well, only inquirer when you are being treated badly." Turning to the Captain he added, "If possession of the key adds to your comfort, it will be done." Glancing back at Pierre he added, "Despite the rudeness of its request."

"Youthful impatience," Captain Rochelle said, "sometimes masquerades as rudeness. But it is youthful impatience, and not middle-age prudence, that enlivens the world." He smiled.

"And rudeness masquerading as youthful impatience leads to misunderstanding." The Sheikh's expression brightened. "But please enter; our meal will arrive shortly."

Crossing the threshold, the Captain said, "And we will not exaggerate Pierre's infraction. Exaggeration only leads to misjudgment."

With a laugh the Sheikh said, "If your purpose is to assure me your colleague is not a boorish oaf, I need no additional evidence."

"For this I am relieved," the Captain said. "We can now discuss issues of importance."

"Such as," Pierre injected, "where we're headed."

The Sheikh turned a dismissive glance toward Pierre before speaking to the Captain. "As we agreed, Tenerife. Planning beyond that will depend upon what I learn after landing."

Pierre asked, "So you'll continue to attack ships?"

"To ignore an opportunity for profit is to laugh in the face of Allah since every opportunity exists as His expressed will. To ask His help and then ignore what is sent is worse than folly."

The Captain said, "But would you not agree that God sometimes sends temptation under the guise of opportunity simply to test our submission to His will."

"I can see no way to distinguish one from the other until it is revealed by His light."

Following a quiet knock the door opened and two men entered, each carrying a large tray of food. As they were set down the Sheikh gestured his visitors to seats of stacked pillows.

The meal resembled the one at midday, except there were more enticing aromas and more startling flavors and all of it was artfully arranged. As they ate, the Sheikh and the Captain discussed the nature of religion. When Captain Rochelle suggested Christianity was superior to Islam by virtue of its antiquity, the Sheikh shook his head. "The Prophet recognized those ways Christianity had failed. By His grace and His deep understanding, the Prophet purged Greek rationalism from the Hebrew message. He understood that the seduction of reason leads inevitably to heresy and blasphemy and thereby invites doubt to crush the believing heart."

The Captain said, "But reason has brought us the miracles of science."

Again shaking his head the Sheikh smiled. "An intriguing suggestion, but are you certain it is this science that brings ideas to men's minds? Might it instead be by Allah's direct will and inspiration? Could it be these so-called discoveries are eternally present in the mind of Allah, and that it is a direct result of His choice that they become present in the minds of men?"

The Captain sighed. "I confess I find that thought thoroughly disconcerting."

"Disconcerting because it questions the power of reason to reveal that which Allah does not wish revealed? Certainly, I can see how one might find that disconcerting."

"But reason is that tool which enables us to challenge our sensations. We have no other criteria by which to distinguish truth from error."

The Sheikh shrugged. "That tool is at hand and available to all; it is the Holy Koran."

"And if the Koran is flawed, how will we recognize those flaws except through reason?"

"The Holy Koran is not flawed," the Sheikh said flatly. "It is perfect because it is the direct expression of the thoughts of Allah as communicated to his most favored Prophet."

Pierre added, "But can a human creation be perfect? Suppose its writer made a mistake?"

The Sheikh turned glaring at Pierre. "The mercy of Allah does not permit such mistakes. He would not deceive us. He controlled the hand of each scribe so that every word is His word."

The Captain said, "Pierre has cultivated an unhealthy skepticism from which I hope no insult results. His is not an intentional blasphemy, and his skepticism extends even to the Bible. I can only account for it by his youth and lack of experience in the real world."

"With respect," Pierre said, his patience for condescension beginning to fade, "my skepticism is rooted in those errors exposed through reason and scientific investigation."

The Sheikh sighed with impatience. "Errors of the most trivial nature. If I mistake the color of a house, do you then doubt that the house exists or that I have seen it?"

Pierre said, "You claim the Koran has no errors yet what, to you, counts as an error?"

The Captain looked at Pierre uncomfortably. "There is a difference between errors of quantity and of quality. If one concludes Noah's ark was some number of cubits larger or smaller than its description in the Bible, that is different from whether it existed or it was built by Noah or that he built it by the direct inspiration from God."

Pierre said, "So you acknowledge there are mistakes but no errors."

The Sheikh laughed. "Such sophistry puts dust into the heart of the believer. You may believe in disinterested research, but every question is driven by some self-interest."

"To be fair," the Captain said, "particular efforts have yielded startling results. Consider that Italian, Galileo, whose instrument has revealed worlds beyond our own. And the Dutch lens-grinder who has found an entire world of tiny animals within a drop of pond water. These are not even hinted at in either the Holy Bible or the Holy Koran."

The Sheikh folded his hands across his stomach and turned his smile from the Captain to Pierre. "A passage in your Bible states that Allah wills the mysteries of the world to confuse those burdened by hubris. Perhaps those men mistake the curious for the profound."

Pierre said, "They've replaced faith with observation." His impatience had grown beyond the point of caring. "No fact displaces belief unless the believer permits it. In all human endeavors there is the element of stubbornness."

The Sheikh laughed. "And one could not point to a better example than you offer."

The Captain said, "The Lord would not have given us reason if he had not assumed its use. We must use it according to His will. I am certain my friend tries to do just that."

This remark made Pierre even more angry, but somehow it placated the Sheikh and his expression relaxed. "As I think about it, a member of my staff exhibits similar habits of mind; a physician obsessed with this so-called science. His name is Mohamed"

Startled, Pierre said, "We have met, for I believe it was he who treated my wound."

"Then so much the better for you," the Sheikh said. "He is a skillful healer. Right now I believe he is aft in his quarters." He turned to Pierre. "Perhaps you would enjoy visiting with him."

The Captain added, "I assume he will need help making his way to his quarters."

"And nothing could be simpler," the Sheikh said, "nor give me greater pleasure." He turned to Ahmed standing beside the door and spoke quietly. To Pierre he said, "Follow Ahmed and all will be well." He grinned at Pierre as at a burden he was about to abandon.

Pierre stood to follow Ahmed. When he turned back he saw that the Sheikh and the Captain already had their heads together engrossed in some new conversation.

Ahmed led Pierre forward along another passage until they stopped before a narrow door of darkly polished wood and knocked softly. The opened door revealed a tall, thin man Pierre did not recognize. Ahmed spoke quietly and the man in the doorway disappeared, replaced by that man Pierre remembered as Mohamed. Seeing Pierre, the man's face lit with a smile.

"Ah, our courageous Christian." He stepped back inviting Pierre to enter as Ahmed turned and disappeared back along the passageway. Inside, beside the man who had opened the door another man sat cross-legged on pillows. All sat gathered around a device looking like the one he had seen in the Sheikh's cabin, though this was crafted of bright brass and dark wood. As with the Sheikh's, four flexible tubes sprouted from the base and each ended with a brass mouthpiece. A burning ember in its bowl released a wisp of gray smoke and the smell of a dankly sweet incense. Each of the men held the brass end of one of the tubes. When one drew on the tube, a bubbling sound came from the base as the ember at the top glowed bright. Gesturing toward a vacant pillow, Mohamed said, "Join us, please!"

Pierre did as was suggested, folding his legs as the others and relieved to find himself comfortable.

"Let me introduce you to my colleagues and dearest friends, Ali and Javad." The men nodded smiling to Pierre and a more unlikely looking pair of friends he found hard to imagine.

The man introduced as Ali had opened the cabin door. Taller than Pierre, he was reed-thin with a long, narrow face and dark circles around his eyes and his thick black beard reached his chest. The contrast to Javad could not be more complete. Shorter than Pierre, his arms and legs appeared afterthoughts added to his round body. His beard, although also thick and black, was trimmed close to his face. Even his expression was different, as if perpetually offering a round-cheeked grin. And where Ali's voice was low-pitched and morose, his was pitched high and reedy as if about to burst into laughter. Mohamed continued, "You arrived in the company of Ahmed so your visit is important. I hope there is no difficulty with your wound."

Pierre shook his head. "I'm here because the Sheikh claims we're of like mind and wants us to meet. His suggestion came in the course of a discussion of science and religion."

Mohamed's laughter was bright with pleasure. "Discussion is a generous label; our captain is intolerant of every idea except his own. In fact, I am certain it was nothing less than a battle, at least within his mind."

Pierre shifted uncomfortably. "It seems he mistook my questions for blasphemy."

"Happily, you are not one of his crew; he never argues calmly."

Ali added, "More than one sailor has had to swim home after such a disagreement."

Javad said, "And we know of none who has reached that other shore." He drew on the brass end of the tube at his lips, the lower container bubbled as smoke drifted from the brass cup. Taking it from his lips he exhaled loudly, releasing a gray cloud. "At least not in this life."

Mohamed offered the mouthpiece of the unused tube toward Pierre. "Please join us."

Pierre hesitated, but remembering Captain Rochelle's advice he did as the others and put the mouthpiece to his lips. The moment the smoke entered his throat he began to cough. Unprompted, Mohamed filled a goblet and passed it to Pierre. Between spasms of coughing Pierre drank greedily, relieved to find it filled with water. He realized the others watched him with concern and mild amusement. Mohamed said, "I will guess you have never smoked before."

Pierre struggled to suppress his coughs so he nodded. Mohamed continued, "In everything, we practice in anticipation that an experience will become pleasant." Drawing on his own mouthpiece, he held the smoke in his chest a moment before exhaling its cloud. Ali and Javad drew on their own mouthpieces and seemed to enjoy the experience, so Pierre tried again. The smoke irritated his chest but he exhaled a cloud without coughing. His companions grinned.

Pierre repeated this once more and found the experience pleasant and with a surprising sense of relaxation, and he did not need to suppress a cough. Gradually he became intrigued by the way the light slanted through the porthole, the way surfaces scintillated and colors deepened, and the movements of the ship seemed a pleasurable caress.

"Now you must tell us," Mohamed said, and his voice startled Pierre from his reflections, "about this controversy you became entangled by with Sheikh Mustafa."

Pierre heard the question and understood what he had been asked but as he gathered his response he remembered additional bits and reflected upon his answers, and then about how he should have responded, and then the questions he should have asked in turn, and also how that would have led to other questions plus how their answers would have been received and then how impressed his companions would have been by his subtle reasoning, finally convinced by his power of thought and...

"My friend," Mohamed suddenly said leaning toward Pierre, "are you all right?"

Startled, Pierre looked around to see the others staring at him and he flushed with embarrassment. "Sorry; guess I got carried away. Could I have more water?"

Mohamed passed the flagon of water to Pierre saying, "Let me tell you about an argument I once had with the Sheikh. As always, it was brief but it had to do with invisible forces and the principle of action-at-a-distance. And as you have discovered, he abhors the idea of invisible forces unless they are direct extensions of Allah's will."

Pierre was certain he heard every word spoken and understood each, yet the light and colors along with the motion of the ship, the quiet creaking of timbers and splash and slap of the sea against the hull, all deflected his attention for whole instants until he discovered he was thinking something else.

"My friend," Mohamed said with a note of concern, "are you certain you are all right?"

Startled once again, Pierre looked about confident that Mohamed had said something but unable to recall what that was. So he said, "What bothers him is the idea of mechanism. He refuses to admit that all actions in the material world can only be the result of the mechanical action of one material object upon another. He sees the world divided between material and non-material, and it disturbs him to think invisible forces are mechanical and not spiritual."

Again Pierre looked about but this time the faces around him bore expressions of surprise. Mohamed said, "I had not thought of it in that way but hearing you, suddenly it seems remarkably accurate."

Ali added, "You have described perfectly his discomfort. Whether we discuss the nature of the heavens or the forces of the earth, he insists each is a mask disguising the hand of Allah."

Javad said, "It appears you have given considerable thought to these questions. Which university did you attend and who was your master?" Pierre found himself embarrassed to confess he had little formal education and had never attended a university.

Mohamed expression immediately became serious. "That seems so unlikely. So tell us how you acquired such knowledge outside the halls of a university."

Pierre hesitated but recognizing the earnest curiosity of his companions he told them about Augustus and how he had helped at his workbench. Then he recounted the story of Dr. de Montpellier and his work on-board the Revenge. Finally he told them about the creature. In the end, he felt he had spoken about himself for a long time.

His companions listened in a silence only broken by the occasional burbling of the pipe. When he finished, they scrutinized him as if suspicious he had come from another world. After a pause Ali said, "An extraordinary tale; each moment is more astonishing than the last."

A smile wreathed Mohamed's face. "As astonishing as the study your father has chosen."

Javad said, "But most remarkable is your account of that creature. We have heard rumors, but you are the first we have met who claims to have seen it."

"That thing tried to eat me!"

Mohamed grinned with embarrassment. "Javad meant that others have claimed only to have heard of it, whereas you have seen it."

Pierre looked away fearful he would need to admit to others what he believed; that an awareness lurked behind the creature's actions since where there is a will there must be an intention, all of which demands a consciousness and so Pierre was forced to assume it was aware of his existence.

Suddenly, with a low, rumbling laugh Ali said, "Perhaps the creature likes you."

Javad added, "That's it! This creature wants to be your friend." He began to laugh and Mohamed joined and then Pierre laughed, and they all laughed so long and hard their laughter seemed to distort time and space into a fabric which drifted about them as a breeze ripples a cloth hung out to dry.

Suddenly Mohamed said, "I am hungry." Hearing these words Pierre discovered that despite the meal, a hunger laid coiled like a creature inside him and those words set it free.

"Yes," Ali said, "I am hungry, too. I am very hungry."

From a shelf behind him, Mohamed bought down a small, dark wooden chest. Its opened lid revealed a cache of dried dates that sparkled like nuggets of dark amber. Their appearance seemed to Pierre more thrilling than if that box had been filled with sparkling jewels. Ali and Javad reached into it for handfuls of dates, and Pierre joined them.

When the first date passed his lips its flavor seemed to explode on his tongue and its sweet pleasure startled him so it was all he could do to resist shoving more into his mouth. Overwhelmed by these sensations, he announced, "I've never tasted anything so wonderful!"

Mohamed grinned. "From the date-trees of glorious Baghdad, and none are more sweet." They resumed eating in silence and the experience left Pierre glowing with pleasure.

But finally Ali said, "Please tell us more about the investigation your father pursued."

The wooden chest beside then was half-empty and Pierre's hunger had subsided. "The aether," he answered, "and whether it moves in waves through material objects, and particularly whether it would pass along a length of metal. When he left our home he had become curious about the lodestone and something that he thought he recognized between its power and the aether." Pierre realized his eyelids had become heavy and he suppressed a yawn. "Suddenly, I seem very tired."

Javad and Ali smiled, but Mohamed looked earnestly at Pierre. "Do not be concerned. The leaf offers a delightful somnolence." Turning to the others he added, "But if you wish, we will be pleased to accompany you to your cabin."

Ali said, "And so prevent you from becoming lost."

Pierre looked from one man to the next as sleep seemed to move through his body like a slow-acting fever. "Perhaps that's a good idea." He placed his hand flat on the floor and began to stand only to be startled that the room moved around him. But instead of panic, he simply laughed. He tried to stand again but his folded legs seemed entangled, and he had to sit again to rearrange them. On his third try he stood, and looked about oddly proud.

They proceeded along the passageway and Pierre followed with a fragrant glow. His euphoria let him to suspect his feet trod along the back of a large, soft animal, and with every step his toes curled into its dense fur.

He followed these men certain they knew what he did not and that their knowledge would assure his arrival. But they seemed to walk a long time until Pierre wondered if they had decided to make a game of it and a fool of him. Time and space took on material weight, his feet seemed covered in molasses and he struggled to keep up, wondering why walking was not as difficult for them. But then they stopped. Mohamed turned to him smiling. "We have arrived!"

Startled, in a moment he recognized the cabin door with its lattice opening. "Thank you for your help and for your delightful conversation."

Ali said, "I believe we enjoyed it even more than you did."

Javad added, "And with the grace of Allah, we will enjoy your company again."

"Yes," Mohamed said. "I have spent some time exploring the aether and have succeeded in demonstrating its progression along metal similar to what you have described."

Pierre was again startled by this and wondered why Mohamed had not mentioned it earlier. But by the time he arranged his question within his mind, they were gone. Alone now in the passageway he could think of nothing else to do except enter the cabin.

Finding the cabin door unlocked he was surprised the Captain was not there. Pierre went to his bunk and laid down on his back thinking about the aether and how it might progress along solid material, but before any of this reached a useful conclusion he fell asleep.

Or was it sleep? Because his thinking seemed to continue, though his thoughts swirled within a churning sea of notions sometimes colliding with other notions as a stew of ideas, with some large and solid and others small and soft. This half-dreaming and half-thinking spiraled into a darker space until he could no longer distinguish any thought from any other. Black objects in a black pool that became a black tunnel of voices saying he must be killed he is a burden the Captain is worth gold but he is not worth salt but must die in a way he does not suspect us perhaps he will fall overboard such things happen even on clear days he must not live all life ends in death but do we dare can we be certain suppose he resists these voices echoing as if through a dark cave there must be light somewhere if the Captain discovers our plan what will we do he will not discover our plan if it is a good plan and besides there are always chains and Mohamed says but he knows the creature and the other voice says you mean he knows of the creature and he says no the creature knows him and the voice says that is not possible.

Suddenly, Pierre realized he was awake in his bunk and those voices were just beyond the door. And just as suddenly he endured an urge to sneeze so powerful it overwhelmed him and it sounded as an explosion. The silence that followed was sudden until it became footsteps moving softly away as Pierre sighed both relieved and frightened.

Relieved because they were gone, but frightened because they would return. Could he be certain of what he had heard? And who should he ask and who could he tell? And would he be believed? And even if believed, what might be done to protect him? Those voices seemed to warn him of something. Was that warning sufficient, or would he be sprung upon in the dead of night, or cornered on the main deck and silently tossed overboard, abandoned again to the whim of the sea and still unable to swim? If there was a plot against him and its origin was Sheikh Mustafa, how could Mohamed avoid reporting Pierre's words to his master? So he wondered again who he might trust and that question did not ease his sleep.

CHAPTER TWO

AMBLING ALONG THE gunwale, Pierre scrutinized each face he saw determined to discover which was observing him. He could not report to the Captain what he could not prove, while the Sheikh need only laugh in Pierre's face, assure him no plot existed and then go about whatever he planned to do.

Annoyed and despondent, he came to a stop beside the foremast. Under a sharply blue sky specked with small white clouds Mohamed appeared suddenly from below and approached smiling. "I trust you are enjoying our journey?"

Ignoring the pleasantry Pierre described the conversation he believed he had heard, but even before he finished, Mohamed began to laugh. "Surely you have dismissed all of that from your mind. There can be no truth in what you have imagined."

Pierre gritted his teeth to stifle his annoyance. "Perhaps you're right. So tell me about your experiments with the aether."

Mohamed blushed. "Compared to what you have described, they have been primitive."

He found Mohamed's coyness irritating but as if recognizing this, Mohamed added, "Join me in my workshop and allow me to show you." Pierre had given up attempting to navigate the interior of the ship, resigned that his ignorance was eternal and simply his lot. Following Mohamed, they reached an unmarked door. When it opened, Pierre's surprise froze him in place.

Devices of bright brass and dark wood stood carefully arranged on shelves that were clean and polished and which nearly circled the cabin. At their sight, he recalled the shelves surrounding Augustus and those surrounding the Scientist, all cluttered with bits and scraps and thoroughly baffling simply by their confused appearance. With an embarrassed smile Mohamed said, "Excuse this disorder as I have been working and have had no opportunity to return them to their proper places."

Pierre circled the cabin recognizing several devices while others were new to him. With a mildly embarrassed tone of Mohamed said, "Although elementary to you, I draw your attention to my current experiment." He nodded toward an apparatus on his workbench. Suspended across two slim, wooden mounts of a lathe that could be turned with a hand-crank was a cylinder of what resembled polished amber. Mounted so that the amber rotated beneath it, a piece of dark fur as wide as the cylinder was encased in a cage of fine wires so that its hairs just touched the surface of the amber. Those fine wires converged into a single wire which ended with a pointed piece of metal. Separated by a narrow space, another piece of metal was attached to a thick wire whose end was submerged in a glass container of clear liquid.

"Sea water," Mohamed said watching Pierre's eyes. "I have varied the conditions yet the effect appears consistent." He began to turn the crank. "Watch the gap between the points." After six turns a spark leapt between the points accompanied by a loud crack that startled Pierre.

"What happens when you continue to turn the crank?"

In response, Mohamed resumed and the spark and its sound appeared after only four turns. He continued and the spark and sound occurred after three turns. He said, "I hypothesize that flowing aether finds it increasingly easy to pass along the metal."

Pierre asked if he had varied the distance between the points. Mohamed nodded, explaining that as the distance increased he needed to increase the number of rotations. Just then the door opened and Javad entered. Surprised to see Pierre he said, "So Mohamed has enticed you to review his work. I can vouch for his long hours of effort."

Pierre nodded. "Perhaps he'll accept my collaboration."

"We should have time," Mohamed said, "to conduct several experiments before we reach port. Your assistance may even prove superior to that of Javad." At this both men laughed.

There was another knock on the door and Ali entered. Glancing at the three men he said, "My timing could not have been better. Have you already begun?"

Mohamed nodded. "Pierre has kindly offered to assist my experiments."

Pierre added, "So much of this is new to me and I can't see how I might help beyond observing."

"And perhaps killing more animals," Ali added.

In response to Pierre's obvious confusion, Ali said, "Mohamed has demonstrated that the aether from his device is not entirely benign." Glancing about he added, "He speculates he may even have found direct evidence of the hand of Allah at work in the world."

Mohamed shrugged. "Merely a curiosity which deserves investigation. Its implications are hardly so far-reaching."

Pierre asked, "And what might all of that have to do with the aether?"

Javad and Ali turned to Mohamed who said, "It began with an accident, as so much valuable science does. While operating the crank my finger slipped between its points triggering a discharge of the aether that resulted in a burning injury. Since I could neither explain it nor dismiss it I have attempted to pursue its implications."

Pierre waited but it was Ali who added, "Tell him about the birds."

Mohamed blushed. "Assuming," he said reluctantly, "that the aether is present in the atmosphere, and since birds travel through that same atmosphere, I wondered if they were vulnerable to its discharges." He looked aside, embarrassed. "I assure you they are."

Ali and Javad laughed and Pierre looked from one to the other. Javad said, "The diligence of his efforts has strewn the sea with the carcasses of birds."

Mohamed shrugged as if admitting something unpleasant. "Having discovered this device could cause injury I needed to learn whether this was the result of a special sort of aether and how dangerous it might be. For that purpose I built a cage of metal wire to confine a small bird and placed the cage between the two metal points with each point touching the metal of the cage. This form of the aether followed the metal elements to attack the bird, although I needed to crank quite a few turns before the bird was injured fatally." He looked down. "I have needed to repeat this experiment several times."

Pierre was puzzled. "And have you surmised the nature of this effect?"

Looking about at the others Mohamed said, "We each have a different hypothesis. For myself, based on the Aristotelian notion of like-to-like, I inferred that bits of amber are embedded within the fur, but are not also present in a bird's feathers. I speculate that in nature, the rabbit nibbles on amber unless amber forms somehow within its gut and then travels through its body to fuse with its fur. I further speculate that upon contact of like-to-like, the flow of the aether results from contact of amber to amber."

Ali sneered and Javad studied him quizzically. Turning to Pierre, Javad said, "We have substituted dog fur and cat fur for the rabbit's, and all generate identical effects. We also crushed amber and fed it to a bird before submitting it to the aether, but found no difference."

Mohamed shrugged. "I am convinced a solution will be found along those lines."

Ali said, "Where the result fails its prediction, either the execution is flawed or the hypothesis is wrong."

Pierre turned to Ali. "Do you have a hypothesis of your own?"

Ali bowed in mock respect. "The aether only flows while the amber and fur are in motion against each other, so I suggest it concentrates the way ice forms on a freezing pond. From this I assume the tips of the fur concentrate some vapor of aether hovering over the amber like a fog. Thus, that flow only becomes visible when the tips of the fur disturb that aether cloud."

Ali grinned but Mohamed simply shook his head. "Ali is the most clever of us, but his theory is too amusing to be satisfying. It is unclear how his analogy reflects the behavior of the aether, since moving water takes longer to freeze than still water." Hearing this Ali grimaced.

Pierre turned to Javad. "I assume your hypothesis is just as intriguing."

Javad looked sheepishly around at the others. "But not nearly as satisfying." He hesitated as if anticipating contradiction. "I assume the aether surrounds us and infer that the intersection between the fur and the amber directs it so that, concentrated, it must explode. I liken it to an imbalance that only returns to balance through violent discharge just as a volcano discharges heat within the earth to allow the earth to retain its balance." Mohamed studied Javad with sympathy and Ali looked at him with an odd humor.

After a moment Pierre said, "Perhaps that imbalance is sustained in the air such that the aether discharges only in contact with something touching the sea."

Javad's eyes became large. "That is my suspicion, though I have been unable to conjecture a suitable test."

Mohamed laughed. "Perhaps we should send Ali up the mainmast in a thunderstorm."

Ali smiled with embarrassment. "Though I believe my height accomplishes half that task, if you surmise that such a test will prove useful I am happy to assist."

The others realized Pierre had not joined in their amusement and they became serious. Pierre then described his experience aboard the Laguna of being struck by lightning. Though he told his tale in a casual tone, at its end the others looked at him astonished. Ali asked, "You experienced a lightning discharge and have lived to speak of it?"

Mohamed asked, "Can you tell us what it was like?"

Javad simply said, "Allah be praised."

He recounted what he had been told about those moments he could not remember and particularly the way his muscles had become rigid. To Mohamed he said, "So I believe I have an idea of how to test your hypothesis. But we will need one of Ali's thunderstorms."

While Ali studied Pierre with concern, Javad's expression suggested relief. Pierre added, "It may even give us useful information." The others watched him as if expecting an explanation. Instead he said, "Consider where we might find a length of metal wire braided into a thin rope along with a cage made of metal and wood."

Mohamed said, "Abdul our carpenter can build such a cage."

Javad added, "That cord of metal and twine we will need to make ourselves."

To Mohamed, Ali said, "Abdul provided the metal wire you used; perhaps he has more."

Javad said, "Still, we will need to braid that twine and wire."

Pierre said, "We'll also need a place on deck where we can set up our experiment."

Ali's expression darkened. "For that we will need the Sheikh's agreement."

Javad added, "He will expect assurances of safety for his ship and crew."

"That won't be difficult," Pierre said. "After all, how dangerous could any of this be?"

Javad asked, "But might we repeat the disaster you experienced aboard the Laguna?"

Pierre said, "Certainly the aether can injure but only with very peculiar circumstances."

Mohamed looked from Ali to Javad and then asked Pierre, "Are you certain?"

"I'm so certain, I'll conduct the experiment personally."

Javad said, "That should prove sufficient even for Sheikh Mustafa."

After wishing the men well, Pierre left their cabin and managed to make his way to the main deck, all the while considering how to conduct an experiment that began gradually forming in his mind. Looking about, the only clear place appeared to be the quarterdeck beside the tiller. He wondered then whether to share his plan with the Captain. To gain the Sheikh's agreement he would need the Captain's support and so he began to search for him. Failing to find him on deck Pierre assumed he was with the Sheikh and made his way to his cabin.

Turning to descend the gangway he saw one of the sailors on the quarterdeck watching him. He continued below as if preoccupied. He decided a detour in his path would prove useful.

When he reached the passageway he turned and followed it as if confused. At the next intersection he turned and continued until he reached another turn, but then he stopped. After a moment, footsteps quietly approached. When they had nearly reached him, he stepped out. The startled look on the sailor's face almost made Pierre laugh.

"I'm trying to find the Sheikh's cabin," Pierre said. The man looked at him startled but said nothing. Pierre said, "The Sheikh's cabin; which way?" But the man simply stared certainly confused. Pierre assumed an impatient tone. "Sheikh Mustafa; which way?" The sailor looked about as if eager to escape. Pierre let his impatience shade into anger. "English? You speak English?" The sailor's expression bloomed into full panic.

Pierre began to laugh until the man smiled with him. He pushed the sailor hard against the bulkhead. "Next time I see you, you better speak English!" He pushed him hard again, stepped past him and retreated back along the passage. At the first turn he glanced back to see that the sailor was gone. He returned to his path to the Sheikh's cabin. At the Sheikh's door Ahmed stood guard. Stepping past him Pierre knocked loudly. Ahmed glared but did not stop him when he opened the door.

Inside, the Sheikh and Captain Rochelle reclined on pillows with the smoking device between them, a mouthpiece in each of their hands and the cabin fogged with blue, sweet-smelling smoke. At the sight of Pierre they both smiled.

The Sheikh said, "I so hoped to continue our conversation. Please join us." He gestured to pillows beside him. Pierre hesitated but then sat down. The Sheikh offered one of the pipes, but he waved it aside.

"When you have someone follow me, be certain at least he speaks English."

"And why," the Sheikh asked with mild surprise, "would I wish to do that?"

"So he can help me find my way below-decks."

"You misunderstand my question. Why would I assign someone to follow you?"

"You're the only one to answer that."

The Sheikh laughed. "We are aboard a ship in the middle of the ocean. Where could any of us go?" His smile appeared so benign Pierre was embarrassed by his own suggestion.

"That's another question only you can answer."

The Captain said to Pierre, "Your suggestion seems ungrateful."

"My gratitude I'll reserve for what I'm given, though I'm uncertain what that is."

Still smiling, the Sheikh said, "Surely this conversation has taken a dark turn. Let us deal with your original intention, since I am certain you came here with some purpose in mind."

Pierre suspected he had been outmaneuvered even while he was unsure how. "I've spoken with Mohamed and I've come to ask permission to conduct an experiment on your quarterdeck." The Sheikh's eyes narrowed and Pierre added. "It will not endanger either your ship or crew."

The Sheikh's expression became quizzical. "But as it is an experiment, how can you be certain there will be no danger?"

Pierre shrugged. "You must depend on my sense of responsibility."

"Assuming the first, the second remains, shall we say, problematic."

The Captain spoke as if from the bottom of the ocean and gasping for air. "I will vouch for his integrity. Though I am ignorant of his experiment, I do not doubt his common sense."

The Sheikh looked from one man to the other until his smile returned. "What exactly do you need from me?"

"The others are gathering elements for the experiment," Pierre said, "but we need your carpenter to build a cage of metal and wood large enough for an animal the size of a small dog."

Sheikh Mustafa and Captain Rochelle studied him a moment but finally the Sheikh nodded. "I cannot imagine what you have in mind or to what use this might be put, but I assure you the more I learn, the more curious I become. Abdul will fabricate whatever you need." Turning to the Captain he added, "I only hope this exercise proves at least amusing."

Pierre was so startled by this prompt response he could offer only a nod of gratitude.

Several days passed until Pierre stood on the quarter-deck beside Ali, Mohamed and Javad, all looking up to a dark, cloud-cluttered sky. With relief Javad said, "Finally, your storm is on the horizon."

Mohamed said, "Forgive my ignorance, but considering the effort it has demanded to make the metal twine and build this cage, I remain unclear how it will test the aether?"

Pierre grinned. "How can I impress you if you know what will happen? But I promise you'll be glad you saw it."

Ali eyed him curiously. "But as it is an experiment you cannot know what will happen."

Pierre said. "If those experiments you've performed and those I observed are useful, this should confirm the aether's ability to do violence."

Javad stood to one side looking curiously at the device Pierre had carried from his cabin. "Have you made anything like that before?"

"They're considered playthings," Pierre said, "but it's the first I've made, though at home I've watched children make them. It's called a kite, and on a windy day one will soar and dive in the sunlight. With this rising wind, we should see just how useful this one might be."

He then watched Sheikh Mustafa emerge from below, followed by Captain Rochelle. They nodded in Pierre's direction and climbed to the quarterdeck. Following close behind, two sailors carried between them a small cage made of iron and wood enclosing a dusky and unhappy lamb.

At the sight of the gathered crew and the open sky, the lamb began to bleat with concern.

Holding the coil of that string braided with metal, Pierre climbed to the quarterdeck, the kite already bouncing rebelliously in his hand in response to the strengthening breeze. Taking a spot beside the caged lamb, Pierre turned to the Sheikh and the Captain and nodded toward the opposite rail. "It's probably best you stand over there." With patient smiles they did as he asked.

To the Sheikh, Pierre said, "Can I have some help from one of your sailors?" Without turning he called out for Ahmed, and he stepped up to join them on the quarterdeck. To Mohamed, Pierre said, "Better observe this from a distance." He hesitated and Pierre said, "I've got all the help I need." Mohamed turned reluctantly and descended to the main deck.

The clouds became thick overhead, the wind blew harder and then near the horizon lightning flashed. Ahmed held the kite as Pierre wound the free end of the metal twine to one of the metal bars at the bottom of the cage, and the other to the controller strings of the kite. The metal twine followed the center of the kite to a thin metal rod protruding from its apex.

With the metal string coiled at his feet, Pierre took the kite from Ahmed's hand and nodded him aside. The kite now struggled against the breeze as if desperate to escape. He stepped to the rail and loosened his hold releasing the kite out over the ocean. Snatched by that wind, the kite leapt from his fingers. The uncoiling metal string cut across Pierre's palm, and as it rose into the bleak sky, drops of his blood fell into the sea. Soon the kite careened high above the ship.

Pierre released the rest of the string gradually, and its weight soon stabilized the kite as it continued to rise. The wind blew stronger and he braced his feet to keep his balance. Thunder became loud as lightning strikes drew close. Wrapping the end of the twine on a hand-spike mounted to the rail, a sudden gust grabbed the kite pulling hard on the string. Struggling to regain control, he nodded to Ahmed for help. He approached and Pierre handed the line to him.

The sky was now black, the crack and rumble of thunder and flashes of lightning played near the ship. Metal string secured to the iron cage and the lamb bleating continually, Pierre stepped back. Satisfied, he reached toward Ahmed for the metal string and Ahmed offered it toward him. Pierre watched Ahmed's hand and the metal string emerging from it, and his own hand extended about to take control of it, when a flash of light surrounded their hands blinding Pierre.

In the next instant he found himself on his back and looking up stunned and unable to move while rain poured onto his face. Then the faces of Mohamed and the Captain were looking down at him. Their mouths moved yet he heard nothing beyond a high-pitched whistle. Hands under his shoulders lifted him until he stood upright. With his feet beneath him, his limbs returned to his control and the hiss of the falling rain became distinct. And then he saw Ahmed lying motionless on the deck. Sailors knelt all around him. Inside the cage, the lamb lay on its side, wisps of pale smoke drifting from its four stiff legs. Pierre felt himself smile.

The Sheikh stepped to him with an expression darker than the sky. "So much for your assurances!" Glancing toward the prone Ahmed, he added, "I assume this was not the objective of your experiment."

"Dead?" Pierre asked, his voice merely a harsh croak.

The Sheikh nodded. After a pause he asked, "Was your experiment successful?"

Still dazed, Pierre was uncertain how to respond but Mohamed appeared by his side. Through the wind and rain he said, "We regret this tragic result but we have demonstrated a principle unknown even to the Ancients. Allah be praised, our world has grown larger and we have been its witness."

Looking hard at Mohamed, in a low, flat voice the Sheikh said, "Not all of us are able to enjoy your triumph." He turned to watch Ahmed being carried by four sailors below deck. To Pierre, he said, "That man stood by my side more than ten years and I trusted no one as I have him. I can only hope the value of your experiment is high because its cost also has been terrible."

The Captain stepped forward. "By my lights there is no fault to be found here. Pierre took the same risk your sailor did, and was struck down by the same stroke of lightning. Though it may appear otherwise, he does not control that lightning."

Looking from the Captain to Mohamed and then to Pierre, the Sheikh's expression softened and he sighed. "Indeed, it is Allah alone who controls the lightning as He controls all things. I will not blame this man, for we must believe Ahmed has died as and when Allah decreed. But forgive my disappointment. He was as dear to me as a son, and I will never know his kindness again." Turning to the Captain he bowed, then turned to descend from the quarterdeck when suddenly, all heard an angry roar, deep and distant and yet clear, from far out at sea. After a moment the roar repeated.

All on the deck and in the rigging looked in the direction of its sound. When it repeated a third time, all turned to look to the Sheikh. With frantic urgency Pierre said, "Hang all the sail you have and as quickly as you can. We must get away from here and not delay even a moment." The rain had begun to weaken.

The Sheikh turned a furious look at Pierre. "You presume too much! You commandeer my ship for your experiment and thereby risk its destruction. You kill my most valuable sailor and claim Allah is responsible. And now you tell me how to sail my ship. Allah forgive me, but I am too close to throwing you to the sharks."

To Pierre's relief, the Captain spoke up. "At the risk of being condemned beside my friend, I urge you to do as he suggests. This is also something he knows."

In a voice that barely contained his fury, the Sheikh said, "I weary of all of the esoteric knowledge your sailor claims to possess."

Pierre said, "We've just heard the voice of the beast. Unfurl your sails if you value your life."

Turning to the Captain, the Sheikh said, "I am reluctant to do so, yet on your good counsel I will do as he says. But just remember that it is by your advice."

Glancing at Pierre, the Captain said, "Whatever his knowledge, on this I am certain he knows whereof he speaks. Our ship once was the subject of the same threat and I believe he preserved us."

The Sheikh looked from the Captain to Pierre and then back to the Captain again. "I have no desire to test his knowledge since even the slight chance I am wrong may prove costly. I only hope Allah plans no more surprises." He turned and barked orders; within moments sailors in the rigging began to unfurl canvas from every yardarm with loud thuds and snaps. To the Captain he said, "A word, please, in my cabin." He turned and joined his crew carrying their dead mate below deck. The Captain turned to Pierre. "Life is short for those who are wrong when they must be right." He followed the Sheikh below deck. The rain had nearly stopped.

When they were gone, Mohamed, Ali and Javad joined Pierre beside the cage and its dead lamb. Mohamed clapped Pierre on the shoulder. "Praise be to Allah, I have witnessed the unthinkable and it is the result of your intuition. I congratulate you."

"Without your help nothing could have been accomplished; this is your success as well."

Ali grinned. "If nothing else, you have discovered a new way to kill a lamb."

Javad simply looked at Pierre as if he was seeing him for the first time. "You are certain what we heard was that creature." He spoke flatly, as if confirming what he already assumed, but aloud so others knew what he knew and that he knew it. Pierre simply nodded. Javad asked, "But how can it know we are here? And why might we be its target?"

Pierre glanced down at his bleeding hand. "If I'm correct, I'm even more afraid than you are." At that moment he understood what he knew, and that knowledge cast all he had witnessed into a horrifying light.

Pierre turned to Mohamed. "Let's return to your workshop." To Ali, he said, "Can the lamb to be brought there?" When Ali looked at him curiously he said, "We must know how the aether took its life."

When they reached the workshop, Pierre asked for quill and ink and paper. Soon Ali arrived carrying the dead lamb on a pewter platter and placed it on the workbench.

Concerning the moment the lightning struck the kite, Javad explained that the kite burst into flame and fell into the sea a smoking ember and that the lightning severed the string which also began to flame. Javad speculated the lightning contained enough heat to set the kite and the string on fire, yet the mechanism of the aether''s travel along the metal string was a mystery.

With his notes complete Pierre asked that they examine the dead lamb. Mohamed brought out a knife and with a series of cuts exposed portions of its internal organs. Pierre was impressed by the skill he demonstrated. So it did not take long for them to determine that only the lightning, a dagger of the aether after all, had taken the lamb's life and nothing more.

Pierre scrutinized the carcass. "Might we perform a similar examination of Ahmed?" He was surprised when they turned to him with horrified expressions.

After a moment Javad said, "We share your curiosity and even agree that useful knowledge might be derived. But the Sheikh will never permit such desecration." He glanced to Mohamed and Ali as if for confirmation. Both appeared embarrassed nodding their agreement.

Caught up in enthusiasm for the experiment Pierre asked, "And what objection could there be?"

His question was followed by another long moment of silence until Ali said, "Aside from offense to Allah and to the spirit of Ahmed, I assure you he will not tolerate its insult to his dead friend." Expressions of the others confirmed his assertion.

"I wish no insult," Pierre said, "but we'll miss the chance to confirm our hypothesis."

Solemnly Mohamed said, "Some opportunities, though apparent, cannot be pursued. We must be satisfied with what this lamb has provided."

Pierre nodded. "Let's hope another opportunity appears we're able to profit from." He was surprised when the others appeared relieved.

Ali said, "With our examination concluded, the lamb can be given to the ship's cook and prepared for a proper meal."

"And so we'll receive an additional benefit from the experiment," Pierre added. Though wishing to seem agreeable, he was disappointed at losing the chance to inspect Ahmed's corpse.

Mohamed suddenly laughed. "We deserve a celebration."

Ali brightened. "And our chef will transform this victim into a delicious feast."

Javed said, "Already I smell a wonderful meal."

To Ali, Mohamed said, "Please escort our prize to the chef and be sure he understands the significance of the occasion."

Ali grinned, took up the platter and left.

Pierre turned to Javed. "As we're unable to make an internal examination of Ahmed, is there a chance for us to make a superficial examination?"

Javad glanced at Mohamed. "Undoubtedly his body is now being prepared for burial."

Pierre asked, "Is burial at sea permitted by your religion?"

"The Holy Koran," Mohamed said, "is specific concerning the disposition of the bodies of those who die at sea and the ceremonies which must be fulfilled."

"Sounds like these ceremonies are elaborate and complicated."

Mohamed said, "Their intent is to prevent the dead from corrupting the living even as the living honor the dead. Washed and anointed, his body will be dressed in burial clothing. He will then be sewn into a canvas shroud weighted to sink to the bottom. In the morning he will be brought on deck for those prayers for the dead that will be offered by the Sheikh. After he has been released to the sea, his mourning will continue for three days."

"Be assured," Javed added, "the Sheikh will make certain he is sent properly on his way."

Mohamed added, "So let us remember Ahmed with gratitude as we enjoy our victory. Meanwhile," he said, "this is a perfect occasion to light the lamp."

Javed asked, "Should we await Ali's return?"

Mohamed shook his head. "An additional surprise awaits him." From a small brass and wooden box he brought out a fragment that could have been a piece of dried mud and put it into the brass cup at the top of the pipe. Javed sat on a pillow beside the pipe and took up one of the tubes. Mohamed put a lighted taper to the bowl as Javed drew noisily on the tube. Soon, that fragment glowed orange as a sweet-smelling blue cloud began to fill the cabin.

By the time Ali returned carrying their meal of a cooked lamb, Pierre discovered he was famished beyond measure. Mohamed went to a hidden cupboard and brought out what Pierre suspected was a bottle of wine. Noticing his recognition, Mohamed said, "Wine is prohibited yet I believe on this occasion Allah will look the other way." Pierre looked about to see the others grinning.

Whether it was the sumptuous food or the delicious wine or the sweet smoke or the company of his companions, Pierre could not recall ever enjoying a meal as much as this. His companions seemed to compete among themselves to share the most astonishing adventures in their service to the Sheikh while repeatedly offering Pierre praise for his accomplishment. At the end of the meal Pierre departed so thoroughly euphoric he could not remember reaching his cabin, and knew only that he enjoyed a deep and dreamless sleep.

As Javed had predicted, the Captain roused him early the next morning to witness Ahmed's burial. Pierre hesitated to join the crew since he was held responsible for his death, but the Captain advised him he was obliged to be there. So, burdened with a miserable hangover, Pierre joined the Captain and the crew as the Sheikh offered prayers for Ahmed. At their end, Ahmed's canvas-shrouded body slipped from a plank on the deck and dropped into the sea. With this done, the crew disbursed, but the Sheikh stood alone beside the rail looking out over the sea. Pierre considered joining him to offer words of consolation and regret. But in the end he decided that no matter how earnest and well-intended, his words were unlikely to be received well. Over the days that followed, Pierre avoided the Sheikh's company and Sheikh Mustafa no longer requested his.

CHAPTER THREE

DAYS PASSED FOLLOWING Ahmed's burial at sea and then one morning when Pierre was attempting an experiment with Ali and Mohamed in the workshop, the call went out of all-hands on-deck. Ali and Mohamed put down their tools and disappeared through the door and Pierre followed.

On the main deck a knot of sailors stood at the port-side gunwale staring out to sea. It took a moment but Pierre made out three black specks on the horizon that soon became five, and then six, and though still far off he was certain they were turning to sail in their direction. The Sheikh climbed to the quarterdeck followed by Captain Rochelle. At the tiller the helmsman handed the Sheikh his spyglass. After a quick observation he passed the spyglass to the Captain, then turned to the helmsman and spoke. He then stepped to the rail and addressed the crew. His speech was brief, and while Pierre did not understand his words, by tone and expression he guessed it was serious. He glanced to Mohamed. "He believes," Mohamed said, "that convoy has unfriendly intentions. As we are outnumbered he has ordered a change of course."

"Is there any way I can help?" Pierre asked.

Mohamed looked at him surprised. "Should the necessity arise, I am sure you will recognize it. Now, I must take up my post." He then made his way forward. Pierre looked up to see Ali and Javad already moving through the rigging. Captain Rochelle remained on the quarterdeck beside Sheikh Mustafa and the helmsman. The ship turned hard to starboard to put the convoy behind them, but Pierre watched those ships also turn as if determined to pursue. They closed the distance until he could distinguish their masts and yardarms and then the Sheikh's vessels quickly were within range of their cannons.

The Sheikh barked another order and Pierre watched the helmsman turn hard to direct their port guns on the advancing ships. The ships had approached close enough for Pierre to see the tiny figures of their sailors clambering through the rigging and moving along the gunwales. He turned to discover Captain Rochelle standing by his side, an unsheathed saber in his hand.

"You should take this," he said and Pierre saw that he held another in his right hand. "We are about to defend our captors. At the very least, we should prepare to defend ourselves."

"Won't they just blast us out of the water?"

"They will take down our masts with their cannons and kill as many of our crew as they can but they want our cargo. It will have no value at the bottom of the sea."

The convoy maneuvered quickly into position opposite the Sheikh's vessels. But then, and even though for a moment it seemed an optical illusion, Pierre saw, in the midst of these converging ships, a sea-swell like an enormous green-glass bubble appear and grow. Startled, he turned to speak to the Captain when at its center appeared the huge head of the creature. It tipped back its head and then opened jaws releasing a roar. Terror froze Pierre to the deck as, for a moment, the sea, the ships and crews, the wind and even the light itself all seemed to pause.

Covered by greenish black scales that surrounded enormous eyes red as a blacksmith's hearth, its head arose until its neck was exposed. Though a distance away, it turned in Pierre's direction as if to look directly into his eyes. Again it opened its mouth, huge, bone-yellow teeth flashing in the sunlight, and roared. Then it turned on the Sheikh's vessel.

As quickly as all of this transpired, the cannons of all of the ships together began to fire at the creature. Singly and in batteries, furious foes were instant allies; cannons all fired until their explosions merged into a continuous roar. In response, the creature simply lowered its head and continued toward Pierre's ship. Round after round of cannon shot struck glancing from its skull to bounce high or splash into the sea. But then, as the creature opened its mouth, the Sheikh's starboard battery fired a volley striking its face so that some shots entering its mouth.

As if startled, the beast closed its great jaws and shook its tremendous head sending huge waves at the ships around it. With a furious snarl it turned upon a ship that had drifted close, lifted itself until a huge, clawed forelimb came down on the unlucky vessel amidships to shatter the center of its hull to the keel and toss screaming sailors into the sea. The ship immediately began to sink. Seeming excited by this, it turned upon the next ship in the line. That ship had begun to steer away but the creature's forelimb crashed down on its quarterdeck, lifting its bow high and shattering its stern sending more sailors into the sea. The other ships continued to fire and the creature turned to roar and snarl at each in turn.

The cries of sailors floundering in the sea and sight of portions of the crushed and shattered ships finally released Pierre. He climbed to the quarterdeck and when he reached the Sheikh he brought his face close to his ear. "Flee now, while the creature's distracted. Take to your heels if you hope to save your ships."

But the Sheikh was looking past Pierre's shoulder and Pierre turned to see Captain Rochelle standing behind him. To his surprise the Sheikh appeared confused. He repeated, "Flee now while you have the chance." The Sheikh hesitated and the Captain added, "There is no victory here, nor prize to be won." The beast turned to attack another ship. In moments that ship was reduced to planks and timbers and those sailors still alive flailed in the sea screaming for help. But this seemed finally to awaken the Sheikh. He barked orders and sailors in the rigging dropped canvas into place until sails billowed and the ship began to move away. From the quarterdeck they watched the creature thrash about among the remaining ships, striking out at any within reach while the cannons of the others continued to fire.

The Sheikh's vessel gained speed as the other surviving ships finally turned to withdraw. The creature appeared suddenly confused, as though unable to decide which ship to pursue, and roared furiously as each of the departing ships sailed away.

Though now more than a mile from the beast, Pierre was only relieved when he saw it turn to pursue another ship and move further off. The Sheikh's vessel reached cruising speed, its sails now filled. But the Sheikh's face betrayed a furious rage. Captain Rochelle said, "There is no disgrace in flight from an overpowering enemy. You have saved your ship and crew and all the treasure it carries."

The Sheikh turned to him with a bitter smile. "I have lost one ship and a full crew of men. As for cargo, that ship carried enough black powder and shot to fit out a small armada. Your consolations are better directed to the bottom of the sea with those men who have died."

Pierre said, "Be content; you could not have defeated the creature."

The Sheikh turned his expression on Pierre. With flat certainty he said, "You brought that creature to us. Though I have no idea how, you conjured its appearance." Glancing toward the Captain he said, "You have proved exceedingly expensive captives."

"Appreciate the irony," Pierre said. "If that creature hadn't appeared, your ships most likely would have been captured or sunk."

The Sheikh looked again from Pierre to Captain Rochelle. "Yes, I must make a note of that. And when I console the widows and orphans of those lost sailors, no doubt they will be grateful to know that." His glance fixed on Pierre. "On the other hand, perhaps I would have saved them all if I simply had given the creature what it wants."

Pierre hesitated. "And suppose you had been wrong? Suppose you tossed me into the sea but the creature continued to pursue you? You'd have brought about my death for a mistaken belief. Seems unlikely Allah would smile on your decision."

After a moment the Sheikh offered his own smile. "Yes, there is that to consider." Turning back to the Captain he said, "Meanwhile I remain burdened with you both." He paused. "At least for now." Certain his message had been understood he bowed. "I will return to my cabin and pray we have seen the last of that beast. And I suggest you both do the same."

When he was gone the Captain turned to Pierre. "You know about all this and a good bit more."

Pierre hesitated. "I think I'll follow the Sheikh's suggestion." As he descended the gangway he looked back to the quarterdeck. Captain Rochelle remained staring hard out to sea as if watching for the creature, or something even more dangerous.

Preoccupied by what had happened and shaken by the Sheikh's conclusion connecting him to the creature's appearance, Pierre made his way back to their cabin. Though he would never have admitted it, he had all but reached the same conclusion, even while accepting that it demanded each of his past encounters had occurred because that creature knew of him as a unique being. For the creature, as for the Christian God, Pierre existed individually. As he followed the passageway he tried to consider that notion in the light of material evidence. If it pursued Pierre uniquely, by what material effect had he achieved an existence within its awareness? And more, was this evidence the creature even possessed a mind? Because if no mind lay behind these acts, what force of intuition was at work?

Pierre's confused thoughts left him so distracted that he looked up to discover he had walked far beyond the door of his cabin and entered another passageway he did not recognize. He was about to retrace his steps when he discovered he was hearing voices and their sound came from further ahead. Curiosity overwhelmed his concern. He stepped past several closed doors until he recognized that those voices deep in discussion included the Sheikh's.

"I believe our encounter has provided all the proof I need."

To Pierre's surprise the next voice was Mohamed's. "Though I am inclined to agree I remain unconvinced."

"If we are to agree," a third voice said, "we must assume it is possible for him to compel a dumb animal to do his bidding." Pierre was startled to recognize it belonged to Javad

The Sheikh's response was impatient. "I simply need to know that it is true so that I can decide how to proceed."

"But that is the point," Javad responded. "How might this have come about? If he is able to call the creature, why put himself in danger by doing so? And why risk the lives of innocent sailors? Could he possibly be so cold-blooded?"

"I agree with Javad," Mohamed said. "However depraved a heathen, I cannot believe he condemns innocent men to the beast's attack on a whim." At these words Pierre sighed in thanks for Mohamed's generous thoughts. "On the other hand," he continued, "perhaps he is so adept at subterfuge he perpetrates the deepest crimes without any purpose beyond the misery that results. If so, he has fooled all of us and is worthy of the most hideous death." Hearing this, Pierre guessed he had heard more than he wanted and now needed to leave. Shifting his weight to move, a plank beneath his foot groaned. The voices behind the door became silent and that silence continued for a long and discomforting moment. Fearing what would follow he took two quick steps back, found that the door beside him opened without a sound and slipped in closing it behind him. At almost the same moment, Pierre heard the door to that cabin open. He held his breath. Mohamed quietly laughed. "Guilt exaggerates every fear."

"And you are too easily amused," the Sheikh responded with annoyance. Pierre heard the door close and then heard Javad say, "Captain Rochelle's presence complicates our situation, so I ask again if his ransom will be that rich."

The Sheikh sighed heavily. "You raise a delicate point without delicacy. With the loss of my ship, the cost of his ransom has increased and the chance of full redemption diminished until the field of individuals able to redeem his ransom has narrowed to just one."

Mohamed said evenly, "You are referring to that scoundrel Mezzanotte."

"Complicating," the Sheikh continued with a resigned sigh, "an already complicated situation. After all, why send his ships against us? Our collaboration has been mutually beneficial. Why risk its benefit with an impulsive and destructive action?"

After a pause, Javad said, "Perhaps another player has entered the game; one of whom we are unaware but whose involvement will prove decisive."

Mohamed added, "Perhaps one of his captains has chosen to pursue his own interests and without Mezzanotte's knowledge. We do not yet know the reason for all this, but the beast's attack allows us to pursue the issue with him."

Javad said, "Our young friend proved surprisingly acute when he suggested we be grateful for the creature's timely arrival. Loath as I am to admit it, he described our situation with startling accuracy. For a colonial, he seems inexplicably intelligent."

"Or perhaps," Mohamed added dryly, "he is merely good at guessing."

The Sheikh said, "If Allah has favored him with a fortunate soul, we must not dismiss his gift."

"However that may be," Javad said, "we should sail to Mezzanotte's lair and confront him directly. Ignorance and confusion over his intentions grants us no benefit."

Mohamed said, "A strategy of naive directness will benefit us even less."

After a silent pause Javad said, "It is unfortunate we did not capture one of his commanders."

"It is optimistic," the Sheikh said, "to assume such an individual would provide us with the truth or even possessed the truth."

"Be assured," Javad said, "that with the use of Mohamed's aether device we would learn everything he even suspected was true."

Mohamed said. "Proper application of the aether-generating device elicits responses from even the strongest will." He laughed quietly.

"Belief," the Sheikh cautioned, "is not knowledge. One must accurately estimate the veracity of an assertion. That device brings forth statements without assuring their accuracy."

The silence that followed seemed to drift along the passage until Mohamed said, "Perhaps we should apply the device to our young friend."

A chill ran through Pierre that made his knees go soft and tightened his throat.

With dripping sarcasm Javad said, "With due respect, that lightning strike he survived was far more powerful than anything your device could create. Besides, though a clever bumpkin, he is more ignorant than any of Mezzanotte's sailors."

Mohamed said, "I resist giving him more credit than is his due, yet I believe he knows more than we acknowledge."

The Sheikh said, "The issue is not whether he knows something, but whether he knows enough for us to risk displeasing the Captain in an attempt to find it out. Once his interrogation begins, the Captain will learn of our lapse in hospitality."

Pierre felt the silence that followed creep down his throat.

"He could not make such a report," Mohamed said quietly, "if he were dead."

Startled, Pierre stepped from the wall and once again a plank creaked loudly. He froze. After another moment's silence the Sheikh chuckled. "Be of good cheer; it is sufficient to endure guilt over our deeds. Guilt over our thoughts is simply misplaced."

With a note of annoyance Mohamed asked, "Have you decided how you will proceed?"

The Sheikh said, "Though I have no faith in the tactic, we will proceed as you suggest and confront Mezzanotte directly. Otherwise, we merely pile clouds upon clouds."

“To compel such a revelation,” Javad said, “we will need a powerful lever.”

“This attack,” the Sheikh added calmly, “allows us to demand explanation. Though he may deny responsibility and dissemble concerning his involvement, facts are facts because they cannot be denied. But we will only judge his response when we have heard it.” Movements toward the door to the passageway sounded from the other side of the bulkhead.

Javad asked, “Have you decided what you will tell Captain Rochelle?”

The Sheikh laughed quietly. “I can dissemble as well as any Christian, so he will only know what I wish him to know.”

Pierre listened until the door to their cabin closed and then footsteps passed along the passageway beyond his door, yet he hesitated. Just a single pair of footsteps moved past him. After a few moments he heard Mohamed quietly say, “It appears he still does not know.”

Javad responded, “That must be true or we would already be dead. But he is a fox, as old as he is, and dissembles as well as any Christian, just as he says. We must assume he suspects what he does not know. Happily, Mezzanotte pays us well-enough to run this risk.”

“And perhaps we will learn why he sent those ships against us. He knew our position and course; why add to our complications?”

“And you are the victim of pointless optimism. He feels no greater obligation to us than to his lowest servant. Still, I remain confident our loyalty and cooperation will be rewarded.”

“We must hope so,” Mohamed said warily. “There is no turning back from here. We must make certain these Christians do not betray our scheme, even by accident.”

Javad added, “The only guarantee against betrayal is death.”

After a pause Mohamed said, “So I am relieved we dissuaded the Sheikh from using the aether-generator against him. It is unlikely Mezzanotte would be grateful to learn that his prize had been tortured.”

Javad paused. “The young man believes he is more clever than he is. An untutored intelligence has a certain charm among the jaded elderly. From what I have learned, perhaps that is the source of Mezzanotte’s interest in him.”

“It would certainly be better if his skills were mathematical.”

“We should be relieved he is competent at reading.” Both then laughed quietly.

Mohamed said, "I believe we have given the Sheikh enough time to reach his quarters. We will return to the deck and congratulate our guest on the impression his creature has made."

"Particularly among Mezzanotte's sailors already on their way to tell him their tale."

Mohamed added, "You mean those who survived." Again, both quietly laughed. Pierre listened as they left the cabin and followed the passageway. Their sounds faded with their retreat and their laughter continued to chill him.

Pierre found himself breathing heavily and his legs suddenly weak as a moment of vertigo shifted the cabin around him. His fate once again was being decided by others and since flight was impossible, his temptation again was to remain hidden. Too many forces were in contention, and protection from one simply left him vulnerable to another. He needed to abandon every fantasy of rescue and plot escape. Ear to the door he heard only silence, so he left and quickly made his way to the main deck.

Under full sail over a calm sea and now far from the scene of their battle with the beast, their ship crested lazy waves with an easy roll. The crew went about their tasks and none seemed to pay particular attention to Pierre. Not finding the Captain on the main deck, he was about to return to their cabin when Mohamed stepped up. Bright with relief he said, "I feared misadventure had ended our friendship."

That overheard conversation still fresh in his mind, Pierre grinned in nervous embarrassment. "It seems I remain among the living and hope to continue."

"Javad and I were just speaking of you. These events have piqued our curiosity. We hope you will add to our knowledge of that creature."

"There's little for me to tell. The beast remains as baffling to me as ever." He glanced about hoping to end their conversation.

"Surely, with your experiences you have speculated upon its nature."

"It's more likely you and Javad have conjectured something more intriguing than I could." Pierre then saw the Captain step out onto the main deck. From his expression he guessed the Captain was eager to speak with him. He excused himself and moved toward Captain Rochelle.

The Captain watched Pierre approach with a dark look. "The Sheikh seems to suspect something dangerous about you."

But before he could continue, Pierre asked, "What do you know about a rogue named Mezzanotte?"

The Captain's eyes widened. "Where have you heard that name?" Pierre said nothing, and the Captain said, "He is a vile, godless and notorious cut-throat; why do you ask?"

"I've heard of him from different folks at different times so I've become curious."

The Captain studied him with a wary expression. "What I can tell you comes down to the fact that he is as bad as are made. Sheikh Mustafa claimed those ships that attacked us were his. If that is the case, we just escaped a fate as deadly as attack by the beast."

Pierre was about to speak when he noticed Mohamed watching them. "Let's continue where we're unlikely to be overheard." He led the Captain further along the gunwale. Though obviously confused, the Captain followed.

Looking about, Pierre said, "From what I've heard his power is enormous."

"Powerful and evil," the Captain said flatly. "To believe the tales, he has a hand in everything illicit in the Mediterranean, and his ambition reaches even into the Caribbean. It is said the Pope himself owes his position to his machinations."

"With all those ships about to attack, he must have a grand fleet at his disposal."

"His nefarious activities are wide-spread and his ships are available to the highest bidder. There even are times when elements of his forces align on both sides in the same battle. Though only conjecture, he is implicated in assassinations of royalty and in the dynastic battles that follow. It is alleged nearly every slave traded out of Africa passes through his organization. His agents are said to crisscross the Atlantic to maintain his web of alliances. Such an alliance may last a day or fortnight or a year, but invariably it ends with someone's death. He tortures priests at the request of bishops and procures whores for cardinals. Since his army of bastards intrigue to slit each other's throats for his favor, even his own family is vulnerable. It is said the bottom of the Mediterranean is littered with the corpses of more of his relatives than his rivals. If a more vicious man exists I hope I never learn his name. Now," he said looking hard into Pierre's eyes, "tell me where you have heard of him."

Appalled as much by the vehemence of the description as by the acts described, Pierre said, "I'm surprised tales of his exploits never reached our tavern."

"Given his reputation I am surprised as well." When the Captain's suspicious look did not soften, Pierre asked, "And just what do you know of his background?"

The Captain glanced down as if embarrassed by his knowledge. "Though some insist he is a direct spawn of the Devil, it is said he was born in the city of Naples but recently moved his headquarters to Catania on the island of Sicily. They say the grandeur of his residence rivals that of the Pope in Rome; a compound of buildings that includes an entire palace for his harem, for he regards himself a potentate of the Moslem style. And all surrounded by miles of farms and vineyards and the artisans and manufacturers for his devices. He operates that city as his personal port with dry-docks and shipyards for his fleet while the vice-governor in Palermo rules as his lapdog. His allies insist even Mount Etna erupts at his command." Now with more curiosity than suspicion the Captain asked, "You say you never heard his name?"

Pierre shrugged. Recalling what he had heard of Augustus's involvement with Mezzanotte, he found it difficult to believe. Yet instead of inquiring further, he asked, "So what does the Sheikh suspect about me?"

The Captain blinked hard as if to refocus his thoughts. "Though I have tried to dissuade him, he believes you are a sorcerer capable of conjuring the creature at will. Beneath his cultured exterior our Sheikh is a peasant in mind and heart. He intends to have you examined by his own chief magus the moment we arrive in Tunis."

Pierre laughed and then glanced toward Mohamed who stood beside the rail watching. "I could no more control that creature than I could compel a fish to fly."

"Agree with you as I might, the beast's appearance has shaken him to his soul and I have failed to dissuade him."

"He seems a reasonable man," Pierre pleaded, "yet that is an irrational belief."

"I have argued as much but to no good result."

Pierre hesitated. "So why are you telling me all this?"

"He believes himself clever and his techniques will force the truth from you." The Captain looked down embarrassed. "I am here to convey his message but to warn you as well; he will have his confession and will pursue the Inquisitor's path if he must."

Pierre could not stifle another laugh. "So I should prepare to be burned at the stake?"

"He is confident his subtle mind makes the infliction of pain unnecessary." He added, "Do not assume I enjoy playing his errand-boy, but he is our host and you have been summoned."

Pierre nodded, "So there's no help for it; let's go." The Captain turned and led the way. Mohamed watched them go.

At the door to the Sheikh's cabin the Captain quietly knocked. With the Sheikh's response he opened the door, ushered Pierre inside and closed it behind him. Pierre was relieved this would be a private audience.

The Sheikh reclined within a mountain of brightly colored pillows, and seeing Pierre he smiled. "Thank you for this interview. I have already apologized to Captain Rochelle for what must seem an unpleasant request, but you must admit that with recent events I might find myself curious. I expect he has informed you of what I hope will be the result of our conversation. Still, I am optimistic we will reach a meeting of minds that results in clarity on my part but also conveys the sincerity of my intentions. I hope I make myself clear."

Pierre simply nodded.

"Can I offer you tea?"

"For the moment I'll refrain."

The Sheikh sighed. "Still mistrustful; perhaps our conversation will dispel that."

"We won't know that until we get there," Pierre said.

Nodding the Sheikh said, "So let me ask how you are able to summon the creature?"

The bluntness of this question stunned Pierre. "Simply put, I don't; it seems to possess a will as free as yours or mine."

The Sheikh nodded again. "A pleasant fantasy unfounded beyond its assertion."

"It should be sufficient the beast became confused when those ships scattered. Confusion results from thwarted intent, and intent assumes self-direction. But that's all beside the point because your question begins with a false premise. After all, you can't prove the freedom even of your own will, and every gesture to do so collapses with a moment's reflection."

"Still, if that creature's will is somehow constrained, how can that be demonstrated unless the constraining force is identified? Thus we find ourselves in a rhetorical cul-de-sac."

Pierre shrugged. "I'm free of that doubt yet powerless to dissipate yours; ask another."

"Instead, let me suggest that you personally constrain the creature's will. How you manage this is beyond my understanding. My question is whether you do so consciously."

"You insist on my responsibility and are only uncertain whether it is intended or accidental. Do I have that right?"

"We progress more quickly than I could hope. Feel free to answer your own question."

"Since you're convinced of my responsibility, I can only insist any influence is unintentional."

"Fair enough, at least for the moment. But consider this more closely. We agree it appears to respond to you. Can we describe the conditions under which that response occurs?"

"Since this conclusion is yours, I await your conjecture."

"Reasonable but I would rather hear your thoughts."

"In that case, I repeat I've never consciously wished its appearance."

"So I have only your report for that. If its actions are outside your will, it nonetheless proceeds in a way that protects your interests. Can we conclude it acts to defend you when you are in danger?"

"Consider your question. If it intends to defend me, wouldn't it be lurking outside right now? Like a watchdog, wouldn't it travel by my side vigilant against my least danger?"

The Sheikh's eyes became bright and he smiled. "Now that is an experiment easily arranged, do you agree? After all, I would simply need to hold a knife to your throat." In a swift and sudden gesture, a bright dagger appeared in the Sheikh's hand and pointed toward Pierre. "Like this?"

Pierre grinned. "But that gesture would only be effective if I was convinced you'd thrust that blade. Otherwise, the creature would remain unperturbed and therefore invisible."

Just as suddenly, the Sheikh's smile disappeared as the dagger returned to the folds of his robes. "Another cul-de-sac and I am compelled to admit it."

A trickle of sweat traced its way down his back as Pierre began to breathe again. "There's nothing to any of this without a certain threat of death behind it. You put the Captain up to convincing me I'd be harmed if I didn't answer as you wished. You need me to believe you're ready to use that knife, so that either I confess my power over the creature or that my terror causes it to appear. How am I doing so far?"

Still smiling, the Sheikh leaned back and sighed. Pierre did not wait for his response. He stood now furious. "I've been chased by a monster, so unless you've got some better ideas, this is our last tea-party."

After a pause the Sheikh quietly said, "Be careful not to over-play your hand, young man. More things are arranged in the shadows than could be encompassed by your philosophy."

Pierre shook his head. "You've just admitted you can't risk killing me because you don't know how the creature will react. So until you do, I'm in the clear." He strode to the door, grabbed the handle and opened it. Outside, he found the Captain standing red-faced with embarrassment. Pierre turned back toward the Sheikh. "And don't bother me again until you know what you're doing!" Crossing the threshold he slammed the door behind him. In the shadow of the passageway he grinned at the Captain before he walked quickly away.

At the first turn he stopped to catch his breath. He looked down to discover his hand was shaking and he realized he could not make it stop.

CHAPTER FOUR

DAYS LATER PIERRE stood beside the port rail daydreaming over a sea of undulating green glass. The steady wind had softened to a mild breeze so that the sails billowed lazily against a sky flat as blue paint. Their ship drifted ahead without conviction, nearly becalmed and compelled to wait until Nature resumed her enthusiasm.

Following their encounter with the creature, the Sheikh and the Captain seemed to avoid Pierre, and even Mohamed and Javad appeared reluctant to look squarely into his eyes. He merely surmised all of this, yet nothing he saw contradicted it and he came to wonder if all was for the best. He had achieved that isolation he had wished for and without needing to be confined. The air on-deck undoubtedly was better than that in the brig.

When eventually all that sunshine pouring down upon him left him sweating and uncomfortable, Pierre climbed to the quarterdeck hoping to catch whatever moving air remained, and he chose a place near the helmsman. Below, dolphins chased the weak, creamy wake of the ship, their glistening bodies caressing the sea's glazed surface as they passed. Under that bright sky and looking out over a featureless sea, Pierre reminded himself this was likely a calm before another storm. He turned then, startled to find Ali suddenly towering beside him also watching those dolphins at play. Ali's sigh was warm with contentment.

"They are so beautiful." His smile appeared as lazy as every other motion around them. "Such careless grace, one might believe they propelled themselves by mere thought." He turned his smile on Pierre. "Whatever you told them seems to have frightened them." He paused but Pierre resisted a response.

Over the preceding days Pierre's trust in others had evaporated until now, under this broad bright sky, he felt only slightly safer than he would in the dead of night. His freedom, he knew, was only apparent, and any challenge might send him swimming with those beautiful dolphins. Glancing up at the flaccid canvas sails he asked, "How long until we dock?"

"Another two days perhaps and certainly hardly more. This," Ali continued lifting his chin toward the sails, "often occurs as we approach Tenerife. Happily, we are still too far off for a swim." He grinned at his own joke. "Full sails will bring us to port quickly. Already, gulls fly about us crying for our return."

"More than anything," Pierre said, "I look forward to standing again on dry land." He turned to offer his cleverest smile though he remained wary of Ali. He recalled how often their opinions conflicted, and how often Ali's sarcasm had left him uncomfortable. But he was now curious that, of all the crew, Ali was willing to engage him in small talk. Pierre asked, "When we reach shore, what do you most look forward to?"

Ali tipped his head back until his face was exposed fully to the sun. "Being beyond the voice of authority and the need to respond to orders."

Pierre nodded. "I guess I take my position for granted. Though Captain Rochelle commanded our ship, I am now answerable to no one."

Ali's smile disappeared and he shook his head. "Believe that and you will come to harm, of this I am certain. Power is all around you; it pools in some places while leaving other places with only a thin sheen, but there is no place where it is not. Even here, you forget the Sheikh, whose power over you is so absolute you continue to breathe only by his indulgence. As your Aristotle insisted, no such vacuum can exist."

"My Aristotle?" Pierre asked amused and curious.

Ali shrugged. "An inspired thinker no doubt, but limited, as all such thinkers must be."

"Is there no one whose thought inspires you?"

Turning again to face out to sea Ali said, "Beyond the blessed words of the Koran, inspiration is where one finds it. Like imagination, inspiration is a capacity. While only some of us are capable of being inspired, its capacity is more broadly spread than we recognize. A lowly farmer is as capable of an inspiring thought, a dissolute chambermaid is as capable of an intriguing idea. Certainly, men like Aristotle generated more interesting ideas than most. But the conjuring of interesting ideas did not end with him, nor will any man bring that pursuit to a conclusion. Reading a thinker like Aristotle too closely assumes his limit is the limit of the world." He turned his smile to Pierre. "Even you are capable of an idea as interesting as his."

Pierre shrugged uncertain, if Ali's attempt at flattery was calculated, and if so, what his motive might be. "Mohamed and Javad certainly have interesting ideas."

"They speak little of themselves and make no great display of their thinking. So you should not be surprised to learn that at the University at Salamanca, Mohamed studied medicine and Javad pursued religious history. For myself, I attended the University of Cadiz and studied the law. The Sheikh inflates his vanity by surrounding himself with men of learning, perhaps to glean the subtleties of their thinking, but more likely merely to enjoy their ornament. But do not doubt he holds such learning in great respect." He turned. "Even though his behavior appears otherwise."

"And what distinction has brought you on-board?" Ali shrugged and Pierre added, "Intrigued by men of distinction, you must possess a distinction of your own."

Ali said, "Perhaps simply a life-time's career as a skeptic. Close study of the law sharpened my sense of contradiction. Every assertion possesses its counter-argument and in recognizing each of those I am well-trained." He bowed smiling. "Please accept my skepticism as a complement to the subtlety of your intelligence."

"Can I hope at least you don't believe I am able conjure the creature?"

Ali's sudden and loud laughter relieved Pierre. "Certain assertions are unlikely and others are ridiculous and still others are ludicrous. Concerning the claim a man might direct the action of a brute creature, if there is an assertion more absurd I would enjoy hearing it."

"Thanks for that," Pierre said because he believed Ali's words and his relief was genuine.

"Though I respect your intention, that gratitude is misplaced. My skepticism is not personal; I would laugh were that same assertion made about anyone."

"Still, I am its beneficiary and I'm grateful. Unfortunately the same can't be said for the others."

Again Ali shrugged. "Like the rest of us, while they retain the power of reason, they agree to what they are told by those with power over them. If that is not always justified, it is certainly safe. Concerning power, we must recognize where we stand and who stands above us."

"And do you see yourself exceptional in this regard?"

"Despite what some say, there is no obligation to acknowledge all that one believes about everything one believes in." He added, "The fox lives longer than the lion."

"Is that true?" Pierre asked. "Pardon my skepticism."

Ali's laugh was wide and filled with relief. "It is true in practice even if not in principle."

"And do Mohamed and Javad believe the same?"

"Being more intelligent than I, it would be surprising if they believed otherwise."

Pierre said, "They confuse me. At the risk of admitting disappointment, I had regarded them as friends, yet I've come to suspect otherwise."

"Like most men, they reserve a portion of their friendship for strategic advantage."

"And is that how you regard friendship?"

"Do not mistake blunt speech for friendship. Your exile by the Sheikh is a result of his delusional belief, but it is exile nonetheless. He knows I am content to ignore political advantage, at least in most instances, because he understands this is the result of neither political ignorance nor disloyalty. But never doubt you are being observed."

"Since you understand politics so well, tell me about Mezzanotte."

Ali's eyes widened just enough to catch Pierre's attention. Ali turned and stepped along the rail to a spot farther from the helmsman and Pierre followed. Leaning his elbows upon the rail, Ali resumed staring out to sea. "The question is not what I know. The better question is, what is it I know that might prove useful to you. Such men are not discussed casually and he has ears everywhere. Even so far out to sea, discussing him carries risk."

Pierre hesitated. "You're certain his hand reaches everywhere as well?"

"His reach is only limited by wealth and his wealth is greater than even I can imagine. So assume his reach is only less than that of Allah Himself."

Pierre again paused. "Fair enough. For reasons I can't fathom it appears I've become an object of his interest."

"Tread carefully and assume such interest is not without purpose. Go about as if under his direct gaze. Ignorance is no virtue and will not protect you if you impede his designs."

Pierre considered this. "Could that interest also involve the creature?"

Ali shrugged. "Your beast likely threatens his enterprises so he may have decided to resolve its threat. Anyone who assists that acquires special interest. If you can influence the creature, you can also remove its threat. So assume his interest in you is serious."

"And would he also take an interest in my father?"

"If the father is a gateway to the son, then of course." He turned to look at Pierre. "Do you believe this is the case?"

"That suggestion's been made by someone with no reason to lie."

Ali's eyes again widened. "Then do not concern yourself. If Mezzanotte wants you, he will find you. Though devious and corrupt, he is not entirely without honor, or so I have been assured."

"Suppose there are some on-board who plan to put me within his reach."

"Assume that belief to be accurate and proceed accordingly."

"Proceed?"

Ali smiled. "I misspeak; to find yourself in his hands, it appears you need do nothing."

Finally Pierre laughed. "I was afraid you'd say that." When Ali turned to him with a quizzical glance, Pierre continued, "I mean, that the only thing to do is nothing."

Ali's laugh was loud and high-pitched. "Describe your suspicions and perhaps I can help."

Pierre shook his head. "The lion and the fox, remember?"

Ali nodded. "Then let me offer this. Like Mezzanotte and like most men, the Sheikh forms alliances based on what he perceives as his needs. When those change he reconsiders his alliances. It would be best if men always made the wisest decision serving their highest interest, but they almost never do so. You can only trust those who must depend upon you."

"So I shouldn't expect loyalty from someone who has no need to be loyal. You tell me this as if telling me something."

Ali looked away. "Fine and fair enough. So I will confirm, at least according to what I have heard, that the Sheikh and Mezzanotte have agreed to some arrangement although I am ignorant of its terms. Those terms may not matter however since they likely change with the phases of the moon. Understand that if the Sheikh is convinced you have influence over that creature and his conviction is communicated to Mezzanotte, prepare for his interview." Ali turned and stepped away from the rail. "Our conversation has continued long enough to stimulate every curiosity but I hope it has gratified at least yours. Meanwhile, I offer best wishes for the rest of our voyage and whatever may follow. May Allah, most blessed and merciful, smile on you and bless you." He watched Ali descend to the main deck.

Pierre recognized that even if only some of what he had been told was true he should prepare for the worst. He looked up gratefully at the flaccid sails with their promise of delay, but as he watched, with a rising breeze they began to fill and stiffen. And as the wind picked up so did activity on the deck and in the rigging, and even this simple desire was just that easily disappointed. Pierre would receive no help from Nature.

After two more days of sailing and just past sunrise the pale mountain tops of the Canary Islands surrounding those blood-red roof-tiles of Tenerife broke a hazy and gray horizon. At their sight, Pierre returned to his cabin to consider his options and wait. He did not need to wait long. Near mid-morning, a guard arrived who summoned him to Sheikh Mustafa.

Pierre entered the Sheikh's cabin to find Captain Rochelle sitting to one side and looking as gloomy as a criminal before the gallows. With a polite smile the Sheikh said, "Let me first assure you this voyage has proved the most curious I have sailed. Were I so inclined, I would be tempted to commit its account to paper. But I am not, so I will not. However, be assured that others also have found our voyage intriguing. My imperfect account of its details has only led another to wish to learn its true particulars. Rather than attempt to elicit those from you, you will be put off this ship and onto that of a man eager to hear your account directly from you."

It took a moment for Pierre to recover from his surprise; Ali had been correct. "Let me guess," Pierre said with what little swagger he could find. "You're pushing me off to your buddy, Mezzanotte." The Sheikh's expression froze into something close to annoyance.

Voice pitched low with consolation, Captain Rochelle said, "Do not be concerned. Your transfer has been carefully negotiated and your security and comfort assured. Your assistance is needed in a matter of the greatest urgency by a man of exceptional power and influence. I have received the Sheikh's promise you will be well-treated as an honorable man."

"That's as may be," Pierre said, "but shouldn't I receive some assurances from Mezzanotte? Maybe he agrees with the Sheikh and the moment he sees me he tosses me overboard in some deluded belief his gesture will prevent another attack by the creature? Otherwise, what's in all of this for me?"

"Melodramatics aside," the Sheikh said sighing, "I am assured your value is such that you can expect the luxury of your accommodations commensurate with that value."

"And if I refuse to cooperate?"

The Sheikh rolled his eyes and called out, "Yusef!" In a moment one of the Sheikh's guards entered the cabin. To Pierre he continued, "This interview now ends. You are an interesting but tediously annoying person. I would do my best to correct that if I were you. But I am not you and you will not. So let me simply offer you my best wishes and the grace and blessing of Allah upon all your endeavors. But one word of warning; not everyone you encounter will find your impertinence amusing." To Yusef, the Sheikh said, "Take him."

The Captain stood and shook Pierre's hand. "Good luck, old man, and mind how you go. The open sea is no man's friend." Yusef took hold of Pierre's arm and led him from the cabin. They followed the passageway until they stood together on the main deck.

Pierre was startled to see a fully-rigged galleon close by, and so large it appeared to tower over the Sheikh's caravel. The wind had dropped to a fresh breeze and both ships rocked easily at anchor. The sun had burned away the haze so that the green hills and dusty tan crags of the island stood out in sharp relief. Looking down, he saw that the Sheikh's crew had already lowered a longboat and four sailors sat within at its oars.

Pierre climbed down to the longboat and Yusef followed. He took a seat near the prow while Yusef took the tiller. The oarsmen pushed off and began to row across the placid sea for the galleon. Under that bright sun, the rowers from time to time turned to glare at Pierre.

The galleon's sails were reefed, its rigging and gunwale stood empty of sailors and its gun-ports appeared closed tight, all as if the entire ship lay asleep or abandoned. He turned to question Yusef, but the man stared ahead with a determined glare. Pierre glanced back at the Sheikh's vessel recalling a saying about preferring the Devil one knows as their boat moved forward as relentless as Death.

Within some yards of the ship's towering hull, the rowers hauled in their oars to allow the longboat to drift the remaining distance. When its prow knocked against the hull one of the rowers forward grabbed a line that hung from the galleon's rail. Pierre stood to take hold.

Suddenly, from above Pierre's head, the crack of a musket shot cut the air. At the same moment a weight fell against his back nearly pushing him overboard before that weight rolled to one side. He looked up to watch the long, black muzzle of a musket barrel, still smoking and just visible beside one of the gun-ports, slowly retreat. At the rail above that gun-port, a man's face appeared staring down at him. Confused, Pierre turned to see that Yusef now lay beside his feet at the bottom of the boat, a bloody hole the size of a fist torn and gaping open in his throat. Then he saw the glint of a short, broad knife still gripped bright in his hand.

Calling down to the crew of the longboat, the bearded, red-faced man at the rail of the galleon cried, "Take that heathen carcass back to your heathen captain with our Christian compliments." Mouth gaping with a loud laugh he added, "It's too bad he's already on his way to Hell and won't be taking the rest of you blaspheming buggers with him." Turning to Pierre he called out, "Climb aboard and be quick if you like your skin about you." Another man holding a musket appeared at the rail beside him and watched Pierre as well.

Pierre took hold of the rope when one of the sailors in the longboat asked, "Are you certain you wish to do that?" Another said, "You saw what they did to Yusef. What do you think they will do to you once you are on-board?" Pierre looked about.

The sailor at the rail above called out, "What's keeping you? We got things to do." Pierre still hesitated and he asked, "Think them heathens'll like you better with that bloody mess at the bottom of your boat?" Pierre scrambled up the rope and climbed over the rail.

When finally he stood on the deck, the first man said, "Welcome aboard.

The name's Jensen and you can thank our Captain your throat ain't been cut." He grabbed Pierre's shoulder and turned him to show a portion of his shirt-tail to him; it glistened with fresh blood.

Jensen muttered, "Better his than yours." Turning to the man holding the musket he said, "Go below and have Simpson fetch us a clean shirt from one of the crew." Pierre looked back to watch the Sheikh's longboat being rowed back to his ship, the guard named Yusef undoubtedly still motionless in its bottom. As if following his glance, Jensen said, "They'll have a pretty tale to tell, you bet. Now, do as you're told. We sail as soon as the anchor's weighed. That dead sailor and all that blood'll likely upset the Sheikh, and we don't want to be here if he decides he's due."

They crossed the main deck, and as they approached the passageway an older sailor about Pierre's own height, and who he guessed was named Simpson, stepped forward offering a shirt that once had probably been white. Jensen said, "Makes sure when he's changed that shirt he sees the Captain." He turned then and headed toward the quarterdeck.

"I seen it all," the man said to Pierre. "Damn good shooting, don't you think?"

Pierre stripped off his bloody shirt and was about to toss it overboard but the man snatched it from his hand. "No need for that, young man. Just a little blood; never know when it'll come in handy." Pierre drew the fresh shirt over his head. "There you go," he said, "good as new." He held out his right hand. "If you ain't guessed it yet, the name's Simpson." Pierre was startled to see that his right hand was missing the last three fingers, but his thumb and forefinger gripped Pierre's hand like a crab's pincers and surprisingly hard. He assumed Simpson meant to convey a message. Pierre shook it awkwardly. Nodding toward the passageway Simpson continued, "Better go below; Captain Harris wants to talk to you."

"And I want to talk to him."

"Ain't it grand when things work out. Down that gangway and to the end of the passage, you can't miss it."

Pierre followed the directions until he reached a door he found closed. He knocked firmly, but instead of hearing a greeting, the door swung open suddenly to reveal a short, round, elfish man dressed in an elaborate uniform, pink cheeked and with thick, black eyebrows, his head shaved to a pale and glistening shine. At the sight of Pierre the man smiled revealing a mouth lined with gold-capped teeth.

"Ah, you must be our esteemed passenger and guest. Welcome to my ship, the Petaluma, and a more beautiful ship has never floated upon Neptune's realm." He bowed at the waist. "Allow me to introduce myself; Captain Benjamin Nathaniel Harris, honored master of this gorgeous vessel. Please be so kind as to enter my humble abode." He stepped to one side.

Pierre crossed the threshold and entered a tiny, cluttered cabin that, despite the broad window at the ship's stern, remained dimly-lit. The Captain closed the door and then gestured toward a chair. "Please," he said smiling, "this is the most comfortable chair on my whole ship." When he sat down, the Captain stepped around his chart table and sat down in the chair behind it. He grinned brightly and the fingers of his folded hands seemed to Pierre to resemble a cluster of pink sausages. "Comfortable?" he asked. Pierre nodded.

"Very good. Events begin well, don't you think? When things begin well, they're so much more likely to end well, don't you think?" Again, Pierre nodded.

"Good, good, good," the Captain said tapping the desk lightly with his finger as punctuation. "It is such a world that when things don't begin well, they are so much more unlikely to end well. Do you see my point? By this I mean, a poor beginning propels us inexorably downward, so that any effort to end well must be almost Herculean. But I am certain," he continued flashing his gold teeth, "you have had similar experiences, have you not?" Pierre could only nod. "But of course, this is the nature of life after all. Nothing to be done about it. Must simply persevere in the hope that higher powers will intervene on our behalf. Am I right?" Again Pierre could only nod.

Captain Harris puffed out his cheeks and thrust forward his chin. "I myself am captain of this grand vessel simply as a result of chance, that same chance which tosses seashells upon the shore. We are all such playthings of life and time. We choose a path as though life was an accumulation of decisions and reason governed all. But the drift of life makes plans for us of which we cannot know, except by hindsight. Like corks bobbing in a storm-tossed sea. Imagine a cork with the power of will." The Captain rolled his eyes skyward as if looking for an answer, his smile nearly wistful. For a moment the silence hung within the twilit cabin like a green fog.

Pierre said, "Mind if I ask a question, just to satisfy a curiosity?"

The Captain's eyes grew large with startled surprise. "Indeed no, of course not. That is to say, of course. Curiosity is an appetite which gnaws unbearably at our minds. Please, of course, ask what you wish and I will do my best to satisfy that hunger. After all, what is a captain if he cannot answer questions? Am I right? The great Pico della Mirandola once remarked that each question is a door which, once passed through need never be passed through again. Such a wise and honorable thought. But please, ask your question and I will make certain you will not need to pass through that door again." He finished by peeling back his lips to expose his glittering teeth.

"Where are we going?"

The look of shock contorted the Captain's face. His smile disappeared, his eyes grew large, he half-stood but then immediately sat again. His hands flopped over each other again and again like dying fish. He tried for a moment to smile and failed. "Where are we going? You ask our destination? Where we will go when we have departed?" His hands flapped, his glance moved around the cabin, searched each corner and then passed along the ceiling.

Pierre said, "Just as a matter of curiosity so that I'll know with some likelihood when we've arrived. You can, of course, understand the urgency of my curiosity."

"But of course, of course! I certainly see from whence that question might arise. And I can also see why such a question might contain a certain urgency. Yes, of course, I can see that instantly. Yes, it is obvious." His glance again moved about the cabin and over the ceiling until Pierre said, "Well?"

"Yes," the Captain said. He cleared his throat. "Yes, indeed. Undoubtedly it appears to you this question is straight-forward, its response a unitary answer and unambiguous. Yes, indeed, of course. But let me begin by reminding you the apparent is not always obvious, and a complete answer must begin at the true beginning. Which itself must take us back many months, to the moment when this wonderful ship was first captured and put under my command."

"Please spare me the ancient history, Captain." Pierre found his impatience expanding. "I'm here against my will and it seems I'm taken under orders of a man named Giovanni Mezzanotte. I simply demand to know if this is true, and what our destination is. After all, I have a right to know."

The Captain's mouth suddenly dropped open, his eyes grew huge with shock. He stood then and, hands locked behind his back, began to pace behind his table. "Right? He asserts a right?" He muttered as if he was alone. "Aboard my ship he insists he has a right?" He shook his head from side to side. "Unheard of," he said. "Truly, this is remarkable." He paced staring straight ahead. "Insistence. The assertion of a right. No, no, this will never do, not do at all. No, there is nothing in Vico or Machiavelli or even Dante himself. No, nothing like this has ever occurred on my ship, under my command. Insistence, indeed. And a right. From whence could such a right arise?"

"It was only a manner of speaking," Pierre said, his impatience turning suddenly into panic. "Just a way we colonials have of talking." The Captain continued to pace and mutter.

"Where can it all logically end? This insistence upon a right to insist upon a right to insist upon a right. A logical hall of mirrors, I become dizzy simply by its contemplation. Truly, this cannot be borne, it is beyond tolerance, a bottomless pit opens darker than midnight."

As concerned as he was confused, Pierre said, "A simple request for inconsequential information."

Turning suddenly to Pierre with eyes afire, the Captain said, "You, sir, are cargo, pure and simple, and cargo has no rights and never insists on what it does not possess. I do not know from whence your delusions arise, but if you do not understand what I am saying, pretend that you do and act accordingly. You are to be delivered into the hands of another. You now know all that you need to know, and certainly all I must tell you." He stopped suddenly in his tracks. "Patterson!" Then he resumed pacing and muttering.

"Cicero?" he muttered to himself. "Plato? Erasmus? I am at a loss. Aghast and stunned. A quagmire, a perversion. He dares to insist to me, the master of this ship, as if we are equals, as if he and I are at the same level. He insists upon telling me what I must do and when and how. Such temerity, such impertinence, it cannot be endured." Again he cried, "Patterson!" as if his patience had reached its limit. The cabin door opened suddenly. A tall, broad-shouldered and thick-necked young sailor entered. "Captain?" he asked.

"Take this man below and confine him; clearly he has gone mad. Take him now!" The man grabbed Pierre roughly by the arm and jerked him from the chair. Pierre opened his mouth to speak and the Captain added, "Be sure he is shacked and kept from the rest of the crew. It's likely this man's delirium is contagious!"

"Yes, Captain," Patterson said.

When they reached the door, the Captain added, "As we do not wish our guest to die of loneliness, make sure there are extra rats. He has a right to extra rats!"

"As you order, Captain." Patterson pushed Pierre through the door. Even with the door closed Pierre could still hear the Captain pacing and muttering. Further along the passageway, Patterson relaxed his grip. "Things didn't go well, I take it."

"Could have gone better, I suppose," Pierre said.

"Ah well, everyone has their place," Patterson said and smiled. "Now you've discovered yours." After a moment he added, "Be of good cheer, you no longer need to wonder."

"Yes," Pierre said with a loud sigh. "Lucky me."

CHAPTER FIVE

PATTERSON LED PIERRE along passageways until they arrived at a door of dark, rough-finished wood, thick and with deep pale scars that could have been saber slashes. A narrow opening covered by a small latched door was cut at eye-level into its center. To Pierre's surprise, they were greeted by the sailor named Simpson. "Fancy meeting you here," he said appearing surprised himself. "You being down here only means one thing; its good thing I kept that shirt, it'll come in handy as a pillow."

"My luck is without limit."

"Shackles," Patterson said. "But not too tight. He won't give no trouble."

Sarcastically Pierre added, "And don't forget the extra rats."

Simpson's eyes widened. "Didn't know you was a special guest." He grinned. "Consider it done." He brought out a large iron key and used it to unlock the door. The main door swung open to reveal a series of small wooden doors to cubicles each hardly larger than a single man. Simpson unlocked the door to one revealing a pile of darkly rotted straw covered by a stained and dirty portion of canvas. Simpson watched Pierre's expression and laughed. "I hear the king of England sleeps on one just like it. Believe me, you'll sleep like a dead man."

"Why don't that make me feel better?"

"Why, indeed. Feeling better is something we're all working on. But cheer up; like everything else in life, you'll get over it if it don't kill you." Nodding toward the wall of tiny doors he added, "It's where we keep them slaves what we sell. Just be glad this ain't the brig."

Simpson attached black iron shackles to his wrists and ankles, Pierre crawled into the cubicle and Simpson attached the shackle chains to a ring in the bulkhead. "If you can't sleep like a king, at least you can sleep like a hero."

As the door closed, Pierre said, "Thanks for that. I'm already feeling better."

Pierre heard Simpson laugh. "You're a funny one, you are. You and me'll get along just fine, you'll see." The footsteps of the two sailors then faded away.

Except for a grayish light from the corridor seeping around its closed door, his cubicle was utterly dark. But Pierre was relieved by this. He need only listen to the rats scrambling and squeaking around him instead of having to watch them. In that darkness and lulled by the roll and sway of the ship, after a time he dozed and then awoke in a series of fitful sleeps. He could not guess how long this continued, but suddenly the small window in the door opened, filled by Simpson's face.

"Rise and shine, buttercup; hope you're hungry." He passed a platter of something hot and watery with a piece of what he guessed was bread floating in it. "We're a bit short of cutlery," he said apologetically, "and fingers was created before spoons; am I right?"

"Someone else told me that once," Pierre said, "but it's always useful to be reminded. I just can't remember how to eat soup with my fingers." He took up the soup-soaked piece of bread.

Simpson said, "Sounding a bit blue in there. Can't be the lack of lively company."

"Just the opposite. It's so crowded I can't hardly get a word in."

"And how is the conversation going?"

"One-sided but stimulating nonetheless."

"Glad to hear. We're proud of our accommodations."

"Understandable. But do me a favor and remind me, because it's hard to keep track; is the sun coming up or going down?"

"It's always going down for somebody."

"Elliptical answers answer questions that haven't been asked."

"It ain't elliptical, it's spiral. But because you're the curious sort, and because I'm a nice guy, I'll tell you it's about an hour after sunset and we're two-days sailing to the Gates of Gibraltar. You won't be down here no more than five days. Well, maybe six and a half."

"Spoken like a man who knows his way around."

“I done this run so many times we could trade places and I’d still know where we are.”

“Then you can tell me where we’ll land.”

“See, that’s the problem with you young guys; always in a hurry to get to the end. Take an old guy’s advice and enjoy the journey. Nothing like an ocean voyage to cleanse the mind.”

“And when we’re finished with the clearing and the cleansing, where will we be?”

“Finished yet?” Simpson asked. “Give me your plate.” When he passed his plate through the window Simpson said, “Learn to love surprises; life’s full of ‘em.” He slammed the door over the window shut. The darkness returned.

“Thanks for the reminder,” Pierre called out.

“Don’t get used to it,” he said from the other side of the door. “You’ll only get yourself all disappointed.” Footsteps moved away accompanied by a whisper of laughter.

After a time Pierre took his suggestion. Freed of every obligation and powerless to change any of it, he began to think. He wondered about the creature. Had it actually followed him? And would it follow him into the Mediterranean, since that was the direction they seemed to be headed? What purpose could Mezzanotte have in mind for him? Time passed for Pierre but nothing resolved, and gradually sleep overwhelmed him. He slept and woke and thought and then slept again. Occasionally, he changed his position to the clank and rasp of his shackles, though even remaining motionless was its own unsubtle torture.

The next time the door that covered the window opened and Pierre heard Simpson’s greeting, he said, “At least you can tell me why that man was ready to kill me.”

The silence from the other side was like deep, slow breathing, and seemed to last a long time. Then he heard a brief snort of laughter. “Here,” he said shoving the platter of gruel through the window. Pierre just caught it but spilled some onto the deck. “You’re so dumb I’m amazed you’re still breathing. Maybe you’re even too stupid to realize you’re dead. Maybe you’re dead and too dumb to stop breathing. You give me a lot to think about, and I’m not much good at that.”

“So thinking isn’t something you spend a lot of time at?” Pierre began to eat.

"Only when I have to and it can't be helped otherwise. Of course, that's likely the reason I ain't much good at it, I grant you that. I figure it's something to practice at if somebody expects to get good. But I don't, so I don't. And the thing is, I hear there are fellas who actually get paid to do it. I'll bet if somebody offered to pay me, I'd get good quick. Any of this making sense to you?"

"No," Pierre said between sips of his soup. "But I don't expect that's the point."

"Well, there's that, I suppose. My guess is you spend a lot of time at it. And my other bet is you spend a lot of time around people who do a lot of it, too."

Pierre asked, "How do you figure that?"

"Just by the way you talk. Quick-like. Like, if you didn't say it right away, somebody else would say it first and that would piss you off."

"Sounds like you been sitting on my shoulder for a long time."

"Just a guess, mind you. For myself, I can't remember the last time somebody was curious about what I thought. Not that it costs me sleep, if you get my meaning."

"Sometimes you can be asked what you think but then get somebody mad when you tell them."

"I suppose that's true though it's never happened to me. That's one place where I'm safer than the likes of you."

"So you spend a lot of time thinking about what you're not thinking about."

"That would cover a lot of territory."

Pierre said, "Reminds me of that old question of whether we're measured by the miles or the years."

"That'd be something I'd try to think about and then come to the wrong answer."

"When you're not thinking about what you're not thinking about, what do you do?"

"Bit of this and a bit of that; pretty much whatever I'm asked. There's no end of little jobs in this life nobody else wants to do. Me, just tell me where to show up and when."

"I expect you're busy all the time."

"There's only being busy or being dead. And I just ain't ready for the other. I figure after I'm dead I'll have a lot more time to think."

"Let me know when you figure that part out. Meanwhile," Pierre said passing the platter through the window, "I'm finished with this."

Simpson again laughed. "Good, because for dessert I'll tell you what you ain't figured out yet, smart guy. For instance, did you really think the Sheikh was going to let you go without a scratch after what you did to Ahmed?"

Mention of Ahmed and the suggestion Simpson knew of events on the Sheikh's vessel startled Pierre. "How did you hear about that?"

"The Big Guy finds out what the Big Guy needs to know and you can bet on that and never lose. The rest of us just pick at the crumbs left behind; kind of like pigeons. Seems he's had his eye on you for a while. The Sheikh was ready to pass you on without a blink, but you had to make it cost him. Him and Ahmed were close like I can't explain. You really jammed yourself up with that stunt."

"But it was an accident. I never thought the man would be hurt."

"Dead is dead," Simpson said with a laugh. "Distinction without a difference."

"The difference is the intention. The experiment demonstrated a principle of nature. What happened to Ahmed wasn't part of the experiment and wasn't necessary for its result."

"Are you sure about all that? I'm probably the least educated man you ever met, so I'm asking you. Are you sure about all that?"

Pierre hesitated, trapped and suddenly no longer certain. "Yeah, I'm sure," he lied.

"Okay, if you say so," Simpson said. "But just think for a minute about where you put the Sheikh. On the one hand, he'd already promised to pass you on to the Big Guy in good shape and no harm done. But after what happened to Ahmed, I expect he wanted to kill you dead on the spot. Suddenly that deal he made had just cost him way too much. His best friend was dead and he had to do something about it. He had to show his crew he'd stand up for them. And he had to show the Big Guy there were things he couldn't just let go by."

"So you're saying killing me was in his best interest?"

Simpson laughed. "I don't say it were clever and I don't say it would've got him what he wanted. Delivering you holds up his half of the deal. But the Sheikh knew there was no way the Big Guy could make up for Ahmed. I expect he ordered that sailor to kill you, and afterward he'd hand him to the Big Guy for punishment. He'd say it was all that sailor's idea, that it was the sailor getting his revenge for Ahmed. So the Sheikh gets his revenge and still keeps his hands clean. Everybody ends up unhappy. Now, he's even unhappier than the Big Guy, but that was pretty much inevitable since the Big Guy's smarter than the Sheikh. The Sheikh's unhappy because the Big Guy's getting what he wanted all along. Tell me if I'm going too fast for you."

"You think your Captain Harris has figured all this out?"

"Who knows what he's figured out. He ain't very smart and he sure don't share his thoughts with me. But he was the one who ordered Higgins to the gun-port with a loaded musket. Maybe, somehow, he just guessed you'd end up dead otherwise and if that happened he'd look seriously bad to the Big Guy and maybe even end up dead himself. And here, educated smart guy that you are, you never suspected. It's funny how smart people always believe what they're told. Talk about too stupid to live." Simpson laughed and Pierre heard something like a foot-stomp from the other side of the door, followed by a snort. "That sailor was dead the second he got into that longboat and maybe he even knew it. Maybe he said to himself, I'm dead, but I'm taking this one for my captain and I'm taking this guy with me. And you? I must be giving you too much credit as a smart guy. Walking around with an empty pot for a skull, you must sleep like a rock you got so little up there to bother you."

The door to the window slammed shut and Pierre called out, "Wait!" After a pause it opened again and Pierre said, "One question? What does the Big Guy think I'll do for him?"

"Ah," Simpson said and slowly closed the door over the window again, "ain't that an interesting question?" The door's latch clicked into place and Pierre listened to Simpson walk slowly away muttering, "That is such a good question."

Pierre slumped back against the bulkhead certain he had been told something that had turned into nothing. How could he understand a question whose opacity only grew thicker? To understand, he would need to guess, but the only guess that seemed to fit the question was one he did not like.

Meanwhile, the gruel he spilled excited the rats far more than it had excited him. They brushed against him and he pushed them away, but they were unimpressed and leaned against him like cats on a winter night. He was disgusted but could not move without brushing against them yet he could hardly stop moving. He rattled his shackles to chase them away but they behaved as if that sound was music. They scrambled and squealed as if the chamber was their playground and Pierre a new amusement. Eventually he dozed, and then he must have fallen deeply asleep, the darkness around him growing even darker, until suddenly Josiah Rollins was speaking to him, the gambler who had told him about Augustus, but Pierre could not understand what he was saying, and then Rollins began to laugh as he got smaller, and the more he laughed the smaller he became, and then he was an ink-blue pool that Pierre tried to move away from, except that the pool managed somehow to follow him. Or perhaps he was circling around it unaware and he turned to discover he had not moved any distance from it, or maybe he had but then lost his direction and returned to it again. Suddenly, as if coming from very close by, he heard the creature's roar. Then he woke up.

"Hey Buttercup," Simpson said, "you need to stop that screaming. At least a few of us has got feelings and it's making us upset." The window in the door opened and the sudden light, though feeble, hurt Pierre's eyes. "You must be asleep because you've been screaming like there was somebody in there with you."

"Did you hear it?" Panic from the sound coursed through him.

"Hear what? I heard just you and you scream pretty good for a young guy."

"No, the creature. Did you hear it? Like a thousand lions an ocean of blood couldn't satisfy."

"Well," Simpson said. "Somehow we've brought out the poet in you. Either that, or fear of permanent death. Take your pick, eh?" His laughter calmed Pierre.

"So you didn't hear it," he asked flatly, unsure whether he was relieved or disappointed.

"Listen, mate; down here you're so safe even your mother'd be happy. Safe is what you are, and safe is what you're going to stay, you and your furry friends. We got a delivery to make. But we're pleased you all are getting along in there." He held the platter to the window. "Almost forgot; here's your grub."

Pierre took the platter certain at least the rats would enjoy it. "How much longer?"

"Not so much. From where you are, hardly any time at all. In fact, to you I expect it'll seem quick. Anyway, not so long you'll starve or go crazy." After a pause he added, "Well, at least you won't starve, that's for sure."

Fragments of his dream left Pierre's mind cloudy. He ate what was on the platter, doing his best to not share with the creatures around him. Or were they all over him? Even that distinction had become hard to make. He said, "Tell me what you know about the Big Guy."

"The Big Guy?" Simpson said, but in a voice so soft Pierre was uncertain whether he had actually heard it or the slough and wash of the sea beyond the hull. "What's it you want to know?" Pierre detected an unlikely caution in his voice.

"Anything," Pierre said. "Tell me anything I might want to know."

Simpson hesitated. "First, I never met the man. I mean, he's the guy who signs the checks, you see my point? Orders come from him, but I only see guys like our Captain Puff-n-Poop. I get the bug's-eye view, if you see my point. I hear things, you know, from time to time. You should talk to somebody who knows things. Me, I'm the guy who knows enough to get through 'til tomorrow and that's about all I need. See my point?"

Pierre laughed and its exercise felt good. "C'mon; I'm the guy who doesn't know anything, remember? Anything you tell me is more than I know. Wise me up, be a pal. I don't give you trouble. Help me out here."

"Ah, well, I don't know about that. I better get going. Got work to do top-side." He paused and silence drifted from him like damp smoke. "All right, listen," he said as if in a rush, "one story I heard about him. Once he killed a man with his bare hands; that's how it was told to me. Shoved his two thumbs into the guy's eyes so hard they went into his brain. But the best part? The guy was his brother-in-law, married to his sister. The story is the Big Guy caught the brother-in-law staring at some woman. Said the brother-in-law had dishonored his sister. Anyway, that's what I heard. Now go to sleep and sweet dreams to you." With that he slammed the door over the window with a crack. Pierre listened to Simpson hurry away.

Bound in darkness, Pierre needed to catch his breath. Simpson had spoken so quickly he waited a moment to be certain of what he heard. It demanded an effort to imagine the scene, to visualize furious brother confronting arrogant brother-in-law as tearful sister/wife is sent from the room, brother barely containing his rage, smirking brother-in-law certain his fury will pass, brother's lieutenants on a signal step suddenly forward to pin brother-in-law by either arm, brother stepping close and in a mutter between clenched teeth pronouncing sentence on gradually terrifying brother-in-law. And almost in slow motion brother raising his hands thumbs forward and in one forceful move brings them to brother-in-law's eyes, leans forward eliciting a howl of pain that grows louder and higher, and the fluid of his eyes spurts suddenly and his pitiful howl becomes even louder, brother grimacing presses forward, neck knotted and arms tight, until a final, audible crack and brother-in-law slumps between his captors. Pierre sucked in his breath thinking this was the man who controlled his future, the man into whose hands he was about to be delivered. His furry companions suddenly seemed like friends.

But Pierre did not sleep or even doze. He thought about Josiah Rollins, the man who had told him Augustus was working for Mezzanotte. He wondered about Augustus and whether he was still in Mezzanotte's service or if he was even still alive. Or had Mezzanotte regretted his decision and disposed of Augustus, quietly and discreetly but completely? Either Augustus was alive and held in some dank cellar, or he was dead and disposed of. Pierre preferred he was alive and miserable but assumed the odds for that were not good. And his own fate?

What, he wondered, could he expect from Mezzanotte? And so Pierre began to wonder about this world he was about to enter and whether there was room in it for him. Yet eventually he found himself wondering if anything he had seen or done had justified leaving poor Gabriella. He imagined her at the tavern fretting night after night that she had married one faithless man and then given birth to another. Shackled and surrounded by squealing, squeaking, nibbling creatures in his darkness, Pierre was relieved she could not imagine this plight. There was always the chance that soon he would be dead, especially considering that creature seemingly chasing him, an element, after all, that Gabriella could never have guessed.

He found he could not sleep for thinking about the creature and how it had managed to find him and only him. Why was it that, whoever he met—sea captain or sailor, fisherman or pirate—each could only report having heard a rumor of the creature, but none had seen it? Nearly all those who had been with Pierre and had seen the creature were dead. While it seemed absurd, he was forced to assume this creature was entirely his own and had come into existence exclusively for him with some infernal or even mystical link to bind them together. But what could be the purpose for any of that? Even more confusing, how could he account for a sympathy that seemed to enable their connection? Could it have something to do with the aether? Were he and the creature emanating some aether waves to enable their resonance? And how could any of that be the case if these aether waves were destructive, a power whose danger Ahmed had demonstrated? Pierre found himself finally confused, and his confusion made him sleepy. In the end he could be certain of one thing; if that beast had followed him into the Caribbean and then into the Atlantic, surely it would follow him now. So they would meet again; it was simply a matter of time, unless it was a matter of fate.

CHAPTER SIX

SIMPSON CALLED OUT, "Rise and shine, Buttercup." Pierre awoke startled but also relieved. Trapped in a downward spiral of dark conjecture, his appearance was a reassuring distraction.

When the window in the door opened Pierre said, "Tell me something; how is it the Big Guy manages to operate from Sicily? Doesn't the island belong to the Spanish?"

Once again, Simpson hesitated as if Pierre had asked something other than what he had expected. Finally he said, "And that's a pretty tale." He passed the platter through the opening. "I'll tell you now and for your own good, when you're with the Big Guy, don't say nothing good about the Spanish unless you're ready to become thoroughly dead."

"So they don't get along."

"The Big Guy gets along with anybody he can't kill and right now the Spanish're still too big for that. Ever heard of the Sicilian Vespers? When the day comes that the advantage's gone to the Big Guy, the streets of Palermo'll run with Spanish blood, and he'll dance in it with his bare feet."

"Why don't the Spanish do something about him?"

"Same reason he don't do nothing about them. For the moment he's just too big; too many ships and too many guns and too many friends. Besides, their hands are full with the British and the French. The New World's bleeding gold, and a long time ago those countries got tired of it all draining into Spanish buckets. They bide their time and the Big Guy takes his bites whenever he can, and so the Spanish see snapping jaws whichever way they turn." Then he stopped. "By the way, you ain't related to any Popes or anybody like that? Ever since Pope Alexander died, the Big Guy's been fishing for a replacement."

"If I'm related to any Popes, somebody forgot to tell me."

"Yeah," Simpson said, "me too. Just figured I'd ask." He sighed. "I wondered if maybe that's why the Captain's stuck you down here."

"And how much longer you figure I'll be down here?"

"You know, I'm thinking maybe two more days. The wind's been good, not that you'd notice down here, and we ain't seen another ship for a while. Besides, he's got a date with a Viking wench so he's got his own big hurry, if you get my meaning. I'd say two days, maybe two and a half, but not likely three."

"That's a relief," he said passing the platter back through the opening. "I don't know how much longer I can take all this good food."

"Yeah, kind of grows on you, don't it?" Simpson said and laughed. "But I know you can't be complaining because something is always better than nothing."

Pierre said, "Always is a strong term, but I take your point."

"Think of it this way," Simpson said, "whatever you're being fed, when you get to the Big Guy's palace you'll eat better than the King of Sicily. Unless he kills you first, and then none of this'll matter."

"And you figure that's, what, a fifty-fifty chance?"

Simpson hesitated. "Make it seventy-thirty. Unless you got some talent playing the guitar. I hear the Big Guy's crazy about guitar music. If you can play a guitar, he'll take good care of you. Other than that, watch your back."

"Thanks, I'll remember that." Then he asked, "By the way, you don't happen to have a guitar? Seems I've got some time to practice."

Simpson laughed again. "You know, you're a pretty funny guy. It'd be too bad if the Big Guy had you killed."

"Yeah," Pierre said and then sighed. "I won't be so funny when I'm dead."

"And you won't have much chance to practice your guitar either," Simpson said. "Meanwhile, I'll be back with the best news I can gather. And don't bother locking the door, I'll let myself in." Pierre listened to him laughing all the way down the passageway.

Two more days, Pierre thought. The dank and motionless air confused him even as it soothed him. With the constant beat and wash of the sea against the other side of the hull he had lost his sense of time's passage. Adrift and shackled motionless in complete darkness, his only reminder of time's progress was Simpson's appearances. The movements of Pierre's furry friends provided no help there. But with Simpson's conjecture over the length of his confinement, he found himself impatient for it to end. Finally he was tired of waiting for his fate to be decided. A decision had been made and now he wanted to learn what it was.

But what, given his circumstance, did it mean for him to want? Was there any value in his desire to know, and could that desire change what was about to happen? Was his impatient uncertainty worse than being devoured by the beast? Suddenly he recognized what he was thinking and quietly he laughed. There is being foolish and then there's being stupid; one was merely annoying, the other was death itself. Soon he will come face-to-face with the Big Guy, and he will ask what all this has meant and how he should understand it.

"Your destiny approaches."

He heard those words though he suspected they were inside his head. He discovered all the rats suddenly huddled pressing against him as if for shelter, and they were trembling.

"Forces gather."

He decided he had heard those words, though he could not recognize where that certainty came from. The rats pressed their bodies still harder against his.

"The wind moves you forward; all of the secrets of your fate will be revealed."

He looked about, but his darkness seemed thicker than black wool.

"The creature dwells in darkness and hungers for light. Your mountain awaits, the site of battle chosen. Fires will fill the sky. Allies gather, your weapons are at hand. Though it prepares to die by your will, the creature demands battle and will not retreat."

Pierre shifted and the rats clung to him as if begging not to be left alone.

"Step forward, offer yourself, expose yourself. Defy your fear, ignore your terror. Challenge the creature as you do yourself. The power of the universe that passes through you will destroy the beast. The universe looks to you for salvation through that creature's destruction. Fear nothing except your own timorous spirit. Your path is clear, let no man interpose himself. Though you will perceive turns, know simply that your path is straight."

Pierre listened until he realized there would be no more. Fragments of what he had heard came to his mind, yet made no sense. Like bits of paper scattered by the wind, phrases swirled about him but without a suggestion of purpose. Was he being informed or warned? Either way, its exercise had failed; he felt neither informed of something he understood, nor warned in a way that would enable him to avoid danger. But all of it had to do with the creature. Now certain he would see that creature again, perhaps he had been warned of what he should expect. Suddenly he realized the rats had scattered and no longer pressed against him. At least they seemed to feel reassured.

In fact, those cunning and furry creatures had begun to lick at his ankles, if those things he imagined he felt at the ends of his legs were in fact his ankles. Would those rats eventually become bored with him, or might his movement upset them, make them angry so that they would then attack him? On the other hand, if he made friends with them, could he persuade them to chew through his shackles? His shackles were made of iron, of course, and he wondered how a rat might chew through iron. He found himself perplexed, caught in that ill-defined space between doing one thing and doing another and doing nothing at all. Or was doing nothing the same as doing something, something and nothing being the same thing? He found he did not like his thoughts and wished he could begin thinking something else. Or better, think hard about nothing at all. Would the Big Guy see a difference between doing something and doing nothing, or acknowledge that thinking about nothing was to think about something? On the other hand, might the Big Guy always be doing something, so that even doing nothing accomplished something? Pierre suddenly hated what he was thinking; it was making him dizzy and nauseous, and just as suddenly he envied Simpson.

"Hey, Buttercup." The voice and the rap on the door startled him and he awoke to discover he had been asleep and his thoughts had in fact been dreams. He recognized Simpson's voice and was so relieved by its sound he began to smile. But this time his greeting was accompanied by the sound of metal scraping against metal.

The door creaked open, the sudden flood of light blinded Pierre, and then he recognized Simpson standing before him. He smiled at Pierre, exposing his rotted teeth, but then his expression became perplexed.

"Don't we look the sight?" Wide-eyed with concern, Simpson sniffed loudly. "And we don't smell none too good, neither." Holding a large ring of keys in his hand he leaned down. "The Captain won't want you meeting with anybody looking like this. Or smelling like this, now I'm thinking about it." The shackles dropped away from Pierre's wrists and ankles, and he had the sudden sensation of feeling lighter, as if he might, like a balloon, drift up to the ceiling.

Leaning further down, Simpson said, "Put your arm around my neck and we'll get you standing up." He grunted and Pierre felt himself rise. Inexplicably, he had to resist the temptation to kiss the man on the cheek.

"Get your feet under you, boy, there you go. One foot after the other, that's the way, just like you was a baby." The chamber, the brig, the world, everything seemed to move around Pierre as up and down lost distinction and his certainty evaporated. "Come along, it ain't so tough. Just do like I say and we'll be out of here in a jiffy." He clung to Simpson harder.

"Whoa, boy, not so tight. Choke me dead and where will we be then, eh?" He laughed.

"Wait," Pierre said. "I should say good-bye to my friends."

"Still the funny one, ain't you," Simpson said and again laughed. "Let's just get you out of here before the natives see you've gone." Pierre felt himself move forward. It took another moment to discover he stood in the passageway. He wanted to stop and catch his breath but the fresh, salty aroma of the sea caught him. He tried to rush forward but, stumbled and nearly fell.

"Not so fast, boy. Seems you need a bit more practice at this walking business. Stay with me; one step at a time and we'll get there." Pierre did his best but his legs began to throb and tremble beneath him until he badly wanted to sit down.

"Oh no you don't!" Simpson said with startled urgency. "Don't quit on me now. You've got a date with the Big Guy and it's my job to make you presentable. Let's you and me get out of here and we won't do no more dawdling."

Step after step the light around Pierre grew brighter and the smell of the sea stronger until they reached the passageway leading up with its steps needing to be climbed. He held back but Simpson pushed him forward. "This ain't the place to be stopping, boy. Just a few more steps and you're home free. Fresh air and sunshine for you, and there's nothing you can do about it. Now, up you go." Pierre lifted his leg and then lifted the other. The steps seemed to float up to meet his feet as each brought still brighter light. He watched his feet though they had lost sensation and he could just feel them touch the dark wooden steps. He looked up to see so much blinding light he became frightened. Simpson's hand once again pressed against the middle of his back to push him forward. "Almost there," he said, "just keep going, almost there."

Suddenly Pierre stood on the main deck. Green sea and blue sky and patches of pale and fleecy clouds were everywhere he looked, so it took a moment before he saw the others. Sailors, he realized; men of every age and race and all staring at him.

From behind him Simpson said, "Don't mind them. You just keep going like you belong here and know what you're doing." He nudged Pierre's back once more. "Over there, beside the rail." He steered Pierre forward until he stood against the rail. Looking down at the sea so far below left Pierre dizzy. Then he was spun around by his shoulders to face Simpson.

"There you go," Simpson said. "Brace yourself right there, your hands just like that." He lifted a dark, wet bucket. The water that poured over Pierre stung his skin like needles of ice, and he trembled and gasped for breath.

"That's the thing," Simpson said. "Just what you need. Feels pretty good, don't it?"

Still panting, Pierre looked around again. "Maybe. I suppose so."

"Good," Simpson said. He leaned down reaching for another bucket. "Get ready." More water, sea water Pierre realized tasting the salt on his lips, poured over his head. This time it did not feel as cold, and he tipped his face up to receive the last of it. He sputtered the water from his mouth and with his hands cleared the water from his eyes. Finally the ship seemed to gather itself under his feet, solid and sturdy.

"One more?" Simpson asked.

"Sure," he said nodding. He watched Simpson toss the bucket over the side holding its rope with his right hand, and then haul it up splashing full. "Turn around," he said and Pierre did as he was asked. This time the water poured over his head and down his back.

"Now, strip out of them clothes and we'll do a couple more." Pierre pulled off his shirt and trousers as Simpson again tossed the bucket over the side. "Garcia!" Simpson called out. "Go below and bring this man something to wear." He hauled in the bucket and to Pierre he said, "Use that shirt to wash yourself down with." Simpson poured but more slowly, until the bucket was empty. Pierre did as he was told feeling the world still solidifying around him.

As Pierre rubbed himself with the shirt, Simpson said, "So you've just had yourself a taste of what them slaves go through. But only a taste, mind you, just a hint. Think about where you was, being down there inches from the guy next to you, chained together for a month and more. Hour after hour, day after day. Just think about that, but maybe not too hard."

Simpson filled the bucket once more, and this time poured the water more slowly over Pierre as if to make certain no part of him was not washed. When he finished, Pierre stood still beside the rail, the breeze flowing over his wet skin finally assuring him that he was certainly alive. The man who he guessed was Garcia stepped up beside him with folded fresh clothes stacked in his hand. Simpson handed Pierre a piece of dry canvas. "Here; rub yourself off with this first. When you're dry you can put these on." He rubbed himself down and then pulled on the fresh clothes. As he did so, he looked down to discover bleeding red and purple bruises at his wrists and ankles.

Simpson watched him. "Don't worry about those, boy. They'll heal in a few days. Never be ashamed of scars honestly earned; they show you've been someplace and done something."

Pierre felt suddenly very tired and very hungry. As if guessing his thoughts Simpson said, "When you're ready we'll go below and get some proper food in you. And then you'll get some proper rest."

He turned about to follow Simpson but then stopped. "No, let's stay here a while longer."

Simpson grinned with surprise. "Good lad and stout fellow. You'll want the sun and the air for a time. You rest here a bit and I'll report to the Captain and then I'll come back for you."

Pierre smiled. "Captain Puff-n-Poop."

Simpson laughed and clapped Pierre lightly on the back. "Just the thing." In a quieter voice he added, "Don't worry, boy, you're all right now." He turned then and disappeared. When he was gone Pierre looked around. The other sailors on deck continued to stare at him, and he could not decide if it was mere curiosity or deep suspicion or simple pity. But after a time he found he did not care and he turned back to stare out to sea. The reflected light from the water seared his eyes and he found himself blinking hard in the hope they would adjust.

"That's Sicily," a voice over Pierre's shoulder said. He turned to see a sailor standing behind him. Young, dark-haired and broad-shouldered, his large, dark eyes seemed to smile regardless of the expression of his face. Pierre looked past him to see that the rest of the crew had resumed their activities. He looked out again and saw a tan strip of land just shading the edge of the horizon. The man said, "We'll reach port before nightfall."

Simpson appeared suddenly behind them. "Nothing better to do than bother the passengers, Giuseppe?" he asked. The man turned and walked away. To Pierre, Simpson said, "Can't trust these dagos to do a lick of work without you stand right on top of them all the time. Anyway, the Captain wants a word before your meal. I spoke to the cook. You'll eat well and sleep like a babe. Ready to go?" Simpson nodded toward the gangway.

Moving his legs proved more challenging than Pierre had expected. He laid his hand lightly on Simpson's shoulder. "How long did you keep me down there?"

"Does it matter?" Simpson asked.

"Shouldn't it?"

"Come along. You need food and rest, but you'll need to speak to the Captain first."

When they arrived at the door to the Captain's cabin, Simpson opened it without knocking, urging Pierre before him. The Captain half-rose from his chair behind his chart table to greet them, but he did not smile and did not step forward. "That will be all, Simpson," the Captain said. To Pierre he said, "Please, take a seat." He gestured to the same chair Pierre had sat in during their first meeting.

"Since this'll be brief, I'll stand," Pierre said, though he was unsure how long he could maintain that position.

The Captain nodded and resumed his chair. "As you must have noticed, our ship's quite crowded and comfortable accommodations are few. From time to time, other areas must serve as quarters for our guest's. I trust you have otherwise found your journey pleasant."

"I demand to know what any of that has to do with why I was held under lock-and-key."

The Captain's expression hardened into a mask while the color of roses appeared at his throat and moved toward his eyes. "You are an extremely valuable passenger and I cannot always vouch for the momentary disposition of each of my crew."

"And the shackles?" Pierre asked holding up his wrists.

The Captain's color deepened as it moved toward his glistening skull. "Simpson!" he called out. The door opened in an instant and Simpson filled its frame. "This man is clearly suffering from a prolonged exposure to the sun and he has not quite resumed all of his faculties. See that he has a meal and is permitted bed-rest until we reach port. And be certain he has no contact with the rest of the crew." Though the Captain's face was now red as a sunset, he looked down and resumed his chair as if he were now entirely alone.

Simpson lightly touched Pierre's arm. Pierre hesitated but then turned and left the cabin so quickly that Simpson had to hurry to catch up. Simpson said, "Now I know why you never considered a career as a diplomat."

"I'll talk to Mezzanotte the moment I see him."

Simpson grabbed Pierre's arm stopping him in his tracks and then spun him around to stare hard into his eyes. "Never assume the Big Guy don't know; that would be bad for your health and suggest ineffective supervision." He held Pierre's arm an instant longer and then he smiled. "Now, let's you and me go see what the cook thinks is good food."

When they reached the galley, they discovered three platters piled high, steam rising from each, a thick, tan loaf of bread between them, a large, bright pewter flagon and goblet beside the platters. At the back of the galley stood a tall, thick, black-haired man wiping his hands on a bright towel and grinning at Pierre. Simpson said, "I'll leave you to it and be back in half an hour. By then you'll be ready for a long siesta." He clapped Pierre on the shoulder and left.

By the second mouthful, Pierre realized he was famished and could hardly move the food quickly enough to his mouth. Once he paused to look up to see the black-haired man still watching him, his grin still huge. "Prego, signor, manga." Without being certain what he had been told, Pierre ate even faster. Simpson returned to find Pierre had cleared most of all three platters. Seeing this, he nodded approval. "You should sleep like a saint. Ready to go?"

Pierre stood. The black-haired man reappeared. "Thank you," Pierre said earnestly. The black-haired man shrugged and smiled. "De nada, signor, mon plaisir."

He followed Simpson forward until they stood beside an empty bunk. "Here you go," he said slapping the upper with the flat of his good hand. "Five hours before we dock."

Pierre climbed, his eyes already becoming heavy. "Thanks," he said.

Simpson looked at him a long moment. "Just remember me when the time comes." He turned then and left. Pierre followed him with his eyes, and when he laid back he wondered what Simpson could have meant. But that thought disappeared from his mind like a wisp of smoke in a wind storm. His sleep was bottomless and velvet black, as though he floated on undulating feather pillows and the whole rest of the world swayed easily beneath him.

CHAPTER SEVEN

"TIME TO GO."

The voice beside Pierre's ear woke him with a start and he opened his eyes to see Simpson. Turning, he saw men standing behind Simpson dressed in elaborate, dark blue uniforms and each wore a grim expression. The man standing beside Simpson was tall enough to need to stoop slightly in the close quarters. His face was devilishly sharp-edged, eyes large and piercingly dark, his mustache and beard were glistening black and precisely trimmed. He grabbed Pierre's wrist and brought it close to examine. With a scowl he released it and muttered to a man behind him who then turned and left the cabin. He then turned back to Pierre smiling.

"Please, signor, forgive the suddenness of our appearance. We are here to accompany you to a man eager to meet with you." Pierre blinked hard at the sudden light, shook his head and then stepped down carefully from the bunk. His feet touched the deck and the taller man took him lightly by the arm and led him along the passage. Leaning toward Pierre, quietly he said, "I will not ask how you enjoyed your voyage but will only assure you that better accommodations await you." Pierre glanced back to see that Simpson remained behind.

At the gangway up to the main deck, the tall man stopped and turned to face Pierre. His sudden smile contained all the good-natured charm of a younger man. "It has just come to my awareness that my manners have fled me. My name is Commander Vitullio Amadeo Genovese and it is my privilege to accompany you to the palace of the esteemed Signor Giovanni Archangelo Mezzanotte. He has looked forward to your arrival with great anticipation." His English was heavily accented but precise and clear. "Now, with your permission let us proceed." He turned and with a dignity that impressed Pierre, he began to climb.

When they reached the main deck, Pierre was startled by the blast of sunlight, but his eyes adjusted and he saw the crew gathered as if waiting. The cluster of sailors parted allowing their entourage to approach the main mast where Captain Harris stood. Commander Genovese stepped forward. "Captain Harris, be so good as to accompany Sergeant Luciano. Captain Pettruchio will assume command of this vessel." Then he turned to Pierre. "As all is now in good order, we shall depart."

"But Commander," Captain Harris said moving to block his path, "this cannot be by Signor Mezzanotte's orders." The sudden panic in this voice startled Pierre. "My loyalty is beyond challenge. I have followed his command and delivered this man as quickly as conditions permitted. I insist upon speaking with him personally. When he has learned the true facts of our voyage he will find no complaint against me."

The Commander turned to him with an expression as blank as a dinner plate. "Insist as you wish, my orders come directly from him. But you are correct, he plans to speak with you, eventually. Now, we must delay no longer. Follow my officers." To Pierre he said, "Our carriage awaits."

Pierre smiled at the cringing stupefaction on Captain Harris's face though there seemed something almost too pathetic there. Despite his anger toward his treatment, he felt embarrassment over that pleasure.

He and the Commander were followed by two officers and then Captain Harris and then the rest of the Commander's men as all descended the gangplank to reach the dock. Mounting a horse, Captain Harris glanced furiously at Pierre before he turned to accompany the others and they rode off. The Commander led Pierre to a shining black open carriage displaying a large and curiously colorful crest on its doors and drawn by two enormous, ink-black horses.

The driver turned the carriage and they began to move forward. Taking this opportunity to look about, Pierre recognized that their ship had docked at a seaport as busy as any he had visited. Noticing his interest, with a smile hinting pride the Commander said, "Welcome to the Kingdom of Sicily and to the city of Catania, our loveliest port. Shall I assume this is your first visit?" Pierre nodded. "Then it is my privilege to introduce you to the most beautiful island in the world."

The carriage and its single outrider horseman turned away from the docks to follow a wide straight avenue lined on both sides by tall trees that stood poised like broad and dark green parasols. Behind the lines of trees, the avenue was bordered by dun-colored houses two and three-stories tall of stone and plaster. The window-boxes below each tall and shuttered window overflowed with plants flowering with blooms of red and pink and blue and white. Foliage cascaded from those window-boxes thick and dark like green waterfalls, and some reached to the ground. Far off and sharply-etched against the flat blue horizon, a cone-shaped mountain stood dusted white at its top, a pale plume rising from its pinnacle. The outrider led their carriage to turn and follow another avenue also bordered with trees though these boughs met overhead to provide cavern-like shade.

Glancing grandly about at the passing scene, the Commander leaned back in his seat with his arms draped across its back. With a wave of his narrow and elegant hand he pointed. "His Excellency's palace is some miles beyond those hills ahead but we will arrive soon." He turned then to face Pierre. "I will not ask the details of your voyage since his Excellency expects to hear of them directly from your lips. But I hope you will satisfy a personal curiosity; is it true that you have encountered the creature?"

They reached the edge of the city where, between the trees beside this road and extending further off, Pierre glimpsed broad, flat fields brown as toasted bread that reached to hills rising in the distance. "Yes," he said. The easy trot of the horses and the slow rocking of the carriage, along with the dry and motionless heat that seemed to surround them, lulled Pierre into a somnolent indifference.

"Ah," the Commander said with a nod and sounding pleased, "then I will ask nothing more but simply assure you that you are a man of remarkable fortune." As if to change the subject he pointed toward the mountain ahead. "Before you our volcano, Mount Etna. Hidden within it are the forges of Vulcan himself that throw fire into the air and spit rock and smoke. And beneath it, restless Enceladus lies sleeping. When he turns, our island trembles. There are times," he continued, "our island shudders so violently it seems eager to fling all of us into the sea."

"I expect that spectacle's thrilling," Pierre said. "Perhaps I'll be fortunate enough to witness its exhibition."

"With even better luck you will be spared."

Surprised Pierre hesitated but then asked, "And just how did it come about that you joined the service of Signor Mezzanotte?"

The Commander looked away as if reaching for a memory, and the suggestion of a smile appeared about his narrow face. "Our precious island is that gem which every monarch wishes to add to his crown, and so we find ourselves often at war. But this jewel has edges sharp as razors that cut whoever attempts to hold us. Our experience of war is so vast and frequent, at our births we resign ourselves that, although we will live as farmers, we will die as warriors. There is hardly a man among us who does not carry a scar or cannot recount a tale of battle and awful bloodshed. As for myself, humbly I can only report that I do not know what led the Signor to offer me a place in his service. He is a generous patron and my loyalty to him is without limit." He leaned closer. "There is no way for you to know this, but his interest in you does you great honor which I do not doubt is richly deserved."

Pierre laughed. "Put it this way; I've no idea why I've come to his attention so I can only hope that I'll be received as you suggest. Perhaps you know why I've been brought to him."

Turning away with an empty expression the Commander said, "It should be apparent I am not one in whom he confides, but I assure you he does not invest his attention casually." Pierre smiled though he felt no assurance.

The colonnade of trees ended at a wide dirt road that continued into the hills. No longer sheltered by trees, sunlight washed over them suddenly and its intensity startled Pierre.

Squinting against the sudden light, the Commander said, "I promise you this much. His Excellency understands advantage. His own, certainly, but he also understands that to derive advantage he must also provide it. And when his advantage is within sight there is no one more generous."

"I'll guess as well," Pierre said, "there's no one more dangerous when that advantage disappears."

The Commander turned as he nodded. "Have no doubt that, whatever his intention for you, your reward will be generous and any promise he makes as reliable as Holy Writ."

"So tell me," Pierre asked, "does a certain Augustus Chanceux also live at the palace?"

Mention of the name left the Commander puzzled. "Many reside under the protection of Signor Mezzanotte and I do not know all of their names."

Pierre said, "I learned this from a man on the island of Cuba, but that was long ago."

"Is this man you ask about someone you know well?"

Pierre shrugged. "If he's the man I'm thinking of, we haven't met for a long time and he may not even recognize me."

"It is best that you ask Signor Mezzanotte himself about your friend." An uncomfortable silence followed. Pierre thought of no other question he believed the Commander might answer and the Commander seemed to lose his curiosity about Pierre.

The pale and stony dirt road beneath their wheels climbed as the carriage passed beside one dusty, silent and mud-colored village, flattened by the relentless sun, after the next. The carriage traversed what seemed to Pierre a bitterly unforgiving land where life was forced from the soil. Everything appeared coated with fine, yellow dust filtered by a golden penumbral light. Figures in these fields, what Pierre assumed were peasant farmers, stood dressed in that same dark and tattered clothing of all farmers, their faces drawn and beaten and lined as perpetually aged and who, as the carriage passed, stopped what they were doing, removed their broad pale straw hats and bowed, all the while watching with dark and pitiless mistrust. Women dressed in black bowed their heads and crossed themselves and open-mouthed children beside them simply watched.

The path of their carriage climbed gradually to cooler air until a mild breeze finally found them. Climbing still higher, spindly clods of dry grass beside the road became lush and green, and broad leaves of trees dappled the sunlight. They entered a narrow valley whose high and stony sides stood apart just enough to allow the horses and carriage to pass. Becoming suddenly steep, the horses slowed and the driver encouraged them with his whip. When the road then leveled, they perched on the edge of a broad, golden plateau whose solitary trees stood as scattered points of green. In the distance and bright as an ingot of brass, he saw what he assumed to be Mezzanotte's palace, and its view even from this distance startled him appearing elaborate and enormous.

Grinning as if he recognized Pierre's thought the Commander said, "His Excellency is an ambitious man and his palace cannot but reflect that." The pride in his voice surprised Pierre.

The road ahead was now arrow-straight and broad fields on both sides disappeared into the dusty distance. Beyond the palace, patches of gray-green forest marked the hills ahead. The driver coaxed the horses into an easy trot. Reaching the shadow of those pale stone walls surrounding the estate he steered the carriage up a broad stone ramp and then beneath the main gate, its portcullis raised and spikes at its lower edge hanging down as threatening as a monster's black teeth. Men stood at either side of the entrance uniformed as the commander. Without slowing, their carriage passed through to rattle loudly across the palace's cobbled piazza.

At the piazza's center, a broad fountain of black stone with a tall carved leaping dolphin spouted a stream of water that glittered in the sunlight. Window boxes beneath the surrounding windows were filled to overflowing with more brilliantly-colored flowering plants. As he had noticed in the town, these windows were shuttered against the early sun. Their carriage continued around the fountain toward a building of several stories where, in a cloud of golden dust, it came to a stop. With a broad smile the Commander announced, "The palace of His Excellency, Signor Giovanni Mezzanotte."

Gray stone stairs climbed to a wide, dark door Pierre assumed was the main entrance. The Commander stepped down from the carriage and Pierre followed. As they climbed the stairs, the door was opened by a slim young man also dressed in dark blue livery. He and the Commander greeted each other and the young man stepped back inviting them to enter. After the fierce sunlight, the palace seemed restfully dark and cool.

Turning to Pierre the Commander said, "Lorenzo assures me His Excellency is expecting us." The young man the Commander called Lorenzo turned and led them through an opulently-decorated vestibule. Despite the soft light, Pierre recognized that he was now surrounded by elaborate and brightly-decorated furnishings under a high ceiling whose rich decorations seemed to glitter. At a wide, circular staircase of white marble with marble balustrades thick as tree-trunks along one side, they climbed past one landing and then another to the top-most floor. The corridor they reached passed through several more decorated rooms and ended at a closed door. Lorenzo opened it and ushered Pierre through.

Stunned by a blast of sunlight, it took a moment to recognize they stood at the edge of a broad rooftop plaza. Pierre was impressed by its panoramic view of distant hills climbing toward the pinnacle of the volcano, Mount Etna. Meanwhile, at the roof's center and sheltered beneath an enormous red and white-striped awning, stood a tall and broad circular cage comprised of glittering bronze-colored metal bars. Inside this cage Pierre guessed a tall and narrow perch appearing covered by cooing and fluttering pigeons. Blue and gray and tan, these pigeons seemed to ripple in constant motion. The flat rooftop of large, pale tiles otherwise was as empty as a ballroom floor.

Suddenly, Pierre heard a voice call out, "As usual, Commander, you have accomplished your mission with speed and efficiency. I congratulate you." Pierre looked about for the source of the voice until he suspected it had come from within the cage. "I assume," the voice continued, "Captain Harris was perplexed by his reassignment."

Speaking in the direction of the cage the Commander said, "He could not disguise his consternation."

The voice continued in weary resignation, "A good man who has served me well. And yet, as so often happens, comfortable in my good opinion his reach exceeded his grasp and his presumption led to egregious error. A period of time as sub-commander of the garrison on Malta will enhance his prudence. Thank you, Commander. As our guest and I have much to discuss I wish some privacy."

The Commander bowed, retreated through the door and was gone.

In a sudden flurry of feathers the pigeons fled their perch to fly wildly about within the cage, and Pierre saw that their perch was in fact a man. Middle-aged of medium height and muscular, the man's long, dark hair flowed past his shoulders. He wore a brilliantly colored robe whose billowing sleeves hid his hands. Smiling in a wide, dark-eyed face, he stepped toward the edge of the cage while pigeons gradually returned to joust on his shoulders. Several perched on his head and others clung to his garments creating the illusion of a living and moving feathered cloak. In this way Pierre discovered himself standing before the infamous Giovanni Archangelo Mezzanotte.

CHAPTER EIGHT

SIGNOR MEZZANOTTE WATCHED the cascade of pigeons flutter about him with unembarrassed delight. Stretching out his arms at his sides, he turned both of his hands down and from their palms poured golden kernels of dried corn that clattered to the tiles of the floor of the cage. Instantly, the pigeons abandoned him and fluttered noisily down for the corn at his feet. He muttered down toward them as they cooed pecking at the corn. But when finally he looked up at Pierre, his expression was piercingly dark. "I have long looked forward to this meeting. Come closer, please, for we have much to discuss."

Without moving Pierre asked, "Why am I here?"

As if startled for a moment by the question, Mezzanotte glanced down again at his feet. "Pigeons." When Pierre said nothing, he continued with a contented sigh, "Such delightful creatures. Do you like pigeons?" Pierre could think of no useful response. "So clever and intelligent. Charming and beautiful as well, are they not?"

"You have the advantage of me," Pierre said. "You know a great deal about me while I know nearly nothing of you. And worse, from the little I've heard, I can't imagine why I might be interesting to you."

Mezzanotte glanced up again to stare hard at Pierre with sparkling eyes and leaving him startled. His thick, fleshy features became quizzical. "Explorer in the realm of the aether and confidant to the most destructive creature since the time of the Bible, and yet you cannot conceive why I might find you interesting? Perhaps your reputation for intelligence is less than deserved."

Pierre hesitated. "Maybe the better question is how I've come to your attention."

Mezzanotte looked down fondly again to his pigeons still fluttering about in pursuit of the corn. He leaned down and from among the flashing feathers he gently snatched up one in his hand and with the fingers of his other began to stroke its head. He brought it close to his lips, muttered and lightly kissed it. "Pigeons," he said and sighed.

When Pierre offered no response, he asked, "Do you know why we regard pigeons as clever?" Without pausing for an answer he continued, "Once a pigeon identifies a location as its home, it will always return to that location. It could be set free anywhere on the surface of the earth, but eventually it will return to its home." He paused then, adding, "Unlike certain men."

"And what does any of that have to do with me?"

As though whispering into the ear of the pigeon in his hand Mezzanotte said, "Take a small piece of paper and write a bit of intriguing information on it. Tie that paper with thread to a pigeon's leg and then release that pigeon and its information will fly through the air." Mezzanotte then smiled, glancing at Pierre. "Imagine a sky full of pigeons, each with a piece of paper tied to its leg, and you imagine a sky full of information. No doubt one day it will be your aether which will convey that information, but until then, my pigeons do that job rather well."

Pierre hesitated. "You say you learned about me from these birds?"

He glanced warily at Pierre. "So it is true; your reputation for cleverness does exceed its reality." Mezzanotte again paused. "If you are able, imagine further that there are individuals in many locations and at many levels of influence who derive pleasure and profit from passing to me odd bits of information which they suspect may stimulate my interest. Still further, imagine that, unknown to their providers, from time to time fragments of information from widely-separate sources converge on a single subject. Finally, imagine that, having come into possession of these bits of information and having speculated upon their convergence, my curiosity might be so piqued I would be compelled to satisfy it. Putting a still finer point to all of this, imagine that information comes to focus upon a peculiar individual named Pierre and his relationship with an even more peculiar creature." He shook his head and looked away. " Have I begun to address your curiosity?"

After a pause Pierre said, "Pigeons."

Signor Mezzanotte smiled. "We begin slowly, but we progress. I have questions to ask and curiosities you will satisfy, but all of that will take some time. Considering your ungenerous treatment during your voyage, I do not doubt you are in urgent need of food and rest, hospitalities which I am happy to provide in abundance. Let me invite you to partake of both and we will resume this conversation later. There are several individuals residing here eager to make your acquaintance. Does this all seem satisfactory to you?" Before Pierre could respond, the Signor added, "And accept my assurance that any flesh consumed within these walls is of the conventional type. So rest content and consume with confidence; your comfort and security are my most urgent interests."

The door to the rooftop plaza opened and Lorenzo stepped through. Mezzanotte called out, "See that our esteemed guest is provided with anything he wishes." Turning back to Pierre, he glanced up and down and then smiled. "Including a change of clothes; something respectable and befitting an accomplished natural philosopher and courageous world-traveler."

Lorenzo bowed in acknowledgment. Mezzanotte tuned back to Pierre. "Follow Lorenzo and be of good cheer. I have looked forward to your arrival and anticipate many enlightening conversations."

Lorenzo opened the door and Pierre moved to follow him but then stopped. Turning back toward Mezzanotte, he asked, "Among those you describe, might one of them be my father?"

Mezzanotte's eyes grew large for a moment. "So, it appears I am not the only collector of unlikely information." He looked about as if being compelled to answer a question he had not anticipated. "At this moment the man you speak of is in the thrilling city of Naples completing an assignment from me. Perhaps he can be encouraged to join us. I hope that satisfies your curiosity for the moment. A more complete response must wait for another occasion."

Lorenzo led Pierre back along the cool, dim corridor. Grappling with an odd satisfaction of the confirmation of his suspicions along with the prospect of finally meeting with Augustus, he passed nearly oblivious through rooms of elaborate furniture and tall, wide tapestries whose rich colors and intricate designs hung from every wall. The sounds of their footsteps were lost in the deep carpet as a cool and scintillating twilight surrounded them. At the top of the staircase Lorenzo hesitated but did not turn to Pierre.

"His Excellency has spoken the truth, or at least as much as he wishes to share at this moment. A room has been set aside for you and I will be happy to find suitable clothing for you."

Descending the stairs with measured steps he continued, "He has charged me with looking after you and assisting with your needs but also make certain you do not become lost in his vast estate. We endure constant danger from brigands, so His Excellency asks that you remain within the palace grounds. As your safety and comfort are my responsibility, I need to impart this to you in confidence. Were some misadventure to befall you, I would be held accountable, and that would not be to my credit." He laughed quietly as if to make the confidence more serious by making it a joke. "I have other responsibilities so you should not expect to see me often. But whenever you find yourself in need, seek me out and inform me first. I will be most obliging and make every effort in your interest."

When they reached the second floor, Lorenzo turned and led Pierre along another corridor arranged and decorated as the others, until they stopped before a closed door. With his hand on its door handle, he looked into Pierre's eyes. "I hope I have been understood."

Although he had not phrased his remark as a question, Pierre nodded and smiled. "I'm much obliged by your thoughtfulness and promise I'll proceed with discretion."

"I merely extend the compliments of my patron and his hope you remain well and content." He opened the door and stepped back inviting Pierre to enter.

On first glance Pierre was charmed. The room was large, its ceiling high and every surface painted in bright colors in scenes and images of what he could only guess were ancient gods and goddesses at play. Those images were separated by columns decorated with painted garlands, bouquets of flowers and overflowing baskets of fruit, all interspersed between tall, narrow mirrors and sparkling wall-sconces with numerous tall candles. Three broad, high windows, now open to the mid-day sun, offered a view of red-tiled rooftops, and beyond to high hills and pale peaked mountains, and then further to the profile of Mount Etna.

Three chairs, thickly-upholstered in wine-colored cloth, stood around a circular table. Against the near wall was a couch, also upholstered in a wine-colored covering and wide enough to seat four people, and with a chair of the same color standing at each end. In the far corner beside one of the windows stood a painted screen decorated with more of those antique and floral images of the walls and ceiling. But what held Pierre's attention was a bed easily wide enough to accommodate three sleepers. Directly across from the bed stood a cold fireplace with a small tapestry positioned before it.

"His Excellency," Lorenzo said, "is famous for his thoughtful generosity as well as good taste." When Pierre said nothing, he added, "If these accommodations are not sufficiently comfortable I will be happy to arrange for something else."

Pierre walked slowly toward the bed afraid that, dream-like, approached too closely it would disappear. But reaching out his hand, it proved to be thrillingly substantial. Pressing down with his hand he found its mattress thick and soft. Three fat pillows cradled his hand as he pressed them.

"Do you approve?" Lorenzo asked from behind Pierre's shoulder. The sound of his voice caught Pierre by surprise.

"Fine, just fine," Pierre said. There seemed an unbridled sweetness to everything he saw. "Yes, this will do quite well."

"Very good," Lorenzo said with audible relief.

"One favor," Pierre said. "I'm tired and this bed is inspiring. I wish to rest for a time."

"Of course; you've had a long journey," Lorenzo said. "Our evening meal will be served after sunset and I will wake you in time to bathe and change. Will there be anything else?"

Pierre shook his head. "Suddenly I feel like I haven't slept in a year." He climbed onto the bed and stretched out on his back, only noticing the click of the door closing as he closed his eyes. In a moment, images and sounds came to his mind in a flurry of unconnected fragments like the snowflakes he recalled falling outside his window at the tavern. But then it all melted into a silent darkness. His last memory was the sensation that he was smiling.

When he opened his eyes again he discovered, sitting on the wide couch before him Signor Mezzanotte himself, but now dressed in a vaguely-military appearing uniform of dark blue and with a sparkling rapier belted to his waist. He watched Pierre and smiled. "I hope you are not surprised to learn you have slept nearly five hours. The sleep of a hero, and no doubt richly deserved. How are you feeling now?"

Though his eyes were open, sleep clung like strands of wet seaweed to the edges of his mind. "Do you always watch over the sleep of your guests?"

"Only the important ones." His voice was content and self-assured, as if certain that everything he said was believed. "And you are of that tribe who awake surly and disgruntled."

"At the risk of being rude, that's pretty accurate. And obviously unlike yourself."

"Precisely. Each day of my life I have awakened singing. This proclivity so touched my mother and my aunts they called me Angelo. Early in my life I realized that every day provides a new opportunity for adventure and romance."

"And profit?" Sleep drained from Pierre's mind but only very slowly.

"But of course," he responded with surprise. "Profit is the ultimate romantic adventure. Do you agree?"

Finally, Pierre had a reason to laugh. "Not enough chances to form an opinion."

"So you confess that yours has been a youth misspent and overdrawn. It should come as no surprise if I remind you that in the end all debts are paid, either in gold or in-kind."

"Heard that before, and you wake me to tell me?"

Mezzanotte chuckled indulgently. "Ah, the impertinence of youth; how well I remember it. The certainty that one can act in life without concern for consequences. This, I assure you, is a delusion exclusive to the young. But it is also a delusion impossible to dispel, so I will move on with the purpose of my visit." He shifted on the couch as if settling in for a long story. "What I wish to explain will demand more than a moment. Meanwhile, Lorenzo has left fresh water to fill the tub behind that screen, along with a towel and a set of clean clothes which should fit you well. Suppose, while I indulge in this discursive recitation, you take advantage of that bath. I promise I will reach the end of my tale by the time you have dressed."

"There's no avoiding this?"

"On the contrary, I hoped you would be eager to learn why I have taken an interest in you and how I expect you to help me."

"Actually I was thinking more about that bath."

Mezzanotte laughed. "Such impertinence, I have discovered, seems endemic to the minds of you colonials, so I suppose there is no alternative to indulgence. Still, I assure you that one day, inevitably, your people will learn what we understand at birth. And that lesson will prove costly and painful."

Pierre finally stood from the bed. "Since there seems no help for it at least I'll be certain to be clean and dressed."

Mezzanotte said, "Cynicism is a weak disguise for fear."

Behind the screen he discovered the bath and buckets of clean water sitting beside it as Mezzanotte described. To one side, fresh clothes along with a large, thick towel lay folded on a chair. He poured the water into the tub and then took off the clothes he had been given by Simpson on Captain Harris's ship. "All right then," he said, "fire away, I'm all ears."

Invisible to Pierre, Mezzanotte said, "What an odd expression. Ah well, there is no help for it, so let me start at the beginning. More than a year ago I first heard rumors of the existence of a powerful and hugely destructive creature roaming the high seas and plaguing the trade routes. These rumors came to me as I described to you before, by way of my precious pigeons. But as I say, it was entirely a matter of rumor and conjecture. And as is my method in such matters, I put aside the information that came my way and awaited confirmation."

As Mezzanotte spoke, Pierre stepped into the cool water, and using the large sponge at the bottom began to wash himself. He called out, "But you learned those rumors were true."

"Not so fast, young man; no reason to rush. A leisurely pace leads to our destination just as surely as a head-long careen, but our journey will be so much more enjoyable. To resume; within two months I was informed of the attack on the Bristol, of which you know considerable. My agents provided more details than I had possessed, including mention of your name. Over the following months, information concerning subsequent attacks gave me the opportunity to surmise based on evidence. By the way, I hope the bath has proved adequate."

"More than adequate," Pierre said, "and I thank you for this indulgence. It's been a long time since I've enjoyed the like."

"Your gratitude is noted and appreciated," Mezzanotte said, "and speaks well of your sense of honor. But to continue; accumulating further reports, eventually I was able to turn the matter over to minds deeper than my own. You see, among those residing here, it is my pleasure and privilege to provide residence to many possessed of wide and deep learning and who offer perceptive assistance on matters that defy my own understanding. But let me correct myself, for those men and women also provide diverting companionship. It was to these individuals that I gave my accumulated information suggesting they speculate freely on what all of it could mean."

"Should I assume they speculated adequately?" Pierre asked. He stood from the bath feeling unaccountably refreshed. He toweled himself off quickly.

"The process of speculation and refutation was methodical, I assure you, but it proved frustratingly inconclusive. I reviewed separate reports on the attack on Port Royal and then the attack on Cuba. But then I received reports about my carefully designed attack upon the ships of Sheikh Mustafa al Harum. You see, until that point I had convinced him he and I could collaborate together and successfully divide risks as well as gains from predatory adventures, particularly against Spanish shipping. And those efforts proved successful. But, as with all alliances, it also proved temporary, simply awaiting one of us to decide it had reached the end of its usefulness. It just so happened I chose to act on that conclusion before he did."

"And I can assure you of the Sheikh's complete surprise." He pulled on the trousers and then slipped into the shirt, noting how well they fit and silently complimented Lorenzo.

"But of course," Mezzanotte continued. "I would never have initiated the encounter otherwise. In any attack, surprise is the only certain advantage. Be that as it may, the interference in my plan by the creature alerted me to a completely new dimension to be considered. Finally I could account for losses of certain valuable shipments that, until then, had mystified me. And I now understood that I could no more anticipate the creature's interference than I could that of a hurricane or a volcano. This is where consideration of your involvement became paramount. You see, the group of individuals I mentioned had offered the conjecture that some unaccounted-for element was directing this creature's activities. That of course remained a conjecture until descriptions of the attack on the ships of the Sheikh began to accumulate. Several reports again noted your presence during an attack by the creature, so that the simple number of occasions when you were present finally suggested you occupied a position of significance. At first, and as is scientifically responsible, we attempted to account for this by some other force. We considered several variables, including the speed and direction of the wind, air and water temperature, the time of day or season of the year and even the position by latitude and longitude. By a process of elimination we discovered that the only element common to all of these tragic events was you." He paused then as if hesitating. "You likely find this conclusion discomforting, but believe me when I say we made every effort to avoid it."

"Just knowing that makes me feel better," Pierre said and did not hide his sarcasm. "But were you able to account for how this could be anything more than coincidence?"

"We have not yet identified the mechanism, in this you are correct. But we have agreed that exercise is unnecessary. The fact such a connection must exist appears incontrovertible. The how-and-why is simply an intriguing but extraneous detail that eventually must become clear. I wish to give no offense, but simply hope to outline the process by which we reached our conclusion."

Refreshed and comfortably dressed, Pierre raked his fingers through his still-wet hair and stepped out from behind the screen. "Have you decided what all of this has to do with me?"

Seeing Pierre, Mezzanotte grinned. "It is as if the shipwrecked sailor has finally been rescued. I am delighted my facilities have provided such a remarkable change." He stood from the couch. "And yes, your involvement as you call it has yet to be determined and so will give us all a great deal to consider. Meanwhile, dinner is about to be served. Let us continue this conversation on our way to our table."

"Whatever else this is," Pierre said annoyed, "it's not a conversation. But right now I'm starving. Since I'd rather eat, just point the way and I'll get there before you."

Signor Mezzanotte said, "Your bath has improved your mood as much as your appearance." He turned to the door. "I can only hope our meal will prove as satisfying."

"Does that mean you plan to avoid my questions?"

"All questions are avoided until they must be answered and there is no alternative." He opened the door to the corridor. "Shall we go?"

Pierre stepped through the door and Mezzanotte followed behind him. "And I suspect it will be your table companions who will prove most engaging."

They reached the stairs and Mezzanotte took the lead. Pierre said, "I don't doubt any of that." They reached the first floor and Mezzanotte led Pierre along another corridor. Pierre said, "Tell me one thing; why am I confined within the grounds of the palace?"

"Quite simple," Mezzanotte said. "My plans depend entirely on your participation." Leaning toward Pierre, he quietly added, "And the hills around us are filled with the most awful bandits; men who, were they not in my pay, would do the most frightful things." This hall ended at a pair of closed doors. He opened one and stepped aside inviting Pierre to enter.

The dining room was much larger than any they had passed through, and although Pierre assumed he was prepared for the sight, he still hesitated with surprise at the threshold.

Six broad windows along one side of the room that reached to the ceiling stood open to the purple twilight. As in the other rooms, this ceiling was very high and, continuous with the walls, it was decorated in the elaborate style of those paintings and tapestries and mirrors he had seen. Despite the fading light, this room was bright with the flames of the many candles mounted in wall-sconces.

The table at the center of the room and running nearly its length was set with glittering platters, cutlery, glasses and decanters and three tall candelabra of polished silver. But what captivated his attention, as the Signor had predicted, was the company of people already seated. Carefully dressed men displayed their wealth and status beside elegantly-dressed women who offered elaborate costumes and glimpses of flesh pearl-bright to dusky, and all with a cheerful formality. Surveying the company, he only recognized Commander Genovese seated at a chair at the far end of the table. Faces bright with curiosity turned to watch him enter beside Mezzanotte.

"Ah, my friends," Mezzanotte said aloud as he strode the length of the room toward the large vacant chair at the head of the table, "I am so glad you all have managed to join us. It gives me the greatest pleasure to announce our table is graced this evening with a guest whose appearance I have long and eagerly anticipated. His name is Pierre Chanceux and he has survived many amazing adventures, as several among you already know. He and I have spoken at length and I promise you will find him intelligent and articulate and quite clever. In every way he is a perfect addition to our company, but it will be up to you to convince him to share his tales with you."

Pierre stood awkwardly for his introduction, until a smiling, silver-haired gentleman, tall and slim in a green coat signaled him to the empty chair by his side. On the other side of that empty chair sat a youngish, dark-haired woman dressed with exceptional style. Pierre hesitated, but when he realized Mezzanotte had finished with him he took the seat offered.

Standing before his chair at the head of the table Mezzanotte said, "As our company is now complete, I believe it is time our food arrived." He clapped his hands once. At the sound, doors at both ends of the room opened and liveried men entered bearing platters and trays and tureens to begin moving silently around the table.

CHAPTER NINE

SEATED FINALLY, PIERRE could not decide which way to turn or where to look. Whether it was the lighting, or elaborate and garish decorations of the room, or carefully-dressed servants, or captivating aroma of the food in the sparkling serving dishes they carried, or lively and well-dressed company of men and women surrounding him, all of it tugged at his attention and he could never be certain exactly what he was looking at. To his relief, the middle-aged man sitting beside Pierre turned to him.

"Please forgive my rudeness," he said. "I am the Viscount Guillermo Antonioni and I am pleased by this opportunity finally to meet you. Your adventures have been a topic of our conversations for some time, and I promise that what Signor Mezzanotte has said is true; this meeting with you has been eagerly awaited by us all."

The woman to Pierre's right turned to him smiling. "I am likely the least knowledgeable person in this room, yet even I have looked forward to meeting you." He had glanced at her when he first sat down but now sitting close to her, he was charmed by her large, dark amber colored eyes, her thick, dark hair and her pale, heart-shaped face. He hoped her remark was intended as a compliment.

To Pierre, the Viscount said, "Allow me to introduce to you the Countess Val d'Olivo, a woman of remarkable intelligence and pedigree. The rest of us you will soon meet, but we feel quite fortunate to be the first to enjoy your conversation."

The Countess asked Pierre, "And how did you find your conversation with our host?"

“As a conversation,” Pierre said with a nervous laugh, “it was entirely one-sided.”

The Viscount and Countess both laughed, and Pierre found the Countess’s bright laughter musical and enchanting. The Viscount said, “Our conversations with him are usually like that.”

The Countess added, “He is inclined to discourse, and rarely anticipates a response or solicits another’s thoughts.”

The Viscount added, “The Signor is certain of nothing so much as his own ideas, and feels no thirst for new ones.”

“I heard that remark,” Mezzanotte announced suddenly and in a loud voice from his chair at the head of the table. His words were accompanied by general laughter. “And I confess that I largely, though not entirely, agree.” This brought forth more laughter.

A man seated to the right of Mezzanotte addressed Pierre saying, “But we are all well-rewarded for keeping our opinions to ourselves.” The laughter continued.

“And so you should,” Mezzanotte said. “It is a rare person who is rewarded for doing nothing.”

A woman sitting near the middle of the table said, “Not all of us are rewarded for doing nothing.” This time the laughter was louder and mostly female.

“I am told,” said a man sitting across the table from the woman who last spoke, “that some forms of work are their own reward.” This laughter was general and even Mezzanotte joined in.

Food and wine, bright candlelight and even brighter conversation, all of it lifted Pierre’s spirits until he found himself smiling. As he ate and opportunities allowed, he surveyed his companions. At some point he realized that a woman sitting beside Commander Genovese on the other side of the table and near its far end snared Pierre’s attention. Though the two appeared to have much to discuss, there was something about her that seemed to speak to his memory. He reminded himself he could not possibly know the woman and yet she seemed to be someone he knew and so he wondered where he might have met her.

“Her name,” the Countess whispered beside Pierre’s ear, “is the Duchess di Nuova Cento. It is said she is close with the Papal Legate, Monsignor Alberto Maggio.” Pierre turned to face the Countess as she added, “Very close." She held his look with sparkling eyes and a mischievous smile, as if she knew he was intrigued. But mention of the Papal Legate stirred something else in his memory. A confused notion fluttered in his mind like a moth around a light whose source he could not make out.

The Viscount said to Pierre, "At the risk of frightening the Countess, I would like to hear something from you about your beast." This startled Pierre. "Although we have learned something of its size and power, none have provided a description of the creature itself and how it behaves."

"He means," Mezzanotte called out to Pierre from the end of the table, "he wants to hear those details my agents have been unable to provide."

Pierre glanced about to discover the eyes of his table companions now directed at him. And he realized that each had learned something about his encounters with the creature. So, quietly at first, he held the table's silent attention describing the destruction of the convent and of Port Royal on the island of Jamaica. He then recounted his adventure on the island of Cuba at the hacienda of Don Benito Cereno and how it came about that Dr. de Montpellier was killed, and how the creature had waited for Pierre outside the cave. Then he paused.

Suddenly it seemed he was speaking about one thing, but his thoughts had leapt to something else. He hoped his companions assumed his hesitation was an excess of emotion at recalling those events he described. At that moment he realized why the Duchess stirred his memory.

But his hesitation lasted only a moment and he resumed, quickly bringing his tale to a conclusion. His audience remained silent until Mezzanotte said, "It should now be clear why I have been eager for this young man to join our company. His experiences involving certain matters of great importance to my organization undoubtedly will prove enlightening." He smiled. "And I assure anyone who doubts his veracity that his accounts tally with everything I have learned from my agents. So, at the very least, his lies are not those of an ordinary sailor." Laughter rippled over the table to Pierre's great relief.

When he turned to face the Countess, her eyes sparkled with an unaccountable excitement. Breathlessly she said, "You must be a terribly brave man."

"Not at all," Pierre responded uncomfortably. "I just ran faster than anyone else."

The Viscount leaned toward Pierre. "Only those who are truly brave can trivialize their bravery. I congratulate you on your resourcefulness and courage." Pierre's embarrassment grew and he was relieved when the buzz of general conversation resumed.

His companions seemed finally to lose interest in him, allowing him to consider his own thoughts. No longer the center of their attention, he indulged in the elaborate meal before him at least to satiate that clawing hunger. But memories of Abbess Maria forced their way into his thoughts. In thinking them he realized that, since the destruction of the convent he had hardly thought of her. As he ate he remembered those things she had explained to him and that so much of what she said had turned out to be true. His memories of how she stood by him at the convent with her attempt to save his and the Scientist's lives came to mind, and he cringed with anguished embarrassment at his faithlessness and his failure.

He emptied the platter before him and, quickly as a feeding fish, the hand of a servant posted behind his chair removed his empty platter and replaced it with another. His hunger slacked, he ate more slowly, taking the opportunity to glance about at the lilting voices and glowing faces surrounding him. But the stir of memories of the Abbess forced every other from his mind. He wanted urgently to observe that woman he had been told was the Duchess di Nuovo Cento in the hope of catching a glance at her full face and perhaps confirm his suspicion. But she seemed in continual and animated discussion with the Commander. Even at moments when she turned to speak to someone at their end of the table and he expected her to face in his direction, she remained obscured. He suspected her evasion was so successful it could be intentional.

"If you wish," the Countess said quietly to Pierre, "I have no doubt that an introduction could be arranged." Her voice in the midst of his conjectures startled him. When he turned, her eyes revealed something so avid he believed she would enjoy doing just as she suggested.

"Sorry," Pierre said. "My rudeness is showing." He was more embarrassed by his lack of interest in the attractive Countess beside him than his curiosity about the Duchess.

As if guessing his thoughts, coolly she added, "One's curiosity goes where it must. But it is diplomatic as well as courteous to guide one's curiosity to go where it should." Her cocked eyebrow suggested he was being indulged and her patience was not without limit.

Pierre turned his glance to encompass the table. "I find I'm curious to speak to everyone. But right now, I'd like to learn more about you."

"That is an improvement," she said, her smile becoming brighter, "but only just."

"After months aboard ships," he continued, "my social skills have disappeared. So please tell me how you came to join this glittering company."

"And that, I assure you, is better still," she said. Although her eyebrow remained raised, her full smile suggested he had made progress. She explained that she was a member of a prominent family of Italian nobility, that her family once had owned estates in Tuscany, and that for several years she had been resident of the La Controra convent under the Fathers of the Holy Trinity of Santa Maria di Mercede. There she came to the attention of the Duke d'Espary and soon was invited to join his entourage. It was the Duke who first brought her to the palace and introduced her to Signor Mezzanotte. When he decided to move on, the Countess agreed to Mezzanotte's suggestion she remain. Pierre asked how she filled her days and she explained that she helped Mezzanotte with his voluminous correspondence. "As you must have guessed, he responds to each message sent to him the same day it is received." She added that several at the table did the same. "In gathering the Signor's information we have enjoyed the privilege of reading some intriguing messages."

The Viscount leaned toward Pierre. "You are most fortunate; she has just told you more about her past and work than she has ever told me. By this sign she must think well of you."

To the Viscount, the Countess said, "At least this man has done something courageous and dangerous and worth hearing about and does not put one to sleep or leave one embarrassed."

"You see," the Viscount said to Pierre with a discomforted grin, "it is all but certain she has adopted a special affection for you. Otherwise, she would never feel compelled to defend her curiosity. You are a most fortunate man."

The Countess added, "Some egos can barely be contained within a single body."

"Large, but also necessarily resilient," the Viscount said. "Otherwise, how could one survive your disdain and continual rebuffs?"

"You seem," the Countess said to the Viscount with a touch of acid, "to do well in that area. This is, after all, the first occasion when I have seen you at our table without companionship."

Pierre said, "Pardon me for saying so, but it seems I've walked into an ongoing conversation. I just want to make certain I'm not the source of conflict."

"You see," the Countess said to the Viscount with frigid certainty. "Our guest has been among us hardly one hour and yet already he has displayed remarkable sympathy and delicacy of feeling, while you have caused him embarrassment."

The Viscount responded, "Undoubtedly in another moment you will find a clever way to assuage his discomfort. And then I am certain he will feel gratitude for having been cast onto such embarrassment."

Though the two smiled at each other as if engaged in good-natured rivalry, Pierre guessed a long-lived and ongoing annoyance; this could not be the first time they had engaged in such a discussion.

Suddenly, Mezzanotte cleared his throat and stood from his chair. "As it appears our meal is concluded, desert and liquors should now await us. And added to the good fortune of our newest companion, this evening I have been promised an entertaining musical divertissement. Follow me and we will all go together."

A painted portion of the wall in a corner of the room swung open and a man liveried in dark blue stood to one side. The doorway was just wide enough to allow one person at a time to pass through. Mezzanotte led their glittering and talkative parade. Pierre surveyed the crowd hoping to spy the Duchess but failed. Then he realized the Commander was not with the crowd either. His imagination grasped at possibilities as he followed the Countess.

Standing beside her, Pierre discovered she was taller than she appeared. Stepping still closer and bringing his face near her naked shoulder, rosy under the candle-light, he discovered she smelled of something sweet and warm and ineffable. But nothing seemed to compensate for the disappearance of the Duchess, and he felt a remarkable sense of loss.

A voice behind Pierre said, "I hope you enjoy music." He turned to see the Viscount. "His Excellency maintains a group of musicians in residence. Agents across Europe supply him with sheet music of the most current composers. Though we may appear isolated, we manage to remain quite up to date."

"I do enjoy music," Pierre said, "and I'd be happy to hear something new." He paused. "But I confess that most modern music doesn't excite me."

He tried to remain close to the Countess as the Viscount spoke and they passed through the narrow doorway. When he emerged in the next room, Pierre was again impressed. As with the other rooms, this one was exuberantly decorated though it was smaller and nearly square. On one side stood a cluster of empty chairs arranged in a half-circle, a music stand before each and to one side stood a harpsichord. The rest of the room was arranged with well-separated small tables, each with four chairs around it. At the center of each table stood a small lighted candelabra, a carafe and four glasses.

Looking about for the Countess, Pierre saw that she had already taken a seat among other guests. He looked about for a table to share and chose one near the back wall otherwise occupied only by an older man and a much-younger woman. They seemed to have a great deal to discuss because they did not acknowledge Pierre when he moved one of the chairs to join them. Mezzanotte sat at a table near the front of their gathering and to one side close to the harpsichord. Just one person sat at Mezzanotte's table, a young and gorgeous woman Pierre was certain he had not seen at dinner and who laughed whenever Mezzanotte spoke.

When all were seated another disguised wall-panel opened as a door to reveal a group of men, all but one carrying a variety of violins, violas, violas de gamba and cellos begin to enter. The single musician without an instrument sat down at the harpsichord.

The musicians settled in their chairs and turned to face Mezzanotte. He stood and addressed the room. "Tonight we are promised a performance of a new harpsichord concerto by a famous Italian composer whose name I cannot recall. It is a difficult and complicated piece of music. I know this because I had to kill two of the musicians before I convinced the rest to perform it properly." A response of soft laughter suggested this was a joke heard before. He then nodded toward the man behind the keyboard and resumed his seat. Through all of this, the couple at Pierre's table continued their conversation in whispers as if they were alone. With their heads tipped together, her hand rested motionless on the top of his and lingered. Led by the man at the keyboard, the musicians began to play.

Pierre was pleased by the company he found himself in, but this music seemed remarkably dissonant and irritating, and he wondered if Mezzanotte had not been joking and the musicians had not practiced sufficiently. The man at his table lifted the carafe and filled two glasses and then, as if noticing Pierre's presence for the first time, gestured toward him to fill his glass as well. As the musicians continued to play, Pierre concluded this was all rather boring. He looked around for a door he might disappear through unnoticed.

Suddenly, Lorenzo stood beside his chair. He leaned down and whispered, "Come with me, please." Pierre was so thoroughly relieved he did not wait to hear details. Standing, he noticed that Mezzanotte was no longer at his table and the woman who had been sitting with him had moved to another. The two people sitting at Pierre's table did not look up as he left.

CHAPTER TEN

PIERRE FOLLOWED LORENZO through a disguised door that had opened in a corner of the back wall. The music faded as the door behind them closed. They followed a narrow corridor lighted by distantly-spaced candles giving it a penumbral twilight. Past several closed doors they reached a pair that were tall and narrow of polished dark wood. Lorenzo knocked quietly twice and a voice within said, "Yes." He opened one of the doors and stepped aside inviting Pierre to enter.

Pierre found Mezzanotte seated in a chair behind a wide and dark desk that faced the door. Small and low-ceilinged, this gloomy room's only source of light was a three-candle candelabra on the desk. Instead of the painted decorations he had seen elsewhere, three walls were comprised of floor-to-ceiling shelves overflowing with books and folders of papers. The darkly-carpeted floor was nearly covered by more scattered folders and loose sheets of paper. Aside from the wide desk and its chair, the room was furnished with two large chairs separated by a small, low table. Mezzanotte looked up from the clutch of papers in his hand. Seeing Pierre he stood and stepped from behind the desk gesturing toward one of the two chairs.

"Delightful music," Mezzanotte said brightly, "performed by talented musicians; there are few pleasures to equal it. I am grateful you forced yourself away to join me."

Pierre sat down and Mezzanotte took the chair across from him. He hesitated as if gathering his thoughts. "I apologize for interrupting this evening's entertainment, but information has reached me that demands your consultation. According to my source, four days ago the beast attacked an armada of trading ships approaching Tenerife. It seems two of the ships were destroyed and another severely damaged. Most significantly, all reports agree that, following this attack, the creature traveled eastward." He paused. "I assume it is unnecessary to remind you where that path leads." He leaned back then and watched Pierre.

After a moment Pierre asked, "Why are you telling me this?"

Mezzanotte's expression became quizzical. "You refuse to concede you have some connection to that creature." Pierre offered no response and he continued, "I tell you now I am certain something passes between you and that beast such that, with your presence here, it is bound to reach our shore. And be assured, at that moment I will call for your help. So let me explain what I have in mind." He moved his chair beside Pierre's, learned close and spoke quietly.

"You have been brought here with only one purpose in mind; to lure that creature into a confrontation, but one on my terms. And I do this because I am certain that with your help I will destroy it. I am using you as a lure, as bait if you will, this is true. But I believe what this creature must believe, which is that deep within your mind you already know what will bring about its destruction. You do not yet know what that involves or how to bring it about, but confronted with your own destruction you will recognize what needs to be done and how best to do it." He leaned back. "Now you have seen all the pieces of the puzzle, or at least all that are at this moment in play."

"And what might that mean?"

"As with any card player, I reserve the right to the contents of my own sleeve."

"In other words, there's more in play than you're ready to admit."

"I could not describe your situation better."

Pierre assumed that whatever remained hidden was more important than what he had been told. "On the possibility your delusions don't evaporate by sunrise, exactly how should I accomplish this impossible task without divine intervention?"

Mezzanotte studied Pierre as if debating with himself. "That is what I hope you will conjecture and then explain to my advisers. As they all are far more clever than I, without doubt they will provide more interesting questions and better responses than any I might."

Pierre grimaced. "I've no idea the true reason you've brought me here, but I don't believe that explanation because I, at least, am certain there's no way I can help you."

Mezzanotte's expression brightened as if delighted by Pierre's discomfort. "First, be assured I am certain you can and will help me, and my own certainty is all that has ever mattered to me. But second, I am infuriatingly persistent and utterly persuasive. If you have not already recognized this, know that I am a man who always gets whatever he desires." He leaned closer and quietly added, "Always." He paused then leaned back. "Now, if you believe this creature is formidable also believe I am even more so." His sudden smile was indulgent. "But you have been with us only a few hours. Undoubtedly you will soon come to see all this in a better light. Until then, indulge me, meet with my advisers, answer their questions and consider their thoughts before you conclude we are wasting your time. Will you do that?"

It was Pierre's turn to laugh and he did. "I hardly have a choice, now do I?"

"There is some truth to that." Mezzanotte's tone suddenly hinted injured feelings. "But you are provided with exceptional accommodations, so forgive me if I assume that, were an alternative available, you still would choose to remain and help us."

"As you've said, I reside under your opulent roof, wear your handsome clothes, eat your delicious food and sleep in your comfortable bed, so how might I refuse your request."

Mezzanotte's smile softened. "Exactly as I had hoped. After spending time with your father, I was confident you were patient and generous-minded and in every other way utterly unlike him." Mention of Augustus left Pierre startled, but before he could ask about him Mezzanotte stood.

"It is late and I have a great deal to accomplish before the sun rises again. We will continue this conversation and then you will be introduced to my advisers." He called out, the door swung open and Lorenzo appeared.

To Pierre, he continued, "Get to know us and you will see the wisdom as well as justice of giving us your help. Yet undoubtedly you remain exhausted from your journey so I suggest you make this an early evening. I confess that I look forward to a time when conflict with this creature is behind us and I can return to killing the Spanish and making money." He patted Pierre's shoulder. "Appreciate my impatience and sleep well." He returned to the chair behind his desk and took up a sheaf of papers.

Pierre hesitated, tempted to ask about Augustus, but from Lorenzo's expression, he recognized this interview was over. Together they followed a different corridor until after several turns, Pierre recognized the path to his room. He said, "Bet people get lost in this place."

Lorenzo said, "The layout of these hallways is His Excellency's best security. There are corridors and rooms even I know nothing about. No one knows this building as he does."

At the door to Pierre's room Lorenzo bowed. "I will wake you in time for a morning meal." Pierre watched him follow the corridor and then disappear, relieved finally to be alone and to consider all that he had learned, because he had learned a great deal.

Above all he wondered if, despite what Lorenzo had said, there was some way to escape this palace after all. After a moment and considering his past failures in such efforts, he had to wonder how far he could get before he was discovered and returned to the palace but under far less tolerant terms. Still, unless they knew more about that beast than he did, he could not surmise what purpose a meeting with Mezzanotte's advisers could accomplish. Without doubt they would expect to hear from him those answers they could not provide. So perhaps he should save himself and take his chances with the bandits; better to face them than that beast. Pierre then opened the door to his room.

A small fire burned in the fireplace and threw shifting brass-red shadows across the walls. From the fireplace Pierre took a lighted taper and lit the three candles in the candelabra on the table at the center of the room. A good night's sleep, he reminded himself, changes everything.

What he had learned about the creature's path left him frightened, and after what Mezzanotte had said he knew he should flee as fast as his legs would move. As for Augustus, he could hardly be surprised Mezzanotte seemed to offer a meeting with him as a lure to his participation. Yet, aside from his ungenerous remark, he had offered no proof Augustus was in his employ, nor had he actually promised a meeting. All he had learned left him confused and tired, but he could hope that morning would dispel those shadows billowing around him.

The large meal and this flickering darkness and shifting shadows all left him yearning for sleep and he began to undress as. Glancing at the bed he noticed that the bedclothes lay piled oddly near its center but he assumed this was as he had left them. He stepped to the side and pulled at a corner to flatten them, but the pile did not disappear. With the tips of his fingers he pushed at the bedclothes and felt something firm. He pushed again and heard a yelp. Suddenly, from the edge of the bed, a head appeared.

"You!"

"I know, I know," Abbess Maria, who Pierre had learned was named the Duchess di Nuova Cento, said panting as if startled and upset. Her eyes were red and bleary with sleep. "I wanted to be awake when you arrived."

"Awake!" Pierre said. "You might have said something about being alive!" His shock and startled confusion left him babbling. "Was it you who convinced Mezzanotte to drag me here?" But then he stopped. Words filled his head that refused to cohere so that finally he found himself stunned into silence.

The Abbess looked at him with large, round eyes. "All of these questions; aren't you even a little pleased to see me?" Reaching out her arms to embrace him the bedclothes fell away and her naked skin was luminous in the shifting golden light. A swirl of memories of the Abbess bloomed behind his eyes. "Because I am more than happy to see you again."

Pierre sat down hard on the edge of the bed. He discovered tears in his eyes and something bitter and hard blocked his throat. In the soft firelight her eyes glittered up at his. He managed to mutter, "I thought you'd been killed; I thought you were dead. All these months I've been sure you were dead."

Nodding, Abbess Maria said, "I thought you were dead, too." She bit her lower lip. "I was certain the beast had killed you, too." With a brave smile she added, "It is miraculous we were both wrong."

Pierre leaned forward, wrapped his arms around her shoulders as her arms encircled his neck pulling him tightly to her. Her tears were hot against his cheek. They held their embrace a long time but then abruptly she pushed him away. On her face was a grin of mocking pleasure. "Well, if you are so glad, why are you crying?"

His laugh was a choking sound that resembled a groan. "And I'll ask you the same thing."

In place of an answer she embraced his neck again and again pulled his face against her cheek. They kissed, and for so long Pierre found himself panting for breath. More moments came to his memory; scenes of terror and pleasure, faces and voices and sounds that seemed all to have occurred long ago. Then the face of Dr. de Montpellier; the last moments Pierre had seen him blended with the night he last saw her so that their deaths became bound together. Seeing her reminded him of how much time had passed and all that had transpired, along with all the deaths that had pursued him and interposed themselves at every moment. And as well, that death which the creature carried within it determined to impose upon Pierre. And now, at least according to Mezzanotte, that death approached as relentless as the dawn.

When their kiss ended, he held her shoulders and looked again deeply into her eyes, as if his own eyes were tongues lapping at her cheeks and tasting her skin. Though he smiled, tremors passed through him like waves of fever, and so strong and urgent even she noticed them. "Are you all right?" she asked, concern mixed with amusement in her voice.

"So I did see you at dinner!" She said nothing but simply smiled, Pierre added, "Didn't Mezzanotte tell you I was alive? Didn't he tell you I was arriving?"

Startled and mildly surprised she said, "No, and I do not know why though he must know of our past. But even had I asked, his response would not have been worth the breath it was spoken with."

"And that young man you charmed so eagerly at table? The Commander?"

Her smile became mischievous. "Rather dashing, is he not?"

"That describes all sorts of blackguards and scalawags. Which of those is he?"

Her eyes grew wide with surprise. "That cannot possibly be the voice of jealousy. After all, you are rather late to this party. Just hours ago I was certain you were dead. In any case, I should not need to remind you whose bed I am lying in."

Embarrassed suddenly into silence, Pierre knew what she said was true and he was chagrined to admit it. "So then, how would you prefer I address you?"

She smiled with a wily disdain. "Though I am known by many names I am content that you address me as Abbess. At very least it recalls an intimacy that even in recollection still pleases me." Again he found himself baffled in her presence and delighted with his confusion. He asked how she had managed to escape the convent and the wrath of the creature.

She shook her head with a grim sigh. "A long and complicated story, as you might guess and this hardly seems the best time to review it."

Pierre hesitated with surprise. "Can you think I'll sleep well until I've heard it?"

The Abbess Maria studied him until an odd smile appeared. "I suppose your curiosity right now is your most urgent hunger; not exactly flattering considering our situation and circumstance. Still, looking into your eyes I must suppose none of it can be helped." She drew the bright coverlet tight around her shoulders and sat up straight.

"When you and the old Scientist fled, I used the confusion that resulted to escape the walls of the convent. Guessing your likely path, I chose another. And you can save your gratitude for my having distracted the Mother Superior and her coven from following you; apparently, they found my escape even more infuriating than yours. But I reached the forest far enough ahead of them to find a place to hide and that also allowed me to observe their pursuit and then their retreat when they failed to find either of us. I can only guess at this, but I assume the Mother Superior had a plan to continue their search the next day."

Surprised, Pierre asked, "So you weren't inside the convent when the beast attacked?"

The Abbess shook her head. "The Mother Superior understood how thoroughly I had betrayed her and she needed to preserve the secret of her convent. I had no choice but to hide in the forest with my own plan to return to Port Royal at first light where my allies were prepared to act on my behalf. But there was no defense from that beast. When it attacked the convent, the Mother Superior offered a delusional resistance. Perhaps it was the fury of that resistance which enraged the creature so that it leveled the entire convent."

Pierre nodded. "We hid close by and witnessed the attack. I promise that it frightened us as much as it did you."

"That hardly seems possible, but I must accept your assurance. I waited until dawn before I started back to Port Royal. But you cannot imagine the shock of what I found. Portions of buildings and parts of ships lay mingled and scattered over the yellow sand like the battered toys of angry children and as haphazard as leaves fallen after a storm. But I needed to get still closer before I began to see the bodies."

She hesitated and Pierre watched as she gathered her thoughts. "Some lay as if asleep but most bodies were twisted, lacking an arm or leg or even a head, and all strewn about like broken bits of ancient sculpture. Finding no one alive I took shelter beside a knot of fallen palm trees. And that was fortunate because ships began to arrive in what was left of the harbor. Watching those sailors land, at first I was relieved guessing that rescue was at hand. But quickly I realized they had only loot on their minds, and I watched them brutalize anyone they found alive. So I remained hidden now as frightened by the marauding sailors as I had been by that beast. Eventually ship's officers began to arrive and brought some order. When eventually it seemed safe to do so, I drew the attention of a French officer who invited me to board his ship preparing to sail for Hispaniola. Arriving at Port-au-Prince, I met with the Bishop to whom I revealed my true identity, and he arranged my passage on a vessel that returned me to Nantes. There, I contacted my adviser in the Vatican. Unhappily, as a result of the death of the old Pope and election of the new, I had become politically risky and so a new adventure began. My danger was such that I needed to flee to Palermo in the company of the Papal Legate, Monsignor Maggio, a confidant from a past assignment who had remained personally loyal. To my relief I found it easy to insinuate myself into the good graces of Signor Mezzanotte." Pierre smirked and, in response, the Abbess's expression darkened with annoyance, but she continued.

"I managed to reconcile with the Curia chosen by the new Pope, although in exchange for its protection I was forced to agree to ensure the Signor fails to expel the Spanish from this island and otherwise assist His Holiness's French allies. The new Pope enjoys the economical advantage of a loyal Spanish crown because he recognizes the French crown has become too powerful and His Holiness has no confidence in Louis XIV's desire for conciliation. The loyalty of the Spanish king to the Pope on the other hand remains unquestioned." She shrugged her shoulders and sighed. "Still, I have managed to attract two conspirators among Mezzanotte's associates."

Pierre had followed her recitation as best he could. "Should I assume Lorenzo is among them?" She smiled suddenly and from that he guessed she had left her most exciting adventures out of her account. He hoped this was intended to preserve his pleasure.

He then confessed his conclusion that most of his adventures had been orchestrated by Mezzanotte and calculated to bring him to this palace. He asked if she could confirm that.

The Abbess would only agree to its possibility. "He strategizes as a chess-master. He moves among his many enemies like a shark, destroying one and then moving on to await the moment to snatch the next. He avoids direct confrontation, preferring to stab at the side or the back. He is an enemy of God and a source of much that is vile and evil, yet I confess I half-admire him and continue to hope he will return to the Lord's truth."

"A pointless optimism," Pierre said, "if I'm any judge of men."

She shrugged but then smiled in such a charming way he almost regretted his doubt. As if dismissing his conjecture, the Abbess continued. "Concerning your other question, I promise I have heard nothing of you since that night, despite what the Signor may have said. I was certain you were dead and you cannot imagine my surprise. Otherwise, I can only confirm he has contrived some plot that involves you, though I have no idea what."

"And my father?" Pierre finally asked. "Have you heard anything of him?"

Her eyes became large as if startled by his suggestion and she shook her head. "Why would anyone speak to me about your father? I do not even know who he is?"

Pierre smiled. "So perhaps you're not as well-informed as you believe. I was told by someone far from here that there's some agreement between my father and Mezzanotte, and the Signor mentioned he was in his employ, though I've no idea what that might amount to." He studied her. "I don't suppose you would do a bit of investigating for me?"

She shrugged with indifference. "I know persons who may help. If I learn anything I will tell you." He was relieved that at least she wanted to reassure him even though he did not feel reassured. She glanced over his shoulder. Pierre turned to see though the window that the sky had begun to brighten.

"I must go," she said and he heard a note of panic in her voice. "It would not be good if I was discovered here." She reached forward and Pierre discovered her clothes lay piled beside the other side of the bed.

He watched as she dressed, thrilled by the sight and his recollected desire. He asked, "Do you really believe there are any secrets kept from Mezzanotte here?" He grinned as he spoke but his amusement was not returned. "Can you believe he might know nothing of our meeting?"

"Considering your position in his plans that is my hope." She stood and straightened the last of her garments. "But if, as you suggest, there really are no secrets here and he knows everything, then I am utterly lost."

"It's that bad?" Pierre's enjoyment fading with each garment she put on.

She was about to respond but then paused. "If there are still secrets within these walls, then it is probably better you not know. And if there are no secrets, it will not matter." She smiled finally, as if dismissing every other question. "Either way, I promise I will do what I must to make certain I do not lose touch with you again."

Pierre's smile confessed his pleasure. "That's supposed to be my promise." He sat forward at the edge of the bed watching her move toward the door.

Suddenly, as if she had just remembered something urgent, she rushed back to the bed, threw her arms once again around his neck and kissed him long and hard. Looking deeply into his eyes and seeming breathless with the thought, she said, "We will see each other again, I promise you." She broke away then, rushed through the door and was gone.

He watched the door for a time on the chance it would open again and she would reappear, but it did not and then he decided it would not. Memories churned and spread though his mind as questions without answers drifting as a mist that gradually veiled his thoughts. But then, with the sky turning pearl-gray, he discovered himself softly panting as if he had run very far and for a very long time, and now tired beyond description he needed to struggle to keep his eyes open. But then, after a time he no longer struggled.

CHAPTER ELEVEN

THE COUNTESS VAL D'OLIVO turned her heart-shaped face up with her eyes closed to the hard blue sky, inhaled deeply and then sighed. "Every beautiful day is a gift, but like all gifts it is most enjoyable when shared. So thank you for sharing this one with me." She turned to Pierre. They sat side by side on one of three pale stone benches set into a semi-circle. Sunlight dappled as it passed among those leaves of the trees standing close around them. When she turned away, Pierre was charmed by the shapely elegance of her profile.

Earlier, Pierre had joined several others for an elaborate luncheon presided over by Mezzanotte, and where Pierre had been introduced to more residents of the palace. But he did not see Abbess Maria there and his disappointment surprised him. The Commander had been present although he sat some distance from Pierre. As the luncheon was ending, the Countess appeared suddenly at his side with the promise he would enjoy a stroll through its gardens. The elaborate meal weighed on Pierre, but he had no plan for the day and by her suggestion he hoped to learn more about the Signor and perhaps about Abbess Maria as well.

Descending beneath fierce sunshine to the foot of the stairs at the main entrance of the palace, she led Pierre toward a sand-covered avenue that passed into shade. They followed the path until they reached these benches. Around them stood trees festooned with large, bright oranges among dark and shiny green leaves. A sharply citric scent filled his head like a delicious incense. She turned to face him. "To someone who has endured such adventures, ours must appear a sadly sheltered existence."

Pierre looked away. "The adventures I survived found me and never happily." Discomforted by the subject, he continued, "And the Signor has described your world of intrigues which I'm certain I could never survive. Yet he seems otherwise methodically thoughtful, so I'm grateful to be here."

"His generosity is his most effective weapon." Her smile became mischievous. "He recognizes advantage, and generosity assures that advantage so he pursues it without restraint."

"I got that idea from his attack on Sheikh al Harum."

She turned away as if embarrassed by her own amusement, and treated Pierre to her musical laughter, for which he was grateful. "You witnessed the finale of a long-running performance. As with old lovers, each anticipated the end of their alliance but neither was prepared to pay the price. Only months before, the Sheikh had sent a flotilla to lay siege to Syracusa, but the sudden appearance of a squadron of French galleons convinced him its price suddenly was too high. Unfortunately for him, he had just lost his last chance to best the Signor. Once gone, the next opportunity came to the Signor and he was determined not to fail."

Pierre said, "I'm still confused by how he manages his extensive affairs. He claimed that his information comes to him by way of his pigeons."

She laughed again and Pierre remained charmed by its sound. "He so cherishes those creatures, it is wonderfully amusing. If you hope to cultivate his friendship become friends with his pigeons." She glanced about and quietly added, "I find them filthy animals, and for that I assume I have assured my eventual exile from his inner circle."

"His use of these pigeons seems remarkable, and I'm still unclear how it all comes about."

"In its simplicity his strategy is ingenious. I expect he has explained that his agents constitute a far-reaching network. Messages move along that network in stages, and at each stage a pigeon carries each message onto the next. When a message finally reaches the palace, it is reviewed, sorted and then filed with any previously received that touch on the same subject. Thus, at first the messages that mentioned you and those that mentioned the creature were filed separately. But after a time and perhaps by intuition, the Signor began to request additional information until he had assembled an archive that linked the two of you together. This is how he learned of your exploits."

"How could any of that information help his enterprises? And why would he assume there was a link between me and that creature? And anyway, what could any of all that mean to a pirate?"

The Countess looked down as if momentarily embarrassed by what she had heard. "Those are many questions wrapped together and I am the last person capable of teasing them all apart. But first and most urgent for your continued survival, regarding our host as a mere a pirate misses his deepest ambition, and worse, will lead you to a serious mistake." She glanced up as if coming to a decision and then moved closer to Pierre.

"The threads of intrigue binding our world together are so densely woven they are nearly impenetrable. While there is no way for someone like you to recognize this, the map of Europe is changing yet the forces leading that change are not those that have shaped it in the past. There are rising men, like Signor Mezzanotte, who are neither royalty nor clergy but possess such immense wealth they acquire the power to shape affairs. Recognizing this, clergy and royalty form alliances with such men that will assure their power over their empires." With a quiet laugh she added, "All of that becomes a delicate and convoluted dance, I promise you."

Half-grinning Pierre said, "So Mezzanotte can't overthrow the Spanish empire but he's determined to put it in danger."

The Countess returned his smile. "Attacks against Spanish ships provide his wealth while rendering Spanish enterprises insecure. When no ship can travel safely every captain must find protection. And if the King's navy cannot do so, merchants will find someone who can, even if the individual conducts himself in a piratical fashion."

Suddenly, from around a corner the Viscount appeared in the company of a woman Pierre had seen at the luncheon but had not been introduced to. The Countess leaned toward him. "Discretion is always its own reward."

Approaching, the Viscount nodded. "In the palace of Signor Mezzanotte, every meeting is a conspiracy. I hope this one progresses satisfactorily."

The Countess's smile disappeared. "The success of any conspiracy is judged by its outcome."

"Well then," the Viscount said, "I look forward to reading your next report."

"And I expect the Signor will provide it to you once he has derived its value." To Pierre she added, "He squeezes our reports for information as one might one of these oranges."

The woman accompanying the Viscount laughed. "I thank my good fortune I am spared that dismal chore." At this all three laughed. Pierre smiled to disguise his confusion.

Glancing at Pierre the Viscount said, "We have spoken so often about you that I fail to note those of us you have yet to meet. So forgive my ineptitude and allow me to introduce you to the Marquesa Eleanor of Toulouse."

The Marquesa was tall and very slim with reddish hair, sharp green eyes and a sprinkling of faint reddish freckles across the bridge of her nose Pierre found charming. When she smiled the outer corners of her eyes turned mischievously up so that her expression was both wily and sweet. To Pierre she said, "But the Signor should be pleased to learn of your conversation with his most successful negotiator."

The Viscount added, "Her negotiations have earned universal praise."

The Countess shrugged. "More accurately, my skills are universally exaggerated." Her remark drew quiet laughter from the Marquesa and the Viscount.

Pierre said, "A man I greatly respect once said there's no pleasure like the memory of a misery survived." The laughter of his companions reassured him.

"And in that way," the Countess added, "legends arise."

After a moment's silence Pierre said, "The Signor has threatened to introduce me soon to his advisers." His companions glanced at other in silence.

Finally, the Viscount said, "I expect he has certain individuals in mind who are sophisticated in science and will note everything you say."

The Marquesa added, "Those conversations will prove fascinating."

The Countess said, "And no doubt, from them you will find whatever help you need."

Pierre nodded without conviction. "But help doing exactly what; that's my fear. He insists I know some peculiar way of destroying that creature. But can he honestly believe that?"

A moment of startled silence descended upon them all until the Countess said, "Whatever he tells you, he never exaggerates, so it is safest to take him literally at his word."

Pierre asked, "But why is he determined to confront that creature?"

Again his companions looked at each other in a conspiratorial way. The Marquesa said, "As he has not shared that with you, we can offer only speculation."

The Viscount glanced about as if prepared to offer his own speculation. "The creature's unpredictability creates risks to his enterprises he can no longer tolerate. It has compromised several carefully laid plans just as it did his attack on the Sheikh."

The Countess added, "Having read the relevant reports, I can vouch for that."

Glancing to the others, the Marquesa said, "In addition to his own fleet, the Signor invests in other voyages he believes will prove successful."

The Viscount added, "In fact, he employs a man whose sole responsibility is to calculate the odds for their success using information from the Signor's archive of messages. It seems these unpredictable actions of that beast negate every calculation."

The Countess said, "And yet, it was those calculations which made it possible to discover that a person with influence over that creature must exist. Though he has said nothing about this, I expect it is because of that analysis he has come to believe you will relieve him of his burden."

Pierre was startled to think his father, as director of those calculations, might have seen his name and learned of his predicament. And then Pierre wondered if it had been Augustus, after all, who had brought him to Mezzanotte's domain. "He's said something like that, but can he believe that's even possible?"

They all smiled at Pierre's confusion. The Marquesa said, "If he is convinced of something he acts on that conviction, so have no fear and do not be concerned."

"So I should be frightened because I've no idea how that might succeed."

The Countess said, "Since his conviction is all that matters to him he will be disappointed if you fail. And he does not endure disappointment patiently."

"As there's no way," Pierre said, "such a plan will succeed, I should prepare my escape."

At this his companions laughed loudly. The Countess said, "Put that from your mind. Every person within twenty miles of us is in his employ, and their loyalty is unquestioning."

The Marquesa added, "Concentrate on how to accomplish what he wants you to do."

Pierre searched the faces around him. "Remember that I've seen that creature and witnessed determined attempts to defeat it. Believe that I know what I'm talking about."

The smiles of his companions faded. Finally the Viscount said, "Perhaps it is better to put these questions aside and enjoy the pleasures available to those of us residing here."

"Of which there are many," the Countess added with a trill of excitement. "Not the least is clever and charming companionship." Turning to the Viscount and the Marquesa she stood. "With your permission we will continue our tour of this remarkable garden." To Pierre she added, "Beyond that gate are the Signor's stables and his collection of gorgeous horses pampered beyond conscience and kept for his fleet of beautifully decorated carriages." Pierre stood and she slipped her arm through his. Turning to the others she said, "We will join you at dinner." Steering him by the arm, she led him away. A few paces along Pierre glanced back; the Marquesa and the Viscount continued to watch them and he could not decipher their expressions.

The Countess leaned toward him and whispered, "Our stroll will be general knowledge within the hour, so we should enjoy ourselves." She squeezed his arm then and he thrilled at the intimacy of its gesture with the sensation of his arm pressed hard against her breast.

Their path led them among a cluster of small buildings whose arrangement forced them to turn often. Suddenly the air again filled with the fragrance of citrus. They reached two tall and rectangular pillars of dark stone supporting an elaborate and dark metal gate closed to block their way. The stone of these pillars continued as a coarse wall to surround the garden. The Countess lifted a large, black iron latch, pushed the gate aside and led Pierre inside. Though he saw portions of this garden through the gate he was startled by its elaboration and design. Several sand-covered paths radiated ahead like broad, pale fingers.

Unlike those rectilinear gardens he remembered from his home, these paths appeared laid out in an intentionally confusing pattern, as if to entice the visitor into becoming luxuriously lost. She moved to the path furthest to the right and Pierre followed. Sinuous, narrow beds of dark earth and brilliantly colored flowering plants alternated with thick, dark-green shrubs, and all of it was over-towered by graceful palm trees with their umbrellas of shade. Their path turned and then turned again as they seemed to follow a gorgeously colored maze. Each turn was sudden as if the Countess chose their path without reflection. He broke their silence to ask how she had come into the Signor's service. Her quiet laugh again was sweet.

"Fear and an insatiable thirst for revenge." He looked at her uncertain of what she meant. She added, "Unless one is powerful, it is always best to ally oneself with power. Although a strategy more opportunistic than honorable, my loyalties have moved from powerful individual to more powerful individual until eventually I reached a position that allowed me to exact revenge."

Pierre said, "Considering the difficulty, I assume you pursue revenge for a profound insult." To his surprise she laughed again, but more loudly.

"Profound insult hardly describes what I endured. Were I as powerful as God Himself I could hardly wreak that revenge which is my fair justice." She shook her head looking down at the bright sand and Pierre could not guess her expression. "My family owned an estate and raised cattle, my brothers and sister were educated, but when Charles V's army entered the Piedmont we all were treated worse than animals. Hungry and angry and knowing no law beyond their own appetites, his blood-thirsty soldiers stole what they could and destroyed what they could not. As leaders of our village, my family had taken up arms along with others determined to defend ourselves and our farms, but our feeble efforts simply made his soldiers more furious, and the misery we endured at their hands is impossible to describe."

Their path led them alternately from cool shade into bright sunlight. Sometimes they walked side by side until their path split and Pierre suddenly would find himself alone and he called out to her. Her voice came to him then through a dense stand of shrubs. "I was the youngest of five with three brothers and a sister, and I was perhaps eleven years old." Suddenly she walked beside him again and her pace slowed.

"Though more than a decade has passed, its recollection still terrifies me. When his soldiers had killed every man above the age of reason, they turned on the women." Their path again split into narrower paths and she chose the one furthest to the right. Nodding ahead she said, "This should take us past a bed of roses." He continued to breathe the scent of lemons.

"The older women they beat without mercy and forced to do menial chores, the rest of us fared far worse." Though she continued ahead, she slowed and then sighed. "Sometimes inside barns or within houses, but just as often out in the open, as if knowing no shame of their own and happy to inflict that shame on others, his soldiers clustered grinning around each screaming woman they held down and took a turn. Even now I cannot decide which was more terrifying; the bitter laughter of the soldiers or those wails and screams for mercy of our women." She disappeared behind a screen of bright flowers though he continued to hear her voice.

"But our agony was so deep and misery so wide-spread, even the notion of mercy lost all meaning. Our wretchedness flowed in streams that mixed with our blood." Again he was startled when she appeared at his side. She took his hand into hers. "For reasons I hope are obvious, I cannot agree with your friend about the pleasures of recollected misery."

With another meaningful glance she continued. "They remained among us four days and only fled to avoid the advancing Papal troops." Although he had begun to notice their aroma, he discovered that suddenly they stood before a long and narrow bed of bright and pale roses. Looking down at those flowers the Countess sighed again.

"They are so beautiful. And yet, imagine heartless children beating at them until all are bruised and broken and trod into the soil. There are those for whom beauty is an antagonism and a bitter threat, infuriating in its delight. For them, Nature's beauty is a darkly acrid thing that demands violation and destruction; as if every beauty was an insult." Intoxicated by their sweet aroma they resumed their stroll among the roses. On the Countess's face was an expression of relief.

"Afterward, those who survived and were able to walk moved about our village in a fog of pain and despair. Abandoned by man and god, we went about the grisly work of burying our dead. In a haze of bloody horror I buried my brothers, my father and mother, but worst and most bitterly, my poor, sweet sister. An older woman named Bettina nursed me back to health and hid me from the onslaught of the Pope's vicious army. Days later Bishop Requelia of Torino, sent by the Pope to survey our destruction, reached our village. I had gained a reputation for being clever with words, and whether it was curiosity about that reputation or simple lust, when he prepared to return to Torino he asked me to join his entourage."

She led Pierre around a corner and there they faced a stand of trees each laden with large, bright yellow lemons. Their scent was as over-powering as it was surprising. She stepped into the puddle of shade cast by the trees. In a brighter voice she said, "There is a liquor made from lemons whose flavor is dryly refreshing though its bitterness remains, a reminder there is no sweetness that is not also bitter." Then she looked into his eyes. "Come along; like this garden, my story includes several more turns." She glanced about as if choosing their path. "Along this way there is a surprise I hope you will enjoy." Then she resumed their stroll.

"I was relieved," she continued, "by how easily I gained the Bishop's favor. A year later at a reception for the Archbishop of Bavaria I came to the attention of the Archbishop of Milano. Despite his ardor I did not favor him, and so I was kept in one of his less comfortable residences. But with time and after many inducements, eventually he gained my trust. My affection, however, took longer for him to earn. It pleases me to say that I remained among his favorites for nearly three years. The Archbishop, meanwhile, found himself entrapped in a war with the Doges of Venice that continued as an exchange of brutal and expensive raids. Though their armies fought to a standstill, the Archbishop became convinced eventually he would be defeated so he initiated negotiations. His main negotiator was unable to make progress against Venice's demands. Finally and in desperation he asked for my help. What motivated his choice I never learned, but out of gratitude for his protection and generosity I agreed. Immediately it was apparent Venice hoped to continue the war, since the Archbishop then would be forced to concede far more than he wished; but terms were reached and peace finally was restored." She smiled as if pleased by what she had accomplished.

"My efforts seemed unremarkable to me but the Archbishop offered extravagant praise, and with that my adventure truly began. Shuttling from crisis to crisis, my reputation as a negotiator rose with each resolution until I came to the attention of the Signor. At that time, his troops had surrounded Palermo and its incompetent Spanish Viceroy. Whether out of pride or ignorance, the Viceroy had failed to prepare for the Signor's threat by requesting additional troops from Madrid. I was lent to the Signor by the Archbishop in payment for a favor. Considering the military situation, negotiations proved brief and entirely to the benefit of the Signor. He claimed to be so impressed by my skill that he offered me a treasure to join him. Happily, my efforts continue to satisfy him. I will not bore you with the details, but my tenure has proved both pleasurable and profitable."

Pierre was about to ask her opinion of Mezzanotte when from around a corner Commander Genovesse appeared and approached. Pierre was unaccountably relieved that the Abbess was not with him. The Commander and the Countess exchanged greetings before he turned to Pierre. "Signor Mezzanotte will be pleased to learn that two of his most gifted protégées are deep in conversation since their exchange of ideas undoubtedly will bring him benefit."

"And in that he is correct," the Countess said with a challenging smile. "Pierre has utterly captured my attention." She again slipped her arm through his. "He is certainly privy to esoteric knowledge and if I was not already confident otherwise, I might believe him a sorcerer of the highest order." He was startled to hear this since he had not spoken of his experiments or the beast.

The Commander said, "Having charged Signor Chanceux with a serious challenge he will be delighted to hear this."

"From our discussion," the Countess said, "I have no doubt the Signor has made a brilliant choice and will be satisfied with his accomplishments and enriched by his achievements."

Turning to Pierre, the Commander said, "And is this also the way you see your role here?"

Pierre said, "As his guest I'm obliged to help him in any way he thinks valuable."

The Commander responded, "His generosity is not always so calculated. However, it is a relief to learn that you will help us against this creature." Turning to the Countess he said, "I trust you have introduced him to the beauties of the garden."

"As a matter of fact, I have bored him with tales of my misbegotten youth. Happily, he is a most polite man and has listened patiently as I have led him about."

"Splendid," the Commander said with a rigid grin. "I hope you will also introduce him to our library. I do not doubt it includes volumes that will interest him."

After offering the wish to detain them no longer he bowed and continued on his way. Pierre now recognized the Countess was correct and they were being spied upon. When the Commander was out of earshot he asked, "What relationship does he have with Mezzanotte?"

A playful smile appeared about her lips and she resumed walking. "He is one of the Signor's most trusted advisers. The fact that he accompanied you here says a great deal about the value the Signor places on your presence. Undoubtedly he feels personal loyalty to the Signor but he also has close ties with other magnates on the island and across the Mediterranean. Sheikh Mustafa himself once hoped to entice him to join his officers. I have had only occasional contact with him. Those less generous among us insist his ambition is to displace the Signor." She glanced around. "Of course, what I have said must be shared with no one."

Pierre said, "The more I learn, the more curious I become, but I suspect the Signor is such a clever man he has anticipated each possibility and provided for it."

"So I will concede that my suspicion is no more than that." Her bright smile beguiled Pierre. "But here!" she said triumphantly. "My surprise!"

They had reached a circular, pale stone-bordered pond filled with black and white and golden carp that moved undulating lazily around each other as effortless as thought. Sunshine sparkled with their movements around a burbling spring that spouted from the fountain's center, its water glittering in a plume which never quite broke the surface. In their movements it seemed to Pierre that time had ceased to flow.

"I hope you are delighted," she said. The quiet gurgling of the water was like the sighs of small children. They walked slowly together around the fountain. The air was cool and she sighed deeply before leading Pierre toward a bower shaded by another stand of small trees. But to his surprise they found the Marquesa sitting on a bench there and engaged in conversation with an older man Pierre did not recognize. The Countess seemed startled as well and moved toward them but Pierre took her lightly by the arm and led her away.

Further along, teasingly she said, "You seemed so curious about her."

"A trick of the light, perhaps," he answered as casually as he could. "Certainly an attractive woman, but she isn't the person I thought I recognized."

For reasons he could only guess, this caused the Countess's smile to grow. "Perhaps I overestimate your curiosity about her. I am rarely wrong about such things but this may be one of those occasions. Otherwise, I might suspect you wish to impress me."

He turned to her smiling. "If I knew some way to impress you, I'd certainly try."

"A good night's sleep has had a wonderfully salutary effect on your outlook. You have exonerated yourself of every suspicion."

"My relief is inexpressible."

"Well then," she said, "follow me and we will continue all this in greater privacy." She led him further until they reached a shaded bench where she sat down hidden within the deepest part of the shade. Then she patted with her hand the space by her side. He joined her. "I cannot have gratified all of your curiosities. There must be at least a few that remain unresolved."

"You have found me out," Pierre said laughing nervously. "I still have questions, but my most compelling involve you."

Her expression brightened. "You are far more charming than I had thought likely. If I did not know better, I would suspect you hope to make love to me."

"If I had such a plan in mind," he said, "I'd only go about it if I was confident my attempt would be properly received."

A surprised look came to her eyes. "From such a brave adventurer I would never expect hesitancy or indecision."

"I only hope to avoid offense, no matter how inadvertent."

"Such reluctance is commendable so long as it does not dissuade one from romance."

"And is that now our topic of conversation?"

"If I am wrong, I hope you will tell me; romance is not something one should play at."

He moved closer to her, but then a shadow suddenly filled the entrance to their bower. In a moment he recognized the shadow belonged to Lorenzo.

"Please pardon my intrusion," Lorenzo said. He turned to Pierre. "Signor Mezzanotte has requested that I accompany you to an interview with the Marques d'Ostia."

With the mildest edge to her voice the Countess said to Lorenzo, "You are to be congratulated for having found us. That could not have been easy."

"As the order is from the Signor himself, he would not have tolerated otherwise."

Pierre asked, "This man I'm to speak with, is he part of a plan concerning the creature?"

"I am not privy to that," Lorenzo said, "but I believe he is a participant in that effort."

Turning to Pierre, the Countess said, "It all sounds rather serious and fairly dull. But you are to be congratulated; the Marques is one of the Signor's most powerful advisers and he speaks to hardly anyone. His decision to speak with you is a compliment."

"One for which I'm surely unworthy." Though he had failed to keep annoyance from his voice, Pierre stood and bowed to the Countess. "My disappointment is measureless. I hope we resume our conversation soon."

She said, "Yours is an important meeting, but I promise we will speak together again." Her glance seemed to mean something, and Pierre enjoyed teasing that out as he turned with Lorenzo and walked away.

CHAPTER TWELVE

PIERRE FOLLOWED LORENZO back through the garden along a path he did not recognize. At the gated entrance they continued toward a dark stone building of two stories he had passed in the company of the Countess. At its wide, roughly carved wooden door he turned to Lorenzo.

"You spoke with Commander Genovesse and that's how you knew where to find us."

Lorenzo looked away. "We are such creatures of habit that it is only a question of which overwhelms us at any moment. Suffice it to say I know the Countess's habits."

Nodding toward the front door, Pierre said. "So I have something to look forward to."

Lorenzo bowed. "My wish is that you regard your entire residence among us in that way. Meanwhile, I join the Countess in congratulating you; the Marquis is an estimable and elusive man and your meeting marks you as a person of special regard."

"Then I can only hope I'm worthy of such regard

Solemnly Lorenzo said, "The Marquis d'Ostia rarely makes a mistake." Glancing at the door he continued, "His rooms are on the second floor. I will return for you in one hour." He turned and began to walk back toward the main building.

Pierre paused to watch Lorenzo depart. If all he had heard was true, he assumed Signor Mezzanotte's determination to destroy the creature was sincere, and after just twenty-four hours he was already deeply entangled in his plan.

Closing the front door behind him put the room Pierre entered in a cave-like darkness. He moved to those stairs immediately ahead of him. At the top of those stairs he found a single door and guessed it was the door to the Marquis's rooms. He knocked and a voice called out, "Enter!"

Though brighter, the room he entered was sparsely furnished and its size reminded him of Mezzanotte's office. Despite its twilight, all of its furnishings appeared well-made and well-decorated. But when finally his eyes adjusted, he was startled to see that the stone walls all around were cluttered to the high ceiling with paintings. He stood very still as his eyes moved from one compelling image of bright, pink flesh against flesh to the next, and all these demanded some moments to review. Of various sizes but all in brightly gilt frames, the subject of each was a scene of remarkable lasciviousness. As charmed as Pierre was excited, he was startled to hear quiet chuckling immediately behind him. He turned to find a tall, slim man, his long silver hair swept back and receding to a broad bright forehead. His face was dark and square, and his brown eyes sparkled with good humor. Behind his wiry gray beard he grinned.

Leaning toward Pierre he said, "A trick I learned from the Bishop of Ravenna; tends to detain the visitor and thereby permit observation and judgment."

After a moment Pierre said, "How did I do?"

The Marques d'Ostia shrugged. "Had you expressed shock or distaste I would have seen you as one sort of hypocrite. But by pretending to ignore them, I would have seen you as another sort of scoundrel. Thus, I must assume you are run-of-the-mill and otherwise unremarkable; I hope you are not disappointed."

"Is there any value in being average?"

"The tallest tree always feels the ax first, so yes, there is value in being average."

"You called me here for this meeting so I can't be absolutely average."

The Marques leaned toward Pierre and lightly patted his forearm. "There, there, dear boy, no need to be testy, especially as this is our first conversation. Come," he said and turned with his hand still on Pierre's arm, "follow me. Refreshments await."

He led Pierre through a doorway into a larger and much brighter room also well-furnished and with three tall windows shuttered against the late-day sun but otherwise undecorated. A couch with a single large chair facing it and a small table between; on the table stood a glass carafe along with two small cups. The Marques nodded toward the chair as he sat down on the couch.

Lifting the carafe the Marques gestured toward Pierre saying, "Made from lemons." He removed its stopper and poured small amounts of a pale yellow liquid into each cup. "A specialty of the island and very popular; I hope you enjoy it.

"I was told of this drink by someone else." He took the offered cup. "But I live to learn."

Bringing a cup to his lips the Marques smiled. "The only certain way to draw profit from this life."

Its taste startled Pierre. As the Countess had described, sour lemon blended with a bit of sweetness. With the second sip its flavor seemed less astringent. After the third he decided it was pleasantly refreshing.

The Marques said, "As you have discovered, your arrival has been anticipated and the topic of many conversations. As you have also discovered, if there was as much intelligence as curiosity, certain delusions would be avoided."

"And distinguishing the one from the other suggests a lot of optimism," Pierre said. "Sorting through those distinctions would leave me dizzy."

"Understandable," the Marques said, "considering how delusional some among us are. But our host is certain his problem is solvable so, as he is a generous host, we are obliged to try."

"You have little faith in the project."

"On the contrary, I have no faith."

"What is it the Signor expects you to convince me of?"

The Marques hesitated. "Strictly speaking, he expects me to convince you of nothing. He has asked that I explain the significance of this creature to his future. Having heard my explanation he believes you will recognize the need as well as the value of your participation and will offer your assistance by your own free will."

Pierre laughed. "Quite an assignment."

The Marques shrugged looking away. "Having learned the facts, in the end you will see no alternative except to help. I merely need to convince you that all of his facts are factual."

"Fair enough," Pierre said. "But a word of warning; unless you know something I don't, I possess all the facts I need to make that judgment. And based on those, I'm certain the creature can't be defeated by any device available to man."

The Marques studied Pierre but then smiled. "The facts you possess are considerable, but they are not all of the relevant facts. We can appreciate that you find your experiences compelling and that, so compelled, your reluctance is also compelling. Still, let's review your facts but from a different angle. Is that acceptable?"

Pierre folded his arms and leaned back in his chair. The Marques said, "Let me begin by agreeing that your experiences would convince you the creature is invulnerable. What I simply insist here is that the creature and its actions have such wide-ranging impact it can no longer be ignored. Yet, to accurately recognize the cumulative effect of its actions, one needs the resources of someone like the Signor with his accumulation of reports from around the world. By their review, a pattern of activity has emerged. Are you with me so far?"

Pierre nodded, his impatience beginning to rise though he said nothing.

"Now, in addition to your own encounters with this creature, other conflicts have been reported and by them your beast has destroyed other ships and devastated other crews in situations where you were not present. Still, the Signor remains convinced you and that creature share some peculiar communication. One might assume those widely-separated appearances would contradict such a conclusion if not disprove it all together, yet the Signor is content with his own conclusion." The Marques smiled. "It is precisely because all of this is unlikely that you should find it all reassuring."

"My relief is without end," he said. But the Marques was partially correct; Pierre was surprised by his own sense of relief.

"Very good," he said. "Now, as far as you and I are concerned your reluctance to join his effort, though unjustified, is understandable. The Signor has asked that I simply relieve you of certain anxieties so that you can confidently consider ways of destroying this creature."

Pierre hesitated. "Whatever your intention, the facts you're ignoring remain facts. Most important, the fact I've witnessed desperate efforts against that beast using every sort of weapon available. Even cannon-shot fired point-blank had as much effect on it as a face full of rain."

The Marques studied Pierre and then shrugged. "Your report simply emphasizes the necessity that we discover new weapons. But please," he said refilling both of their cups, "the Signor is certain I will convince you of the necessity of destroying the beast if I describe to you the significance of its threat. In order to do that I must describe certain relations those activities continue to thwart. Still with me?"

Pierre's frustration deepened. "You explain these things as though I was a child and this world a treacherous swamp where I'll make no progress without someone's endless lecture."

The Marques's laugh was bright and this startled Pierre. Catching his breath he said, "I cannot be sure whether your impatience is assurance of your intelligence or the hopelessness of your delusion. You present me with a puzzle. Since you cannot concur with my appraisal, let me add this. A new world has begun to emerge, and with it elements of the past are about to be discarded. Your experiments have demonstrated that what was once regarded as settled knowledge is not merely wrong but resists progress. I remind you many areas of thought remain burdened by the confused ideas of ancient thinkers, and among those is wealth."

Pierre felt suddenly confused, and noticing this left the Marques as much amused as relieved. "Our ideas concerning wealth have always been entangled with notions about God and morality. Yet, just as our knowledge of the natural world is being disentangled from assertions of God's will, and just as the position and movement of the earth has revealed its own laws separate from God's decisions, so also has wealth, its accumulation and its movement. While its rules continue to emerge gradually and only with experiment and experience, it is here that the creature proves most destructive."

The Marques paused and Pierre guessed for dramatic effect, but instead he took that moment simply to refill their glasses. "The clearest expression of these new laws," he continued, "is in the transportation and distribution of goods. And in that, Signor Mezzanotte stands in the forefront. Simply put, the highest price for goods can only be achieved through their widest distribution. Thus, if a French producer only sells his products within France, he is unlikely to receive as high a price as he might by selling those same products in New Spain. But as you know, the King of France and the King of Spain and every other monarch conspires to make certain that never happens, mistakenly believing those restrictions are in their best interest. But now and finally, men like the Signor demonstrate that conclusion is destructively false, and evidence of how false accumulates with each passing day. Yet it is precisely this accumulation of evidence which the beast seems determined to prevent. You may not be aware of this, but the Signor employs a man whose sole task is to calculate the likely success of each of his voyages of trade and commerce."

"Actually," Pierre said, his patience for this lecture near its limit, "that's been explained to me."

The Marques nodded without conviction. "What you have not been told is the person assigned to that role is your father, Augustus." He sat back to watch Pierre. "I hope this news pleases you."

Pierre smirked. "I've already heard that from others and so I look forward to meeting with him. But why didn't the Signor confirm this to me earlier?"

His words seemed to catch the Marques by surprise, but his composure instantly returned. With a dismissive wave of his hand he said, "Ah, and who of us can know the operation of the mind of another. Perhaps he regards such information as leverage to induce your participation. It is best to assume he has reasons he will reveal when their revelation is useful."

His words left Pierre annoyed since he had suspected all of this from the start. The Marques watched him another moment. "But we shall leave that aside and instead let me describe the difficulties your creature creates." He paused and hesitated. "The calculations performed as I mentioned take into account all conceivable variables; from prevailing winds and currents to the likelihood of pirate attack along with the prevailing price for a commodity at various ports. Each condition involves calculable odds along with their variables, and all reduced to numbers. In passing, let me assure you the results of those calculations are disarmingly consistent. Yet, when the beast's activities are included within those calculations, results become all but meaningless." He leaned forward and in a quiet voice added, "This recognition is the result of your father's work." He leaned back then and watched Pierre.

Pierre sipped his drink. "Your need doesn't make the beast's destruction any easier or more likely."

"An interesting distinction," the Marques said, "but in this instance not useful. No doubt its destruction will demand exceptional ingenuity, but the Signor also understands that an extraordinary solution demands a thinker capable of extraordinary thoughts." He paused. "I encourage you to see yourself as that thinker." Once again he leaned back, but now smiling. "I hope the light of understanding begins to dawn."

"That light," Pierre said, "is brutally harsh; especially as it illuminates the conclusion that I'm about to be killed and not in a nice way."

"My boy," the Marques said with an affectionate chuckle, "resist the temptation to think childishly about these matters. This challenge demands subtle consideration unclouded by emotions, least of all by fear. We are all about to die, and only children and fools fail to assume this. You have an opportunity to save not only yourself but the entire world. Think about it; though it may cost your life, your effort will be noble to the point of heroism. Among our ancestors such an opportunity would have been regarded a priceless gift, and not the terrifying burden you believe it to be."

The Marques waited for a response and Pierre recognized this but he was so deeply perplexed he could not find words for his confusion. Finally the Marques said, "I have no difficulty imagining the depth of your fear. But you have read the ancient Greeks, so you know that for them, fear of mere death was ignoble. The only important question is how one dies." He added, "You are on the threshold of a grand enterprise that will lead to a monumental achievement. Surely trepidation cannot rule your mind; surely you put fear behind you as you pursue greatness."

"Funny," Pierre said with a smirk. "You speak casually of my death, and my life is of so little consequence to you that you believe fine words and noble sentiments will lead me to value it as little as you do. That's all pretty funny."

The Marques' expression darkened. "I assure you that humor has no place in your deliberations. If I have failed to convince you of my request, so much the worse for me. But my failure does not mean the importance I speak of does not exist; the beast's threat remains and it is approaching." His frustration with Pierre seemed finally to overwhelm him. "Signor Mezzanotte requested that I convince you to join his crusade. If I have failed, I will report this to him. But I tell you honestly, I do not believe I have failed. Whatever your thoughts are now, upon reflection you will recognize you have no choice but to participate, and any other decision is evidence of cowardice." He spoke so emphatically that Pierre was startled.

"Glory or death," Pierre finally said.

"Glory in death," the Marques said defiantly. "Death is certain and inevitable but glory remains for those prepared to grasp it."

Pierre began to laugh. "Why is it that you judge my life so cheap you're happy to invite me to die and offer thanks for the chance? This creature is keeping you all from making as much money as you wish, so first thing you do, you find a young guy to die over it. And when I'm dead will you offer a reward to my mother? And what if I'm only injured? What if my leg gets smashed and I limp for the rest of my life? Who looks out for me then?" He looked about. "Mezzanotte thinks I'll risk my life to save his wealth, as if that was some sacred cause. Do I have all that right?"

The Marques' expression hovered between frustration and anger. "You are asked to assist for a specific reason; your skills and experience make you uniquely valuable to this enterprise. The Signor cannot, upon your refusal, simply go to someone else. Do not insult our intelligence. You may allow fear to control your mind, but do not pretend that is of no consequence. Besides, you speak as if you could simply walk away from this creature and have nothing more to do with it, even though your experiences insist otherwise. If you abandon this opportunity to change the world I cannot stop you. But that decision will not please the Signor, and what he does about his disappointment you leave entirely up to him."

There was a quiet knock at the door and it opened after a moment to reveal Lorenzo. The Marques turned to Pierre. "Your escort awaits and this interview is ended. But reconsider your decision, if only to protect your father." He stood, walked to a window and, with his hands locked together behind his back, he stared out.

Pierre asked, "What does he have to do with all this? Does my father expect me to help Mezzanotte as well? And what'll happen to him if I don't?" The Marques did not turn or speak, but stared through the window as if Pierre had already gone.

Pierre stood and followed Lorenzo out of the building.

CHAPTER THIRTEEN

OUT AGAIN UNDER the sharp bright sun, Pierre and Lorenzo walked back toward the palace. Pierre now wondered how his refusal to help Mezzanotte might place Augustus in danger. Lorenzo turned and said, "I hope your interview went well."

Pierre said, "Depends on what you think of as going well."

"It went well if you reached an agreement. Do you have another criterion in mind?"

Pierre suddenly began to laugh. "Success is a slippery notion. Mezzanotte's response will tell me if our meeting went well."

"Permitting another to define our success is a strategy full of traps. We should set our own criterion, if only because it invites us to justify it."

Their path took them past the dolphin fountain burbling and splashing in sun-blanched solitude. Inside, Lorenzo led him back through the palace's twilight to the door of his room and then stopped. Without turning to face him, Lorenzo said, "Signor Mezzanotte is a persuasive man, infinitely skilled at resolving difficulties. Like his requests, his decisions are never frivolous or ill-considered. Though it may seem unlikely, in the end you will find your way clear to do as he wishes." He bowed then and left.

Pierre entered his room confused and annoyed but mostly frustrated since he was certain Lorenzo was correct and despite its danger eventually he would join Mezzanotte's plan. And because once again he was reminded there is no negotiation without leverage. He recalled Shark's witless attempt to cheat at cards. Despite his posturing, Shark had to take his beating; there was nothing he could use to negotiate his way out of it. So Pierre began again to wonder if there was a path of escape to save him from another confrontation with the creature.

Sunlight slanted through his window and Pierre went to close its shutters against it. But at the window he found himself charmed by the sight of the countryside spread before him like a tan and green blanket, generous and inviting, and then further on, those mountains reaching into the blue sky beyond. It all reminded him of his confinement. Anything resembling freedom lay just beyond those pale mountains, as seductive as the pleasures portrayed in the paintings he had seen in the Marques' antechamber. Not everyone, he reminded himself, needed his death to assure their personal success. But thinking about the vast world beyond these walls, he reminded himself that the beast was out there as well, still looking for him and for him alone. Whatever else, that creature was out there with an entirely different plan for his future.

He wondered if Mezzanotte was correct after all, and his confrontation with the creature was inevitable, and so in order for Pierre to move ahead in this world he first needed to defeat it. This led him to wonder again about Augustus. Would Pierre's refusal put Augustus's life in jeopardy, and would the Signor then use Augustus to exact revenge? On the other hand, if Augustus's skill at calculation really was that useful to Mezzanotte, would he risk it in order to compel Pierre's help? And even if that was merely a possibility, was it right for him to run that risk in exchange for his own freedom? His own thoughts, Pierre realized, had become circular. Each question implied another and each response was nullified by the next.

He needed time to sort through these conflicts, so instead of trying to force a conclusion, he assumed he had made all the progress possible for that day and some considerations would simply need to wait until tomorrow. Perhaps he now was just too tired to think clearly. Perhaps he had reached his limit for the day and it was now time to put reflection aside. He glanced behind him to the wide, soft bed, and in an instant he knew what he wanted to do.

Pierre stretched out and the bed seemed to embrace him, to enfold him as if the bed was pleased that he had decided to lie upon it. He closed his eyes though a cacophony of voices filled his head. Behind his eyes those voices battled for his attention and he stepped back inviting them to settle things among themselves certain he would need to battle only the one that emerged victorious.

Eventually those voices grew quiet, the darkness behind his eyes became thick and deep, and Pierre felt himself fall in a comforting drift until that darkness took on a deepening red hue. That aura of red gradually became brighter and acquired an orange cast. Growing brighter still, slowly it separated into points of light. Those points became precise and specific and then he recognized them as bonfires, and sensed the presence of people nearby. His sense of their presence grew stronger as they separated into individuals, became numerous and then numberless, all gathered around bonfires of light. Those fires multiplied as the individuals around them multiplied, until Pierre stood in the midst of a plane surrounded by countless enormous bonfires, each itself surrounded by a multitude of people. Suddenly all of those people turned to look at him before turning to stare past him and into the darkness. Pierre attempted to turn but failed. Then he heard the roar of the creature, so loud and clear it was as if he stood beside it. That was when he awoke.

Pierre opened his eyes to a twilight burnished darkly red pouring through his window, and it took a moment to realize the candles on his table were alight and a small fire burned in his fireplace. With a second glance he discovered a meal had been set out for him on the table. Sight of the food awakened his appetite, so he moved to stand, and that was when he discovered a weight laying in the bed beside him.

"Did I wake you?" The voice startled him and Pierre turned to find the Marquesa lying beside him. Beside a cascade of her red hair, her lively amber eyes looked warmly into his and she smiled. "You slept so soundly I tried not to disturb your well-earned rest."

Pierre struggled to disguise his astonishment. "I'm relieved that you failed. I'd count myself the worst of cads if I had not noticed your presence." He glanced about and saw her clothes piled colorfully on the floor beside the bed. Nodding toward the food on the table he said, "It appears Lorenzo brought my dinner, unless that was your kindness. And I'm famished. Would you like to join me?"

"It appears I already have," she said giggling mischievously, and he was reminded of her laughter's delight. "It was Lorenzo who brought your food. Thank you for your offer. I have already eaten, but perhaps just a bite or two to keep you company."

Pierre stood from the bed and, while the Marquesa propped up her pillow, he dragged the table to its side. She took a dried fig from the platter and leaned back nibbling at it as she watched Pierre eat. She said, "The Countess is very charming. I am certain her tour of the grounds was as informative as it was pleasurable." She looked at him with an expectant smile.

"She seemed to know the names of every plant and flower. But she also seems well-informed about Mezzanotte's operation. And she seems to know important participants."

"As should be expected since she is a skillful negotiator. She and the Duke d'Orange form a powerful team; I shall introduce you to him. He and the Viscount contract with those voyages the Signor invests in." She paused. "Have I satisfied all of your curiosities?"

Pierre said, "It's funny the Duke's name never came up in our conversation. But my curiosities are infinite and never totally satisfied, so it's nice of you to think of it. Tell me this; Mezzanotte is a man of wealth and status but can he hope to expel the Spanish from Sicily?"

The Marquesa studied him with mild amusement. "For him, only that mission justifies his wealth and status. His love of this island and its people is without limit. Recalling those glorious decades under the Norman kings, the Signor becomes rhapsodic, and he is determined to revive their glory. He will bring about that new age where Sicily stands as a beacon to mankind's noblest goals and highest aspirations."

Pierre said, "So his commitment to the French king is opportunistic at most."

"He recognizes France's power and how useful it would be to his mission. Perhaps he envisions a time when the French crown will be both ally and protector of an independent Sicily. But independence for this island is his ultimate goal, whatever else any alliance might offer."

"With himself at its head, of course."

"Of course." The Marquesa's smirk was as charming as her laughter. "He is confident that since he has both fought for and paid for this island's independence, and since he has the best interests of the island in mind, he has earned that privilege."

"This is just a guess, but I'll assume there are other landowners just as certain they deserve that position and its prestige."

"Large landowners certainly and of course, but also those who own no land at all. We have no shortage of families certain their prerogatives reach back to Caesar Augustus himself, even though, confronted by Signor Mezzanotte's wealth and force of arms, such claims tend to fade into self-flattering rhetoric. But as you suggest, success in expelling the Spanish alone will not bring about that glorious era of peace and freedom of which he dreams."

"Should I assume the Pope is less than enthusiastic about this plan as well?"

"In fact, His Holiness is ambivalent. On the one hand, he is certain the Signor is a godless heathen and an offspring of Satan. But on the other, he recognizes that both Spain and France have grown too powerful for his office to dominate. Removal of Sicily from either of their realms would cut at least one of them down just a bit. An independent Sicily, whatever its power, would remain vulnerable to Papal interference. Although His Holiness has no doubt Mezzanotte would resist his interference in the island's affairs, he knows others on the island who would encourage that interference."

"So Mezzanotte's prepared to expend blood and treasure to free the island from all of their influences just as long as his own influence replaces it."

"And only as long as Sicily's independence is not illusory. He will tolerate nominal involvement by others as long as his own control is literal and material."

Pierre had nearly finished the meal and now he leaned back with a sigh. The Marquesa watched him with a coquettish smile. He said, "Well tell me this, then; what role in this plan does Commander Genovese occupy?"

The Marquesa's eyes grew large but slowly her smile returned. "An excellent question and to be honest, there is no consensus on its response. The current rumor is that he was discovered conspiring with an island chieftain and against the Signor's interests. Although young, the chieftain in question died suddenly and under unlikely circumstances and nothing was charged against the Commander. Some believe the Signor simply bides his time and follows the old proverb of keeping friends close and enemies closer."

Pierre could not resist smiling. "And is that how you see your own situation?"

The Marquesa shook her head although her smile remained. "The Commander is charming and widely regarded as clever and certainly far more clever than I. And although he presents himself as a dedicated patriot, it is possible his notion of patriotism justifies an alliance with someone other than the Signor in a simple grab for power. Others have suggested his ambition is grander than he will ever admit."

"Exactly what responsibilities does he have within the palace?"

The Marques laughter was suddenly warm and bright. "Signor Mezzanotte has made him responsible for his palace's security. That may sound unlikely and even counter-intuitive, but in fact, with that responsibility the Signor is more easily able to observe him and judge his loyalty."

"And what about you?" Pierre asked. "How would you describe your loyalty to him?"

She turned and sighed, her smile faded as she looked beyond Pierre and out through the window. After another moment she turned back, her face nearly without expression. "To burnish his credentials as a supporter of the people and savior of his nation the Signor has confiscated idle land and given it to ambitious peasants. So merely for that reason and its insult to the divinely decreed hierarchy, there are many among the clergy and aristocracy who look forward to spitting into his dead face. The aristocracy particularly has become prosperous and content in support of Spanish rulers, and so will actively resist its disruption. But, having noted that, there remain some who cultivate patriotic sentiment hopeful independence will add to their holdings and fortunes. Whether that is justified only the Signor can say with certainty. But for myself, I confess that I believe appeals to freedom and independence lead inevitably to enslavement and oppression. When it comes to the affairs of men I am no optimist. Whatever else, the Sicilian aristocracy has entered a phase of profound degeneracy and the Signor's activities have stimulated certain portions of that aristocracy, even if only to fight to preserve their own wealth and privilege. So, while I have no enthusiasm for his program, his presence on the island has had a salutary effect. Above all, he has reminded every family that change comes quickly and not necessarily to their benefit. His presence has awakened the patriotic impulse, or at least its simulacra; for good or for ill."

"And what else can you tell me about the Commander?"

The Marquesa looked at Pierre a moment as her smile turned to mild surprise. "I hope the Commander is flattered when he learns of your curiosity."

"And will that happen?"

"That all depends."

"Depends on what?"

"On whatever happens next."

Pierre smiled and moved closer to the Marquesa. "Tell me just one more thing and I promise it will be my last question. You know that Signor Mezzanotte believes I can destroy that creature for him. Do you think I should take up that challenge?"

Suddenly her expression seemed to suggest surprise that Pierre would even consider the question. "You are right about one thing; that question supersedes all others." She paused. "Obviously I am no expert on the creature, though I have learned something about it through reports I have reads. Men are superbly capable of killing each other and have no need of assistance from any other creature. At the same time, valuable goods as well as the lives of hard-working men are sent to the bottom of the ocean. Merely with that, I agree this creature does great harm and without any corresponding good and conclude the world will be a better place when it is destroyed. At least then, the grand game of political power will advance without interference by any unaccountable players. The future has yet to be written, but there is no doubt that future will be clearer, if not also brighter, without the presence of the beast."

"So you think I should do as Signor Mezzanotte has asked?"

"Yes," the Marquesa said. She smiled then, pressing against him. "But not right now."

CHAPTER FOURTEEN

PIERRE OPENED HIS eyes to watch Lorenzo place a platter of bread, cheese and fruit beside a flagon of water on the small table. He struggled to wake himself but when he turned to find he was otherwise alone he was not surprised, though he was impressed by his own sense of disappointment. Beyond his window, the sky was gray with low, continuous clouds billowed like plumped wool. The air was cool, thick and damp, and worse, Pierre's head throbbed as if he fought a hangover. "What time is it?"

Lorenzo looked over to him startled, as if he had been caught at something he should not have been doing. "You have slept deeply," he said. His alarm was replaced with a smile. "Though one might not believe it from the view through the window, we are approaching mid-day. The Signor suggested I wake you earlier, but you slept so soundly it seemed cruel to do so."

"For some reason I found it difficult to fall asleep." Rubbing his eyes he wondered if Lorenzo recognized his lie but his expression betrayed nothing.

"No doubt," Lorenzo suggested, "the result of the excitement of the last several days."

He yawned again and stretched. "Whatever the reason, I'm hungry and thirsty so I'm grateful for what you've brought."

"The Signor would not accept anything less. He asks that you prepare to meet with his advisers. It seems there have been disturbing developments and he wishes them to discuss the situation with you."

"More bad news about the creature, no doubt," Pierre said. He stood and made his way to the table.

"Quite likely." Lorenzo stepped toward the door. "In an hour I will return to escort you to the meeting." Pierre sat down to his meal and watched as Lorenzo left.

He ate pondering what this news would amount to. He did not look forward to this meeting. He would be asked questions he could not answer involving matters he did not understand. Having nothing useful to add he was certain he would disappoint those he did not make angry. And with that, Mezzanotte would question the value of his presence. But Pierre still might learn something about Augustus, and so he might benefit from this meeting after all. He finished his meal and washed and changed into those fresh clothes he found set out for him. Soon after, Lorenzo appeared at his door.

He led Pierre out of the palace and across the plaza past the dolphin fountain splashing noisily under that chill and gray sky to a narrow, three-story building built against the higher compound wall. Beyond the front door they climbed a brightly decorated staircase to its top floor and a pair of tall, wide doors, one slightly opened revealing a group of men seated around a large round table. Lorenzo glanced at Pierre. "It appears the others have gathered. Good luck." He turned then and left.

As Pierre entered the room, all heads turned. A silver-haired man Pierre recognized as the Marquise d'Ostia stood at the head of the table. "Gentleman," he announced, "our guest of honor has arrived." He then introduced Pierre to the others providing names Pierre would not retain before he gestured to an empty chair to his right. Pierre made his way to the offered seat as the Marquise continued.

"Our host has asked that we gather to discuss a piece of information concerning a profound threat to his enterprises. For this discussion Signor Chanceux has been invited to join us. He possesses certain knowledge derived from direct experiences of the beast and our host is confident he will assist our deliberation. And to be clear, our deliberations have gained urgency with new information which amounts to this: the creature has been seen approaching the Pillars of Hercules. Thus, we are asked to plan for its arrival on our shores within just a few weeks. Time is passing, gentlemen, and delay will prove fatal." Nodding to the man seated directly across from Pierre, he said, "I suggest that our colleague, Dr. Ginesterra, begin."

A gaunt, angular man with large, hollow eyes and a narrow and stringy black beard, Dr. Ginesterra had a large book open before him, a pen in his hand and a container of ink beside it. He wrote and then, with his pen poised, asked if Pierre believed the creature was mortal. The simple bluntness of this question stunned him. He answered that he had harbored doubts, but then described the battle involving the ships of Mezzanotte and the Sheikh. He asserted his belief that some element of the fusillade of cannon-fire had caused the creature to change its intention, and that this suggested it experienced physical pain which suggested it was mortal.

The next man, Father Danton, a plump, round-face and fair-haired man, asked whether the creature moved across land as easily as through water, and how such movement was accomplished. Pierre described the beast's two enormous and powerful legs and its forelimbs though relatively small and of limited use. He then described its thick and long tail that it used with devastating effect, and described the way it moved that tail with tremendous power.

His questioning passed to Count Regurio, a meek-looking, quietly spoken man with piercing blue eyes, who asked if Pierre had observed anything which might repel the creature. When Pierre acknowledged he had seen nothing like that, the table became silent and even Dr. Ginesterra stopped writing. The next man, Brother Alphonso, a broad-shouldered and thickly-bearded man, broke their silence asking if he believed the creature was a direct creation of Satan. Startled again, Pierre's response was emphatic that he saw no reason to suspect such a thing.

Dr. Ginesterra followed by asking if Pierre observed that the creature had an equal taste for heathen and Christian flesh. Pierre described how it appeared to devour men indifferent to their religious convictions. This response created even more consternation.

Professor Marconi, a trim, thickly-muscled man who had sat in a contemplative silence, then asked bluntly if Pierre had any ideas of how the creature might be destroyed. It seemed to Pierre that everyone around the table then held their breath. After a long pause he said, "Although I haven't reached a conclusion, a strategy has occurred to me that might prove effective."

Silence froze the room until Dr. Ginesterra asked, "Can you elaborate on this idea?"

Pierre hesitated unsure of what among his thoughts he should reveal. "The beast is enormous and powerful and if this strategy fails, even more death and destruction will result. What I have in mind is unprecedented as is the danger it's designed to confront. Further, it will likely demand considerable resources and many men. For the moment, I will only say I'm prepared to work with you and even put my own life at risk, if that will somehow assure success."

When he finished the silence that followed descended like a wool blanket over everyone until Dr. Ginesttera said, "You say your strategy will prove dangerous and expensive yet you offer no promise of success. Putting aside whether your life need be held ransom, is there anything more you are prepared to tell us?"

Trapped now by his own words, Pierre looked around the table again. "Two days hence I'll offer my proposal and it will include quantities and dimensions of material and number of participants. Will that prove sufficient?"

Nodding heads seemed to assure general approval. "When we meet again I'll invite you all to scrutinize my plan." He stood then and left the room.

Outside he found Lorenzo standing beside the door. He said to Pierre, "From your expression I trust this meeting went somewhat better."

"Well enough," Pierre said though his thoughts were dark with anxiety. Lorenzo led their way along the silent corridor and toward the stairway. "Meetings are easy," Pierre added, "killing monsters is hard." About to descend the stairs he reached out for the rail and glanced down at his hand; it was shaking.

When they reached Pierre's room he asked Lorenzo to bring quill pens, a straight-edge, large sheets of drawing paper and a large-scale map of the area. Lorenzo agreed and left.

Pierre struggled to order the thoughts that might describe and elaborate what was beginning to appear a glimmer of an idea. But an even larger doubt confounded him; could any idea bring down a creature broader than the largest palace, taller than the highest hill, and more powerful than the mightiest army?

Seated at the couch and staring out to the gray sky and darker hills, Pierre wondered until Lorenzo arrived with his arms full of the equipment and paper he had requested. He asked that Lorenzo return with candles and that, still later, bring his evening meal. Pierre assumed a long night of work so that, deep into the night, it would be best that he run out of nothing.

Lorenzo returned with Pierre's meal to find him lying on his back on his bed. His sarcasm was good-humored. "I hope I am not disturbing your contemplation."

"I have an odd question," Pierre said still reclining. "Mezzanotte's a man of power and wealth but do you admire him? I mean, do you believe him to be as just and honorable as he is powerful?"

Lorenzo hesitated as if sorting through his thoughts. "He took me into his service as a very young man. You see, my father had died leaving my mother to care for my younger brother and sister as well as myself. But her tiny plot of land could never quite support us, even in times of plenty, and many nights we went to bed hungry. Often we were rented to neighboring farms as help, in exchange for small amounts of food. But after I joined the Signor's household, my brother was accepted into the priesthood and my sister was well-married with a substantial dowry, and now my mother lives in comfort and security; all of that was a result of Signor Mezzanotte's guidance and generosity. Despite the wealth of our country, poverty among us is nearly universal. If he has not generally provided the one, he has spared many of us at least from the other."

"But at least as far as you're concerned, is he a man who will keep his promise?"

Lorenzo again hesitated. "If he has made a promise, be certain he will keep it. Has he made such a promise?"

Pierre stood from the bed slowly as though determined to shake off a deep confusion. "He will if he expects my help." Pierre moved to the table, sat and began to eat. "Just one more thing; I'm told he imagines himself an old-style patriot determined to lead an independent Sicily. Is that how you see him?"

Lorenzo looked at Pierre with an expression he had not seen before; mistrust and something that resembled hostility. "If our island was determined to free itself from the misery of foreign occupation, we could choose no better leader. And if he organized an army to expel these foreigners, I would join instantly and feel honored to do so. And were I to die in his service, I would regard it as a heroic death on behalf of my people." He looked about as if embarrassed. "Your question draws upon deep sentiments. If I have not answered your question, I hope at least I have caused no concern." His expression softened and he moved toward the door.

Pierre said, "Nothing of this need leave this room."

Lorenzo nodded and then asked if he needed anything more.

"Please return around midnight. By then I'll need more of just about everything."

With that Lorenzo bowed. "It will be my pleasure," he said and then he was gone.

When he finished his meal, Pierre cleared the table and spread out paper and drawing equipment. His idea to defeat the creature remained both vague and peculiar. He scrutinized the map as if something there might offer a suggestion. Uncertain of his strategy, he searched for a location sufficient at least for the scale of his task. His idea, he was certain, would need to be grand if only to match the grandeur of his adversary. Eventually he began to sketch and figure.

He covered a sheet with lines and numbers, balled it up and tossed it aside, covered another, balled that up and tossed it aside and then began a third. After several hours he found himself finally lost with his head filled and nothing resolved. Suddenly, he heard a quiet knock at his door. Remembering Lorenzo's promise he called out, "Enter." So he was startled when the door opened and the Abbess appeared carrying a tray. Seeing his expression she smiled.

"Lorenzo is invaluable," she said, "and I cannot think what we would do without him." She carried the tray toward the table, saw the clutter there, put the tray carefully on the seat of an unoccupied chair and then sat down on the couch.

Still startled Pierre said, "I've no doubt you have many helpful friends." Her arrival finally pleased him despite his surprise and its distraction and interruption.

"Are you disappointed I am not Lorenzo?" Her tone of hurt feelings confused Pierre. "I will happily fetch him if you prefer his company." But Pierre reminded himself he was dealing with a woman of unconventional outlook and that he should be glad of that fact. He glanced down at what he had been working on and resigned himself that events for the moment had escaped his control. There are times, he reminded himself, when conversation is the better part of valor.

"No, just the contrary. Besides, this seems a perfect time to rest."

"If that is your way of saying you have looked forward to my visit and cherish this opportunity to spend time in my company, I am flattered and relieved I chose to do as I have."

"And I'm relieved you've so thoroughly guessed my thoughts."

"Good!" she said and her expression was finally pleased. "Tell me how your work is going."

Shaking his head Pierre tossed the quill onto the table, leaned back in his chair and sighed. "I began with a nearly nonexistent idea, so I should be satisfied with the little I've accomplished, or at least relieved I've accomplished anything at all."

"And yet you sound neither satisfied nor relieved."

Pierre was stung with embarrassment. "Fair enough, you've caught me; I'm good at complaining about what doesn't exist rather than being satisfied with what does."

"The beginning of self-knowledge, an accomplishment by itself."

"And yet I'm no closer to my objective."

"Rumor has it you promised to present a plan to Signor Mezzanotte's counselors."

Startled, Pierre again sighed. "Word gets around; I should remember that. In thirty-six hours I've promised to offer a plan to a group of men, each of whom is smarter than the smartest I've ever met, and which will describe how to defeat a creature more powerful than any ever encountered."

Sympathy fell like a shadow across the Abbess's face. "You sound as though you could use some rest, so it is indeed fortunate for you that I arrived when I did."

Finally Pierre laughed. "You've got me again. Having demonstrated that you, too, are smarter than I am, would you please take over this project?"

Surprise close to shock appeared on her face. "If that is intended as a compliment it has failed and I am not flattered. You possess experience and knowledge, in fact far more of both than anyone who will review your plan. But be that as it may, you have made your promise and now you must keep it." Her expression relaxed. "Perhaps describing your plan aloud might clear your thoughts. I have no advice, but the mere exercise might prove useful."

Her suggestion tempted Pierre but not enough to agree. "Thanks, but I'm probably better off wrestling with this daemon alone. So tell me how you've spent this lovely day." He cleared the table and moved the tray of food onto it and then watching her, he began to eat.

Whether she was startled by his suggestion or pleased by his curiosity and this opportunity to talk about herself, as he ate she described a conversation with Cardinal Arugulas concerning an uprising of peasants in Calabria, and then a stroll through the garden with Commander Picolloni of the Venetian navy. The Commander described his concern over the deployment of his fleet in anticipation of a challenge from a flotilla stationed on Crete. Her best suggestion was that he should speak with Lautramont de Perpignan, the Cypriot ambassador and someone she assured him would likely prove useful for his problem.

Finally nearly finished with his meal, Pierre said, "An impressively productive day; I congratulate you for providing useful counsel to such eminent men."

The Abbess shrugged though she smiled obviously flattered by his words. "I was a bit jealous to see you walking with the Countess." She then confessed disappointment at not seeing him at dinner. His absence had led her to speak with Lorenzo, and thus her decision to visit him. "Destiny will not be denied."

"Since we're together by your decision, I'll confine my gratitude to the agent responsible."

A look of urgent concern came into her face. She leaned toward him, took his hand into hers and caressed it. "Can you doubt we have been destined to meet?"

He enjoyed having his hand held by her and found himself thrilled by her excitement, but her insistence bothered him. "Destiny's a topic I'm eager to avoid. If our meeting is a result of destiny then so are my encounters with the creature. If destiny exists, I must wonder if defeat of the creature is also destined. Otherwise, all of these plans are useless. Besides meeting you, destiny has not proceeded in my favor." He laughed to disguise his anxiety and his effort failed.

She sat back scrutinizing him with a quizzical look. "After a long and dangerous journey with all of its trouble, you find yourself here, and now that creature is catching up with you. So instead of finding shelter, you must prepare for battle and consider your own death. I do not know whether to admire you or pity you."

Pierre was so startled by her summary of his situation he laughed. He had not recognized himself until she described all of that, and now he was unsure whether to be grateful or embarrassed. She observed him in a way that made him uncomfortable, and he wondered how he might redeem himself from seeming to her both ludicrous and pathetic. Looking into her large, dark eyes he hoped she would recognize his honest confusion. Suddenly he wanted her to remain beside him even if only for a bit longer. And realizing this, sadness washed over him.

Perhaps she recognized all of this because her expression softened. She looked down at his finished meal and then at the paper and map and drawing equipment and balls of discarded paper scattered about the room. She stood, walked to the bed and sat on its edge. Then leaning forward she began to unfasten her shoes. "Your project, I am certain, will benefit from a short rest." Then she reached behind to unfasten her bodice.

He glanced at the drawings and calculations he had scrutinized for so long and then decided she was probably so right that nothing more needed to be said.

CHAPTER FIFTEEN

PIERRE AWOKE TO a sky beyond his window again filled with clouds the color of wood ash, thick and unyielding, and once again he was alone. He rolled over and buried his face in the hollow the Abbess' body had left inhaling its ghost of her flesh. His papers and map remained on the floor beside the table but he could not return his mind to their problem or that possible solution teasing the edge of his memory. As if at the margin of his vision he glimpsed a solution, but turning his attention fully to it, that notion evaporated like dew at sunrise. He stood from the bed, wrapped its blanket across his shoulders, returned to his chair at the table and retrieved his papers from the floor.

Elements of a plan gradually had acquired shape but how each would connect to the next evaded his thoughts. Staring out to a sky whose brooding reached to the horizon, he mused about connection and linkage though those thoughts swirled without a center. He visualized ways small pieces might connect to other small pieces to form a flexible and durable network, like so many small nets bound to larger, each connecting to the next in such a way that, repeated many times, those pieces would connect across space like a tapestry whose network resembled a rug. And thinking all of this, an idea formed as a sort of chain, a kind of network itself, links leading one to the next, tiny links bound together in a metal tapestry spread across the ground. A rug of such metal but large enough to cover the floor of a valley, even grand enough to cover the plain of Catania but so sturdy it could be trod upon by the largest creature on earth. But even more; large enough to trap and hold that creature so that it must go where it is dragged. Such a net would need to be more powerful than that creature it constrained, stronger in fact than the strongest net ever made and constructed to confine the largest creature ever conceived.

He leaned back eyes wide and breathing fast, a little astonished by what drifted before his eyes like those dusky dark clouds passing slowly toward the east. The enormity of the object that had begun to form within his mind startled and then frightened him. He stood from his chair, pulled the blanket more tightly across his shoulders and walked to the window.

The red tile roofs of smaller buildings in this damp and muted light tinted gray led his eyes to the far walls of the compound, and then further to roofs of buildings beyond his walls, their cascade receding into pale brown fields and the green points of umbrella cypress trees. There his eyes met misty, gray hills one after the next until they reached the crest of the furthest hill and crepuscular hilltops beyond. Recalling the map, he knew that beyond those hills lay the plain of Catania.

Against this backdrop his mind's eye saw the head of the creature in profile move majestically forward, vicious and defiant, its power unmatched by any on earth. So he again recognized that it was one challenge to trap a creature and another to dispose of it. His eyes followed rising hills until, misty in the distance, they were caught by the white-capped peak of Mount Etna with its lazy plume of pale smoke.

And the volcano seemed to stare back quizzically at Pierre, as if it too wondered how he might resolve his problem, a passive observer unimpressed by either Pierre or any other creature in this world. With half-lidded eyes it stared back at Pierre content to wait indifferent even until the day after the end of time. He turned from the window and looked back toward the paper scattered and spread across the floor and the table, and then he knew; in that moment, he knew.

His plan, or at least what was coming to seem a plan, appeared so suddenly its pieces interlocked behind his eyes with a nearly audible click, like the links in a network of chains, each connecting to the next larger and in a sequence itself precise and operating like gears in a clock, wheels within wheels, part to part. With the blanket still tight around his shoulders he returned to the bed and stretched out on his back. Just before he closed his eyes he saw that the sun had begun to work its way through those clouds and a brightening light came to paint the ceiling.

"It is nearly mid-day, sir, and I have your meal." Pierre recognized Lorenzo's voice. He opened his eyes to see him standing at the foot of his bed sharp-edged in the daylight.

"That's good of you because I'm starved." Pierre sat up and discovered himself smiling. Lorenzo put the tray carefully down on the only clear space on the table. Pierre stood pulling on his trousers and when he reached the table he swept it clear of the papers and moved the tray to its center. "Starved," he announced as if his hunger startled him. He fell easily into the chair.

Lorenzo glanced down at the paper scattered across the floor, the hint of a frown about his lips. "Should I assume your evening proved disappointing?"

At the question, Pierre's smile became a grin. "On the contrary, it couldn't have gone better. There's more to be done, but from here it's just a short walk down-hill."

Lorenzo looked at him curiously and took up the tray the Duchess di Nuovo Cento had left the night before. "I wondered about another aspect of your evening." At that Pierre began to laugh. "I meant," he added with mild embarrassment, "I hope I did not make a poor decision."

"Your decision was excellent, as was its timing. I'm grateful for your thoughtfulness. My only regret is that I can't think of a way to return that favor."

"I am pleased simply to have chosen well. Will there be anything else?"

Pierre reached for the food before him and then stopped. "Just one question; how is it that you know the Duchess?"

Lorenzo's eyes widened. "That answer would take us into complicated terrain. Suffice it to say both by personal inclination and political position, it is in her best interest to know as many people as she can. I would not betray her confidence but since I understand that you know each other well, I assume she has explained her role as a member of the Papal legation. I hope I do not betray a confidence by admitting that here, she operates as the Pope's eyes and ears to warn him when politically complicated events are about to transpire."

"As you say, we know each other rather well and she's described her considerable responsibilities; I'm just curious to know what those responsibilities currently are."

Lorenzo glanced down and Pierre assumed he was making a careful selection of his words. "As I said, I would not compromise her mission, but I believe I can safely tell you the Pope is eager to know where Signor Mezzanotte's allegiance will fall should the German Hohenstauphen princes advance against the Spanish Hapsburg house. His Holiness is well-aware of the Signor's antipathy toward the Spanish crown. Unfortunately, the Spanish have provided valuable support for the Roman cause in Germany; thus, our enemy remains his ally." Lorenzo looked cautiously about. "But please ask no more. Though it must seem unlikely, the problem you are aiding the Signor with is temporary and minor in comparison with others." Pierre found this surprising and Lorenzo must have recognized it. "Understand that when the beast has been disposed of, our island will still lay at the center of the Mediterranean."

Pierre nodded. "And the Duchess di Nuova Cento will still be in the service of His Holiness. I'm grateful for this reminder and for your willingness to share this confidence."

"A confidence I trust you will maintain." He glanced about. "If there is nothing else I will resume my duties. And unless you prefer otherwise, I will return later with your meal." Pierre thanked him again and Lorenzo was gone.

Though he reminded himself he had no right to be disappointed, Pierre found that he was. Whether he needed to imagine himself the Abbess's protector or rescuer or simply her escape from unpleasant situations, he needed to remember she was a skillful agent in the service of a powerful patron. More likely he had greater need of her help than she of his. And despite all that he had survived, he was as little capable of helping her as ever. So however the coming battle turned out, their paths would part and he must be prepared for that. In the end there was only himself and the creature, and the rest of the world would observe from a distance.

Clutching a crust of bread in one hand he reached to the floor and began to sort through his notes because finally he began to see his project complete to its edges. His meal finished he cleared its remains from the table, brought out a blank sheet of paper and began to draw a fair copy of the plan. He progressed slowly, confirming calculations and revising designs of each element. Even in its drawings, the structure with its connections appeared absurdly large, though he recognized that in the presence of the beast, even this would be dwarfed. He drew and revised and recalculated until there was a knock at his door.

His hopes rose suddenly only to be dashed when in the open door

Lorenzo appeared carrying a tray. He must have suspected the source of Pierre's disappointment. "Perhaps she has been detained," Lorenzo said. "Or hopes to avoid interrupting your work." He approached the table, but then set the tray on the seat of a chair by Pierre's side.

Pierre laughed. "That's considerate of you; to conjecture a reason for a failed assignation in order to spare my feelings. I'll certainly mention your thoughtfulness to Signor Mezzanotte."

"It did occur to me you hoped for a visitor other than myself."

"That's likely true although perhaps not as much as you may assume."

Lorenzo glanced at the sheet of paper beneath Pierre's hand. "And I will guess you have made progress today."

"That's a very good guess, indeed."

"And can I also guess you have nearly finished?"

Pierre shrugged. "Will that be reported to others?"

Lorenzo's eyes widened. "And who would that be reported to?"

Pierre studied him a moment but Lorenzo's expression was as opaque as a fog-bank at night. "That would depend upon whoever was curious to know."

Lorenzo shook his head. "That describes no one I know. But does it concern you?"

Pierre hesitated. "Since I'll offer this plan to Mezzanotte's committee tomorrow, I suppose it shouldn't."

"So in principle," he suggested archly, "this conversation is of no consequence."

"In principle, that is true, though in practice the result might prove different."

"I promise to keep that in mind," Lorenzo said with a touch of frost. "Will there be anything else?"

"Only that I'll anticipate your return in the morning." In response, Lorenzo bowed and with the tray from the previous meal in his hands left the room.

Pierre ate slowly as he reviewed his work. Design of the most complicated parts seemed finished and he simply needed to be certain he had missed nothing. But eventually he recognized a deepening suspicion; by this exercise he had merely deluded himself, and none of what he had drawn and figured would accomplish what he needed.

He struggled then against the suspicion this was merely a collection of clever gestures toward a device of no worth and ultimately this plan must fail. After all, the whole contraption might prove impossible to assemble, but even if its larger parts could be fabricated and assembled, the many smaller parts might prove impossible to join together with sufficient strength. And even if all were successfully manufactured and assembled, deploying this contraption might prove fatally unwieldy. But worst of all, having manufactured and assembled the parts, and having managed to deploy the mechanism, there was that possibility it would fail to accomplish what he had needed and leave the creature unaffected; it might not even notice that it was in danger. If the beast used all of its enormous power to struggle against confinement, could Pierre be certain these parts would continue to hold? If the most powerful creature under God's sun pressed hard against them, would his devices fail?

So he wondered if there was a way to test his plan; some useful way to simulate the power that would be pitted against it, a way to rig this device to make certain it would hold. On another sheet of paper he sketched possible tests he hoped could be assembled quickly. Time moved beneath Pierre as his quill moved over the paper. When several sheets were filled and discarded he looked up to decide there really was no more time for any of this. Just as it had come from his head and then appeared on paper, this was his only plan and it must work. The creature approached and there would be neither a second chance nor room for error.

But further and more complicated, he needed to trust that Mezzanotte would find the craftsmen to do those things he needed them to do; men who would successfully take a two-dimensional plan and conjure it into this three-dimensional world. And he had to trust that Mezzanotte would do all of this in a way that all would converge with the arrival of the creature.

Pierre was already awake the following morning when Lorenzo arrived to place his meal on the table. Lorenzo said, "I have been asked to accompany you. There seems considerable interest in your plan and the Signor is eager to hear the opinions of his counselors."

Pierre shook his head. "That's an awful lot of people to disappoint and I'll hate doing that." He ate quickly, rolled his plans to carry under his arm and they descended the stairs together. Crossing the plaza he still wondered whether there was some way his plan could be tested but he had failed to recognize an answer when they reached the door of the meeting room. He squared his shoulders and turning to Lorenzo he said, "Wish me luck."

Lorenzo smiled. "But you will not need luck; you have a plan." Then he leaned past Pierre and opened the door.

All eyes turned to follow Pierre as he crossed the meeting room. He had nearly reached the far-end when he recognized Commander Genovese seated with the others. As if noticing his glance Dr. Ginesterra said, "I believe you know the Commander. At Signor Mezzanotte's request he has kindly agreed to advise us on your strategy and help us to evaluate your plan."

Pierre smiled hoping to disguise his surprise. "I've had the honor and pleasure of his acquaintance and I'm flattered that he is willing to offer his wise counsel. I'm sure it'll prove useful." Turning to the others he said, "If you'll permit, I'll dispense with preliminaries and move to the purpose of our meeting." He unrolled his drawing on the table to its full length.

"What I propose is to slay the creature and then use a sort of trap to dispose of it. To accomplish this I've designed a device unlike any that's ever been seen." The men around the table stood from their chairs and gathered around Pierre to look at his drawing more closely. "This device will demand significant resources to complete and a large body of men to construct. Yet I assure you the principle behind its design is simple and elemental and therefore certain to be effective. Finally, although this plan is thorough and based on a principle as familiar as sunlight, in order to accomplish its purpose we'll need the assistance of fickle Nature."

"You'll notice," he continued, "that it's composed of two elements; the first is a mat made of chain-maille and designed to cover an area roughly a thousand yards wide and two thousand yards long. The second and more unusual element is a collection of one thousand kites, each connected to the chain-maille at points five yards apart along either of the sides. I propose all of this be laid-out on the plane of Catania, with one end of the mat anchored beneath the waves and the other unrolled to its full extent in the direction of Mount Etna." He paused, but his words were met with only bemused silence so he continued.

"Before I review the drawings of the mechanical devices, I'll explain that simply stated, these kites will divert lightning to strike the chain-maille mat. And before you ask, all of this is certain as proved by experiment that the lightning's force must certainly kill the creature. Once dead, the mat will then be secured to surround the creature's corpse so that an army of oxen and men will haul it to the top of Mount Etna and propel it into the heart of the volcano."

The faces around the table looked up from the plan startled. After a long pause Professor Marconi said to Pierre, "An audacious plan, ingenious in its conception and ambitious in its execution. I am certain I speak for all of us when I congratulate your imaginative approach to an unprecedented problem." He paused again and looked around at the others. "But I for one remain unclear how you expect to divert lightning by any means other than magic."

Though stung by the question Pierre said, "You'll note that each of the kites includes a design to weave a metal wire into the length of each string with one end connected to the peak of the kite and the other to the mat of chain-malle. The principle employed is that the aether within the lightning will follow the metal wire and defuse through-out the chain-malle. With the beast standing on the chain-malle mat, as lightning strikes these kites their aether will travel directly to the creature and its cumulative effect will undoubtedly cause its death."

The silence that followed caught Pierre by surprise. But then Count Regurio spoke up. "This is the most audacious proposal I have ever heard. But I simply must question your assertion that lightning can be diverted through base metal. The conjunction of a base material with an aetherial force defies all logic, and I know of no author who supports this claim."

Father Danton added, "At least offer an experiment to assure this plan will succeed."

Pierre said, "Unfortunately, documentation for all of that is aboard the ship of Sheikh Mustafa and is thus unavailable."

"That is convenient," Brother Alphonso sniffed, displaying his irritation and distrust.

Father Danton said, "The fact is, you assert an effect without an underlying principle."

"My principle is sound," Pierre said his irritation constructing his throat. "While I lack the documents, I have assisted in experiments proving this will succeed if Nature cooperates."

"Nature and this creature both," Brother Alphonso said with a derisive chuckle. "You will need the creature to enter your so-called trap and then stand quite still until it is dead." With a smirking smile he looked around at the others. "So we must hope your beast is at least patient. And just how do you propose to attract it and then confine it to your device?"

Pierre said, "If Signor Mezzanotte's information is accurate the creature is approaching these shores. Beyond that, as in all things we will depend upon God's will." He heard himself say those words and instantly endured a wave of embarrassment.

Dr. Ginesterra said, "It is good that we all acknowledge the will of God."

Hopeful his words had mollified this audience Pierre added, "The Lord is the author of all things, including lightning and beasts. The devices I've designed are based upon the operations of this world as our Lord created it. Nature dictates my course, and the experiments I witnessed followed a trail revealed by Nature. I promise that every subsequent step has been suggested by Nature's actions."

Professor Marconi said, "But at least admit this attempt to confine and direct the lightning using base metal is, at best, far-fetched. By what principle do you believe it can be channeled in this manner?"

"Belief is unnecessary. I've participated in the experiments so I'm certain by experiment that the aether of the lightning is merely an extension of that vortical concentration of aether which flows all around us."

Father Danton asked, "So the principle of the vortices underlies this assertion. Can you reproduce any of those experiments you mentioned for us?"

"With the appropriate equipment and in the presence of a thunderstorm, of course. But our time is limited so that such a demonstration does not appear possible."

Count Regurio asked, "You insist we approve your plan without a shred of proof or any form of demonstration to assure us it has even a chance of working?"

"As I said, with sufficient time I'm certain I could provide a demonstration that would convince all who witnessed it. But I remind you the creature we need to destroy approaches. With respect, I ask that you take my word for the principle of Nature I've described. It's true that I can't guarantee the result, but just as you must accept the existence of a beast none of you has seen, you must accept this principle I've described." By the expressions he saw around him, Pierre realized he had convinced no one.

Finally Commander Genovese spoke up. "You say the principle you describe is beyond doubt. What is also beyond doubt is that your plan will prove expensive and complicated and will demand the help of an army of men and oxen." He paused and looked over at Dr. Ginesterra. "Do not misunderstand our apprehension which you must admit appears justified. In any case, despite the Signor's conviction I suspect that reports of this creature are exaggerations and conjectures."

Pierre's impatience leaked into his voice. "With these eyes I've seen cannon bounce off that beast as if they were balls of cotton. But I will not debate its existence. If you reject my plan and it arrives you will need something powerful against it." He felt his anger rise and he decided to let it show. "Signor Mezzanotte has assigned you the responsibility of judging the best way to defeat the beast. I promise you this is the only strategy likely to succeed. If there's another plan I'd like to hear it." He looked around the table but no eyes returned his gaze. "Since there are no more questions I'll assume this meeting is over. Please inform me when you reach your conclusion. Otherwise, take it or leave it, because I have no better to offer." He stepped from the table and turned to the door. "You know where to find me." He opened the door and left, slamming it closed behind him.

Lorenzo stood just outside. After a moment he asked, "Your meeting went well?" But Pierre had already turned and was striding along the corridor.

"Better than I expected," Pierre said as he walked. "No one laughed." They continued in silence to Pierre's rooms.

When they arrived he asked Lorenzo to bring him a large container of wine. Lorenzo looked at him oddly and Pierre said he felt very thirsty. When he had gone Pierre paced tense and furious before the wide window reviewing the particulars of the meeting, pondering each of his words and every question he had been asked, certain that at every moment he should have been clearer and conveyed an absolute sense of conviction. As he reminded himself, his plan was based on his knowledge of Nature's behavior and habits as he had observed them. He found himself conjuring the words he should have used to demolish each argument and overwhelm every objection, and he berated himself for having failed.

Lorenzo soon returned with the wine. Pierre took the carafe from his hands, filled his goblet and drank it greedily down at once. Lorenzo asked if he needed anything more and Pierre told him that he would once again take his evening meal in his room. Pierre refilled his cup and drank it down as Lorenzo closed the door.

After either the third or fourth cup, Pierre was not certain, he discovered he had stopped panting and his body began to relax. He fell back onto the couch with an uncanny sense of sinking, as if he drifted down into the padded upholstery until his flesh merged with its padding.

Gradually the world became quiet, the light softened, even the air offered a caress. So although the knock on his door surprised him, he had become nearly indifferent to whoever might enter. Recognizing Lorenzo carrying his evening meal, he enjoyed a kind of contentment, as if Lorenzo had divined without being told just how hungry he was, and had taken it upon himself to relieve him at least of that. Placing the meal on the table, Lorenzo offered the wish that he enjoy it and smiled as he asked if there was anything more. Pierre replied that he would be grateful if Lorenzo woke him early the next morning. He promised he would do so and wished Pierre a peaceful night. By the time the door closed Pierre felt exhausted.

He sat for a time wondering about the Commander's unexpected appearance and what it might mean. Had Mezzanotte changed his mind? Or did it signal his abandonment of Pierre? This world, he decided, was as opaque as ever and still he was not clever enough to sort it all out.

He stood to cross the room for the meal Lorenzo had provided and was startled at how unsteady the floor seemed and how uneven its surface. Recognizing Lorenzo's effort and his concern for Pierre's comfort, he moved to the table and sat to enjoy it. As he ate, memories of the tavern and Gabriella came to him and he thought about how far from all and everything he now was and how complicated everything had finally become. Then he wondered again about Augustus and continued to wonder until his plate was empty.

Meal finished, with another full cup of wine in hand he sat heavily on the couch. He glanced over to the bed but managed to resist its temptation to repose. He folded his hands, closed his eyes and released a great, loud sigh. His plan to trap the creature was now in the hands of Mezzanotte's advisers and thus beyond his responsibility. Even Professor Marconi had acknowledged he had done remarkable work. And unsurprisingly, none of those eminent thinkers had offered an alternative plan. The idea that men without understanding would pass judgment on the unprecedented made him smile. He assumed that modifications would be requested but he was certain that in the end they would be forced to accept his plan. This thought left him content, as if the candles on the table burned bright and still just for him.

Phantom images of his plan drifted about him. He envisioned the defeat of the beast, its demise brought about by the ingenuity of his thought. He watched in his mind's eye as the great creature stumbled and in a roar of agony crashed to the ground. And then after a moment of motionless silence, another roar arises but this of approval from the multitude gathered to admire his effort and congratulate his success. Dignitaries and potentates applaud while Signor Mezzanotte grins with proud pleasure. From the midst of the crowd Augustus suddenly pushes his way forward smiling with pride to embrace and congratulate him. And then the Abbess steps forward, kisses his cheek and then stares up into his eyes with glittering admiration. He sees all of this happen again and again, each time the crowd's adulation a bit louder, more enthusiastic and more prolonged.

And so he dozed smiling, a haze of gratified success filling his head, until the door to his room suddenly crashed open with a bang that nearly threw him from his seat.

Instantly he was awake though confused. His fog-shrouded vision revealed Signor Mezzanotte filling his door with Pierre's carefully drawn plan crumpled in his right fist, and on his face an expression of absolute rage.

CHAPTER SIXTEEN

"ARE YOU MAD? Have you gone insane? You dare make a fool of me?" Signor Mezzanotte strode across the room until he stood glowering down over Pierre.

Pierre wondered at first if this was part of another dream he did not recall. He looked up waiting for this dream to change, to shift into something pleasant, but no change took place. That figure appearing to be Mezzanotte remained towering above him, his snarl revealing teeth ready to bite.

"Answer me!" Mezzanotte slapped the paper crushed in his fist onto the table.

Pierre decided he was actually looking at the man and regretted this was not a dream. "There must be some mistake." His throat suddenly was tight and his voice cracked. "I did what you asked; this plan will rid you of the creature. Why are you angry?"

Trembling, Mezzanotte studied Pierre. "You expect me to believe this ludicrous contraption will do anything but dissipate my wealth and render me the laughing-stock of the Mediterranean?"

Fog drifted slowly from Pierre's befuddled mind as under a brightening sun. "I've conducted the experiments that prove this plan needs only the cooperation of Nature to succeed."

Mezzanotte continued to look down at Pierre, his fury fading into something near pitying astonishment. With a sigh of confused exhaustion he fell heavily into the couch opposite Pierre. "I begin to believe you are an earnest and dedicated imbecile, well-meaning but utterly and fatally addled. Perhaps your experiences have shriveled your mind, I cannot decide. Your delusional scheme can only be the product of the broken and imperfect thinking of a crippled brain. And most astonishing, I begin to believe that you believe your own idiotic claims."

Pierre said, "This plan is your only chance to free yourself from the creature's threat."

Mezzanotte leaned forward and propped his elbow on the table. "Do you have even an inkling of the cost all of this will demand? This enormous piece of chain-maille alone will equal the price of a small garrison. For the cost of your whole scheme I could purchase, outfit and man an armada. And I will need to employ every blacksmith and armorer within fifty miles. But worse than all of that, my advisers insist there is no principle of Nature to account for your ridiculous claims. It cannot surprise you that some suggest you are a conscienceless charlatan in the pay of the Spanish crown. Now I ask you, if my trusted advisers remain unconvinced, how can I consider spending the tremendous sum of money your plan will cost? You offer me almost nothing and demand from me almost everything."

"I assure you of one thing," Pierre said, his irritation rising. "The principle of Nature upon which this plan is based is sound and incontrovertible."

"Why should I believe any of this when you are unwilling to conduct even a single experiment sufficient to convince my advisers?"

"It's the beast who decides how little time we have. If you insist I prove all of this to your advisers before you begin work, time will be lost and according to your own sources the creature will be upon us. Any more time spent in debate and suddenly it'll be too late. You must at least concede that point."

Seized suddenly with an uncontrollable exasperation, Mezzanotte stood and, hands locked behind his back and staring at the floor, began to pace before the couch. Seconds crawled forward with each of his steps until suddenly Pierre said, "I want to see my father."

Mezzanotte stopped in mid-stride and looked up startled. "What?"

"You told me he was in Naples and would return here soon. When will I see him?"

He stared at Pierre as if shocked by his insistence. "What could he have to do with this?"

"That isn't important; I want to know when I'll see him."

Mezzanotte hesitated but then sat again on the couch across from Pierre who studied him certain his answer would not be the one he wanted. In a quietly pacifying voice Mezzanotte said, "A meeting with your father demands planning. His presence in Naples is vital to my project and I did not expect his return until after this business had been resolved."

"Are you using him as a hostage?" Pierre asked and he did not disguise his annoyance.

Mezzanotte glanced up with a quizzical expression. "If I did not know you better I would resent that suggestion. I need this problem resolved just as urgently as I need a successful outcome to his project in Naples, and I cannot abandon the one to pursue the other. But as I look at your stupid face, I begin to suspect that as a counter to my supposed ransom you have decided on blackmail. Are you about to tell me you will not help unless I produce Augustus?"

"Why would I risk blackmail when I can't control the outcome? That would just confirm my stupidity. Besides, it was you who insisted sentiment has no place in a business negotiation. In any case, can you expect me to trust you when you don't trust me? What would you do if you were in my shoes?"

Mezzanotte leaned back as a small smile appeared about his lips. "First and foremost, I would never be in your shoes, as you describe it. Being in your shoes is your first problem. Did you not abandon your mother and your country to find what you were unsure even still existed? Anyway, by explaining all of this I must also admit I find myself embarrassed to occupy the shoes I now find myself in. That is, utterly dependent on someone as addled and irresponsible as you. I console myself that unlike you, my position is not entirely a result of my own ineptitude. The presence of this creature is neither a result of my own actions nor a strategy of my many enemies. Still, none of that cures the ill. Take my word, I resent finding myself in a position without alternative. Certainly not checkmate, but clearly in check." His smile faded. He leaned forward clasping his hands together and turned to stare out the window. "All right; tell me what you expect me to do. I need this done and you seem to be the only man to do it. The return of Augustus aside, how can I convince you to offer me something that at least resembles a reasonable plan?"

After a long pause Pierre said, "You could simply ask; as a personal favor."

The Signor turned from the window as his eyes grew gradually large and then he burst out laughing. "That is true! I could do just that. And as I think about it, I am surprised that never occurred to me. I must wonder if

I have overestimated your guileless inanity, because if so, I suffer additional embarrassment." He looked past Pierre and his expression darkened. "All right and fair enough. Though it galls me to confess it, I need your help. You and only you can spare my kingdom. Does that admission please you? Whatever is done must not fail because all I have or hope to achieve rests upon it. Does all of that satisfy you?"

Pierre shrugged. "Since that's the case, why are you unsatisfied with my plan?"

Mezzanotte glared. "A complicated, elaborate and expensive plan that educated men tell me cannot succeed? How else should I respond?"

"Considering both of our situations, you should assume I'd only offer a plan that had the best chance of success. Simply because your advisers are unfamiliar with its principle shouldn't negate its value. And despite their dismissal, I assume they've offered none of their own. I would expect you'd insist on that. They fail to understand what I offer yet offer no alternative."

Mezzanotte's expression turned to suspicion. "But you offer neither explanation nor demonstration. It is a fine thing for you to demand more than that from others."

Pierre leaned forward unaccustomed to a sensation of authority. "Remember, time is not on your side. Were I to plan and execute a demonstration sufficient to convince them, the only result would be your admission that I know what I'm talking about. By then the beast will be on your doorstep. This may irritate you but you'll have to believe me, and worst still, trust me."

Mezzanotte looked at Pierre as though he was a door without a door handle and he knew that behind that door was something he could not live without. His eyes seemed to grow heavy, a relaxed somnolence veiled his expression and Pierre wondered if he might fall asleep. Pierre added, "I'd gain nothing by setting you after a useless scheme. How would I benefit from that?"

"You know," Mezzanotte said in a tone of voice as if his mind had gone far away, "I have many enemies. Not simply rivals or business competitors. No, there are individuals ready to assassinate me. Each would slit my throat gleefully and wash his hands in my blood, because for our island and our people I have aspirations. I see my people rising up to command the entire Mediterranean, beholding to no empire and equal to the greatest.

Unfortunately for some, the realization of that ambition will be their death-knell. Especially for the clergy, my ambition is heretical, poisonous and all but Satanic, deserving nothing less than punishment. And I assure you, on this island there is no punishment without blood nor victory without dismemberment. So the enemies of my people plot my death from sunrise to sundown." His expression sharpened as his eyes became bright. "I have wondered since your arrival whether you might be just such a person. My spies have been about you, by your side and even in your bed. I have inquired and cast about for indications of your true intent. So when you refuse what appears a reasonable request for demonstration, my distrust only grows. Do you see my point?"

Pierre studied Mezzanotte a moment and then burst into laughter. "Pardon me," he said, "but the idea that someone could mistake me for an assassin is too ridiculous to consider. Please, put aside your fear on that score."

Suspicion coloring his eyes, Mezzanotte said, "You murdered an unarmed man; struck him through the heart with a knife." He paused watching Pierre's reaction. "Do not deny another man's blood has covered your hands. In principle, you are no more innocent than I."

Pierre was utterly startled. "That's not how it happened. I defended myself and he came at me and..." but suddenly he stopped, overwhelmed with anger. "Think what you like and do as you wish, but unless you come up with a better idea you have two choices. Put my plan into action or take your chances with the feeble weapons and useless strategies that have failed the others."

Mezzanotte paused. "You omit a third option." Pierre looked at him genuinely curious. "I could have you killed and leave your body for the creature."

This suggestion stunned Pierre. In a tone of indifferent curiosity he asked, "But can you be certain that will satisfy the creature? Instead, that action might drive it to greater fury. Admit you simply cannot know." He paused as his smile returned. "But you've already discounted that or you'd have killed me long before this."

Mezzanotte's own smile grew slowly. "This is true and it is perceptive of you to realize it. Still, you must admit it is the less costly option."

Pierre stood. "Only if it works." He shook his head, his patience running low. "I'm no good at dancing as you must have noticed. I've given you my best plan and the rest of this talk is getting you nowhere. Unless your advisers have another idea you'd better organize your resources. Time is passing and the beast approaches."

Mezzanotte leaned back and looked up at Pierre. "Patience is a young man's virtue and an old man's vice. Assume I am prepared to devote my resources to your scheme; is there nothing you can offer to assure even a possibility of success?"

Pierre studied Mezzanotte and after a time decided the man would not be dissuaded or proceed without a concession. Snatching a blank sheet of paper and quill, as he drew he asked, "What're the chances of a thunderstorm over the next few days?"

Mezzanotte watched Pierre's hand move. "We have entered the season where they are frequent but nothing is on the horizon. Why?"

"Our time is short and the demonstration you seem to need can't wait for one." He continued to draw and figure. Mezzanotte stood, stepped to the window and stared out.

As best as he could recall, Pierre attempted to reproduce the device Mohamed had designed aboard the Sheikh's ship. When he finished he called Mezzanotte over and pushed the paper toward him. "When your craftsmen have constructed this gather your advisers." He hesitated, looking from the drawing to Pierre. "I'll provide you the demonstration you need." Pierre sat back in his chair and stared hard at the Signor. "Now, I'm tired and I want rest."

Mezzanotte scrutinized the paper, his eyes flicking past it from time to time to look at Pierre. Then he rolled up it and stood. "You will be summoned. Now, I leave you to your rest." In a moment the door closed behind Mezzanotte and Pierre was relieved to be alone.

A sudden exhaustion overwhelmed him, he staggered to his bed and laid down feeling as though he had just run miles. He closed his eyes wondering why he even bothered with all of this but sleep overpowered him before he found an answer.

So he was startled when he opened his eyes to discover Lorenzo glowing within morning sunlight at the foot of his bed. "Your meal awaits," he said. "Signor Mezzanotte expects your company within the hour. I will return to provide your escort."

Seeing Lorenzo after what he had learned from Mezzanotte was like seeing him for the first time. Lorenzo turned toward the door but before he reached it Pierre asked, "And just how is he this morning?"

"Skeptical," Lorenzo said and then he was gone.

Pierre dressed and ate quickly, and Lorenzo arrived just as he finished. He led Pierre out to a small, brown canvas pavilion tent beside the dolphin fountain. Passing beneath the flap of the tent Pierre found Mezzanotte standing beside the Commander and surrounded by his advisers and several others Pierre had not met, all in a semi-circle around a wide table. On the table was the contraption Pierre recognized as the one he had drawn the day before.

Seeing Pierre, Mezzanotte smiled. To the others he said, "Our master scientist has arrived." To Pierre he said, "We are grateful for this demonstration."

Pierre moved to the device and took his time determining that each part conformed to his design. He tested the crank, made certain the fur just touched the surface of the cylinder of amber and that the field mouse chosen as the experiment's victim was closely encased within a metal cage. In his design he had assumed the mouse to be roughly the size of those birds Mohamed had used on Sheikh Mustafa's ship. "Your craftsmen are highly-skilled and they are to be congratulated." Addressing the others he said, "This experiment substitutes the contact between the amber and the fur for a bolt of lightning. This metal device will supply the aether and mimic its flow concentrated by the kites in the lightning."

Mezzanotte said, "If we are convinced by your demonstration, my craftsmen will execute your design to perfection."

Pierre began to turn the crank. After several turns a spark appeared across the metal points and the mouse squealed and twitched within the cage. Several around the table gasped with surprise. Pierre stopped and the mouse stared back at him wide-eyed with terror, its nose and whiskers twitching. He resumed turning the crank but more rapidly and for a longer period of time. Once again a spark appeared across the gap between the points, and again the mouse squealed but this time only briefly. Its eyes grew wide and its body froze. Pierre continued to turn the crank sustaining the spark between the points until a wisp of gray smoke drifted just above its fur. He stopped turning the crank. The mouse slumped in the cage eyes shut and it did not move again.

Mezzanotte and his advisers moved to the table staring as wide-eyed as the mouse had. With an expression of disbelief the Commander prodded the mouse with his finger but it remained still.

Grinning, Mezzanotte turned to the Commander. "Tell Hericulo to alert the copyists. The program will commence and with all speed." Then he turned to Pierre. Taking his arm into Mezzanotte's own he said, "Walk with me, please." The others spoke quietly among themselves as Pierre accompanied him out from under the tent and they continued in silence.

They passed beyond the gates of the garden before Mezzanotte spoke. "I confess I had prepared myself for almost anything. I took the time to study your drawing and assumed I knew what to expect. But you have surprised me, young man, and that by itself is an achievement. Heartily I congratulate you." To Pierre's surprise, he smiled as broadly as a new father and lightly patted Pierre's forearm. "I believe I now understand the heart of your plan and this comes as a great relief. I have only one more question although I suspect I already know its answer. Please explain to me again the purpose of the numerous kites your plan demands."

"The dart of aetherial force that results from the moving contact of the amber against the fur is identical, except for its scale, to the dagger of lightning that accompanies a thunderstorm. Several among those many kites will attract darts of lightning so that the aether is concentrated and directed to the chain-maille mat. And just as the mouse is nearly nothing in comparison to the creature, so the aetherial discharge of that device is nearly nothing compared to the power of a bolt of the lightning."

Mezzanotte chuckled. "As I suspected, though I am grateful for that explanation. But time is fleeting and there is much to be done. I hope that after our mid-day meal you will ride out to visit my chief blacksmith, inspect his work and confirm he proceeds according to your design. Until this project is complete, a carriage and driver will be available so that you can assure the work being done at our workplaces. As the designer of this project, I hope you will accept the responsibility for supervising its progress."

"As you wish." Pierre said. "But since time is short, it is vital that progress be rapid."

"My workers are aware of this and will proceed with all possible speed."

They walked in silence for a time before Pierre asked. "And my father?" Mezzanotte said nothing and Pierre added, "You've got my design and my agreement to help. I have only that one request."

Mezzanotte continued to stare down at the ground as he walked. Pierre was about to repeat his request when Mezzanotte said, "He has been summoned. Although my orders travel through the air, men do not. He should arrive within ten days. But tell me one thing; what will you do when he arrives? Perhaps the answer is obvious but I confess my curiosity."

His question, so direct and unvarnished, caught Pierre off-guard. He had not put that question to himself as directly and he struggled to be certain of his own thoughts. "Augustus has experimented in this field far more deeply than I, so his participation can only prove valuable although I don't believe it's necessary for its success. Is that what you're asking?"

"You believe he will confirm your theory; do I have that right?" When he simply nodded, Mezzanotte asked, "But is there any possibility that, upon consultation, you will discover you are wrong and your scheme is a colossal waste of time and resources?"

"I assumed I just answered that. As I said, I've seen this effect in operation."

"Yes, of course," Mezzanotte said but he seemed to remain uncertain. "My ignorance of these matters is complete. I am simply curious to know how you might collaborate."

"Augustus is a true scientist while I am merely a technician. I've only used obvious connections to design a device for immediate use, so I hope this all will prove interesting to him. I'd be content if my work advanced his."

"You admire your father," Mezzanotte said flatly.

"And you seem surprised by that," Pierre said.

Mezzanotte shrugged and then chuckled nervously. "Considering his abandonment of you and your mother, I suppose admiration is the last thing I would expect you to feel."

"Augustus is a brilliant man driven from his home because he found no way to gain acknowledgment for his achievements. Had his world been larger, I am certain he'd have been the kind of father he expected himself to be. It's too bad he needed to leave us to accomplish what he hoped." Then he stopped and turned. "But you've spoken with him about me, haven't you."

He looked into Mezzanotte's eyes.

After a moment's pause Mezzanotte said, "I can only say your family never came up in our conversation."

"What has he been doing for you?"

Mezzanotte looked down and away and then resumed walking. Pierre decided he would not be told anything he wished to know. "Your father came to my attention through a mutual friend. In addition to his expertise in science he demonstrated an uncanny ability, through the manipulation of numbers, to advise me on future prices of certain goods along with the probable success of certain voyages. Happily, most of his predictions have proved startlingly accurate. By his efforts I have enjoyed significant profit which I have generously shared with him. He has explained his practice but instantly I become confused beyond all hope of understanding. Still, he has proved himself startlingly accomplished and capable."

"Why was he sent to Naples? I assume he rendered some unique service there."

"His mathematical technique has proved so useful I have asked that he instruct others in its esoteric knowledge. My hope is that he will provide me a group of advisers all equally capable of his magic and thus I will benefit from trade in a variety of commodities always assured a sizable profit." He grinned briefly before he continued.

"Do not misunderstand. My difficulty with that beast is real and its threat to my enterprise is substantial. You came to my attention as a result of your experiences with it. The fact that Augustus is also your father is incidental and something I only discovered later."

Pierre was relieved he had drawn this admission from Mezzanotte, though he could not gauge its value. Mezzanotte looked up and squinted as he smiled. "Your plan will cost me a fortune. I hope that, at least, gives you some perverse pleasure." He stopped then and turned to look at Pierre. "Even as we speak my messengers are on their way, and soon the hard work will begin. Be of good cheer, the worst is still before us." He clapped Pierre on the shoulder. "Join me for the midday meal if time and opportunity allow; I will look for you." Then he walked off, leaving Pierre beside the thickly-fragrant bed of roses.

As a rich, heavy aroma filled his head, his conversation with Mezzanotte left him alert as the success of his experiment left him exhilarated. Something had been accomplished and a small mountain had been climbed. He decided to return to his room to wash and change and accept Mezzanotte's invitation to lunch.

He followed the path leading out of the garden, and passing through its gates he continued until he approached the now-abandoned site of his experiment. The dolphin fountain splashed loudly and his experiment remained on display. He walked toward it content to admire his own handiwork. He looked over the mechanism and then glanced at the mouse. Whiskers twitching, the mouse stared back. Looking about to see if he was being watched Pierre picked up a small wrench lying beside the cage and with one move struck the mouse's head. Its eyes closed and its whiskers stopped moving. Pierre held his breath, made a mental note and continued to his room, Mezzanotte's luncheon suddenly and certainly on his agenda.

CHAPTER SEVENTEEN

MEZZANOTTE SAT AT the head of his grand table for the mid-day meal seeming unable to resist regaling his guests with the tale of Pierre's experiment and how impressed he was. His account seemed exaggerated to Pierre and he wondered who else at the table felt that way, so that he found himself trapped between pride and embarrassment. Whether because of what Mezzanotte described or the way he described it, Pierre was never asked to confirm details or add elaborations, and for this he was relieved. The principle of Nature his experiment involved had proved difficult to explain to Mezzanotte's advisers; for the elegant sybarites sharing this table it might be mistaken for magic. When the conversation finally moved to another topic, Pierre sat back relieved to resume his invisibility.

The awnings shading the windows of the room against the piercing sunlight now cast the dining hall into an odd twilight allowing golden shards of light to cut through gaps and throw scintillating, irregular shapes across the table and against the painted walls. Bored, Pierre watched those fragments of light crawl with infinitesimal slowness across the surface of their table. Thus, boredom set his mind to wander until he found himself wondering about Augustus.

According to Mezzanotte, Augustus somehow had achieved the status of mathematical savant. From his description, he wondered if he described the same man Pierre had known as at best clumsy with mathematics and at higher levels of complexity vague and befuddled. But recalling his own experiences before the mast, Pierre reminded himself that many things will happen in ten years of even a circumspect life. Augustus had changed residences several times and his only letter had placed him in Amsterdam, far from both Naples and Sicily. So Pierre had to assume that somewhere in Augustus's travels he had managed to acquire something nearly miraculous that turned him from a numerical inept into a mathematical adept.

It was one thing to calculate weight or distance or speed, or size; entirely another to manipulate likelihoods and conjectures. If Mezzanotte's account could be trusted, Augustus accomplished this not simply with skill but with exceptional success. This in particular left Pierre puzzled. According to the Signor, Augustus had acquired such skill that he taught men already well-versed in the numerical arts. Something seemed not quite right about all this but its recognition eluded him.

Pierre's own ignorance of anything more sophisticated than addition was a wall he could neither climb nor circumvent. Even to glimpse that terrain which Augustus seemingly had conquered was as unlikely as his traveling to the moon. Confronted by another barrier decisively separating him from Augustus, his sigh of frustration was so loud the well-dressed young man sitting beside him at the table turned appearing concerned. Pierre offered him a reassuring smile and resumed picking at the food on his platter and silently conceding his own failure.

To cheer himself, Pierre recalled that the challenge of this creature was sufficiently great, and perhaps even greater than that which Augustus had overcome. In the end he could only hope he would acquit himself as successfully as Augustus apparently had.

Like a long swim against a raging torrent this meal dragged on, but finally Mezzanotte seemed to tire of hearing his own voice. When he stood from the table Pierre's sense of relief was sincere. He followed the other guests as they filed out of the dining room but when he stepped into the corridor he was startled to find Lorenzo waiting for him.

Lorenzo bowed. "Signor Mezzanotte has asked that I accompany you to the carriage provided for your excursion."

"Please assure him I didn't forget my assignment and I'm ready to do as we had agreed. And I hope you're relieved to see I've learned to navigate these halls alone."

Lorenzo appeared hurt and vaguely embarrassed. "I have enjoyed your company and have looked forward to our meetings."

"Have we become friends?" Pierre asked.

Lorenzo's startled expression surprised Pierre. "It may seem presumptuous but I confess a certain enthusiastic acquaintanceship."

Pierre said, "I'm flattered you regard me as something of a friend, but do your services to Mezzanotte include spying for him on your friends?"

Lorenzo looked about confused and his expression of shock left Pierre regretting his words. "Observation is not the same as spying." His expression became blank. "The Signor charged me with assuring your comfort and I have done no more than that. If I have caused you concern, I regret that." Formally he added, "As you are certain you can carry out your assignment without my assistance, I will wish you a good journey." He bowed then, turned and left.

Pierre watched him suddenly certain Mezzanotte had once again made a fool of him, because instantly he felt foolish. He guessed he had been lied to and that he owed Lorenzo an apology. In the next moment Lorenzo's retreating back turned a corner and was gone.

Pierre followed the corridor and descended the stairs to the main doors without losing his way. Stepping out into the hard sunlight he saw the horse and carriage Mezzanotte had promised waiting for him. To his surprise the Commander stood beside it, and from his shoulder hung a large, black leather satchel. When he reached the carriage the Commander did not smile. Before Pierre could offer a greeting, the Commander said, "Signor Mezzanotte has requested I accompany you to our workplaces and protect you against the bandits infesting these hills."

Pierre attempted to disguise his mistrust. "I'm honored by your assistance and relieved by your concern. In your company I'm sure the time will pass quickly and very pleasantly."

The Commander responded, "And I am honored to accompany such an educated and accomplished man. But time is passing and we should go." He opened the carriage's door and stepped aside inviting Pierre to enter.

They took seats across from each other as the driver turned the carriage. Passing under the main gate put them onto that road Pierre recalled from his arrival but the driver turned the carriage to follow a road heading east. The Commander said, "Signor Mezzanotte suggested that since your device will be laid on the coast and near the volcano, it would be best that you visit that location first."

"A very good idea, Commander, and I'm grateful for the recommendation."

The Commander shrugged. "He has planned this excursion and it is simply my role to carry it out." He turned away then as if the passing scenery of jagged, sun-blanched rocks, stunted bushes and skeletal trees was more interesting than Pierre.

After traveling for some time Pierre said, "As a fighting man trained for strategy and combat I expect this is tedious for you, so I offer my personal thanks for your assistance."

His words might have caught the Commander by surprise but he continued to watch the passing landscape. "In carrying out the Signor's orders nothing is tedious." He paused. "But it is kind of you to regard my help in that way and for that I am grateful."

"These bandits you mention make me curious. I was told that loyalty to the Signor is universal and unswerving."

"On our island, no loyalty is unswerving." He added, "Except, of course, for my own."

Pierre said, "Such loyalty would be precious anywhere. Yet, if loyalty is fleeting and unstable, how is it that he is convinced he can unite this island into an empire?"

The Commander hesitated and Pierre could not guess whether he was annoyed by the question or confused by it. "Above all, the Signor understands that loyalty is acquired through either money, flattery or sex but that only the first is likely to endure. Thus, to assure that loyalty he must have a constant flow of treasure. The Signor is certain there is no way to assure a flow of wealth as long as that creature remains at large. Thus, he justifies this expenditure as an investment whose reward will greatly exceed its risk of loss. Unfortunately for him, his advisers are divided and therefore useless. He has concluded he has no choice but to risk everything on this roll of the dice." He turned to look at Pierre. "I do not envy your future should your plan fail." His expression was as featureless as a new moon.

Pierre shrugged and smiled. "On that point we both agree." To his relief they continued in silence; some things Pierre did not need to hear described.

They traveled east and then north until, passing along a road between high hills, they emerged onto a great, broad plain eerily flat, its soil gray to nearly black and without vegetation. In the distance, a line of dark blue told Pierre they approached the sea while to the north stood the cone of Mount Etna. Pierre said, "I stared at the map for hours and never realized how close the volcano stands to the sea."

"Do not be confused; its peak is further away than it appears." He then spoke to the driver. Turning to Pierre he added, "We will continue to the edge of the sea where, as I recall, your device begins."

Reaching the plain, the carriage moved smoothly, and Pierre hoped once the creature was bound up this terrain would offer little resistance to its movement as well. At the edge of the water they stopped and he was surprised to see that these waves lapped gently at the shore. The Commander seemed to notice this. "Except during a violent storm," he said, "the sea will cooperate with your plan."

Pierre stepped down from the carriage and followed the shore until he reached a point that appeared particularly flat and began a gradual incline toward the volcano. He built a small pile of stones there and then paced off the width of the carpet where he then placed another pile of stones. He turned to survey the terrain leading back toward the volcano, relieved it appeared uninterrupted by anything more than a scattering of gravel. The Commander stood beside the carriage watching Pierre with distracted indifference.

Pierre returned to the carriage and asked, "Do you know of any obstacles further up?"

The Commander was silent as if searching his memory. "I recall that your plan is for the creature to be dragged to the volcano's summit. I believe the path remains uninterrupted far up the volcano's side but perhaps it is best we ride in that direction to confirm this."

Back in the carriage, the Commander spoke to the driver and they followed a path that climbed toward the volcano's summit. Suddenly they approached a wide and deep ravine. From his seat, Pierre saw that beyond it their path appeared to continue ahead smooth and even. He turned to the Commander. "Can your men fill that?"

The Commander scrutinized the ravine. "It could be done but it will demand additional time."

"How much time?" Pierre asked.

The Commander stepped down from the carriage and walked to its edge. "As in everything else, that will depend on the number of men put to the work."

"So we need to begin soon." He spoke as if he was thinking aloud. To the Commander he said, "And what are the chances of that?"

"All depends upon the Signor. If you assure him it must be done for this to succeed, he will find it difficult to refuse." From his satchel the Commander brought out a large sheet which he unfolded onto the seat beside him revealing a map. He then brought out a small stick of charcoal and made a pair of black marks. "These are the points you made with those piles of stone. This marks the endpoint of your survey. We are now standing here, and as you see, nothing here indicates that ravine. Otherwise, there seems nothing else to show additional obstacles but it would be best if we confirmed this."

Pierre looked more closely at the map and then asked about three other marks that might threaten their path, but the Commander assured him they were widely-spaced and could be maneuvered between without difficulty. Pierre was dubious. "I'll need to travel that path to be certain but bridging that ravine seems sufficiently difficult." He refolded the map and handed it to the Commander. "The day grows late. While there's daylight we should visit the foundry."

The Commander spoke to the driver and the carriage turned west and south. As they traveled, the Commander explained that the foundry had been built and organized by Signor Mezzanotte several years before to assure his supply of armaments, that it was a grand establishment and included twenty forges employing more than one hundred men and supplied all of his metalwork, from chamber-pots to swords to body armor and cannon. Charcoal to smelt the iron came from oak forests further north and west, and iron ore came from rich mines in those mountains near the center of the island. "According to the ancient writers," he said, "our island once was famous for its wheat and wine and olive oil. Invasion has forced us to exploit other treasures. Now, invaders lust for our minerals as much as for our women." He smiled bitterly. "Undoubtedly, one day they will attempt to steal our sunlight and wind. Though we may possess a thing in abundance, nothing ever belongs to us for very long."

Pierre asked about the skill of the workers and the Commander explained that they employed techniques as old as Byzantium itself and their skill was the glory of the Mediterranean. Pierre then asked if he believed there were sufficient workers to complete the task on time. The Commander shrugged claiming he had no doubt Mezzanotte would gather all the men needed. "He can be irresistibly persuasive when he finds something he wants. In any case, there is hardly a man within fifty miles who has not worked for him before and would not consider himself fortunate to accept his coin again."

Their carriage climbed until Pierre spied the red roofs and powder-gray walls of a compound of buildings, most with blackened chimneys attached, and all secure behind a high, thick wall. A cloud of gray-black smoke lit from beneath into a golden haze by the declining sun hovered over the compound. At the main gate, a guard beside it glanced at the Commander as he stepped aside allowing them to pass. Within, that ear-piercing clang of metal pounding against metal that Pierre had been hearing from far-off nearly deafened him to speech.

The carriage stopped before a single-storied building of pale yellow stone roughly twice as large as the others. The Commander stepped from the carriage and a short, solidly-built man appeared at the building's door. His hair was thick and curly black, and sharp blue eyes peered from a wide face black-bearded where it was not smudged black with soot. The Commander introduced him to Pierre as Luigi Castiglione, master craftsman of the foundry.

To the Commander, Castiglione said, "The Signor's messenger arrived earlier with these drawings. We will do as he asks but his request appears monumentally difficult."

Pierre spoke up. "He insists yours are the most skilled artisans to be found and he is absolutely confident you will succeed."

Castiglione's expression of angry mistrust startled Pierre. "We are masters at the manufacture of many things including chain-maille and our work has protected the bravest knights from Paris to Tripoli. Yet none has ever seen this design. And more, the quantity demanded is beyond our experience."

The Commander growled, "The Signor has promised this man he will have all that he requires. If his request is extraordinary, be assured his need is also extraordinary. If completion demands more workers, hire them, but time is short and completion is a matter of life and death."

Castiglione's dark look told Pierre he was not satisfied by what he had heard, so Pierre explained that, as indicated in the plans, separate portions of the chain-maille would be brought to the foot of Mount Etna and bound into increasingly larger sections. "In this way each portion will be bound to form a single, complete piece."

By his expression Castiglione appeared mollified though his confused mistrust remained. "Thank you for your effort to explain. Some of what you describe is clear from the drawings but I cannot conceive the purpose for all of this. What need could all of this chain-maille fill?"

Pierre said, "By your efforts a terrible threat to your people will be defeated."

Castiglione's expression again flared in anger. "You tell me nothing because you believe me a fool. Surely we who sweat and struggle can be told if we fight the French or the Spanish or the Turk. Tell us who our enemy is and we will work that much more fiercely. By knowing our enemy, our hands will be directed by our hearts as well as our minds."

The Commander suddenly stepped in front of Castiglione. "You are being paid generously for your work. Do as you are told and allow your greed to direct your hands."

Pierre began to worry; the last thing this project needed was an army of disaffected craftsmen. "God will reward your work because it is God's enemy who threatens your families and your homeland."

"God does whatever He wishes," Castiglione said bitterly, "but men are not so free. You see grand schemes while we see long hours of hot, hard work. Your castles are in the air, but it is our hands that bleed, our backs that ache, smoke burns our eyes and fills our lungs. Surely you can tell us what it is that calls for such work."

The Commander spoke as though his patience had reached their limit. "You only need to know what it is that the Signor needs done; more than that can be of no concern to you."

Castiglione recognized he would receive no satisfaction from the Commander so he turned to Pierre. On a rough wooden table beside the door Pierre unrolled his copy of the plan. Pointing to the design of the links to the chain-maille Castiglione said, "This is unlike any I have seen." He stopped then and looked at Pierre.

"That design increases the strength of the chain-maille ten-fold. If it helps, imagine that I have designed chain-maille strong enough to confine a galleon under sail."

From Castiglione's expression Pierre guessed that while he remained dissatisfied, he had finally heard enough to visualize an intention behind the design. He glanced from the Commander to Pierre as if resigned to his task. "Return in two days," he said flatly, "and assure yourself we proceed as you wish."

With a curt farewell the Commander led Pierre outside to the carriage.

Their carriage eventually reached the main road which would return them to the palace. Pierre asked, "Why can't those workers be told the purpose of their work? Surely it's a better way to inspire their effort."

The Commander turned a surprised expression on Pierre. "Can you seriously expect those men to believe in the existence of a creature which even I doubt?" He paused. With casual indifference he continued, "For those who toil, poverty is their inspiration. Empty stomachs and squealing brats send them into the fields every day. Their hearts belong to God but their backs belong to Signor Mezzanotte and nothing more needs be thought about it."

"And you?" Pierre asked mildly annoyed. "What brings you to do your work?"

The Commander's laugh was snide and condescending and Pierre's irritation rose. "Certainly you intend no insult comparing me to those who labor. It has pleased the Signor to retain me in his service for more than five years, but were I in the service of another, though the reward be as ample it would provide less honor. He is superior because his actions arise from his love of his people. Our island is as near to his heart as his own mother."

"Just so I understand," Pierre said, "you say it's his heart that makes him worthy of your loyalty yet you can't say the same for the men at the foundry."

The Commander straightened looking away. "Peasants work for their bread by God's will just as it is written in the Bible. Do not mistake them for true men nor assume they possess the nobler faculties. You from the western colonies cultivate delusions about the fates of men but those will pass with time. I pity you for their burden yet I sympathize with your confusion. But the day will come when you will recognize your error." He paused and turned to face Pierre. "Of course by then it will be too late. The rabble will command and noble spirits will be despised. The worst, greediest and most insolent will possess the greatest power and will wield it with remorseless self-interest." His grin of finality irritated Pierre but also frightened him.

Following this road, Pierre was struck again by the sight of people they passed, dusty and threadbare but invariably pausing to bow to their carriage, ignorant of whom they bow beyond the emblem on its door, nor seeming to need such knowledge. He wondered what they would do if they knew the sort of people they bowed to and how little they themselves were valued. But then it occurred to him they might already know, and that thought caused him to tremble.

He said, "Though I disagree with your conclusion I'm grateful for your candor. It's a pleasure to travel with a man so clear-thinking and well-informed. Let me ask that, if it's convenient for you, we travel tomorrow to the village where the kites are being made. I will look forward to another conversation to dispel my ignorance."

The Commander leaned back into his seat and Pierre's words had the desired effect because his expression revealed a man so content with his own thoughts that an expansive generosity suffused his face. "In that journey, the pleasure will be entirely mine. I am delighted to introduce a sympathetic person to the glories of my country. And that journey will be brief since that village is close to the palace. I can only hope what we find there pleases you."

"I've just one more question; I'm curious to learn about the weather and in particular how often thunderstorms strike."

The Commander looked at him curiously and then looked away as if giving his question earnest thought. "I believe at this time of year such storms are more frequent."

"Is there someone in the Signor's retinue who has special knowledge of that?"

The Commander's expression turned to annoyance. "In fact there is and he maintains extensive records of just such things. Count Pagliaro has a passionate curiosity for winds and storms, gathers their information and maintains their records. I expect at the Signor's request he will be happy to speak to you." As if relieved his interrogation was over he turned away. Their journey continued in silence until the carriage stopped at the gates of the palace.

There they found Lorenzo waiting. Seeing him, the Commander said farewell to Pierre and walked away. Lorenzo turned to Pierre saying, "Signor

Mezzanotte has asked to speak with you. It seems he is eager to hear your observations. Please follow me."

At Mezzanotte's door, Lorenzo ushered Pierre inside. When he saw Pierre, Mezzanotte smiled and stood and stepped around his desk. "Well-traveled and unharmed, I hope your journey was as reassuring as it was informative."

"Your workers appear skilled and capable and their workshops well-organized, so I'm confident the work will be finished in time. And the Commander has agreed to accompany me tomorrow to observe the construction of the kites. Otherwise I hope to speak with Count Pagliaro and learn of the chances for a lightning storm. I'm told his observations are subtle and their record extensive."

"This is quite true and I hope he answers all of your questions. But I have an entirely different question I must ask." He gestured toward a chair.

Pierre sat and Mezzanotte came to stand before him. "I repeat my gratitude for your demonstration; my advisers and I were all impressed by it. You made your point and the principle you revealed may accomplish our goal. I have just one question." He leaned forward and in a quiet voice asked, "Did you kill the mouse or was that done by another?"

Pierre was stunned into silence. From the expression on Mezzanotte's face, he understood he had trapped Pierre. "I didn't intend to mislead you. My experiment was exactly as I described, but by a minor miscalculation of the mouse's weight it did not proceed as I expected. When I returned to the apparatus, it was clear the mouse was not dead but mortally injured and in severe pain. I simply put it out of its misery. The experiment was not perfect yet it demonstrated my hypothesis." He was sweating and hoped it was not obvious.

Signor Mezzanotte rocked on his heels grinning down at Pierre. "Your experiment was indeed interesting and certainly stimulated a curiosity. As for your hypothesis, you must admit it supported only part of it and that poorly. The element connecting lightning and your parlor trick remains only your assertion. Yet on the strength of what I took to be an honest demonstration I have committed considerable resources. I do not begrudge you your fun but considering the generosity of my support you owed me an accurate report." He returned behind his desk and sat down. "Unfortunately for me I have given my promise and from that there is no retreat, so let me insist that as this work progresses you give me honest appraisals. You need to explain how your minor failure affects the completion of this project."

Pierre continued to sweat and he no longer cared that it was noticed. "I hadn't expected that development but I remain certain a large number of lightning strikes will slay the creature. To assure that event my design includes chain-malle rings strong enough to bind up the creature's carcass so that when it is struck dead it can be dragged to the top of Mount Etna and thrown into the volcano. What you witnessed simply makes it more important that, whether dead or only severely wounded, it is bound up so that it presents no additional danger. You see, this plan takes into account every conceivable contingency."

"Every conceivable contingency," Mezzanotte purred in distracted disbelief. "One contingency your plan does not account for is that the beast does not even notice those pinpricks you insist your device will draw down from the heavens."

"I repeat that I've witnessed those results just as I've described them."

"And your assurances are worth far less than they were yesterday." He folded his hands looking down at his desk and sighed. "There seems little point to continuing this debate. You have the material you say you need so it is now up to you to fulfill your promise. I await your results with urgent curiosity."

He looked up at his desk and shuffled those papers spread over it, and so Pierre guessed he had been dismissed. He stood and stepped to the door, but then stopped. "And Augustus?"

Mezzanotte looked up. "What about him?"

"When will I see him?"

Mezzanotte leaned back in his chair looking at Pierre with vague surprise. "His ship approaches the Straits of Messina, which means he is still several days away. When I learn anything more I will inform you. This interview now is finished and I await your next report."

Pierre was about to leave but again he stopped. "By the way, in our journey we discovered a ravine cut into the side of the volcano that needs to be filled-in. The Commander has the relevant details. Please be sure it's repaired." He turned from the door and left.

Outside in the corridor he felt a sudden chill and discovered that perspiration had soaked through his clothes. He made his way to his room to change, but when finally he reached it, exhaustion overwhelmed him and he laid down for a rest.

Something about the sea, or perhaps standing on the deck of a ship, and he felt movement, he was moving, his body was moving, and he turned and opened his eyes to see eyes liquid blue and cunning and looking into his. It demanded another instant to realize he was looking into the eyes of the Abbess lying beside him. She laughed softly in a way that made him smile. "For a moment I thought you might have died."

"I hope you're not disappointed." Fog clung to Pierre's mind that only drifted off slowly.

She sat up. "I can hardly count the ways that sounds unpleasant." He discovered then that she was naked.

"Then I must be a very talented sleeper," he said.

"And a very fortunate one."

"I expect I'm also clever to fail to latch my door."

"Is that because you awake so often with a beautiful woman lying beside you?"

Stung, Pierre replied, "Not nearly as often as I'd like."

"Ah ha! So this one is not enough?"

Through his smile he sighed with exasperation. "You can't awaken a man from a sound sleep and expect clever answers to every question."

"Perhaps it is not cleverness I value."

"That's reassuring since clearly I'm at a loss. But what else could you be looking for?"

"Perhaps honesty?"

Surprised, Pierre said, "You'll be flattered to learn that's a preference you share with Mezzanotte. Still, admit that clever answers are so much more amusing."

"Some say that bear-baiting and bull-fighting are amusing but I abhor them both."

"Tell me then, what is it that most amuses you?"

Her mischievous smile returned. "Watching young men squirm out of their own idiocy."

"Then you are amused every day. And happily I know now what brings you back."

Finally she laughed; high pitched and bright and Pierre was thrilled. He added, "Shall I assume that in addition to your amusement you have observed me for the Signor?"

Her smile faded, replaced with curiosity and mild annoyance. "Why would I do that?"

"Because he has asked you to, and because you cannot refuse his request?"

She shook her head as if dispelling an unpleasant aroma. "Even assuming his request, are you certain I would do so?"

"I'd be surprised if you didn't." He realized she was now off-balance and he enjoyed it.

"And how exactly should I understand that?"

"He has wealth and power and holds a significant influence over your life. Were he to ask, you would have no choice except to agree. Beyond all of that, what is there to understand?"

"That assumes I provide assistance he cannot receive from another. Since that assumption is unlikely, it is just as unlikely he would make such a request." Her smile returned and Pierre guessed she had regained her footing.

"So there's no truth to the suggestion that I've been observed since my arrival, and my words and behavior have been reported to Mezzanotte?"

She scrutinized Pierre as if expecting him to say more but when he did not, she laughed. "Congratulations; you are convinced you are important to Signor Mezzanotte."

He could not resist a sense of embarrassment and looked away. "He's gone to considerable trouble keeping me well-fed and charmed with affectionate companionship. Tell me if I've missed anything."

"Is that how you regard my presence here beside you? Perhaps, in fact, you are far too humble and fail to note that along with his harem, the Signor has mobilized his entire organization. He even ignores his closest advisers in order to accomplish your plan. For the moment at least, you are his golden boy." Something dark and ungenerous entered her eyes. "Of course, your failure will not go unnoticed."

"Success and failure," Pierre said pretending an indifference he could not embrace. "An experiment supports or contradicts a hypothesis. If my hypothesis frames the real world and its experiment is well-designed, it can't fail. On the other hand, if it fails, that must mean my hypothesis does not reflect the real world. Thus for a scientist even failure, by yielding new clues to the nature of our world, offers success."

The Abbess's laughter chilled Pierre. "I hope you do not believe any of that. There is only one incontrovertible rule; success is rewarded because it is success, and failure is punished because it contains no success. Everything else is decoration to aid those who have failed to endure their failure. If you believe anything else you will die alone, unremarked and poor."

"Nothing much to look forward to there."

"Even the noblest failure lacks the most valuable ingredient; success."

"It may beg the question but I believe it's possible to fail successfully."

"Such a belief is suitable only to virgins, children and fools. Since I cannot see you as any of those, that belief is mere self-indulgence."

"You've given me a lot to think about. So tell me what you know about my father."

Her smile was sudden and wide with a coquettish shape to her lips. "As little as you do."

"And how would you know how little I know?"

"You could only know as much as Signor Mezzanotte wishes you to know. And since you are working for him, I expect he has shared very little."

"Does he believe I'll work harder the less I know?"

"You'll prove yourself more reliable. He needs you to see this to its end. He does not trust you and may not even like you but he needs you to succeed, just as with your father."

"And why go to all of this trouble? If he believes I influence the creature, why not just tie a log to my feet and set me adrift? Let it have what it wants and leave him alone."

Her smile disappeared as her expression became serious. "You have never really spoken with him, have you? I mean a long and thoughtful discussion." When he said nothing she continued. "He is certain that regardless of your connection to it, the beast remains his personal burden, whether as punishment for his insolence or reward for his bloodthirsty ways. He is confident that even if he allows it to have you, eventually it will come for him. Believe me, he has searched the world for someone to help him and only you have come to his attention."

Pierre found all of this frightening. “Either the creature is confused or Mezzanotte is. Can he be certain the creature is after him yet just as certain it is after me?”

“And you are not among those confused?”

Pierre was startled to hear his position with Mezzanotte so bluntly described. “Yet he remains reluctant to help me reach my father. Does he see an advantage in keeping us apart?”

She appeared surprised by the question. “Is that what he is doing; keeping you apart?”

“How else should I understand it?”

Her smile turned to patient amusement. “A battle is coming and as a commander, that is all he thinks about. The creature approaches and he recognizes he is defenseless except for your help. He has committed all of his resources to this conflict and yet its outcome remains in doubt. He has risked his empire with this one turn of the cards and he knows he has no second line of defense. I suspect your father is low on his list of concerns. When you deliver his victory, the question of your father will rise in importance to him.”

Petulance entered Pierre’s voice. “So this is a hostage and ransom situation after all.”

“With all he has put at your disposal, it seems unfair to demand more, or to expect it.”

Whether it was the Abbess’s relentless insistence or his own exhaustion, Pierre found he had to concede defeat. “Perhaps you’re right and I expect too much.”

“Too much from Signor Mezzanotte,” she said as a smile returned to her voice, “but perhaps not enough from life.” She leaned forward and nuzzled his cheek. “Have you eaten?”

“No,” Pierre said, “not recently.”

“Good,” she said and drew closer to him. With her arms enfolding his neck she pulled him against her. “I would not want a large meal to slow you down.” And then she laughed.

CHAPTER EIGHTEEN

WHERE THE CONSTRUCTION of the chain-maille carpet demanded close coordination between individual craftsmen to assure its portions linked tightly together, the creation of the kites and their wire cords was organized very differently. Accompanied by the Commander, Pierre visited those workshops and their choruses of women.

Aside from the attachment of a metal tip at each kite's apex and a strip of metal from that tip to the anchor for the metal cord, the variety of the designs of the kites appeared endless and involved an exotic range of colors and figures. While the men at the forges struggled to work to a single and repeatable design, these kite-makers and their kites, constructed nearly as tall as themselves, competed to stand out and with no two of their painted designs the same. Many of those designs were portraits of the saints of the Church calendar but others were images of wild beasts, natural and mythical, while still others appeared abstract and the product of a free creativity. Although the variety of their designs was wide, their shapes were limited to triangle, diamond or rectangle.

Where the men at the foundry worked in small teams accompanied by the piercing clang of metal striking metal, these women worked in pairs and to the sound of quiet speech and laughter, their rivalries and competitions announced with their insistence that a particular design would never fly or a particular saint would never permit it to fly. Competitions were launched when each kite was finished so that the shop emptied and the women gathered outside to see if this ingenious design would ascend to the sky. Each test then elicited high-pitched cheers of congratulation or jeers of loud mockery and heartfelt condolences; all of this in contrast to the darkly muscular and furiously energetic determination of the men at the foundry pounding metal against metal.

The contrast between these workplaces and that shop where the cords that tethered the kites to the chain-maille could not be more stark. This shop was also made up entirely of women who spun hemp into twine and wove it with metal thread delivered from the foundry, all to create a sturdy umbilicus linking the sky with the earth. Within this shop, however, the only sound was the whir of the spinning wheels as twine and metal embraced. Yard upon yard, cords then were wound onto large spools in such a way that they would unreel with little effort. And unlike that shop where the kites were made, these women all were young, their close work demanding young eyes and slim, nimble fingers. Engrossed in concentration, each appeared to Pierre serenely beautiful, and they sat bent over their work so earnestly he was moved to respectful silence. He drew confidence from his visits to the other workshops; the concentration, determination and ingenuity of each assured him he had planned well. But his visits to the weaving shop filled him with a certainty his project proceeded with irresistible grace.

Yet beneath the reassurance of these excursions, Pierre endured that chill and constant wind of the creature's approach. Whenever he found himself entranced by the energy of all of this collaborative effort, he only needed to remember his last sight of the Scientist as he was devoured by the creature to recall the significance of what was being carried out.

After many days of effort the work of each of these shops with their different assignments and disciplines and workers began to converge.

Each day a portion of the chain-maille arrived by ox-drawn cart at the site beside the sea and Pierre supervised its placement. Once laid, men using small anvils and portable forges worked to bind that portion to the others. Under the furiously blazing sun, shelters of wood and canvas protected them as they heated and hammered each link into place, the clang of metal striking metal resounding sharp from the far hills. To supervise their placement Pierre constructed an observation platform near the base of the volcano and from there he called out adjustments to compensate for the terrain. Viewed from there, that sparkling, shimmering carpet appeared to grow like a puddle of quicksilver, and soon it dwarfed the men working around it.

More pieces had been set in place when the spools of cord began to arrive. Working beside the carpet, men measured off lengths of cord which were then rewound with one end bound to its own ring at the edge of the carpet which was secured at the mat's edge by a heavy stake of wood driven into the ground. Colored by the cloudless sky, the carpet lay as a silver blue scintillation which appeared to hover above the wheat-colored earth like a pond of glistening fog.

Portions of cord were still being attached to the mat when the kites began to arrive and each of those was then attached by its cord to the carpet. Pierre decided it was time he spoke with Count Pagliaro. He hoped that some natural principle behind the weather's changes made its behavior predicable though he assumed its phases were as arbitrary as a roll of dice.

Early one morning Pierre crossed the plaza to the Count's tower and its narrow, wooden door, weather-beaten gray and with gaps yawning between its planks. Stepping out of the fierce sun and crossing its threshold he found the room utterly dark and cool, musty yet dry and without furniture or decoration. To one side a rough wooden stair climbed the wall to a floor above. There seemed no alternative but to follow, and so he did.

At the top of these stairs was another closed door, smaller and just as narrow as the entrance but also as gray and worn. He paused and then raised his hand to knock when a hard, dry voice from the other side called out, "Dragonslayer, enter! You are expected!"

Startled, Pierre looked about. After a moment the voice called out, "Slayer of dragons yet fearful of entering an old man's hovel?" This was followed by a sound like two rocks being rubbed together that could have been laughter.

Opening the door Pierre found himself at the threshold of a wide room with a high ceiling. Against the opposite wall stood a chair whose wooden back nearly reached the ceiling and whose seat appeared wide as a bed. Then he noticed a small, wizened and old man sitting in its seat. The front of his head was nakedly bald and shiny, while at its back stood a tall halo of wiry gray-black hair swept upward as if buffeted by a strong wind. This small, bright head perched atop an inexplicable conflation of tattered dark cloth and bits of worn animal pelts, as if the sitter dressed constantly for bad weather. Sharp black eyes scrutinized Pierre with an expression that might have been a smile if his mouth contained more teeth. He repeated the sound of rubbing rocks followed by hiccups like the snapping of dry twigs.

Pierre hesitated. "Count Pagliaro?"

"If the answer to that question," the old man croaked, "has any urgency to you, you are in worse trouble than you can possibly know."

Pierre took a moment to look around at the several maps hung from the rough stone walls and filling the space between four small windows. Beneath the maps stood rough wooden shelves to a height just above Pierre's head and each was filled with thick, dark-brown volumes. Completing the room's furnishing were three tables on which large sheets of paper were spread. One of these tables stood immediately before the old man and his enormous chair.

"Signor Mezzanotte told me..." Pierre began.

"Yes, yes, yes," the Count said waving a pale and skeletal hand. "That bloated sack of excrement befouls our precious atmosphere by his open mouth with distressing regularity. Worse for you if you are compelled to his presence."

Pierre hesitated. "Perhaps I've arrived at an inconvenient moment."

"And perhaps you have been born into the wrong century. Fortune favors few, and none for very long, but that is not my fault. As I see it you have two choices; shut up or end your own life. My suggestion concerning suicide is, never hesitate since you can only live to regret it."

Pierre fought his impatience. "He assured me you have special knowledge of weather."

"Nearly everything that puss-bucket says is a lie, but, unfortunately for me, that is not."

Pierre said, "Pardon me for saying this but I suspect a certain animosity for the man."

Instead of an immediate answer, the diminutive Count emitted such an emphatic combination of the sound of rubbing rocks and snapping twigs that his body slid from the chair to form a twitching puddle of fur and clothing on the floor that roiled like the surface of a lake in a storm. This continued and Pierre resisted the temptation to leave until eventually the pile began to leak a sort of soft mewing he guessed was the old man's effort to regain his breath. The Count then unraveled himself and awkwardly regained his seat. "Much has been said about you, young man," he wheezed, "but no one warned me you were capable of such cutting sarcasm."

"I've been accused of many things, this is true," Pierre said, "but eloquence has never been one of them."

The Count released the horrible sound that passed for laughter again. Pierre's eyes followed another staircase of roughly carved wood that climbed the far wall at an angle and ended at an opening in the ceiling. The Count must have watched his eyes because he walked toward the staircase, his gap-toothed mouth opened in what Pierre hoped was a smile. "Come, follow me and I will show you where the magic happens."

Nimble as a monkey, in a moment the Count reached the top of the staircase. The small, narrow steps were hard to negotiate but Pierre eventually reached the opening to find the roof flat, open and exposed to the sky. The view he enjoyed was unobstructed in every direction to the farthest hills and with a grand view of the volcano. At the opposite end of the roof stood a small, partly-covered wooden shelter. Standing beneath the shelter, the Count waved his small hand for Pierre to approach.

Drawing nearer, Pierre noticed projecting above the shelter's roof a device made up of four horizontal rods that each ended with a diamond-shaped piece of perpendicular metal. The whole contraption spun slowly in the weak breeze. Waving toward Pierre the Count called out, "Come, come and see, come and see."

Beneath the shelter Pierre saw a telescope and beside it several devices he did not recognize although one seemed startlingly familiar. Gleefully the Count said, "See what marvelous devices I have! Look, look, look!"

Perched on a wooden stand was a wide glass tube about two feet high sealed at both ends and filled with a clear fluid. Floating at different levels within it were eight spheres each filled with a different colored fluid. The Count avidly watched Pierre's face. "Do you know what that is? Have you seen its like before?"

When Pierre shook his head, the Count repeated that awful sound. "Of course, how could you? In all of Sicily, there is only this one. In all of Italy, there are only seven. In all of Europe, there are not twenty. Stand in awe, young man, stand in awe. You are in the presence of a miracle of the human mind shaped one hundred years ago by the hand of none other than the divine Galileo Galilei. He named it the thermoscope because by noting which sphere has reached its top one can learn how much phlogiston is in the air. Is that not wonderful?" The Count danced from one foot to the other. "The brilliance of the Italian mind is all around us, my boy, all around us."

Turning then, the Count wheezed, "And this, just look at this!" He pointed to a device mounted to the wall resembling the face of a clock except having only one hand. Surrounding its face like hours were numerals ranging from one to seventy. The Count placed his own face beside it as if he might kiss it. "A product of the hand of the glorious Leon Battista Alberti, whose cunning mind remains unmatched since the days of Leonardo himself. It is attached to that device on the roof and is called an anemometer, from the Greek anemos, meaning wind, and by its action it reveals to us the speed of Aeolus's gift as it passes." He clapped his small hands together as he grinned.

"But here," the Count said suddenly turning to point to a thin tube that appeared to be filled with a silver fluid attached vertically to the wall and having marks along its length, "you see the true glory of our age and the crown jewel of Italian genius. Product of the incomparable mind of Evangelista Torricelli, I am certain you cannot possibly know what it is."

"In fact," Pierre said casually, "I've seen one before." At his words the Count's expression froze into a startled awe. Pierre continued, "It's called a barometer and indicates a pressure of the air." The Count's awe turned to annoyed amazement and then to surly resentment. Fists balled-up he appeared tempted to strike Pierre. Instead, he stormed past Pierre, reached the stairway and in an instant disappeared. Pierre followed him but at the top of the stairs hesitated, mesmerized by the glorious view, until the Count suddenly cried from below, "Touch nothing which you see and come down here now!" Pierre shivered with annoyance but did as he was told.

At the bottom of the stairs he found the Count muttering angrily while he scanned the papers spread over the tables. Suddenly he snatched up a single sheet and turned, bumping into Pierre who had come to stand immediately behind him. In an instant the Count brought his heel down on Pierre's foot. "Too close!" he screamed. "Too close! Too close!"

Annoyed more than injured, Pierre took two steps back. "Keep your distance, you oaf, or I feed your balls to my dog!" The Count appeared to have no dog but Pierre's gesture seemed to mollify him. He turned muttering and carried the sheet of paper to that table which stood before his enormous chair and climbed back into its seat. In a quieter voice he said, "Come and see what I have." When Pierre appeared to hesitate, the Count added, "Come, come, come. Do as I say, just not so close." Pierre's sore foot tempted him to leave but his curiosity got the better of him and he followed the Count's request.

On the paper he saw wavy lines beside a series of numbers along with what he guessed were calendar dates. The Count asked, "Do you recognize what you are seeing?"

Pierre shook his head and the Count's smile returned. "Do not feel too badly, young man, you are looking at something few men have ever seen. These here," he said pointing with a finger like a dry and withered root, "I expect you recognize as dates. But look here, just look. This number represents the level of heat in the air, this the pressure of the atmosphere, this the speed of the wind, and this letter indicates the direction of that wind's origin." He leaned back into his chair, his expression contorted into a grin of pride. "You see here recorded the progression of minute atmospheric variations that provide our weather. And these volumes," he added with a gesture of his rake-like hand toward the bookcases, "contain similar lists reaching back years. You should be profoundly impressed, my friend, profoundly impressed. And do you know why?" Without waiting for Pierre's response he added, "But of course you do not. How could you? How could you understand what so few men have even seen?" In a voice dripping with patience he said, "With these observations I am in the enviable position to assure you that the day after tomorrow it will not rain." He leaned back and his expression was of unembarrassed pride. "Is that not marvelous? Are you not astounded? You can only be shocked into mute astonishment." He waited for Pierre's response. When he offered none the Count said, "Go ahead, you have my permission, confess your astonishment."

"I'm astonished," Pierre finally said.

"Of course you are, my boy, of course you are. How could you be otherwise? No shame there, nothing to be ashamed of. Truth cleanses the soul as it clears the mind."

Pierre stared at the numbers a while longer. "You really can do that?"

The Count slipped his shoe off and began to clean a toenail with his finger. "Do what, dear boy, do what?"

"Can you really predict the weather? Storms and such?"

The Count glanced up with mild surprise. He released his naked, misshapen foot and made that awful sound again that Pierre hoped was laughter. "Of course I can! This is the modern world, my boy. We have moved far beyond our ancient ancestors. We no longer slice open a chicken to find the weather among its entrails; we slice it open simply to eat it."

Pierre returned his attention to the sheet divided by columns of numbers. The Count said, "We have learned to correlate those numbers you see to activities in the sky. For example, I can tell you positively that because the strength of the wind is moderate and is arriving from the south, the pressure remains high and the temperature remains high, it will not rain for the next three days. But if the wind comes from the north, its strength is strong and the pressure and temperature are low, my advice is to watch the sky since the likelihood of rain has increased. Do you understand?"

Pierre's eyes remained on the sheet of paper. "But how are these things related? What about all of this is likely to produce rain?"

The Count shrugged skeletal shoulders. "How should I know? Certain of these things remain unclear, I confess, but their relationships are utterly consistent. Sites equipped like mine are spread from Paris to Warsaw and down the peninsula to Cutigliano, each reporting its observations to Florence, where all are compiled and then sent to me. By a close study of these measurements it remains consistent that a storm which strikes Paris propelled by a wind from the north will eventually appear in the sky over Florence and then here. And because I receive these reports once each week, I can tell you that a significant storm is on its way, although whether it will reach us and exactly when remain uncertain. The Englishman Edmund Halley has claimed to trace a consistent direction for the moving air which he has labeled the trade winds. Those maps on my walls which you have successfully ignored are my attempt to chart possible similar winds as they pass over our island from the four points of the compass."

Pierre said, "Wait! You say a storm is approaching us here?"

The Count hesitated. "Yes, why?"

Instead of answering the Count's question, he asked, "And do you believe another will follow soon after?"

Annoyed the Count answered, "You do a poor job listening, my boy and that will not advance your fortunes let alone your existence. Perhaps you should take a moment to clear your large and obviously stupid ears. I am not reporting beliefs; I report facts as they are conveyed to me by my instruments and those of my colleagues. I simply pass along to you what I have learned from others. I repeat; these predictions are based on reliable measurements made by knowledgeable men. Not like those silly and ignorant conjectures your father makes." His mouth opened and he resumed his horrid noise.

Pierre looked up. "What?"

The Count studied his face a moment and then resumed his noise only louder and more emphatic. "That old fraud; of course I know about him. It should be some relief for you to know that at least one of us in this room is not a complete fool." When Pierre continued to look at him with his own mouth half open in surprise, the Count continued.

"He and that windbag Mezzanotte deserve each other, they truly do. Each deludes the other and both walk away content." He paused to shake his head. "It defies the imagination! The old reprobate goes alone into a room, flips a coin a few times, scribbles something on a piece of paper and passes it off to Mezzanotte as his closely-considered prediction. Please! What science is there in that? Tell me!" The Count's parchment-colored skin began to flush red. He brought out a piece of dirty cloth from under his clothes and wiped his high forehead. "It bewilders one that the Good Lord has not struck them both with a plague of boils, if He remains the Good Lord. But it is a perfidious and deceitful world, my friend. Instead, your perverse and perverted father becomes rich and lives in silks surround by a harem and all of it at Mezzanotte's expense." He paused once more and turned his mouth-twisted smile on Pierre.

"Your father is Mezzanotte's punishment, I swear to that as I sit here." The Count made his terrible noise again, but then stopped and a look of mildly startled surprise appeared on his face. "Please do not tell me you did not know all this!" He paused again and his tiny black eyes grew larger. "Please do not tell me you are not part of your father's scheme to empty Piss-bucket's pockets. Please do not tell me you believed what you have been told."

Stunned into confusion Pierre continued to stare at the Count. The Count's surprise turned to astonishment. Suddenly his horrid sound became that of metal scraping against metal, the sound of a rusty metal hinge being forced open. He clapped his hands, stepped down from his chair and began to dance around the room, his small hands clapping together, his gnarled feet slapping hard on the wooden floor, clapping and slapping his spinning, cavorting movements so quick and antic Pierre became dizzy keeping him in view. Finally he slowed, wheezing as if out of breath.

Leaning forward with his hands on his thighs, the Count said, "Oh my, oh my, oh my. I have not laughed like this since the death of my own dear father." He moved slowly to stand before Pierre. "I hereby confess to you without embarrassment that I am grateful for this visit. You have brought me more joy and pleasure than a house full of whores." He reached up and lightly patted Pierre's shoulder several times. "If I live longer than Methuselah I will always be grateful to you. You have reminded me that there is a form of stupidity that is almost charming. So should you ever, in the midst of your useless and pointless life, find yourself in need of a favor, never hesitate to find me." He looked earnestly up into Pierre's eyes, but after a moment he stepped away making his horrid noise again.

Pierre was overwhelmed by a blizzard of tangled questions but as with a horse gone off at a gallop, he pulled firmly on the reins of his mind until he remembered his purpose. "I need to ask this again; are you certain about the accuracy of your prediction of an approaching storm?"

The Count brought himself to his full height. "Sir, my predictions concerning the weather are nearly one hundred percent accurate." Then he looked more closely at Pierre. "Why? What is the purpose?"

Pierre was about to describe his plan but decided to save himself from further mockery. "Perhaps you already know about as much as you need to know. At least for the moment."

The Count squinted suspiciously but then his mouth twisted into a smile. "So sly, I was right, cautious and sly. Very well, I have made my promise and I will not retract. Ask anything, my boy, any time, and it will be yours without question or condition."

"You'll hear from me soon and perhaps at short notice. Meanwhile, I'm grateful for your time and this conversation. My responsibilities call me elsewhere but we'll meet again."

With the Count's mouth presenting a twisted opening he said, "I will hold you to that as a promise and look forward to its redemption."

Pierre reached the door and looked back. The Count had returned to his chair, his head shaking back and forth, his mouth still open as that sound of rubbing rocks filled the small room.

CHAPTER NINETEEN

SEVERAL DAYS AFTER Pierre's meeting with the Count Pagliaro and with the carpet approaching completion and more of the kites attached, Signor Mezzanotte appeared at the work-site suddenly and unannounced. He hoisted his bulk up the observation platform's rickety ladder and joined Pierre. Under a piercing sun and stretching away to the edge of the surf, the glittering silvery carpet and its colorful talismans disappeared into the creamy fringe of the lapping blue sea. Surveying its expanse, the Signor grinned. "For this aesthetic achievement alone I congratulate you. A monument to science, it is so utterly beautiful it cannot fail to work."

Pierre shrugged. "Aesthetics won't impress the creature."

"And you are certain this beast will follow your carpet onto land."

"My single certainty is that it's heading this way because it is unable to do otherwise."

He turned to Pierre amused. "So just one element to your plan remains in doubt."

Pierre nodded. "The creature and the storm must arrive together."

"And there is no way this can be assured," Mezzanotte added pensively.

"Count Pagliaro insists a storm approaches, but you're right, that's no guarantee." Nodding toward Mount Etna, he added, "We'll move this observation post to the side of the volcano where a lookout will signal the creature's approach."

Mezzanotte sighed. "And yet even our Count's storm may not be enough."

Pierre nodded, frustrated he could only describe probabilities. "Yes; we must hope the storm includes lightning."

Mezzanotte quietly laughed. "Hope is an unreliable anchor to any scheme. What do you propose to do if the creature arrives and the storm does not?"

"Amuse it until our storm arrives."

"Any ideas about how that might be accomplished?"

Pierre looked out over the carpet with its kites now recognizing it all as work completed perhaps for no good purpose. "I'd lie if I said yes, but something will occur to me."

"How unfortunate; I assumed you prepared for every contingency."

Pierre felt the sting of his suggestion. "Remember that by your insistence of a connection between me and this creature, that opportunity must come."

Mezzanotte sighed. "The confidence of youth; nothing is accomplished without it."

After a moment Pierre asked, "And will Augustus arrive before or after the creature?"

Mezzanotte turned annoyed. "His ship is on course and will arrive as God permits."

"I've accomplished the task you kidnapped me for, so offer me something more."

Mezzanotte's voice resounded with frustrated patience. "Your task will be accomplished when the beast is dead. Forgive my concern but I can only hope your father's arrival does not distract you since undoubtedly you and he will have much to discuss."

Pierre smirked. "Hope is a poor anchor for any plan."

Mezzanotte glanced at Pierre. "Hope sustains me in an ocean of uncertainty."

"And timing's everything," Pierre said brightly.

"Including the arrival of your storm."

Pierre turned away. "So your plank of hope is really just a sliver."

"As hope is God's gift I will not speculate upon its dimensions."

"You've recruited the men and oxen so that the beast will be disposed of as we agreed?"

Mezzanotte seemed relieved to reach firmer ground. "Many more than enough."

Pierre shook his head turning away. "That task will demand every man you can reach."

Mezzanotte's impatience returned. "Look about you and have no fear."

Pierre hesitated. "Then I promise that within a few more days, everything will be ready."

Mezzanotte appeared relieved their conversation was finished and smiling he descended the ladder to his carriage. In a cloud of dust his carriage disappeared among the hills.

Finally Pierre could admit his own fear. Nothing would be resolved until the beast arrived, but at that moment the world would witness either his success or his failure. Suddenly his desire was to curl up in bed and never need to do another difficult thing again. Instead, he descended from the platform and went to those last sections of the carpet being staked down to check its end-rings. In his imagination, both the creature and the storm drew closer.

Turquoise twilight soon thickened the air around him. With their work day ended, Pierre watched men step away from their tools and climb into their carts. Their lowing oxen lumbered into the hills to return them to their homes trailing a fog of golden dust that swirled about them catching the day's last brassy red light. The rising songs of insects sheltered within the underbrush made the silence around Pierre deeper, while the edge of the darkening sky began to sparkle with broken shards of light. At the far edge of the carpet, Pierre could still make out that pale filigree that marked the churning surf. With only a soft, dry breeze whispering past, all that was about to happen still appeared to him unlikely. Catching himself in this revere, Pierre decided he needed to return to the palace and be among people again, along with whatever reality he might still grasp. He would only clutch at straws if straws were all that remained.

At the palace Pierre stepped from his carriage and entered a doorway different from one he usually used. Over time he had become confident walking these halls so he was certain that, regardless of the door, he would find his way to his room. He followed the first floor corridor with hardly a thought, and he did not panic when, after one turn and then a second, he still did not recognize where he was. After more turns he realized he had become lost with no choice but to wander. Turning another corner he heard a mutter of voices and a short distance further he was startled to find himself on the threshold of the palace's kitchen, a place he had never visited before.

The size of this room impressed Pierre. Wide with a high ceiling, against the wall opposite its entrance two open fireplaces stood side by side burning low, their embers' red eyes disguised by the dark ash piled around them. At this room's center stood a long and broad pale-wooden table still half-covered with brightly-colored scraps of food. Side-by-side along the ceiling hung blackened pots and pans of different sizes, some enormous, along with other cooking implements. Against another wall were deep wooden bins piled high with foodstuffs, and above these, thick wooden shelves bowed under great wheels of pale or dark cheeses. At the far wall, skinned parts of animals, raw, pale and bloody, were suspended from thick, black metal hooks. In the midst of this shadowy and smoky world, three women in the pale costumes of servants moved about, one older and two much younger, speaking quietly among themselves. Pierre stopped, inexplicably intimidated and waited to be noticed. In a few moments the older woman turned to see Pierre.

"Ah Signor!" she said in an eager, high-pitched voice. "Welcome. Please enter. What can we do for you?" At her words the other women stopped and turned.

Pierre hesitated. "Forgive my interruption but I've become lost."

Short and round, the older woman wiped her thick hands on her long white apron and stepped forward, earnest concern on a face nearly as round as her body yet eternally cheerful. Her wavy dark hair, revealing strands of gray in the light of the fires, was tied tightly in the back.

"Do not concern yourself, Signor, we are happy to help." The younger women came to stand beside her and stare at Pierre with curious concern. Both were slim and in the subdued light their long hair was the color of honey. "And who might you be, if I may ask?"

Pierre introduced himself and the eyes of all three grew large. One of the younger women said, "You are the foreigner who'll save us from the Devil."

Pierre smiled but then caught himself and became serious. The older woman turned a dark look on the younger and hushed her. "Pardon our rudeness," she said. "I am called Josephina, and these are my nieces. The impertinent one's name is Maria, the other is Angela."

Maria said to Pierre, "But you are the one who has come to save us, aren't you?"

"I'm not a priest," Pierre said, "and I don't know if it's the Devil who threatens us, though I wouldn't be surprised if it was."

Angela said, "But with the Signor's army, surely you will defeat this monster."

Maria said, "You must be terribly brave." Her eyes glowed in the firelight. "Will you slay the beast with a sword or with arrows or with a club?"

Josephina turned with impatience. "Forgive these questions, Signor. These young ones know so little."

In a loud whisper Maria added, "And the old ones know hardly more." This made Angela laugh as it drew a dark look from Josephina.

Turning a suddenly sweet smile on Pierre, Josephina said, "You are in luck. Continue along this corridor to its end and then turn to the right and you will reach a set of stairs. Climb them to the top and you will find your way from there."

Pierre smiled again and bowed. "I thank you for your help." He turned to go but then stopped. "Once more I must ask your pardon, but I've missed the evening meal. If it would prove no trouble, perhaps some food could be brought to my room. A bit of bread, some cheese perhaps and fruit and wine. I'd take that as a great kindness."

"Think nothing of it, Signor," Josephina said, her smile brightening. "It shall be done and just as you request." She curtsied and turned her back; he caught a wry smile from Maria.

He followed Josephina's direction and as she had promised he reached his corridor. Approaching his door he saw Lorenzo coming toward him. Pierre stopped him and asked if he would contact the Duchess di Nuova Cento. He looked at Pierre as if uncertain, but said he would try and then turned and left. Pierre was surprised by his own disappointment.

As with so many others, this day had begun early and Pierre had worked hard under a hot sun, so reaching his room he washed and changed his clothes before bringing out his notes and sketches of the day's progress. But sitting at one end of the couch with the plans spread on the table before him, he found himself struggling to keep his eyes open until eventually he failed and nodded off. So the knock at his door startled him awake. Before he could respond, the door opened and, to his surprise, Maria appeared carrying a tray of food. He stood intending to take the tray from her hands but still drowsy he bumped into a chair and stumbled.

Maria laughed warmly and moved the tray away from his out-stretched hands. "I have had more practice." He stepped back allowing her to carry the tray to his table.

He bowed. "Thank you for bringing this."

With a flattered smile she said, "It allowed me to get out from under my Aunt's thumb."

"She seems to run a tight ship." Pierre returned to his seat on the couch

"If you mean her eyes are everywhere and her tongue is sharp, you have it nearly right."

"Can I guess that Angela gets along well enough with her?"

"She's shy, but I like talking with people. That's why I'm always in trouble."

"Your Aunt must trust you at least a little or she wouldn't have sent you here."

"She didn't send me," Maria said with a hint of pride. "Lorenzo did."

This surprised Pierre. "I didn't realize he had such authority."

"He is upstairs staff."

"I guess I'm just curious why he would send you."

She smiled again as if flattered by his interest. "Perhaps he regards me as more reliable." Then she said, "But more likely he simply had something important to do."

"Pardon my suggestion but there can hardly be much skill to carrying a tray of food."

Maria's smile turned into a scowl but it was so pretty and charming he ignored his own insult. "A task skillfully done always looks easy. But perhaps you will carry this tray back to the kitchen when you have finished." She turned toward the door.

"Sorry," he said to her retreating back. "I didn't mean to offend you."

Maria stopped and turned, her smile resumed. "I am always curious to see if someone like you worries about the feelings of a person who carries a tray of food."

"What kind of person do you think I am, unless you've already answered the question?"

Maria studied him and then shook her head as if choosing which question to answer. "I have stood here this entire time. Do women in the New World stand and only men sit?"

"You've now embarrassed me twice," Pierre confessed, startled because she was right. "Or should I say I've embarrassed myself. Please, kindly have a seat."

Maria sat down at the far end of the couch facing Pierre, her hands folded in her lap and amusement around her eyes. She nodded toward the table. "I carried this from the kitchen. Aren't you even a little hungry?"

"I don't want to add to my insults," Pierre said. "Will you join me?"

She shook her head. "I ate some time ago. Besides I like to watch people eat. It's a public intimacy, like weeping. Besides, after a day among the workmen you must be hungry."

Once again she surprised him. "You seem to know a lot about my day." He picked up the loaf of pale dense bread, tore a piece from the end and then sliced a piece of the cheese.

"Everyone here knows what you plan to do."

Startled, Pierre said, "So everyone also knows about the creature."

"We know the Signor believes it exists, though only you have seen it. This has made you mysterious but also terribly important."

"That seems unlikely. Other than Mezzanotte, I've only spoken to his advisers."

Maria shrugged and looked away as if Pierre had said something remarkably stupid. "Walls have mice and mice have ears. You must not believe that something which involves so many people will remain secret. And if I know of it, there is no one in the palace who does not."

"I don't know whether to be flattered or frightened. So it must also be well-known that a man employed by Mezzanotte is my father and that he is traveling here."

Maria's dark eyes grew large with surprise. "So it is true; he is your father. But that man has been among us perhaps for a month."

A storm of panic blew suddenly through Pierre. "That's not possible! The Signor said he was in Naples and promised to bring him here."

Startled, Maria shrank back into her seat. "I only say what I have heard."

His panic turned to anger. "If that's true, why would he keep it from me?"

Maria chuckled and its sound brought to mind clear water passing over large rocks in bright sunshine. "If you wonder at that, you are not nearly as smart as people say. If you and your father were to meet, would you remain eager to fight the Signor's beast?"

Pierre did not try to answer her question. "Where I can find him?"

"Ah," Maria said and slowly stood, "that I cannot say. I do not know where he is, but even if I did and the Signor did not want you to know, telling you would only make trouble for me."

Pierre's suspicion turned suddenly toward Maria but he shook himself. "Fair enough, but if Mezzanotte expected to keep that information from me, why allow others to know?"

"Remember those mice and their ears." She gnawed her lip. "I begin to think I have said too much." She turned and stepped toward the door.

"Don't go!" Pierre said, surprised by his own request. "I've enjoyed listening to you."

"Enjoy my company and perhaps a bit more, is that it?" Though she sighed with disappointment her smile remained. "You mean well but this is not flattering." She looked about. "It is late and soon there will be trouble for me."

Pierre leaned forward. "Don't worry; I'm sure I'll clear things with Josephina."

Maria burst into bright laughter and this time Pierre did not enjoy its sound. "You are so appealing when you are silly, but you must not believe that. I know you wish to be nice to me and I am flattered but Josephina will not be fooled. I am not so invisible like your beast."

As she stepped closer to the door, he asked, "Then tell me when you will finish."

"When my help is no longer needed."

"Promise you'll return?" His urgency surprised him. "I'll wait the whole night."

Again she laughed and this time its sound delighted him. "Are all those of the New World so eager to make love to servants?" She paused but then added, "Still, though I do not believe you, it is nice of you to say." As if suddenly feeling sorry for him she added, "If I finish early I will return." She nodded toward the tray. "I can always say I am returning for that."

The sound of the door closing behind her left Pierre disheartened in a way he could not understand. He turned to his meal and filled his glass. The light in her eyes and the trill in her voice clung to his mind as if he could have listened to her all night. Besides, he was certain she knew much more and wondered if any of it might be what he needed to know. Though he hoped his promise to wait would mean something, he decided he would not see her again that night. So he ate slowly with a heaviness in his mind until his thoughts returned to the beast.

Recalling the way the kites sometimes collided above the carpet, he wondered if they would survive the violence of the thunderstorm he needed to arrive. Just as suddenly, he decided he should have considered this earlier and wondered why he had not. The more he thought about this question the more uncertain he became. Suddenly his project seemed vulnerable to difficulties he had failed to consider.

He pushed aside the rest of his meal, cleared the table and unfurled the sheet bearing his design. He needed to review his plan again and recognize whatever remained vague and therefore vulnerable. He scrutinized the sheet making notes of elements he suspected might fail. He found it difficult to think about what he had not thought about, so he could not pretend surprise when difficulties appeared which he had not considered. He tried to weigh and recognize those most serious, along with what might be done about them. In this way his despair grew.

Pierre lost all sense of the passage of time, so a light knocking on his door startled him. Suddenly hopeful that Maria had returned after all, he stood and opened the door. To his surprise the Abbess stared back at him.

"Well, this is interesting." Annoyance lay just behind her smile. "If I did not know better I would suspect that expression was disappointment." She stepped past him and then turned. "But that could not possibly be the case."

Pierre disguised his confusion with a wry smile and closed the door behind her. "I asked Lorenzo about you earlier. Perhaps it's just surprise, since it's late and I'd given up hope."

Curiosity appeared around her eyes. "You and I are connected at the deepest levels of our beings or have you forgotten. Be content and have no fear. You will see me when you need me." Her look softened and she looked about. "Would you mind terribly if I sat down?" Hearing this question startled Pierre. "And perhaps you will offer me something to drink."

"How is it you're always right and I'm always rude? Take a seat as I pour some wine."

"Lovely," she said. She sat down on the couch and straightened her skirt. "Just as you say, I am here because Lorenzo said you had asked for me." She glanced at the papers spread over the table. "Despite the late hour, it appears

I have interrupted something."

Pierre filled a goblet. "Can I ask you something?"

"As we are friends you may ask anything you like."

He handed the goblet of wine toward her. "Where is my father being held?"

Hand suspended in the air beside the goblet, she looked at him with flat, expressionless eyes. "Why do you believe he is being held anywhere?"

"Come along." He watched as her hand finally took the goblet. "Everyone speaks to you, including Mezzanotte. I can't believe there are any mysteries for you here. I want to believe what you tell me, but this one's a puzzle."

She glanced at him over the rim of the goblet and sipped. "You flatter me even when you insist I know what I do not. The fact remains, I know nothing about him."

Pierre hesitated. "Suppose I tell you I've learned of his presence from someone who has no reason to pretend otherwise."

She shrugged. "An unlikely source does not assure accuracy. Just where has this information come from?"

"This person doesn't have access to the sources you do, yet I believe it's true."

Her expression softened and grew sad. "I did not come here to argue. I had something far more enjoyable in mind. But here you are, prepared to spoil things merely over a rumor."

"I haven't made myself clear. Whatever else I'm doing, I'm here to find my father. Since you're my friend, please tell me what I want to know."

Suddenly sympathetic she asked, "Can you doubt I am your friend?" She reached out to put her hand lightly on his forearm. "If I knew what you seek I would certainly tell you. So if I do not, please believe it is because I cannot."

"Because you don't know or because you're not permitted?"

She smiled as if in agreement. "Is there a difference?"

When he did not answer she sighed as if their conversation had become tedious. "If I am constrained against sharing my knowledge, it is just the same as not knowing."

"But you are my friend, so in that case it should be different."

"You surprise me," the Abbess said. "You insist you are my friend yet you wish to put me at risk." Impatience filled her voice as if she were compelled to explain the mysteries of existence to a child. "Assume I possessed such a confidence. If I betrayed it, that person would never share another with me again. How would I benefit from that?"

He enjoyed a rush of triumph. "So you admit you know something. Don't forget how far I've come and all I've survived. Can you believe any of what you say is enough for me?"

Her sudden bright laughter startled him. "So much drama over so little. I tell you again; I only know what you know. He is traveling from Naples and will arrive any day. Why might I jeopardize my position over the difference of a day or two?"

Pierre could no longer hide his frustration. "Because you are my friend."

"So this is no longer about your father; it is your test of my loyalty and our friendship."

His frustration overwhelmed him and he shook his head. "I suppose we've reached an impasse."

The Abbess' laughter this time was filled with relief. "Oh, but not on everything." She slid closer across the couch, leaned toward Pierre and returned her hand to his forearm, this time caressing it from wrist to elbow. "It took so long to find each other and our reunion was so unlikely it would be a shame if we lost touch again." Her eyes became soft and he felt himself begin to fall into them as his impatience drifted away. He leaned toward her, her mouth so inviting he could already feel her lips against his, but a knock on the door stopped him. The Abbess leaned back as if to see whether he would ignore it. He hesitated but then he stood.

He opened door to find Maria. She smiled. "So you managed to remain awake." Bright surprise was in her voice. She entered his room but seeing the Abbess she stopped. Her voice went flat. "I've come for that tray."

"I expect that you have," the Abbess said. Then she stood. "No need to hurry; our conversation is finished and I am about to leave."

Suddenly there was another knock at the door. He opened it to find Lorenzo. He stepped into the room, saw the two women and then stopped. Turning to Pierre he said, "The Signor wishes you to know the creature has been seen. Please come with me."

Glancing at the Abbess and then at Maria, Pierre sighed, relieved to follow Lorenzo since it was only the creature that awaited him. He wondered then what the weather would be like.

CHAPTER TWENTY

ENTERING MEZZANOTTE'S SMALL room lit by three flickering candles, Pierre found him seated behind his desk with the Commander standing by his side. His advisers stood ranged behind them in quiet conversation. As he entered they became silent and their eyes turned on him.

Looking up from his desk Mezzanotte offered Pierre an ominous smile. "Well, young man, it appears your moment has arrived; the creature has been seen." He turned and gestured with his hand behind him. "These gentlemen are determined to convince me your scheme offers nothing beyond the cost of many lives in its failure. In your defense I have reminded them you have experience of the beast and that experience is the source of your plan. Be that as it may, the deed has been done and your trap has been set, while they fail to offer a convincing alternative. So as the hour approaches, tell us; are you prepared to lead us forward?"

From the expressions of the advisers' faces, Pierre could guess their consensus. "Where was the creature last seen and how long before it reaches us?"

The Commander said, "Two days ago it approached Messina. Sources report the turbulence of the strait forced it onto land which resulted in devastation to the city and terrible loss of lives. It then re-entered the sea and continues south. At its current progress, in no more than three days, and perhaps in two, it will arrive off our coast." He looked for confirmation from the rest of the advisers.

Mezzanotte glanced at Pierre and then stood. "By your estimation, does this leave us enough time? Will we be prepared when it arrives?"

Pierre knew he could give only one answer to this question. "Of course.

Perhaps a half-day's work but no more and all will be ready."

Mezzanotte stepped from behind his desk, glanced at his advisers and then at the Commander. "Then nothing more needs be said."

To Pierre, the Commander suddenly said, "Assume your devices are all in place and the creature arrives; is it not the case there is an element still necessary for your success?"

"You're referring," Pierre said patiently, "to the presence of a storm."

"Not just any storm, but one that includes lightning. Is there any way we can be assured this will happen?"

"You're right, the plan depends on that. Count Pagliaro assures me a storm approaches and will likely arrive soon. But you are correct; there's no guarantee of its timing or strength."

The Commander looked around at the others. "A thin reed to append an ambitious plan. Suppose this storm is insufficient for your needs, what will you do?" Though Pierre had been asked this question before, the Commander's smug grin conveyed all that his words did not.

Despite himself Pierre smiled. "We will simply temporize as we improvise."

The Commander snarled, "In fact, what you confess is that confronted by the beast you do not know what you will do."

Mezzanotte glared at the Commander. To Pierre he said, "The Commander has convinced my advisers of what he believes is a more likely strategy. It concerns me that you have experience of the beast and yet were not consulted." Glancing behind him the Signor said, "Now that its arrival is imminent, it seems best that you hear him out."

The Commander said, "First, our plan is less complicated and less expensive."

Pierre asked, "And thereby far less likely to succeed?"

The Commander glared. "Be so kind as to hear me out before passing judgment. In any case, since your plan has already been put in place, it seems the question of resources is beside the point. Our plan's virtue is that it deals with the creature as we would with any animal. If, as you suggest, it is not possible to kill the beast, our plan is certain to drive it away and regret its encounter." Pierre shook his head, a trace of a smile about his lips as the Commander continued. "We propose that a series of bonfires be set along the shoreline with batteries of cannon positioned at intervals between them. Undoubtedly this will discourage the beast from coming onto the land and a fortunate shot may inflict a mortal wound."

Pierre's quiet laughter seemed to rise from deep in his chest. The Commander turned annoyed toward Mezzanotte and then to the others. Pierre asked, "That's the best you have? That thread-bare plan is the product of all these very eminent minds?" He turned to Mezzanotte. "Only someone with no experience of this creature would offer that." He paused. "But let's consider the likely outcome. The Commander concedes that it's all but impossible his plan will result in the creature's death so his best hope is to drive it away. Unfortunately, that'll simply demand that you repeat this exercise and only hope the result will prove useful." He paused and looked at the Commander. "Forgive me if I'm unimpressed."

"Gentlemen," Mezzanotte said with a false joviality intended to relieve tension, "we will agree we have reviewed this proposal even though on the surface it seems to offer slim promise. Thus my decision remains and the time to act is now. The plan put into operation enjoys my confidence since it offers the likelihood of the creature's destruction, which must remain our ultimate goal." Turning to the Commander he said, "We are deeply grateful for your effort." Turning to the rest of his advisers he added, "And yet, in a spirit of compromise let me offer this. Implementation of the Commander's plan in no way need interfere with Pierre's, so I propose we include its elements to supplement Pierre's effort."

Pierre could not hide his annoyance. Appearing to notice his discomfort, to Pierre, Mezzanotte said, "Give this some thought. It would be a great advantage if these fires were built close together along the shore, leaving a gap to act as an invitation for the creature to enter. And if it appears reluctant to cooperate, might the cannons drive it in the direction we wish?" He paused with the expression of a man intrigued by his suggestion. He looked about. "So we will combine these plans and hope to assure ourselves the greatest likelihood of success."

A moment of silence passed. Mezzanotte looked from one face to the next as if waiting to be challenged. Pierre glanced at the Commander and then spoke up. "I'll concede the Commander's suggestion may have value. We've already moved the lookout post to a place on the volcano that'll alert us to the storm's approach, so there are workers now free to assist him."

The Commander's irritation colored his voice. "This does not solve your problem of the storm's arrival."

He spoke with such authority that Pierre was startled. He hesitated and then glanced at Mezzanotte. "Let's put this in terms we'll all understand. Disturbing as it is for me to admit, the Signor insists it's my person attracting this creature to your shores. Assuming that's true, if it proves necessary for our success I'm prepared to offer myself as a lure to hold the creature's attention until the storm arrives and I hereby accept all the risks this may entail." He looked about challenging contradiction or protest. "My one condition is that you produce my father." He paused again and then added, "Immediately." He looked about at the others.

Most had expressions of mild surprise or confusion, but none returned his gaze. Only Mezzanotte's face displayed annoyance shading toward anger. Pierre said, "If there's nothing left to discuss I'll return to my room and look forward to my father's arrival within the hour." With a glance he looked to confirm that his words had been understood and then turned. As he reached for the door, the Commander said, "You still have not resolved the issue of the storm." Pierre stepped into the corridor slamming the door behind him. To his surprise, Lorenzo stood waiting. He strode past Lorenzo who turned and trotted to catch up.

"Your meeting was brief," Lorenzo said. "I hope it was productive."

"Blunt exchange produces clarity and that is precious in all affairs."

Hurrying beside Pierre along the twilight-dim corridor Lorenzo asked, "And when do you expect to learn if your efforts have succeeded?"

"Soon I'll know a lot more than I know now." Finally he slowed and they continued in silence until they reached the door to his room. Lorenzo seemed startled when Pierre thanked him for his help as if dismissing him, entered the room and closed the door. He stood for a moment inside panting for air. He had not expected either woman still to be there and so he was not surprised to find himself alone.

He paced about his room relieved. The gauntlet had been tossed and it was Mezzanotte's turn to respond. Hope and fear washed over him like waves in a storm-tossed sea; anticipation of meeting with Augustus alternated with concern with the creature, each offered its own humiliation, misery and taste of failure.

Time inched forward. He paced and then sat and then paced, stood for a time at the window to stare at the bright moon afloat in a black and cloudless sky before retreating to his bed to lay back. Moments crawled over his prostrate body like an army of ants. An hour passed and then a second evaporated and then another crept by. Had his challenge to Mezzanotte accomplished anything beyond irritating a man who controlled his life?

At a knock at his door he hesitated but then stood and rushed to open it, and was startled with disappointment to find Lorenzo at his threshold, a tray of food in his hands. "Pardon this interruption but I assumed despite the hour you would enjoy something to eat and drink." His look of concern surprised Pierre.

He stepped from the doorway. Lorenzo carried the tray past him to the table and set it down. "Any word from Mezzanotte?"

Lorenzo looked up. "It seems he has sent men to the observation platform."

Pierre sighed. "Watching for the creature. I guess he hates surprises as much as I do." Lorenzo offered a questioning look but Pierre said nothing more. He asked if he could bring anything else and Pierre shook his head as he thanked him. The door closed quietly.

He sat down, poured wine into a goblet and began to eat. His sudden hunger surprised him. Events moved forward and he wondered if all the cards finally were on the table. Mezzanotte must have recognized his determination to see his father and his threat to abandon his program, but an exchange of threats is a dangerous game. If Mezzanotte chose, he could simply order the Commander to take up the battle. The elements of the plan were all in place and Pierre's help was now likely irrelevant. Yet he continued to insist Pierre had some ineffable connection to the beast. Pierre finally had to admit that he depended on that conviction. As Mezzanotte had said, Pierre at least had seen the creature. But all of this could change in an instant. If Pierre's insistence became a burden and Mezzanotte decided he was a liability, Pierre could find himself suddenly dead, if not worse. The Commander was a fool yet he still enjoyed Mezzanotte's confidence. Pierre wondered if his battle with the beast would demand battle with the Commander, and the defeat of one could only come about by the defeat of the other. Mezzanotte's production of Augustus would tell him how determined he was to keep his trust.

Though he had been hungry when Lorenzo first delivered his food, his thoughts drove his hunger away until he sat picking at his meal with distracted indifference. He pushed the meal aside and refilled his goblet. He had challenged Mezzanotte to produce Augustus and now he was obliged to see if he would follow through. He sipped from the goblet and when it emptied he refilled it. The wine proved stronger than his will so that sleep overwhelmed him.

Thus, Pierre lay sprawled on the couch when a knock at his door woke him. He opened his eyes to a room flooded with light. He forced himself to stand, but before he reached the door it opened and Lorenzo appeared with a tray of food in his hands. "Reluctant as I am to wake you," he said, "the morning is passing and I took the liberty." Seeing the remains of the previous meal hardly touched he said, "I hope I have not presumed too much."

Pierre yawned and stretched and then shook himself. "Mustn't sleep the day away; my promise to Mezzanotte demands better." He stepped behind the screen and began to wash. "Heard anything of him this morning?"

"He was seen leaving the palace in his carriage in the company of the Commander."

This surprised Pierre. He stepped around the screen. "Know where they're going?"

Lorenzo shook his head. "The Signor never informs me of his intentions unless he must." He placed the tray of food on the table and took up the one from the previous night. "Doubtless it was urgent and likely involves your beast. Beyond that, the mystery remains." He asked if Pierre needed anything else and when he said he did not Lorenzo turned and left.

Pierre finished washing, put on fresh clothes and returned to his table, but his appetite battled with his curiosity. Beyond the window, the morning sun was still low in a cloudless, flat blue sky promising a hot and windless day. He finished his meal quickly, made his way to the plaza and asked the waiting carriage to take him to the work-site.

Dust from the iron-clad wheels of the carriage hung in their wake an ominous cloud. Scanning the sky Pierre wondered about the Count's promise of a storm. This day appeared unlikely to cooperate so he hoped the creature's progress would be slow and its arrival delayed. But hope, he reminded himself, is a poor prop for any ambition.

He had made this trip so often he did not need to guess its duration, but when the carriage climbed the last hill and he looked out over the work-site, its changes startled him.

Dark wooden carts drawn by oxen and loaded with long, roughly-cut logs snaked along a path that followed the coast from the south. As each cart approached, soldiers directed it to the beach alternately north and south. When a cart reached a predetermined spot, workmen emptied it and that cart then moved off. Other men climbed over logs that, from a distance, appeared as piles of black matchsticks, and set them up into pyramids. Away from the activity by the shore and near the edge of the metal carpet stood the Signor's open carriage with the Commander seated within. Pierre asked his driver to take him there. As the carriage moved forward he gathered the questions he would ask.

Nearing the carriage the Commander stepped down from his to stand beside it. He called out orders and directions as Pierre stepped down from his carriage and joined him. The Commander greeted Pierre as if this was an annoying obligation and then resumed calling out instructions. Pierre's irritation filled his throat but he forced it back. "What's the plan?"

The Commander hesitated and turned a look of pained patience on Pierre. "Simply what I agreed to carry out for the Signor." He turned away then as if certain Pierre's curiosity had been satisfied.

"Glad to hear it," Pierre said. "But I'm curious to learn something more specific."

The Commander no longer disguised his impatience. "As we discussed, to confine and direct the creature to enter your trap." He turned back to observe the activities around them. "I hope these preparations are satisfactory."

Pierre said, "And these are the bonfires. When will the cannons arrive and where they will be placed?"

The Commander turned suddenly, impatience replaced by anger. "I am a military man, Signor, and you are not. I have offered the Signor my opinion of your ludicrous strategy. He has heard me out and reached his own conclusion. He has given me my orders and it is now my obligation to carry them out. I assure you all will be in place by sunset. Now, I ask that you stand aside and allow me to do my work." He turned away then as if Pierre had ceased to exist and resumed calling out instructions.

Pierre could barely contain his frustration but he knew he had learned all the Commander would allow. If he wanted to know more, he would need to ask Mezzanotte. Once again, he would need to speak with Mezzanotte or be satisfied with his own ignorance. To the Commander's back Pierre asked, "Can you tell me where Signor Mezzanotte's gone?"

Without turning he replied, "The Signor does not consult me on such matters."

"And my father, what about him?"

Still turned away from Pierre he replied, "Why would I know such a thing?"

"Because my assistance is conditioned on his appearance."

"And yet you are here," the Commander said with smug contempt.

Fury overwhelmed Pierre. He grabbed the Commander's shoulder and spun him around to face him. The Commander glared, shoved Pierre to the ground onto his back and in a moment the tip of his drawn rapier was pinned to Pierre's chest just over his heart and pressing hard.

"Fool! Fool! You dare lay your feces-covered hands on me!" The Commander's eyes blazed. "And without a sword of your own, nor the wit nor character to wield it." The tip pressed harder; when it penetrated his clothes and pierced his skin Pierre winced. "If your life means so little to you it means even less to me." A flick of his wrist and in the next instant the rapier disappeared into its sheath. The Commander turned his back on Pierre.

Gathering his feet slowly beneath him Pierre stood. Touched to his chest his fingers came away bright with blood. Gritting his teeth, to the Commander's back he said, "I look forward to our next meeting." He clenched his fists trembling but turned slowly and returned to his carriage. Tempted to challenge the Commander, he reminded himself there was someone else he needed to speak with. He asked the driver to return him to the palace.

Caressed by a hot, dry breeze the carriage rocked over the uneven ground as the sun beat down leaving no shadow as a refuge. Pierre touched the wound at his chest again contemplating revenge. Yet even thinking this, he knew there was nothing he could do. The Commander was bitterly correct; he had neither rapier nor skilled hand and he could imagine no future where that would change. Still, he could not smother his own fury or sense of insult and betrayal.

Mezzanotte had agreed to produce Augustus, but perhaps he had done so simply to humor Pierre, his threat as transparently empty to him as it had been to Pierre. As he thought about it, all of them likely had enjoyed a good laugh after he left, and his sudden departure had only deprived them of the pleasure of laughing in his face. Had the Commander wanted to award

Pierre with a token of his contempt, Pierre had given him the opportunity and the man had succeeded. His wound grew slowly to a flame of pain.

Passing beyond the next hill the palace came into view and Pierre felt an odd relief. The sight reminded him he had other issues to resolve, greater enemies to slay, and he was determined to equip himself to succeed. Besides, once the creature was slain he could demand the Commander's apology, its dead carcass a challenge more powerful than any rapier.

The driver hurried their carriage through the main gate and at a trot brought Pierre to the Count Pagliaro's tower. Even before it stopped Pierre leapt down, let himself through the heavy dark door, thudded up the stairs and swung open the door to the Count's chamber, but the Count was not there. He turned looking about when from overhead he heard the cry, "Flatfooted blockhead, arise!" He climbed the narrow stairway to the rooftop and found the Count standing near the shed and beside his telescope grinning at Pierre.

"I have watched you," he called out as Pierre approached, "since your carriage passed between those hills." Nodding toward the horizon he patted the telescope on its tripod like a favorite dog. "There is no sense as certain as sight." His eyes moved to the small, bloody tear on Pierre's shirt. "I hope your opponent has paid dearly." Pierre winced as much from the unintended rebuke as the pain.

"Revenge must wait," Pierre said. "A truly dangerous enemy approaches."

The Count nodded. "One enemy at a time, a wise strategy. So your creature is near."

Pierre looked up with surprise. "How have you heard?"

"The urgency of your visit tells me everything. The world of lies is less a barrier than a net allowing the large to pass through while capturing the small. So tell me, where and when?"

"Messina two days ago and heading in this direction."

The Count squinted toward the horizon. "And now you need to know the likely appearance of your storm."

Pierre hesitated. "I won't ask the obvious; I've had too much practice at that."

The Count patted him lightly on the shoulder. "Come, my boy, it cannot be as bad as all that. Follow me and we will see what can be done." He turned toward the stairs. "Like most of us, you likely have better luck than you deserve."

CHAPTER TWENTY-ONE

PIERRE NEGOTIATED THE stairway and when he reached the room he found the Count standing before one of his wall maps. "Come, my boy; you need to know where you stand." Pierre recognized the map's outline of Western Europe but every other line and mark was a puzzle. "I will spare you an explanation of this esoteric notation and simply tell you this map arrived from Florence early today and bears observations accumulated from across Europe. Although there is no way for you to know this, the goddess Fortune does not merely smile upon you, she beams." He chortled at his own joke. "You see that line right there?" Though the Count's finger lay directly upon the map Pierre could not distinguish any line from any other, but to avoid disappointing the Count he nodded. "That tells me we can expect a superb storm; a storm anyone would be happy to call a storm."

Pierre nodded. "I told Mezzanotte I'd only continue to help him if he produced Augustus. But he hasn't and now Mezzanotte's gone. You wouldn't know where, or if it has to do with Augustus?"

The Count turned away. "As remarkable as this may seem, no one tells me anything."

"Then how did you learn about the creature's arrival and the need for this storm?"

"I said no one tells me anything; that is not the same as not knowing anything." His rasping laughter followed. "I do you a favor by not disentangling all of that for you. Know simply that indirect knowledge is still knowledge. The movements of men reveal even more than their words, and who they speak with reveals their thoughts. Of course, none of that bears on your concern. But as I look at your face I detect a question more urgent though unspoken."

"You're right. When will the storm arrive?"

To Pierre's surprise, the question startled the Count. "When? Are you asking the hour of the storm's arrival?" He turned back to the map. "According to this, it should reach us soon." He paused. "You see, this line indicates prevailing winds, but this suggests those winds are shifting toward the east. Another current threatens to deflect these winds but it does not appear strong and may weaken further. On the other hand, winds may arise from the south to deflect the storm unless they shift to the west. Though unlikely, that could weaken your storm." His voice trailed off. He brought his face closer to the map then shook his head slowly from side to side. "Soon," he said vaguely. "I believe your storm will arrive soon." Leaning even closer and squinting he added, "Yes, something should arrive soon."

Pierre leaned forward to scrutinize the map. "Is that the best you can do?"

The Count straightened himself to his full height. "That is considerable! My assurance is considerable. And I defy you to find better."

Pierre stifled his frustration. "Fair enough. As that's the best you've got, it'll need to be enough. Meanwhile, would anyone else in the palace know where Mezzanotte's gone?"

The Count thought for a moment. "Perhaps the Commander." He glanced at Pierre's shirt. "But perhaps he is not the person you most wish to speak with right now."

"Asking him got me this for my trouble." He gestured toward his chest.

The Count nodded. "An experienced but dull-witted man. So events are entirely in Mezzanotte's filthy and treacherous hands and will remain so until their conclusion. Be comforted that it is merely an assistant to the Devil you must deal with."

Suddenly Pierre realized he was hungry even while it felt as if the entire weight of the day had fallen onto his shoulders. "I'll return to the palace and wait for events to play out."

"You could do worse, dear boy," the Count said with unexpected sympathy, "and likely will."

"That's probably more good advice I'll never use."

"Think nothing of it," the Count said. "There is always more where that came from and none of it worth the breath."

As Pierre reached for the door the Count said, "And when you see your father, please do not pass along my greetings or best wishes." Again he emitted that sound Pierre assumed was laughter, though it no longer seemed quite so irritating.

By the time he stepped outside the sun had passed its midpoint and begun its approach to the horizon. During his conversation with the Count he had considered returning to the site of the trap but looking up he guessed he would only arrive with little time before full darkness fell.

Pierre crossed the piazza and entered the palace through the main entrance. Just within he met Lorenzo and asked that a small meal be brought to his room. Soon after he reached his room Lorenzo arrived with a tray of food. He ate slowly still baffled by his conversation with the Count. Combined with the heat of the day his meal left him exhausted and he fell onto his bed. The cacophony of his thoughts slowly became quiet, his eyes fluttered closed and all faded into darkness.

But a knock at his door again startled him awake. A glance through his window told him that night had fallen. The table had been cleared and a single candle burned at its center. Confident this all had been done by Lorenzo and that he now stood outside his door with his meal, Pierre stood, moved to the door and opened it. But the person he found there was not Lorenzo.

By weak candlelight from the corridor, the older man who stood before Pierre appeared nearly his own height. His dark brown eyes searched Pierre's as a smile grew slowly on his lips. Pierre stepped backward and the man followed him step for step until both reached the center of the room. For an instant he wondered if he was staring into a mirror that showed himself years in the future. Pierre's jaws locked, his mouth did not move though words filled his mind. He could only stare at this face he hardly recognized and yet knew suddenly and utterly. Still awash in the confusion of sleep, it took a moment to realize the man facing him had begun to scowl, an expression he recognized instantly though he could hardly recall the memory.

"Happy now?" the man growled. "This what you wanted? Are you happy now?" Instead of turning to walk away, the man stepped around Pierre and sat down on a chair that faced the couch. Pierre dumbly followed, sat down on the couch facing him, blinked hard once but could not dispel his surprise.

Augustus seemed somehow smaller than Pierre remembered him; not shrunken but reduced and narrowed. Where Pierre remembered thick waves, a fringe of pale reddish hair encircled his reddish brown head just above his ears, his bald head marked by large and dark brown freckles. The brown eyes Pierre remembered staring down at him with surly impatience now appeared surrounded by thin wrinkles, slightly sunken, watery and opaque. He remembered a thin-lipped mouth and sharply pointing chin that now was surrounded by creased rolls of flesh and supported by a throat that, where it did not sag, appeared strung with sun-baked cables. Though he had no idea why or what he might do, his arms rose and he leaned toward the man. But Augustus's expression changed from annoyed impatience to eye-widened horror. He leaned back into his chair waving his wiry hands.

"Stop right there, boy. No point getting familiar all of a sudden. For reasons we don't need to talk about I'll be leaving just as soon as I've taken care of this business. You made a lot of fool threats to Mezzanotte about needing to see me. You must be a hell of a guy to convince that old crapper of anything except what he's already decided. I know why you're here and what you think you'll do, but I tell you right off I ain't as gullible as him. I've my own ideas as I expect your mother's been telling you for years." He paused. "By the way, how is she?"

"She's fine," Pierre said. "At least last time I saw her."

"Which is what, two years ago now?"

Pierre hesitated, forcing words from his throat. "It's good finally to see you."

"No doubt," Augustus said. "But how could you leave her all alone with that shitty hole of a tavern on her hands? How d'you think she's gotten by without you there? What were you thinking, if that's what you're still calling it? What could possibly possess you?"

"I came looking for you," Pierre said. Suddenly his sheepish, ten-year old self squirmed out from under all the subsequent years of knowledge and experience to speak in his place. For an instant his answer seemed to take Augustus by surprise.

"Why? Just to say hello? Think I've got some money to give you? D'you think you'd horn in on my good thing? Or did you think you'd drag me back? Twist my arm until I stood behind that bar again with those idiot assholes braying in my face day after day, night after night, about the price of potatoes and what a bitch it is getting old? Just because they know how to milk a cow the world's mysteries are solved. Like wearing shoes proves their higher powers. Talk to me, boy, because I can't imagine your mother put you up to this. Did you come here thinking you'd tell me some story of broken hearts and I'd run back like my ass was on fire?"

With the man's eyes piercing his own, Pierre sat vaguely dizzy, the room moving beneath him like the deck of a rolling ship. Eyes wide and unblinking, he stared at the man he had pursued just as the man's memory had pursued him. His mouth began to move in an uncontrolled stammer until he heard himself say, "I've crossed oceans, been attacked and starved and near drowned more times than I can count, all just to find you." The whining tone of his voice did not embarrass him. Augustus finally smiled.

"Good for you, boy. Now at least you've got something to brag about." But his smile disappeared as quickly as a thought. "Are you satisfied? You've seen me. Here I am, not yet dead, if that's what was bothering you."

"But you don't understand..." Augustus cut him off.

"Understand? Is that all you can say to me? You telling me all this has something to do with understanding? And that I don't get it? Listen to me, boy. You're so far from understanding, if understanding was a tree you'd be just a pile of broken bones from falling so far down so often. I come all the way from Naples on a godforsaken wreck of a ship and sea-sick every day just because that child-bugger Mezzanotte insisted. Somehow you convinced him to bring me here, so here I am. What you don't understand is the situation I've got going. Finally I'm getting paid big money, live in a palace near big as this, got servants coming out my ass, eat the best food, drink the best wine, got hot and cold running whores, all because I can do clever things with numbers. Get over yourself. You think I'll give that up for anything, you're so far wrong, if being right was a river you'd die of thirst. I don't know what you've been using for brains all these years but you ain't getting your money's worth."

Finally something inside Pierre trembled. "What I understand is you left your wife and son for a reason you never would explain. What I understand is I spent near two years chasing your shadow half-way around the world. And now that I've found you, all you do is insult me and run away."

Augustus finally laughed. It was a sound Pierre remembered well and without pleasure. "Not running away, boy, running back. There's a world of difference. Like I said, if understanding was a warm coat, you'd have froze to death long ago."

"What I understand is that you left us to fend for ourselves. And you never wrote, never tried to find out whether we were okay."

"Not true! I wrote once, otherwise how could you find me? And I wrote to be sure there weren't no concern wasted. Not that I believed there was concern to begin with."

"But you didn't write looking for us to answer. Mother cried. You know that? She cried for years. Did you even care?"

"You're mother ain't the sentimental type. I know her well enough for that and there's nothing you can tell me otherwise. And you can't tell me there wasn't a man or three to keep her warm on a winter night. Don't try to sell me that because I ain't buying."

"What are you saying?" Memories piled up in Pierre's mind like rocks in a stream-bed. "What do you mean?"

"One thing I know about your mother. She's a woman, flesh and blood right down to her toes. Human she is, just like you or me, is all I'm saying. By the way, did you ever get married?"

This question startled Pierre. "No, not yet."

"Good for you, boy. Reduce the misery in the world and be sure you stay that way."

"She loved you and missed you."

Augustus laughed so suddenly and so loud it startled Pierre. "Listen, I left her owning her own house and a business that couldn't fail. A tavern in that town is a money-machine. Set for life she was though I wouldn't set foot in that place again with a gun to my head."

Pierre finally felt his annoyance rise. "But what about me? Why did you leave me all alone?

Augustus paused and looked ruefully at the floor as though that question had caught him by surprise. He sat a long moment and sighed. Very quietly he said, "Best thing I could've done for you."

Again Pierre trembled. "So many times I wanted you to be there, by my side. To tell me things and answer my questions and tell me I was doing well."

Augustus shook his head thought his eyes would not meet Pierre's. "And you're a better man for it, believe me. If I'd been there to answer every one of your stupid questions with my stupid answers, there's no telling how stupid you'd have got. As it is, you've got yourself stupid enough without my help. Be glad things worked out as well as they did."

"I don't know how you figure things worked out well. After all I've gone through..."

"...is nothing to what you'll go through before you're dead. Don't kid yourself, there's no pleasure like a misery survived. Whatever it is you've survived, you'll keep surviving until you're dead, which most of us don't survive so well. Like this thing you think is chasing you."

Pierre felt his head spin. "Wait! What do you mean? What do you know about it?"

"Seems more than you do. Unlike yourself, I've been thinking. And from what I've heard you've set yourself up for a big disappointment. This creature you think you're going to destroy has been trying to protect you all along and getting no credit for the effort."

"What?"

Augustus shrugged and leaned back folding his arms across his chest. "I know that you're thinking you're going to kill it, and I promise you right now you'll fail."

"What do you mean the creature's been trying to protect me?"

"And it's done at least a fair job. I mean, we're sitting here, right? Having this little talk and all, ain't we? So this beast or whatever it is has done a pretty good job."

"That creature tried to eat me!"

Augustus laughed with a snarl. "If it wanted to eat you you'd already be on the inside and that'd be the end of it." He sighed and looked away. "Anyway, it don't matter. That tangle you talked Mezzanotte into building couldn't kill a flea. But it looks great and should provide hours of fun."

"What d'you mean?" Pierre felt his head spinning again but in the opposite direction. "It's designed and built according to scientific principles; it can't fail!"

Again Augustus laughed. The sound cut through Pierre's chest. "A fake science of your own creation is what you mean. But that's all right too because eventually something'll be true, and then you'll know what it is you think and where you went wrong."

"What are you saying?"

Augustus waved his hand. "Don't worry about it. Take it from me; mistakes are more useful than even the best guesses."

"But where did I go wrong?"

Augustus finally looked at him and then shrugged. "There's a question we all ask ourselves all the time, so get used to it." He stood. "Anyway, I've got to go." He held out his hand. Pierre looked at his father's hand, gnarled, wrinkled and twisted by the passage of time, as if it was the only object in the world. It demanded a moment before he reached out and shook it. "It's good seeing you and really, I wish you luck." Still holding Pierre's hand he leaned very close and into his ear whispered, "I never thought you'd get this far or succeed this well." He turned then and headed toward the door.

"But wait," Pierre said. "There are things I need to ask you."

"I don't doubt that because you keep thinking I know something. I'm flattered but thinking never made anything true. So it's better you don't even ask because I could only confuse you." He paused then as if something surprising had occurred to him. "But I'll tell you what; how about I send your mother some money? I think she'd like that and it'll make you feel better. Otherwise, do yourself a favor. When you're finished with this colossal waste of time, go home. All sorts of things'll work out better if you do. And you'll get famous for the great stories you'll have to tell." As they stood together beside the door there was a knock. Pierre gestured but Augustus opened it to reveal Lorenzo and his expression was grim. To Pierre he said, "You had better come."

Augustus turned to Pierre smiling. "You see, I told you. Timing is everything and mine couldn't be better." He stepped past Lorenzo into the corridor. Pierre reached the doorway just in time to watch his back fade and become swallowed by the long, dark hallway.

Pierre moved to follow Augustus but Lorenzo asked, "Are you ready?" Pierre hesitated wondering about that question and whether he could answer it at all and if so, would his answer be sufficient. But then his confusion passed. To Lorenzo he said, "Where's Mezzanotte?"

"He waits for you with his carriage; follow me." And Pierre did.

CHAPTER TWENTY-TWO

AT THE FOOT of the palace stairs Pierre saw Signor Mezzanotte seated in his carriage, its shining black horses pawed at the cobblestones. Behind his carriage and bathed in the same crimson golden light, another open carriage waited filled with his advisers. All of them watched Pierre descend the stairs with grimly shadowed eyes. The evening's air was hot and thick and ominously still. Mezzanotte called out, "It has been seen just beyond the shore and moving this way."

Pierre stepped up into the carriage. "Is there a storm on the horizon?"

"Not yet," Mezzanotte said. Despite the light of the torches his face appeared anguished and deep-lined. "We should go."

The carriages passed through the palace gates in a single file and followed that road Pierre had come to know well riding hard into the violet black night. Pierre said, "I spoke with Augustus."

"Of course," Mezzanotte said indifferently as if preoccupied. He stared out to an invisible horizon. "I hope your anticipation was well-rewarded."

"Our visit was brief," Pierre said.

"And undoubtedly more valuable thereby." He turned. "Are your preparations complete?" Pierre's throat was tight with anxiety so he simply nodded; something was about to happen.

At the last rise approaching the site, the horizon ahead showed a hellish orange glow and Pierre guessed the bonfires had been set. At the top of that ridge their drivers stopped. Though he thought he had prepared himself, this sight left Pierre mute with astonishment.

Beneath the black canopy of night, bonfires flamed red-orange above the expanse of pale sand like a strand of blood-amber pearls, and their fires licked the sky. Those fires followed the beach in both directions nearly as far as he could see. More fires formed a horseshoe to surround the carpet whose metal reflected their gold-orange light as a scintillating promenade. At each end of the horseshoe and positioned between the bonfires along the edge of the surf stood groups of ink-black cannons and in their shadows stacks of shot and casks of powder. Shadowed men clustered further back.

The broad gap at the center of this line of fires offered an entrance to the chain-maille carpet which, reflecting the light from the fires surrounding it, formed an iridescent golden path before disappearing where it reached the creamy pale waves.

Pierre was so dazzled by what he saw that he needed a moment to notice that behind the line of fires, still more dark shapes of many men stood beside their teams of lowing and nervous oxen. Arriving from the surrounding villages, their crowd continued to grow around golden puddles of torchlight. Looking farther off into the hills, Pierre saw that even more people approached and their torches inscribed snaking and sinuous paths like rivulets of lava to carve serpentine lines of molten red light upon the black earth.

In the wide space between those blazing bonfires and that metal carpet the fires surrounded, men stood in groups of three beside each of the kites anchored to the ground, waiting to send them into the sky. A rising breeze from the sea kept these kites trembling.

Pierre stood in the carriage stupefied, overwhelmed by the recognition of the completion of what he had imagined. At Mezzanotte's prompt they stepped down together from the carriage; an officer carrying a torch came to stand beside them. The advisers stepped from their carriage and joined Pierre and Mezzanotte until all stood within the light of the torch. Viscount Guillermo Antonioni stepped up beside Pierre and pointed. In the opaque blue-black distance and far beyond the pale thread of surf Pierre could just make out a small but darker shape. Looking more closely, it appeared to move slowly toward them.

Pierre nodded. "Send the kites aloft."

The officer held his torch above his head and waved it from side to side. In moments, the clusters of men began to move among the kites. Enlivened by the strengthening breeze, those brightly-figured and eccentrically-shaped kites began to dance in their hands. One by one a man from each cluster ran along the edge of the mat until his kite began to rise. The wires within the tether-lines glittered with shards of firelight as each line reached its maximum length and then swayed and drifted. Seen from below, their shapes dipped back and forth illuminated against that black sky, and seen from their floating undersides their images glowed like shreds of fiery confetti. The whole arrangement deployed beneath that oily darkness appeared a demonic carnival of red and golden light. As Pierre watched, he realized that in their gorgeously erratic movements, some of the kites approached and nearly touched each other.

His face ablaze with that devilish light, Mezzanotte turned to Pierre. "What now?"

Without turning Pierre said, "We wait." He looked beyond the thread of surf to that shape gradually becoming larger. "Has the lookout been posted for the storm?"

Mezzanotte nodded toward the volcano. "Arrived before we did." Pierre saw a tiny point of yellow light. The Signor added, "One of my best men."

From out of the darkness and traveling across the surf, a deep and rumbling roar suddenly filled the space around them. Every face turned to follow its direction. Though distance left its sound still weak and hollow, Pierre shivered, its memory more familiar than a bad dream. He looked back to the volcano disheartened that he saw no signal. His offer to entice the creature had been his gesture of bravado intended to silence debate. Now he wondered what he might need to do before he saw the sun rise again.

With a death's-head grimace and darkness filling his eyes, Mezzanotte said, "Finally we all will see your creature face to face."

"I've run so often to avoid its clutches it's like a visit from an old friend."

"One must never become attached to what one hopes to kill." Mezzanotte paused and his smile disappeared. "And God-willing, in that you will succeed."

Pierre again looked around at the gathering crowd. Success or failure, the result of this encounter would be witnessed by all. Suddenly, the Abbess came to his mind and he wondered if she stood somewhere in that crowd, a curious observer to his triumph or his death.

The creature roared again and this time its sound was louder and deeper.

Unmistakably it had drawn closer.

As if impatient for its arrival, Mezzanotte asked, "What can it be doing out there?" The tremor in his voice caused Pierre look harder. He turned to Mezzanotte's officer and asked for the telescope. Seen through the telescope, its head stood out from the inky sea profiled against the black sky by the infernal light of the fires and moving just above its surface. Even at the distance, with that light from the bonfires its yellow-green eyes glittered.

Pierre handed the telescope to Mezzanotte and pointed. He put the telescope to his eye and instantly gasped. Mouth half-open he took a step back. As if determined to dispel any chance that what he saw was a mirage he looked again, and then slowly lowered the telescope.

With a tone of satisfaction Pierre said, "Finally you meet your adversary. I hope you're impressed and you're satisfied that everything I've said is true." Mezzanotte said nothing but Pierre assumed that for the first time he was seeing this man genuinely frightened. He looked back at the cluster of his advisers, their eyes turned toward the Signor. "And I hope you see why these preparations have been so elaborate, and the Commander's insufficient." Though he did not see him, he wondered if the Commander stood just as shaken by that same shock of terror. "Where have you assigned him?"

He turned to pass the telescope to one of his advisers. "Directing those batteries; he awaits only your signal. Perhaps it is time they were employed." The tremor in his voice caused Pierre to look harder.

"We need to wait until they'll be most effective."

The creature had finally moved close enough to the shore so that it plowed the sea, pushing a fringe of surf to break as a higher wave against the beach. Step by step the upper part of its body gradually became visible until it was easily seen from the shore. Then the murmur of panic growing among the gathered crowd became a rumbling roar, with some voices crying out in fear. When finally its towering bulk was visible to its haunches, the creature stopped.

Glowering with a grumbling growl, its enormous body swayed from side to side lighted by the bonfires against a blacker sky, as if the beast was bemused by what it found. Seeming to contemplate the shore's demonic scene it appeared to look for something, or perhaps wait for something. The lurid and wavering light from the torches and the bonfires cast a red-orange glow onto its greenish black shape. As if hesitant and confused but then perhaps angered, its bilious yellow eyes scrutinized the crowd gathered within the light of the fires. Under its baleful gaze the crowd seemed suddenly to step back in a noisy panic of gasps and screams. In a trance-like monotone Mezzanotte asked, "Should we not do something?"

Pierre shook his head. "Until the storm arrives there's nothing to be done." But just as he spoke, a breeze gusted and then stiffened to send a flutter through the bonfires, a powerful breath tossing a blast of dancing orange sparks into the black sky. The flames from the torches leaned away from the sudden rush of coolish air. Pierre looked back toward the volcano with relief; a pinprick of light moved slowly from side to side. To Mezzanotte he said, "Looks like your man is signaling."

Mezzanotte turned and astonishment appeared about his eyes. "The Good Lord appears determined to smile upon your efforts. Or perhaps Count Pagliaro has finally justified the expense of his keep." Just as suddenly, from the darkness the hollow rumble of distant thunder rolled overhead.

Pierre turned back toward the creature. "More likely someone's looking for a good laugh." The wind stiffened and grew steady. Torch flames folded, flames from the bonfires leaned hard as more sparks swirled about to be sucked up into the sky. He looked up to watch the kites bright against the black sky begin to swoop and careen.

Mezzanotte followed Pierre's gaze. "Is this something we should be concerned about?"

"Yes," Pierre said. "We won't miss one or two, but if too many fail, our trap will no longer be a trap."

"Are you prepared for that?" His tone of concern surprised Pierre.

"The men controlling each kite should be able to keep them from colliding or becoming entangled. But if any get into trouble, they have orders to cut the line and let the kite drift off. It's simply chance if enough remain to communicate the aether to the creature."

He offered Pierre an admiring smile. "You have given this considerable thought."

"It's what you asked." Suddenly, thunder rumbled again but louder and much closer and both men looked again to the sky.

Mezzanotte asked, "You know, it is possible this storm may pass without lightning."

Pierre said nothing. The creature remained in shallow water just beyond the edge of the surf and glowering toward the shore.

Mezzanotte turned to face Pierre. "The Commander's cannon were deployed precisely for this contingency. Shall I give the signal?" Pierre hesitated. "Otherwise, you have agreed to play the goat tethered as bait. It would be unfortunate if your offer proved necessary." A sudden flash of lightning followed by the crack and boom of thunder caused them both to look up. Mezzanotte smiled. "On the other hand, a providential Lord appears prepared to provide whatever help is needed."

The wind strengthened suddenly and the kites began to swoop and dive until their crews struggled to control them. When two became entangled fluttering like golden birds in battle, their crews called out and began to curse each other screaming directions.

Mezzanotte asked, "What are they doing?" Control of their kites became hopeless. Both crews abandoned their tether-lines and began to exchange blows. Men from nearby lines abandoned theirs and rushed in to break up the fight or join it, but under that light nothing was clear.

Furious, Pierre called out, "This won't end well."

Abandoning Mezzanotte he ran down the slope toward the crews shouting. At the carpet he reached for the abandoned tethers, but before he could grab them their entangled lines pulled hard on the edge of the carpet. Stakes popped out of the ground as if shot from the earth. Still attached by their rings, the edge of the carpet began to lift. Lines to the adjacent kites added to the strain. Pierre seized the tethers, his drawn knife flashed in the firelight, and cut both with one stroke. With the knife held high he charged into the melee of fighting men, kicking and calling out as he punched at those closest. Confused, the men reeled back from his assault until the creature's sudden roar turned all heads in its direction and froze everyone in place. Pierre called out orders and the scattered men returned to their assignments, although each kept an eye on the creature looming still just beyond the surf.

Somehow the brawl excited the creature. It became restless and began to move about. When its tail beat against the water it sent foamy pale geysers into the black sky. The curl of a large wave appeared suddenly and rushed toward the shore. When the wave broke upon the beach the bonfires along the beach winked out and darkness threatened like a rising tide. Only the bonfires immediately around the carpet continued to burn providing the remaining light.

Screaming to be heard above the rising wind, Pierre moved from group to group. Mezzanotte came to walk beside him as if to assure his authority. The next lightning stroke flashed simultaneous with the crack of thunder, and its blinding dagger struck one of the kites. That kite exploded into flame, fluttered and then drifted before careening down. But the crew tending its tether had already fallen, their bodies lay motionless on the ground spread like petals of a black flower.

Over the whistling wind Mezzanotte cried out, "So your hypothesis has been confirmed."

Men from neighboring crews rushed to help the prostrate men. The wind had begun to whip and swirl, another flash and blast of lightning struck another kite, but its crew had already stepped away from its tether. The men watched astonished as that kite dropped like a flaming stone and scattered from its blazing debris.

The remaining kites swayed and swooped wildly, but despite the danger their crews held tight to the tethers. Pierre rushed from one group to the next but the wind grew stronger, a tether snapped and its kite sailed off to disappear into the darkness, followed by another.

His mouth agape Mezzanotte watched the kites disappear into the black sky. "Are we lost? You must do something!"

"They're vulnerable in this wind," Pierre bellowed, "and helpless against the violence of Nature. That's why we deployed so many."

"Will there be enough left to slay our daemon?"

Another blast of lightning struck a kite, followed by another that struck a second, their explosions blinding and deafening. More men stepped away from their tethers and their kites released to the wind suddenly swung and swooped with terrifying abandon. Winds stirred a chaos that gradually overwhelmed Pierre's creations. He looked back out to sea. Glowering furious and bemused, the creature remained just beyond the surf. Its low rumbling growl of impatience throbbed through Pierre's feet.

Mezzanotte pulled at Pierre's arm. "We must fire the cannons!"

Pierre turned toward the ridge and began to wave his arm. It took a moment but a torch poised on at the ridge began to wave. In rapid succession cannons then fired, one after the next.

Despite the rain that had begun to fall and the darkness, Pierre watched as the first shots splashed harmlessly around the creature, but when one struck its body, the creature hardly turned. Gradually more shots found their mark. The creature snarled and began to swat with its short upper claws at those cannon shot. The cannons soon began to fire so quickly their reports overlapped into explosions that rivaled the blasts of thunder. The cannonade continued, but seemed to do little more than annoy the creature. Blast followed blast but the creature hardly moved. Gradually Pierre came to believe something more would need to be done. A glance skyward reminded him that soon, few of his kites would remain aloft. Mezzanotte's thoughts must have followed his. "We must not allow the storm to pass and the creature refuse our challenge."

"The cannons are not helping," Pierre said. "So much for the Commander's plan."

The wind swirled howling about their ears. Men stood in clusters away from their tethers as much from exhaustion as fear, and watched the remaining kites swoop and dive against the black sky. Whipped by the wind, the rain struck Pierre's face like small stones. Men began to move away from the carpet to join groups gathered beyond the bonfires, fleeing the edge of the firelight and into the safety of darkness.

Mezzanotte pressed down on Pierre's arm until his lips were level with Pierre's ear. "Do not forget your promise. I have given you what you requested, including your father. You must honor our agreement." He smiled grimly, then turned to retreat with his advisers to the ridge.

Pierre looked about to discover himself alone. Surrounded by the fires and the torches and the kites and the lightning and the thunder and buffeted by wind and rain, he stood at the edge of the carpet alone. Having exhausted their ammunition, the cannons became silent. The gathered multitude waited, and Pierre realized even the creature now watched him as though it had always known what Pierre now discovered. Panic, like a malodorous gust, suddenly filled the space around him. Something of sulfur yet more organic; the odor of rotting flesh but bitter like the taste of metal or a mouthful of seawater.

Under flashes of lightning and rolling thunder and pelted by the rain, Pierre made his way through the clutter and mud until he stood alone at the apex of the carpet. Surrounded by the hundred fires, he faced the glowering creature. With a glance to the black sky and swirling kites, he strode five paces out onto the carpet.

The beast seemed to watch him but then appeared to hesitate, as if debating whether to accept this challenge, and as if recognizing that by doing so, their final act would begin. But its indecision lasted less than a moment. It tipped back its massive head, opened its jaws to display its wide red throat and monstrous ivory teeth, and released an ear-piercing roar so deep and strong the ground beneath Pierre's feet reverberated in echo. Then, as if with conscious deliberation, it took a step forward, followed by another. Each step caused the ground to tremble until finally the beast stood clear of the water and at the very edge of the carpet. But then it stopped. Another roar from the creature tore the air. Pierre looked from the creature to the kites and the black sky beyond, waiting for the dagger of lightning that would kill him as certainly as the creature. Fear like molten mercury seared through his limbs.

The creature snarled and growled and took another earth-trembling step forward, followed by another. Now the creature stood on the metal carpet; Pierre watched as it grew to obliterate more of the sky. Suddenly he recognized that those kites continuing to fly about dipping and swaying in the wind like golden wildflowers hardly reached as high as the beast's shoulders. He took one step back and the creature stopped.

The beast glowered, its nostrils flared black as twin caves as if waiting for Pierre to move. When he did not, the creature dipped its massive head toward Pierre and took another step forward.

Glancing again at the sky, Pierre wondered if the heart of the storm with its bolts of lightning had already passed. The creature took another step forward and Pierre looked about for a path to escape. The creature advanced another step and Pierre took two steps back, but the creature continued to advance now and approached the carpet's center. Pierre stepped further back but the creature was now close enough to tower directly over him. Looking about, Pierre saw that the field behind him had been abandoned, the crowd had retreated further, although in the distance he could still see that all faces remained turned toward him. His next step brought him nearly to the edge of the carpet. He looked up as fearful of the lightning as the creature. A figure broke from the darkness running toward him. But as if it watched that advancing figure as well, the creature roared.

Pierre took two steps off the carpet when suddenly he was blinded and deafened as lightning struck. When his sight returned he saw that some of the remaining kites continued to fly. The creature lifted its head and cried out to the sky, but this time its cry was of pain. Blinded by another stroke of lightning, Pierre stumbled further back just able to watch this bolt of lightning strike the top of the creature's skull. The beast looked down and its eyes seemed to lock onto Pierre's. Another lightning bolt nearly blinding Pierre struck its head again and this bellow was of agony. The creature looked about at the sky as if searching for the source of its torment. Pierre stumbled back more steps. Two bolts of lightning struck the creature at the same instant. His ears throbbed and he again found himself blind. The creature moved to turn as if intending to retreat to the sea, but another bolt of lightning struck. The creature screamed, lifted its foot to stagger away, but lightening struck once again, this time leaving a wisp of pale smoke to drift from the crown of its head. When the sound subsided, the beast's jaws remained open but it made no sound. Another stroke of lightning struck and the creature remained as if frozen.

When Pierre's sight cleared he noticed suddenly that very slowly the creature had begun to lean forward, its shape above Pierre darkening the sky and stirring the stars with its shadow. It leaned further forward and Pierre realized its enormous head was falling toward him. But panic left him frozen and unable to turn or move his legs. The black void of the creature's head above him grew larger and drew closer, and Pierre held his breath. Suddenly there was a sound behind him he did not recognize. Eyes fixed on the creature's descending head, that sound behind him grew louder until he was struck powerfully in the middle of his back. Startled, Pierre stumbled to one side and then fell just as the creature fell to the earth with a resounding thump that reverberated through the ground. But then, something heavy fell onto Pierre.

Blows, he finally realized, rained down on his back and shoulders. A screaming voice cried directly into his ear, "Are you stupid?" The blows continued to fall as the voice screamed again, "Are you crazy? Are you an idiot?" The weight on his back pressed his face into the mud. Finally the blows and screams subsided, the weight shifted and Pierre turned over.

The Abbess' face hovered over his, red, wet and tear-streaked, frantic and smeared with mud; her small fists landed blows at his chest. His arms now loose, he managed to deflect a few. "In a hurry to die? Kill yourself and leave the rest of us out of it! Just kill yourself and do the rest of us a favor." Hysterical hiccups of rage finally exhausted her and she collapsed onto his chest. He was breathing hard and fast and, with her lying on his chest, he feared he could not catch his breath. But then he looked past her trembling shoulders.

The gigantic black shape of the creature's head towered behind her and over them both.

And it did not move.

But then, another roar startled Pierre.

CHAPTER TWENTY-THREE

PIERRE COULD NOT take his eyes from the creature towering above him; its mountainous black head, its enormous, cave-deep nostrils, its tremendous incisor fangs pale and orange in the firelight. Gradually he managed to untangle himself from beneath the Abbess. When he stood he discovered the roar now battering at his ears came from thousands of throats accompanied by the rumbling thunder of thousands of footsteps rushing forward to surround him. Smiling and grinning faces gathered about Pierre as countless hands reached forward to grasp his arms and his shoulders. Looking up into a black and brilliantly star-specked sky, he recognized that sound surrounding him as cheers and laughter.

Snatched up within this surging crush of bodies, his own body arose supported by numberless hands and illuminated by the red-golden flames of the torches. Joy and celebration rang in his ears as hands reached slapping at his arms and shoulders in congratulations. A riotous and jubilant crowd carried him past more reaching hands and grinning faces until the sea of bodies surrounding him parted. He was returned to earth to face Cavalier Giovanni Archangelo Mezzanotte whose smile was brilliant and eyes glittered with the golden glints of the torchlight. He grasped Pierre by the shoulders and kissed each of his muddy cheeks several times, and with such urgent ecstasy that Pierre's shoulders hurt.

"Conqueror of monsters," he cried out, "and worthy of all acclaim, on behalf of these and all of my people I congratulate you and thank you! A true hero, accept and enjoy our praise!" He turned to face the crowd and its roar of approval filled the sky.

In a still louder voice he continued, “And this day will be recounted beside every hearth and across the ages to the very end of time. Not since Ulysses himself has our island seen such a hero. Your courageous actions will forever remain hallowed in our memory. Your ingenuity and determination gave us hope, but it is your bravery that has spared us. In grateful chorus with my people I say humbly again, thank you!” Mezzanotte bowed deeply. Another roar reverberated into the sky, hysterically cheering men and women embraced each other laughing and shouting. Pierre was speechless with astonishment while Mezzanotte simply grinned.

With a more somber expression Mezzanotte again held up his hands until the crowd became quiet. “But our work is not yet complete!” He waved an arm toward the creature. Calling out to the crowd he said, “There remains the carcass.” Turning to Pierre he said, “We will be grateful if you will lead our effort.”

But already, appearing like ants crawling upon an enormous log, men had begun to climb about on the beast. Others along either side gathered the end-rings of the chain-maille as ropes and chains were tossed up to surround its body. Hands that had congratulated Pierre began to push him toward those men lifting and hauling the chain-maille and prepared to cover the creature’s body. More men and women rushed forward to join the boisterous crowd, and suddenly Pierre realized he had begun to give orders and provide directions.

Wrapping the chain-maille like an enormous silver net about the creature and then securing its edges with more chains, by the time the carcass was entirely encased, the stars overhead had winked out as at the eastern horizon the sky began to brighten. Dark shapes moving between the hills soon were revealed to be even more men and women, all rushing eager to join the work. Pierre guessed that news of his battle with the creature had spread until surrounding villages began to empty of those eager to join the army already at work. At the far-edge of the crowd, teams of oxen bellowed beside neighing and restless horses.

Running from one group to the next Pierre urged all to work quickly. The drovers and teamsters began to harness their teams to those chains attached to large iron rings along the edge of the chain-maille. Additional chains then were threaded through these rings and attached to each other as threads of a spider’s web until, like a dense fan, those heavy chains finally spread from the creature and each chain was bound to a team of animals.

More teams arrived dragging huge logs shaved pale of their bark. These were laid parallel to form a path leading upward toward the volcano. Ropes as thick as a man's thigh were attached to the lowest points of that shimmering chain-maille cocoon that now encircled the carcass of the creature, and then teams of oxen and horses were harnessed to those rings. As part of his preparation, Pierre had plotted the smoothest path to the volcano's summit, and now working from his memory he described that path to the drovers and teamsters. Villagers continued to arrive, and as the sky grew pale their crowd became tremendous. While the creature's metal cocoon was being rigged and the animals harnessed, the rest of the men moved those logs across its path. Drovers took their places at the heads of their harnessed teams.

At Pierre's signal, whips cracked loud as pistol shots. Against that brightening sky the lowing of oxen along with neighs and cries of horses all harnessed to those chains leading to the chain-maille cut through the air. Crews of men manning more ropes along each side and bound to the metal cocoon prepared to keep the creature on course.

Chains creaked and groaned, oxen bellowed and horses screamed in response to the men among them. But with a sudden lurch, the metal-wrapped carcass began to move, and the crowd once again cheered. As the metal cocoon passed over each log, other men carried that log forward to the front of the path. In this way, and despite the increasing incline, the carcass of the beast gradually climbed the side of Mount Etna.

With this effort begun, Pierre moved among these teams determined to find the Abbess. As he was being lifted and carried off, he had watched her face disappear, swallowed and devoured within the raucous and surging crowd. Called upon by every person he saw, Pierre remained certain that in the next moment he would see her. So when the creature began to move he stepped away and resumed his search for her in earnest.

Running from one cluster of people to the next, by the time the sun was about to peer above the horizon he decided she was gone and he had no idea where or how to find her. From the top of the ridge he spied the group of advisers surrounding Mezzanotte standing together and watching the astonishing procession in silence. Pierre broke from the crowd and made his way to where they stood.

When he reached them, the advisers with Mezzanotte at their center were in deep conversation. He pushed forward to stand before Mezzanotte. "Where is the Duchess di Nuova Cento?"

At the sound of his voice Mezzanotte looked up as if awakened from a deep sleep and startled to see sunlight. But then he smiled. "Ah, the hero of the day. Each element of your plan fell nicely into place, and even as we speak our difficulty is being resolved. You have dispelled every doubt, vindicated my trust and in every way proven your worth. You are a credit to your father and your mother and your nation."

"Kind words aside," Pierre said as his patience drifted off, "I need to find the Duchess."

Mezzanotte looked at him bemused and uncertain and then looked around. "I must say I assumed she was with you. Perhaps she has returned to the palace. Have you gone there to check?"

When Pierre shook his head Mezzanotte said, "Well, there you are then. I am certain she has returned to the palace and looks forward to congratulating you personally."

Pierre stared at Mezzanotte as if seeing something behind his eyes he had not seen before. Almost gasping for air Pierre said, "She saved my life, you know; I'd be dead without her. So I ask once more; where is she?"

Mezzanotte's expression soured as if he was tired of these questions and had finished answering them. "As undoubtedly you already know she responds to commands other than my own. She comes and goes as she must. If you need to find her you must consult others." His brief smile was thin and dismissive. "Is there anything else I can help you with?"

Instead of answering, Pierre turned and walked away. Though his impulse was to resume his search, the progress of the creature's climb to the summit of the volcano had begun to slow. Lines harnessed to animal teams were becoming tangled as the path grew even steeper and then the carcass began to slip to one side. Pierre ran from crew to crew barking out orders and waving gestures. When he looked back, Mezzanotte and his advisers had climbed into their carriages and in the next moment those carriages turned to return to the palace.

By now morning sun stood clear of the horizon. The work of hauling the creature continued; teams of fresh horses and oxen along with armies of well-rested men replaced those that had tired. Further and further up the slope, past and around obstacles, the exhausting work continued under a baking sun. Groups of women moved among the workers dispensing water, but recalling the fate of the mouse, Pierre could not allow any to pause for food or rest. By the time the sun had passed its zenith, the incline of the creature's path along the volcano's side was steep. The closer the beast approached the edge of the crater, the more treacherous its path became, as there was less room to maneuver those teams of animals along with their crews. But Pierre's preparation had anticipated this as well.

Along the rim of the crater, workmen had sunk the ends of thick logs deep into the soil and positioned well-apart. The sun approached the horizon as their teams reached these logs. Their crews looped the chains and ropes over them, and then turned their teams back down the side of the volcano. With this, the creature's carcass continued to move upward. Yet their progress slowed even more, so that it was nearing twilight by the time they approached the edge. Still more lines were attached to metal rings at the back end of the creature's shimmering metal cocoon and other crews began gradually to turn the beast to lie sideways. Although Pierre had been confident about this strategy, movement of the creature's tremendous bulk demanded a fierce struggle as men and animals competed to scream loudest. Even more daunting, being dragged further toward the crater, the creature's weight was being taken up by fewer and fewer lines. Then, and just as suddenly, the enormous carcass began to slip to one side.

But word of this great battle and the creature's death and then the herculean effort that followed had traveled to villages even further off and, eager to see what had happened, its news attracted even more villagers so that the size of the crowd was truly enormous. Thus, a cry for help brought hundreds more well-rested and enthusiastic hands and strong backs determined to control the off-setting lines, and these managed to balance the effort of others. Pierre stood to one side watching groups of people continue to arrive to join this effort. Looking about, he regretted Augustus could not witness all of this. And thinking of his father he recalled his startling guess that the creature's efforts all had been to protect him. Despite the titanic effort in progress and right before his eyes, Pierre knew he would need to find Augustus and ask what it was he had meant.

The effort to haul the creature to the edge of the volcano's crater had demanded most of the day, so that as it approached the summit, the bronze-colored light of the setting sun scintillated from its silver cocoon. Finally, and with enormous strain and effort, the beast inched past the edge of the volcano's rim and began to rise. Approaching its equilibrium, for an instant its carcass lay poised at the rim of the crater like a beam-balance. And for a long and breathless moment, Pierre and the crowd and the rest of the world paused and hesitated and waited.

Then that moment passed. The fore-edge of the creature's metal encasement tipped slowly downward, then more quickly, until in the next instant it dropped completely forward, its back-end tipped up just before disappearing below the rim's edge to fall free trailing its ropes and chains that caught the dying sunlight to glisten like golden streamers before crashing into the tremendous cauldron of red-orange fire. Striking the bottom, an explosion of blazing rocks reached back up as if the gods of volcanoes had approved and then devoured their sacrifice.

At that moment a cry erupted as if from one gigantic throat; a chorus of all the hundreds who had gathered, and its sound rivaled the cry of the beast itself shattering the deepening twilight. Some remained at the rim of the volcano gazing down in wonder, still stunned by what they had witnessed and participated in. But, as if liberated by that final burst from the mouth of the volcano, most people raced back down the side of the volcano to gather beside an enormous bonfire that had been lighted as sunset approached. And thus began a great celebration.

Even as the work was reaching its climax and the creature being prepared to be hurled into the volcano, others villagers had continued to arrive, and while they had not participated in that great collective effort, they joined in the celebration of an event they knew and recognized as monumental. Against the gathering darkness, more fires were lighted to join the ones already burning as the full darkness of night approached. Among those newly-arrived, guitars and horns and drums appeared, and soon their music cut through the soft and placid air. Pierre was reluctant to join and had all but decided to return to the palace and search for the Abbess when a passing group of excited young men and women grabbed his arm in the most friendly fashion, and suddenly he found himself surrounded within a swarm of laughing and dancing people.

Caught up by their excitement Pierre grinned at all who came near. Sprouting suddenly like mushrooms from the depths of the earth itself, gigantic table after enormous table appeared, piled to the point of collapse with more food than he had ever seen accompanied by countless bottles and jugs of wine. A dozen hands pushed food from every table toward Pierre and he could not refuse. Surrounded by joyous strangers, instantly he was caught in their delirium even while their high spirits embraced him as warmly as if he was surrounded by his dearest friends. Word spread of who he was and what he had done, so that quickly he became the focus of all attention. Men stepped forward to embrace him and praise him, comparing him to mystical animals, classical heroes and saints. From every side hands reached out eagerly to touch him and women offered alluring glances as if eager to catch his attention. He was jostled from one table to the next, encouraged to eat and drink before moving to the next, only to be further praised and lauded and invited to eat and drink still more. Thus, before Pierre could even realize it and despite his exhaustion he was thoroughly drunk and utterly enchanted.

Women jostled each other for the opportunity to dance with him as the clapping hands of others kept time. The swirl of music and dancing left him dizzy and disoriented and added to his intoxication so that he could not contain his laughter. The embrace of each woman and every man, their glowing smiles and glittering eyes, all spun as a kaleidoscope of bright and dark; faces flashed by only to be replaced by new faces, new eyes and new smiles. Beneath that black canopy of night sky the red-golden light of a hundred bonfires flashed upon face after face. More wood was added and the fires grew higher and brighter as still more people arrived to join this celebration. Exuberance and excitement was a river that flowed over and all around Pierre until time became a breeze drifting without notice, and he sang and shouted with the others all bound together by passionate hysteria, breathless and delirious.

Pierre once again and finally looked up to discover the sky had begun to brighten as a new day approached. At that moment he turned to look about, startled to discover that just as suddenly, aside from a few very drunken revelers, the boisterous and now exhausted crowd had turned about and begun to move off, the hills beyond now specked with their gray-black shadows moving slowly upward and away. Those hills that had disgorged these reveling villagers now began to take them back, their shadows drifting into larger shadows as all were swallowed back into those hills and their worlds, those worlds from which they had come, from which they had been released to gather and participate in an event that would transcend each and of their lives.

Breathless and still delirious, Pierre recognized himself resigned finally that this party had concluded. Snatching at those few people who passed, Pierre tried to convince the less drunk men still nearby to give him a ride on the back of a horse and return him to Mezzanotte's palace. Each ignored his request with loud, bright laughter as if Pierre could not be serious and then he staggered away.

But then another man, tall and slim and dressed in black with an oddly conical hat tipped to one side and with a particularly piercing and sparkling light in his eyes approached Pierre as if he recognized him. To Pierre's relief he agreed to take him back to the palace, insisting Pierre drink with him first. He agreed reluctantly, and then became violently sick, so that instantly he regretted it. His companion seemed to find the sight of this muddy, bedraggled and vomiting hero terribly funny, and the sound of his laughter struck Pierre as familiar and unnerving. He struggled to recall this man and failed. But finally he helped Pierre onto his horse. Pierre recalled nothing of their journey, as though perhaps they may even have flown through the sky, but all that had transpired evaporated within its moment and Pierre was startled to discover himself standing at the foot of the stairs to the palace, the man and his horse an amorphous black shape disappearing into the chill, gray morning haze.

Even more exhausted than he was drunk, Pierre made his way to Mezzanotte's room and entered to find the Signor seated surrounded by his advisers and all in deep discussion. Mezzanotte looked up to see Pierre and instantly an odd expression came over his face. Before Pierre could speak he said, "You look terrible. Wherever have you been? And whatever are you doing still here?"

Startled by these questions, the morass of Pierre's baffled mind could conjure no useful response.

A wry smile came to Mezzanotte's face as he recognized Pierre's confusion. "Your things are packed and await you on-board the Virgil. It's another sea-voyage for you, my boy and nothing to be done about it." The Signor glanced out the window. "And if I am not mistaken, your ship will weigh anchor very soon." He turned to one of his advisers. "Make certain a carriage is put at our guest's disposal. Time is short and he has far to travel. On your life, make certain he arrives in time to catch the tide." Then he returned to his counselors.

Exhausted and drunk and now even more confused Pierre asked, "Have you found the Duchess di Nuova Cento?"

Mezzanotte looked up annoyed now as if he had already answered every useful question. "I remind you that she answers to powers higher than my own. She is where she is supposed to be, or at least on her way." He sighed with exasperation. "I promised I would reunite you with your father and I have done so. As for the Duchess, she is neither my charge nor my responsibility. The Virgil will take you to Naples where I believe Augustus planned to return. Though I can claim no certainty, I expect the Duchess has departed to return to Rome and her confessor."

"After all I've done for you," Pierre whined, "that's the best you can do for me?" He could not tell if his anger was a result of his exhaustion or his impatience or his intoxication.

Mezzanotte no longer bothered to disguise his annoyance. "If you are determined to find her you will need to take up that search without my help. I repeat my suggestion; begin your search in Rome. Even if she is not there, it is a very nice city with many nice women. Otherwise, for all I know she may already be headed elsewhere. You must go forth and find her without my assistance." Pierre opened his mouth to ask another question, but Mezzanotte cut him off, his voice edged with impatience shading toward anger.

"Believe me, young man, we are eternally grateful for your help and for what you have achieved and the way it has been accomplished, but your time among us is now finished. You have vanquished your enemy and you have located your father. Your victory is complete and your fate has been fulfilled; at least this portion of it. But you are a young man and there is undoubtedly much still to be achieved. Enjoy this victory, sleep the sleep of a hero and move on to whatever life offers you next."

Pierre felt certain there was something more he needed to know, but words and their ideas kept slipping from his mind and he looked down to see them piled around his feet, and now he was simply too drunk and too tired to lean down and pick them up.

"Go now!" Mezzanotte said. "Your ship and your fate await you, and time and tide wait for no one; not even a hero, not even you."

In this way Pierre was utterly and thoroughly dismissed. When he turned toward the door, no one looked up.

He made his way down the stairs to the courtyard where he found the carriage waiting for him, all of this without seeing Lorenzo and for a moment he regretted that. No sooner had he climbed into the carriage and sat down than the driver cracked the whip, the horses bolted forward, and Pierre was thrown backward to begin the wildest ride he had ever experienced. The world flew by painted with the blue-gray light of morning and he gripped the sides of the carriage certain that in the next moment he would be tossed from it. The driver leaned forward and never looked back as if he was certain he was being chased by the Devil himself.

The sky continued to brighten although the sun had not yet appeared, and they trailed a cloud of dust that seemed to disguise and then erase the hills surrounding them. When the carriage reached the stone-paved road leading into the town of Catania, the horses sped forward clattering even faster. Bathed in that early morning light, soon they were careening past silent and darkened houses toward the harbor and he watched those buildings fly past that he remembered seeing at his arrival. But finally they reached the harbor, and at the foot of a gangplank to a ship, the driver reined the carriage to a sudden and noisy stop. Trembling, Pierre managed to stand and then carefully descended from the carriage. The moment his foot touched the cobbles of the dock, the driver turned the carriage, cracked his whip and was off, departing even more quickly than he had arrived. Pierre stood bewildered and looking about when a voice from the deck of the ship called out, "Naples?"

He looked up to see a dark-skinned and shirtless young man wearing a pale turban looking down at him and smiling. Pierre nodded.

"Come aboard then and be quick. The tide is turning and the sea awaits."

Beclouded by his confusion he stepped onto the gangplank and began to climb. But then, halfway along the gangplank he stopped and turned to look back once more. In the distance, placid Mount Etna stood cool to the point of indifference, but now suffused in his mind with a sudden fondness, and so for a moment his departure became tinged with trepidation.

"Hey," the voice above him suddenly cried, "tell me if you'd prefer to swim because that can be arranged." Pierre turned and resumed his climb.

When he reached the deck, the man introduced himself as Captain Aldi. He looked hard at Pierre. "A cabin's set aside for you and a good thing; you look like you could use the rest. And don't worry; you'll be summoned for meals." Smiling, he leaned close. "People say you're real famous and done something real important."

A sailor stepped up beside the Captain and spoke. After a moment the Captain said to Pierre, "Follow this man and he'll take you to your cabin. We'll get you where you're going and don't you worry about that." He turned then and gave orders to get underway. Exhaustion finally overwhelmed Pierre and mechanically he followed where he was lead below decks until he reached his bunk. He climbed into it and stretched out on his back. As he closed his eyes, it occurred to him that finally he was ready to dive into the pity of life and prepared to swim.

And in the next moment Pierre slept the sleep of a hero.

Fifty years later a man in Philadelphia repeated the experiment to great acclaim.

The career of the creature resumed centuries later and is well-known.

A. W. DEANNUNTIS lives in Philadelphia, Pennsylvania and has published short fiction in more than twenty journals, including *Timber Creek Review, Los Angeles Review, Pacific Coast Journal, CrossConnect, North Atlantic Review, Mobius, Philadelphia Stories, The Evansville Review, Mind in Motion, Cimarron Review,* and *Coe Review*. In addition, he has published the novels, *Master Siger's Dream* and *The Mermaid at the Americana Arms Motel*, and also the collections *The Final Death of Rock-and-Roll and Other Stories*, and *The Mysterious Islands and Other Stories*. The novel *Terror Island* is his first publication with Giant Claw.

www.ingramcontent.com/pod-product-compliance
Lightning Source LLC
Chambersburg PA
CBHW020602310726
48979CB00008B/1314/J

* 9 7 8 1 7 3 3 3 7 8 9 9 4 *